# ORANGE SKY

## J.E.GAUDET

*First printed in the United States of America 2017*



Front cover image courtesy of;
Marie Ferlings and Jake Snowden
www.mariefeandjakesnow.com

TRADE PAPERBACK ISBN: 978-0-9954459-0-1
EBOOK ISBN: 978-0-9954459-1-8

for Dustin and Hunter
*...both brave and true.*

# PROLOGUE
## - SOUTHERN CALIFORNIA -

July 2014

OKAY IVY, I want you to relax. Breathe in…and breathe out. I'm going to begin in five, four, three, two, *one*…

Ever get that feeling of wanting to walk peacefully through the sunshine with your eyes closed?

Well, close your eyes. Do not open them. Be in this moment right now. In the sunshine. Let the universe carry on around you. It always will. Take your time. Follow the sun. Wherever you may be … be still.

Feel the earth beneath your feet. Its warmth. Its life. You are a part of this earth. Feel it. Own it. Remember, do not open your eyes. Nothing can hurt you here. Unwind. Listen to the universe, for it has so much to tell you. Listen to nature, there is peace there. Wisdom. Do not open your eyes. Feel the sun. *See the dark.*

Contemplate in the darkness as it is here you can see everything most clearly. Do not be afraid of the dark. Learn from it. Find your fear here. Find your strength here. One cannot be without the other. To know your true strength is to understand your fear. Do not let your fear define you. Learn to find your strength in the dark. Your light. It may be small, but even the smallest light can withstand the darkness. Find *that* strength. When you find it, nurture it. Now imagine your light growing inside of you, filling every inch of your body until it reaches your fingertips. Until it reaches your toes. Until it fills your lips and has nowhere else to go. Feel it burst into your surroundings and imagine yourself glowing in the dark. Your light is growing bigger and brighter, it is radiating into all that surrounds you. The land. The trees. The ocean. The sky.

The world needs that light. *Your light.* Not your darkness. Not your fear. It is our light that manifests the glory in this world, and it is our light that can withstand any darkness within it. Look at you now. You shine so bright. You are a shining piece of this universe. *The universe is a shining piece of you.*

Now open your eyes, Ivy. Open them. Be in this moment right now. In the sunshine. Let the universe carry on around you. It always will. Take your time. Follow the sun, and wherever you may be…

…be still.

# Part One

## - LIBYA -

*"Build me a son, O Lord,*
*who will be strong enough to know when he is weak,*
*and brave enough to face himself when he is afraid,*
*one who will be proud and unbending in honest defeat,*
*and humble and gentle in victory."*

Douglas MacArthur

1880 – 1964

## Chapter 1

# - BENGHAZI -

## May 2014

### 1

"Another perfect day in the desert. Our paradise in hell."

The soldier threw his arm over his friend's shoulder and hit him affectionately on the chest. Midday had meandered by and the desert was peaking at a scorching 125.6 degrees Fahrenheit. The two men were making their way back from a call-out to oversee administrative loading at the Seaport of Benghazi, Libya, two kilometers away from their rendezvous with the other four special operative soldiers in their unit who were waiting for them at Il Liberta Square, in town. For three years their elite team had patrolled the sunbaked cities and sands of Libya, and in less than forty-eight hours they were slated to head home to the United States for some long-awaited leave from duty.

Their unit went by the name Phoenix, a six-man, special operations detachment team, deployed directly to Libya from Afghanistan at the end of 2011. They were originally sent here as intelligence operatives to monitor the uprisings among loyalists to the previous notorious government, which was overthrown during the civil war before their arrival. Phoenix was assigned the delicate task of integrating these militia groups into the Libyan Army without igniting fresh controversy—a risky and probably futile task. The groups stood restlessly at the threshold of war, while the rest of Libya trembled in suspense of the looming conflict. Another civil war was inevitable, and as a result, their team's operation was dutifully extended without leave. With the nation's political unrest, their position and knowledge proved too valuable an asset at such a critical time.

While based at a small U.S. camp a short distance outside of Tripoli, the nation's capital, Phoenix had moved around the country with the Libyan ground troops, training them in specifics about weapons and tactics. The U.S. military moved this particular split-team unit around the world for this very reason ... Foreign Internal Defense. These soldiers were renowned for being the best in their field; each man was flawless in linguistics, each cross-trained with a different infiltration skill, all highly focused and agile with exceptional intelligence, and most importantly, for the local civilians and ground forces, the soldiers possessed enduring patience and extremely affable personalities. These men surpassed all other units for their uncanny ability to be socially accepted by people around the world. Citizens of war-torn nations warmed quickly to their compassion and easygoing charm. The people loved them, and so the U.S. Special Operations Command back home also loved them. The USSOCOM—the big boss.

"We should swing by the Esplanade and sneak in a quick paddle before we get back to the boys," Oliver beamed at his brother-in-arms.

"Oh, buddy, stop. You're killing me!" Hart groaned into the sky. He closed his eyes under the harsh sun, then he lifted his rifle into the air and wiped the sweat from his darkly tanned forehead with his forearm.

Oliver laughed at Hart's anguished austerity. It didn't take much to stir his men these days, and with their service drawing to an end, the soldiers handled his banter as more of a teaser for what was soon to come. He smiled to himself, grateful his men were getting the time off they deserved. Three long years of in-sufferable heat and grueling hours spent protecting the people of Libya had taken a toll on his men.

Their leave didn't come without some degree of infamy. Oliver was forced to beg for his team's leave with the USSOCOM still reluctant to send another team in their place. Too nervous about Libya's instability as it perched on the brink of civil war. Libya's future was restless. Oliver knew that, but it would be pretentious of him to believe their presence over the next few months would prevent decades of conflict, and Phoenix was anything but pretentious. He had to convince the USSOCOM that his men had grown weary, which was not entirely a lie. Three years living in the memory of the Western world was breaking their spirits. They were fatigued men preparing for fresh combat. The walking dead, in every sense, being led to their graves by the very people who were supposed to protect them.

In his final bid, and losing morale, Oliver offhandedly threatened his superiors with Phoenix's inadvertent neglect of engagement due to exhaustion should they be forced to stay on ground without leave. Two months leave was allocated to his team. Two months only. However, for his men, two months was plenty of time to relish the world that lay far beyond the deserts…and far beyond the brutality of war.

Hart stopped at the side of the road under the shade of a date palm and leaned his rifle against its trunk. Oliver followed and did the same. The men had been walking for a couple of hours now, stopping in the shade occasionally to escape the extreme heat. They squinted their eyes and peered across the sunburned land as it rippled in the afternoon heat, then they looked at each other wordlessly and smiled.

Hart opened his water bottle and took a long, breathless drink, then poured the water over his face and let it wash down his chest. The water soaked through his t-shirt and he welcomed the temporary relief of it against his hot skin, even though it was too warm for his liking.

"I'm driving to Mexico when I get back. You in?" Hart asked, taking another sip. He winced at the warm water as it washed down his throat.

"Hell yeah! Pascuales, Colima?" Oliver answered cheerfully, taking a sip of water.

"Yeah, Pascuales."

"Perfect waves, fresh seafood, tequila shots on the sand…," Oliver reminisced dreamily. He sat down in the sand and leaned against the palm tree with an excited grin.

Hart smiled at his friend and sat heavily beside him in the heat. They were both strikingly handsome men, often mistaken as brothers for their tall, strong builds and eye-catching smiles.

They had tanned, olive skin from years spent under the desert sun, and a warmth in their eyes exuded kindness, illustrative of their gentle natures.

Oliver had spent most of his childhood at the army bases across California—surfing, fishing, and living a relaxed, beach-influenced life. His hair was sun-bleached blonde as a child and seemed to remain that way into his adult life. His gaze sparkled a dazzling, crystal blue, and he possessed an inspiring energy and passion for life that people were drawn to. Oliver was the best friend every man wanted in his life, and women found him mesmerizing, besotted by his bright enthusiasm and good looks. No one was immune to Oliver's effortless charm.

Then there was Hart, with his dark hair and rich brown eyes that were perpetually drenched in kindness. His eyes creased at the sides when he smiled and alluded to an endearing humility that people instantly warmed to. He seemed imperturbable to the point of insouciance, but there was something about Hart that only those closest to him knew; on the surface, he was exceedingly calm, but deep within, there ran a strong undertow of incredible power, fierce loyalty, and a determinedly strong will. Hart was the guy his friends talked to when they needed someone to listen. His comforting presence in Phoenix had become a crucial lifeline among the close friends. Hart was dependable and compassionate, with an unyielding, honorable heart. His unassuming nature and laid-back humor captivated women all over the world. He was alluringly intriguing. They yearned for his rumored intensity to love, but he rarely shared it. In fact, Hart hadn't been with a woman in over three years, like the rest of the Phoenix men.

Hart breathed out tiredly. "I'm looking forward to a sweet, ripe—"

"Woman?" Oliver interrupted.

"Mango," Hart corrected him, grinning. "Papayas, coconuts, the scent of Heliconias while you're sleeping. Surf all day, sleep all night, and maybe, *maybe,* a gorgeous woman."

Oliver laughed softly and leaned his head back against the palm tree, smiling to himself. "Man, I can't wait."

"Me neither." Hart glanced at Oliver, whose musing expression mirrored his own. "Two more days."

The two of them sat next to each other in cheerful content as they spoke about their plans once they had landed in America. It temporarily masked the thirst, dirt, and drenching sweat, but there was still no relief from the heat.

"Think the boys will join us?" Hart asked, turning to Oliver.

"Walker and Benji will. I think Taym and Abad have other plans."

"Taym said they might head back home to Afghanistan."

Oliver narrowed his eyes in thought, "Yeah, he told me."

"They offered him and Abad an American passport and flight back to the U.S. with us, why didn't they take it?"

"They took the passports," Oliver replied, screwing the lid back on his water bottle. "After serving with us for ten years, I think they earned them. Those twins have been fighting in wars since they were eighteen. Taym said he wanted to get back to his girlfriend and I don't blame him. It has been a long time since any of us enjoyed the pleasure of a woman's company." Oliver laughed.

"Too long," Hart grinned, rubbing his chest meekly. "At least he has someone to go back to."

Oliver smirked in disbelief. "Coming from the man who leaves a trail of women in his unassuming wake. I don't think you'll have any trouble finding love back home, buddy."

"I don't know. I am out of practice." Hart rubbed his jaw and smiled.

"Hey, remember that gorgeous brunette in Cabo? Rosalinda?" Oliver asked, grinning.

"Shit, Ollie, you remember her name?"

"Are you kidding, she was an eleven-out-of-ten." Oliver shook his head and laughed. "She followed us around all night begging you for it, Hart, and you gave her nothing. *Bastard.*"

Hart smiled as he remembered. "She was beautiful."

"Beautiful? She was perfect."

"You know I couldn't do anything. I had a girlfriend back home." He heard Oliver laugh beside him and Hart pushed the sand around with his boot, feeling a little foolish for his weak response.

"I thought you two broke up before we left for Cabo?" Oliver asked.

Hart looked at him and smiled. "Shit, it's possible, she was always breaking up with me."

Oliver shook his head and laughed. The two of them sat quietly for a moment, each in their own thoughts, thousands of miles away from Libya.

Hart continued to push the sand around with his boot, thinking. Maybe he should have slept with the Cabo woman. His girlfriend at the time had told him to go fuck himself if he chose to return to Afghanistan rather than stay with her in the States. She wasn't kind, or gracious, but she was sexy as hell with a badass, wild spirit and she liked to fuck, which is all he wanted from her at the time. But times had changed. He hadn't been with a woman in so long that it almost didn't matter to him anymore … a thought that frightened the hell out of him.

"You know, these last few years have ruined me," Oliver said quietly into the silence.

Hart glanced thoughtfully at him. "I know."

Oliver grabbed a handful of the warm sand they sat in and let it glide out of his closed fist like sand in an hourglass.

Hart watched the sand slide through his friend's hands like he had done a hundred times before today. He found it relaxing. Comforting almost. Oliver's pensive stillness meant they were safe. He saw the wonder in what everyone else considered commonplace, and Hart envied it. Hart didn't notice the purple skies after sunset or the black silhouettes of palm trees along the esplanade at twilight. His strength was people, not the natural world. Not animals. Not mountains. Not skies or oceans. That was Oliver's strength, and he saw all of it.

"Look, I know it's a lot to ask…." Oliver said, interrupting Hart's thoughts.

Hart looked at him and waited.

"I've already spoken to Walker and Benji about it…." Oliver glanced at Hart, a little despondent, but his bright-blue eyes still sparkled through the dirt and sweat on his face. He paused.

"What is it?" Hart asked, concerned.

"If anything happens to me," he continued, brushing the sand from his hands, "can I ask you to find my sister and make sure she is okay. Will you do that for me, Hart?"

Hart frowned at his friend's sudden somberness. "We're going home in a few days. What could possibly go wrong before then?"

"Yeah, I know. Just promise me you will check on her for me." Oliver looked at him seriously. "Please protect her. If I don't make it home."

"Of course," Hart replied on demand, deliberately ignoring the sentimentality of their conversation to protect his feelings. The thought of losing one of their team so close to the end was too disheartening to comprehend. "I promise I'll check on her, and I promise I won't leave her until she's begging me to go."

"No, Hart, she would never do that," Oliver smiled knowingly. "She will ask you to stay."

Hart shrugged, smiling. "So, I'll stay. Whatever she wants, Ollie, you have my word."

"Thanks, buddy." Oliver flicked him a smile, but it quickly faded.

"Where is all this coming from?"

"I don't know." Oliver laughed softly at himself. "I've been watching the guys lately, and something's changed. I don't know what it is, and I should. It's my job to know." His brow furrowed in concern and he rubbed his forehead. "I guess it's made me think about things I wouldn't usually."

Hart considered him as he spoke, unsettled by Oliver's wariness. Oliver was a decorated war-hero, renowned for his uncanny assessment of the enemy. His sharp intuition had saved countless lives in the past, including their own, and it was for this reason USSOCOM appointed him as the Captain of Phoenix. It was uncharacteristic of Oliver to question his men. The group's dynamics *had* shifted, and it hadn't escaped Hart's attention either, but he put it down to their oncoming leave—nothing more than nerves. Anxious excitement to return to a world they felt so removed from.

"Hey, it has been a long three years, and we're so close to going home," Hart reassured him. "It's an unfamiliar feeling, and I think we're all getting our heads around it in our own way."

"I know, you're right."

Oliver smiled at Hart without conviction. He removed his cap and ran his hands through his hair, thinking about what Hart said. His thoughts shifted to home and his sister, and he thought about her future without him, without their parents, and it worried him more than anything. Death never frightened him; it was those he left behind that did. He wondered who would be there to brighten the darker hours for her or make her laugh. *Really* laugh. Like he could. Her being alone in this world was his biggest fear, and Oliver sighed inwardly at the thought. Suddenly their presence in Libya seemed insignificant. He felt guilty asking this of his men, but he knew they would honor his wish should anything happen to him … and he found comfort in his request.

Oliver leaned his head back against the palm tree and stared into the hazy, afternoon sky. A knowing smirk crept across his solemn expression as he thought about his sister. Her sweetness. Her innocence. Her beauty. He would send his men to find her, but the decision to leave would be hers in the end. His soldiers were strong, yet none possessed the strength to withstand her breathtaking enchantment. No man did.

Oliver fought to restrain his grin.

Hart smirked, studying his friend's expression. "What is that? You know something I don't?"

"Yeah," Oliver chirped. "I do."

Hart narrowed his eyes suspiciously at Oliver who was tucking his water bottle into his backpack and lifting himself to his feet.

"Are you going to tell me about it?" Hart asked, peering up at him.

"Nope."

"I didn't think so."

Oliver extended a hand out to Hart. "We should head back. They'll be expecting us soon."

Hart took Oliver's hand and jumped to his feet. They collected their rifles and started back to their meeting point in Il Liberta Square with a lighter step.

The streets of Benghazi were a little less crowded than usual. Both men noticed the subtle variance, but neither one commented about it to the other. Benghazi was an ancient city and no stranger to war. Each war brought a different reign of power and it was most evident in the distinct differences of the architecture surrounding them. Outside of the city, some of the smaller buildings had become so dilapidated after the civil war that they seemed to be standing not by any solid foundations, but by the stronger buildings they leaned against. Hart imagined pulling one away and watching them fall upon each other like a row of dominoes. Here in the city, the majority of the landscape boasted grander, Eastern-inspired structures that dated back to the early 1900s, and it was the architecture of these buildings that the men likened to art. Historical monuments sat proudly among more modern, contemporary buildings raised after the destruction of World War II. Palm trees towered gracefully along the streets in front of the buildings, reaching stories high with their lush green fronds contrasted beautifully against the light, sandstone facades. It was a remarkable city, perpetually struck down by the politics of possession.

Hart and Oliver continued along the road by foot, with rifles in hand, but they were taken as no threat by the people that moved around them. They had become a familiar presence in the local area. Music chorused from the cafés along the strip that led toward Il Liberta Square. Women foraged through market stalls filled with silks, dates, olives, and grains, and the divine smell of freshly baked bread wafted lazily on the warm air. The children played on the street, laughing and singing with each other in the sunshine as though the heat didn't faze them at all. The soldiers had learned to read them as an innocent indication of the city's temperament; if the children played, it was a good sign that the city was settled.

Oliver gazed pensively into the sky. As the sun lowered, a haze of pale pink encircled the horizon leaving the center of the sky a faded, dusty blue. The colors of the desert never failed to impress him. Each day the sun would glide across the sky with its changing light, and as it rose and fell over the horizon it illuminated its deepest, richest shades. Even in the midst of heavy combat, the sunset still glowed magnificently above them, unfazed by the mortal destruction that lay beneath it. On the ground he walked amongst death and destruction, but up there in the breath-taking, burning orange sky, Oliver could be anywhere he dreamed.

He remembered sitting with his sister on the beach before his deployment. They had spent the entire afternoon with their friends on the beach outside their home in Southern California, drinking, swimming, and bathing in the glorious golden glow of the sunset. His sister's concern for him that evening came back to haunt him now. He hadn't thought about it in twelve years. She tried to hide it from him that day, but after losing their parents a few years earlier, he recognized the fear in her crystal eyes.

*"What if I lose you, too?" she whispered.*

*"Ivy, if I die," he pointed into the sunset, "then look into the orange sky, and I will be standing there. You will never be alone. I promise."*

"You okay?" Hart asked, noting the distant look in Oliver's eyes. After serving with each other for over twelve years, he had come to know his friend almost better than he knew himself.

"Yeah, I'm okay," Oliver replied. He looked up at Hart. "Do you want to meet her?"

"Who? Your sister?" Hart smiled. "I feel like we've already met."

Oliver looked at him and grinned. "She says the same about you."

A contentment flashed through Oliver's eyes, and Hart smiled curiously at him.

"Benji will fall head over heels for her," Oliver continued. "I'll have to keep an eye on him, make sure he behaves."

"Yeah, younger sisters. They're the ones you're forbidden to touch yet are always excruciatingly attractive." Hart chuckled and rubbed his chest. "They know you've been told not to go there, so they'll try their damn hardest to tempt you there."

Oliver smirked. "You sound like you're speaking from experience. Maybe I should be keeping an eye on you?"

"I don't know, is she beautiful?" Hart teased.

"Sure she is, she's gorgeous! She is the Queen of Hearts. Kind, sweet, thoughtful, and passionate." Oliver smiled to himself. "I've been pushing men away from her since she turned fourteen."

Hart laughed and shook his head. "I would never do it to you, buddy."

"I know you wouldn't." Oliver looked over at him with a playful, but pensive grin. "I think she'd like you."

"Me!? No," Hart exclaimed. He bowed his head, slightly uncomfortable with the conversation.

"Why not? You two remind me of each other in a way."

"We do?"

"Yeah," Oliver thought to himself for a few seconds. "You both have this mysterious depth to your soul that is beyond me." His expression grew serious, then he turned to Hart and smiled.

Hart laughed humbly. He couldn't imagine talking to a woman he was interested in, let alone his best friend's sister. The thought of impressing a woman these days genuinely terrified him. His heart was already pounding frantically inside his chest, nervous for a moment that may never happen. His sister wouldn't find him appealing, she would find him awkward and out of practice. He hadn't been with a woman in so long that he would certainly let her down. It would break his friendship with Oliver, and these guys meant everything to him. They had fought side by side and kept each other alive for over twelve years. He would never risk losing his friend for a woman.

"It's kind of you to say, but I'm not touching your sister," Hart stated eventually. He glanced at Oliver, who laughed.

The soldiers entered a lane that ended at the south end of Il Liberta Square, known as the Italian Quarter. Three-story apartments mirrored each other down the length of the lane, casting a shadow over the entire Quarter. The buildings sat atop a marketplace that skirted both sides of the lane, and lamps hung from the pillars outside, drawing a dotted line down the edge of the street that glowed in the afternoon shade. The soldiers stepped into the Quarter, feeling instant relief from the sun's blistering heat.

A few locals ambled across the street, but it was not the usual buzz of the Italian Quarter that the men were accustomed to. On any given day, the markets underneath the buildings were filled with locals, music, and life, but today, only a handful of people rummaged through the stalls. Hart and Oliver strolled side by side down the middle of the street, both wary of the change and vigilantly surveying their surroundings. When they were halfway down the lane, the men's pace slowed until they came to a complete stop. They paused and looked at each other, equally as baffled by the unusual stillness.

"It's too quiet," Oliver muttered. He scanned their surroundings without looking at Hart.

"Maybe it's the heat?" Hart suggested, raising an eyebrow at

Oliver. He gripped his rifle instinctively to his body.

"I hope you're right. Let's move," Oliver commanded, his wary eyes searching for anything out of place.

Hart moved on command, adhering to the familiar transformation of his best friend from the laid-back comic they adored to the unsmiling, commanding rank they respected. He was their appointed leader, and they would follow him anywhere. Oliver had earned the respect and admiration of his men long ago, and he honored their devotion with great leadership. He valued his life less than the lives of his men, and his uncompromising commands were the decisions of a wise and compassionate man who fought only for the survival of his friends so that he could lead them into another day. Hart, like the rest of his unit, knew precisely when to act on his orders.

The two of them jogged to the end of the lane and stopped before it opened up into the square. They stood together on one side of the street, pausing before entering the square. A woman walked past them into the lane and hesitated when her eyes caught their rifles. She peered up at Hart with an unmistakable fear etched into her expression. Hart recognized her. She lived in the apartments above the lane.

"Hey," he nodded at her.

The woman frowned and turned toward the lane again.

Oliver laughed. "Maybe you are out of practice."

Hart frowned to himself, then glanced at Oliver and shrugged his shoulders at the strange encounter. Seconds later, there was a gentle tap on his shoulder.

"Soldato?"

The soldiers turned to her.

"Signora," Hart replied.

"I know you. I have seen you before … here," she continued.

"Yes, you have."

"Be careful," she breathed, glancing warily at a man who strolled past the three of them. "There is new trouble here." Her large eyes flicked around the lane.

"*New* trouble?" Oliver repeated.

The two soldiers glanced at each other, and when they turned back to the woman, she was gone.

The men frowned at each other before Oliver peered out

carefully from behind the wall into Il Liberta Square. He furrowed his brow quizzically at Hart who also had a brief glimpse. Hart looked back at Oliver and shrugged his shoulders … the area seemed unruffled by the disquiet atmosphere that plagued its exterior. It was everyday business as usual, so Hart stepped confidently out of the eerie stillness of the Italian Quarter and into the cheerful chaos of the square.

*"Attenzione! Bastard!"*

Two young men shouted at him as they swerved past on their scooter, barely missing him, and Hart fell back into the lane again, visibly rattled by the close encounter. The driver leaned on his horn, and the man on the rear of the scooter looked back at Hart and waved his arm madly in the air, reeling out his anger in swift Italian as they sped off down the lane way.

Hart raised his hand in apology.

"Sorry! Mi dispiace!" he called out to them, a little embarrassed. He rubbed his jaw in residual shock, and then he heard Oliver laugh behind him.

"Shit!" Hart exhaled loudly to himself, then he turned to Oliver and laughed.

Il Liberta Square was its usual thriving ambiance on a Saturday afternoon. A balmy desert evening lay in store for Benghazi tonight, and the atmosphere buzzed with festive music and excited voices from the multitude of cafes and restaurants that sprawled out from their buildings into the empty car parks outside. Markets lined the perimeter of the square, and the soldiers could smell the array of incense and street food on the air. The square measured a hundred meters in length and width, and each meter between was filled with bustling, exuberant life. As evening approached, crowds of locals swarmed into the marketplace. Large date palms glowed in the afternoon sun and people dined at the tables beneath them, indulging in the delicious local cuisine.

Hart and Oliver headed toward a mosque with a large, green dome on its roof. Their rendezvous was at the far-left corner of Il Liberta Square at a small seafood restaurant that sat adjacent to the back wall of the mosque.

"Well, this is more like it," Oliver spoke to Hart. His blond hair glinted in the scattered rays of the setting sun as it peeked through the buildings.

The two soldiers walked through the crowd with an effortless cool, though heavily laden with gear. There was a relieving drop in temperature as the sun drifted out of the sky on its way to the horizon, and they glanced at each other and relaxed. A bright smile swept across their exhausted expressions as Il Liberta Square's excitement washed over them, then they reached a small but quaint restaurant with a hand-made sign that read ALFATAH

Hart checked his watch as they entered the restaurant. "1600 hours. Right on time."

Phoenix often met here, esteemed for offering the freshest seafood in town, straight from the Mediterranean Sea. In the garden, fifteen small tables surrounded the base of a date palm that had fairy lights spiraled up its trunk and strewn through its large fronds. Light music played over the voices of the people dining here, and it was surprisingly busier than any other night they had visited the restaurant, contrary to their expectations earlier.

A tray of fresh, grilled octopus and fish soup whisked past Oliver and Hart, and they watched it until the waiter placed the mouth-watering dishes on a table nearby. It was there they found the rest of Phoenix.

"Welcome back, fellas!" The men stood from their seats to welcome Oliver and Hart.

They greeted each other with closed fists and pats on the backs and ecstatic grins that were all a little more exuberant due to one unfathomable occasion—their service was drawing to an end. It was increasingly difficult for the soldiers to contain their mutual excitement.

One of the men grabbed two extra chairs from the table behind him and swung them around to the table beneath the palm. Oliver and Hart sat down beside each other with a long sigh, thrilled to be back with the four friends who comprised their unit. Two ice cold bottles of Coke were handed to them by a young boy who waited eagerly for Hart's recognition, so Hart pulled the child's cap down over his face with a gentle laugh and guzzled the Coke in his other hand.

Around the table sat the other four men in their unit; Split-A

Detachment Team Phoenix. Desert rats, together for over twelve years. Each an expert in their field with a specialized infiltration skill, and each cross-trained in the other due to the nature of their split team operation. Making them one of the most highly-trained, and deadliest group of men in the world.

To the left of Oliver sat Josh Walker, Special Operations Weapons Sergeant and Aviation Officer, dressed in his khaki-cotton tee, dog tags, and combat pants, leaning precariously back on his seat with his large, black boot up on the table. He was casually shooting out smoke rings in rapid fire across the table from a cigarette he took from his treasured pack of Samsun's. Walker always looked disinterested in the conversation, but it couldn't be further from the truth, his cool, easy-going temperament belied the unfeigned depths of his sharp personality. Walker was exceptionally intelligent and incredibly perceptive, and an expert in both his fields. He was capable of operating all U.S. weaponry and the majority of foreign weapons, but his true passion waited for him back at the camp near Tripoli in the form of a UH-60 Black Hawk. Walker doubled as a helicopter pilot. He was personally plucked out of the Night Stalkers, a U.S. Army aviation regiment, by USSOCOM itself and consigned to the elite Alpha-Team Phoenix. If required, he could lead and coordinate operations using a range of Army helicopters, including Chinooks and Apaches, but the Black Hawk he had at camp was his pride and joy, his 'Bird.' She gave him the ability to fly while directing undetected heavy assault on the enemy. To this day he would rather be in the air than on foot, but he was, and forever will be, grateful for the boys he met twelve years ago who still sat by his side today.

Walker was tall with black hair and brown, furtive eyes framed by dark eyebrows. His dark features and wry grin made it seem like he was either infiltrating your thoughts or planning his next dangerous move. He had a steeliness about him that men wouldn't dare to mess with, but women were hopelessly drawn to. His rugged good looks and brooding veneer earned him a bad boy image that he never seemed to shake, but Walker didn't mind because it allowed him to get away with much more than he should, especially with women. He smoked, and he cursed a lot, but his friends knew he had a good heart. He was loyal and dependable, and they trusted him with their lives ... as he trusted them.

"How did the administrative loading go at the Port?" Walker asked, pulling his boot from the table and leaning in to join the conversation.

"We're waiting on a few light armored vehicles and an MRAP that are coming in from Tobruk tomorrow morning," Oliver replied. "They planned on picking them up on their way out, but the Captain is apprehensive about pulling into the harbor there. They can't guarantee safe anchorage."

Oliver had been quietly watching each of his men around the table as they ate and laughed. There was a small smile on his face as he listened to their usual playful banter, and he was grateful for their cheer ... it lessened the unease he had sitting in the pit of his stomach. They were heading home in a few days, but a foreboding awareness still troubled him. He spun the empty Coke bottle slowly in his hands as he stared blankly into its bright, red label. A small piece of a Westernized world in a nation swarming with those who condemned it. Oliver couldn't quite work out if the bottle contradicted his time here, or reinforced it.

Hart looked at Oliver. His grave expression reminded him of their conversation earlier.

"Hey, Tobruk is only another 250 miles from here." Hart glanced at Ollie and smiled, attempting to lift his spirits. "You know, it is quicker this way. I'd say it's a decision made on convenience and less on concern. Everyone's keen to get the hell out of here, am I right?" He grinned at the boys.

"Before they change their minds again!" Benji remarked with a dimpled grin.

Sitting to Hart's right was Benjamin Swift, or as they affectionately called him, Benji. He was the guy who softened life's hard edges. He had endless reserves of energy, and most of it was spent on being the entertainer when life became too serious. He was a comic, joker, prankster...you name it. Benji's way of dealing with life's hardship was to find the humor in it, and the boys were quietly thankful for it. He reminded them not to take life too seriously. A soldier witnessed plenty of suffering and adversity, but Benji showed them that happiness was not decided by the people around you—rather it was manifested within yourself. Even in the darkest depths of battle with barely a hope for survival, Benji still had a knack for making them smile.

He had kind, blue eyes and tanned, dimpled cheeks, and hair that had turned a sun-bleached, sandy brown in the desert. Born and bred in New Orleans, Benji talked with a strong southern accent that complimented his playful yet cheeky charm, which the ladies couldn't resist. Flirting was his quintessential element. His be all, end all. Whether it be the harmless wink of an eye or a lingering kiss on the lips, Benji innocently alluded to what may have been had they met under different circumstances. He knew all too well the effect he had on women, and he was the first to admit the effect they had on him. He was always falling in love, often falling hard, leaving a trail of frustrated women around the world. They always wanted far more than he could ever offer them, but Benji was a soldier first and foremost. Benjamin Swift, Special Operations Communications Sergeant. Responsible for all conventional and unconventional warfare communications. Proficient in all systems to transmit and receive radio messages through different means of communication; burst code, waves, or voice. It was his extraordinary talent that boasted his surname, Swift, which awarded him legendary recognition throughout the Armed Forces—Benji was as quick as they come, not only with his sharp-witted humor but with his astute, swift delivery in combat. He was clever and calculating with razor-sharp skills, and this is what earned him his rightful place at the table.

The four soldiers grew up as Army brats moving from base to base every few years as children. They all had that one parent that may have been a little too hard on them, but with age came the realization that they more than likely deserved it. Other than that, they each enjoyed a free-range childhood roaming the bases with the other children, playing games and finding themselves in all kinds of wayward mischief.

But with the ups came the downs. They were all familiar with the loneliness of starting again in a new base or town. Moving away from your friends was tough, and for these men, it helped them realize what they were always desperately searching for, and that was one friend who could never be replaced no matter how many times you moved. A friendship that lasted a lifetime, no matter what happened. This is what they had now ... Oliver,

Hart, Walker, and Benji. They were brothers-in-arms. Brothers for life. Unbreakable. *Inseparable.*

Between Walker and Benji sat Abad and Taym Malak. Twin brothers who were trained by these four soldiers while Phoenix served in Afghanistan. They were only fourteen when their parents, alleged members of a notorious brotherhood, were killed after the United States and coalition forces bombed a U.S.-owned arms depot that the militia group had overrun and occupied as their own. There were dozens of casualties on the ground, all whom in some way or another had been linked to the initial raid.

Abad and Taym were picked up on their return to the depot and escorted to a U.S. military camp in Afghanistan by Oliver Rose himself. The brothers knew their parents were affiliated with the brotherhood and had expected the grave outcome. After being thoroughly grilled about their involvement with the group, the boys were cleared and offered a position in the camp that would see them trained by Oliver and his men in tactics, communications, and weaponry. USSOCOM planned to use them as undercover intelligence operatives who would remain in Afghanistan, but Abad and Taym were smart kids who learned quickly and proved to be too valuable to be left behind. Once they turned eighteen, their devotion and loyalty to America paid off, and USSOCOM declared them special operatives in the Afghanistan unit. Given that they were trained by the esteemed commander, Oliver Rose, they progressed into Detachment Team Phoenix while the unit served in their country.

The affable twins, with large, dark eyes and smiling faces, had talked their way into everyone's hearts, and now here they were, twenty-five years old and still a secure part of the elite unit currently based in Libya. To this day, not a single word had been exchanged between the soldiers and the twins regarding whether Oliver and his team were responsible for the operation that killed their parents that day at the depot.

"Benji, did you get in touch with Base?" Oliver asked. "What's news in Tripoli?"

"They are rearming," Benji told him reluctantly.

"Rearming! Why?" Oliver replied, annoyed.

Benji shrugged apologetically. "They believe an attack is

imminent. I wouldn't be surprised if they call off our leave and order us back to Tripoli."

Hart and Oliver exchanged concerned glances.

"What is it?" Walker asked, catching their wordless exchange.

Oliver sighed to himself.

"Ollie?" Walker frowned. He looked to Hart when Oliver didn't reply.

Hart's high spirits plunged in Oliver's silence. He knew exactly what Ollie was thinking, because he thought it too—Phoenix was never leaving Libya.

"Something didn't feel right in the Italian Quarter on the way here," Oliver replied. He turned to Walker, who was leaning toward him across the table, keen to hear what he had to say.

"We thought something had happened in the square," Hart added.

"Like what?" Taym asked.

Abad glanced nervously at his brother when he spoke.

"I don't know it just seemed … *quiet*," Oliver replied.

"An Italian woman told us there was new trouble," Hart smiled meekly. "I think she may have spooked us."

"An Italian woman? Man, I bet she was gorgeous. Was she gorgeous?" Benji chirped. An impish grin beamed brightly on his face.

"Ah, Benji," Oliver laughed, shaking his head.

"What!?" he replied, throwing his hands in the air at the smirking faces around the table.

"You know who you remind me of?" Hart chuckled. "That howling wolf on those old Tex Avery cartoons."

"The one who's getting aroused watching Red Riding Hood sing in a nightclub," Oliver added.

"Yeah, yeah, I know the one," Benji replied reticently. He tapped a bottle cap on the surface of the table with a hurried excitement, and nodded with a meek smile. The soldiers laughed.

"Well, you know those young, Italian women," Benji added in his defense, "if they're not trying to seduce you with their dark eyes and smoking hot bodies, then they're warning you about something like…like their father's temper, for example."

"Of course, you would know all about that, hey Benji boy,"

Oliver teased him, grateful for the upbeat change of topic.

"Why is it that you always get caught with your pants down?" Walker asked, laughing gently.

"And picking women with overprotective fathers," Hart added.

"I don't know. I don't know," Benji shrugged his shoulders and rubbed his chest, slightly embarrassed by the truth of it all.

"Remember that time back home when you had to jump out the window of that woman's bedroom on the second floor, and you were stark, fucking naked, scrambling down the roof?" Walker grinned behind the cigarette in his lips.

The soldiers laughed, remembering the event well.

"I wasn't completely naked," Benji added with a sheepish smile.

"No, even better, you were wearing a singlet and your fucking dog tags, but no jocks," Walker added. "You had nowhere else to go except down that old oak tree and you only got halfway down by the time her father was underneath it with the hose on you."

"I know! Shit. I got my God damn balls impaled on a bunch of twigs," Benji grimaced at the painful memory and rubbed his pants. "Fucking hurt."

"We told you not to go up there," Hart added.

"He can't help himself," Walker grinned wickedly at Benji.

Benji shook his head with a defeated grin. "Alright, alright, we get it … I'm a fool for beautiful women." He put his hands up in surrender and laughed with his friends at his expense.

"Ah, Benji, aren't we all?" Oliver looked at each of his friends with a revitalized cheer in his blue eyes.

The soldiers' laughter settled down, and an unfamiliar noise over the bustle of the square caught Hart's attention. He paused to listen as the soldiers continued to talk. A faint, low hum of an aircraft grew louder in the sky, evidently flying toward them, and Hart searched the afternoon sky.

"Hey, quiet," he hushed the boys. "Listen." Hart pointed his finger into the air and stared soundlessly at the soldiers, as one by one they heard what he was listening to.

The six men glanced wordlessly at each other in concern. Nothing left the ground around here without their knowledge. Even the Libyan National Army couldn't send a chopper into the air without informing them first, and the militia groups around here were confined to ground force attacks. Over the music and voices of the square, identifying the aircraft proved to be a challenge. The locals around them continued with their meals, oblivious to the strange, oncoming noise that the soldiers had picked up. Phoenix, on the other hand, had been trained to detect even the slightest discrepancy in their surroundings.

"What do you think it is?" Abad asked. "Should we be concerned?" He fidgeted with the empty Coke bottle in front of him. His dark eyes connected with Oliver's, anxiously awaiting a response.

Oliver watched Abad carefully and thought about his unease concerning the group's dynamics. It was his role as commander to pick up on any degree of incongruity within his men. Oliver couldn't see the change, but he sensed it, and after confiding in Hart about it earlier, the glitch within Phoenix seemed more evident now than ever before.

Oliver stared back at Abad, wary of his peculiar edginess all of a sudden.

"Well, it isn't a chopper," Walker opined coolly. He dropped his cigarette and ground the burning ember into the dirt. He looked up at the waiting eyes that stared at him from around the table. "Or a jet."

"Then what is it?" Abad asked, knocking his empty Coke bottle onto the table with his elbow. He glanced quickly at Oliver.

"Abad! You idiot!" Taym glared at his brother.

The soldiers watched the bottle spin between them, each engrossed with identifying the sound of the aircraft. Except for Oliver. He watched Abad and Taym, who sat opposite him, curiously examining their suspicious behavior this afternoon. The brothers were agitated with each other, more so than usual, and so he listened to them argue under their breath across the table from him—until Taym met his heedful eye with a cold, unblinking expression.

Oliver narrowed his eyes without looking away, and Taym shifted uneasily under his intimidating gaze. Taym pulled his hands from the table and dropped them into his lap. Oliver waited judiciously for him to make a move. The others, still focused on the unidentified sound, were oblivious to their silent confrontation, but Oliver preferred it that way. He wasn't quite sure what was unfolding before him anyhow. The air between the two of them was blatantly tense, and a wave of distrust swept through Oliver.

Taym slid his rifle onto his lap like he had done a thousand times before, but something was different this time. It was unsettling. Taym tapped his heel on the ground with an agitated, hurried twitch, but it was his white knuckles that gave him away … he gripped his weapon in a way that concerned Oliver.

Oliver calmly reached for his rifle. Following his lead, Hart, Walker, and Benji did the same.

Abad took a few seconds to notice the subtle conflict happening next to him at the table. He glanced at his brother and saw Taym's finger anxiously rubbing the trigger guard of his rifle. Abad's eyes widened and, with his nerves getting the better of him, he leaped impulsively to his feet, pulled his rifle into position, and aimed it directly at Oliver's head. In the blink of an eye, all six of the soldiers were up from their seats with their rifles aimed at one another across the table.

The surrounding diners fell off their seats in dumbfounded surprise, and it didn't take long before the restaurant transformed into a scene of hysterical chaos. The locals scrambled out of the area, fearing the deadly stand-off between the six soldiers.

Abad panted frantically as he and his brother stared down the barrels of four unwavering rifles.

"What the *fuck* is going on, Abad!?" Hart's voice boomed down his rifle over the commotion they caused around them.

Each soldier was as baffled by the clash as the other, but each remained steadfast in their critical position. Abad didn't answer. He stood behind his weapon and whimpered weakly at the sudden face-off that he had initiated.

Oliver stood silently with his rifle fixed on Taym, who glared straight back at him along the barrel of his rifle. Mayhem rushed over the square within seconds, but the men consciously ignored the disorder.

"What's wrong, Ollie?" Taym sneered. "Abad making you nervous?"

"You have something you need to tell us, Taym?" Oliver responded powerfully and unblinking, his finger perched calmly on the trigger.

"Nothing you want to hear," Taym replied. His thin lips curled into a pretentious grin.

The men held their positions, and in the silence of the confrontation, the noise they heard earlier was almost upon them. A small, unmanned drone hummed through the golden sunlight over the square, and the six soldiers flicked their eyes to the sky and back, before the drone disappeared over the top of the mosque behind them.

"What the fuck is a UAV doing out here!?" Benji asked, staggered by the unfamiliar sight, yet unflinching from his rifle.

"Anyone else getting a bad feeling about this?" Hart asked.

"I am," Walker replied darkly, shifting his aim from Abad to Taym.

"Boys, boys, boys, why are you so nervous?" Taym smiled, slowly lowering his weapon. "Abad is a fool. He worries like his mother did."

Taym smacked his brother on the back of the head and pushed the tip of Abad's rifle to the ground.

"We have been friends for ten years now, Ollie, don't be like this!" Taym laughed and raised his hands, but the men failed to see the humor.

Hart looked out the corner of his eye to Oliver, who was deathly still, and analyzing Taym.

"It's your call, Captain," Hart said.

Oliver held his breath and considered the circumstances. He didn't trust Taym. Ten years no longer mattered. Something right here, right now troubled him. He didn't know what it was, but for now the only option was to let it be and trust his instincts for when the time came. His breath was deep and controlled, but the decision weighed heavily on his mind. Hundreds of miles separated the soldiers from their base in Tripoli, and if Taym chose to play innocent, then there was nothing he could do at this point in time.

Oliver lowered his weapon, and one by one, Benji, Hart, and Walker put down their rifles in accord with his decision.

"Well, that was intense," Taym sighed in relief, feeling his adrenaline wane. "What the fuck is wrong with you, Ollie!?"

Oliver didn't reply. He wiped the tension from his face

with his hand and turned to Hart, inwardly contemplating the dilemma he now found himself in. Oliver nodded at Hart, wordlessly handing over the reins to his second in command.

Hart nodded in return and glanced at the rest of the team. Oliver's actions had sparked his suspicion of the twins, but he let it slide for now.

"Right! Abad, Taym, I want you on the other side of this mosque with Walker, see if you can locate that drone. Benji, get on the radio and contact Base, see if there are any authorized UAVs in the area. Meet in the courtyard of the mosque at…." Hart paused to check his watch, "1630 hours. You've got twenty minutes, boys, find us some answers!"

Walker was already fifty meters away from the restaurant, jogging toward the back door of the mosque, when Hart called out to him. Walker stopped and looked at him. Hart lifted his right hand and pointed at Walker, then with two fingers he pointed at his own eyes and directed them toward Abad and Taym, who were oblivious to their interaction as they ran to catch up with Walker.

*"Watch them!"* Hart mouthed with a profound seriousness etched into his expression. Walker nodded and left.

Hart turned and tapped Oliver on the shoulder. "Let's go."

"Where are we going?"

"We're going to find that Italian woman. I believe she knows more than she'd like to." Hart frowned.

Hart and Oliver jogged toward the lane through the crowds of locals, who were noticeably settling down once they realized the soldiers were leaving.

"Hey, what happened back there with Abad?"

"It's Taym we need to worry about," Oliver replied.

"You think so?"

The two of them stopped running when they reached the laneway.

"I don't trust him, Hart. He…." Oliver paused. He stopped talking and followed Hart's gaze into the sky.

A high-pitched whistle ripped through the air, growing louder as if coming closer to them. Hart and Oliver looked at each other, and three seconds later the square exploded into a deafening fireball, propelling the soldiers backward into the lane with shattered concrete and flying debris.

2

HART WOKE TO a severe ringing resonating through his ears. He rolled over onto his stomach in excruciating pain and pressed his pounding head into the concrete beneath him. He coughed into the ground and groaned.

Hart rolled back over with another painful groan, then sat up. The silent chaos unraveled before him. An enormous cloud of dust gently settled over Il Liberta Square and the wounded laying around him. Hart rubbed the dust from his eyes and peered at the aftermath of the attack. The missile had wiped out everything within a fifteen-meter radius just south of the center of the square. People wailed past him like a herd of frightened livestock into the lane, but he couldn't hear anything, just the harrowing shrill that resonated through his ears.

"Oliver!" Hart called out through the deafening silence, scanning the immediate area for his friend. Hart then checked himself over, wincing at the stabbing pain in his upper leg. Seeing the tattered, blood-soaked fabric, Hart reached through the hole in his pants and felt around the wound for the object that had embedded itself in his thigh. He growled in agony as he tried to dislodge a piece of metal with his bare fingers. His warm, slippery blood made it difficult to remove, but he managed to yank the metal free. Hart took one glance at the steel in his fingers and hurled it away. He inspected his injury, grateful the shrapnel hadn't caused any real damage. He used his rifle to leverage himself to his feet ... and then a second missile hit the square.

Hart didn't hear the incoming whistle of the second missile, nor did he hear the explosion, but he felt it. The shockwave knocked him through the air with a blast of burning heat, and he hit the ground again in the lane. He rolled over on the concrete until the debris settled once again. This time he was able to recuperate much more quickly. Hart pulled himself up with his rifle and scoured the area for Oliver. He looked at the ground when he felt it shake, narrowing his eyes at the concrete rubble bouncing between his feet. The trembling grew, and Hart glanced down the lane away from Il Liberta Square. Three Leopard Tanks forced their way destructively through the Italian Quarter, and behind the tanks trailed a line of swerving jeeps filled with armed men who hung perilously off the sides. They were shooting any unsuspecting soul who stood exposed to the terrifying convoy, many of them already wounded in the missile strikes.

Hart was forced to suspend his search for Oliver to seek cover. He entered the marketplace under the building beside him, weaving in and out of the stalls until he reached a safe distance from the lane to stop and consider his options. *Oliver.* They would have been separated in the sudden rush of locals escaping the square. There were no dead surrounding him, so Oliver was alive, along with the rest of Phoenix, seeing as the missiles hit the south area of the square. If the soldiers were still alive, then they would head to the courtyard of the mosque, their last planned meeting point.

He stopped at one of the stalls when he reached the right side of the square, so he could analyze his surroundings and determine a quick route out of the clutter of the marketplace. The afternoon light was noticeably dimmer in here. Somehow the locals had made it out, so Hart looked for an exit along the back of the marketplace with no luck. His eyes caught the fragmented light of the lowering sun that pierced through the holes in the tin wall, and Hart considered kicking his way out through the frailty of the metal, but the noise would attract unwanted attention.

He passed under an open window overlooking Il Liberta Square and stopped to steal a quick glance of the group that had established itself in the area. The square was littered with rubble and bodies, with half a dozen jeeps and the three tanks parked in the center. Hart guessed there were close to forty men, all armed and wearing black balaclavas, and firing their weapons randomly into the air with a seemingly bewildered excitement. It seemed nothing more than an overzealous group of terrorizing fanatics who decided to meet at the same place, at the same time, and happened to achieve far more damage than they originally anticipated. But the longer Hart examined them, the more he acknowledged that there was a united disorder among them. A shared victory. The missiles were too precise. The UAV was too coincidental. The attack was premeditated, and Hart guessed the insurgents were backed by a discerning and sagacious leader.

A few moments later, as he had assumed, a masked man

walked through the raucous crowd and climbed his way onto the roof of one of the jeeps and hushed the group. With waving arms, the man appointed smaller groups of masked assailants and sent them off in different directions around the square. He pointed at Hart who dropped to the ground beneath the window.

"Shit!" he breathed.

Adrenaline burst into his veins, sending his astute intellect into full speed. He wiped the sweat from his forehead and vigilantly scoured the area in front of him, then something caught his eye. Hart squinted his gaze and studied the shadow beneath a grains stall only meters in front of him. Once he realized what he was staring at, Hart rubbed his jaw and closed his eyes in exhausted surrender.

Two women were staring at him, an older woman who was mumbling to herself, and a younger woman who had her hand pressed to the older woman's mouth. They watched him cautiously, unblinking, unsure where else to look.

Hart put his finger to his mouth and hushed the mumbling woman, but there was no response. He exhaled frustratingly and wiped the sweat that dripped down his temples. The air was inconceivably hot beneath the sun-scorched metal roof of the market. He could smell incense and smoke, and his head still throbbed from the blow to the concrete during the missile blast. He needed to move, now, but the decision to take the women with him weighed heavily on his heart. He couldn't leave them here to die.

The afternoon sunlight filtered through a door frame on the exterior wall of the market, catching Hart's eye. A fresh wave of hope swept over him, but it was short-lived, as the voices in the square were almost upon them. He considered the hand grenade in the pouch of his backpack to give him more time. It was only a concussion grenade, but with the insurgents almost upon them, it was his only chance to exit the back of the building with both the women.

Hart tightened his lips and considered the woman who was still mumbling to herself. She was going to get them killed any minute now if she didn't quiet down. Keeping low, Hart shifted across the floor to them and reached out his hand to the quiet woman, who was much younger than he initially had thought. She looked up at him with wide, frightened eyes and hesitated to trust him.

"Take my hand," Hart whispered flawlessly in Arabic, his brown eyes pleading with her. "I'll protect you."

The girl glanced at his rifle, and slowly but surely, she placed her small hand within his. Hart took her hand and slid her swiftly across the sandy concrete and into his arms. She crawled around Hart and kneeled behind him to wait for her friend. He felt her hands rest on his shoulders and her light breath next to his ear. He felt her innocent, young life in his hands. In his capable hands, he told himself. *I've got this.* Hart reached out his hand to the second woman, but she recoiled from him into the darkness beneath the stall.

"Please. Take my hand," Hart whispered determinedly.

The woman shook her head.

"You will die if you stay here!" Hart breathed.

"Afina! Take his hand!" The girl whispered over his shoulder.

The older woman looked up at her friend and shifted her petrified gaze to Hart. She considered the soldier in front of her, then she shook her head again and wailed into her hands.

Hart wiped his face and cursed.

He stared at the woman as he listened to the voices drawing nearer in the square behind them. They were running out of time. She covered her ears when she heard them, and Hart nodded with empathy. These women were no strangers to war. He felt sorry for her. Apologetic almost.

"Afina, you must take his hand," the girl whispered behind him again.

The woman blinked her eyes open. She peered at Hart, who still had his hand outstretched. She reluctantly reached for him, and Hart grabbed her before she could change her mind, pulling her effortlessly from underneath the stall toward him. They kneeled in front of each other, face to face. His brown eyes fixed intently on hers. Hart put one finger to his mouth to remind her to keep quiet, then he nodded reassuringly at her.

A man shouted a few meters from the window, and the woman sprung to her feet.

"Get down!" Hart exclaimed.

"Afina!" The young girl went for her friend, but Hart forced her back against the brick wall below the window. He leaned forward to grab the woman, but she looked out the window in front of her, and an instant pallor washed across her beautifully tanned skin. The frenzied voices in the square brought their lethal attention to the woman in the window, and Hart growled furiously to himself once he realized she couldn't be saved. He fell back against the wall beside the girl and peered up at the woman, catching a silent prayer leave her lips before a merciless shower of bullets tore into her.

The woman shook violently on her feet. Hart grabbed the girl beside him and tucked her into his chest, shielding her from the woman's blood and the gruesome image that would haunt her for the rest of her life. The girl was screaming in his arms, but it couldn't be heard over the ear-splitting sound of the gunfire. He kept her there until her friend's body collapsed awkwardly away from them. When the shooting ceased, Hart leaned over the girl and reached into the pouch of his backpack for the grenade. Without a second to waste, he pulled the pin with his teeth and hurled the grenade through the open window into the square. Hart waited a few seconds and when the grenade exploded, he scooped the girl into his arms and headed for the back door.

The sun was blinding when he finally forced his way through the locked door. Hart searched the sandy yard for insurgents, then he hurried to a small doorway in the building opposite the markets.

He moved inside and sat the girl down against a pillar inside the building. Inside was far more contemporary than anything he had seen since arriving in Libya. It was light and open, with a large area in the center of the hall where the ceiling reached over three stories high. A tall, brass palm tree stood in the middle of it, and circling the base of the palm was a polished concrete desk. The brass glistened in the sunlight from the surrounding windows, and it threw golden shards of light throughout the hall. It was one of the most impressive buildings he had ever seen, but he had never seen it before now. As he surveyed the room, Hart noticed the building's occupants hidden amongst the shadows. One by one they hid their eyes when he looked at them, terrified of him and his weapon.

Hart bent down to the girl, who was now sobbing on the

ground.

"Are you okay?" Hart asked.

The girl nodded. He lifted her to her feet and moved her quickly to a nearby door. He forced the door open and met another wide-eyed group of people who wailed at the sight of him.

"I won't hurt you. I'm a commander in the United States Special Forces," Hart spoke reassuringly. He threw his hand into the air toward them to settle the agitation his presence caused in the room. "I need you take this girl for me."

"I'll take her." A young man with a British accent walked over to Hart.

"Thank you," Hart nodded at him.

"We're locking the door. She will be safe here."

"What building is this?" Hart asked.

"This is the International Exhibition Centre," he answered. An anxious smile appeared on the man's face, then he looked up at Hart. "Should we be concerned?"

"Just keep the door locked, and keep quiet," Hart responded, unsmiling.

Hart willed the girl to enter the room. She looked at the man who waited for her, then she shook her head and threw her arms around Hart's waist.

He looked down at her and unraveled her slender arms from around him, and sighed. "You are safer here without me."

He pulled the girl easily from him, and with light force, he pushed her through the doorway. The British man grabbed the girl to foil her attempt to run back to Hart. She looked at him with a deep-set angst in her dark eyes, and Hart suddenly felt guilty. Apologetic. Her friend's life had been in his hands, and he had let her down. The grave thought distracted him.

He shook his head and refocused on the task at hand. Hart shut the door and ran to an exit on the east side of the building, toward the mosque. He concealed himself behind a pillar in the courtyard outside and grabbed his intra-team radio to touch base with Phoenix. The fact that Oliver, Walker, and Benji had not been in radio contact yet concerned him. He imagined they were confronting similar conflicts individually around the square. Splitting the elite team was a success on its own. As conceited as it sounded, he couldn't help but feel the attack was a personal assault on Phoenix. But by whom? Hart had his suspicions.

His lips brushed the device when he spoke. "Phoenix, this is Hart, do you read me?"

Hart's dark gaze scanned the courtyard in front of him, studying the area for any lurking threat or route of escape. In the background, he could hear the occasional explosion and the ominous rumble of jeeps in the area. Either the insurgent's numbers had increased, or they were on the move.

"Phoenix, this is Hart, do you read me?" he repeated. Again there was no answer.

Hart bowed his head and rubbed his eyes as he waited. "Come on boys, touch base with me, fellas."

He waited a few extra seconds before giving up, then decided to head to the mosque anyhow. Hart tucked the radio away and carefully descended the steps into the courtyard. As he did, a faint voice mumbled incoherently through the static. He repositioned himself behind the pillar and grasped the radio tightly in his hands, pressing it gently to his mouth.

"This is Hart. The signal is weak, please repeat."

He waited patiently for a reply. He stood quietly in the silence, listening to the heavy, agitated beat of his heart. When no one responded, Hart bowed his head and sighed into the back of his hand.

*"Hart ... this ... Oliver ... you read me?"*

Hart breathed a long sigh of relief. He leaned his head back against the pillar and closed his eyes, then he pressed the radio to his lips again and smiled. "Goddamn it, Ollie, am I glad to hear your voice."

Hart took his thumb off the button and ran his hand back through his hair. He heard Oliver laugh through the radio.

*"Hart ... where are ... have ... Walker ... Benj...."*

"I'm in the courtyard east of the International Exhibition Centre, and to the south of Il Liberta Square. I've had no contact with Benji or Walker."

Hart paused for Oliver's reply.

*"Hold your position. I'm coming to you, I am ... Square. I repeat. Hold ... position. Do you copy?"*

"Copy that."

Gunfire rattled the air inside the Exhibition Centre, and Hart ducked instinctively. Cries and deep voices resonated through the building and echoed into the courtyard where he stood. He searched the area in front of him. Tall concrete columns and empty terraces encircled a tiled courtyard. In the center was a tall, bronze statue shaped intricately into a woman. There was no ceiling, just a glorious, late-afternoon sky that stretched across the courtyard.

Excluding the statue, the courtyard was rather bare. Hart twisted his mouth in thought. Without an exit, the columns seemed his only chance of concealment. He hurried down the steps, setting his sight on the opposite side of the courtyard to take cover. He paused halfway, behind the statue, who gazed down at him with a smooth expression of commiseration that troubled him. As he moved past her, a small scuffle behind him caught his attention and Hart swiveled in his position, dropped to his knee, and aimed his rifle past the statue at the perpetrator standing at the back door of the Exhibition Centre. A masked assailant stood in Hart's aim at the top of the stairs, and in his arms, he held the girl Hart had saved earlier from the marketplace.

His heart dropped when he saw her. The assailant had her neck locked securely in his arm and concealed himself strategically behind her with his handgun pressed into the back of her head. Hart studied the dark eyes that burned through him from behind the balaclava, and he wondered if the face cover was a prop to intimidate the civilians, or a means to conceal identity.

Hart narrowed his eyes at the man.

Negotiations. This is how things usually panned out in futile predicaments such as these. Hart was no stranger to a hostage situation, but he'd never faced one alone. There was little chance of the girl surviving a second time, and Hart sighed into his rifle at the somber thought. He fixed his steady gaze on the masked man in front of him and rested his finger comfortably on the trigger.

"Don't move, or I will shoot the girl!" The man shouted in his native tongue.

Hart ignored the threat and rose from his knees in a slow, careful manner. He breathed steadily down the barrel of his gun, feeling his sweat trickle down his jaw. The man glanced back through the doorway he had come from and Hart assumed he was hoping for back up.

Without a clear shot of the assailant, Hart redirected his aim to the girl's head.

"The girl is your only protection," Hart spoke in Arabic. "You shoot her, I shoot you. Do you understand?"

"Put down your weapon, or I will shoot her!" The man shouted again, his voice splitting with fear.

Hart sighed impatiently. "Release the girl, and I will let you walk away, unharmed." He kept his voice calm. The more agitated the assailant became, the more unpredictable his behavior, and Hart still had no clear shot past the girl.

The man considered Hart's offer. "Okay."

"Okay?"

"I will let her go," he smiled, "...if you take her place."

Hart considered it for a second. A curious request from the typical belligerent assailant who rarely negotiated. Hart studied the girl through the eyepiece of his rifle and guessed she was around twelve years old. She watched him peering out from behind the bronze woman. From behind his weapon. Her big eyes weren't pleading with him like most did in these situations. She didn't cry. She didn't beg for him to save her. The girl stood ruefully in her confinement, mentally and physically defeated.

"My life for hers ... that's how you want this to go down?" Hart reiterated the proposal, carefully considering the exchange of souls.

"Yes."

The assailant's offer to trade made Hart wonder whether the man recognized him, recalling his earlier suspicions. "You know who I am, don't you?"

An unnerving excitement ignited in the assailant's eyes. "You are Phoenix!" he shouted across the courtyard. "There will be only great things for me if I bring you back alive. It is not my honor to kill you, Commander Johnny Hart."

Hart hesitated when his name rolled off the assailant's tongue.

Phoenix *was* the intended target, he thought, meaning their very presence in Libya may well be the catalyst to spark another civil war. This assault undermined everything Phoenix had striven for these past few years, which was a thought Hart struggled to wrap his mind around.

"I am not afraid to die," the assailant professed loudly, contradictory to his cowardly behavior.

Hart believed him, and now his own options were dwindling fast. He breathed out wearily as the weight of the young girl's life bore down on his honorable heart. There was no negotiating with a man who exhibited no regard for his own life.

The girl cried out when the assailant bent her backward to rack the slide of his handgun. He repositioned himself at the top of the stairs behind the girl, and pressed the barrel of the gun into the soft flesh under her chin. She cried out in the scuffle and a fateful decision was forced upon Hart. There was no doubt in his mind—the man was going to shoot her any second now.

"Okay!" Hart growled across the courtyard. *"Okay!"*

Hart pressed his lips together and stared down his rifle at the girl … and the rest of the world seemed to fall away. He saw her young, innocent eyes gazing back at him through the soft strands of hair that wisped past her eyelashes. Her future balanced on his final decision and a strange feeling cast itself over his heart and stripped him of any sentiment, as though he no longer existed.

Hart dropped the rifle from his eye and lowered it to the ground. Then he stood with his palms faced forward in the air so that the assailant could see he was defenseless. With his rifle on the ground, Hart felt more vulnerable than he ever had before.

"Now let her go," Hart ordered calmly.

The man clung to the girl.

Hart clenched his teeth together and growled. "Let her go! We made a deal!"

The man snorted arrogantly and shoved the girl down the stairs in front of him, keeping his gun trained on Hart. The girl toppled down the steps and scurried fearfully out of the court-yard somewhere behind Hart, disappearing without a single glance back. Hart watched her leave, then returned his resigned gaze to the gun that remained fixed on him.

The man's penetrating eyes selfishly lingered on him as though he'd caught a prize-winning catch that was far too marvelous to share. A deal made with the enemy didn't always go to plan, and Hart sighed in the warm air. Here he stood with no cards left to play, but he would die a thousand deaths before allowing a child to die in his place. It was his honor as a soldier. His honor as a man. Then a gentle pride gradually consumed his fear of death.

"I've changed my mind," the man sneered, readjusting his grip on his handgun.

"You shoot me, and they will kill you for it."

Hart knew the man wanted to claim his kill—too vain for his victory. It was an extraordinary moment the assailant had never anticipated, and now his impulsiveness threatened to overcome his intelligence. An unfortunate turn for Hart. He considered the handgun strapped to the calf of his combat pants, but he knew he'd be dead before he reached it.

"It is not you, specifically, that they want." The man shrugged, pulling the balaclava from his face.

A mop of shaggy black hair fell around the man's face. Hart was half expecting a smug grin to be plastered across the assailant's face, but instead, a seriousness carved itself deep into the lines of his brow. Hart could see the man was of two minds about killing him, but he didn't doubt for one second that the man wouldn't end his life right here, right then.

Hart searched his feelings, surprising himself with his lack of fear for what was to come. He could barely remember a time before the war. This moment was always around the next fucked up corner. This is how he had predicted it would end, laying on the sun-warmed ground, gazing into the desert sky … anticipating his last breath. He thought about Oliver, Walker, and Benji, and how hard they would take his death. Then he waited for the man to shoot him. He waited to leave the desert. He waited peacefully to leave the war.

An intensity swept across the man's face as he pulled the trigger. "Fucking Americans!"

Hart heard the ear-splitting sound of the bullet. It reverberated through his entire body and he waited for it to enter him and tear him away from the world, then a hole appeared in the forehead of the assailant in front of him, and the man was thrust backward through the air.

Hart blinked as he watched the man fall to the ground. Everything had slowed to a pace that left Hart progressively catching up to what was happening before him. Then he felt the air move behind him, and time sped up again. Hart spun around and dropped to the ground, pulling the handgun from its harness on his right calf. He cocked the hammer as he landed on his back with both arms raised and ready to fire at the person who stood behind him.

The man threw his arms up in the air with the gun still gripped in his right hand.

"Whoa, whoa, whoa! Hart! Don't shoot!" Oliver shouted.

"Shit Ollie!" Hart lowered his gun and dropped his head back on the hard ground in exhilarated relief.

Adrenaline raced through his veins, and Hart groaned at the sudden sensation of his blood rushing through his heart. He felt the heat of the sun still lingering in the tiles he laid back on. Consoling him. Reassuring him. He drew in a long breath of warm air, and breathed it out slowly, treasuring the sound as it left his lips. Hart gazed up into the desert sky … alive. The glow of the sun caught the tips of the columns that surrounded the courtyard, and its orange color evoked a soothing solace that calmed his racing heart.

Hart's eyes flicked to the bronze woman who leaned over him sadly. Her lifeless eyes drowning in sympathy. He breathed out in relieved exhaustion.

"Not today," he whispered to her.

"I leave you alone for fifteen minutes and look what happens," Oliver beamed, reaching his hand out to Hart.

"Shit, I thought that bullet was the one," Hart replied as Oliver pulled him up. "How long have you been standing there?"

"I arrived when he had the girl."

"Are you fucking kidding me!?" Hart replied, exasperated. "You were there all along! Why didn't you take him down?"

"Why didn't you?"

"I couldn't get a clear shot."

"Neither could I." Oliver grinned apologetically. He could see his friend was still rattled by the incident. "You are pretty convincing when you have to be, Hart. I knew you would talk him into letting her go. So I waited." He shrugged.

Hart smiled faintly and took another deep breath. He leaned over, slid his handgun securely into the holster strapped to his calf, and picked up his rifle.

Oliver patted him on the back, and Hart noticed his friend giving him the once over to see if he was okay after the near hit on his life. Oliver's gaze lingered on the wound on his leg.

"Piece of shrapnel from the missile blast," Hart told him.

"Did you get it out?"

"Yeah."

Oliver looked at him and smiled, beaming with relief and incredulity.

"Did you have to wait until he was right about to shoot me? Shit, Ollie!" Hart laughed finally.

"Honestly, I did hesitate for a moment," Oliver replied, frowning. "I mean, I expected your decision to die for her because that's the type of guy you are, but you, Hart, you almost looked ready to die."

Hart shook his head. He didn't want to think about it anymore. He wasn't ready to die. He also wasn't the type to analyze his own feelings … so he left what he thought were his final moments behind him.

"Thanks, Ollie, I owe you one," he breathed, glancing warmly at his brother-in-arms.

Hart held out his hand to Oliver, who grabbed it and pulled him in for a quick hug, ruffling up his hair as he pushed him away.

"You would do the same for me," Oliver replied, dismissing his friend's gratitude.

Oliver led him behind a wall and ducked through a large hole in the bricks at the far end of the courtyard. The two of them kept low as they hurried to the next building in the direction of the mosque.

Hart followed him around the perimeter of a small building, both scouring the area for danger as they ran. Oliver hurried ahead of him, and there, waiting in the distance and huddled against a half-crumbled wall, sat Walker and Benji. Hart sighed in relief as he and Oliver joined them.

"Hey, look who got an invite to the party!" Benji grinned.

"Good to see you, man," said Walker quietly, patting Hart as he crouched into position with them behind the wall.

Hart kneeled, wincing slightly at the pain in his upper leg. "So did I miss anything?" he asked, a playful grin sweeping across his face.

"Nope, just another day at the office," Benji joked. "Although, I did get that secretary's phone number. She was the one who got her breasts out at the Christmas party last year. I'm hoping she's going to take me to the print room and fu—"

"Benji!" Oliver interrupted without looking, peering over the wall behind them with his rifle. "Focus, Sergeant!"

Benji grinned impishly at Walker and Hart.

Hart chuckled, but mainly at Walker who sat beside him and stared at Benji with a bemused expression, shaking his head. Benji winked at Walker, playfully stirring him.

"Benji, get in touch with camp in Tripoli, we need a Hawk here ASAP," Oliver commanded, ignoring the silent banter between his team. He repositioned himself behind the wall again. "Have you received any information on what the fuck is going on here?"

"Nothing yet," Benji replied. He began to construct a small communications device in his lap.

"We need to get back to the concrete plant. Something's wrong, we should have heard from camp by now," Hart declared. The abandoned concrete plant was serving as their temporary base away from Tripoli. It was their only chance of extraction if something went horribly wrong. Like today.

Oliver contemplated what Hart said. "Their silence is not a good sign."

Another explosion shook the ground. A section of the wall about eight meters away from them crumbled, and the men glanced warily at each other but held their position.

"What the fuck are they doing out there?" Walker shouted over the commotion.

*"Phoenix … copy? I repeat, Alpha Team Phoenix, do you copy? This … Officer West on board … USS Winston … of … United States Navy."*

A deep, familiar voice buzzed through the static on Benji's radio. Benji hooted in response as he fiddled with the device until the man's voice was clear through the white noise. The soldiers waited patiently for Benji to respond.

"West! Man, are we glad to hear from you! This is Phoenix, go ahead," Benji replied.

"*U.S. Camp 21 Tripoli has been seized by a militant group yet to be identified. Do not return. There are violent clashes between the Libyan Army and the insurgents. U.S. military has been evacuated, so far no casualties. I need your location for extraction.*"

"Your timing is impeccable, as always. Sending you our coordinates now." Benji tapped in the coordinates and waited.

"*Are you ready for extraction?*"

"Yes, we are." Benji peered up at the boys, each one eager for the sweet confirmation of their exit out of this mess.

"*We are unable to evacuate you from your current position. Can you make it to the concrete plant?*"

The four soldiers discussed the route to the concrete plant; it would mean passing directly through the insurgents who currently occupied Il Liberta Square and the surrounding area.

"Port Benghazi is more ideal," Benji added.

"*Negative. The port has been closed by the Libyan Army. We've sent a Black Hawk to lift you out from the Benghazi Concrete Plant at exactly 1800 hours. Do you copy?*"

"Copy that."

Benji frowned at the men.

"*Hey, Benji boy?*"

"Yeah, man?" Benji stared at the device and waited for his friend to speak.

"*Don't be late.*"

Benji sensed a trace of humor in his voice. "You taking me on a date, Westy?" He grinned deliberately at Oliver and waited for a reaction.

Oliver rolled his eyes on cue.

The man laughed heartily down the radio. "*Parmigiana, baby! Like I promised!*"

"Ah geez, West. You know the way to my heart." Benji smiled to himself as he pulled apart the device. Another explosion rumbled the earth beneath them. "1800 hours at the concrete plant! We have a bird in the air," he shouted over the noise to the others.

"Well I'm reading 1700 hours," Walker shouted. "The plant is three and a half miles from here! We won't make it!"

"We'll only just make it if we move now," Hart added, facing Oliver.

"You really think we'll get there on time?" Oliver asked him in the sudden silence.

Hart did the math in his head. It was possible. "Yeah, I do."

Oliver nodded. "Then we better get moving, fellas. Let's do this."

The four of them beamed at each other, psyching each other up to face the action that lay ahead of them.

"Let's go home," Hart said, grinning from ear to ear.

"Back to the land of the free," Walker quipped as he transferred a handful of 40mm grenades from the front pouch of his backpack into a pocket hanging on his belt.

They smirked at his dry humor.

Oliver looked at his men. "We're going straight through the square. It's too large an area to go around. We haven't got the time to take the scenic route. You all agree?"

The soldiers looked at him and nodded. They agreed it was the only way back to the concrete plant in time for their extraction.

Oliver peered over the wall they leaned against with his rifle ready to shoot any threat approaching, but the area was free of both insurgents and civilians.

"All clear! Benji, you're on!" Oliver commanded.

"Finally some action. Time to get our dicks wet, boys," Benji smirked at Walker, who furrowed his brow disturbingly at him.

"You need to get laid as soon as possible," Walker smiled, quietly impressed by his friend's unflappable good mood. "The rest of us have good reason to worry if the bad guys are starting to turn you on."

Walker shook his head at Benji and then rolled his rifle into his peripheral vision to reload his magazine. The half-empty cartridge dropped to the dirt between his feet, and within two seconds he had replaced it with a new magazine from his belt pocket. He racked the slide at the back of his weapon and rolled the rifle back to his side, then he pulled his Beretta from its harness. Walker pressed the magazine release and replaced the mag with a new one from the pocket of his backpack in an array of hurried, precise clicks.

Benji sighed pleasurably beside him. "Fuck the enemy, Walker, you're starting to turn me on."

"Benji, you're a clown. Now get outta here!" Walker snorted, pushing him away.

Benji grinned and blew him a kiss, then swiftly jumped the wall behind them and ran toward the crumbled building positioned between them and Il Liberta Square.

All three soldiers had their rifles resting on the brick wall behind them, vigilantly scouring the area to protect Benji's exposure. Benji reached the wall of the dilapidated building. Keeping low, he scurried beneath an open window and ran along the length of the wall toward a dark, door-less entry that led into the abandoned building. Benji checked the entry for any danger, then disappeared into the building out of sight.

The men held their position and waited for his signal.

"Walker, you're up next," Oliver commanded without looking away from the telescopic barrel on his rifle.

Walker nodded and concealed himself behind the wall again and began to pull out the 40 mm grenades that he had placed in his pockets earlier. There was still no sight of Benji, and Oliver and Hart grew anxious for his safety.

"Come on Benji," Hart muttered to himself.

A few seconds later another ground-shaking explosion rumbled through the earth, a little too close for comfort. The soldiers held the wall to keep their footing, taking cover for a brief moment until the rubble settled around them. The three of them peered over the wall with their rifles and searched for Benji. The door-less entry and its adjoining wall suddenly crumbled to the ground in a cloud of dust.

"Ten seconds and we're going in after him, prepare to move," Oliver commanded.

Walker's dark eyes frantically searched the area through his scope, then Benji's dimpled grin appeared in the open window. He jumped gracefully through the window and crouched underneath it, then pointed at the boys and communicated with them through a flurry of hand signals.

"That's my boy." Hart breathed out in relief. He looked over at Walker who smiled back at him, shaking his head with a relieved, but tense, expression.

Oliver responded to Benji's signals without delay.

"No civilians. Walker, front," he ordered.

Benji ran back toward them, keeping low and out of sight. He leaped over the wall and fell into position with them again.

"Distance?" Walker asked Benji as he passed him.

"90 meters."

"Walker, indirect fire. Six rounds," Oliver ordered. "At my command."

Walker moved to a clearing in the wall that had fallen earlier in the blast. Kneeling, he effortlessly attached a grenade launcher to the bottom of his rifle. He propped it on his right shoulder and delicately adjusted the rear sight aperture with the tips of his fingers. He considered the exact angle and distance to fire the grenades in order to clear the building that obstructed the distance between them and the enemy congregated in Il Liberta Square. Walker couldn't hit his target directly, but all he needed was to pinpoint the square with the consideration of the blast radius accuracy and ammunition scatter. The afternoon was still balmy without a hint of a breeze, so he was thankful he didn't have to deal with a wind factor.

"Ready when you are, Captain," Walker shouted into the launcher.

Hart held his breath. This was it. Right now they were moderately safe. Once the grenades launched, it was time to move in on the enemy. Hart listened to the disquieting silence before each launch, never grasping if the surrounding noise disappeared, or if it paled in comparison to the madness the grenades caused.

"Fire!"

They listened as their covert attack whistled through the air toward the square. Before the grenades had reached their unsuspecting target, the four soldiers had soundlessly moved from their position behind the wall.

The soldiers followed each other in single file, darting silently around walls and through empty buildings. Exchanging wordless commands through hand signals and nods. Each as silent, agile, and dangerous as the other. An hour ago they talked about their return home to the United States, but now it was a matter of staying alive to see out the rest of today.

They heard the explosions of their grenades in the square, but the soldiers didn't trade a single glance to acknowledge it. They hurried along a narrow street lined with identical, quaint, two-story villas. Hart and Oliver skirted down one side of the street, while Walker and Benji flanked the other. They followed a long line of green front doors that opened onto a small footpath beside the road. Hart imagined it to be an upmarket neighborhood usually buzzing with life, but now it was unnervingly quiet. He could almost feel the apartments trembling with their terrified inhabitants. The street itself led toward the back of the marketplace that adjoined Il Liberta Square, and there was bound to be trouble lurking close by.

Oliver threw his hand up to the others, warning them to take heed. He slowed to step over a civilian's body, and Hart did the same. The four men exchanged concerned glances, then the door next to Walker swung open unexpectedly.

Oliver and Hart stood on the opposite side of the street and raised their rifles in readiness to fire. Walker flattened himself against the wall only centimeters from the open door. Without taking his eyes from the doorway, Walker passed his rifle back to Benji and pulled out a Strider combat knife from a zipped pocket in his pants. He gripped the closed knife in his right hand and waited patiently for someone to emerge from the apartment.

A masked man casually stepped out of the building and zipped up his pants, oblivious to the threat surrounding him. He immediately set eyes on Oliver and Hart who stood before him with their rifles in position, but were reluctant to shoot—disinclined to bare their location around the square. The assailant gasped at the sight of the two soldiers and fumbled comically for the rifle hanging loosely by his side. Walker tapped him on the shoulder, and as the man peered up in bewilderment, Walker gave him a sharp, powerful hit to the nose with the back of his elbow. He flicked the blade of the knife open as he swung it upward and sunk it into the soft flesh of the man's neck, then he silently lowered the man's quivering body to the ground. Walker scanned the dark room beside him for danger before pulling the lifeless militant back through the open door. He used the man's shirt to wipe the blood off his knife, then snapped it shut and slipped it into his back pocket. He stepped outside again and gently closed the door behind him, then he nodded to the others with an indifferent look in his eye, as though he'd innocently stopped for a cigarette.

Oliver, Hart, and Benji looked at each other blankly in the silence, grateful for Walker's deft skills, quick thinking, and utter dispassion for the enemy.

As Oliver neared the end of the street, the barrel of an automatic weapon appeared just centimeters from him behind the wall. It was aimed at Walker who stood on the opposite side of the street, and Oliver launched himself in front of the rifle, managing to deflect the barrel into the air before it could fire. He pulled the perpetrator toward him with the strap of the rifle and spun him in the soft sand that bordered the market, then Oliver pulled the rifle up under the assailant's neck so powerfully that he began to choke.

Oliver stood head-to-head with the man who was madly eye-balling the rest of the insurgents concealed behind the same wall, who, one-by-one, comprehended the altercation taking place beside them. They began to shout hysterically and their voices resounded against the walls of concrete on either side of them. When they lifted their rifles to shoot at Oliver, he turned to them with the man still in his arms so that the assailant caught a chest full of friendly fire. Oliver felt the forceful hit of each bullet that penetrated his human shield. He prayed one didn't make it through. He returned fire using the assailant's automatic rifle, killing all seven of the men before Hart gripped him by the collar of his shirt and yanked him back behind the wall again.

Oliver released the assailant, who fell from his grip like a dead-weight, landing face first and lifeless into the sand, then he ran his hands down his body to check for wounds.

"Any holes?" Hart asked, having already looked over his friend.

"Surprisingly, no."

"Good."

"Thanks, buddy!" Oliver patted Hart breathlessly on the shoulder, then bent over to catch his breath.

"You would do the same for me," Hart replied.

A wide grin swept across Hart's face, and Oliver laughed.

"We're still going to head through the marketplace to the mosque and go around the square that way. Agreed?" Hart suggested.

"The whole area is swarming with the enemy!" Walker replied, joining them on their side of the street.

"We're going to face them any way we go," Benji added beside them.

"Benji's right," Hart agreed. "We're surrounded."

"If someone gets to the Black Hawk before the others, then you keep the bird grounded until all four of us are on board. Do you hear me?" Oliver said, looking at his men. "If we are leaving Libya, then all four of us leave together."

The soldiers looked at each other with an unfamiliar seriousness and agreed. With so many insurgents and only four of them, they were bound to be separated eventually. They looked at each other with the dire hope of this ending how they hoped, but Phoenix would never go down without a fight.

Hart glanced at each one of his friends and nodded reassuringly. "Let's move, boys!"

The men dashed across the sand to a door at the back of the market. Once inside, they moved in the direction of the mosque. The insurgents' voices grew boisterously louder, becoming a collective chant in the square as though something had gone in their favor.

"What the fuck is going on?" Walker asked, ducking behind an abandoned bread stall.

"Maybe they seized Tripoli?" Hart added.

"I don't care," Oliver answered them. "We'll worry about Tripoli from the safety of our Black Hawk. I've had enough. Bad fucking timing, that's all it is. Three fucking years in the desert and this shit happens days before we go home."

The three soldiers watched Oliver stare furiously through the market ahead, his expression engrained with a steely and incensed anger. He was pissed off. Pissed with the insurgency, pissed with Abad, pissed with Taym, and pissed with the USSOCOM for not letting them return home months ago as they were promised.

Amid the riotous noise of the square, a masked man emerged undetected a few meters in front of the soldiers, startling them with a shot that split the air between them. He grinned down the barrel of his gun, but before he had the chance to fire again, Walker shot him dead.

"What the…! How did you do that?" Benji asked, stunned by Walker's speed and precision.

"What do you mean? I just shot him," he replied frankly, pointing at the dead assailant with the tip of his rifle.

"Yeah, but no one even saw him!"

"Am I quicker than you now… *Swift?*" Walker jested, laughing at Benji, who rolled his eyes.

More men appeared from between the stalls further in front of them and began shooting at the soldiers.

"What about them?" Benji yelled, hiding behind a stand of newspapers.

More shots ripped through the air, and tattered newspaper fluttered through the air like confetti. Benji ducked for cover, hiding his head in his arms in the deadly chaos. Walker watched him protectively through the rainfall of newspapers. When the gunfire slowed, Walker leaned over the bread stand behind him and started shooting the assailants one by one. Oliver and Hart kneeled beside him and did the same.

As the soldiers fought their way through the marketplace, the inevitable transpired; Phoenix's united front had split. Hart stood alone at the entry to the mosque. He looked back for the others, panting with exhaustion, and instinctively he went back for his friends.

He only got a few meters before he was grabbed around the neck from behind. His assailant pulled him off his feet, and Hart gasped for air as he was dragged backward through a doorway into the mosque. He felt the blood pound nauseatingly in his head, and he reached hopelessly at the person whose arms wrapped around his throat. They passed a gathering of masked men, who immediately dropped what they were doing and followed him through the mosque … his trail of incompetence. Hart growled to himself in frustration. He fought to free himself, but with the insurgents in tow, his retaliation was repaid with a few brutal kicks to the ribs. Without oxygen, the task to free himself seemed impossible, then, without warning, Hart felt the crashing pain of his head being slammed against the concrete. The last thing he saw before he lost consciousness was Taym's complacent grin staring down at him.

3



Hart blinked his eyes open. He managed to regain his bearings quickly, the mumble of voices pulling him from the darkness.

A gentle voice lulled over his pounding head, "Let Hart return home safely, you know how much we've all been looking forward to going home. Including yourself."

"Pity he is not awake to witness your heroism. Hart has no part in this—Abad, leave him!" Taym ordered. "Now hand me your gun, Ollie."

Oliver gave up his weapon. "Why are you doing this?"

"Why!? See, you never gave a shit, Ollie!" Taym chided. "This treachery has been in the making for ten years and you still have no idea what my motive is! You are a fucking disappointment."

Before moving, Hart opened his eyes the merest crack and scanned the mosque's lavish yard and all its occupants. The far end of the courtyard opened onto the street, which appeared to be empty. Abad was standing a few meters away with his back to him. He stood between two masked men, and all three of them had their handguns hanging by their side. Through Abad's legs, Hart saw Oliver with a gun pressed to his temple, his own gun—held there by Taym.

Revenge entwined itself eternally around his heart.

Gunfire outside the mosque proved that Walker and Benji were still putting up a fight. Phoenix still possessed some degree of control, Hart thought. Not all hope was lost.

"An eye for an eye, you know how it goes," Taym taunted.

Hart heard Taym cock the hammer on Oliver's handgun.

"Sweet dreams, Ollie."

Hart was quick to react. He pulled the handgun that was strapped to his calf and while he lay on his side on the concrete, he fired a shot through the legs of Abad, hitting Taym in the knee before he got the chance to shoot Oliver.

Hart shot the man to the left of Abad, and caught a glimpse of Oliver who had promptly reacted to his unexpected recovery. Oliver snatched his gun from Taym's grip, then he turned and shot the second militant who had turned to aim at Hart. The man collapsed on the concrete just meters from Hart, who sprung to his feet.

Hart fixed his gun on Abad, who shuffled anxiously between the fallen men, uncertain whether to help his brother or kill the men who had become his closest friends. Before Abad could decide, Hart appeared behind him and pressed his gun into the back of his neck, forcing Abad to freeze in the commotion.

Taym crumbled in agony to the ground with his shattered knee. He peered at his leg and growled at Oliver through his teeth. Pieces of bone sat in small pools of blood around him on the concrete, nearly sizzling in the residual heat from the sun.

Taym growled into the sky with enraged frustration, "Oliver!"

"It is over, Taym," Oliver panted. He pressed the tip of the gun firmly between Taym's eyes.

"Stop!" Abad called out suddenly. "Ollie, please!"

Oliver glanced at Abad, and in his hesitation, Taym launched off the ground with a small, concealed pocket knife and buried it into Oliver's stomach. Oliver roared in pain and ripped Taym's arm away, feeling the blade slide out of his flesh. He kept a firm hold on Taym's arm, then he pulled the knife toward him again and snapped Taym's elbow against his knee. Oliver released Taym and watched him slump forward on the concrete again with a gut-wrenching groan.

Taym gasped against the ground, but something soon caught his attention. Oliver and Taym paused, detecting the quick-paced fight between Abad and Hart in the near distance. Abad had the advantage, given Hart's leg wound, and within seconds Abad had him in a headlock, with his handgun pressed to the back of Hart's neck.

Taym took the fleeting opportunity to reclaim the advantage over Oliver, who was now distracted by Hart's predicament. Taym reached for the handgun he had concealed in his combat pants and aimed it at Oliver, who simultaneously directed his gun back at him in their second lethal standoff.

Taym kneeled on the ground in front of him, and Oliver acknowledged the gun in his hands. He narrowed his eyes at Taym. Then, without warning, Oliver shifted his aim to Abad and shot him straight through the back of the head before he was able to kill Hart.

"No, Abad!" Taym's gruff voice growled through the dry, desert air.

Taym watched his brother's lifeless body land with a sickening smack against the ground. He kept his shaking gun fixed on Oliver's chest and gasped breathlessly in his misery.

At that moment, a jeep pulled up outside the courtyard and a group of masked men jumped off. They quickly positioned themselves along the edge of the courtyard in an orderly manner, then aimed their rifles at Oliver and Hart and waited for Taym's command.

Hart panted and turned around. He saw Taym kneeling on the ground with his gun aimed at Oliver, but Oliver's gun was aimed at Abad. Hart glanced down at Abad's body. It took him just seconds to realize that Oliver had chosen to shoot Abad instead of defending himself, and his heart sunk gravely through his soul.

The two soldiers stared knowingly at each other across the courtyard of the mosque. They were significantly outnumbered. Home had never seemed so far out of reach.

"Drop your fucking weapon, Oliver!" Taym spluttered, visibly shaken by Abad's death. "Drop it and get down on the fucking ground!"

Oliver raised his hands into the air and released his gun so that it swung upside down on his finger, and it hung there until one of the insurgents took it from him.

"Get down on the ground!" Taym commanded fiercely.

A masked man helped Taym to his feet as he watched his former commanding officer turn around and lower himself gently to the ground.

Oliver laid on his stomach. He pressed his cheek into the warm concrete and gazed soundlessly at Hart who stood underneath a magnificent orange sky. Then Oliver smiled peacefully at him.

Taym shuffled his broken body awkwardly to Oliver. His snapped elbow swung loosely by his side, and he groaned hideously as he moved. Taym leaned down and pressed the tip of his gun into Oliver's temple and moaned through his teeth, either in pain or fevered excitement. Both, Hart assumed. Taym looked up at Hart and smiled wickedly, cementing a solid foundation of hatred between them.

Oliver saw the sudden anguish in Hart's expression across the courtyard. His desperation. His helplessness. He saw Hart's chest rising and falling with his panicked breath, frantically searching his intelligence for a way out of this calamity. For the first time—they were defenseless. Powerless. This was the end, but Oliver smiled reassuringly at his friend. He remembered the time they met in the desert of Arizona, both eighteen years old with their whole lives ahead of them. He had warmed to Hart instantly when they met. He knew at that moment what the past fifteen years had only confirmed; they were brothers-in-arms and brothers for life. Unbreakable. *Inseparable.* Until Taym fired his gun.

"No!" Hart exhaled sharply. Oliver's crystal, blue eyes closed before him. *"No, Ollie!"*

Hart's breath quickened uncontrollably, panting fiercely through his clenched teeth. Taym signaled his men to shoot Hart, and so he closed his eyes and prayed for his end so that he could leave this world with his best friend. But his prayers were denied. Walker and Benji appeared from behind him and fired at the insurgents, killing three instantly and sending the rest cowering for shelter in the jeep, along with Taym. They sped away in a red cloud of dust which hung in the air and cast a rich, auburn glow over the sun, and as the dust settled lazily on the ground in the sudden silence…the world fell still in mourning under the orange, setting sky.

Hart dropped to his knees and bowed over Oliver's lifeless body. Walker and Benji kneeled down on either side of Hart, both breathless and in utter disbelief.

Oliver was never going home.

# PART TWO

## - CALIFORNIA -

*"One does not become enlightened by imagining figures of light,*
*but by making the darkness conscious."*

Carl Jung

1875 - 1961

*Chapter 2*


# - SAN DIEGO -
## July 2014


"Ivy, open your eyes."

Ivy drifted back to where she was and blinked her eyes open. The sunlight filtered through the tears that still lingered on her lashes, dazzling the darkness behind her eyes with its spectral glow. She squinted through the light at the palm trees towering over her in the bright-blue sky. She listened to their glossy leaves rustling gently above her. She heard the slow, rhythmic lapping of the ocean waves against the sand. She breathed in the salty air and smiled, then closed her eyes again. In the distance she could hear the squabble of seagulls, opportunistic creatures, no doubt mobbing a perfect, unsuspecting picnic on this beautiful afternoon. She smiled at the thought, and it warmed her soul. Soothing sounds of serenity. A thousand memories of a lazy, beach-side life. Familiar and calming.

Her fingers caressed the soft towel underneath her on the sand as she peacefully rediscovered the beauty that surrounded her. Never forgotten, but temporarily overlooked in grief. It was time. The world beckoned her to return, and in the tranquil silence of this moment, the message was loud and clear. It had been too long, and she was ready to be set free once again.

Ivy sat up and took in her surroundings. It was beautiful. The air was warm, and the ocean lay before her like smooth, deep blue glass stretching to the horizon. People walked in and out of the water with gratitude after a long, hot day ... a refreshing tonic for an exhausted spirit. A light mist climbed the tree-covered ridge that surrounded the bay, and the sun fell toward the horizon with a bright, golden halo, the same way it always did on these balmy, summer afternoons. Ivy gazed into the sky. The sunset would be spectacular tonight.

Taking in a deep breath, Ivy closed her eyes again and breathed out the fear that clouded her heart. This is how she remembered the world. Before Oliver left it. It was still peaceful and breathtaking. The world had not changed—she had.

"How are you feeling?"

Ivy's eyes sprung open in surprise. She turned to her friend who knelt patiently beside her with a warm smile and her hands resting in her lap.

"Helena," she answered.

"You forgot I was here, didn't you?"

"I did, sorry." Ivy smiled meekly.

"Don't apologize. That's a good sign, believe me," Helena replied. A bright grin swept across her face. "I'll take it as a compliment."

"You should. I feel different ... clearer ... *happier.*" Ivy bit her lip. "Thank you."

Ivy rested her hand on Helena's and gazed thoughtfully at her friend. She had to admit, she had the courage to face the world again, but Oliver's cheerful grin remained resolutely in her thoughts. An irrevocable memory that lingered torturously in her mind. One day she hoped she could return his smile.

"I think you may have listened to me this time," Helena observed her friend carefully, and then smiled to herself. "Plus you didn't fall asleep."

Ivy pushed her brother out of her thoughts.

"No, I didn't fall asleep," she replied, blushing. "I guess it is more effective if I stay awake."

"It helps!" Helena laughed. "You are sleeping again, though. I didn't hear you get up once these past few nights. Maybe that's why?" She grabbed her water bottle and her cell and began packing away her belongings into her brushed cotton beach bag.

Ivy smiled at Helena in response, but it quickly faded as she considered it. She didn't realize she had been sleeping again. Since Oliver died, she had come to endure a grueling, nightly routine fleeting between the labyrinth of her cruel nightmares and the painful, awakened reality of losing her brother. Sleep was an unbearable torture, as though losing him wasn't enough. Tragedy had always defined Ivy, but she refused to let it destroy her. She nurtured a willingness to appreciate the natural world around her. The serene scene before her was the unvarying constant in her life. Sure, the ocean lay impassive to her heartbreak, but it was inexplicably consoling. This is where she would find sanctuary from her grief once again, in the simple, ancient beauty of a complex, modern world.

Ivy rubbed her palms along the smooth skin on her thighs and peered up the beach toward the cliffs. She took a deep breath and slowly filled her lungs with the warm, afternoon air, then she exhaled and smiled cheerfully to herself.

She turned to Helena. "Sure you don't want to stay one more night in La Mar?" Ivy asked, drenching her crystal eyes with foolish hope.

"Oh, Ivy," she frowned. "Don't tempt me!"

"I know, I know. Work. James. Big city life. I understand." Ivy thought about Helena's new job in Las Vegas, the one she had to put on hold so she could come here.

Helena looked at Ivy. A sad concern lingered in her expression. "I would stay if I thought you couldn't make it on your own, but I know you, Ives. Better than anyone. You'll be fine. You always are."

With a small, convincing smile, Ivy nodded her head. "I will be fine."

"Now, I'm going to head back to the house. Are you coming?" Helena asked, standing with all her things.

"Yes. You have a long drive, and I don't want you leaving too late." Ivy reached out her hand so Helena could pull her up.

Helena was gorgeous, in an animated kind of way. Like a cartoonist scribbled out a life-size drawing into the air and Helena magically appeared. Her eyes were big and dark and too large for her face, but it brought every expression of hers to life. She had a button nose and sweetheart lips, and jet black hair that hung on a sharp angle only inches below her ears. It was a style

Ivy could never pull off, and she envied the way Helena executed the look so effortlessly.

Helena was also smart, fearless, and rather brash. Never one to shy away from confrontation, she loved a good argument. She had a cynical tongue and a savvy personality, and a confidence that encouraged her to pack her bags and move from sleepy La Mar, to study law at Harvard University on the opposite side of the country. Helena wore her skeptical heart with pride and allowed it to steer her through the convolutions of life in the fast lane. A disbelieving mind was essential for Harvard Law, and for survival, so she liked to think.

With an almost identical upbringing to Ivy's, the life-long friends couldn't be more contradictory in nature. Ivy inspired Helena to make peace with her more vulnerable side—the part of her that didn't trust the world she lived in. Helena grew up watching Ivy interact with the natural environment as though it were created just for her. As though Ivy owned the forests, and the oceans, and all the creatures within them. Her friend possessed a strength that disregarded everything Helena thought she knew about life. Ivy had lost everyone, and still her spirit was indomitable. It was something Helena didn't have, an indomitable spirit.

Helena's crossroads literally had come to her when her truck broke down at a four-way intersection in the Nevada Desert on her journey back to Harvard. This mechanical failure came after a soul-searching summer spent with Ivy on the coast of California. She didn't plan to search her soul, it just happened. Ivy had that kind of effect on people. Helena thought she had acquired some immunity to her friend's enchantment after all these years, but apparently not.

Two men stopped to help her that day at the crossroads. One offered to tow her a few miles further along the highway to a local mechanic, and the second man offered to lead her off the highway to Las Vegas to visit a different mechanic. The men played no part in her decision; it was her soul that seemed to be digging its heels into the highway, reluctant to go forth into the known. With less deliberation than she expected, Helena chose the second option and left the highway for Vegas. A turn no one saw coming. Least of all, Ivy. That year, Helena quit law to study meditation and self-help in a renowned school in Las

Vegas, and she released a successful book one year later. It was a summer that changed her life, and Helena understood then that she would forever be in awe of Ivy's *magic.*

Ivy ran her slender fingers through her long, wavy hair, and flicked it all over to one side. Helena looked on enviously. She wished for hair like Ivy's. In fact, everything about Ivy created a similar stir among the women in town. Ivy was the quintessential American sweetheart. Young and gorgeous with a heartwarming smile that engaged her entire body from the inside out. She had cherry-red lips and flawless skin, and her eyes were a pale crystalline blue framed with dark lashes. Ivy was reasonably tall with long legs that were always beautifully tanned from her bare feet all the way up to her lean thighs and cut-off denim shorts. But it was her hair that seemed to catch everyone's attention. Her golden, sun-bleached locks cascaded down the entire length of her back in soft waves that fell weightlessly around her and shimmered brilliantly in the sunshine. People would stop on the street and wait for her to pass them, momentarily seized by her beauty. Ivy was not entirely oblivious to the effect she had on those around her, but she found the attention discomfiting. She discovered at a young age that men worshiped her, and women undeservedly despised her.

Ivy threw on a white dress she plucked from her beach bag, and the two friends strolled barefoot into town.

"Helena, do you mind if we swing by the boutique? I should check on the girls and see how everything is going."

"Oh, please do. Can I shop without money?" Helena sparkled with excitement.

"Of course! Take whatever you want."

Helena shrieked happily.

Ivy owned a small boutique in town which offered her very own line of organic skin care. All of her products were one hundred percent natural, and with every product she sold, she gave a substantial part of the profit back to charity. It was more a hobby than a source of income; her family had great wealth, but they were also dedicated humanitarians. After her parents had died, Ivy threw herself wholeheartedly into the idea of a philanthropic business that bore no burden on the world, and as a result, ALCHEMY was born on the main street of La Mar.

Ivy opened the glass door and a sweet chime announced her arrival. Helena followed her in. The shop itself had whitewashed timber flooring with three surrounding walls stacked to the ceiling with white shelves. Each wall had a tall, white ladder that slid along a track on the ground making even the highest shelves accessible. Quaint, tan glass bottles lined the shelves, each filled with her concoction of oils, salt scrubs, and balms. Luxurious potions for the mega-rich, a status of clientele that La Mar certainly was not short of.

Central to the room stood her counter, along with a laptop, scented candle, and always a vase of fresh flowers hand-delivered by her many satisfied clients. The boutique was small and intimate and smelled like lavender and bergamot.

"Oh my, it smells divine in here," Helena breathed.

Ivy looked back at Helena who stood by the door with her eyes closed. Lost in a tranquil state of bliss.

"There are no free products on the door mat," Ivy said, smiling.

Helena's eyes shot open, eager to start shopping.

"Ivy?" A young, fresh-faced girl in a white apron peered up suddenly from behind the computer. She had her hair tied into a scruffy bun on the top of her head with long, wispy strands that sweetly framed her heart-shaped face. She slid off the stool to her feet and rushed over to Ivy. "What are you doing here?"

"Hey, Casey, how are you?" Ivy replied. She tucked a lock of hair nervously behind her ear—she hadn't seen Casey since her brother died.

Ivy held her breath and glanced fleetingly at Helena.

"Oh my God! I am so sorry about Oliver. He was beautiful, and so full of ... *life* ... and now he's gone, just like that!" Casey embraced Ivy. "Are you coping?" She pressed her hands theatrically into her chest and waited with a somber, open-mouthed expression for Ivy to speak.

"Coping?" Ivy repeated.

She quietly contemplated the meaning of the word. Coping suggested she was managing her grief. It signified some kind of control over her feelings so that she could accomplish the more straightforward tasks in life, like eating, for instance. She wasn't eating. Her emotions were in a state of constant anarchy, selfcontrol fleeing at the first sign of weakness. Every wakeful minute moved by at an agonizingly slow pace, and then Ivy realized she had been surviving each minute by foolishly convincing herself that the next might be an Oliver-free one, if only she tried hard enough. That wasn't really coping, was it?

Helena's hand glided reassuringly down the back of her arm, and Ivy glanced up at her. Her expression softened with empathy.

"Yes," Ivy replied with a sweet smile. "I'm coping … just."

"Oh, you're incredible! I would be a complete wreck! Miserable. I can't even put my head there….."

Ivy tilted her head and watched Casey speak. She was so innocent. So guileless. So untouched by tragedy. So *unjaded*. Ivy smiled to herself. She had been that way, once.

" … my friends would have to drag me out of bed and convince me to carry on with life! Force me to get dressed, to eat, and take a shower. I don't know how you do it." She shook her head and stared pitifully at Ivy. "How do you do it, Ives?"

"Well," Ivy took a deep breath, "I have this beautiful girl by my side." She threw her arm around Helena's shoulders and gave her a grateful kiss on the cheek. Helena beamed in the attention. "Casey, this is Helena. An old friend."

Helena shook Casey's hand. "Pleased to meet you."

"Pleased to meet you, too," Casey replied, watching Helena with suspicious eyes. "Old friend, huh? Not as old as the friends you usually like to keep. How old are you, Helena? Like, twenty-eight?"

"I think she meant that we have known each other for a *very long time*," Helena answered, exaggeratedly clear.

"No, I know. I'm just teasing Ivy," Casey replied. She winked at Ivy and walked back to the counter. "I haven't seen her hang out with anyone in town much younger than seventy."

"Hey, don't say that!" Ivy narrowed her eyes and glanced behind her at the door, concerned someone might overhear them talking. "They're not seventy. They're more like … late fifties."

Casey rolled her eyes. "Relax, no one will hear us."

"Oh, I know what you mean," Helena replied, matter-of-factly. "No girls our age like Ivy. They never have."

Casey smirked at Ivy. "See!"

A small smile twisted on Ivy's face. "I'm sure they liked me at some point?"

"Oh please!" Helena threw her hands into the air to dismiss the old news and began shuffling through a shelf of salt scrubs. "Remember in the fifth grade and that girl, you know, the ugly bitch who had no friends…."

Helena stopped sifting through the bottles to look at Ivy. She had a wicked grin that anticipated Ivy's disapproval, and she waited for Ivy to shake her head before she continued.

"…yeah, you know exactly who I'm talking about," Helena smirked. "She told you that you were far too pretty and God likes balance, and so one day you would be uglier than a horse's ass."

"That one has stuck with me through the years," Ivy laughed sweetly.

Helena shrugged. "Now you know why she had no friends."

"It honestly made me worry. I was so young, I believed her."

"A horse's ass?" Casey repeated as she re-tied the bun on the top of her head. "I had a horse when I was a kid, and it had a beautiful ass."

Ivy burst out laughing.

Casey glanced sincerely at Ivy. "What? I'm serious."

Helena frowned. "You're missing the point."

"Oh, did she mean the horse's actual," Casey stopped talking and made a circle with her fingers, then screwed up her face in disgust.

Helena hit her forehead with the palm of her hand, and Ivy laughed again.

"Girls don't like Ivy," Helena added frankly. She placed another bottle down on the counter rather firmly. "They never have, they never will. She is too good to be true."

"Well, I like you, Ives."

"Thanks, Casey," Ivy replied, amused. There, she thought, a minute passed without any piece of him.

"Men *really* like you Ivy," Casey added.

"Okay, let's move on," she blushed. "Let's talk about business—"

"Tommy came in looking for you again," Casey interrupted.

"Tommy?" Ivy frowned. "He knows I haven't been in here

for months."

Helena grinned, "Yet here you are."

Ivy stared at her friend as she thought about it.

"You know he's head over heels in love with you. *Tommy*," Helena spat out his name distastefully.

"What's wrong with Tommy?" Casey asked, smiling. "I think he's cute."

Ivy pressed her finger to her lips. "Hush, I swear he can hear us. He always shows up when we talk about him. It's so weird."

"And now *you* are weird." Helena frowned unpleasantly at Ivy. "You're starting to worry me."

"That's not weird, it's creepy," Casey replied, slightly afraid.

Helena glared at Casey. "Stop encouraging her."

The girls stood around the counter and stared soundlessly at each other, anticipating Tommy's arrival any second … and when the door chimed loudly in the silence, Helena yelped in fright.

"Ivy Rose," a woman's voice spoke eloquently from behind them.

Ivy's heartbeat slowed down in relief, and she turned around. "Amy."

Amy sighed dramatically and glanced at her friend beside her with an exasperated expression that confused Ivy. She looked displeased. Provoked. Like it was unreasonable that Ivy should even be here.

"I'm sorry, I didn't realize you were here," Amy responded eventually.

"It's no problem," Ivy replied.

Amy stared at her for a few moments, then peered past Ivy to speak to Casey. "We'll come back later." The two women turned around and headed for the door again.

Ivy raised her eyebrows at Helena, who rolled her eyes.

"Amy, I have everything here ready to go," Casey called out.

Amy paused reluctantly with her hand on the door handle, then she spun around on the spot with a forced smile and headed back to the counter, brushing past Ivy to collect her purchase.

Ivy stepped politely out of the way.

Casey leaned into the cupboard below the computer and

pulled out a brown paper bag and handed it to Amy. "The receipt is in the bag."

"I wouldn't have come if I had known you were here," Amy said, glancing uneasily at Ivy.

"Why are you doing this to yourself?" Ivy asked. "It's been seven years." The weariness in her tone didn't go unnoticed by the others.

She saw Amy wince in the memory. Amy had barely had a chance to date Oliver because he only had a few months leave at the time. Ivy remembered the night they broke up; Amy was hysterical, she didn't want it to end. She had fallen madly in love with Oliver, but her love was unrequited. Amy was determined for a fight that night and Ivy had never seen her brother so angry. The sound of his aggravated voice, thundering down the hallway, sadly stuck with her throughout the years.

Ivy sighed inwardly at the memory. It saddened her more so now than ever before. It was a peculiar emotion—to feel protective of someone who no longer needed your protection. She didn't know how to shake that one. Maybe it would never go away?

Only one girl ever captured Ollie's whole heart, and her family moved her across the country when they were just seventeen. Ivy understood her brother. He flourished in female attention. He was never short of women in the few months he had between deployments. He was a natural charmer, but he never loved any of them like he had loved the one that got away. Oliver didn't have it in him to settle for anything less. Then Amy moved into town and things suddenly changed. She was mysterious, like most outsiders who moved into a small town like La Mar. Oliver was smitten, but it didn't take long for Ivy to realize that Amy had one, discouraging resemblance to the rest of the women in town. The same disgruntled envy all his past flings had shown; Ivy had Oliver's unconditional love. Oliver detested any jealousy toward his younger sister, especially after their parents died, and Amy hated her. Loathed her. No matter how hard Ivy tried to please her, Amy clung to her jealousy right up until the day Oliver left her. Her heartbreak weighed heavily on Ivy's shoulders ever since, and Amy was determined to keep it that way.

"Just seeing you makes me feel wretched again," Amy muttered.

Ivy exhaled sharply.

"Amy!" Helena scorned.

"No, you don't understand! You remind me so much of him. Your eyes, your skin, your smile," Amy explained. "I see him when I look at you and I still can't believe he's gone."

Ivy lost her breath. *Gone....*

Her heart skipped a few panicked beats, and she grew faint in the unsteadiness. Each person's grief was her undoing. Ivy relived the reality of his death each time someone else cried. This is why she avoided town.

Ivy breathed herself through the pain.

Amy wiped a small tear away from her cheek with her manicured nails. Her friend rubbed her back with sympathy, and Amy flicked her a shadow of a smile.

"You must miss him terribly," Amy said. She looked up at Ivy through her tears.

Ivy bowed her head and closed her eyes tightly. No words came to her.

"Anyhow," Amy added, as if discarding her grief with a simple flick of her hair. "I will see you tomorrow evening at the Annual Silver Moon Gala. I have written a check for one hundred thousand dollars for the charity you picked."

Ivy just looked at her.

"Oh, and I wondered—did you choose the charity before or after Oliver died?" Amy asked blandly.

Ivy sighed. "Before."

"Hmm. It's funny how the world works sometimes." Amy stared at her in thought.

"I thought about changing it in light of everything that has happened, but I couldn't do it," Ivy mentioned. "They need the support." She breathed out sadly and ran her fingers despondently through her long hair.

"The way I see it is that all things happen for a reason," Helena said, standing by Ivy. "You chose the charity because it is close to your heart, even more so now because you lost Oliver. I think tomorrow night will be a huge night for you, Ives."

"It will be for me," Amy added. "I plan on getting hammered. I need to drown this grieving heart in a bottle of Bollinger."

Helena furrowed her brow at Amy. "I don't mean *huge* as in getting wasted. I mean therapeutic," Helena responded. "The world stole something from you, Ivy, and I feel like tomorrow night at the gala…it will give you something back."

Amy scoffed.

"What?" Helena glanced impatiently at her.

"So the rumors are true then." Amy turned to Helena.

"What rumor?"

"You gave up Harvard Law to preach the principles of life." Amy smirked. "Bold move."

"I don't preach."

"Well, it sounds like you're preaching."

"If I were preaching, I'd be looking at you, Amy!" Helena replied. "But I wouldn't waste my breath…they are lost words on your empty soul."

Ivy opened her mouth to speak, but Amy raised her hand.

"No, it's okay, Ivy," Amy stopped her before she started, "we have to go anyhow. I'll see you tomorrow night."

The girls waited for Amy and her friend to leave, then all three of them turned to each other and breathed out a collective sigh of relief.

"What did Oliver ever see in her?" Helena shook her head, genuinely perplexed.

Ivy shook her head and grinned, amused by it all.

"She had *great* boobs," Casey replied, indifferent to the encounter with Amy. "I'm serious. I could barely take my eyes off them."

Ivy and Helena studied Casey's detached expression, then they glanced at each other and laughed. Unjaded Casey. She was right. Oliver was the kindest, brightest, and most thoughtful man Ivy ever knew, but he was still just that … a man.

Helena and Ivy left shortly after and reminisced about their time together as they walked home, enjoying the warmth of the sunshine on their tanned, salty skin. Summer was well and truly upon them, and it brought a blissful cheer along with it through the orchestra of insects and the tiny birds that twittered above them in the trees.

Ivy ran her hand along a lavender hedge that bordered a rock wall on the gentle climb back to her house at the top of the hill. She loved the feeling of them tickling her palm. She picked a few of the purple flowers and dusted the petals across her top lip, sniffing their soothing fragrance and dissolving her grief. She tapped in a code at the front gate, and the two of them waited for the large, iron entry to crank open, like a draw bridge descending from its castle.

"I still can't believe you live here. You have this enormous, extravagant estate all to yourself," Helena said, staring ahead of her in admiration.

"I know. I love it here."

"I can help you go house shopping," Helena offered.

Ivy glanced at her as though she were mad.

"To get something smaller," Helena explained. "It would be so much fun because you could buy anything you want, Ives— shit, you are loaded! If I were you, I would sell this one and buy smaller properties all over the world." Helena's eyes glimmered at the prospect.

"What? No. I couldn't leave this place. This is my home, all my sweetest memories are here." Ivy gazed nostalgically toward the house.

Helena frowned. "Don't the memories make you sad?"

"Sometimes ... but the memories also keep them alive."

Ivy peered fondly down the driveway toward her family home. Large trees lined the length of the driveway, their leaves gracefully floating to the ground as the friends ambled back to the house. Her home was a luxurious, sprawling estate perched on a cliff above one of the most secluded shorelines in San Diego's northern suburbs. It had a stone stairwell carved into the side of the cliff that led down to a stretch of sand and rock pools. With cliffs on either side of the beach, the shore was exclusively hers. Inaccessible by the rest of the world.

The home itself was designed by her father, who instantly fell in love with the seaside town during a visit to the Marine Corps in San Diego. What was supposed to be a one-night stopover resulted in an elaborate nine-bedroom, twelve-bathroom estate, overlooking the endless azure of the Pacific Ocean.

Her parents had loved it here. They had entertained guests all the time, and Ivy had discovered great comfort in the sound of their parties. Her father had imported a large glass orb from a renowned Australian artist based in Indonesia. It had been her father's favorite piece on the estate, and in the wake of his death, the orb became one of her most treasured belongings. The glass sculpture was built into the foundation of the home, which meant if she ever moved, her father's orb would have to stay. The orb was shaped like a coconut and sat nestled into the grass at the base of the palm trees growing next to the pool. Besides being a sculpture, the piece doubled as a lamp. As a child, Ivy found it fascinating. It responded to touch, and the light would take on different shades depending on how long she lay her hand on it. Oliver and Ivy spent a lot of their childhood lying on their backs in the grass with their feet resting on the glass on warm summer nights, unwrapping dessert chocolates they had stolen from their parents' dinner parties. They loved to lie there and listen to their parents' voices over the music and the laughter, and for as long as they rested their feet against the orb, it would cycle continuously from dark to light, and back again, and they would gaze contentedly together into the starry night sky. Happy and complete.

The gardens were lush and green and perfectly manicured thanks to the aging gardener, Alejandro. He had turned eighty last year, and his labor had slowed, but he found peace in the garden, and Ivy didn't have the heart to fire him. His knowledge of botanical life was rather impressive, and Ivy loved to listen to him. So he was here to stay. The backyard had a twenty-five meter lap pool, and at the end of it lay a dense, luxuriant, green wall of tropical trees and vines that bordered the north edge of the property. The wall of plants cascaded down to the pool, and the tips of the leaves swayed dreamily on the water's surface. Between the pool and the cliff there was a circular stacked-stone fire-pit that had breathtaking views of the ocean, and this is where she spent almost every sunset. Alone.

When they reached the house, Helena paused to inspect her white, 1970's Dodge parked near the fountain which was encircled by the driveway.

"Wow, my car looks like a heap of crap parked out the front

of your place," Helena joked.

"The Dodge? I love your car," Ivy responded affectionately.

"Me, too," she agreed.

"But you know it's a heap of crap out the front of anyone's place."

Helena laughed at the truth.

"There is no way I would have pulled through without you." Ivy gave her a big hug. "Thank you, Helena, for everything."

"Should we make this a quick goodbye?" Helena asked with a sad smile.

"Very quick. I'll still cry," Ivy laughed through the lump in her throat.

"I'll miss you," Helena spoke through her tears.

"I'll miss you, too."

The two friends separated in silence, choking on their sadness and unable to speak. They looked wordlessly at each other and then laughed at their inability to keep it together.

Helena threw her beach bag and towel carelessly through the open window of her Dodge and climbed into the driver's seat. She revved the old car to life and pulled a twisted face at Ivy when the engine threatened to surrender to its old age.

"Runs like a dream," Helena called out sarcastically. She raised her eyebrows and twisted her face as she putted past Ivy.

"You sure you're going to make it back to Vegas?" Ivy asked, concerned. "You broke down once before!"

"And look how that turned out!" Helena laughed and blew a kiss to Ivy. "I'll call you when I get home!"

"If you don't, I'll worry! Drive safe! Thanks again!"

She waved until the Dodge slowly bumped its way off the end of the driveway and disappeared down the street with a few happy honks of the horn.

Ivy stood there for a minute in the silence.

"Alone again," she whispered to herself. She peered into the sky. The sun was setting.

Ivy raced up the steps behind her and hurried inside. She slid her beach bag across the floor of the entry hall and ran toward the kitchen. The hall looked like a small ballroom to Ivy, elegantly framed with two staircases that curved up to the second floor on either side of her. She ran underneath them to a door that led into the kitchen. Once in the kitchen, Ivy scooted around the island bench to the refrigerator and pulled out a cold bottle of chardonnay from Sonoma Valley. Her favorite. The orange-colored sunlight blazed into the kitchen through windows that framed a wall-sized view of the ocean. She reached up into the cupboard for a wine glass, then rushed to the glass doors that opened onto the pool and the back of the estate. Ivy slid the doors wide open to let the sunset in and hurried down the white marble steps and past the pool to the cliff.

She saw the sun setting on the horizon when she reached the fire-pit. The sky burned a brilliant orange above her, and the air was still, and it was warm, and the ocean rolled calmly below her. She breathed a long breath of salty air…and relaxed.

Ivy sat on one of the benches that faced the ocean and poured herself a glass of chardonnay. She sipped the cold wine and watched the sunset dance on the deep-blue water before her. Then she spoke softly to the sunset.

"Hey…," Ivy bit her lip and gazed into the sunset, "… so I'm going to talk to you as though you are there, just like you said you would be, in the orange sky, remember?"

Ivy smiled nervously and took a deep breath. She looked around her instinctively. She knew she was all alone, but even she felt ridiculous talking to the sky.

She took another sip of wine, bowed her head in thought, and then glanced up at the orange sky again. "So tomorrow night is the Silver Moon Gala. It looks like I'll be going alone…again. Tommy asked me. You know he does every year, but I don't want to encourage the poor guy. I think he's hoping one year I'll just get tired of saying no. We all know what he's like when he wants something," she smiled beautifully into the sky. "I just wish it wasn't me," her voice faded.

Ivy gazed wistfully into the sunset and thought about Oliver; wondering if he was really there, listening to her gentle voice drift off the cliff and across the ocean to him in the orange sky. Ivy felt the last of the sun's warmth against her face, and she tried to find comfort in it. Refuge for her breaking heart. She ran her fingers back through her long hair and exhaled a slow, controlled breath through her pursed lips.

*"God, I miss you, Ollie,"* she whispered.

Her heart crumbled. Ivy fought back her tears and took another sip of wine. The sharp, cold chardonnay soothed her tight throat. She breathed in deeply and bit her quivering lip, and then she gazed back at the sea with glistening eyes that reflected the burning ocean.

"Oh, Ollie," Ivy smiled through her tears, quickly wiping them away as they fell, "I'm trying to be strong without you but look at me, I'm a mess," she laughed at herself. "I know I shouldn't talk to you like this because it hurts so much, but I just … I…." her voice broke before she finished. Her strength shattered. She shook her head and peacefully ran her thumb through the condensation around the outside of her wine glass. Oliver really was gone.

Ivy looked back to the house. It was so quiet. So still. There was nothing but an empty home full of sweet memories of an entirely different life. She had nothing left. She had no one.

"You promised I would never be alone," she whispered, searching the sky.

The last of the sun sunk soundlessly below the horizon. A flock of terns flew silently past in the distance. They were beautiful, as always. She drew in a long, sad breath, then drained the rest of her glass and sat it beside her. She pulled her knees up to her chest and wrapped her arms tightly around them, and thought of Oliver's promise to her all those years ago; *Ivy, if I die, then look into the orange sky, and I will be standing there. You will never be alone. I promise.*

Her breath shook as it left her lips, "I've never felt more alone in my life."

A cool breeze rose over the cliff and kissed her cheeks, stealing the sun's warmth, and so Ivy buried her face into her arms and cried underneath the setting sky.

## Chapter 3

# - FORT BRAGG, NORTH CAROLINA -
## July 2014

"You'll be fine, Johnny. What's the one thing I need you to do for me?" she asked with a prim, British accent.

"Keep quiet if the shit starts to hit the fan," Hart replied, without looking at her.

"Good. Because it will." She sighed heavily. "I've been in meetings all week with these men, and it isn't pretty, believe me."

"Commander Johnny Hart and Doctor Hannah Arnett, the board is ready to see you now."

An expressionless woman dressed in a black suit and sky-high heels directed Hart and the military's clinical psychologist through an office door and into a narrow boardroom with a long, mahogany table running the length of the room. Around the far end of the table sat twelve representatives for USSOCOM, including General Bob Garvey at the head, one of the highest ranking officers at Command. It was his idea to create Alpha-team Phoenix, using four of the best soldiers in the United States military. He had hand-picked these men himself from across the country. Phoenix was his pride and joy. A loyal force to be reckoned with. When the unit proved itself to be an invaluable asset to the United States, Garvey had earned himself instant recognition as one of the most distinguished leaders within the military, and he couldn't be any prouder of his men. He had three beautiful daughters with his wife, all who were much older now and had left home. They had spent years trying for a fourth child, desperate for a baby boy, but it was never meant to be. He had rounded up the Phoenix men just a couple of years out of their teens, and hence Garvey had developed a close bond with the boys. Oliver, Hart, Walker, and Benji became the sons he never had.

He had a worn, downcast expression today as he watched one of his finest soldiers enter the room. Hart gave him a quick nod of acknowledgment, and General Garvey managed a warm smile in return.

"Take a seat here," the woman ordered. She laid one finger on the empty chair sitting at the opposite end of the table to General Garvey and the representatives.

Hart did what he was told.

"Doctor Arnett, please take a seat with the rest of the board. Thank you."

The woman walked to the door behind Hart and waited for two heavily built security guards to enter the room. They positioned themselves on either side of the door with crossed arms and cold expressions that declared they were callous, merciless savages, should anyone decide to step out of line.

Hart noticed the sudden shift of attention from himself to the door, so he turned in his chair to look behind him. He faced the boardroom again with a poker-faced facade, contrary to how he felt about their demoralizing presence. Hart silently deliberated what stood behind him, but more so, *why* they stood behind him.

He shot Hannah a perplexed look, and she quickly averted her attention to her seat at the other end of the room. She squeezed her way along the left-hand side of the table, passing by eight empty chairs, then pulled out a chair beside one of the representatives. She sat down and opened her notebook. She pulled her platinum-blonde hair back into a tight bun, and with a quick click of her pen, she looked up at Hart who sat on his own, watching her intently.

Her heart skipped in the steady gaze of his warm, brown eyes. He would never admit it, but she could tell he was nervous. She smiled reassuringly at him, and without taking his eyes from her, Hart flicked her a small smile in return. Hannah bowed her head into her notes to conceal her blushing cheeks; God forbid she gives herself away while sitting in the presence of the

General. She was sure she could feel his authoritative gaze on her, and she nibbled the tip of her pen in the discomfiting silence. Johnny Hart was more than just handsome; he was gracious and admirable, and incredibly selfless. Hannah promised herself not to analyze her feelings for him—quite the challenge for a psychologist who had a bothersome tendency to overanalyze everything in her life. She loved Hart, but she loved him as a friend more than anything. At least, this is what she told herself since his return two months ago. Ethically it was wrong to feel attracted to her patient, but it was something she had learned long ago to disguise. Hannah was too professional to ruin her career, or her friendship with Hart.

She glanced at him again while she waited for the debriefing to begin. His head was bowed, and he stared at his hands in his lap. He looked lonely and anxious sitting by himself at the end of the table, and her heart went out to him. Hannah considered going back to sit beside him, but the room's eyes were on her, so she wisely remained seated.

General Garvey spoke first.

"We are here today for the third and final debriefing of Assistant Detachment Commander John Hart," Garvey spoke in a low, gentle voice as he read out his notes. "I take it you are all now very familiar with the nature of the betrayal within Phoenix, specifically with Taym Malak and Abad Malak. Abad Malak now deceased, killed in action by Commanding Officer Oliver Rose. Oliver Rose also killed in action by Taym Malak."

Garvey glanced briefly at Hart, then continued.

"Taym is still at large. We believe he is currently located in the Misrata District in Libya. Mr. Crawley, I assume these findings are still correct?" Garvey casually looked up from his notes and over the top of his reading glasses to a young man sitting on his left. He waited patiently for confirmation.

"Uh, affirmative. Taym Malak was last seen making his way through the Misrata District only yesterday," he pronounced. "We believe he is on his way back to Tripoli to bathe in his victory. We aim to have a Special Forces team standing by in Tripoli over the next few months to apprehend him and hold him accountable for the death of Commander Rose."

Hart sighed. He grew anxious at the thought of seeing Taym

again, but he longed for the meeting.

The man nodded proudly at Garvey when he finished talking. Hart guessed he was an intelligence analyst or administrative officer of some sort. He looked too fresh-faced and enthusiastic to be of any higher ranking.

General Garvey was staring at the young man with a deadpan expression, as though he required a more informative reply, and Crawley began to twitch nervously under Garvey's intimidating gaze.

Hart smiled to himself.

"Uh, uh, also…." the young man stammered and flicked aimlessly through his notes.

Garvey raised an eyebrow at him.

"…unfortunately, the last positive confirmation of Taym Malak was, uh … the 15th of May, and therefore we cannot verify that the man we are following is actually Taym Malak."

The board erupted into a disgruntled mumble of voices.

Hart took a long, deep breath. Adrenaline burned excruciatingly in his veins as the world, once again, weighed down on his shoulders. His reprieve from the relentless grief of losing his best friend lay in the apprehension of Oliver's killer. There was only one, clear path forward that Hart considered for his future, and that was to find Taym and bring him to justice. But now Taym walked freely as a worshiped leader amongst the underbelly of Libya, while Hart stood perpetually bound to the shameful guilt of being alive when Oliver wasn't. Forever burdened by the culpability for his best friend's death—and his unyielding hatred for Taym. It festered within him like a black hole that gradually consumed his soul, but he didn't care. He longed for the eternal darkness. Revenge kept him going. It was all he had thought about since Oliver gave his life for him. Now Taym had slipped through their fingers, and Hart was furious.

"But that was two days after we lost the commander of Phoenix," a woman added.

"Yes, you are correct, ma'am," Crawley sniffed awkwardly.

"I'm sorry, so you're saying you *lost* Taym Malak almost eight weeks ago? Who the fuck have you been following since then?" A silver-haired man scoffed ludicrously across the table from Hannah.

Hart glared at Crawley and hoped for a more informative answer than ones he had given so far. The boardroom didn't respond well to his sheepish demeanor; in fact, no one stopped talking to hear his reply.

"We ... we do have reliable sources, which ensure it is, most likely, Taym Malak," he mumbled.

No one paid any attention to him. Except Hart. Each word from this man resonated deep within him. He caught Hart staring at him with a somewhat tranquil fury, and Crawley nervously buried his eyes back into his clutter of papers.

"Okay, okay, settle down!" Garvey's deep voice ordered control over the boardroom. The board took a while to calm down, and when they did, the General spoke again, "It seems Taym Malak has escaped our watchful eye for now, but we have more pressing matters at hand with the increase of clashes within Libya. This militia group not only set their sights upon our very own commanding officer, but intelligence has now advised us that the group intends to spread this destruction far beyond Libya's borders. The United States, no surprise, being their number ... one ... target."

General Garvey threw his notes on the table and leaned back into his chair. He pulled his reading glasses off and put one of the arms into his mouth and glanced at each representative around the boardroom table with a serious, contemplating expression.

With no response, Garvey continued without his notes, "We need more people on the ground. Without our presence, the Libyan government fears the insurgents will seize even more than they have already acquired. They need assistance. They need our men on the ground."

"Have you lost your mind? It is too dangerous!" The silverhaired man declared again. "We put our troops back on the ground, and we may as well be throwing them straight into the fire!"

Hart vaguely recognized this man from the news these past few weeks. If he remembered correctly, he represented the White House and the President himself. Richard Hanes, he recalled.

General Garvey didn't respond.

"May I remind you, this terrorist organization has spoken publicly and demanded an immediate assassination on any known

U.S. representative within Libya," Hanes continued. "In the past few weeks, there have been six assassinations of Libyan Army officials. Officials that *our* Special Forces trained personally. If we put our troops in there, the group will retaliate."

"He's right. We should wait," a woman added. "There was talk of the United Nations intervening."

"They're retaliating either way. If the UN goes in, then we're going in," said a self-assured man with a Texan accent. Until now, he had been sitting calmly at General Garvey's right hand.

Hart had fought beside this man once in Afghanistan. His name was Damien Derulo, nicknamed Diamonds because he had remained uninjured for the entire length of his fifteen-year service. Not even the slightest graze to his skin. He was scratch-resistant right up until he became wounded in Afghanistan after his vehicle hit an improvised explosive device at a narrow point on the road. The wheel triggered a massive explosion, and Damien spent months in rehabilitation learning to walk again, but his nickname seemed to stick no matter. His knowledge and expertise proved invaluable to the military, and now he assisted men like Garvey who hadn't served in active duty for quite some time.

Damien was a resilient, gutsy soldier who despised people's trepidation. He indulged in the adrenaline of combat, and he found it difficult to settle into the quiet life now that he was out of action. Damien's thrills solely revolved around his friends' heroic tales when they returned home from service. It was evident to him that Hart wanted to avenge his fallen comrade because he would want the same. So he made it his priority to get Hart back to Libya … back to hunt down Taym Malak.

"No. Our intervention is not an option," Hanes disagreed, indifferent to anyone's opinion.

"Actually, Richard, it is an option, and that's why we're here today. Phoenix knows what they're doing. Libya is their playground, and we need to decide if we're ready to drop our boys off to play," Damien stated, winking at Hart.

Hart was stunned. This was exactly what he wanted. He glanced excitedly at Hannah who was watching him, waiting for his stupid, eager anticipation to return to the war. She had told him it was highly unlikely that he would return to Libya, not after everything he had been through. Now here they were, arguing over the decision to send him back to fight. He saw her shake her head in quiet disapproval.

Hart's eyes flicked back and forth between the representatives at the other end of the table who bitterly debated his future.

"We're here to continue with Commander Hart's debriefing, not talk about starting a God damn war!" Hanes protested.

"Are you keeping up with the conversation, old man?" Damien replied, brazenly. "We all know what went down with Phoenix in Benghazi, and now we're deciding whether or not to rally our troops and—"

Hanes cut in. "The President will not allow—"

"The President!?" Damien overruled the interruption. "You're playing the President card already? How about you listen to what we're trying to propose before you go throwing your President bullshit across the fucking table! God damn ass kisser."

"Language, gentlemen, please," Hannah interjected, rolling her eyes.

"Fuck you, you little dipshit!" Hanes shouted at Derulo. "Where did you get this kid from, Garvey? Are these the kind of people you have advising you these days? Shit, no wonder everything's spiraling out of control around here!" Hanes slammed his pen down on his notepad and glared at Damien.

Hart watched Hannah sigh and lean her head on her hands, rather unimpressed by the unfolding events. Hart, on the other hand, still had a spectacular chance of returning to Libya. He was thrilled. His heart pounded along with the fast pace of their heated conversation.

"Alright, Mr. Hanes. That's enough," Garvey spoke gently.

"All I'm saying is that the President wouldn't approve!"

"Approve of what exactly?" Damien glared at Hanes. "You're shutting us down before we've even had a chance to deliver our proposal. This is why we're still sitting here, arguing like a bunch of women!"

"Excuse me!?" Hannah interrupted abruptly. "I would like to point out that the women in this boardroom are the *only* ones who are not arguing. Those types of derogatory comments are for cavemen, Mr. Derulo. I suggest you leave your chauvinistic tongue on the asphalt outside the building before you next decide to enter it and offend the professional women at this table, or any other woman for that matter. It's called evolution, *Diamonds,* jump on board before you get left behind."

General Garvey slowly shifted his gaze from Hannah to Damien. A trace of humor lingered in his tired eyes, and Hart knew Garvey couldn't wait for Damien's response. Hart chuckled to himself. He admired Hannah's fearlessness as she sat at a table filled with the most esteemed men in the country, although their behavior would suggest otherwise.

"I sincerely apologize, Doctor Arnett. I meant no personal attack on women. My frustration got the better of me. Please forgive me," he relented in his southern accent. He glanced sheepishly at the women around the table. "I am truly sorry if I offended you."

When the debate picked up where it left off, Hannah squinted at Damien with a wicked twinkle in her eye. He stifled a subtle grin in return.

There were only a handful of people who knew they were sleeping together. In the boardroom, she managed to keep him on his toes, but in the bedroom, he kept her on hers. Hart detected the insatiable hunger in Damien's eyes during his apology, all thanks to Benji. Hart had heard all about these two over the past few weeks. Benji knew everything there was to know about anyone worth knowing at Base. He had been gone for three years, but in two months he had acquired all the gossip at Fort Bragg.

"Thank you, Mr. Derulo, for the light entertainment this morning, but now we need to get down to business." Garvey gave Damien a stern look to pull his behavior back into line. Damien lowered his eyes to his unopened notebook.

"I appreciate everyone's feedback, but last night, after considerable deliberation, we came to the agreement that Phoenix may be deployed back to Libya as early as next week. For now, they will act as the requested U.S. presence during this conflict, and their first mission is to locate Taym Malak and bring him to justice for his treachery against the United States of America," Garvey announced.

The room erupted with loud protest from several of the representatives.

Hart was elated. He tried his hardest not to give away his excitement, keeping himself calm and composed at his end of the table. He couldn't wait to tell Walker and Benji the good news. None of them expected they would return to Libya so soon. If they wanted to find Taym, then time was of the essence.

Garvey understood Hart's motive. He glanced around the room, satisfied with the stir he had created among the representatives. He met Hart's watchful eyes with a serious, rather grave expression, and he gave him a slight nod. A silent command.

The subtle exchange went unnoticed by the rest of the boardroom, and Hart understood what Garvey asked of him. The General wanted Taym Malak *dead*. Hart narrowed his eyes. There it was—his permission to kill. The thirst for blood unfurled within him like a sweet, black smoke. The darkness entombed his tormented heart, slowly and seductively, and he surrendered himself to its cold fury. The road ahead would be traveled without seeing, driven blindly by his hatred through the blackest of nights until he found his revenge, until he found his peace in Taym's dying breath.

Hart nodded to the General.

"You can't send him back!" Hannah protested. "He has been through a severe psychological trauma, and he needs time to recover! Why didn't you inform me of this decision prior to the meeting?"

Hart glared at her, but she purposefully ignored him.

"I'm sorry, Doctor Arnett, the last two debriefing sessions have concluded that Commander Johnny Hart is fit for active duty," Garvey answered.

"Quite the contrary, General Garvey," she declared, outraged. "How can you say this after what we spoke about earlier? He is not ready!" Hannah glanced worriedly at Hart.

Hart was baffled by her reaction. Frustrated by her unexpected tenacity to keep him from fighting. He wanted to go back. He *needed* to go back, so Oliver's death was not in vain.

The voices shouting across the table were growing louder, and Hart struggled to hear himself think.

"I am ready!" he shouted. Hart stood up at his end of the table and leaned his fists on the desk in readiness. "Send me back. I want to fight!"

The boardroom fell quiet.

Hannah saw the genuine hope in his brown eyes. He was shaking with anticipation, and she noted the unmistakable desperation in his body language that answered a question which had lingered on her lips for weeks. One question that was pivotal in her assessment of his trauma. One question she had yet to ask because the answer was so important—and so final. *Did he feel responsible for Oliver's death?*

Hannah already knew the answer. She saw it in the angst that drenched Hart's pleading eyes. Her heart plummeted into the pages of her notes. His future lay in their hands, and he would have to convince all of them that it was the right decision to send him back. Emotionally, Hart had been through hell and back, yet here he was, pleading for his right to return and avenge his best friend. Hart wanted Taym so badly, and it hurt her to watch him suffer like this, but she knew killing Taym wouldn't help him move past Oliver's death. He didn't understand the severity of what he was suffering. He needed time. Time away from this volatile environment.

"I am ready," he repeated. His voice was calm and reassuring. "Send Phoenix back to Libya, sir. You will not be disappointed. I promise."

"You can't go back, you only have half your team," Hanes answered.

The board looked at Hart with sympathy. Except for Hanes, who wore a patronizing grin to belittle him instead.

"What does that matter?" Hart replied. "You have no idea what we have accomplished in the past with only three of us. We have never failed to deliver. You all know how good we are."

"I agree," General Garvey praised. "These men are of the highest physical and mental caliber. Yes, they are a man down, but the loss of Oliver Rose has affected their high spirits, not their renowned capabilities. What we need in Libya, right now, is Phoenix. This is what we've trained them for."

Damien nodded enthusiastically beside him.

Hanes snorted in denial. "Right now they're weak! Damn right they never fail to deliver … they delivered us their *dead* commander!"

Hart exhaled sharply and bowed his head. He bit hard on his

bottom lip until it bled, forcing himself not to strike back and lose Libya for good. He glanced at Hannah, who considered him carefully. She seemed unusually calm, but Hart knew her better than that—Hannah wasn't blinking. He swore he heard her screaming at him from across the boardroom with her sweet, decorous, British accent, imploring him to keep quiet ... *the shit is most definitely hitting the fan!*

"We failed because we were betrayed by one of our own," Hart's voice was quiet. It hurt him to say it out loud, and it didn't escape Hannah's attention. "We can do this. Just give us another chance to prove ourselves."

"I think we should hand it over to another team," Hanes replied.

There were a few solemn nods of agreement around the table.

Hart shook his head, his eyes wide with disbelief.

"I believe so, too," Hannah gazed sadly at Hart. "I'm sorry, Commander Hart."

"I agree with Doctor Arnett," another woman spoke up.

One by one, the rest of the representatives, aside from Garvey and Derulo, agreed with Hanes.

Hart breathed himself through the sudden shift in his future and questioned how the table had turned on him so quickly. Hart glanced disappointingly at Hannah before looking to General Garvey for his support, but Garvey remained silent with a weary, thinking expression.

Hanes looked at Garvey. "Another team will be just as good."

Garvey considered what he said, but he didn't answer.

"How can you say that? No one knows Libya like we do," Hart added. He spoke directly to Hanes. "We possess invaluable knowledge of the cities, the towns, the people, the local army— and the enemy! Phoenix lives and breathes Libya! What do you think we've been doing over there for the past three years? Scratching our asses?"

Hanes frowned angrily.

"Why are you even here?" Hart asked. He looked at the General without waiting for an answer. "Why is he here?"

Garvey sighed to himself, and Hart frowned curiously in response. If he didn't know any better, he'd say Garvey was under pressure from the President himself. It was only a debriefing, but Hart was positive the President made sure his little lap-dog was here to relate to him, precisely, what went down. Hanes was the only one putting up a fight against Phoenix's return to Libya, against him. Without Hanes, Hart would be sharing the good news with Walker and Benji right about now. He didn't take well to the man's sneering attitude. No one did.

Hanes laughed derisively at Hart. "Do you talk to all your superiors in this tone?"

Hart shoved his chair away in anger. The security guards moved behind him, but he stood resolutely in his place, anticipating their overzealous attack.

"Whoa, at ease, soldier!" Hanes snorted.

"Don't speak to me like that," Hart said coolly. He glanced at the security guards as he retrieved his chair and sat down again.

"Johnny's right," Damien interjected, glaring at Hanes. "I can't sit here any longer and not defend our boy here. Everything you say is fucking offensive!"

Hart glanced at Damien, grateful for his presence in the boardroom. Hart noticed Garvey roll his eyes, but he didn't stop Damien talking.

"This man right here," Damien leaned forward and pointed at Hart at the other end of the table, "puts his *life* at risk every day and every night, so you can sleep, eat, drink, and take a God damn shit in the freedom of this country. He lost his Captain fighting for you. Fighting for your partner. Fighting for your children. Fighting for *our* America. You should be on your knees thanking him and not treating him like he's a worthless piece of shit, you fucking...."

"Mr. Derulo!" General Garvey warned.

All eyes in the boardroom considered the shattered soldier at the end of their table. Damien's loutish explanation still managed to provoke an unexpected, mutual gratitude throughout the representatives.

Hart didn't look at anyone while Damien spoke; it was difficult for him to accept praise when it came to his role in Phoenix. He bowed his head and thought about Ollie. Hart felt defeated. He stared at his hands in his lap and watched anxiously as they began to tremble. He had no control over it. It was something he was learning to live with these past few weeks. Along with everything else that had suddenly altered in his life. The tremor shuddered violently through the depths of his soul, and he could hear it on his shaking breath. Hart pressed his lips together to stop it. He groaned lightly to himself and closed his eyes. Oliver was dead, and it was all his fault. Now they were taking Libya from him. Taking Taym.

Hart clenched his trembling hands into tight fists, took a deep breath, and suppressed the weakness that tried to claim him. He lifted his eyes and met Hannah's worried gaze.

"Where's your respect for these soldiers who fight for your America?" Damien added.

"My respect!?" Hanes scoffed. "The fucking nerve—"

"Gentlemen, enough!" Hannah shouted.

Before the meeting, she had taken Garvey aside and warned him that today's debriefing was not in Hart's best interest. He was too vulnerable in the wake of Oliver's death, and Hannah was concerned the meeting might cause him more harm by exposing him to unnecessary conflict, including the petty bickering among the boardroom. More importantly, she had yet to inform Hart of his condition.

"Look, Phoenix is a mess," Hanes stated plainly. "The fact is, you have only two elite soldiers left in the unit. This one here is suffering post-traumatic stress disorder and doesn't even realize it. He's a hazard…."

Hannah glared at Hanes.

"…it is too risky!" he continued, ignoring her. "We'd be putting Sergeant Walker and Sergeant Swift in danger by sending them to the front line with this soldier here who has his Stars'n'Stripes flying at half-fucking-mast."

Hart stood up furiously at the end of the table.

"Mr. Hanes!" Hannah protested. She despised the White House man's insolent behavior.

Hannah glanced behind Hart at the guards. She noted their restlessness. They were itching to take Hart down, while they still maintained some degree of control over him. She had learned that it wasn't so much Hart's size that intimidated men with insufferable egos, it was his laid-back sagacity that seemed to unsettle them. The extraordinary strength in his composure…

up until now, she thought.

Hannah looked back at Hart. She saw his eyes boring holes into the back of Hanes's head. She imagined his blood boiling with rage, and Hannah could almost feel the heat radiating from his body.

"You know what, fuck you!" Hart declared. His eyes darkened with rage. "I don't have to sit here and listen to your bullshit!"

"Commander Hart is right," Hannah added in his defense. She glared at Hanes across the table.

"Then leave!" Hanes sneered. "It's much easier to talk about you when you're not in the room. Come on, Garvey, dismiss the soldier and let us move on." He raised his eyebrows at Garvey, who had been quietly considering everyone's point of view.

"Mr. Hanes, I think we all have a clear understanding of your thoughts regarding this matter," Garvey stated. "I would appreciate your silence from this point forward, so I can consider what the rest of the board has decided."

"Of course," Hanes replied, complacently.

"It pains me to say this, but I have to agree with Mr. Hanes," said a young man beside Hannah. The entire board turned their attention to him, including Hart. "I understand why Commander Hart should go back to Libya, but after listening to Doctor Arnett talk at the last debriefing, I still believe he is not ready to return. I'm very sorry, Commander." He shrugged apologetically at Hart.

Garvey nodded in response, giving nothing away.

Hart leaned on the table and bowed his head, expecting the worst. He stared coldly at the table between his hands, as one by one, he listened to the board vote against his return to Libya.

Hannah felt sick to her stomach. It was horrible for her to witness his pain. Returning to Libya meant everything to him. These soldiers were her friends. She knew their dreams, their plans, and their fears. It broke her heart to witness it all come crashing down around him at such a critical time in his life. She could see the muscles ripple in his arms as he leaned on the end of the table, his fury pulsing through them with every beat of his enraged heart. His strength was incredible, and Hannah couldn't help but marvel at him. Any other man would have given in to defeat and left the room, but not Hart. Hart possessed a deeper kind of power. He had a strong, unwavering heart that beat fiercely for what he believed. Somewhere inside of him was a source of strength that he managed to tap into when he really needed it. Like today. As a psychologist, Hannah found it remarkable to witness him in action like this. Here he stood, literally trembling, begging to return to the source of his nightmares. For years she had tried to get this kind of emotion out of him, but for years he just smiled kindly at her and told her he was fine. Hart was determined to get to Oliver's killer, and she knew he would find him eventually—to finish what Taym started.

"Well, it seems the boardroom has come to a unanimous decision." General Garvey demanded attention with his deep voice. "Phoenix will not be returning to Libya."

Hanes nodded in delighted agreement.

"*No,*" Hart breathed in disbelief.

General Garvey stood and placed his reading glasses into his chest pocket. He regarded Hart with a disheartened frown. "I'm sorry, Johnny."

It had been a long four weeks. The General couldn't bear Hart's imploring gaze any longer. He wanted to send him back; for Libya, for Taym, for Oliver, for his own peace of mind. Taym needed to pay for his betrayal. Every part of the mission would be executed proficiently and without error if they positioned Hart in Libya. Commander Hart was still the best soldier they had … but the decision was no longer his.

"We will have a break," Garvey ordered. "The meeting will resume in fifteen minutes without Commander Hart."

The people around the table began to gather their belongings.

"No." Hart's gentle voice broke the quiet scuffle in the room.

Everyone stopped.

"General, you have to let us fight, please. It's all we do. Send us back. You have to send me back," Hart pleaded. He pushed his chair away and began to make his way toward the other end of the table.

The General didn't reply. He examined Hart as he shuffled around the table to get closer to him. To convince him to have faith in him still. Garvey frowned. The son he'd never had … he had already lost one.

"Sir—" Hart started.

"Johnny, please," Hannah interrupted, concerned he would make things worse for himself.

"No, you don't understand," Hart exclaimed. He shuffled behind the empty chairs toward the representatives who were still huddled at the other end of the room.

The two oversized guards caught his eye.

"What are you doing?" Hart asked. He glanced at the guards innocently, curious as to why they were shadowing him, but they didn't answer.

The woman nearest Hart grew tense as he drew closer. She was still in her seat, and smiling curiously beside her was Hanes. The two of them subtly slid their seats closer to the younger man who sat on the other side of Hanes, nervous of Hart's approach.

"Johnny," Hannah said again, but Hart ignored her.

"Commander Hart, please take your seat," General Garvey ordered.

Hart stopped immediately at the General's order. He took a deep breath and rubbed his jaw, then he sighed resignedly into his hand and turned back toward his seat at the far end of the table.

"Relax soldier," Hanes called out, "use the time off to take a holiday."

General Garvey rolled his eyes.

"You!" Hart growled, pointing a finger at Hanes, who began to flick through his papers without purpose.

"What?" he shrugged. He glanced around the room with a forced smile.

Hart sensed his fear.

"This is all your doing!" Hart shouted. "What the fuck kind of representative are you anyhow? I know the President. I've met him, and he's an intelligent man. It makes me wonder why he's got a spineless jerk like you working under precarious conditions such as these." Hart moved swiftly up the right side of the table toward Hanes, who was now shielding himself with the woman sitting beside him.

Hannah gasped. "Commander!"

"Precarious?" Hanes questioned.

"Yeah, precarious!" Hart repeated with a mocking smile. "Because you've successfully pissed off a highly trained killer!"

Hannah mouthed the word *killer* to herself, before she looked up at Hart who was now across the table from her. He was striding toward Hanes, who panicked and fumbled his way out of his chair.

"Johnny!" Hannah called out in vain. She glanced at the General who had no intention of stopping him.

"Security!?" Hanes cried out. His voice broke in its peculiarly high pitch. "Don't just fucking stand there!"

One of the guards wrapped his arms around Hart's shoulders before he reached Hanes. With a few swift strokes, Hart had the man pinned against the wall behind him, and the room fell silent. When Hart turned away from the guard, the boardroom watched in stunned silence as the guard's eyes glazed over and he slid down the wall, unconscious. He hit the floor with a heavy thud, and the room suddenly broke out in a fearful commotion.

"Hart! Please stop!" Hannah shouted over the chaos.

Hart knocked away the grasping hands of the second security guard. He reached past the woman for Hanes as she howled in terror beneath him. Hart grabbed Hanes roughly by the collar, and then the guard threw himself on top of Hart. Sensing their fall, Hart rolled the woman's chair away from underneath them with his foot; then they crashed onto the surface of the table where she had been sitting a moment ago.

The woman escaped the altercation unharmed, but Hart didn't notice. The guard pressed him into the table and lay down on him with all his weight—one hundred and forty kilograms of it. Hart breathed laboriously into the timber under the weight, and he had no choice but to let go of Hanes. He growled as the dress shirt slipped out of his fingers, and Hanes's ashen face disappeared from Hart's view.

Hanes sighed in relief and flattened his tie against his chest. He peered around the room with a brazen smile that proved his insolence.

The guard managed to secure one of Hart's wrists with handcuffs, but Hart continued to resist. There was no way he was letting Hanes leave this room untouched by his torment. Hart gritted his teeth, seething with hatred. For Hanes. For Taym. Then the darkness finally consumed him. The black smoke twisted its way through his soul, and he felt a dark creature emerge from it with wings and sharp claws, and it curled itself around his pounding heart, and his heart began to bleed. *Oh Oliver.* Hart's cheek throbbed against the solid timber. His friend lay down beside him and pressed his cheek into the concrete, and looked at him. Hart grunted when he heard the bullet. It sucked the air right out of him, and he groaned into the table, wincing at the pain that gripped his bleeding heart.

Through the darkness he heard Hannah's voice calling out his name, begging him to stop, but he couldn't. He didn't want to. Hart growled fiercely. He pushed himself up from the table under the weight of the security guard. When he was high enough, Hart flipped himself over on the table and kicked the guard away from him into the wall. The guard came for him again, but the back of the chair that Hart had kicked into the air caught the guard under his chin, sending the man crashing to the floor.

Hart no longer felt the tremble in his hands, or the violent shudder that coursed through his veins. He didn't feel the suffering or the grief that he had succumbed to these past couple of months. There was no pain when he fought back. There was nothing but his immeasurable hatred for Taym.

Hannah couldn't believe what was happening. This wasn't Hart. The security guards pulled themselves up from the floor and made their way back toward him, but they were too late— Hart had already reached Hanes again. Hart swung his arm back and delivered a powerful strike to Hanes' right eye, sending him spiraling onto the boardroom table.

Hannah gasped in shock with the rest of the representatives. Hart fell back against the wall in exhaustion and Hannah studied him amidst the chaos. He'd gone easy on Hanes, and it gave her the smallest reassurance that he was still in there, somewhere.

Damien slid across the table and positioned himself between Hart and Hanes to suspend any further conflict. The security guards managed to pull themselves to their feet to salvage what little dignity they had left, and they launched themselves at Hart and bent him over the table again with an exaggerated aggression, payback for their humiliation. They bore down on

Hart with their combined weight, nervous of his strength, and he panted into the table's surface without resisting his arrest.

Hannah sighed into her shaking hands. Hanes had it coming, but she could never condone Hart's actions. The security guards hoisted Hart off the table, and the bigger of the two locked his arm around Hart's neck. Hart's head tilted back awkwardly in the guard's arm. She saw his chest heaving, exhausted both mentally and physically. Hart met her gaze from across the table, and his anger instantly softened into shattered repent. A tear rolled unexpectedly down her cheek, and she brushed it away in surprise. Hannah tried to mask her distress but she was too late—Hart had seen her. The room seemed to pause in his apologetic gaze. Hart whispered a soundless *sorry* to her before they ushered him out of the room in his handcuffs.

Hannah exhaled loudly, quickly wiping away another tear. Tears of shock. Tears of fear. Tears of compassion. She wasn't sure why they came, but it was Hart's reaction to her tears that made her want to sit back down and cry hopelessly into her notes. Hart knew he had failed her. He had failed himself. Now he had failed Oliver, *again*.

~

"It's only twelve months," she said softly.

Hart didn't respond. His exhaustion from the past few weeks had finally caught up with him.

"They're sending Walker and Benji with you," she added.

Still no response.

Hannah looked down at her unopened notebook, which sat in her lap and began to tap her pen idly on its surface to break the silence between them.

Hart sat on the edge of the black leather chaise in her office, facing Hannah in the chair opposite him. He leaned forward with his elbows on his knees and his head bowed into his hands as he stared impassively at the dark gray carpet between his boots. Her office was hot and muggy. The fan that whirred tiredly at its highest speed in the far corner of the room offered little relief. He listened to the summer storm that thundered through their silence. The rain against the window. Hart tried to remember the last time he had seen the rain.

"You were lucky," she said.

He laughed quietly to himself at how absurd her comment sounded. Hart rubbed his jaw pensively, as he always did when he was lost for words. He looked up into her penetrating green eyes, and she gave him a weak smile.

"I got your attention at least," she teased.

Hart smiled at her. He knew she was worried about him, but her attempts to lift his spirits were rather futile. Hannah had been there for ten years now, and she was well accustomed to the detrimental effects the war had on even the most resilient of human minds. Hannah was right about most things—but he knew he wasn't lucky.

"What is it I have again?" Hart asked, without looking at her.

"Post-traumatic stress disorder."

Hart smiled to himself, shook his head, and gazed out the window. The rain cascaded down the glass, and he wanted to go out there, to feel the rain against his skin.

"What is it?" she asked.

He frowned. "See, that doesn't sit right with me. Maybe I don't? Maybe I'm just dealing with his death like everyone else would if they lost their best friend? Why label it? Is it because I'm a soldier?"

"Johnny, what you witnessed was inconceivable. For anyone! No one should ever have to go through what you have. Not only do you suffer the loss of a friend, but you suffer the way he died," Hannah breathed.

She swallowed, louder than she'd intended. Hannah glanced at Hart, but he didn't seem to have noticed. Her emotions were getting the better of her once again. In all her time at Fort Bragg, she had never come across a soldier more broken than Hart, yet so resilient at the same time. She picked up the notebook and placed it on the lamp table beside her, then she studied Hart carefully.

"I can deal with death. I see it every day," Hart said without emotion.

"No, it is not the same. Those people weren't Oliver."

Hart glanced uneasily at her and rubbed his forehead.

"Post-traumatic stress disorder, I admit, can be difficult to diagnose," she explained, "but I have been a clinical psychologist for the United States military for over ten years; I am more than familiar with the signs. You can try and hide it from me, Johnny, but I can see the defeat in your eyes."

Hart sighed. He had difficulty accepting anything was wrong with him. He was feeling tired, but then he had attended countless meetings and debriefings since his return from Libya two months ago. There had been little time even to consider moving past Oliver's death. He didn't want to, anyway. His suffering was the fuel that kept him going. His grief paved the way back to Taym. Without it, Taym would get away with everything. Everything he had planned for the past ten years since Oliver took Taym under his wing, where he schemed Ollie's death and the destruction of Phoenix. Hart didn't want anyone's support; he wanted revenge. He had fire in his blood—and he liked it.

"Look, you may not feel different, but your mind is coping with a significant, psychological trauma and your body will soon follow suit. If it hasn't already," Hannah explained.

Hart looked up at her knowing gaze and sighed into his hands.

"If we don't take the necessary precautions and do what is best for you now, then your health will take a turn for the worst. We all want you back here doing what you do best!" Hannah said.

The room fell quiet when she stopped talking. Her heart thumped heavily inside her chest. She desperately wanted to help him, but Hart's unwillingness to share his feelings about Oliver's death was starting to frustrate her. She could see the rage swimming in his unguarded, brown eyes and it hurt her to know that he was bottling up emotions and thoughts that deeply troubled him. It was more than Oliver, and it was more than Taym, but Hannah realized she could never force Johnny Hart to share with her what he didn't want to.

"Why are you fighting this? I'm trying to help you," Hannah exclaimed. She quickly wiped away a tear before he noticed it.

Hart looked up at her and frowned. He didn't want her hurting like this. Hannah had become too invested in his wellbeing. Hart put his anger for Taym aside, so he could ease Hannah's concern. She had devoted all her time and energy to him these past few weeks, the least he could do was cooperate.

"I understand what you're saying, Hannah, but I don't want you to worry about me. I'll be fine, I always am." He smiled warmly and sat up straight. "Ask me anything, and I'll answer you honestly."

Hannah rolled her eyes. "Oh please, don't say things like that. When have you ever answered me honestly, Johnny?"

"Well, today will be a first for both of us." Hart grinned playfully at her.

Her doubtful expression dissolved into one of curiosity.

"I promise," he added. "I will answer anything you need to know."

"Are you being serious?"

"Anything."

"Alright," she hesitated. Hannah picked up her notebook from the table and opened it. She smiled quickly at the blank pages and then gathered her composure. She peered up at Hart who had been watching her.

"Where do I start?" Hannah shrugged. "I have so many questions."

"Good. Lay them on me, Han."

"Okay." Hannah looked at him. "Do you sleep at night? Do you have nightmares? Do you think about Oliver? Do you think about what he would be doing if he were still alive? Do you relive the memory of how he died?" She paused and gazed attentively into his brown eyes. Hannah went to speak again, but hesitated.

"Why do I get the feeling you haven't finished?" Hart asked.

A boyish smirk lingered on his lips, sending her heart into a shameful flutter.

"Do you...." Hannah paused again and dropped her gaze to her notebook. She took a quick, deep breath and looked at Hart. "Do you feel responsible for Oliver's death?"

Hart waited.

She smiled meekly. "Oh, sorry, that's it. I'm finished."

"That's it, huh?" he asked, amused.

"For now."

Hart laughed humbly to himself, then he rubbed his jaw again and sighed aloud as he considered her questions.

"Okay." His smile faded, and he leaned forward on the chaise. "I am sleeping, mostly, except when I wake with nightmares. Just the one nightmare, the same one every night." Hart laughed softly at himself, slightly embarrassed….

"I do think about Oliver, a lot, especially the way he died. But it doesn't hurt … it just makes me angry." His voice lulled sadly. He had a small smile, but it quickly faded. Hart looked down into his open hands and rubbed them together before he spoke again….

"I think about how we should be surfing together in Mexico—" he stopped talking. He tried to continue, but his lip trembled before the words escaped him.

Hannah breathed sadly. "It's okay."

"Yeah," Hart nodded. He exhaled sharply and smiled through his grief.

Hannah heard his voice shake, but he kept his composure. She didn't. The tears welled shamefully in her green eyes. She had waited ten years for this soldier to open up to her. His mystery always intrigued her, but now his raw sincerity made him even more fascinating.

She waited for him to go on, pleased with his unexpected progress.

"I hear that bullet over and over and over, and I can see him lying there with his face pressed against the concrete," he paused, "and I see his eyes closing in front of me and I know that I will never see them open again." He heard Hannah take a deep breath, but he didn't look at her. "I think about this every day. More times than I can count."

Hart smiled faintly at her, to show her that he was okay, but he had a distant look in his eye. Hannah remained silent and patient, but she was eager for him to continue. She saw him look out the window, and an emotionless calm fell across his handsome face. She knew Hart was deep in thought and contemplating whether or not he should answer her final question. Hannah expected this from him. It was the only information she needed. The only information that really mattered, and his reluctance to answer proved he understood how much weighed upon its revelation. She watched him carefully. He was a thousand miles away from her, in the terrifying depths of his tortured soul.

"Yes …," Hart looked at her and breathed out resignedly before he spoke, "I am responsible for Oliver's death."

Hannah breathed out suddenly, stunned by the remarkable man who sat in front of her. Everything that had been hanging in the air around her since his return had now settled in its place, and she could finally see a clear path appear through the fog in front of her. Hannah stared at him, baffled by his effortless ability to impress her.

Hart smiled at her. "Isn't this the part when you start scribbling away frantically in your notes?" His eyes were kind and weary, and he rubbed his hands together timidly as he waited for her to respond.

"Yes, I guess it is," Hannah answered. She stared at her blank page for a few seconds, then glanced up at Hart. "Thank you, Johnny."

"For what?"

"For being so honest. I know how hard it is for you to share your feelings, but they are in good hands. I promise."

"I know they are," he smiled, visibly glad it was over. "Now you know why I need to go back to Libya. I need to find him, Hannah, to right the wrong I am responsible for."

"No. Listen to me," Hannah leaned forward to Hart, "you are not responsible for Oliver's death."

Hart laughed to himself. "Shit, I knew it."

"What?"

"I trusted you with the truth, Hannah. Please don't use it against me." Hart rubbed his face tiredly, he felt mentally and physically drained.

"Listen," Hannah ignored him. "You have twelve months leave that you are being forced to take. You don't have a choice in the matter, you can't go back to Libya."

"I can if you help me! You're the doctor, just tell Garvey I'm fit enough to return!"

"No!" Hannah replied in refutation. "How dare you ask this of me, I could lose my job! You must believe me when I tell you that I am only doing what is best for you!"

"No, you're not, you're treating me like I'm a different person! Everyone is! *Shit!*" Hart ran his hands through his hair in despair. "I am half the man I was two months ago! Everyone tiptoeing around me as though I'll break if they tread too hard—"

"That's not how we feel about you," Hannah interrupted.

"Yeah, okay," he snorted in disbelief. He ran his hands back through his hair again and then looked at her without smiling.

"Is that what you think?" Hannah asked. "We see you as weak?"

"No," Hart replied. "I don't know."

Hannah waited for him to go on.

"All I know is that I need to get back to Libya and fight. I need to get back to the desert to remember who I am … or who I was."

Hannah frowned and shook her head in heartrending disbelief. "You don't need the desert to remind you of who you are, Johnny," she breathed. "I know who you are."

Hart twisted his mouth and glanced at her fleetingly before he stared out the window again.

She continued in his silence, "You're the warmest, most compassionate man I have ever met, and you always will be. You suffer like this because you have too much empathy. You put everyone's feelings above your own and it is one of your most admirable traits, but this time I need you to put yourself first. You care about the people in Libya, but you can't help them if you lose the battle inside of you."

Hart bowed his head into his hands.

"So much has changed and you're feeling lost. Your best friend died, and the two of you were inseparable. Everyone knew they couldn't get one of you without the other," Hannah smiled when she thought about them. "It must feel so unnatural not to have him by your side, and to make it even harder, you are back in America after being overseas for three years, and it is a new and foreign feeling that will take some time to adapt to. Every part of this takes time."

Hart looked at her without speaking. Her relationship with the Phoenix soldiers was different from those she shared with anyone else at Fort Bragg. They encouraged her to show them more than just the clinical, unemotional doctor she was supposed to be, and Hannah often found it difficult to keep her emotional distance from them when she was alone in their presence. With any other patient, her method was strictly professional.

"Hannah, Libya—"

"No, Johnny. No more Libya, please!" she cried out. "We lost Oliver. I can't bear the thought of losing the three of you as well. You are not strong enough to fight yet. Your decisions will be based on anger, and you will get yourself killed."

"Hannah—" Hart spoke softly, leaning forward to her.

"How can I clear you to go back to the war in Libya, when I know you are at war with yourself?" She fought back her tears.

Her British accent was strong, and for Hart, it was a telltale sign that she wasn't coping. Hannah was their friend before she became the clinical psychologist at Fort Bragg. She trained with them a few times in Arizona when she was forced to partake in military units outside her psychology major. She was slightly younger than they were and she became an instant friend to all four of the soldiers. Hart hadn't once stopped to consider her feelings after losing Oliver, and he felt awful for it. Phoenix had been so far away, for so many years, and he forgot people like Hannah were still here thinking of them. Like Oliver had told them before he died; they were becoming too separated from this part of their lives. This is why they were coming home in the first place.

Hannah was right…it was going to take him some time to remember who he was here. She had always had a strong mind and a big heart, and she could take care of herself, but it didn't stop him worrying about her. Right now, Hannah didn't look a day older than the day he met her ten years ago.

"I'm sorry," he whispered. Hart knelt on the ground in front of her and when she went to push him back onto the chaise, he grabbed her by the wrists and resisted her attempt to cast him away.

A stray tear rolled down her cheek. It had been a long day of wild emotions. She struggled to free her wrists from his strong but gentle hands—Hannah didn't want him to see her tears. She looked down into the brown eyes that gazed up at her in angst. His skin was still dark from the desert sun, and his lips were smooth, and he smelled like the sand and the sun and the earth. Hannah sighed and stopped resisting him.

"Listen to me," she breathed in defeat, "trauma shatters your innocence."

"There is little innocence left within me to be concerned about," Hart smirked handsomely, trying his best to coax a smile from her. He couldn't leave her feeling wretched on his behalf.

"I'm serious. I don't believe we should have debriefed you at all, but it's all we've been doing since you returned home. The USSOCOM feels responsible for what happened, and they needed every little piece of information you had. Now I'm worried it has made things worse for you." She looked down at him. "You got so angry today. I've never seen you like that before."

"I know. I'm sorry," Hart frowned. "Everything will work itself out in the end. I'll be fine. I always am."

"You will be," she replied, "because I'm sending you away with Walker and Benji. You need to find your safe haven, Johnny, find somewhere that brings you peace. Move past the trauma of Oliver's death…away from here. Then you can come back to us and return to the war if you need too, but please, forget Libya, forget Taym, forget—"

"Hannah, Hannah, Hannah, stop. Just listen," Hart interrupted, trying to calm her. He held her hands and gazed into her sad eyes. "You're right. I'll leave. I'll go and I will find my safe haven." He smiled beautifully at her. "Doctor's orders."

Hannah stifled a smile at the breathtaking man who kneeled before her.

"Don't you worry about me," he said again.

She laughed feebly, "I do. I can't help it."

He let go of her hands, then stood up slowly. Hart walked to the door of her office and then turned back to look at her. "Will you be okay?" he asked, concerned.

Hannah nodded silently and smiled at him in thought; it should be her asking him that question, not the other way around, but she already knew his answer. It was always the same. He flashed her a warm smile and left the room, closing the door gently behind him.

Hannah sighed loudly in the privacy of her room. She took a few deep breaths to compose herself and then picked up her notebook and placed the tip of her pen on the paper, then she paused in thought and stared at the door. The Phoenix men affected her in a way that she would never admit to herself, or anyone else. They were intelligent, powerful, and incredibly handsome, but most of all, their compassion for others was beyond comparison.

She threw her notes on the chaise lounge where Hart was sitting, and thought about their conversation. Hannah got up and walked over to the window, and stared through the summer rain over the quadrangle on the Base below her. She thought about the last few weeks and her time spent with Hart. He said he was fine, but she knew he was lying to her. There was one exceptionally beautiful and humbling thing about him, which separated him from all the other men she had ever known ... it was his eyes. They gave everything away.

*Chapter 4*

"COME WALK with me, son." His white teeth glowed through the fog.

Hart could only see a few meters ahead before the mist became too dense to see anything. He could just make out the dark shadows of the pines surrounding him, stretching toward the sky and encircling the white, hazy glow of the sun.

He stood on a frozen bed of pine needles in a small clearing at the base of the pines, like an offering to the gods. He squinted toward the sun and assessed his location. He saw the condensation on his hot breath, and an unnerving chill ran through his body. He'd spent his entire life in the desert—Arizona, Afghanistan, Libya—and the desert felt like home no matter where he was in the world. The dry sands were his lifeblood, but here in the forest and its freezing air, he felt out of place. The pines were unsettling. Unfamiliar.

Survival instinct. Hart stood motionless in accord with the eerie silence that surrounded him. He sensed a thousand eyes on him from underneath the pines, yet through the fog he saw nothing. He was no offering to the gods ... he was easy prey.

Someone whispered his name.

Hart reached for his rifle that wasn't there. He threw his hands out in front of him and searched the fog beneath the pines, anxiously waiting for someone to appear, but no one came. It was time to move.

"It's not far. We'll be there before dark." The man patted him firmly on the shoulder as he walked past, startling Hart. He paced steadily into the fog, dissolving into the murky air.

"Wait!" Hart shouted. He stared at the faded silhouette between the pines. The shadow gradually darkened and the man appeared again.

"Let's go, son! Night brings the dark, and I ain't talking about the shades of the day!" he commanded.

"Okay," Hart replied, confused. "I'm coming."

The man considered the forest around them with a grim expression. He separated his glove from his sleeve to check his watch, and his eyes widened at the time. Hart sensed his sudden urgency to move.

"Let's go, Commander!"

He was an older man. His face was marked with mud, sweat, and deep lines, and he looked shattered. A disheartened witness of a world with no reprieve. He wore a helmet, wrapped tightly in a scarf that rested just above his eyes. Blue eyes that were patiently fixed on Hart and waiting for him to move. A demanding presence filled the air around him, yet Hart felt entirely at ease with this man. He was dressed in combat uniform, but his gear was distressed and unkempt, and Hart guessed he had been in this place for far too long.

The man pulled his scarf up over his nose and mouth as he waited. Hart recognized the black pattern and tassels on the beige cotton of the scarf: a Shemagh tactical scarf from the deserts of the Middle East. He had a few of his own, which offered protection from the extreme temperatures they faced in the deserts. The man wore a Special Forces tab on his arm and a few badges decorated his shirt, but before Hart could identify any of them, the man turned to make his way up the hill.

Hart tried to follow him, but his legs wouldn't move. He glanced down at his feet, past a pristine, stainless combat uniform, not a day spent in the war. Hart tried to step forward again, but his boots were too heavy to move. He peered up at the man who watched him struggle. The old man's eyes creased in compassion, sympathetic to Hart's burden. He strolled back down the hill to the commander and placed his hand on his shoulder. He rested it there and studied him briefly.

"Alright, you can stay here."

"What? No. I don't want to stay here!" A sickening fear overwhelmed Hart. One he had never felt before in all his years at war. He felt vulnerable. Weak. He sensed his imminent end.

"Just keep your eyes forward, okay, son. Never look back, and that is an order."

The man looked directly past Hart into the forest and returned his blue eyes to Hart. He gave him a few encouraging pats on the shoulder, and reluctantly, he left. He ascended the hill through the pines and faded into the fog.

"Wait!" Hart pleaded. "WAIT!"

Hart panicked. He stared down at his legs that remained frozen to the forest floor and he growled through his teeth in frustration. None of this made any sense. He crouched to the ground and wrestled with his boots. The fog grew thick with black smoke and a decaying stench reeked the air. Hart gagged once or twice before he noticed the smoke surrounding him. Burning embers floated lazily past, and Hart peered quizzically into the sky. A thick, blanket of smoke cascaded down to him from the white mist, then the sun disappeared.

Hart untied the laces on his boots, then realized his hands were smothered in fresh blood and soot.

"What the f...?" He stood quickly.

Large, smoldering holes burned through his combat shirt, as though he'd run straight through the flames of a fire. It sizzled his flesh and Hart tore off his shirt and threw it on the ground at his feet. His chest rose and fell in the frosty air, and he stared at his bloody hands outstretched in front of him.

Hart searched the forest ahead.

"Don't leave me here!" he yelled.

The smoke ripped coarsely through his throat. Hart coughed suddenly, the air burning him from the inside out.

"One foot in front of the other, son!" A voice echoed through the forest. "It's all there is to do!"

"Shit!" Hart whispered to himself.

He picked up his combat shirt and used it as a fire blanket to extinguish the small spot fires in the pine needles around him. He took off his white singlet and wrapped it around his face below his eyes to slow down the smoke inhalation, but the waft of decay still managed to seep through the cotton. Hart wiped the burning ash as it landed on his naked back, cursing in pain as they burned his skin. Then the forest started to whisper to him.

Hart lifted his hands in defense and glanced between the shadows of the pines. The whispers multiplied and cooed over his frantic breath, growing progressively louder around the clearing. Hart trembled in the cold, in the unknown. The ghostly air drifted past him through the fog, until the whispering finally settled in the forest behind him.

"Keep your eyes forward," he told himself.

Hart stared straight ahead and clenched his hands into tight fists on either side of him, determined not to turn around. He never disobeyed a command, but the whispering was torture. It hissed through his ears until he couldn't take it anymore, then suddenly, they stopped.

A dreadful silence hung in the air.

Hart listened to his panting breath. *Fear.* It weakened him. It was all he could feel, besides guilt. Hart closed his eyes and shook his head. A shadow of the man he was.

He turned around, and then he saw them.

A wave of nausea overwhelmed him, and Hart bent over and groaned into the icy air. Piles of bodies littered the ground beneath the pines. Black smoke curled away from their charred, lifeless figures, into the ethereal sky above them, and Hart fell on his knees and choked in the toxic fog. He ripped the singlet from his mouth and gasped for fresh air, but the putrid taste of burning human flesh suffocated him.

The smoke grew heavier and darker until he could barely see his hands, clinging to the forest floor. The pines circled him, and Hart spun mercilessly in the center of the clearing. He took a deep breath of thick, foul smoke and held onto it for dear life, certain it was his last.

The pine needles crackled beneath the boots that suddenly appeared in front of him. Hart pulled himself off the forest floor and sat exhausted on the hard heels of his boots. He peered wearily up at the tall figure standing over him, his panting breath loud on the crisp air.

"Get up!" the man ordered.

Hart grabbed the hand that was offered to him and pulled himself off the ground. Oliver stood there in front of him, unsmiling. Hart's eyes softened. His best friend's familiar blue eyes stared back at him through the smoke, and he sighed in relief. Oliver raised his gun and aimed it at Hart, and shot him straight through the heart.

Hart stood in stunned silence, feeling the hot bullet entomb itself in his cold, naked chest. He peered down at the blood that pumped out of his body in thick, rhythmic waves, and Hart collapsed heavily onto the bed of pine needles behind him. He stared at the white halo that encircled the sun above the clearing, and he gasped desperately in the freezing air.

Oliver looked down at him, blocking the sun and shaking his head. "You promised me," he said balefully. *"Never,* look back." He turned away from Hart and disappeared into the pines.

"Ollie," Hart breathed softly. "Ollie, please, don't leave me here." With his dying breath, he growled furiously into the sky.

Hart sat up in bed, panting.

It took him a few moments to gather his bearings in the dark. The room was unfamiliar in his confused wakefulness. Colorless curtains drifted in the midnight air. The darkness flashed faintly in the flickering streetlight that beamed through the open window beside him. Hart studied the motel room door, which had five different types of locks attached to it, but not a single one was locked. He relaxed when he recalled laughing with Walker and Benji about any unfortunate intruder who decided to break into a room full of special operations soldiers. Benji snored lightly in the double bed beside him, and Hart smiled at the familiarity of the noise. Things were usually pretty safe if Benji was snoring.

The three soldiers had been flown from North Carolina to a training base in Monterey County, California, yesterday morning. They had been driving all day in Hart's black, 1967 Pontiac Firebird that he kept safely tucked away under sheets in one of the plane hangars at the base. It was a road trip that he was reluctant to take, but Walker and Benji had been looking forward to it since the decision was made to carry out Oliver's final wish—to check on his younger sister, Ivy.

Hart remembered turning off the interstate late last night on their way to Oliver's hometown just north of San Diego. They stopped at a rundown motel around 0200 hours, and the three of them fell asleep soon after. He lit up the luminous green light on his watch: 0312. He had been asleep for a whole hour.

Hart watched the curtains flutter beside him. The sea breeze cooled his sweating skin, and after years spent in the desert, the sensation stirred an uncomfortable nostalgia in him. He didn't know why. He rubbed his face tiredly and stepped out of bed with a mindful quietness, so as not to wake Benji. Hart walked toward the bathroom, moving soundlessly past Walker who was asleep in the other double bed. He rolled open the sliding door and closed it gently behind him before turning on the bathroom light.

Hart leaned on the sink and sighed heavily into its dirt-stained depths. He looked up at the tired man who stared back at him in the mirror, and he shook his head in pitiful disapproval. The scars on his stomach were darker than usual, or at least he thought so. Beads of sweat dotted his forehead, so Hart flicked on the tap and washed his face in the cool water. He dried his face with one of the motel towels, then reached into his canvas toiletry bag and shuffled around until he found what he was looking for; a small, orange container filled with dozens of tiny, white pills. He held it up and read his name on the label, along with Dr. Hannah Arnett's.

Hannah had given these to him before he left North Carolina, much to his displeasure. Hart took them to keep her happy. He never believed he would take one, but the nightmares were becoming relentless. There was no longer any refuge from his grief, day or night, and so he finally succumbed to his suffering and followed the advice of his doctor … his friend.

With a nervous breath, Hart fumbled with the sealed lid until the entire container emptied itself into the sink.

"Shit!"

Hart caught a couple of pills that rolled around the bottom of the unclean sink and threw them quickly into his mouth without another thought, then he flicked on the water again and drank straight from the tap.

Hart breathed loudly with a nervous energy as he bent

over the sink with his hands resting on either side of it. He was never good at taking medicine. He hated the thought of taking something that altered his vigilant state of mind. Hart stared at himself in the mirror … the competent soldier he once knew was regrettably shaking hands with the devil. He shook his head and tried to comprehend that this was his life now. Hart knew he was lost in a vague shroud of reality these past two months, so anything had to be better than the hell he was barely surviving each day.

*Two pills. That's it.*

He pushed himself off the sink and turned the light out so he could no longer see his sorry reflection in the mirror. He pulled open the sliding door and quietly made his way back to bed through the dark.

"You alright?" Walker asked him quietly.

Hart stopped. Walker's thoughtful gaze examined him through the dark. He was sitting on the edge of his bed, his elbows on his knees, as though he had been contemplating whether to come and check on him.

"Yeah, I'm fine," Hart replied softly.

Walker heard him climb back into bed beside Benji. He had seen Hart wake from his nightmares every night, and every night he had waited patiently until Hart fell asleep again. Walker sighed quietly to himself and thought about his friend's pain. He couldn't believe it. Johnny Hart was the fearless soldier who was heroic even in the darkest depths of war. Nothing frightened him. *Nothing.* But Walker was witnessing Hart's strength crumbling before him, and it troubled him deeply.

He looked over at his friend, asleep beside Benji. He pressed his lips together in concern. Hannah had told him it was bad, but it was worse than he had thought.

## Chapter 5

# - SOUTHERN CALIFORNIA -
## July 2014

THE FIREBIRD'S ENGINE PURRED loudly as they rolled down the main street of La Mar. People stared at them, mostly with curiosity, but a few disapproving glares forced Hart to ease his foot off the accelerator. It was not his speed so much as the deep rumbling of the engine that caught their attention. His Firebird couldn't drive much slower than it already was.

The town itself was small and quaint. Sycamore trees lined the streets, forming a lush canopy overhead, and luxury cars bejeweled the road below them. Immaculately dressed locals ambled between the cafes and upmarket boutiques, seemingly delighted by one another and the idle, summer afternoon. The soldiers thought of it as San Diego's version of The Hamptons. Overall, it was green and tranquil, and Hart could already feel himself relaxing in the peacefulness of this luxurious seaside town.

Beach towels draped over locals' shoulders as they strolled into town from the beach. The soldiers could smell the salty air. They could just make out the sparkle of the sapphire sea through the trees at the end of the street. It had been three years since their last swim in the Pacific, and each was eager for the refreshing relief of the salty water against their parched, desert skin.

Benji was beside himself with excitement in the back seat of the Firebird. "Remember that sunburned feeling on your skin in the evening after spending the entire day baking on the sand and swimming in the ocean?" Benji reminisced. "Man, it reminds me of Mexico and summer and all the places I want to be *right now*."

The three of them thought about it fondly.

"Why don't we just travel the Californian coast for the next twelve months?" Benji asked excitedly.

"It'll take one month to travel the West Coast," Walker answered from the front seat. "Two months if we stretch it out."

Hart smiled at Walker.

"So we'll scoot over to Hawaii. Or Australia," Benji replied. "You know I read somewhere that Australia has this animal called a platypus. They say it is the cutest little critter, but if it feels threatened, then it has this sharp barb, concealed in its thumb that releases a venom which can incapacitate its victim." Benji grinned.

Hart nodded, impressed.

"Cute, but deadly, eh?" Walker laughed. "That is you in a nutshell, Benji."

"I like that idea," Hart smiled. He glanced at Benji in the rear-view mirror. "It's not like we have anything else to do, right?"

"Why not? I'm all for it," Walker agreed.

"We'll check on Oliver's sister for a few days, see how she's doing. Then we'll head south along the coast to Mexico, what do you think?" Hart asked. He grinned cheerfully at Walker and Benji, who both agreed.

"I'm sure she's doing okay," Benji added, gazing out his window. "I mean, look at this town, it's an exclusive hideaway rolling in cash."

The plan excited Hart. He didn't want to stay here in La Mar. Sure it was beautiful, but the thought of meeting Oliver's sister literally made him sick with anxiety, and he didn't know why. Fear was a new emotion for him since Oliver died, and Hart was still trying to get his head around it. No doubt there was a way to conquer it, but he wasn't sure what frightened him in the first place. He didn't like to think about it for too long, it got him frustrated and short-tempered, and it was Walker and Benji who suffered for it. He felt bad enough for their undeserved leave; twelve months from service because of his behavior.

Each day their presence played on his guilty mind, so Hart tried his damned best to ignore his anxiety—which is exactly what Hannah told him not to do.

Hart pulled into a gas station to fill the Firebird, and so Walker could ask where to find Oliver's sister. It was a small town, and they hoped someone would know her. Hart pulled in next to a young guy who was filling up his white BMW convertible. He leaned confidently on his car and coolly inspected the rumbling Pontiac Firebird and the car's three occupants. His conceited expression made Walker sigh, and Hart looked at his friend and smiled.

They were no strangers to animosity, especially when they moved around as a team. Men always picked fights with them. Hart could never decide whether these guys were insecure or simply testing their brawn on something more life-like than the boxing bag they had hanging in their basements. He guessed a bit of both. Alcohol was usually involved. Nothing like a night of drinking to make a man believe he was built like Hercules. There was also nothing quite like the mortified look on their faces when Walker made their thumbs disappear into their assholes without a single bruise to their bodies. He knew a bruise to the ego was far more ruthless.

That is why Walker was on his final warning. One more incident and he would be out of the military. Hart had never been involved with a citizen, right up until his debriefing in North Carolina that is, and he was certainly paying for it now. Benji had one or two when he first joined the Special Forces, but he soon learned to laugh off his frustration. Walker, however, found it more difficult. He'd been in countless clashes with citizens who got off on trying to provoke him, to the point where he was finally court-martialed five years ago, and USSOCOM nearly had to pull him from Phoenix. It was General Garvey who risked his revered reputation to defend him, and Walker had been on his best behavior ever since.

It was tedious to avoid confrontations when such men worked so hard to pick a fight, but the soldiers did so at all costs. They recognized a fight before the guy even knew he had it in him, and there he was, innocently filling up his sports car with his quaffed hair, Tod's loafers, and Tommy Hilfiger jacket.

"Here we go," Walker muttered under his breath.

The soldiers ignored the stranger who leaned casually on his car and eyeballed the three of them as they pulled up. Hart nodded at the man and climbed out of the driver's seat.

The man nodded in return. "Hey."

"Hey, how's it going?" Hart replied, politely. He unscrewed the cap on the gas tank and inserted the nozzle into the car.

"Sweet Firebird. 1966?" he asked.

"Close, '67," Hart replied with a warm, but cautious approach.

"I have a 2014 Pontiac Solstice back at the house. She's sitting in my garage. She's a dream to drive, black just like yours." The man grinned roguishly. "You know, I always say that if you love the same cars, then you love the same women."

Hart laughed. "Okay, interesting. So do you have a girlfriend?"

"Why do you ask?"

"Well, I have yet to find my perfect woman. Maybe your theory could help me find out who I've been searching for all my life." Hart glanced away and frowned, concerned with his genuine intrigue.

He heard Benji chuckle in the backseat, and he smiled to himself.

"Yeah, I have a girlfriend," he answered proudly.

Hart picked up the vagueness in his tone. He was lying, but Hart didn't care.

"Okay. So what type of woman is she?"

"Ah, man, she's perfect," he praised.

Hart could tell he was speaking from the heart now. Maybe he wasn't lying?

"She is the sweetest, little thing with the biggest heart, and you've never seen a sexier woman than her. Long blonde hair and a body to die for." He spread his hands in a "what are you gonna do" gesture and smiled at Hart. "She just doesn't know a good thing when she's got it."

"Trouble in paradise?" Hart asked.

"No, not for me. For her. She's been through a lot lately, and now everything is just how I needed it to be. I couldn't have planned it better myself. The stars have aligned," he crooned.

"So she's been through a lot in a good way?" Hart asked,

confused.

"No man, shit, she's been through hell. It's easier to win them over when their hearts are breaking," he exclaimed. He secured the nozzle back in its place and screwed on the cap.

"I don't understand?" Hart was pretty sure he did understand, he wanted to give the guy a chance to avoid being a complete jerk.

"You can comfort them when they're vulnerable, it makes them easy." He winked smugly at Hart.

Hart furrowed his brow in disagreement, but he didn't say anything. He turned away and hung the nozzle back in its place, a little more roughly than required.

"So do you agree?"

Hart bowed his head before he turned around, reluctant to answer. "I don't think so."

The man shrugged, unimpressed with Hart's response. "So are you guys just passing through?"

"Yeah, we are. We're on our way to Mexico, and we thought we'd stop in a few places along the way," Hart lied. They were well accustomed to keeping the specifics down to a need-to-know basis.

Walker opened the passenger door and stood, stretching. He looked at Hart without acknowledging the man he was talking to. "You want a Coke?"

"Yeah, buddy, thanks," Hart replied.

Walker bent down to look at Benji who gave him a thumbs up in the backseat. He walked past the man without looking at him and entered the shop.

Hart noted the man's eyes lingering on Walker, practically pleading for his attention, but Walker remained indifferent to him. Hart could tell it pissed the guy off.

"What's his problem?" he asked. He turned to look at Walker who was talking to the man behind the till.

"No problem," Hart answered. "We've been on the road since yesterday morning. He's just tired, I'd say."

The man nodded warily and returned his attention to Hart. He reached out his hand. "I'm Tommy, by the way."

"Johnny, pleased to meet you."

Hart shook his hand, and Tommy squeezed it with an over-zealous force.

"You guys part of a football team or something?" Tommy asked, subtly rubbing the blood back into his fingertips.

"No, just friends," he answered. Hart faced the car to screw the cap back on the gas tank. He shot Benji a quick wink.

Tommy climbed into his car and leaned out the window. "Well, enjoy Mexico. Hey, if you get a chance, drop in at the Ritz Hotel in Cancun and drop my name. They'll give you a sweet deal."

"Ah, okay, thanks," Hart replied. He had no intention of ever visiting Cancun.

"The waves are spectacular, the women, even more so. I mean the tourists, by the way. Cocktail wasted sluts in bikinis who just want to…." he mouthed the word *fuck,* then winked at Hart.

Tommy flashed him a cocky grin and slapped the side of his own convertible. The BMW roared out of the gas station and into the main street of town.

"Charming!" Benji called out from the back seat.

The white sports car accelerated obnoxiously through town and skidded around the first right turn, barely missing a couple who were crossing the street.

Hart leaned on the open window of his Firebird and looked at Benji. "What a nice guy," he said sarcastically.

Benji grinned. "Money can't buy everything."

They heard the BMW fang it up the hill in the distance and they shook their heads and laughed. Walker emerged from the store only seconds later, relieved the guy had left.

"Any luck?" Benji called through the open window to Walker.

"To get to Ollie's we take the first right turn, and his place is at the very top of the hill at the end of the street. Not far at all. His place is called *La Jolla,*" Walker reiterated.

Benji and Hart gave each other a knowing glance and rolled their eyes.

"What?" Walker asked, sensing their unspoken concern.

Hart smiled. "Get in the car."

Walker climbed into the passenger seat. As Hart walked

around the car, a cloud of concern for Oliver's sister shrouded his short-lived happiness. He thought about the swim they had planned, but the thought of that jerk with Oliver's sister made him anxious. He wanted to get to Ollie's and make sure Ivy wasn't the heartbroken girlfriend the guy was bragging about. If she was heartbroken, Hart knew why. The last thing she needed was that asshole taking advantage of her.

They pulled out of the gas station and headed toward the beach.

"I think we should check on Ivy before we take that swim," Benji suggested.

"You read my mind, Benji boy," Hart replied.

"Did I miss something?" Walker asked, glancing at the two of them.

"I hope not," Hart sighed, steering right off the main street where Tommy had turned earlier.

The road to Oliver's place was beautiful. Majestic, even. The lush canopy from town continued up the steep hill, and in some places it cascaded down to the footpath on either side of the road. They passed mansion after mansion, and occasionally what appeared to be small castles.

Walker peered quizzically at Hart. "Did you know Ollie had money?"

"Not this much," Hart replied. A small smile curled on his face.

Hart slowed down when he reached the end of the street. He pulled into the last driveway and stopped at the large, iron gates that blocked the drive. On the wall beside the gate were curved letters that read LA JOLLA.

"The Jewel," Hart read aloud. He peered through the gate along the driveway that was lined with picturesque, weeping trees. He watched the leaves float weightlessly to the ground, and Hart imagined an old castle sitting grandly in the distance.

"Shit, no!" Benji whooped.

"I have to admit, I didn't see it in him," Walker said in surprise. "I'm impressed."

Hart glanced at Walker, perplexed by the lack of his usual sardonic tone. He searched Walker's expression for a hint of jest, but he continued to stare, unblinking, at the lush estate in front of them. Hart smiled to himself and glanced back up the driveway. Things were changing faster than he had anticipated, but it felt good. He was grateful to have Walker and Benji here beside him.

Hart studied the security keypad outside his car window. There was a shiny, silver button that he guessed was the intercom for the estate, but he hesitated to push it.

"Push it," Benji ordered.

"I will," Hart replied abruptly.

He didn't. Hart felt their eyes on him, and he rubbed his jaw in thought.

"We don't have to do this today, Hart," Walker said, sensing his anxiety. His dark eyes filled with compassion for his friend, remembering the nightmare that woke Hart last night, and every other night before that.

Hart considered coming back another time. Maybe he would never be ready to meet Oliver's sister. Then the gates cranked open.

"What did you touch?" Benji asked.

Hart opened his hands above the steering wheel. "I didn't touch anything." He saw a white BMW driving toward them from the estate, and his heart sank. He cursed under his breath, leading Walker and Benji to look up the driveway ahead of them.

"No, she's not seeing that asshole, is she?" Benji exclaimed, his expression falling.

Hart entered the gates and drove as far to the right of the driveway as he could, hoping to avoid confrontation. Tommy approached them slowly, no doubt recognizing the Firebird. He glared through his window at Hart when they passed each other. Hart waved and kept driving, keeping the encounter to a minimum, then Tommy's break lights came on in Hart's rearview mirror.

"Keep driving, kid," Hart muttered.

Walker checked his mirror. They didn't want trouble.

Hart kept a vigilant eye on the vehicle behind him as the Firebird rumbled slowly toward the estate. The soldiers were quiet as they waited for Tommy to make his decision. Hart tapped his finger on the steering wheel as he conjured up a plan should Tommy decide to pick a fight today, then the brake lights flicked off, and the BMW continued along the driveway onto the road. Hart held his breath until the gates closed securely between them.

Walker smirked at the boys. "He didn't look too happy."

"Yeah, but he didn't stop. If he were Ivy's boyfriend, he would have pulled us up, right?" Hart concluded. "Wouldn't you?"

"Definitely! Us three striking fellas pulling up to your girlfriend's door…," Benji grinned. "It would raise a few questions."

"Oh, he had questions, he just didn't have the balls to ask them," Walker added, narrowing his eyes.


Eventually, the trees opened up, and they had a clear view of Oliver's home. The three of them laughed in disbelief as they drove around the fountain in front of the estate. The place was even bigger than they imagined it to be. Hart pulled up at the base of the marble steps, and all three of the soldiers remained seated in the Firebird, taking in the grandness of Oliver's remarkable estate from their car window.

"Holy shit. Are you seeing this?" Benji breathed in awe. "Ollie owned a fucking palace! Oh, we are most definitely staying longer than a few days!"

"A few days, Benji," Hart reinforced firmly. "We're checking to see if she's okay, and then we're on the road again."

The boys climbed out of the Firebird and strolled up the stairs to the front door. Hart ran his hands nervously through his hair, then rubbed them together as he took in the lavish estate. When they reached the door, the three soldiers stood side by side and stared anxiously at the intercom bell, each patiently waiting for someone else to step forward and press it.

When no one moved, Benji pushed Hart toward the door.

"Ring the bell, man!"

Hart regained his balance and frowned back at Benji. He turned around and reached toward the bell. He lingered there for a moment or two before he pushed it, thinking about Oliver and why he wasn't standing beside them. *He should be here.*

"We shouldn't do this," Hart breathed, changing his mind. He turned and stared at the guys.

"What?" Benji frowned.

Walker's dark eyes squinted thoughtfully at Hart. He slid his hands into his jeans pockets and silently studied his friend in front of him.

"What is it?" Hart asked him.

"Nothing," Walker replied calmly, without judgment.

"I just don't think we should be showing up out of the blue like this. Maybe we should have warned her we were coming?" Hart shrugged his shoulders. The thought of meeting Ivy stirred something deep inside that he couldn't explain. Hart thought about how much he'd suffered since he had lost his best friend. He was trying to put Oliver's memory to rest, not reignite the dark hell he had been living these past couple of months.

He stared back at Walker who was still quietly reading his thoughts. Walker understood how he was feeling. He didn't have to tell him. Walker's intuition was razor sharp, but he remained diplomatically furtive about it, as always.

"We've come this far, buddy," Benji encouraged, "just push the bell."

"I don't think I can."

"What is wrong with you?" Benji asked, exasperated. "Push it!"

Hart sighed. "Benji."

Walker quietly laughed at the two of them.

"You've made bigger decisions than this before, man, see that silver button there, just fucking push it."

"I can't, I'm sorry."

Benji's face grew serious. "Do you remember that time we were trapped in that tiny warehouse in Kabul and the only way out was through that roller door where the enemy was sitting and waiting for us? Remember that?"

Hart nodded and stared intensely at Benji as he spoke.

"Walker, you made that lob bomb out of an empty gas can and a car remote, fucking genius, and you, Hart, were the one in charge of pushing that button to initiate the IED and blow our way to freedom through those assholes!" Benji stared at him with wide, serious eyes. "Did you hesitate to push that button? No. You didn't, and you killed fifteen extremists who had decapitated dozens of innocent civilians ... and it gave us a clean exit out of that scorching steel coffin."

Hart rubbed his jaw as he comprehended where Benji was

going with this.

"*That* was a decision, Hart. See that button there?" Benji pointed at the doorbell. "That button will send a sweet chime through her home and into our hearts, instead of blowing the whole fucking estate sky high. There is no decision to make here! We are meeting Ollie's sister, *today,* now push the God damn bell before I lose my fucking mind at the absurdity of your decision-making skills these days!"

Hart glanced at Walker, amused, and the two of them grinned at Benji, who was remarkably serious for the first time in his life.

Hart shrugged. "Okay, point made. I'll push the bell. What could possibly happen right?"

"Well, his sister might answer? Imagine that," Walker answered sarcastically, goading Benji for a smile.

Benji pulled his cap down over his face and sighed into it, and the three of them laughed. Hart turned back to the door, pushed the bell, and stepped back into line with the others.

Ivy looked at the time. Her driver was early. She went to the front door, and before opening it, she checked her gown and her hair in the over-sized mirror hanging on the wall in the entry hall. The theme of the Silver Moon Gala tonight was Vintage Hollywood, and her dress was designed by an old family friend who once worked for Chanel back in the seventies. The pale gold dress shimmered in the sunlight that shone through the windows above the door. The gown itself was an intricate golden lace with a high neck that exposed her smooth shoulders and hugged her figure right down to her hips, where the lace evolved into a golden silk. The gown had a split that revealed her left thigh, and the rest of the silk cascaded down around her legs and flowed elegantly to the ground behind her.

She ran her hands down the warm silk around her hips and turned to look at her back, which was entirely exposed. The lace met at the back of her neck with a delicate button made from mother of pearl. Ivy traced her fingers along the sheer lace on her lower back, admiring how it flawlessly shifted to silk and fell away from her hips in a weightless, golden waterfall. She had never seen a more beautiful dress.

Her hair was pulled to one side and hung in blonde waves

down her left shoulder. Ivy did her makeup herself, her usual bare minimum: a brush of blush, a faint sweep of gold eye shadow, and plenty of mascara. She had opted for bright red lip stick to complement the Hollywood theme, considerably bolder than her natural tinted gloss.

Ivy breathed out a long, controlled breath, apprehensive of the long night ahead.

"Ring it again," Benji suggested.

"Do you think she's home?" Walker asked.

As Hart reached for the bell again, the door opened. He swiftly stepped back into line with Walker and Benji, and the three soldiers stood tall, as though standing at attention, each nervous as hell to meet Oliver's sister.

Ivy opened the door. Standing in place of her driver were three young men, and her heart fluttered unexpectedly in her chest. They were strikingly attractive, and she grew uncharacteristically nervous in their presence. Ivy opened her mouth to speak, but no words escaped her.

The three soldiers saw Oliver staring back at them in her crystal blue eyes, and it rendered them speechless, captivated by her compelling beauty and the resemblance to their late commanding officer. The soldiers and Ivy stood wordlessly before each other, as though the universe had paused to witness their meeting, irrevocably binding the four of them together without their knowledge.

"Hi," she managed, her cheeks blushing. "Are you looking for someone?"

Walker and Benji scooped their jaws off the ground and managed to divert their eyes to Hart, who stood a million miles away between them. He was oblivious to the attention on him, and so Walker gave him a gentle nudge with his shoulder.

"Uh, hey," Hart cleared his throat to speak and stepped forward. "Hi, yes, we are looking for you, I hope. I mean, I hope it is you because we're looking for you, not *I hope* it's you because you're beautiful." Hart cringed at his inability to string a sensible sentence together in front of a gorgeous woman.

He laughed humbly at himself and rubbed his hands against his thighs. He felt Walker and Benji's eyes on him, and he knew they'd give him a ton of shit for this later. He peered back into the crystal eyes that studied him from the front door of Oliver's home.

"So you are looking for me." She grinned sweetly, amused by his awkwardness. "I'm curious, if you didn't know what I looked like, then how do you know who I am?"

Hart thought about her question, and it confused him. He had been in the desert for too long.

"Good question! Spit it out, soldier," Walker teased, hitting Hart playfully on the back.

Ivy shot a glance at Walker. *Soldier?*

Her heart jumped anxiously in her chest.

"Are you Ivy Rose?" Hart recovered. He gazed into the crystal eyes in front of him. Oliver's eyes. The eyes he thought he would never see again.

She looked at him cautiously. "Yes, I am."

Hart sighed in relief.

"Well, this here is Josh Walker." Hart grabbed Walker's shoulder, and he nodded at Ivy and smiled. "Benjamin Swift," he continued, resting his hand on Benji's back, "And I am Johnny Hart." Hart smiled beautifully and reached his hand out to her, but Ivy didn't take it.

She stared at him as she went over the names one by one in her head. She examined each one of them briefly, then something within her faded before their eyes. The blood drained from her cheeks. She closed her eyes and rested her face on her hand, mentally processing the three soldiers who stood before her. *Oliver's soldiers.*

"Are you okay?" Hart asked her. The boys looked at each other in concern.

"Walker, Benji, and Hart," she lamented softly to herself.

"You've heard about us through Ollie, haven't you?" Hart asked, as comprehension dawned on him. He stepped into the doorway and reached out to hold her, then decided against it.

Ivy nodded behind her hand, overwhelmed by the biggest part of her brother's life standing before her. Right here, right now, at her front door in southern California, far from the deserts and the wars that lay on the other side of the world. They were her heroes in a parallel universe. Brave men who existed only in Oliver's tales of courage and comradery. Strangers whom she had known for many, many years, whom she dearly loved but thought she would never meet—especially now that he was gone. Yet here they stood in place of her brother, and Ivy's heart broke. She wished for Oliver to be here beside them in the infinite space he once gloriously filled. He was the one who was supposed to introduce her to the men she adored from afar.

Ivy's bare shoulders rose and fell with her short breath. A rushing sound filled her ears, and the world seemed to fade away. Before she knew it, she was falling into darkness.

Hart noticed the color drain from her rosy cheeks just moments before she fainted. He scooped her into his arms as she fell, and the boys moved swiftly into the house to find her a comfortable place to lie down.

"So, do you think she's happy to see us?" Benji quipped. He slipped past Hart into the estate.

Hart frowned as she lay unconscious in his arms. She seemed to weigh less than most of the weapons he hauled around the deserts on duty. Her silk dress felt warm against his skin, and it floated weightlessly in the air behind him as he followed Walker and Benji through the doorway and into her home. He looked down at her sweet face as he carried her. She was beautiful. Breathtaking, actually. She smelled like the ocean, and the sand, and sweet coconuts, and exotic flowers, like she was born to the tropical isles across the world. She reminded him of the waves and hot, summer nights sleeping by the ocean. She embodied everything he hadn't seen or experienced in so long, and Hart was suddenly overcome by her. He knew he would meet her one day, but never like this. Even unconscious, she cast a spell over him, and he fell hard and willingly into her enchantment. The past couple of months had been his darkest, and her presence embraced him like a halo of light. It felt incredible, but she was obviously hurting. They had never met, but they had lost the same man. If his loss was hard, then her loss was even harder. Oliver was her brother. Her only family. Hart knew she had no one left.

He looked away from her and took a deep breath, and tucked Oliver's sister protectively into his body.

*"Ivy. Open your eyes."*

Ivy breathed in deeply and opened her eyes as she was told. From the sofa she saw the soldiers in her living room, watching her closely with equally pained expressions. Hart kneeled in front of her on the carpet and rubbed the back of her hand gently with his thumb.

"You're still here?" she whispered weakly. She sat up on the white leather sofa. "I'm so sorry—"

"No, don't apologize. We should have warned you we were on our way," Hart replied. "It was a lot for you to take in. We're the ones who are sorry, Ivy."

Ivy watched him pull his hand away and sit beside her on the sofa. She rubbed her hands together, feeling his warmth still linger in her palms.

"I've never fainted before." Ivy smiled self-consciously. She glanced around at the men who still considered her with beautiful, worried faces.

"Hey, don't worry about it, Ives. Hart has that kind of effect on women," Benji laughed cheerfully. "That way they don't have to tell him they're not interested."

Hart smiled at Benji's uncanny ability to turn any heavy situation into a lighter one, usually at his expense. He peered into her smiling eyes beside him and was pleased to see her laughing.

Hart rubbed his jaw bashfully. "Don't you listen to Benji, we keep him around for the entertainment only."

His voice was soft and tender, and Ivy caught herself staring at his smooth lips.

"His accent is more than enough to keep me entertained," Ivy teased Benji lightheartedly.

"See there you go, she has you figured out already, Benji boy," Hart jested. Walker laughed.

"Hey, hey, hey, come on now, Ivy! You don't like my accent? Shit, I thought all the women loved my New Orleans charm."

Benji shot her a mesmerizing grin that struck Ivy like an arrow through the heart. His dimples creased into his cheeks when he smiled, and there was an easy contentment in his bright, blue eyes that gazed at her, unwavering, from across the room. He leaned back in his chair and winked at her harmlessly.

Ivy shook her head and smiled. He was fresh-faced and playful, and he was incredibly sexy. She couldn't deny it; his charisma was off the charts.

"No, you're right," Ivy grinned, narrowing her eyes at him. "You do have that Orleans charm working for you. I like it."

"See, I told you, fellas!" Benji sat forward in his seat and pointed enthusiastically at Walker and Hart. "Thank you, darlin'."

"So how are you feeling, Ivy? Can I get you a glass of water?" Walker asked, still a little concerned by the pallor under her light make-up.

Ivy glanced at Walker, who sat opposite her on one of the oversized armchairs with its back to the glass wall of the living room where the Pacific Ocean rolled majestically behind him. He had a steely, intense expression, but his dark eyes were gentle, and she could see that he had a kind heart.

"Yes, thank you," Ivy answered. "Here I'll get it, but I think I need something a little stronger than water."

Ivy stood quickly. She was a little wobbly at first, but she recovered nicely. She saw the soldiers rise out of their seats in response to her fleeting instability. They were just like her brother; tall, gorgeous, and undeniably compassionate, but these men weren't her brother. Ivy could barely look in their direction without blushing, so she hurried to the kitchen.

"What do you guys drink? I have everything," she asked on her way.

"I would love a beer," Benji answered happily.

"I have beer. Do you two want one?" She looked at Hart and Walker, who nodded together.

The three soldiers followed Ivy into the adjoining kitchen like silent, protective shadows. She turned away from them and screwed up her face, cringing at herself for collapsing in front of them earlier. Ivy was mortified. She moved gracefully around the island bench to the refrigerator, her dress sweeping behind her. Hart moved toward her from the other direction around the island, gently sliding his hand along its stone surface. She thought about his warm skin against her, and her body melted hotly in his nearness again.

Ivy buried her head into the fridge and cursed silently into its cold depths. She pulled out four Budweisers and slid them across the island to the boys, who leaned casually on its surface. They laughed with each other as though they had arrived weeks ago, not minutes ago. There hadn't been a scene like this since Oliver had lived here. A small flame ignited inside her, and she soundlessly thanked the universe for sending her his soldiers. Their timing couldn't be more perfect.

They raised their beers over the center of the island.

"Here's to Ollie ... and to finding another Rose," Benji grinned.

Ivy and Hart caught each other's eyes, and the four of them took a long, refreshing sip of the cold beer.

"So what brings you all this way down to Southern Cali? Are you guys on leave?" Ivy asked.

"Ah, you could call it that," Hart answered.

Ivy saw him glance furtively at the boys, who clearly had a silent understanding of his vagueness. She studied him carefully as he spoke. He was hiding something behind those tranquil, brown eyes.

"We are on our way to Mexico, and we wanted to swing by and pay our respects," Hart added, steering the focus away from their leave.

Her heart sunk. She didn't want them to go. They had just arrived. They were Oliver's soldiers, and she felt they belonged to her, in a strange, hopeful way. She thought about how lonely she would be once they moved on, but she dismissed the thought before it tainted her brief happiness. Ivy glanced around the island at them. She hadn't been this attracted to a man in her entire life, and now she had three breathtaking soldiers standing in her kitchen.

"So, where are you staying tonight?" she asked.

"We're going to check in at a bed and breakfast we passed on our way into town," Benji answered.

"Why don't you stay here? I have plenty of beds ... and breakfast." Ivy looked at them with wide, hopeful eyes. "Ollie wouldn't want you staying anywhere else while you're in his hometown. Please, stay as long as you like."

"Are you sure? We wouldn't want to intrude...." Hart stopped talking and looked toward the pantry.

Ivy had noticed Benji disappear into the pantry without Hart or Walker's knowledge, but she liked that he felt comfortable enough with her to help himself. She smiled at their displeased expressions and waved away their concern. While they focused on Benji, Ivy stole the moment to admire her childhood heroes. She adored how many traits they shared with her brother. Ivy imagined them in the desert for years at a time, living in each other's pockets and relying on the tight cohesion of their team for friendship, commitment, and unswerving trust. Their separate lives ultimately blending as one. She thought about the three of them losing Oliver that day in Libya, a huge piece of themselves tragically ripped away. They stood bravely before her, but their hearts were still healing. Like hers.

Ivy breathed out sadly and tucked her hair behind her ear.

Benji emerged with a pack of salt and vinegar crisps in one hand, salsa dip in the other, and a bag of nacho chips hanging in his teeth. Walker rolled his eyes, and Ivy laughed.

"I'm sorry, Ives, we haven't eaten since the Interstate. I'll replace them tomorrow I promise," Benji mumbled around the bag of nachos. He dropped it on the island.

"No, please don't buy more, there's plenty in there. I don't eat a lot these days anyhow," she replied.

Hart glanced at her, and she caught his concern, then he jumped up and sat on the kitchen counter beside the refrigerator and looked at her, his brown eyes filling with a warm compassion.

*God, he was handsome.* Ivy breathed out suddenly. She quickly faced the island again, hoping he didn't catch the desire in her eyes. There was something about Hart that intrigued her. He seemed calm and content, but his eyes were drenched with a sad torment that made her want to take his hand and lead him somewhere safe. She remembered Oliver telling her that Johnny Hart was the bravest of them all ... so why did he seem so afraid?

Ivy tapped her finger on her Budweiser, thinking.

"You know, Ollie used to get that *exact* look in his eyes," Walker commented. "Usually when something troubled him."

"Did he?" Ivy dropped her gaze to her drink and smiled timidly to herself.

She felt Hart's eyes on her again. She went to speak, but her arm knocked her Budweiser off the stone surface. Walker lunged down beside the island to catch the bottle as it fell. He scooped it up in his right hand, spun on the spot, and hurled the bottle at Benji.

Benji reacted on cue. He threw his hand out in front of him and caught the flying Budweiser, which came to a dead stop in his left hand. A small amount of beer splashed into his eyes, and he screwed up his face in response. With his eyes still closed, Benji smiled and casually continued to crunch on the handful of nachos he had placed in his mouth only seconds before Walker rescued Ivy's beer.

"Wow," Ivy gasped at their swiftness.

Walker and Hart burst into laughter, and Benji nodded at their amusement. He blindly handed the beer back to Ivy and lifted his t-shirt to wipe his eyes.

Ivy glanced fleetingly at Benji's rippling abs.

"Thank you," she said sweetly, taking the bottle from him.

"No problem, Ives." He shot both Walker and Hart a mutinous grin that Ivy read as a warning to watch their backs. She tried not to laugh and was thankfully saved by a loud knock on the door.

"Oh no!" Ivy exclaimed. She turned and grabbed Hart's wrist and read the time on his watch, then looked up at him with big, blue eyes.

"Where are you headed?" he asked, conscious of her nearness.

"The Silver Moon Gala, I have to go!"

Ivy hurried to the front entry hall to collect her things. She reached into her clutch and misted her wrists and her neck with perfume, reapplied her lipstick, then opened the door for her driver.

"I'll be one minute!"

He smiled contently at her. "Take your time, Miss Rose."

"Yeah, I've heard about it," Walker mentioned to the boys. "They close the beach and throw a marquee and dance floor on the sand. All the rich and famous across the country attend and donate their money to charity. The tickets are thousands of dollars a pop."

Benji and Hart glanced at each other in disbelief. They stared at Walker, baffled by his knowledge of an event they had never even heard of.

"How the hell do you know all this, Walker? We've been walking Libya for the past three years!" Benji asked in awe.

"I read it once at Alfatah," he shrugged, remembering the restaurant in Il Liberta Square. "A girl handed me the *Los Angeles Times*. They knew we were Americans, but don't ask me where she got it from."

Ivy returned to the kitchen with her silk clutch and smelling like sweet perfume. Hart's strength dissolved again in her presence. If she were any other woman, he thought, *any* other woman. Not Oliver's sister. He sipped his beer and tried to stifle his desire.

"Rich and famous, hey," Benji grinned at her, raising his bottle. "Sounds like a rather prestigious event. I didn't realize you were famous, Ives! What do you do?"

"Oh no, no," she laughed, "I'm not famous."

The soldiers looked at her.

"Or rich. Well, I do have money … ugh." Ivy winced. "I'm sorry, that sounded so vain."

Hart smiled to himself, humored by her sweetness. She bit her bottom lip, and he forced himself to look into his beer. Ivy stirred something within him that he had never felt before. Oliver told him that she would like him, but he didn't say anything about how he'd feel for her in return. Where was the cautionary advice from his best friend? Her exceptional beauty and untainted innocence called for at least some advance warning so he knew what he was walking into. Oliver never once mentioned in all their years, that one day, when Ivy opened the door to him, he would never be able to close it again.

"Why don't you come with me?" Ivy asked, interrupting Hart's thoughts.

He looked up into her crystal blue gaze, and for the briefest moment, he thought he was looking into Oliver's eyes. It struck him like a bullet to the chest.

"Ah, Ives, I don't think they'll let us in." Benji laughed, tugging at the black cotton tee that clung pleasingly to his body.

She sighed inwardly at his dreamy physique, which she had noticed they all shared. Ivy found herself being won over by all three of them, and her cheeks warmed with desire.

"I have suits," she told them, forcing herself to focus. "I

mean, Ollie has suits, heaps of them. We had to go to these things all the time when we were younger. You're all the same size as him, and I know they'll fit."

"I think Benji means we're not invited, Ivy," Hart responded politely.

"Oh. You don't need an invite, you have me," Ivy replied.

The soldiers looked at her, confused.

"Ollie never told you? The Silver Moon Gala is my event." She smiled. "You are the three friends that Oliver thought the world of … and it would mean the world to *me* if you were there."

Ivy bit her lip nervously and waited for their answer. The soldiers looked at each other wordlessly, and she wondered if they were communicating like they would in Phoenix—when silence was necessary for survival.

"Why not?" Benji smiled cautiously. He looked to Hart for a reaction.

Hart stared back at him with an indecipherable expression.

Ivy beamed at Hart for a moment and then dropped her hopeful gaze to the floor while she waited for his response; she didn't want her eagerness to persuade him if he was reluctant to attend.

Hart glanced at Ivy with his musing brown eyes, and then a gorgeous smile swept across his face. "Okay," he replied warmly. She looked up at him, and he nodded happily in surrender to her.

The three soldiers grinned cheerfully and Ivy's heart beat faster with sweet anticipation for the night ahead. Only half an hour ago the house was empty, she thought. Hollow. Like her heart. Mourning the dead silence that floated around its walls. How quickly things can change for the worse … or for the better.

"The Gala starts at 6 p.m. Your names will be on the guest list," she told them.

She caught Hart's eyes before she left the kitchen, stirring a deep yearning inside of her. One that had lain dormant and un-touched in the depths of her being until now. Ivy sighed as she walked to the front door, allowing herself an elated smile despite the grief and fear that had haunted her these past two months. Hope reigned foolishly within her heart, but she embraced it for now. Soon hope would leave her indefinitely, along with Oliver's soldiers.

Walker and Benji stared at Hart across the stone island. The three of them leaned on their elbows and fidgeted with their beer bottles. They waited for Ivy to leave before speaking again.

"You okay, buddy?" Walker asked.

Hart looked at him for a moment or two and then groaned into his hands, rubbing his jaw in thought.

"What? I thought that went well?" Benji responded innocently, taking another sip of his beer.

"She's just like Ollie; kind, thoughtful, happy. What is it?" Walker asked.

"Nothing. Nothing at all." Hart sighed. "She's gorgeous."

"So are we really going tonight?" Walker asked Hart, still unconvinced, but smiling.

"I'm all for it!" Benji replied.

Hart stared at Benji and Walker for a moment as he contemplated their eagerness to do something pleasant for a change. He needed to leave this town before he discovered what it was that pulled him so strongly toward this girl he didn't know. The last thing he expected to do was attend a gala with her. Hart knew from experience that nights like these never went to plan, and he was already feeling sick with anxiety. The tremor rattled him deep within, but he smiled through the pain.

Walker looked at his friend and waited for him to answer. No matter where they were—the desert or home—he never questioned Hart's motives. He trusted him always. If Hart needed to leave La Mar, then he would go with him gladly.

"I think we should go with Ivy," Benji said into the contemplative silence. His smile disappeared. "Let's go and enjoy ourselves without the threat of being shot at if we ain't paying any fucking attention. Be young and reckless for once in our lives. Seriously, we haven't done anything like this in years."

Hart finished his beer and looked at Benji. "That's what worries me."

*Chapter 6*

# - SILVER MOON GALA -
## July 2014

### 1

IVY LEANED AGAINST the balustrade at the end of the dance floor and gazed wistfully into the golden light that cast itself across the ocean. Oliver was there tonight, in the orange sky. She sensed his comforting presence in the stillness that kissed the glowing sea. In the nostalgic shrills of the terns that glided along its glassy surface. In the sun's rays that sparkled in her crystal eyes and splintered through the dark void that had consumed her heart. Oliver was *alive*. She saw him today … in Benji's cheer, Walker's protectiveness, and Hart's warmth. He was in the delivery of soldiers she never saw coming.

She took a deep breath and smiled excitedly at the sky. The Silver Moon Gala was in full swing, buzzing cheerfully with its three hundred guests, twenty-five wait staff, ten chefs, eight bartenders, two bouncers, and one journalist from the *Los Angeles Times*. The standard, uninvited news crew set themselves up hours beforehand on the sand further along the shore, eagerly inching closer to the event and her list of elite guests. For an hour, her bouncers manned the beach to prevent the unwelcome attention, but her guests never complained about the distant invasion, so it didn't concern Ivy. In fact, most of them appreciated the publicity.

The Gala sat tucked away toward the quiet end of Town Beach, closer to the cliffs, where no one liked to swim because of the dangerous rocks in the shallows. It was for this reason that they had the beach to themselves, an exclusive party on the sand.

Timber steps led from the dancefloor to the sand where Ivy had arranged a few bonfires blazing for her guests. It had been Oliver's idea. She loved the formality of the Gala itself, but the informality of the bonfires created a festive ambiance later in the evening. The flickering flames enticed the guests onto the sun-warmed sand, and everyone looked forward to kicking off their shoes at the end of the night and drinking around the fire. It was her favorite part of the evening, losing herself in the tall, spell-binding flames that licked the night sky. Ivy loved watching her guests drink expensive champagne in their elegant dresses and rolled-up suits, standing barefoot by an open fire beneath the stars. Good music, beautiful food, and exciting company always amounted to an unforgettable night.

It was a perfect evening for it, too. The sun shone rich and golden across the beach as it neared sunset. The misty air hugged the cliffs. She could smell the salt in the air, and Ivy breathed in the calming scent of the ocean to settle her nervous heart before turning back to the Gala.

The Gala itself consisted of two large adjoining party tents that sprawled out from the side of the cliff. Inside one of the tents was an eye-catching cocktail bar whose back wall was the cliff face itself. A live band played in the other tent, and this year she had managed to wrangle one of the most popular bands touring the nation. It was never difficult to enlist the help of celebrities. It was for charity, and everyone knew of the Silver Moon Gala. Ivy would dial a number and mention her name, and the person on the end of the line would say yes before she even asked them for a favor. This time of year made her a popular commodity amongst the rich and famous, but Ivy loathed the attention. She couldn't think of anyone less suited to this position than her. She was awful at public speaking, and the thought of making a dozen phone calls made her wretchedly nervous. It was for charity, however, and the Silver Moon Gala was fortunate enough to raise inconceivable amounts of money for those who had none. So, Ivy dealt with the awkwardness of her introverted nature, because it was her privilege to do so.

Ivy admired the café lights strung through the large Ficus tree that hung over half the dance floor. She silently praised her team again for their effort. The entire structure of the Gala was only temporary, but it had been pieced together meticulously. All their hard work had come together magnificently once again.

Her guests mingled pleasantly among the live music and popping bottles of Bollinger. Ivy listened to the excited mumble of voices around her on the dance floor, socializing in the golden glow of the descending sun. She felt rather at ease for such a big event. Years of experience had taught her well, but a trace of disappointment still jaded her happiness; the soldiers still hadn't arrived. Ivy took a nervous breath and faced the setting sun again.

"Ivy?"

She jumped. "Tommy! Oh, hey, how are you?"

"I'm good." His blue eyes took her in. "You look beautiful, Ives."

"Thank you."

Tommy smoothed his suit and fidgeted with his tie, waiting for a compliment.

"You're not so bad yourself," Ivy replied, without looking. She searched the guests for the soldiers.

Tommy wore a white sports coat and beige chinos. His short blonde hair was gelled meticulously into a quaff above his forehead, and his blue eyes sparkled in the afternoon sun. He had a wide, attractive smile, but she hadn't seen it very often lately. He was undeniably good looking, but his behavior toward her these past few years made him less attractive in her eyes. The women in town adored him, and therefore they despised Ivy— his desire for her was no secret in La Mar. Still, he managed to keep the women satisfied so as not to lose their affection entirely. He was a notorious love rat, and the women of La Mar were, surprisingly, rather forgiving. On the rare occasion that he came across an embittered female who sought his devotion, his fake tears for Ivy drew out their compassion. They excused Tommy, and blamed Ivy. Only she had Tommy's heart, black as it was.

A guest passed them and praised Ivy on the Gala. She thanked the gentleman, and a hint of displeasure crossed Tommy's expression. It didn't escape Ivy's attention, but she ignored him.

"Ivy," Tommy spoke firmly.

Her eyes lingered on the guests.

"Ivy!"

Ivy looked at him.

"How were you this afternoon after I left you?" he asked.

She smiled at another guest. "I was fine. Why do you ask?"

"Well, you told me you wanted to be alone."

Ivy looked at him. She wondered if he had seen the soldiers arrive at her place this afternoon.

Her smile disappeared. "I did want to be alone."

"See, you said that, but I wanted to know who…," Tommy trailed off.

Ivy searched his unblinking eyes for the rest of his question, but she didn't find it.

He scratched his nose awkwardly and sighed, "I just wanted to know if you were okay after I left."

She frowned curiously at him.

Another guest interrupted their conversation to praise Ivy, and Tommy acknowledged them with a look of distaste.

"Why wouldn't I be okay?" Ivy ran her fingers through her hair and sighed. She knew where this conversation was leading. "Please don't start this now. Not here."

"You said you needed space."

She tightened her eyes and rubbed her forehead.

"Tommy—"

"What? Don't be mad at me, Ives."

"I'm not mad," she said quietly, aware of her guests. "You have been checking on me every day since Ollie died, sometimes more than once. I just don't want you to get the wrong idea about us. We've talked about this."

Tommy twirled a lock of her hair between his fingers and leaned into her to talk. "I care about you. You know how much you mean to me."

"I know," Ivy placated. She turned her head to discourage him. "But you know how I feel in return."

Tommy took a deep breath and stepped away from her. Ivy watched him from the corner of her eye. He stood unmoving for a brief moment while he considered her, then she looked up and recognized the same deflated expression that she had witnessed in him almost every day since Oliver died. No matter how many times she rejected him, he never gave up.

Ivy sighed wearily. "Tommy, please."

"It's fine. You said you needed time alone, so that's what I'll give you. I won't give up on you, Ivy Rose. You are one in a million."

Ivy sighed despairingly and watched him walk away with his usual confident arrogance. It was like breaking up with someone over and over, yet never dating them in the first place. Something had to give, eventually.

"Miss Rose?"

Ivy jumped in fright and turned to the waiter standing beside her. He smiled and lifted a tray of drinks to her.

"Champagne?" he asked.

"Yes, thank you. Excellent timing." She needed a drink. One slightly stiffer than champagne. Nonetheless, she lifted a flute from the tray and smirked. "Don't go far. I'll need another one of these in five minutes."

The waiter laughed. "I'll keep an eye on your glass, Miss Rose."

Ivy turned around and leaned on the balustrade again. The sun was finally setting, yet the night was still young. She tried to lift her spirits, but as she sipped her champagne, she thought about Tommy and his erratic behavior. He was becoming unpredictable and increasingly angry, and his possessive behavior was beginning to frighten her. Ivy took another sip of her champagne to dismiss her sudden somberness.

The ocean spangled gold and dark blue under the sunset, and she thought about the three soldiers who had obviously declined her invitation. It was a lot to ask of them on their first night here. She was nothing but a stranger to them. Just Oliver's younger sister. They came here to offer their condolences, and now they were free to go.

Ivy sighed. Her heart sunk with the sun as it slipped peacefully over the horizon, then she finished off her champagne in one lugubrious gulp. When she turned back to the dance floor, the waiter was standing in front of her with a sparkling flute of champagne. She glanced at her empty glass and laughed, then handed it to him when he reached for it.

"I should have said two minutes," Ivy screwed up her face, embarrassed.

He shrugged his shoulders and smiled without passing any judgment. "You obviously needed it."

Ivy sighed. "You have no idea."

"I believe a message has been left for you at the front door, Miss Rose. They would like you to see to it when you can, but there is no rush."

"No, I'll go now, thank you."

She predicted a note from the soldiers, politely rejecting her invitation. The waiter left her and Ivy ran her fingers through her hair. She took a deep breath and looked back at the orange sky ... *they're not coming, Ollie.*

Ivy threaded her way across the crowded dance floor to the front entrance under the main tents. The band was loud inside, in a happy, chaotic way. It was dark, and the atmosphere was exciting, but she couldn't feel anything but the foreboding disappointment that waited for her at the Gala's entrance.

A man bumped into her by accident and Ivy stopped walking. Her heart seemed to have lodged uncomfortably in her throat, and she considered not going any further. If she didn't get the message, then there was still a chance they might come. She seriously considered it, for a few seconds longer than she should have, Ivy sighed again. It was too perfect. Too lucky having three, thoughtful soldiers arrive on her doorstep in the wake of her brother's death—she never needed them more. Ivy's frown drifted dolefully in a sea of smiles. It crossed her mind that they may have moved on to Mexico after she had left for the Gala. She did put them on the spot after all.

"I am such an idiot!" she shouted. No one heard her over the music, but it seemed to affirm the statement when she said it out loud.

Ivy reached the front entrance, and the doors were closed. The two men in charge of security seemed at ease, casually chatting without a care in the world. Then she remembered the waiter had mentioned there was no rush.

"Hey Richie," she interrupted.

"Ives! How's your night been, gorgeous?"

Richie had been one of the Gala's security guards ever since she started the event seven years ago. He lived in New York with his young family, but he flew back to San Diego each year especially for her. He was six-foot-four and built like a buffalo. His eyes were dark and sinister, and he wore a few mean scars that carved across his face and attested his durability. He naturally frightened people from most walks of life, which was convenient for his profession. Unbeknownst to most, however, Richie had a heart of gold, and she loved him for it. The night wouldn't be the same without him, at least not for Ivy. Besides herself, Richie was the longest standing member of staff.

"The night has been good, so far," she replied.

"Just good? Damn it, Ives! You want me to come in there and dance with you?"

"No, no, no," Ivy grinned. "I've seen your moves."

"What are you talking about? You love my moves," Richie cooed, cozying up to her.

Ivy bowed her head into her hands and laughed.

Richie stopped dancing and threw his arm around her shoulders. "Yeah, alright, later then. What can I help you with?"

"I heard there was a message left for me?" Ivy looked at him and tapped her fingers together nervously.

"A message?" Richie twisted his face. "No, no message, but now that you're here, I do have a minor quandary out the front that I do need your assistance with. I can't get rid of them. Persistent little buggers. They've been out there all night!"

"Okay," she hesitated. "Is it safe to go out there?"

Ivy remembered the past years of trouble at the door. People would fly in from all over the country to wait near the entrance and catch a glimpse of her guests and the Gala, and some years it got a little out of hand. She dreaded to think what might have happened had Richie not been around to help her, and tonight seemed like one of those nights.

Richie walked to the door and opened it for her. The crowd outside usually dissipated after the first hour, and so he appeared comfortable enough to let her go out there alone.

"Are you coming with me?" she asked.

"Nope, you'll be alright. These guys are harmless."

Ivy gazed up at him as she walked past, her crystal eyes pleading for his accompaniment.

"I'll leave the door open, you big baby. They keep telling me their names are on the list, but I've been over it a hundred times, and they aren't on it! My instincts are spot on, Ives, these three gentlemen wouldn't hurt a fly."

"Three?"

"Yeah." He laughed and shook his head, then he moved out of the doorway to let her through.

Ivy's heart raced, and she hurried to the door. Behind it were Oliver's soldiers sitting idly on the balustrade at the bottom of the ramp. They laughed and talked as though they didn't have a care in the world, and Ivy smiled to herself and watched them from the doorway. America's most highly-trained killers ... wouldn't hurt a fly, eh?

Oliver's suits fit them perfectly. They were heartachingly handsome, and Ivy's heavy spirit lifted weightlessly off the ground. The night was young again.

"Hey," she called out.

Walker ditched his cigarette into the sand behind him, and the three soldiers stood instinctively to attention.

"Oh," Ivy threw her hands over her mouth in their response. "I didn't mean to startle you like that."

"Ivy!" Hart laughed softly. He walked up the ramp toward her. "We're always up to no good when we get caught off guard like that."

She smiled playfully. "You three? I don't believe it."

"Don't believe it, Ives, we're saints," Benji replied. He hit Hart on the chest with the back of his hand as he pushed past him up the ramp to greet Ivy.

"How long have you been waiting out here?" Ivy asked.

The three of them looked at each other and shrugged.

"An hour and a half, maybe?" Benji replied.

Ivy pulled a face and dropped her coy gaze to the timber ramp beneath her.

"You forgot to put our names on the door!?" Benji exclaimed.

"I am so sorry!" Ivy tried not to laugh. "I was overwhelmed

with the three of you showing up at my house, and when I got here there were so many things that needed my attention, and I thought I let Richie know about you … but clearly I didn't, and—"

"Ivy, Ivy, hey," Hart stopped her and smiled, "we were fine out here, don't you worry about us."

"Yeah. Hart's right, we could hear the band from here, so we just hung out and talked," Walker added.

"It's not often we get to relax without the threat of being killed. We even contemplated going for a swim." Benji grinned. "We haven't had a decent ocean swim in years."

"Years?" Ivy frowned. "You guys should go for a swim. Don't worry about the Gala."

Hart smiled to himself. Her innocence was endearing. "We'll swim tomorrow. Should we go inside? We don't want to keep you from your guests."

"Oh. Actually, I'm a little nervous to go back inside," Ivy said sheepishly.

She leaned against the balustrade and fiddled with the head of a bolt strung through the timber. Her silk dress draped over the side of the ramp and brushed the fine white sand below her. Ivy looked straight up into the heart of the Ficus tree and took a deep breath.

"I have to do a speech in five minutes," she said.

Ivy seemed to go pale again, and Hart moved toward her in concern. He recalled the moment he caught her in his arms only hours before. When her light burst through his wounded heart and into the darkness that plagued his soul. A moment that he would never forget, and that she would never know.

He could smell her coconut scent when he got closer to her. Her shoulders were sun-kissed and smooth, and the golden sky made her skin shimmer like tanned silk. Hart already knew more about her than any other woman he had ever known. Physically, that is—he had catalogued everything about her, including the dark freckle that sat sweetly under her left eye, like an eternal tear. Every part of her intrigued him. Every part of her was irresistible to him.

She looked up at the soldiers and blushed. "No matter how many times I do it, speaking in front of a crowd seems to scare the hell out of me."

"Well, you're not alone there," Walker agreed.

Ivy looked at him and smiled.

Hart tucked his hands into his pockets when her color returned. "I imagine you're pretty good at it," he mentioned.

Ivy looked from Walker to Hart. "No, I don't think I am."

Hart's brown eyes caught her gaze, but a coy charm forced him to look away. Ivy smiled, besotted by his humility. She melted divinely in the simmering warmth he evoked within her … it made her incapable of thinking about anything else but him. He strolled past her to the Gala door and his delightful scent lingered on the air. She felt the space between them, as though every particle that separated them ignited with heated passion. She was falling in love with a man she had met just a few hours ago—it was senseless and irrational, but she couldn't help herself. These men were thoughtful and sweet, and remarkably unruffled by the world around them. Ivy imagined what horrors they had witnessed in the past, and she shivered when she thought about Oliver.

"Come on. We'll be there waiting for you when you're finished." Hart took her hand and encouraged her toward the door. Walker and Benji followed closely behind.

Ivy felt dizzy with nerves. Speaking in front of three hundred people was intimidating enough in itself, but it was her choice of charity that made her stomach turn uneasily. These soldiers weren't supposed to be here tonight. Walker, Benji, Hart … *what if they run?*

She considered finding someone else to talk. Her assistant, maybe? Taylor was far better at this kind of thing anyhow … then her thoughts drifted to Hart's hand in hers, for the second time today. She mused over it as she walked behind him, sighing inwardly, struggling to keep her thoughts hidden. His hands were boyish and sexy, and strong. His skin was tanned and smooth, and he held her ever so gently. She wondered if it were his hands that made him such a capable soldier; handling his weapons with such careful precision and lightness.

Ivy's breath deepened at the thought. She imagined the warmth of his steady hands gliding up her stomach, pressing her against the wall with a firm but gentle strength, mindful not to hurt her … lifting her summer dress around her hips and breathing into her neck with his hot, hungry desire … then a small groan escaped Ivy's lips.

The soldiers huddled around her with wary expressions, and Ivy nearly died with embarrassment.

"Are you okay?" Hart asked.

"I'm fine," she lied. "Just nervous."

"You're not going to pass out again, are you?" Benji asked.

"No," she answered too quickly.

"You're losing color, Ives," he frowned.

Ivy smiled and buried her eyes into her hand, cringing at her excruciating behavior. Her actions were out of character, and she blamed the soldiers. She was glad the nerves drained her color because she felt her cheeks burning a scarlet red under their watchful eyes.

She laughed timidly. "I promise I won't faint."

Hart let go of her hand, and she tucked her hair behind her ear and took a deep breath. Ivy stared back at the men, who watched her with their doting concern, each so handsome.

The door beside them flung open, and a woman threw herself out of it impatiently.

"Ivy? Ivy!" Her eyes widened. "What the fuck are you doing out here? I've been looking all over for you!"

"Oh Taylor, I know, the speech! I'm coming now! I'm sorry, I … I got caught up out here."

Taylor glanced at the three good looking men who stood chivalrously around Ivy, and her jaw dropped. "Oh, my. Is this a photo shoot for the Gala?"

"A photo shoot? No—" Ivy answered.

"Why didn't you tell me about it?" Taylor interrupted.

Ivy looked at Hart and grinned.

"Hang on, there are no cameras?" Taylor frowned, looking around.

Ivy laughed. "It's not a photo shoot, Taylor."

"Who are these guys then? They're draped all over you like you're in a fucking Calvin Klein commercial."

The three soldiers took a mindful step away from Ivy.

"Oh, look at them move in sync like that, adorable," Taylor

sniggered contentedly at their reaction.

Ivy laughed. She looked up at the soldiers, who were mildly embarrassed and a little confused.

"Walker, Benji, Hart, this is my assistant, Taylor. She keeps this whole event running smoothly, because if it were up to my organizational skills, we'd be dancing on the sand with bonfires and bottles of champagne." She laughed.

"Sounds perfect," Walker responded.

"I'm sorry, what did you just say?" Taylor asked, strutting down the ramp toward Walker.

Her hair was pulled back into a long, glossy, black ponytail that flicked devilishly behind her when she walked. She wore bright red lipstick, and her lash extensions were long and dark and Ivy could tell Walker was caught off guard by her small stature yet commanding presence. She wore golden Louboutin stilettos that gave her a few extra inches, but she still stood a good foot shorter than Walker when she reached him.

"I, uh, liked the sound of the bonfires," he replied weakly, put off balance by her prickly personality.

"I worked my perfect ass off to pull all this together tonight! No offense, Ivy, you helped a little," she winked at Ivy and then glared back at Walker, "and you mention you'd rather sit on the sand next to a fucking bonfire. This is a prestigious event you are attending! Maybe you don't deserve to be here?"

The three soldiers looked at each other, Hart and Benji amused at Walker's situation. Walker responded with a few weak noises that the guys had never heard before, then he closed his mouth before he got himself into any more trouble. He fought back a smile that made Hart and Benji start to laugh.

Ivy chuckled and received a horrified glare from Taylor.

"Oh, now you're laughing, too?" Taylor rolled her eyes.

"Taylor! Please," Ivy stopped her kindly, "I invited them tonight because they were good friends of Oliver's. They served with him in Afghanistan and Libya for over twelve years."

Taylor's behavior changed instantly in light of her new knowledge. She threw her hands up to hide her face.

"Fuck, I'm so sorry, but you can't blame me! Ivy, you should be inside on stage, and instead, you're gallivanting out here with these ... these *incredibly* good-looking fellas!" Taylor rested her hands on her hips and eyed the three men. "Look at you three, no way you're soldiers?"

"I'm afraid so, ma'am." Benji winked at Ivy.

Taylor looked at him. "And you are Ollie's boys?"

"Now and always," he replied.

Taylor smiled pleasantly at Ivy.

"I really should get back inside," Ivy said apologetically, looking away from Taylor and attempting to conceal her similar delight.

"No, no, it's okay," Taylor waved Ivy's concern away, peering up at Walker, "they're having the time of their lives in there, we have a few minutes to spare."

Ivy smirked.

Taylor rested her hand on Walker's chest. She rubbed his suit collar between her forefinger and her thumb, then glanced at Ivy and dropped her jaw in theatrical excitement.

"What's your name?" she asked, peering back at him.

Having regained his composure, Walker looked down at her with an unflinching, subtle amusement. "Josh Walker."

"Will you save me a dance tonight, Josh?"

Walker smiled. His dark eyes lingered on her for a brief moment, then he sunk his hands calmly into his pockets with her small hands still resting against his chest. "Maybe."

The desire smoldered in Taylor's dark eyes when she turned back to the Gala. She could wrap a man around her little finger with a single glance, but she had no control over Walker, and it visibly rattled her confidence. Ivy recognized the intimidation in her friend's eyes, because she felt it, too.

Ivy waited for Taylor to enter the tents and then grinned at the soldiers. "I'm so sorry about that."

Benji hit Walker. "What happened there, buddy? I ain't ever seen you lost for words before."

"I'm not sure," Walker grinned. He rubbed his chest. "Do you think she loves me or hates me?"

Hart laughed. "I'd say a bit of both."

2

THE LIGHT faded on the horizon as night fell. One by one the stars lit up the sky. The air was warm and still, and the cliff face danced with the flames and shadows from the bonfires. Ivy wanted nothing more than to kick off her shoes and slip away to the sand with her three soldiers, but her appointment as hostess kept her from doing so.

"Excuse me," she spoke softly into the microphone.

The Gala hushed to listen to her talk.

"Hello, everyone," she said.

The guests turned to look at Ivy with pleasant, waiting smiles. Ivy stood in front of the band, which took up most of the stage at the far end of the two large tents. The light was dim, and she heard the faint hum of voices diminish as everyone eventually caught on to the silence.

When everyone fell quiet, Ivy started her speech.

"Hi, I'm sorry to interrupt your night. I can see you're all having a wonderful time. Well, I hope you are—are you having a great night?" Ivy asked boisterously.

The guests raised their glasses and cheered.

"Good, I'm glad. I am, too. I hope you all enjoyed Alex Gravelle's heavenly menu tonight." She scanned the Gala for Alex. "Where is that guy?"

A man waved at her from behind the bar. He had a glass of red wine in his hand and a heartened grin on his face.

"There you are! Behind the bar, of course. If you're not in the kitchen, you're behind the bar."

The guests laughed, and Alex shrugged proudly.

"I hope they're not making you work back there?" Ivy grinned. "You're done, Alex, go and put your feet up by the fire!"

The guests cheered Alex, and Ivy laughed.

Hart couldn't take his eyes off her. Captivated, wholeheartedly, by her charisma. By her beauty. By her voice.

"Alex, it was magical, as always," she spoke into her microphone. "He flew in from Alaska, of all places. Forget taxis—this guy had to take a snowmobile, two seaplanes, and an American Airlines flight to get here and feed us tonight…."

The guests cheered again, and Alex nodded appreciatively.

"….a simple thank you isn't enough. You are amazing, and you know how much I love you." Ivy blew him a kiss, and he blew her one back in return.

Hart, Walker, and Benji looked at each other, clearly impressed by Ivy. Her sweetness lit up the room. If Ivy smiled, the room smiled. If Ivy crinkled her nose with delight, the guests did, too. It was extraordinary to witness. She had the room under her spell, and the soldiers fell willingly under her enchantment.

"Oh, there are far too many people to thank tonight, and you all know who you are. *Seven* years, can you believe it?" Ivy smiled proudly. "Without you, this event could never happen. A piece of my heart belongs to each one of you, and I know the world is a better place with each of you in it. My world especially."

The guests and the staff applauded their efforts.

"But now it is time for the bittersweet part of the evening."

The room fell quiet, and Ivy took a deep breath. She glanced at Oliver's soldiers in the center of the room. They watched her in silent awe. Their smiles were soft and content, but they were quicker than anyone else to catch her waning strength. Their cheer faded into concern amongst the smiling faces surrounding them. Ivy ran her fingers back and forth across her forehead and stared blankly at the piece of paper in her hands, deep in thought. Neatly written in front of her was heartache and suffering, and it shook incomprehensibly in her hands. Ivy willed her hands to keep still. They weren't supposed to be here; grief had scarred their bravest of hearts, and she couldn't bear to reopen their wounds—to see them bleed.

Ivy exhaled sharply into the microphone and forced a smile. "I'm sorry."

Hart frowned. He sensed a sudden shift in her mood, and he listened to the unnerving silence that fell dramatically over the marquee. The lively ambiance waned quickly in her sadness, and the guests waited patiently with an empathetic somberness.

Walker glanced at Hart and nodded in the direction of a group of weeping guests. Hart considered them, then shifted his troubled gaze back to Ivy and waited. A woman who had been standing on stage in the background walked over to Ivy and placed her arm around her to encourage her to go on.

Ivy sighed loudly into the microphone and laughed at herself, then she glanced at the guests and caught a sea of sympathetic smiles.

"We come together tonight to raise funds for the Paper Soldiers," she breathed. "A charity that is focused on the families who are left behind after losing a loved one who served their country...," Ivy's voice faded. She bowed her head and bit on her quivering lip.

The room fell silent again. Walker sighed to himself and closed his eyes. This wasn't good for Ivy ... or Hart.

"Like I said, bittersweet." Ivy grinned through her teary eyes, but the room didn't respond. The guests fought back tears of their own.

An older woman leaned over to Hart and whispered into his ear, "It was her brother, Oliver Rose. I don't know if you heard, but he died a couple of months ago overseas in the war. He was a soldier. A true sweetheart. Ivy's hero." She shook her head. "Poor, sweet girl."

Hart nodded in response. *I didn't hear about it ... I was there. I watched him die.* He looked down into his hands. He stretched his fingers in and out, and desperately tried to ignore the tingling sensation that prickled his fingertips.

"Paper Soldiers is an incredible group that is dedicated to providing emotional and financial support to families who have lost a loved one to the war ... to ensure they can keep moving forward at such a tragic time in their lives. They are the shoulders you can cry on, the ears who will listen, and the foundations on which to rebuild yourself. Nothing is straightforward in times of loss. It can be a rollercoaster of emotions. You may be prepared for the climb, yet you can never be prepared for the fall."

Ivy paused for strength.

"One day you're finally moving forward," she continued. "The next day you're hoping the world has forgotten you exist, so no one notices you didn't make it out of bed that day."

Hart listened to the soft eloquence of Ivy's voice. Her words floated over him like a white light that kissed his wounds and fought back against the darkness. He willed her light to enter him, but the darkness was too powerful. *Oliver.* He killed her brother ... if only she knew of his betrayal. There was no world in which he deserved her light.

Hart clenched his numb hands and tucked them into his pockets.

"Jane, the founder of Paper Soldiers, spoke to me yesterday, and she is here to tell you a little about the charity." Ivy turned to the woman holding her hand. "She said that everyone copes with tragedy differently, but one thing remains the same…."

The woman smiled and wiped away her tears.

"….you told me that everyone needs someone to lean on while they're hurting." Ivy smiled to herself. "But letting someone in is a lot harder than it sounds. Believe me."

Ivy continued, "My past has taught me how important it is to have someone standing by you to steer you through the unforeseeable impediments of a broken heart. To take your hand and guide you through the darkness, because they are the ones who can see the light when you no longer can…."

Ivy looked at Oliver's soldiers.

"….if you lose faith in the world, then put your faith in that person. Give them a chance to show you that life, is still worth living."

The guests raised their full glasses and thoughtful gazes to Ivy, but she only had eyes for the three broken soldiers who had walked into her life that afternoon. They watched her with their intense, unwavering gazes. The soldiers hung on every word she spoke, because she was speaking to them. They were here for some reason unknown to her still, but she was certain of one thing; there was an unmistakable torment behind their kind eyes. A suffering. A sense of sadness. *Oliver.*

Ivy wanted to fall to her knees in front of three hundred people and beg his soldiers to stay with her. *Take my light. Take it all. I can't bear to see you suffer over my brother. Stay with me and I will show you, life….*

"Thank you, Ivy. We appreciate your kindness and your courage after everything that has happened over the past couple of months." Jane smiled into the microphone. "I had the great privilege of knowing Oliver. Like many of you, I'm sure."

The crowd nodded in a cheerful grief that saddened Hart.

Ivy stepped away to give Jane the center stage. She caught Hart's eyes. They were dark and uncertain. Something troubled him, and Ivy's heart raced fretfully in his lingering gaze.

Jane continued, "Oliver gave me the courage to start Paper Soldiers, and I dedicate its wonderful success to him, and to you,

Ivy." She turned and took Ivy's hand. "He once told me that a decision made with all of his heart was a decision he could live with. Regardless of whether the decision was the right one or the wrong one, there was always something gained. So I followed his advice and I built a foundation that I believe in, with all my heart."

Ivy looked at the soldiers again. She saw Hart bow his head and wipe his face with his hands, and then he whispered into Walker's ear. She watched them carefully as they talked. Walker considered Hart, then nodded in dejected compliance.

"Ivy. Ivy?" Jane asked.

"Yes?" Ivy blinked vaguely at her.

"I wanted to open the envelope?"

"Of course!" Ivy answered, concealing her concern for Hart.

The guests hushed with eager expressions.

"Okay then, here we go!" Jane shrilled at the crowd. "You should all be excited because this part of the night is all because of your generosity." The guests cheered and waited for Jane to open the envelope.

Ivy saw Walker pat Hart on the back before Hart weaved his way through the crowd and outside the tent. Walker and Benji followed him out. Ivy exhaled, feeling her stomach twist with distress.

"Are you ready!?" Jane asked. Her eyes widened and she gasped before she was able to read out the amount, then she started to sob uncontrollably.

Ivy looked back at Jane and smiled, grateful for the temporary distraction. "Okay. It looks like I'll be the one sharing the good news tonight."

The guests laughed at her comical expression.

"The total funds raised this year ... is two million, one hundred and sixty-two thousand dollars!"

The tent roared with excitement. Ivy grinned ecstatically. It was the most they had ever raised.

Jane squealed with happiness and kissed Ivy all over her face. "You are amazing, Ivy! Look what you have achieved! I can't even comprehend that type of money!" she shouted to Ivy over the frenzied commotion. "Thank you, thank you a thousand times, Ivy! Thank you!"

Ivy laughed with Jane and the band behind them kicked the party into full swing once again, then she snuck away in the flurry of congratulations … to find Oliver's soldiers.

3

AN HOUR HAD PASSED, and the Gala had well and truly settled back into its cheerful atmosphere. The tents seemed to swell with the laughter of the guests. The stars were out. The dance floor swayed. The bonfires crackled. The compliments continued. Everyone was thoroughly enjoying their evening.

Except for Ivy. The soldiers were gone.

She made her way across the crowded dancefloor to the balustrading which overlooked the sand. When she got there, she looked up at the silver moon that shimmered brilliantly across the dark ocean. It rippled toward her like a staircase to the stars, and she sighed at its beauty.

Ivy searched the beach from where she stood on the dance-floor, but they were nowhere to be seen. She twisted her mouth sadly.

"Hey, Ives." A man's voice whispered behind her.

Ivy turned around. "Tommy…."

"That was incredible, two million bucks, you killed it this year!" He hugged her tightly.

"I know, right!" Ivy replied, grateful for his good mood.

"Hey look, Ivy, I'm sorry about earlier. When I worry, I get frustrated, and when I'm frustrated, I get mad, and when I am mad … I say things I don't mean." He threw his hands in the air. "It's a vicious cycle of concern, and I want to apologize for my behavior."

"I understand."

She felt sorry for Tommy. They had been friends ever since they were fourteen years old. Close friends, once, but at some point he fell in love with her, and everything changed. Ivy believed the sincerity of his apology. He never meant her any harm, but ever since Oliver had died, his approach had become rather intense, and he seemed oblivious to his aggression. She found herself questioning his intentions again. Wondering how far he would go to take what he really wanted from her. She quickly brushed the thought aside. Ivy refused to believe he

155

would ever cross that line.

"Dance with me," he told her.

"I would love to, but I'm looking for someone," she lied ... the men she was looking for had left. In truth, she didn't want to encourage Tommy. "Maybe later?"

"Dance with me, Ivy."

"No, I can't."

His eyes darkened. "Whoever it is, they can wait."

"Tommy, stop!"

Tommy looked around at the guests to make sure no one was listening.

Ivy rubbed her arms with her hands, feeling cold despite the warm evening. She looked up at Tommy and frowned anxiously, concerned by the fury of his darkening gaze. Everyone thought of him as a high-achieving go-getter with an impressive university degree and an expensive trust fund. His mother wisely taught him etiquette, and Ivy believed this was the sole reason he was able to bluff his way into everyone's hearts. He wasn't lovable or kind, not anymore at least. He was a trouble-maker and distrustful. He learned how to talk the talk, and, consequently, everyone believed him. It never bothered Ivy before, but then she never had reason to worry until now.

Tommy turned to face her, and Ivy waited, disheartened by his short-lived act of contrition.

He glanced quickly around him and then leaned in to speak to her, "You give me nothing back—"

"Because I have nothing left to give," she whispered abruptly, her voice shaking. "I have lost *everything* ... my mother, my father, and now Oliver. Stop asking me for more, or there will be nothing left of me." Her heart pounded painfully in her chest, so much had happened since this afternoon, and now the soldiers had disappeared...maybe even left her entirely.

An overwhelming wave of emotions washed over Ivy. She turned to lean on the balustrade, but Tommy grabbed her arm to stop her. He dug his fingers into her flesh, and Ivy winced at the pain. She looked up at Tommy and caught him smiling at a couple who walked by them. The sweet sparkle in his eye disguised his enraged heart, and his passive demeanor frightened Ivy.

"Stop, you're hurting me," Ivy said when they left. She

exhaled and tightened her crystal eyes.

"It is supposed to hurt, Ivy. Now you know how I feel," he growled under his breath.

Ivy whimpered quietly at the pain.

Tommy gripped her even harder. "Maybe now you'll start treating me with a bit more respect."

"I give you respect." Ivy glared up at him. "It's what I'm *not* giving you that's making you angry."

Tommy forced her to spin around into the balustrading. He smiled amiably at the unassuming crowd so not to bring any attention to their altercation, and it worked. No one suspected Ivy was in any trouble. To the guests, the pair seemed merely in love.

Tommy leaned against her back and pressed her hips hard against the timber balustrade. She stifled a small cry of pain, and then he gripped the railing either side of her and Ivy was trapped. His warm breath sighed into her ear. It sent a chill down her spine and a sickening panic through her heart. Ivy was grateful for the crowded dance floor. She knew what would happen if they were at her place. Alone. No one ever checked on her. No one knew where she was. Last month she didn't leave the estate for a whole week, and nobody noticed. She had no one left, and Tommy took advantage of her dire situation. Ivy had lost all confidence in the fourteen-year-old boy she once adored; rejection had demolished his decency, and unfortunately for Ivy, she was the source of his rejection.

"You are shaking, Ivy," Tommy whispered into her ear.

Ivy didn't answer.

"I would never hurt you. Just relax. You and me, it feels good, right?" Tommy sighed in pleasure, pushing his hips subtly into hers.

"Please, stop," Ivy said quietly. She would be mortified if anyone realized she was being assaulted at her own Gala. She felt powerless. Ivy had no idea how to stop him without paying for her behavior later. She looked into the night sky in front of her, and begged the black horizon for her brother. She wondered if Oliver disappeared with the sunset. If the darkness emptied the sky of him … or if he was ever there at all?

Ivy closed her eyes at the dispiriting thought. His soldiers had moved on, and now Tommy had her right where he wanted her. Then, all of a sudden … *he was gone.*

Ivy fell away unexpectedly and was wrapped protectively in a man's arms. She felt his heartbeat racing beneath her hands, but his breath was deep and soothing, and Ivy instantly calmed in his presence. She peered up at the man who held her and saw the warm, melting eyes of the soldier she had been missing all night.

"Hart."

"Ivy, are you okay?" He brushed her golden hair away from her face and searched her eyes.

She nodded faintly.

"He didn't hurt you?"

Ivy hesitated before she answered, and she saw him frown.

"No," she answered.

"Good," Hart replied. He appeared unconvinced, but relieved, then he shot a disparaging glare at Tommy in Walker's uncompromising grip.

"What the fuck are you doing?" Walker scorned under his breath. "I saw her telling you to stop from the beach, you asshole."

Walker had Tommy pressed up against the corner of the balustrade, partly out of view from the rest of the party, but only a few feet away from Ivy and Hart. The Gala was too noisy for anyone to hear their argument, but Ivy heard every word. Benji was standing beside Walker, and the two of them stood as a powerful, unwavering force between her and Tommy.

Tommy didn't answer.

"Did you hear me?" Walker shook him.

"Fuck you!" Tommy replied. "Who the fuck are you guys anyhow? I saw you at Ivy's house this afternoon. I know everyone in town and I have never seen you guys around here before!"

Ivy sighed into her hands when she heard him, blaming herself for his impulsiveness tonight.

"What's wrong?" Hart asked her.

"Nothing." She peered up at him, thinking.

Hart studied Tommy. This man knew exactly what he was doing, and Hart didn't trust him. In a way, he reminded him of

Taym. His surreptitiousness. His lack of moral. Tommy presented himself as a genuine threat to Ivy, and Hart's initial instinct was to protect her. Danger had engrained itself into Hart's intuition a long time ago, like a sixth sense. Life had shown him that desperation was hazardous in the hands of the depraved, and he now regarded seemingly irrelevant threats as a forewarning. A precursor to conflict. Hart narrowed his eyes. Ivy had no idea what Tommy was capable of, and he had a feeling Tommy hadn't realized the full extent of his resourcefulness. Just like Taym.

Tommy attempted to free himself from Walker's hands, with no luck. "What are you guys, her God damn security? Let me go!"

Walker let go of him and glanced back at Ivy, who was tucked safely in Hart's arms. He thought about who they were to her; they had only just met tonight, but he had known of Ivy for much longer. She meant everything to him, because her brother had meant everything to them.

Walker looked back at Tommy. "Right now we're her security, and you just crossed a fucking line, my friend. Next time a woman tells you *no,* then walk away and leave her the fuck alone."

Tommy glanced past Walker at Ivy, who had been watching them warily. He looked back at the soldiers in front of him, and pushed his way past Walker to leave the confrontation. He sneered under his breath, "I'll do whatever the fuck I want."

Walker grabbed Tommy around the throat and pulled him back into the corner of the balustrade. There was a small scuffle between them, but Benji was quick to pull Walker off of Tommy.

Benji held Walker back with the length of his arm, "Walker, stop! Take it easy, man, he's not worth it!"

"I'm not worth it! I'm sorry, I didn't mean to hurt her!" Tommy's eyes widened with panic, holding his throat. He noted the danger lingering in Walker's eyes, yearning for him to retaliate so he could quench his thirst for blood. Tommy had no idea who they were, but he could tell these guys were genuine in their quest to protect Ivy … and it pissed him off.

"Walker," Ivy called to him over the music. She went to them. "Leave him be. He needs to leave the Gala, and he'll go without a fight." She gave Tommy a slow nod.

Walker stepped away from him like she asked, and Tommy relaxed. He looked at the three strangers carefully, then stared at Ivy, disgraced. He flattened his tie and puffed up his chest, and walked away, with Walker and Benji escorting him to the exit.

Ivy could tell Tommy was shaken by the confrontation. It was hard to be angry with him when he looked so vulnerable. She closed her eyes when he left, stomaching the residual shock of what just happened.

A hand took hers gently, and Ivy turned around. She warmed pleasurably in his gaze. The music was suddenly deep and slow, and her heart calmed with a sedated desire for the soldier who effortlessly soothed her concern. Commander Johnny Hart. *He hadn't run.*

A bashful grin swept across his face, and Ivy caught her breath; struck all of a sudden by his good looks and humble charm. His olive skin glowed in the soft light, and his lips were smooth and agonizingly tempting. Ivy breathed herself through his unyielding tenderness.

"How are you feeling?" Hart asked.

"I'm okay now."

Hart smiled.

"Thank you for helping me with Tommy." Ivy screwed up her face, suppressing her embarrassment.

Hart looked at her, besotted by her sweetness. "He's bad news."

"I know." Ivy bowed her head. "But he had a good heart once. It's my fault he is like this now."

"Your fault?" Hart repeated.

Ivy heard the frustration in his gentle voice. She nodded and bit her lip, then she looked up at him with large, crystal eyes, and his frustration softened in her gaze.

Hart shook his head. "Only he can be responsible for his actions, Ivy. Your heart is too big. You're going to get yourself in trouble."

Ivy breathed out a long, controlled breath when he spoke her name. His voice was gentle and thoughtful, and it purred soothingly in her ears. She felt her heart race in his attention. His nearness was her undoing.

"May I steal you for a moment?" he asked, unassumingly.

Ivy studied his thoughtful expression. He had stolen her hours ago when he showed up on her doorstep and stuttered his way into her heart. A heart that was shamefully and irrevocably his within seconds. Hart stirred an unbearable desire that threatened to break the little spirit she had left … when he would leave her indefinitely for Mexico.

Hart raised his eyebrow at her when she didn't answer, and Ivy nodded in response, kissing her spirit goodbye without regret. He stepped backward and pulled her toward him, and when she started to follow, he turned and led her through the crowded dance floor.

She gazed serenely at the night sky as she followed him. Beneath the glowing string lights that hung amongst a blanket of stars. A peacefulness surrounded her, and she succumbed to it gladly. Ivy smiled to herself, blissfully lost in the slow, rhythmic beat of the music, then she surrendered herself to the divine mystery of the soldier who held her hand, and led her unknowingly to his beautiful heart.

When they reached the center of the dance floor, Hart turned to her and smiled. Her crystal eyes sparkled at him, and he fell willingly into them. Hart took a deep breath, his tender gaze unwavering. Then he pulled her to him, slid his hand around her back, and began to sway her in time to the music.

Ivy brushed her lips lightly against his shoulder as they danced. There was no pain in his arms. No grief. No loneliness, or loss. She tried not to analyze her feelings for him, nor question how he felt for her in return. He would be gone soon, and it wouldn't matter after that. Hart would forget about her, and things would go back to the way they always were. So Ivy closed her eyes and let herself be swept away, if only for one night, in the arms of this incredible soldier.

A warm light emanated from her once again and he bathed gloriously in her wonder. She was beautiful. *Enchanting.* Her innocence broke his heart, and he could barely fathom her existence. Not in his world of war and betrayal. Hart smiled and danced slowly with her head against his heart, immersed in the feeling of her in his arms. Her beauty. Her body. Her intoxicating sweetness. He glanced over her smooth shoulders, resisting the temptation of them. The thought of her soft skin against his lips warmed his blood. He felt her hand run up his shoulder and rest on the back of his neck, where she softly ran her thumb up and down his hot skin. Her light breath against his neck sent a pleasant ripple through his deserted soul and Hart was suddenly overcome by her again. After years at war, he had become powerless against the tenderness of a woman.

He closed his eyes and sighed on the balmy air. Her coconut scent filled his senses, and he fought the urge to lift her chin and brush his lips against her warm neck, though his body implored him to do so. God he ached for her ... *Ivy. If only you knew. If only you knew I am responsible for your brother's death. Would you dance with me then? Or would you hate me as much as I hate myself?*

Hart stopped dancing and stepped away from her.

Ivy looked up at him. She searched his brown eyes, uncertain of what she saw there.

"What's wrong?" she asked.

Hart knew he didn't deserve her, not after what had happened in Libya. He saw the confusion in her expression. She searched him for an answer, but she would never find one. There was so much to say, yet no words to save her from further heartbreak. He couldn't tell her the truth of what he did. She had suffered enough.

"I can't do this," he breathed. "I'm sorry, Ivy."

He released her hands and walked away from her, leaving her on the dance floor. She watched him dodge through the guests who danced in slow-moving waves around them. Then he was gone.

Hart's intensity left her in a dreamy, exhilarating daze. Ivy breathed out slowly. She looked straight up into the starry sky and closed her eyes, and allowed the slow song to encase her enraptured soul.

4

HART SAT ON THE warm sand beneath the cliffs at the far end of the beach. The full moon cast a silver light around him. He breathed in the ocean air and sighed heavily. He took a sip of the beer he had brought with him and gazed back at the Gala in the distance. The music echoed its way down the beach, and he smiled sadly when he thought about her. He'd never felt like this before with *any* woman. There was an innocence about her that consumed his troubled soul, and it lessened his suffering and the brutality of the war. He felt himself being pulled to her as though a piece of her light was lost inside of him, yearning to go home. Longing to be back where it belonged, in its sanctuary of peace.

His soul recognized hers, though they had never met before tonight. He knew why. *Oliver.* Hart forced the thought of his friend out of his head and took another sip of his beer. The light of the moon cast a somber halo around him. It was hard not to think of his fallen friend under such a perfect sky. How did it come to be that Oliver was no longer here to enjoy this moment with him? There was a time when the full moon's dancing reflection would easily spark his excitement for the night ahead. He was at a glamorous party perched on the Pacific's shore with the most beautiful woman he had ever seen, but as he sat on his own in the darkness, away from the Gala, it all became far too overwhelming.

The light of a million stars shone down upon him from the glorious night sky, but the darkness around him was too much for the stars, their light fading before it could reach his weary soul. There was nothing to look forward to anymore. *Nothing.* He questioned his future. What sort of life lay before him if he no longer felt genuine pleasure in these perfect moments?

Hart wiped the sweat from his forehead. His grave thoughts roused the darkness inside him, summoned the anxiety that continued its stealthy assault on his soul. This was not his first anxiety attack. Since Oliver died, the bathroom cubicle at Base had become his cold, solitary asylum to conceal his torture. No one knew of his attacks, except Hannah. Not even Walker or Benji. It was *his* weakness. *His* burden to bear alone. Now he sat alone in the dark before a cathedral of silver cliffs that rendered him insignificant in size and worth. The fractured moonlight on the sea sent his mind into a vertiginous spin, and he longed for the suffocating fall. He needed it. To remind him of what he did in Libya.

He took off Ollie's blazer and laid it on the sand beside him. He loosened Ollie's tie and undid the first few buttons of Ollie's shirt, moaning quietly with the pain that radiated from deep within. He thought about Oliver, his head pressed into the broken concrete. Contentment resting in his expression, as though they were home in the Arizona desert without a care in the world. His crystal eyes burned with the dazzling reflection of Libya's setting sky as it cast itself over him for the very last time.

Hart closed his eyes tightly.

The sound of the bullet split his ears and resonated deep in his mind, in his body, shaking a destructive path through his veins and becoming a permanent reminder of a tragic day he would carry with him forever.

He held his hand up to the full moon, unclenching his fingers, and watched it tremble in the moonlight. He glanced back toward the party, and there, standing in the sand with his hands in his pockets, was Oliver.

Hart jumped to his feet, startled by the vision. He stared wordlessly at Oliver, his trembling growing fiercer with the confusing apparition. Oliver smiled cheerfully at him. He nodded his head toward the Gala as though he encouraged him to go back to the others, but Hart couldn't move. The anxiety coursed through his veins like black smoke that billowed through his body, weakening him as it spread. Hart rubbed his throbbing head and glanced back toward the Gala ... and Oliver was gone.

He groaned through the sickening feeling of the oncoming attack. Hart peered into the black sky to find comfort in the darkness, and then allowed it to encase him. He bent over, leaning on his knees, and sucked the air into his tight chest. He felt reason give way to panic, so Hart shifted his focus to what existed, something Hannah had taught him before he left Fort Bragg. He closed his eyes and felt the sand beneath his feet. The water around his ankles. He felt the beer bottle in his grip still, and he rubbed the rim of it with his thumb, feeling the smooth glass against his skin. Determined not to let it fall.

*I lived ... I lived, and he died....*

Hart growled into the air and hurled the bottle over the ocean. It whistled through the stars, then erupted into a sky full of fireworks. He groaned into his hands. With each muted explosion, the gunshot sounded and Oliver closed his eyes ... and died.

The world faded in front of him. The darkness gripped its fingers around his tortured soul, and Hart closed his eyes. A numbness stretched across his body, and the world weighed down upon his shoulders, and he knew this was it. He welcomed the immensity of it. The justified punishment. He didn't deserve to be here. He didn't deserve to be happy. Hart bared his vulnerability to the night sky and willed the stars to rob him of his weak soul. Oliver gave his life for him, and there was no going back to life as it had been. This was his pain. His suffering. His sentence. The relentless reminder of losing his best friend, should he ever forget what Oliver did for him.

Grief shattered any strength he had left, and Hart crumbled to his knees in defeat. He kneeled in the wet sand, feeling the waves washed around his legs. Then the merciless darkness he slipped into began to spin, and Hart prayed for the waves to wash him away and end whatever life he had left.

*Let the water take me. Let me die, too.*


5

Ivy's guests sighed and gasped expressively at the fireworks, but she watched on with a heavy heart. Something inside of her was telling her to go after him, but she forced herself to leave him be. It was difficult not to worry about Hart. It felt unnatural to ignore her intuition when he seemed to be suffering so greatly. There was something about her that troubled him, and Ivy knew it had something to do with Oliver.

When the fireworks finished, she frowned at the stars. She felt restless, queasy with nervous tension. Ivy took a deep breath and held it, and listened to her heart. The sudden urge to find him had her shuffling through the crowded dance floor toward the stairs that led to the beach, where she last saw him. The world seemed to push her forward, hastening her search. Something was wrong, she could feel it now. Ivy cursed herself for not looking for him sooner. He was Oliver's soldier, his brother-in-arms, his *best* friend. She had every right to be concerned for him.

When she reached the top of the stairs, she lifted the front of her gown and ditched her high heels, then ran barefoot down the stairs and into the sand. Her heart beat anxiously for him. She could feel his suffering. Wherever Hart was, he needed Oliver. He needed her....

An older gentleman grabbed her hand when she ran by and

squeezed it affectionately. He was a big man, with kind eyes and silver hair. Ivy hesitated but stopped out of respect for her father's friend.

"Flawless, Ivy. Extravagant! It always astonishes me how you are able to exceed our expectations each year!"

She smiled politely. "Thank you, William."

Ivy glanced past him down the beach toward the cliffs.

"Your parents would be so proud of you," his wife said. She reached for Ivy and kissed her on the cheek. "Oliver would be, too. Oh, Ivy Rose … you break my heart!"

She tightened her grip on Ivy's hand and started to cry. "Come on now, Joyce, don't ruin the poor girl's night with your soppy heart."

Joyce smiled through her tears. "I know, I'm sorry. You look beautiful, Ivy. You always do."

Ivy smiled and pulled Joyce in for a hug. They were the closest thing she had to family, and a sharp pain stung her heart in their company. Ivy looked up at William and caught his sympathetic gaze before he got a chance to conceal it. He pointed at his wife's back and rolled his eyes to lighten the mood, mustering a grin from Ivy. The woman reluctantly released her.

Ivy narrowed her eyes and stared down the beach into the darkness.

"Are you okay?" Joyce asked, following Ivy's line of sight.

"Can you see someone there?" Ivy asked without looking at her.

The older couple looked curiously at each other, before peering along the shore toward the cliffs.

"Nothing at all, pet," William replied. "It's too dark."

Ivy saw someone there. By the cliffs in the moonlight. The area was too familiar, even at night, and something was out of place among the rocks on the sand.

"I have to go. I'm terribly sorry." She smiled at the couple so not to cause them any alarm, then hurried toward the cliffs at the end of the bay.

Her silk gown sailed behind her as she raced along the shore, like a ghost caught in the light of the silver moon. When she got closer to the figure in the dark, she saw him kneeling in the sand with his head bowed and the water swirling around him like it was washing his broken soul into the sea.

"Hart!" Ivy cried out as she ran. She whimpered into the dark, fearing the worst for him.

Ivy ran as fast as she could, listening to the sound of her panting breath and her bare feet hitting the wet sand. The light of the Gala had faded, and the moonlight glowed like an aura around him below the cliffs. In Oliver's stories, this soldier had the strength of an immortal. His mind. His body. His spirit. Yet here he was, gradually falling into the sea with the hungry waves wearing him down, as if anticipating his imminent collapse.

She had almost reached him when his balance failed and he tilted forward. Ivy cried out to him again. She threw herself to her knees in the water in front of Hart and caught him in her arms as he fell. Her golden gown twisted fiercely around them in the black, relentless water. She felt it wrap around her ankles and her waist, making her unsteady against the strength of the water. The wave withdrew from the beach, pulling Ivy and Hart into the tumultuous sea around the cliffs. Ivy held him against her and dug her feet into the sinking sand, and when the wave left them, she pushed Hart up onto his knees again and held him carefully so he wouldn't fall.

"Hart, please!" she pleaded frantically.

His head bowed before her and he didn't respond. Ivy whimpered when a smaller wave rushed around them, threatening to drag them farther into the water.

"Hart, answer me," her voice trembled sadly. "What is happening to you!?"

Ivy lifted his head and brushed his cheek with her thumbs to try and get his attention. She saw his face in the moonlight. She saw him staring back at her with empty eyes, and her heart froze with fear.

*"No!"* Ivy shouted breathlessly to the stars. "No, please! You cannot take this soldier, too!"

She heard the wave before it came. Ivy wrapped his strong body in her arms. She buried her face into his neck and held him to her in the dark, and braced on her knees for the wave that came crashing through the rocks behind her. The water rose around her and Hart, and when it reached her shoulders, Ivy took a deep breath and sunk beneath the wave. She held Hart's face as high out of the water as she physically could, and when Ivy thought she couldn't hold her breath any longer … the wave sunk away. She gasped for air, and cried for help.

> *Hart saw her evening gown wash around him in the water like liquid gold. He saw the tears in her crystal eyes. He tried to soothe her, but he couldn't speak. He saw her lips desperately calling out his name, but he couldn't hear her. He tried to reach out and hold her, but he couldn't move. The world was dark, and it was still. Except for Ivy. She glowed like a beacon of light that lingered just out of his reach. Ivy Rose. Untouchable.*

> *Ivy. Ivy, you are here. Don't you worry about me, I'll be fine. I always am. You are beautiful, so beautiful it hurts. I left you on the dance floor because I saw us. I saw us years from now, and I saw how much I loved you. But I am broken, Ivy. Shattered. I will never be the same man I was before he died. I have done something terrible. Unforgivable. Ivy, you are my divine reprimand. My savior, my punishment. You remind me that he died saving me. I am the reason he is gone. I killed your brother. I killed Oliver. I'm so sorry. Let the water take me, Ivy. Let me die, too. If only you knew.…*

Hart closed his eyes, and Ivy cried. She lifted her eyes to the sky and pleaded for help. She was too weak to hold him up any longer. The waves were too strong, too unforgiving. Ivy closed her crying eyes and buried them into Hart's neck, feeling his warm skin against her face. She listened to the ocean, its betrayal against her. Another wave rushed through the rocks behind her, and Ivy held onto Hart as the water sucked them toward the voracious sea. She looked down the beach at the Gala and cried for help again, but her efforts were futile. She was too far away for anyone to hear. Ivy swallowed a mouthful of saltwater and gasped for air, and then a dreadful realization swept over her— *she had to let him go.*

Ivy cried helplessly against his warm chest, and when the wave pulled away from them into the sea again, she leaned into the beautiful soldier and kissed him softly on the lips.

"Ivy!?" Walker's voice boomed powerfully through the night.

"Walker?" Ivy whipped her head around toward the beach. She saw the two soldiers running toward her. "Walker! Benji! Help me!"

She wept with bittersweet relief when they reached her. The two of them grabbed Hart and pulled him effortlessly out of the water, and laid him down on the dry sand further up the beach. Benji hurried back into the water and scooped Ivy into his arms and carried her up the sand, setting her down beside Hart. He removed his suit jacket and draped it over her shoulders and warmed her in his arms.

Walker leaned over Hart's unconscious body and grabbed his hand. "Hart? Can you hear me, buddy? It's me, Walker."

Ivy looked at him through her tears when Hart didn't respond. He spoke with a relatively relaxed voice, considering the seriousness of the situation.

Benji leaned over him to check his pulse, and Walker continued to talk to Hart, waiting patiently between questions for a response. The two soldiers worked with a swift, unruffled calm while they waited for their friend to regain consciousness. Ivy tried to relax in their powerful, soothing presence. She saw the three soldiers as they were, as they had always been…as *Phoenix*. These men were no strangers to trauma. Walker and Benji were handling this situation with confidence and ease, just as they must have done a thousand times before tonight. Unlike herself. She had lost so many of her loved ones, but she had never seen someone die before. Ivy stared at Hart's peaceful expression, and she thought maybe … she hadn't held him high enough above the waves. Maybe he was under the water with her? What if he had drowned in her arms?

Ivy looked back at the waves sweeping up the silver shore and her body began to shake uncontrollably. She sobbed into her shaking hands, and finally succumbed to her shock.

Hart stirred. He blinked his eyes a few times and closed them again, and then a weak smile appeared on his face.

"That's it, buddy. Welcome back." Walker grinned down at Hart and slapped him affectionately on the cheek.

Hart took a deep breath as Ivy continued weeping into her hands. Overwhelmed with relief … *or fear.* She wasn't sure.

Benji rubbed her arms to keep her warm. "He'll be okay,

Ives. Hart is tougher than all of us put together."

Ivy nodded wordlessly in affirmation, too stunned to speak, but she felt her shock subsiding.

Hart looked around to get his bearings, and when his brown eyes met hers, they flooded with his familiar, melting warmth. Ivy took his hand and held it to her.

Walker and Benji talked to Hart about what happened. While their attention was on Hart, she soothed her trembling by gliding her fingertips along an invisible path on the back of his wet hand and over the hard muscles in his forearm, and then traced it back again. Ivy looked up at the stars after a while, waiting quietly as the soldiers talked. She thanked the universe for letting him live, then, unexpectedly … Hart's fingers responded to her touch.

He brushed his fingers across her palm and gently pushed them between hers. Ivy closed her eyes and fell divinely into the feeling of his warm, wanting touch. Her pulse slowed to a steady, tranquil throb, and she opened her eyes. Hart sat up and turned to her. His boyish charm returned, and he smiled meekly at her. His white shirt was soaked through, and Ivy forced herself not to look at his breathtaking body. The sleeves of his shirt were rolled up to his elbows, and his collar sat drenched around his broad shoulders. She glanced at the tie hanging limply against the translucent fabric, and she tried to ignore the tanned smooth-ness of his skin.

Ivy looked away and frowned at herself. How could she possibly be so attracted to him at such a traumatic moment?

"Hey, Ives?"

Ivy looked at him and forced a smile, trying to disguise her fear of what he might say.

"I'm sorry about your dress."

Ivy gazed down at the drenched, disheveled, golden silk wrapped around her body, and managed a small laugh. "Don't worry about it."

"Ivy," Hart sighed into his hands. "Ivy, I get … I … I, ugh …," he paused. Hart sifted through his thoughts, with the next word lingering hesitantly on his lips. He glanced at Walker, who had been watching him carefully.

Satisfied with Hart's look, Walker stood with Benji to give them some privacy.

When Hart looked at her again, his dark eyes filled with fear. He went to speak, but Ivy stopped him.

"It's okay, Hart. You don't have to explain," she breathed. Ivy dropped her gaze to the sand. He wasn't ready to share what it was that did this to him, and she didn't want him to feel like he had to.

He lifted her chin and looked into her eyes with an intense but thoughtful expression. "Thank you," he said.

Hart pulled his hand from hers and rubbed his chest over his heart, wincing as he did.

Ivy smiled sadly, "Does it hurt?"

He smiled warmly in return. "Not anymore."

*Not when I'm with you … Ivy Rose.*

## Chapter 7

HART WOKE UP at 5 a.m.—no earlier than usual. The military had engrained itself into him, into all three of them. Walker and Benji had joined him only minutes later. The three soldiers sat casually around the fire-pit at Ivy's, enjoying the morning sun and the smell of the ocean. There was no better view on the entire estate than the one they had from there. The sky was lightening with the rising sun as they watched, a sparkling haze out to the horizon. Hart, Walker, and Benji sat in a reflective silence, engrossed in the tranquility of the lush gardens, the glimmering lap pool, and the sound of terns in the distance. They watched the swell lines form across the ocean and roll majestically toward the shore below them, and it pleasantly reminded each of them that they were thousands of miles away from the dry, scorching sands of Libya and Afghanistan…and the war.

"So, saved by another Rose, eh, Hart?" Benji smirked and took a sip of his coffee.

Hart laughed gently and glanced at Benji. "Yeah, I guess so."

Hart leaned back on his lounger. He threw his hands over his eyes and allowed the soothing morning sun to warm his face.

"What is that between you two?" Benji asked. "I've never seen anything like it."

Walker smiled to himself and placed his bare feet on the stone edge of the fire-pit, cradling his hot coffee in his lap. He looked up at Hart with a faint smirk and waited for him to answer.

Hart sat up again and rubbed his jaw.

"I have no idea what it is," he replied with a coy smile. "It's intense though, whatever it is."

"I think it may be love, my friend," Benji grinned impishly. He glanced at Walker, who laughed.

Hart stared at the two of them, amused.

"No, come on. I only met her yesterday."

"Hey, it can happen," Walker shrugged.

Hart glanced at Walker, reluctant to speak. His repudiation only fanned the fire. He shook his head and smiled.

"I bet your ego is hurting, Benji boy," Walker quipped.

"It's true, Hart. You're making me feel insecure," Benji teased. "You had her in the blink of an eye. Man, I'm slow off the mark these days."

Hart laughed at him. "Trust me, it is nothing like that. I'm sure she was just concerned about me. Or she pitied me."

"I think it's pretty clear how she feels about you," Walker said into his coffee.

Hart stared at the two of them for a moment, then he groaned into his hands and fell back on the sun lounger again. "Guys, what are we doing?"

"What do you mean?" Benji frowned.

"Well, look at us!" Hart smiled into the sky from his lounger, "we're sitting on a cliff overlooking the Pacific Ocean, *not* a desert. We are staying in the biggest fucking property we have ever seen. We're attending galas, drinking *great* coffee…we are safe, we are home…and we're talking about women, of all things." He threw his hands in the air and squinted at his friends through the sunlight in his eyes.

Benji nodded and grinned. "Things have definitely changed."

"It is a far cry from the war," Walker agreed. He ran his hand through his hair, holding his coffee with the other.

The three of them contemplated where they were just a couple of months ago. There was no comparison, as these were two entirely different worlds. Settling back into life at home had its challenges, and they each found it easier adapting to a deployed location. Home always presented itself with complications they were never concerned with while they were away, women especially, for these particular soldiers. Hart was struggling to wrap his head around being home, because every waking minute he yearned to be back in Libya to hunt down Taym. Taym was a free man, and Hart couldn't say the same for himself, not after losing Oliver. It felt good to be back on American soil, but mentally speaking he was neither here in California nor in Libya. He knew he was hopelessly lost in a darker world between the two.

Hart sighed heavily into the pale blue sky.

"Hey guys, how did you sleep?"

Hart sat up quickly, and all three soldiers stood to greet Ivy. She was a sight to behold in the morning; those light freckles dusted the bridge of her nose, and her crystal eyes reflected the deep blue of the sea behind them. Her long hair fell in waves down her back and she wore an oversized knitted sweater and cut-off denim shorts that showed off her long, slender legs.

Ivy sat down on the bench beside Benji and placed her bare feet on the edge of the fire-pit, gazing dreamily over the ocean. While she mused at the sea, each soldier quietly admired her effortless capacity to enrapture them. She had an unassuming innocence that the soldiers instantly respected, although Benji visibly struggled to contain his appreciation. He forced himself to look away and mouthed a silent *"damn!"* into his fist, earning himself a stern glare from the others. They smiled around the fire-pit with a soundless exchange of pity for one another. It had been a long time since they had enjoyed the company of such a breathtaking woman.

Hart saw Ivy take a deep breath and relax into the stillness of her surroundings. She looked at him across the fire-pit and smiled with a bashfulness that struck his heart.

"It is beautiful here, isn't it?" Ivy smiled wistfully at the boys. She gazed into Benji's kind blue eyes beside her.

"So, this is what you look like under all that Hollywood glamor," Benji grinned mischievously at her. "Disappointing, Ives."

Hart smiled and shook his head.

"Hey, it's early," she smirked, "I'm usually still asleep at this hour."

"Yeah, excuses, excuses." Benji winked.

Ivy laughed and pushed him playfully.

Benji's dimples sunk into his tanned cheeks and Ivy warmed to him all over again. She rested her head on his strong shoulder, and he took her hand and pressed it to his lips.

Ivy looked around the circle at the soldiers—they were shirtless and barefoot and leaning toward her with some degree of controlled enthusiasm. Their chests were hard and defined, and their abs aroused a sinful desire in her which she didn't realize she possessed. *Three soldiers.* Ivy sighed inwardly. They were handsome and tanned, and with the swell lines and palm trees propped seamlessly in the background, Ivy felt like she was on a photo shoot for some kind of surfing magazine.

"Did you all go shopping together?" she asked, pointing at their matching board shorts with a playful smirk.

They laughed, slightly embarrassed.

"We picked them up yesterday at a surf shop on our way into town," Benji replied.

"Be kind, Ivy. We've had nothing but combat gear for three years." A humble smile curled onto Hart's face. "We bought everything there was in our size."

"The girls were very helpful," Walker added.

"I bet they were," Ivy grinned. She imagined the sales assistants scrambling over each other to help the soldiers. The local girls would never have seen men as good-looking and worldly as these three, especially in La Mar. La Mar was full of men like…Tommy. Well, "men" was stretching it, she thought. Lads, maybe. Handsome, but insolent.

"Well, you look good," Ivy smiled, looking away. *Really good,* she thought.

"Can I make you a coffee, Ives?" Benji asked, standing beside her.

"I'd love a coffee. I'll come with you," she replied, standing with him. She looked at the others. "Can I get you guys another one?"

Hart and Walker politely declined, then Ivy left the fire-pit with Benji.

Once she entered the house, Walker turned to Hart. "You should tell her."

"Tell her what?" Hart frowned. "That I'm falling in love with her? She'll think I'm crazy!"

"Ah ha! So you are falling for this girl," Walker's dark eyes sparkled with delight, "but that's not what I'm talking about."

Hart tapped his thumbs together and stared into the blue horizon, realizing Walker was referring to Oliver. He sighed into his hands. "I can't."

"Why not? She'll understand."

Hart stood and walked over to the cliff. He gazed reflectively at the ocean, took a long, deep breath, and then faced Walker again. "How could she possibly understand, when I don't? Where would I even begin?"

"Start by telling her why you're getting these attacks," Walker suggested. "She was terrified last night, seeing you like that."

Hart clenched his fists at his side in thought. He felt awful for scaring her. He was the commander of one of the most elite army units in the world, and last night's humiliating moment perched itself right up there with the rest of his gnawing guilt for Ivy. Soon there would be nothing left of him. A part of him wished she hadn't found him.

Hart groaned softly. "What would I say?"

"Tell her what Hannah said."

Hart looked at him.

"You know, about post-traumatic stress disorder," Walker replied, peering into his coffee. He knew Hart didn't like to talk about it, and he could feel his friend's pensive gaze lingering on him.

"We'll be gone in a couple of days anyhow. It won't make a difference," Hart breathed eventually.

"Maybe it will." Walker looked at him with a soberness in his dark eyes. "Talking to Ivy about what happened in Libya may help you to forgive yourself."

Hart acknowledged what he said and turned toward the ocean again. Walker always had an adept awareness for what was happening around him, and he was never one to get involved until he thought it absolutely necessary. Hart respected that about him, and so he stared at the ocean and considered Walker's suggestion.

Hart had wanted to tell Ivy everything, but he just wasn't sure when to tell her. Or how. He thought about that day in Libya; if he hadn't been caught, then Oliver would never have had to trade places with him in the first place. Oliver would still be alive, and none of this would have ever happened. The debriefings, the nightmares, the grief, the attacks, the darkness … and Ivy. *Ivy* would have never happened. Hart rubbed the side of his neck—he recalled the feel of her warm breath there from their dance under the stars last night. He slid his hands into his pockets and looked up into the morning sky. He felt the warm sun on his back, and he closed his eyes and exhaled across the ocean.

"This is all my fault, Walker."

Walker poured out the rest of his coffee on the grass beside him. He leaned forward with the empty mug between his hands and considered his friend who stood on the cliff at the edge of the world. He knew that Hart wasn't responsible for Ollie's death—Taym was. Walker wanted to tell him this, but there was no way to make Hart believe him. This was a journey his friend needed to make on his own. They could only walk with him so far, and then the rest was up to him.

Walker watched him quietly. Hart's eyes were closed and he looked more at peace than he had ever seen him before, but he knew that deep inside, Hart was fiercely battling the demons who tortured his broken soul.

Benji pushed a few buttons on the appliance inside Ivy's kitchen and patiently waited for it to create his coffee. He lifted the mug and took a sip through the creamy froth and groaned with pleasure.

"Oh, I could get used to this."

Benji's southern accent delighted Ivy. She loved being in his company. Benji was sweet and endearing, and his whimsical charm put her completely at ease. He felt like a friend she had known for years, not days.

Ivy took one of the mugs he passed to her. "I guess it is a bit of a luxury compared to Libya." She pulled herself up on the kitchen island and stared into the depths of her coffee.

Benji noted her silence.

"How are you feeling after what happened last night with Hart?" he asked. He leaned on one side of the island as he spoke, idly rotating his coffee between his fingers on the stone surface.

"I'm okay," she replied, looking up at him. "Last night I thought…" Ivy looked into her coffee again and sighed. "I thought he died in my arms, Benji."

The cheer slid from Benji's expression.

"So much has happened to the people I love, and so I waited for him to die," she breathed. "I expected it." Ivy felt the tears welling in her eyes but she suppressed her sadness. She didn't want to be upset. Not today. Today had started like no other, and so far it was perfect.

She pulled one leg up and rested her chin on her knee.

"I'm sorry," Ivy smiled sweetly to herself, dismissing her feelings.

"Don't be sorry."

She looked up at Benji, who sensed her sadness. His dimples creased into his cheeks along with a boyish grin that suddenly swept across his face, intriguing Ivy.

"At least you know you have some strength in those tiny arms of yours." Benji grabbed her wrist and dangled it loosely in the air. "Look at this skinny thing here, you call this an arm?"

Ivy laughed at him.

"Hey, I mean it, Ives! I don't even know how you can lift your coffee, let alone Hart. Here, check this out." Benji raised his hand in the air. He flexed the muscles down his arm and grinned happily at her. "See? Now this is what arms are supposed to look like."

All three of the soldiers looked deceptively lean to Ivy, but really they were incredibly powerful. The muscles that rippled down Benji's arm from his big, tanned shoulder, all the way down to the muscles in the back of his hand, looked almost like they were carved from stone. He was built like a god. They all were. These men were individually remarkable, and together they were unfathomable. Hart, Walker, and Benji were no longer in her dreams or Oliver's tales… they were here in La Mar, with her.

Ivy smiled warmly at the sweet soldier in front of her, grateful for his light-hearted humor.

"Couldn't help yourself, could you, Benji?" Walker teased him as he walked up the back steps toward the kitchen. He had a wide grin on his face, and Hart was laughing beside him.

Benji winked at them with a proud expression.

As Walker and Hart joined Ivy and Benji at the kitchen island, Walker's cell phone shrilled beside the refrigerator. He walked over to it. When he saw the screen, his smile faded.

Walker glanced back at the soldiers with a seriousness that unsettled Ivy, then he answered the call. "Sergeant Josh Walker speaking." He was silent and unblinking as he listened to the voice on the other end of the line.

Hart and Benji glanced uneasily at each other, and the sudden tension made Ivy nervous. She lowered herself to the ground and leaned into the island with Hart and Benji, waiting for Walker to speak.

"Yes, sir …. Yes, I understand. Yes, sir…right away. Thank you, General."

Walker put his cell down and turned to Benji and Hart with an eager yet troubled expression.

"They caught Taym?" Benji asked, optimistically.

"No, not yet," Walker answered. "They need us back at Base to look at photos and identify leaders of the militia group that attacked Benghazi and Tripoli." Walker shook his head and cursed. "No one knows Libya better than we do."

"I tried to tell them," Hart replied, surprisingly calm.

"We are indispensable. Garvey knows that." Benji rubbed his hands together enthusiastically.

"They have captured the leader of the Tripoli assault," Walker continued. "They believe he was working closely with Taym. His interrogation will begin tomorrow. He is being held at a camp in Libya, but the General wants us to meet him at the training base in Monterey to assist Intelligence when it happens, Libyan time. They are hoping the interrogation will lead to Taym's apprehension."

The world suddenly lifted from Hart's shoulders. Going back to Base gave him direction. A renewed purpose. If he was in Monterey, then there was a better chance he would be deployed back to Libya to find Taym. He started to shake with an unanticipated eagerness to leave San Diego—at least he hoped it was eagerness. Not the darkness. *Not the fear.* He cursed inwardly, desperate to identify what it was that terrified him. Hart tucked his trembling hands into his pockets to conceal them from the exceptionally intuitive friends around him, including Ivy.

Ivy glanced nervously from one soldier to the next. A soberness had replaced their smiles, and she suddenly felt strangely intimidated by them. She could see the hatred pooling in Hart's brown eyes. The warmth was still there, but she sensed the rage within them, and it troubled her.

"Who is Taym?" Ivy asked softly.

The three soldiers gazed down at her with grave expressions, and Ivy wished she hadn't asked.

"Taym Malak. He is the traitor who killed your brother," Walker replied in an apologetic tone.

"Oh." Ivy lowered her crystal gaze to her coffee.

Hart studied Ivy protectively. He watched her consider the name of a man whom she had never met, yet had caused her so much suffering. He thought about her fainting yesterday. She had put on a brave face for them, but it was obvious to him how much Oliver's death still hurt her. Though she hid it well, unlike him.

The soldiers looked across the island at the woman who had somehow managed to win their hearts so easily and without warning. Last night, when Tommy was there with her, they realized an indescribable devotion to Ivy that ran deep within them. An instinctive need to protect her as one of their own. They realized in that moment that they had known Ivy for much longer than one day ... she had been by their side for years, within Oliver.

"Are you okay?" Hart asked her softly.

Ivy looked up at him and tried to smile. She didn't want them to go. Loneliness had already cast its foreboding shadow over her heart. "Life was so quiet, and then you three arrived." Ivy looked at the three soldiers in front of her. "So much can happen in one night."

The four of them stood quietly in thought.

"Think of me as your home away from home. You can stay here anytime. I'd love it," she grinned sweetly, masking the pain that gripped her heart.

Benji threw his arm around her shoulder and pulled her to him, then he kissed her on the side of her head. Ivy put on her bravest face.

"There was something else the General mentioned." Walker

glanced at Hart. "We need to talk."

"Then I'll leave you guys to it," she added, sensing their need for privacy.

Ivy took her coffee out to the front of the estate and sat down at the top of the stairs. She looked out over the weeping trees along the driveway and fell quickly into her thoughts. *Taym Malak*. He killed Oliver. She contemplated this for a while, with a somberness shrouding her short-lived cheer.

The birds twittered about the branches, ignorant in their usual bliss of the pain in the world around them. Their song tiptoed through the grief that clouded her thoughts, pulling her back to the light surrounding her. She closed her eyes in the sunshine, breathed in the cleansing smell of the ocean, and thought about what once had made her happy. Before anyone had ever left her. Hope flickered in her heart and she carefully tended to it, nurturing it in its fragile state. Sure, there would always be uncertainty and fear in this world, she knew this more than anyone, but her love for life would never wane as long as she found peace in what remained constant for her—the ocean, the forest, the sky. That part of the world seemed to understand her pain yet remained admirably impassive to it at the same time. It never apologized to her or showed her pity. It accepted her and all of her heartbreak, and there was a nourishing solitude that came with their mutual understanding of one other. A sense of fullness in a complicated world that left her feeling so empty.

Ivy closed her eyes and laid back on the sun-warmed ground behind her, smiling. Life may become lonely again, but if she paused long enough to listen, the world would continue to keep her company.


"Why the fuck can't I go with you?" Hart growled angrily.

"You know Hannah won't let you come back," Benji replied.

"The important thing is that Benji and I are there and we can keep our finger on the pulse. If they find Taym, then we will be the first ones to know, and trust me, we won't leave the States unless we can convince them to let you return to Libya," Walker declared.

Hart understood what they were saying. It was vital for half of Phoenix to still be at Base. Finding Taym and avenging

Oliver's death was the most important thing to them right now. Walker and Benji needed to be there, even if he couldn't be.

Hart rubbed his jaw, thinking. "You keep me informed, about *everything*," he ordered.

"You are still our commanding officer. You'll be the first to know," Walker said.

"I want updates. Call me every night," Hart added. He stared at Benji and Walker, who nodded at him in response.

"What are you going to do?" Walker asked.

"I don't know." Hart thought. "Maybe I should head home to Arizona and visit my parents."

"And leave Ivy?" Benji asked, concerned. "What about that asshole last night? You think she'll be okay without us looking out for her?"

"Benji's right," Walker added. "That guy is dangerous, and this is Ollie's younger sister. What do you think he would do in this situation?"

The three of them looked at each other across the kitchen island as they considered it.

There was no question; Oliver would never leave Ivy as long as Tommy was a threat to her safety. Hart questioned whether he would have left her had it come down to his decision alone. He caught the look in Tommy's eyes last night. Tommy wanted Ivy. *All* of Ivy. Without anyone in his way, he would take her. It was a thought that troubled Hart. His head told him to stay, but his heart needed him to leave—she would be harder to resist on his own.

He looked up at Walker and Benji who were watching him intently. Waiting for him to answer.

Hart took a deep breath and nodded.

"Okay ... I'll stay with Ivy."


The four of them stood in the driveway and said their goodbyes in the hot, midday sun. Benji threw his pack into the back of the taxi and strolled over to Ivy. He lifted her into the air and planted a kiss on her cheek.

"We'll see you in a couple of months, beautiful," Benji grinned.

Ivy hugged him tightly, "Goodbye, Benji."

"Take care of this big guy here," he added, walking over to Hart.

"I will."

Benji embraced Hart then walked reluctantly to the taxi. "I'll talk to you tomorrow, Hart. I love you, man."

"See you soon, Benji boy."

Walker shot Ivy a wink as he walked toward her to say goodbye. He leaned down to her and gave her a kiss on the cheek, then he slid his hands into his pockets and looked down at her.

"It was an honor meeting you, Ivy," he spoke politely. He glanced quickly at Hart and back to Ivy, then a shade of satisfaction fell over his smile. "I have a feeling this is only the beginning."

Ivy's cheeks warmed in his dark, brooding gaze. "See you soon, Walker."

He turned to Hart and the two of them stood in front of each other without speaking. Saying goodbye was more difficult than they thought.

"Two months, eh," Hart shrugged.

Walker nodded. His dark eyes were serious, but smiling. "We'll be back before you know it."

Hart nodded at Walker, then they shook hands and pulled each other in for a hug.

"I'll be calling to check up on you, buddy," Walker spoke to him as he walked away. "Look after yourself."

"Will do," Hart replied, glancing quickly at Ivy. He thought about Walker waiting up for him in the motel the other night, after his nightmare. He hadn't been on his own, without these men, in years. An anxiety settled uneasily in Hart's stomach.

Walker and Benji climbed into the taxi, which made its way down the driveway beneath the impressive archway of trees. Hart walked behind them until he saw the end of the driveway. He watched the gates close behind them, and they were gone. He stood unmoving in the center of the driveway, feeling slightly lost and somewhat abandoned. He didn't know how he was going to survive the next two months without Walker or Benji by his side...or Oliver. Without Phoenix. They were so removed from where they were just a couple of months ago. When there were four of them. Now here he was, just the one.

After a few minutes, Hart walked back up the driveway toward the estate. He wanted to close his eyes and walk blindly in the sunshine, but there were too many disconcerting thoughts racing through his head. When Hart reached the fountain in front of the house, he stopped.

Ivy was on the top step of the porch, leaning against one of the marble pillars. She was watching him. Studying him. She was wearing sneakers and a pair of black leggings that accentuated her long legs, and Hart sighed at the feelings she aroused. He rubbed his jaw in thought. Two months of resisting the temptation of Oliver's sister. Life was definitely going to get interesting.

Hart walked around the fountain and smiled at her from the bottom step. She smiled beautifully in return, and if he read her expression correctly, she was excited about something.

"What is it?" Hart smirked.

"Can I show you something?" she asked cheerfully.

"Of course. Do I need shoes?"

Hart pointed at her sneakers.

"Yeah," she laughed sweetly, "but we'll need a few more things besides shoes."

Hart smiled. He bounded up the steps and stood beside her, "What do we need?"

Ivy leaned her head back against the pillar and gazed up at him, catching her breath in his warm, brown eyes.

"Well," she hesitated, "we'll need a backpack, fishing rods, bathing suits, towels, flashlights, some food, water—"

"Whoa, whoa, whoa," Hart interrupted, "Ivy, you had me at fishing rods."

Ivy laughed. He threw his big arm around her shoulders and pulled her playfully toward the front door.

"You like fishing?" he asked in surprise.

"I don't mind it," she replied diplomatically and grinned. Ivy didn't mention her inclination to return the fish to the sea after she had caught them. It never went down well with Oliver or her father, and most likely not with Hart either.

"So where are we going?" Hart asked.

"You'll see." Ivy bit her lip with excitement. Today would be fun. Relaxing. He needed this...and so did she.

## Chapter 8

HART WALKED WITH IVY along a remote gravel road that led south out of town. Suburbia seamlessly evolved into large fields of flowers barely ten minutes' walk from Ivy's estate. They walked along an old fence line of decaying timber posts and steel wire that had curled with rust in the ocean air. It leaned precariously toward the gravel road, battered by time. The scarlet petals of the poppies growing around the fence seemed to complement its world-weary appearance. Hart watched Ivy run her hands through the tall flowers as she strolled in front of him, humming to herself. Ivy was a revitalizing escape for a tired soldier. The pure pleasure she took from the earth engrossed him entirely, and a child-like sentiment dashed tantalizingly through his heart—that of *wonder.*

Hart found himself eagerly waiting for her to turn to him, to check on him like she had been doing since they left the estate. Ivy turned around as if on cue. The sunlight caught her blonde hair, and she sent him a smile that stole his breath away and temporarily robbed him of his restraint. Hart gave her a full, unrestrained smile in return, his whole face lighting up with his fleeting freedom from his dark thoughts. When she turned away, Oliver's death rattled his guilty soul. He lifted his face and closed his eyes in the hot sun. It briefly reminded him of the blistering heat on the streets of Libya, but he cast the thought aside before the memory of Oliver jaded his good mood.

Hart wore a white cotton tee, black running shorts, and a pair of black sneakers. He had one of Oliver's khaki packs strapped to his back, filled to the brim with items they needed for the hike to Lights Beach, Ivy's *paradise*. The beach wasn't far from La Mar, yet Hart hadn't seen a single person since they left town. The beach was accessible only by foot, and he figured the trek alone was enough to deter the locals, especially with Town Beach sitting splendidly on their doorsteps.

"Through here," Ivy told him.

She stopped at a point in the fence where the timber posts had crumbled and the wires stooped low enough to step over. A rundown crossing for the wayfaring stranger, and Hart couldn't wait to step off the beaten track. He held Ivy's hand as she stepped over the wires and he leaped over after her.

Hart stood still and marveled at the sea of scarlet poppies, chirping with insects and bowing in waves below a ring of small mountains. A picturesque scene, nestled below a hazy summer sun.

"Pretty spectacular, huh?" She grinned, catching his delight.

"Yeah, I've never seen anything like it."

Ivy smiled proudly and headed toward an opening at the edge of the forest at the far side of the poppy field. Hart followed. He could smell the ocean as they got closer, the salty humidity. He sensed the moisture rising in the air, an instinctual sense that told him a storm was approaching. Hart squinted up at the cloudless sky, wondering if his instincts had become confused by his time spent in the deserts.

The sunshine glowed brilliantly through the delicate red petals of the poppies as he walked through them. Hart listened to the stillness of the earth. He listened to the low hum of bees as they hovered around the flowers. He watched them fly around his legs from one poppy to the next, and the sounds of war began to fall to the trail behind him.

"Falling behind, soldier?"

Hart jogged to catch up.

A pleasant smirk rested on Ivy's lips, then she turned toward the forest again.

Hart followed her without talking. Her long, lean legs stepped carefully between the tall flowers, and he smiled to himself, admiring her body. He smelled the sweet coconut on her skin as he walked through the air behind her, stirring a dormant, carnal hunger inside of him. A beast he shouldn't wake. *Not her. Not Oliver's sister.*

Hart took a deep breath and rubbed his jaw, feeling the anxiety unsettle him, then they reached the edge of the forest.

"They remind me of soldiers," Ivy said quietly, turning to look past him at the field of poppies.

Hart turned around. "The flowers? Why?"

"Well, when they stand together they appear invulnerable," she reached for a poppy beside the forest and bent the stem toward her, "but individually they are fragile, like human lives."

Hart looked at the poppy staring back into her crystal eyes, then Ivy caught his gaze.

"Some of them are strong enough to reach for the sky," she continued, "and the rest bend to the earth as though they are weary or wounded. Nevertheless, each one is remarkably impressive."

Hart stared at the scarlet field behind them, thinking.

"They are truly inspiring," she breathed.

Ivy studied Hart as he stared at the field of flowers, covertly seeking insight into his private and tortured mind. She thought about last night and the anxiety attack that had them both falling into the sea. Commander Johnny Hart—just like a poppy. Once reaching for the sky, now heavy with the aftermath of war. And still, she thought, he was remarkably impressive.

Hart followed her into the forest along a narrow trail that had been worn into the forest floor. It was clear to him that Ivy had been here many times before; he sensed her comfort in the silence of the trees. The stillness seemed to unravel around her as she walked. Hart peered into the green canopy above him, stepping lightly through the dancing fractures of sunlight, enjoying its dappled brightness. He relaxed into his surroundings, losing himself to its tranquility. It was beautiful. *Peaceful.*

The trail met and ran along a shallow river. He thought about wading through the water to cool off from the humid air of the forest. He looked ahead and saw that Ivy had managed to gain a fair amount of distance on him again, so instead, he jogged along the trail to catch up with her. She turned and smiled as he caught up with her. Hart smiled back. She was incredibly sexy. Her long hair seemed to float around her, weightlessly, and when she walked through the sunlight beneath the trees it shone like gold. Now and then she would run her fingers through it and throw it all to one side, usually to glance behind and see if he was still there. Which he was, following her in quiet awe.

Ivy ducked beneath a low-hanging branch and then stopped on the trail to look at Hart.

"You know, you are pretty quiet back there. I can't even hear you following me." She watched him walk toward her.

"I have spent over a decade behind enemy lines," Hart answered. "Moving around without detection is how I stay alive." He ducked under the branch and stood only inches from Ivy.

They caught one another's gaze, both taken aback by their sudden intimacy, the sunlight dancing across their faces through the trees. Hart's brown eyes darkened in her nearness, then he took another step toward her.

Ivy's heart raced. He was beautiful. *Everything* about Hart was beautiful ... his face, his body, his olive skin, his smile. She stared longingly at his mouth, until Hart's inscrutable expression caught her attention. Ivy blushed a hot red and quickly turned up the track, glancing back at him for just a second. She caught him smiling at the ground, and Ivy beamed excitedly at the forest in front of her.

As they trekked along quietly in each other's company, Ivy found herself dissecting the complex soldier behind her. Hart made her excruciatingly nervous, yet his presence was wonderfully sedative. It had a nonplussing effect on her that confused her perception of him, of what she thought she already knew about this man. Hart intrigued her like no other, awakened her like no other. She thought about his fingers running through hers last night. The feel of him. The temptation of him. Her divine yet agonizing desire.

Ivy stopped walking and paused in her thoughts, then she sighed into the treetops to calm her racing heart. She felt the distance close between them as he caught up to her. Her breath deepened in his nearness.

Ivy closed her eyes and whispered, "It is not so much for its beauty that the forest makes a claim upon men's hearts, as for that subtle something, that quality of air that emanates from old trees, that so wonderfully changes and renews a weary spirit."

Hart didn't speak. He stood behind her and listened as she whispered to the forest.

She looked at him. "Robert Louis Stevenson. You know him?"

"Not personally."

Ivy gave him a playful glare, and he laughed.

"Yeah, I know him. *Treasure Island*. Classic. Every boy I knew had a copy."

"Not the girls?"

"Not that I remember."

"Hmm." Ivy turned up the trail again.

"What is it?" Hart asked.

She paused to look at him. "I loved *Treasure Island*. I couldn't put it down. What does that say about me?" she asked innocently.

Hart caught up to her and stood in her crystal gaze. Her skin looked even smoother in the sunlight. He wanted to reach out and touch her face so that he knew her skin was as soft as he imagined it to be.

"I guess it means you have a thirst for adventure… or a wild heart?" Hart's eyes scanned the forest around them. "Given where we are right now, I'd say a bit of both." He looked straight into her eyes, hoping he didn't offend her.

Ivy glanced around the forest. *A wild heart? Was her heart untamed?* Her eyes drifted down to the fishing rod in her hand. Her dad's rod.

Hart followed her gaze. "See, I have never met a girl who knows how to fish."

"Is that bad?" she replied.

"Bad? Hell no, I love it!" Hart grinned beautifully. "I like fishing, but I have no luck when it comes to catching the damn things. I'm hoping you catch our dinner tonight because there's no way I can."

Ivy considered him with a restrained smile.

"What? Why are you looking at me like that—because I can't

fish?" Hart asked warily.

"No, not that. You said you were staying for dinner."

"Yeah?" He narrowed his eyes curiously.

"Does this mean you are staying in San Diego…with me?" Ivy bit her lip in elated anticipation.

"If that's okay with you, Ivy?"

His coy smile melted her heart.

"Of course it is." Ivy's teeth nibbled gently at her bottom lip.

"So…does this track have a name?" Hart asked vaguely, forcing himself to look away.

"The locals call it the Ghost Trail," she replied with wide, theatrical eyes.

Hart casually examined the forest surrounding them, an instinctive habit derived from years of walking the streets in war-torn nations. The mention of ghosts sent a cold shiver down his spine. Not that he believed in them, but he dreaded the eeriness that fell upon the air whenever it came up in conversation.

Hart kept a vigilant eye on the forest as they resumed walking. "Ghosts, huh?"

"Yeah, people see them all the time," she replied plainly. "Everyone has a different story to tell and they are all *very* unbelievable."

Ivy climbed an old log, maybe a remnant of a grand redwood that had fallen decades ago across the trail. There were no other redwoods in the forest, so the tree sat fairly out of place for Hart. Ivy climbed it as though it were a feature of this forest she had grown accustomed to since she was a child. He watched her stand when she reached the top, then she disappeared over the other side.

Hart climbed after her, conscious not to let Ivy out of his sight for too long. Its surface was spongy beneath his shoes. Its length stretched out far beyond him along the forest floor, and he guessed it had fallen long before they were even born, too thick to break down any faster. Hart imagined everything he had done in his life so far, and in all that time, this redwood lay on its side in the tranquil heart of the forest; far from his life amid the unforgiving privations of war. He felt it beneath him, its hibernating heart. An ancient spirit sleeping in a modern world.

"You coming?" Ivy asked, watching him.

Hart jumped off the log after her.

"Funny," he said, picking up from where their conversation left off, "I'd have pegged you as a believer."

"In ghosts?"

"Yeah."

"No. I don't believe in ghosts." Ivy glanced around the forest. "Not the kind that haunt you anyhow. The most common story on this trail is the peculiar feeling of someone or something approaching you, but when you turn to look, no one is there."

"Have you ever had that feeling?"

"No," Ivy smirked at the brave soldier beside her. "You're not afraid of ghosts are you, Commander?"

"Me? No!" Hart laughed unconvincingly. Ivy raised a curious eyebrow at him. "Okay, to be honest with you, and this stays between you and me...," he looked at her meekly. When she nodded, he continued, "I was terrified of ghost stories as a kid."

Ivy made a strange sound in her throat and smiled before looking away into the trees.

"You're laughing at me!" Hart grinned and rubbed his chest in embarrassment.

"Oh no! I'm so sorry, please keep going." Ivy pressed her lips together to stop herself from laughing. When he chuckled sweetly, her heart dissolved with adoration.

"When my friends would tell ghost stories in the dark," Hart continued, "I would sit outside the bedroom door with the hall light on and keep my ear pinned to the door so I could still hear the story. I didn't want to miss out."

"That is so cute," Ivy gushed.

"No, I don't think anyone found it cute."

"Were you afraid of the dark?"

"No."

"Then why didn't you stay in the bedroom with all the kids?"

"I guess being in the dark made the stories scarier than they actually were. Under the hallway light, I realized there was nothing to be afraid of," Hart replied, rather ashamed of himself.

"But your courage shouldn't wane just because the light is out."

"I know, but it was so dark. I couldn't see anything, except for the monsters in my head, that is, and my friends had some pretty wicked imaginations." He rubbed his jaw and laughed at himself.

Ivy stared at him thoughtfully, imagining the twelve-year-old Johnny Hart.

She smiled, "Well if we were friends back then, I would have sat in the hallway with you to keep you company."

Hart looked down into her eyes. Her innocence was extraordinary. Her empathy, even more so. Where would they be now had he met her all those years ago?

Ivy dropped her eyes and ran her fingers through her hair, then turned up the trail again.

Hart followed, watching the forest closely. He didn't believe in ghosts, but it intensified his protectiveness over her. He had spent a lifetime fine-tuning his sharp senses, and there was no deceiving him. If anyone decided to follow them with questionable intentions, then they were risking their lives. Simple.

"Here we are!" Ivy declared brightly.

The trail turned down to the river again, and Ivy was already wading through ankle-deep water with her shoes dangling in her fingers. Hart removed his shoes and stepped carefully into the river. The cold water was relieving.

Hart peered ahead of Ivy. She pushed aside a few low-hanging branches that were brushing the water's surface, and he saw a deep blue sparkling through the leaves in front of them. *The ocean.* Hart felt the spirit of the desert within him awakening from its deep slumber, like it were growing wings and preparing to fly away from him. Liberated. *Relieved.* Grateful to move on. Twelve years walking the hot, dry sands had finally come to its end. The ocean beckoned him. Ivy beckoned him. Then all of a sudden she was gone, snapping Hart out of his reverie.

"Ivy!" he shouted.

The branches fell together like a green curtain across the river. Hart hurried through the water toward the branches, and as he pushed them aside, he unveiled an extraordinary panorama of pristine white sand and turquoise water. Hart was speechless. Terns floated above the crystal sea, glowing splendidly in the early afternoon sun. The scene was a far cry from the deserts he had become so accustomed too—he had never seen anything like it in his life.

"You're going to have to jump!" Ivy shouted at him.

Hart looked down at Ivy. She stood maybe two meters below him in the dry sand, watching him happily. Hart inspected the small waterfall that cascaded down the rocks in front of him. His eyes followed the water as it weaved its way intricately through the sand until it reached the ocean. It was stunning. *Ivy* was stunning. Here, in this sanctuary where the forest met the sea, Ivy was naturally in her element. Long legs, blonde hair, and tanned skin ... she was raw and beautiful as though the forest and the sea had raised her as their own. His heart beat wildly with anticipation for the day ahead. For a day spent with Ivy.

Hart glanced behind him through the trees, thinking about the ghosts that might be following him. It was instinctive. Or foolish. His eyes caught a shadow among the trees that was gone as quickly as it had appeared. Hart blinked in disbelief.

"Everything okay up there?" Ivy called to him.

Hart thought about where he was. This was her world, not his. There was no war here. There were no demons, apart from the ones in his head. He remembered his nightmare the other night when Oliver shot him in the chest. *Never look back.* Hart exhaled hard and tore his eyes from the forest, then, making sure his backpack was still firmly strapped to him, Hart jumped off the waterfall into the sand beside Ivy.

"I can't believe you have all this to yourself," he breathed, enamored by the bay.

"Most of the time. No one really bothers to come out here anymore." She stepped out of the shade of the forest and walked toward the water.

"Except for you."

"Yes," Ivy looked at him and smiled, "except for me."

"Well, it's worth the effort," Hart added. "Now we have the place to ourselves."

Ivy held her breath and nodded, forcing her mind out of the deep trenches of her desire.

They strolled up the beach until they reached a stand of palm trees that bowed idyllically over the sand. Ivy unrolled an oversized cotton towel, and the two of them laid beside each other beneath the palms, soaking in the pleasant afternoon warmth.

After a while, the air grew heavy and hot. Ivy sat up to look at a layer of dark clouds rolling in from the sky behind them. They were in for some rain, she thought, maybe even thunder.

"Looks like rain," Hart said, watching her regard the dark sky.

Ivy nodded happily. "You okay with that?"

"After years in the desert, I welcome it with open arms."

Hart closed his eyes and laid back on the blanket to enjoy what was left of the sunshine. He hoped the rain might encourage a long-awaited drop in temperature.

"I remember swimming in the ocean once when it was raining," he said. "I was only a kid, but I'll never forget how good it felt."

The sun kissed his skin, and he exuded a beautiful calm that soothed Ivy. She loved the way he spoke to her with his eyes closed, facing the sky. He smiled as he talked, reassuring her that maybe, just maybe, this soldier was going to be okay.

Ivy glanced over his body, Hart unaware of her surreptitious gaze. He was wearing his silver dog tags, and she wondered if he wore them as a reminder that he was a soldier first and foremost, in case he lost his way. They laid against the hard muscles of his chest, rising and falling in time with his slow, tranquil breath. Her breath deepened. The dog tags looked like shiny, irresistible pieces of treasure against his tanned skin, and Ivy wanted them. She wasn't sure why. Her crystal eyes followed the centerline of his abs until it reached an arrow of muscles near his hip bones, leading her attention to the laces that tied his shorts. The shorts sat low on his hips. Deliciously low, she thought, envisioning what lay beneath them.

Ivy nibbled her fingertip, lost divinely in her thoughts. She closed her eyes in yearning. Thoughts like these were too unfamiliar for her—a man had never made her feel this way before. It drove her crazy wondering if he was ever going to want her like she wanted him…then she remembered him leaving her on the dance floor.

"So I haven't asked you how you are feeling," Hart interrupted Ivy's thoughts, "about Oliver."

Ivy opened her eyes. His question took her by surprise. She looked at Hart, who was sitting up and watching her. Waiting. *He wanted to talk about Oliver?*

"I miss him," she breathed, eventually.

Hart nodded and looked away.

"I have to keep reminding myself that he isn't here anymore. Especially those times when I need him most…which is a lot lately." She smiled to herself. "He had such a bright soul and it seems impossible that he's gone."

"I know how that feels." Hart smiled faintly. He fiddled with his watch band for a few seconds, then wrapped his arms around his knees. He gazed out to the horizon, seemingly deep in thought.

"I didn't feel him leave this world," Ivy breathed.

Hart looked at her, his heart jolting warmly in her childlike innocence. He wanted to wrap her protectively in his arms and hold her there for as long as she would let him.

"I know we were so far away from each other, but I thought I would have felt that moment when he died." She smiled to herself and looked at the ocean. "I try and think back to what I was doing at the time, to see if I was distracted in some way…but I know deep down that I didn't feel it."

Hart studied her as she spoke, absorbed in her pure perception of things. He liked the way her mouth moved when she talked. The way her eyes caught the deep blue of the sea.

Ivy smiled bashfully in his attentive gaze. "I still feel guilty for it, and I don't know why."

Hart nodded without speaking, tainted by the guilt that still festered inside him.

Ivy breathed out slowly to gather her thoughts.

"How do *you* feel about Oliver?" she asked.

Hart laughed resignedly and rubbed his jaw. "I walked myself right into that one, didn't I?"

She laughed happily. "Yeah, you kinda did."

Hart bowed his head briefly to run his hand back and forth through his hair, then he stared at the ocean again. His eyes squinted at the horizon as he thought about it.

Ivy wasn't sure if he would answer. She turned her eyes away from him, so as not to pressure him. She could almost hear the thoughts screaming through his head. He was so intense. So heart-wrenchingly sad. There was something more to Oliver's death that Hart was struggling to come to terms with. Something that scared him. Ivy could see it in the angst that drenched his soul.

"I have this emptiness that seems to have cast this black shadow over me," Hart said eventually. He rubbed his legs, thinking. "It's hard to explain."

Ivy didn't move a muscle, stunned by his willingness to talk. She held her breath, worried any sound would frighten him. Trigger him to clamp up again. She waited for him to go on.

"It's a shadow I can't step out of, and it feels so unfamiliar. I can't even determine if the shadow is mine, but it follows me everywhere, so I guess it is," he shrugged.

Hart gazed wearily at the ocean.

"He was my best friend, Ivy," his voice broke sadly, dropping with a low huskiness. "All my adult life—my real life—he's been by my side, and now he's gone, just like that."

He looked at Ivy, who fought back her tears and managed a thoughtful nod.

Hart laughed quietly to himself, then continued, "After he died I begged for the emptiness. I begged for the nothingness. I didn't want to feel *anything.* I wanted the darkness to take me away, and it did, but not entirely." Hart stared into her sad eyes. "Now I feel like I'm being eaten alive."

Ivy exhaled into her hands and looked away, unable to restrain her tears any longer. She let her hair fall down the side of her face like a curtain between her and Hart, and subtly wiped away her tears. She looked back at Hart, who was smiling sadly to himself.

Ivy didn't smile. She wanted to cry. His pain was unbearably sad. She breathed through the sorrow that stung her heart, his honesty catching her off guard. One day she had hoped Hart would open up to her, but now she questioned her resilience. She didn't want to cry, she wanted to be strong for him. A pillar of strength. But his sincerity weakened her.

"The emptiness rips away at my soul every day, and every day I have to fight back because it is mine. It's a battle I have yet to win or lose, but I am beginning to see an ending, and it isn't good." He ran his hands back through his hair.

"Hart, what happened over there in Libya?" she asked, swallowing the lump in her throat.

He stared at her for a few moments, then sighed into his hands. "I can't talk about what happened, Ivy. I'm sorry." The fear lurked in his dark eyes.

"That's okay." She smiled forgivingly at him.

Hart considered her for a quiet moment, and Ivy's cheeks blushed in his attention. She forced herself to talk before he caught her desire.

"Oliver's death left me all alone in this world, and then you three showed up when I least expected it." Ivy ran her hands through the sand as she spoke. "It helps to have someone by your side who understands."

Hart sat silently and listened to her.

"Something kept telling me yesterday that this was it, I lost Ollie, but I wouldn't be alone anymore." She looked up at Hart.

"How did you know?" Hart smirked. "At that point in time, we were leaving San Diego and heading to Mexico. We had the whole thing planned."

"Because I asked the universe not to take you away from me."

Hart's smile faded.

Ivy blushed and shifted her gaze to the ocean, inwardly cursing herself for over-sharing. She sounded crazy.

Hart considered her. She watched the ocean peacefully, and a light breeze kissed her skin and caught her long hair. *I asked the universe not to take you away from me.* Hart thought about this. He looked around him where they sat on the sand beneath the palm trees. A blue ocean sparkled to the horizon in front of him. The salty air cast a shade of silver over the rugged coastline behind him. Then there was Ivy, sitting beside him. Beautiful, flawless Ivy. He was worlds away from the war. Worlds away from the destruction and the blood and the tears.

"So I'm in your world now," he grinned beautifully at her. "Where you get to keep what you ask for?"

Ivy laughed. "Something like that."

Hart laughed humbly. "You could have anything you want, and you asked for us, the jaded remnants of war?" His brown eyes filled with bewilderment, enchanted by her breathtaking sweetness. Hart frowned and looked at the ocean. Maybe all this time in the war, they were unknowingly asking the universe for Ivy?

"Yeah, I did." Ivy curled her lip in jest.

"Hey, no, I get it," he teased, scanning the pristine bay around them. "Living in paradise must get pretty monotonous after a while."

"It can be a little repetitive," she laughed, playing along. "Now you are here, and suddenly things are alluringly enchanting once again."

He looked up at her, his brown eyes ablaze with desire. "The enchantment around here is all your doing, Ivy."

She blushed. "I meant to say interesting...things are interesting again. Good interesting, though. You know ... *different*," she mumbled nervously.

Hart laughed softly to himself, touched by her sweetness. "Well, trust me, it always gets interesting with a Phoenix soldier hanging around." He grinned. "There hasn't been a time in our lives that the world didn't throw a curve ball at us, good or bad. I hope you're ready."

"I am." Ivy grinned happily at the thought. The idea of the world throwing something at them together excited her. It didn't frighten her one bit, not if it meant he was still here beside her.

Hart ran his hand through the sand. "So you think there is something bigger out there in the universe that we should believe in? Somebody who listens?"

"It is not about there being something or someone bigger out there that you should believe in," she answered. "It is believing there is something bigger inside of you. If I ask the universe for help with something that is troubling me, then deep down, I know I am really asking this of myself."

Ivy watched him contemplate what she said.

"It sounds ridiculous. I'm sorry," she muttered, shaking her head.

"No, it doesn't."

Ivy squinted thoughtfully at him.

"Ives, how do you manage to keep picking yourself up after losing so much?"

She thought about it. "I guess I see my grief as something that defines me now. A part of me that I can't change, so I've had to adapt to it. It took me a long time, but I have learned to use it as a tool for healing. It sounds contradictory." Ivy frowned to herself.

"So you're saying your pain heals you?" He flashed her a gorgeous, cheeky grin.

"No, I'm saying that this happened to us and now we must try to alter the grief into something constructive we can work with," Ivy explained, smiling. "Because if we don't, then we will live with the same relentless pain for the rest of our lives."

She saw Hart's brow furrow in thought when he faced the ocean. Ivy assumed he was trying to understand her nonsensical explanation. Her cheeks blushed, feeling slightly foolish for opening up to him so unexpectedly today. She was terrible at clarifying her thoughts out loud, but when she thought about it, no one had ever wanted to know this about her before.

"I'm sorry," she screwed up her face and smiled. "I've lost you, haven't I?"

Hart looked at her beside him on the sand. "You haven't lost me, Ivy."

His expression was serious but thoughtful, and Ivy exhaled softly in his striking gaze, feeling her heart thud against her chest. She smiled at him and brushed away her hair, feeling slightly nervous all of a sudden.

"I haven't spoken about this with anyone before, so maybe it doesn't make any sense."

"No, actually it does," Hart encouraged. "You're allowing your grief to evolve into something more manageable."

"Yes. Precisely." Ivy looked at him in pleasant surprise, stunned he understood anything she was telling him. She was even starting to confuse herself.

"It makes sense. I'll email it to the Psych at Base. She might let me come back if she realizes I've become dependent on amateur advice." Hart flashed her a gorgeous grin.

Ivy nudged him playfully and he laughed.

His happiness warmed her to the core, and once again, she melted under his steady gaze. His body was sturdy and strong, and he had barely moved an inch when she pushed him. She thought about how powerful he must be against the enemy and the war. Then Ivy's thoughts fleetingly shifted to the bedroom, her blushing cheeks threatening to give her away.

"It's not advice," she reassured him, subtly cooling her cheeks with her fingers.

"It is *good* advice," Hart replied, his sincere eyes unwavering from hers. "Thank you, Ivy."

Ivy stared at him for a few seconds before turning her gaze to the ocean. She chewed frenziedly on her bottom lip in thought.

"They call you the Queen of Hearts, and I can see why," Hart said, noting her silence.

Ivy looked at him, surprised. "Oliver?"

Hart nodded.

"I've had that name since I was a child. My dad gave it to me. He would return from his service, and I would try and cover his horrific injuries up with tiny Band-Aids. They were useless, but he called me that because I cared. After he died, Oliver kept calling me the Queen of Hearts. Everyone in town knew me by that name," she paused, thinking. "No one has called me that in so long."

"Well, it suits you."

Ivy smiled at him with her eyes.

Hart thought about the older man in his nightmare, his eyes were a crystalline blue, just like Ivy's. He frowned at the thought. Without thinking, he scooped up a handful of sand and let it glide out of his hand.

Ivy noticed Oliver's soothing habit shine through Hart, and it was hard not to believe that her brother wasn't watching over them at a time like this. She smiled as she lay back on the blanket, and closed her eyes.

"At first, you think life will never feel normal again," Ivy said, running her fingers gently over her stomach as she talked. "But the grief will someday snowball into something to lessen the pain, if you can find a way to let the good back in."

"How did you let the good back in?" Hart asked quietly, engrossed in her fingers running idly across her body.

"My parents taught us to appreciate what a lot of other people take for granted, like the sweet smell of a flower, or a beautiful sunset, or the sound of cicadas in the summer. I found reprieve from my grief in the little things like these. In what others find commonplace."

"I don't know if the little things can help me, Ivy."

His tone was soft and sad, and she sat up to look at him. "Maybe not, but it might be a good place to start. Don't you think?"

Hart studied the enthusiasm in her beautiful face. Her crystal eyes reflected the ocean, which was fading into a light shade of gray in the overcast sky.

"Okay," he breathed.

"Okay?"

"Show me the little things. Let's see if they can heal a broken soldier," he said with a warm smile.

"Really?" Ivy narrowed her eyes skeptically. "I need you to believe in me though. I want you to put your whole heart into it, nothing less or it won't work."

He watched her run her fingers through her long hair and brush it off her shoulders.

"It's not in my nature to go half way, it is always all or nothing," he replied. A seriousness swept over his expression. "You have my whole heart, Ivy. I promise."

Ivy paused, lost in his words.

"Good," she managed, dropping her eyes to the sand between her feet. She held her breath until he spoke again.

"So, where do we start?" he asked.

"Well," she breathed, "I found my sanctuary by the ocean."

Hart knew this. He imagined that the earth awakened when she stepped onto the wet sand, as though it had been waiting for her return. He liked the way she lifted her chin to the light breeze, closing her eyes when she reached the water's edge. The way her shoulders lifted as she breathed in the salty air, and with her long breath out, he saw her unwind. Her subconscious ritual of gratitude. He realized that he found himself waiting for that quiet moment she had with the world, fascinated by it. This place of sand and sea was her sanctuary, and he was honored to be here with her.

Ivy turned her body to face him. "I promised myself that I would never take a swim in the ocean for granted. I am grateful each time I feel the salt water against my skin. Are you?"

Hart laughed humbly. "Not exactly."

"No?" An amused frown swept across her face. "Look at the water!"

Hart peered at the ocean with a gorgeous smile that gripped her heart.

"Stand up," she continued, as she got to her feet. "Look. The water is glassy. It's warm. You need to appreciate the peacefulness of the sea. It's saltiness. How it feels against your skin. The way it absorbs the heat from your body." She gazed dreamily at the water.

Hart stood and wondered at her as she talked.

"Do you notice the little fish swimming beside you? Or the seagulls bathing in the water as it washes up the sand? Do you see yourself as a creature on this earth, simply cooling off in the shallows of this vast ocean? Because across the sea, someone is doing the exact same thing as you."

"Like an animal at a waterhole?" Hart laughed softly.

"In a way."

"No, I can honestly say I have never looked at it from that perspective." He laughed again. "You are very different from any woman I have met before."

Ivy screwed up her face and looked away.

"No, that's a good thing," Hart grinned apologetically. "I'm sorry, Ives."

The sun disappeared behind the clouds, but the air was still thick with humidity. Ivy peered into the overcast sky when large raindrops started to fall on the sand around them.

"Should we head home?" he asked.

"No. I want to show you how to *live* again, Hart. Do you want me to?"

The rain drops cooled his hot skin, and he was grateful for the relief from the heat. He heard the rain fall against the leaves in the forest. He glanced at the storm behind them and thought about Ivy's question. He didn't know if he was ready to let go of the darkness. What about Taym? What about his revenge? Hart looked at Ivy, who watched him with her glorious blue eyes, waiting patiently and vulnerably for him to answer.

"Yes," he answered in absolute surrender to her raw and sweet disposition. "Show me, Ivy."

Hart stood there, motionless. Speechless. In her world. Ivy's world. A paradise he would never have believed existed until he saw it for himself, and here he was … basking in the innocent essence of a girl who walked the forests alone and owned the oceans and the sands without even knowing. Unaware of her magic. *Her allure.* Too sweet to realize that she had him completely. Hart wanted to fall to his knees before her in reverence. A knight, worshiping his queen. Silently begging for her forgiveness before she discovered his betrayal. Before she threw his pitiful soul to the gallows where he knew he belonged.

Unless he protected her ….

Vowed never to leave her side until the day he died defending her. This was fair. A *Rose for a Rose.*

Hart held his breath, suddenly nervous of the sun-kissed girl standing in front of him. A blonde lock of hair fell in front of her eyes. Before he had time to lift his hand and brush it away, she tucked it behind her ear. Ivy took his hand and gently pulled him toward her, barefoot and irrefutably breathtaking…then she let him go and turned away. She walked a few meters toward the water and turned around to face him, her wavy hair dancing around her as she walked backward in the sand. She smiled at him, watching him, waiting for him to follow. So he did. She combed her hair away from her face with her fingers and turned toward the ocean again. Everything about her captivated him. Mesmerized him. Ivy was summer's child, born to the coast. He saw the white soles of her feet as she walked through the sand. The whiteness of her fingernails against her silky, olive skin. Her white crocheted bikini was tied loosely around her hips, rousing the hungry beast within him. Hart clenched his jaw, repressing the instinctive craving for a beautiful woman. It had been so long. Too long. He knew she didn't bestow her intimacy upon many men, and so he gladly followed the effortless goddess who walked him down to the azure waters of her ocean. The road he had been walking was long and arduous, and he was tired. *So tired.* Any man would be a fool not to follow her.

Ivy turned to wait for him at the water's edge and smiled. A slow, tender smile that lulled his broken heart. He recognized a reflective thoughtfulness in her eyes, and it reminded him of Oliver. Then, for the first time since Oliver died, Hart was able to remember his friend and smile. *Oh, Ivy.* A stillness fell upon him when he reached her side; it was unfamiliar, but he embraced the feeling whole heartedly.

They stood together in the wet sand, facing the ocean, their hands almost touching. The rain fell across the ocean in front of them, pattering with a soft serenity. The sky was dark, yet the world waited calmly, sympathetic to the suffering that lingered on its shore. A silver shade cloaked the surface of the water and gently lapped their feet, tempting them, luring them into its warmer depths. The mist rose to meet the cooler air that rolled in with the rain. Hart welcomed the absence of heat, the feeling of the raindrops against his desert skin, the way it drummed his body and resonated through his soul. Salvaging his strength. Cleansing him of his concerns. A fleeting moment without pain.

Ivy took his hand and pulled him into the water, slowly. The water was warm, but his hand felt hot against hers. There were a few scars scattered across Hart's stomach, which she had noticed earlier. They were carved into his muscles as he walked toward her, and she looked away politely, sensitive to his feelings. Ivy wanted to trace her finger along them and soothe the nightmare that came with each one, but it was the scars she couldn't see that troubled her more.

She pulled him further into the water, watching him relax. They stood waist deep in the ocean, swaying gently with the water's movement. Ivy caught his soothing gaze taking her in. Desire throbbed hotly in her heart. The sound of the rain evoked an intimacy that neither of them expected. She watched the water run down Hart's forehead and over his eyelashes, dripping past his pensive, brown eyes. A grateful, relieved expression swept across his face, and he looked to the sky and closed his eyes. Her eyes followed the rain as it fell down his body, a body that had been carved by the gods for his time here on Earth. A soldier sent from the heavens to protect those who cannot fight for themselves.

Slowly, Hart's fingers moved through hers. Ivy exhaled heavily in pleasure, meeting his gaze when it returned from the sky. Hart studied their hands, consumed by the feel of her in the water. Lost in her peace. Seized by the tranquility of the ocean, and the rain...*and Ivy.* She was impossible to resist. She was everything he needed right now, everything he didn't have. Ivy exuded a magical warmth to which he was drawn like a moth to a flame. She was sensual and sexy, empathetic and forgiving. She was the antidote for his suffering, but he couldn't save himself with her love. He didn't deserve her. His culpability for Oliver's death ran too deep, and she had no idea of what he had done.

Hart concealed the swelling torment behind the rain on his face…blinking with rain, blinking with tears. *If only she knew.* He looked down at Ivy in the water. Her wet hair clung tightly to her body until it reached the water where it fanned out around her, and for a brief moment, he thought he was floating in the ocean with a mermaid.

When Hart's fingers stopped moving, Ivy pulled his hand out of the water and pressed his palm against hers. She felt the tremor quaking through him. It shuddered up her arm and she frowned. Hart was trembling. Ivy studied his hand until she knew for sure it wasn't her imagination, and then she looked up at Hart. He pulled his hand away from her, but it was too late. He couldn't hide the trembling from her because he had no control over it. The fear had him.

Hart regarded what she saw with a serious, brooding silence, and after a short while, his expression fell.

"It started when I left Libya," he breathed.

"I'm sorry, I didn't mean—"

"Ivy, please, never apologize to me." Hart shook his head, thinking about what he had done to her in Libya. What she didn't know.

Ivy narrowed her eyes at him. Her brother's death had clearly taken its toll on his men. The trauma Hart suffered lingered within him like a slow poison, tracing through his veins, killing him slowly. She swallowed the lump in her throat. *Oh Oliver, look what has happened now that you have gone, look what has happened to your soldiers. The ones you left behind.*

A tear rolled down her cheek, but she was too slow to wipe it away.

"Hey, I'm okay. I can handle it," Hart laughed tenderly. He pulled her into his arms, tucking her into his strong body. "Don't you worry about me, I'll be fine."

Ivy pulled away from him. She looked into his brown eyes, and before her head caught up with her heart, Ivy traced her finger along the faint scar beneath his left eye.

Hart's eyes blinked slowly, heavy with his desire. He sighed resignedly, giving in to her enchantment. He ran his hands back along her wet face and combed his fingers into her hair, then he pulled her closer to his lips. He breathed her in, intoxicated by the sweet scent of her breath. Dizzy with her nearness. He brushed his lips agonizingly against hers, catching the desire in her parted mouth. The rain fell down her face and rolled divinely over her skin, and he sighed lightly on her lips, longing for the taste of her. Then Oliver crossed his guilty mind.

Hart clenched his hands into tight fists on either side of her face. "You need to stay away from me, Ivy."

"Why?" she whispered breathlessly.

"You don't know me," he replied, pulling away from her. "You don't know what I've done."

"Then tell me, Hart! Tell me what happened!" Ivy pleaded. Her crystal eyes searched his face. "What happened over there in Libya? Was it Taym? Was it Oliver?"

Hart didn't answer. He glared at her with his brow furrowed in painstaking defeat, then he dropped his gaze to the water.

Ivy's heart plummeted into the ocean with the falling rain.

"Or is it me?" she asked quietly.

Hart groaned and rubbed his face in frustration.

Ivy stepped toward him in the water.

"Ivy," he breathed, stepping away from her. He thought about the truths that would break her heart. "I don't want to hurt you."

"You can't hurt me, Hart. No one can hurt me. I'm stronger than you think." Ivy remained where she was and brushed her fingertips along the surface of the water in thought. She knew how deadly he could be, but she couldn't imagine it. Hart was too placid to be dangerous. "I know what you do over there, and I know what they ask of you. You would never hurt me."

Hart sighed. "That's not what I mean."

He saw her watching him carefully. Analyzing him. She opened her mouth to speak, but no words left her lips. She was trying to understand him. Decrypt his message. Then she stepped toward him in the water again, her scarlet lips wet with rain.

"Don't tempt me, Ivy. *Please.*"

"What happened to you?"

Hart stared at her for a few seconds, then sighed into his hand. He thought about Taym kneeling on the concrete, with his gun aimed at Oliver's chest. He remembered the contentment in Ollie's eyes after he had shot Abad, the pleasure in knowing his best friend would survive even though he, himself, would not. There was no resentment. No fear. No regret. Oliver sacrificed himself and never came home.

But Hart had come home.

Now here he was, with Ivy, the mystical creature who stood before him in the water. The sister Oliver had asked him to check on in case he died … *and you did die, Ollie. Now here I am, with Ivy, because you couldn't be. I'm here because you died for me. I shouldn't be here. I shouldn't be here. Shit.* Hart tried to wrap his thoughts around the mess unfolding inside his head. Trembling hands were all that was left of him.

He turned away from her in the water.

Ivy's breath shook with concern. "What are you afraid of—"

Hart growled and turned to face her again, "I'm afraid that I will never be the same man I was, Ivy!" He glared at her through the rain. "Because I will never forgive myself for what happened in Libya. *Never.*"

Ivy bravely held his dark, tormented gaze. Her heart thumped madly against her chest, and she wondered if he could hear the fear pounding beneath her feigned composure, spoiling her facade. There was something in Hart she recognized from the Gala last night, when she caught him falling into the sea. A darkness. An emptiness. His eyes were black with self-contempt…*and fear.*

Hart ran his hands back through his hair in distress, then walked away from her into the deeper water. Ivy held her breath as he waded powerfully through the silver ocean, and when he dove into the water, she gazed up into the rain and exhaled loudly into the sky. An impulsive energy bubbled on the surface of the water in the heavy rain, and Ivy soaked it up gladly. This place had never felt so alive. Hart made her feel sexy, and exhilarated, and pleasantly breathless, but also terrified. Terrified of what happened last night at the Gala. Terrified of the darkness that her brother never once mentioned in his stories, because it was new.

Ivy closed her eyes and thought about the spectacular soldier who had completely enthralled her. She felt the rain against her flushed skin, and she listened to the sound of it hitting the water around her. It was all she could hear, and Ivy fell tranquilly and blissfully into the consoling loudness of it as it echoed around the bay. Her heart thumped euphorically, and she smiled into the sky, then she felt something wrap around her legs, and Hart lifted her out of the water into the falling rain.

The wet forest glimmered in the sunlight that peeked through the clouds. She watched it glitter in the distance, feeling Hart's strong body pressed against her legs. Ivy looked down at him and placed her hands on his sturdy shoulders. He was beautifully tanned, and wet. The seawater rolled over the muscles in his chest and down his stomach, and Ivy forced her wandering eyes to meet his.

He mouthed a silent *sorry* to her, captivating her with his sincerity, and Ivy smiled. A playful grin swept onto his handsome face, and Ivy dissolved in his charm. She breathed pleasurably through the sensation of the raindrops rolling down her skin. The feeling of his hard chest against her hips, with his heart against her...*beating against her.* She had always loved this soldier from afar, and now here he was, lifting her weightlessly into the sky. Ivy wanted to run her hands down his wet face and trace her thumb over his glistening lips—but she didn't.

Hart let her fall into his arms, making Ivy yelp in fright.

He laughed. "Don't worry, Ivy. I've got you."

She wrapped her arms nervously around his neck, and he lowered her carefully into the water again.

"You're about as heavy as my rucksack, you know that?"

Ivy wiped the rain from her face and laughed. "I'm sure I am heavier than a rucksack."

"No, you're not. See, along with my rucksack, I throw these huge weapons over my shoulder, just like this." Hart bent over and picked up Ivy again and threw her over his shoulder. "You weigh nothing in comparison, believe me. I could carry you for years, Ivy!"

She laughed as he carried her back toward the shore, reminiscent of summer days spent with her brother. When they reached the dry sand, Hart lifted her off his shoulder and set her down on the beach. Ivy looked up at him. There was a mischief sparkling in his brown eyes, and a playful smile curved to the left side of his face.

"See?" he laughed.

His gentle laugh warmed her heart and Ivy held his gaze with a content smile, appreciating that he didn't look so afraid anymore.

Hart bit his lip and smiled, suddenly bashful. "We should get that fishing line in the water."

Ivy smiled to herself as he jogged up the beach to fetch the fishing rod. This was all he needed, time away from the responsibilities and pressures of life. Unhindered happiness—nothing less than he deserved. Hart spent his life protecting others, throwing himself in the line of fire so that they would survive, even if he might not. She wondered what had prompted him to become a soldier, when he decided that other peoples' lives were more important than his own. He was a devoted servant to his country. To other countries. To this world. Johnny Hart, she thought, the unassuming hero of countless people who now live in gratitude of a man they will never know ... and he asked for nothing in return.

An unexpected sadness gripped Ivy's heart. The world hadn't thanked Hart for his selflessness—it had killed his best friend instead.

"Here you go." Hart handed over her dad's fishing rod.

Ivy took a deep breath and concealed her empathy. "You're not fishing?"

Hart laughed and rubbed his jaw. His warm eyes smiled, and Ivy knew she would never get over how beautiful he was.

"No, remember? I said I was useless at catching fish," he answered, his voice low and husky. "And we want to eat tonight, right?"

"Yeah, we do." She pushed him out of the way, smirking. Ivy walked down to the water with a wicked twinkle in her eye. She planned to throw her catch back in the ocean to see another day, and she couldn't wait to see his reaction.

The afternoon disappeared with the sunset. Hart knelt on the sand beside Ivy and packed away their belongings for the hike back home. As he zipped up the bag he glanced at the ocean, and spotted an osprey plunging into the water. It flapped its large wings on the surface of the water, then lifted itself into the air with a sizable fish in its talons.

"Whoa! Look at the size of the fish he just pulled out of the ocean!"

Ivy searched the golden sky above the bay. She spotted the fish flying face forward, gripped securely in the claws of the osprey high above the sea.

"At least he has fish for dinner." Hart winked at her.

Ivy smirked, then frowned curiously into the sky. "I have never seen an osprey in the bay before." She watched the osprey fly in a large circle around the bay. The fish's scales glistened in the golden sun that still caught the sky high above her and Hart. She watched on in silent awe until the osprey disappeared around the cliff at the far end of the beach.

Ivy thought about the fish. A life spent swimming under the sea, suddenly plucked from the water and lifted into the unfamiliar sky, soaring through the wind into the dark depths of the night. Did the fish recognize the world from that perspective? Did he recognize himself outside of the water? Did he know where he was going, or worse, what was coming?

Ivy stared at the cliff long after the osprey had disappeared behind it.

"What is it, Ives?" Hart asked, recognizing Oliver's concern in her soulful, blue eyes.

"If the fish knew what was coming," she glanced at Hart, "do you think the extraordinary journey through the sky will make it any easier for him to accept what is inevitably going to happen to him?"

Hart felt her curious mind rifling through his.

"Like a glorious misfortune?" he replied.

"Yeah, exactly." Ivy marveled at his perception, astounded once again by his flawless interpretation.

It was difficult for Hart to relate to the fish. He had spent years as a soldier in Phoenix and had no problem understanding the eagle's motive. It was a fearless hunter like himself, but not so much anymore. Hart frowned to himself in thought. He was out of his element now. Out on his own. Swimming aimlessly in the sea.

Hart narrowed his eyes at the cliff where the osprey disappeared. The darkness would consume him eventually, and he had once wanted it to…but now there was Ivy. If he was heading toward his ultimate destruction, then she definitely made the journey there worthwhile.

The thought hit Hart like a bullet to the chest. *Ivy is my glorious misfortune.*

His world had shattered into a thousand pieces after Oliver died, and now here was Ivy, who unknowingly resurfaced all his pain from that tragic day. Each minute spent with her would see him fall to pieces, and simultaneously piece him back together again. It was a torturous process, but he ached for her. Her compelling beauty revitalized his weary soul. Her innocence was his undoing. Her sweetness. Her compassion. Her body. Her lips. *Ivy Rose.* She was here to make his end divinely tolerable… or divinely excruciating.

"You know, if I were the eagle," Hart grinned, forcing himself to lighten the mood, "I'd be unhappy with you for you ruining my appetite."

"Oh, Hart!" Ivy laughed. "I'm sorry I threw all the fish back."

Hart laughed. "Yeah, so I guess we need to think about dinner, eh?"

Ivy laughed again.

He grinned adoringly at her in the fading light and draped his arm around her shoulder, then they walked up the silver sand toward the Ghost Trail.

"We can pick something up on the way through town?" she suggested.

"Sounds great. What do you feel like?"

"Fish and chips."

Hart stopped walking and stared at Ivy with a dry expression. "Are you kidding me? You know where they got those fish from, right?" He pointed over his shoulder toward the ocean and raised his eyebrows.

Ivy giggled adorably as she tied her hair into a long ponytail. A smile swept across his face.

"It is the killing part I don't like," Ivy said. She saw Hart smile at her through the dim light of the forest, but it quickly faded. She felt foolish. "Killing a fish seems insignificant, I shouldn't have said that. I'm sorry, Hart."

"Ivy, I told you, never apologize to me."

Ivy looked at him. This was the second time he'd said this to her today. Nevertheless, she still felt guilty. There was no pleasure in killing for these men, it simply came with the job. It meant staying alive. Oliver used to come home, and Ivy would watch his silent struggle to come to terms with what he had done in the war. It would bring her to tears. Over there it was a necessity, but once Oliver returned home, those lives he ended would come back to haunt him. It broke her heart to imagine the detrimental effects it had on their souls. They were good men, forced to do the unthinkable.

Hart walked along the trail and thought about how innocent she was. How empathetic. He sensed her contemplating his involvement in the war. How would she feel about the countless lives he had ended? Phoenix knew the full extent of the terror that would have progressed had they not carried out their instructions, but their actions still weighed heavily on their hearts.

When Ivy stepped into the poppy field, Hart glanced back along the Ghost Trail and into the heart of the dark forest. The moonlight filtered through the canopy of trees, and in the distance he saw a small green light go out as fast as he saw it. Hart's pulse quickened. Adrenaline leeched into his veins but his focus remained unflinching. The possibility of any lurking threat strangely excited him, and for a brief moment, Hart remembered the soldier he used to be. He allowed Ivy to walk ahead with the flashlight, he didn't want to frighten her. Besides, he wasn't even sure what he saw? *Was it real?* Years spent constantly questioning his safety had obviously taken its toll on his mind. There was no room for imprudence with his level of vigilance, and he found it incredibly difficult to switch off the soldier inside of him. He peered into the woods for another few moments before shaking his head. No matter how long he stared into the darkness, nothing was going to appear ... because there was no one there. Ghosts, he thought. *They are only ghosts.*

Hart gazed at the stars above him as they walked through the field of poppies toward the light of town. Was this it for him, he wondered, always living on edge? Forever doubting the security of the world he lived in, of the world Ivy lived in. He thought about it while they trekked through the dark poppies, their scarlet petals now drained of color in the moonlight, like fading soldiers. He looked at Ivy in front of him. Her white shirt glowed in the moonlight, and she walked happily through the dark, and Hart's mood shifted instantly. Her blonde ponytail bounced over her shoulder as she glanced back to check on him. A playful grin beamed at him in the dark, and she laughed softly. The sound was gentle and sweet, and it sent a shooting warmth through his heart. *Ivy, my angel of light, leading me out of the darkness. Follow her light ... follow her.* This was California, Hart convinced himself as they walked into town. Ivy's world, not Libya.

They strolled beneath the fairy lights that sprinkled the trees along the main street of La Mar, and Hart forced himself to shake off the war. To shake off Libya.

"Hey, Ivy?" Hart smiled down at her tenderly, wrapping his big arm around her shoulder. "Thank you for today, I really needed it."

Ivy looked up at him, her eyes softening with delight. "Me, too."

## Chapter 9

"I AM GOING TO TAKE a quick shower," Ivy called out to Hart as he walked to the kitchen with their dinner. "Start without me!"

"I'll wait," he called back.

Hart checked his cell phone, which he had left in the kitchen this morning. Three missed calls from Walker. He slid his thumb across the screen and called him back. As the dial tone rang in his ear, he walked into the study that adjoined the front hall and sat in one of the chairs opposite the desk. Hart flicked on a lamp and ran his finger down the back of a steel C-130 Hercules airplane model that stood on the corner of the desk.

Walker answered, "Hart, buddy, how are you?"

"Hey, man, I'm good. You guys get to Monterey alright?"

"Yeah, we've been in meetings since we landed. It's doing my fucking head in," Walker spoke gently down the line.

Hart laughed softly. He could tell Walker was smoking.

"How's Ivy?"

"She's good," Hart replied.

"I bet she's pleased you decided to stay."

Hart sensed his friend's smile on the other end of the line. "Yeah, she was."

He heard Walker laugh quietly, and Hart smiled to himself. "Damn, I wish I was in Monterey with you guys, though," Hart added.

"Me, too," Walker agreed, "but you know we'll keep you

informed. Ivy needs you more than we do right now."

"I know." Hart rubbed his forehead uneasily. "It's just hard being here."

"Hard because you want to get back to Libya, or hard because she reminds you that he saved your life?" Walker took a long draw on his cigarette.

Hart thought about the question for a moment. He imagined Walker's steely expression on the other end of the line, furrowed brow and unsmiling, waiting patiently for an answer he already knew.

Hart sighed, "I don't know."

"Hart," Walker said quickly, sensing his friend's despondency, "as soon as we get the go-ahead for Libya, you're on the team. I've spoken to Hannah."

Hart's spirit lifted. "What do you mean? Garvey's letting me come back early?"

"Don't get too excited. I'd say it may be a good six months before Phoenix is even given the clearance to operate again."

"Six months!? Why?"

"They're investigating every single operation we've handled since Abad and Taym joined the team back in 2007. They want to know what went wrong. They're embarrassed, and people want answers. Phoenix is out of action until then," Walker spoke calmly. "At one point they considered shutting Phoenix down permanently, but they can't afford to. They need us. I'm happy with six months if it means we can still operate."

"Yeah, you're right." Hart's eyes narrowed as he leaned forward in his chair. "So what have you got for me?"

"Oh, buddy, no wonder they called us in. They haven't got the faintest fucking clue about what's going on over there," Walker replied with a steely softness.

"What about Taym? Has he been located?"

"Yeah, he has…." Hart heard him pause to draw on his cigarette. "… and they've been patting themselves on the back ever since. Benji's going to lose his shit if he hears the intel crew bragging about it one more time."

Hart laughed quietly.

"Here, I have a recording for you," Walker went on. "You got a few minutes spare?"

"Yeah man, shoot."

"Bar Rafid, remember him?"

"Of course," Hart replied. "Don't tell me he is part of the organization, too?" He rubbed his forehead, disappointed.

"Yeah, he is. I'm sorry."

There was a pause in conversation as Hart fathomed what Walker was saying to him. He sighed heavily into his hand, another kid lost to the enemy.

"What the fuck is happening, Walker?"

"These young guys are being brainwashed," Walker answered. "They're head-hunted because they are easily influenced. You know how you can feel at that age, restless and unworthy, and in the worst cases, marginalized by society. Rafid was the same. These kids are already struggling with their identity, and these organizations are making them feel special."

"They're being used," Hart replied wearily.

"Rafid joined the group last year."

"His family must be shattered." Hart closed his eyes and thought about Rafid's mother and father. They had put everything they had into their son's future, training with the United States military.

"A UK team has Rafid under house arrest in Sirte. We're not sure who the other guy is on this recording, and Rafid is refusing to talk," Walker explained. "We need the identity of this other guy because he possesses the intel regarding the location of the three leaders in charge of this whole organization."

"Right."

"Garvey's hoping you may be able to assist intelligence, seeing as you and Ollie personally trained Rafid," Walker added.

He heard Walker take another drag of his cigarette.

Hart thought about his leave. He shouldn't be here in San Diego. He should be at Base in Monterey because he knew Libya better than all of them put together.

Hart glared at the model of the Hercules and narrowed his eyes. He pushed speaker on his cell and placed it on the desk in front of him.

"Play the recording."

Two men's voices suddenly echoed down the line, mid-conversation in their Arabic tongue. Hart listened in carefully. He immediately recognized Rafid's voice. It was young and animated, but he had no idea who Rafid was talking to. The second voice sounded rather monotonous and forced. There was something peculiar about it. Unnatural. Even the recording itself was of poor quality. Hart frowned intently at his cell as he interpreted their conversation—places, meeting points, people, and a girl. Nothing significant stood out to Hart, except for the faint mechanical hum of what sounded like an aircraft or a train.

The two soldiers listened for a few minutes before Walker paused the recording to speak to Hart, "Did you pick that up?"

"They seem mostly interested in apprehending a girl?" Hart replied.

"Yes, but they refer to her as "the girl" in all the recordings we've listened to so far. We don't understand the role she plays in the Libyan assault. This woman could already be part of the organization, or she could be their next target."

"Maybe the Ambassador's daughter?"

"No," Walker replied, "she was extracted from Libya just minutes after we were."

Hart rested his head in his hands and thought about any prominent women in Libya that may be of any value to the group. Walker played the recording again, and Hart listened.

"Listen, it's faint, but can you hear the other guy is on a plane, or train, maybe?" Hart asked Walker.

Walker pushed pause on the recording approximately ten seconds later. "I hear it. No one's picked that up."

Hart sensed the pleasure in Walker's tone.

"Get intelligence to hone in on that sound. It will open up more leads once they work out where this guy is headed," Hart ordered. "The second voice, it sounds too colorless, no one speaks like that. I want intelligence to look into it. It sounds robotic, like he's using a device to mask his real voice. They've got apps for that kind of shit these days."

"You think he knows we're listening?"

"Maybe. Do we have a team on the ground yet?" Hart asked.

"They will be dropped in Tobruk in a few days. It's a fair way from all the action, but it's too risky to land anywhere else at this stage. Tobruk remains reasonably untouched by the insurgents."

"What happened to the shipment that was supposed to leave the Benghazi port?"

"They seized it."

"Shit! Everything they need is in there! Launchers, heavy weapons, MRAPs …. I can't believe this is happening." Hart's voice dropped to a low whisper, "Things were supposed to go down so differently."

"I know," Walker agreed.

The two of them stopped talking, thinking to themselves.

Walker took another drag on his cigarette, making his voice a little deeper and huskier when he spoke again. "Most of the group has repositioned themselves back in Tripoli. Benghazi seems to have settled slightly, but Tripoli's turbulent. They're not even considering putting our men in there until the demonstrations ease off. It's a dismal sight over there. Fucking bastards."

"So what about Taym?" Hart asked, hopeful for something positive.

"Taym resides in an apartment block in the center of Tripoli, but we're unable to get anyone in there while the ground is hot with the enemy," Walker continued. "Seriously Hart, it's like someone poked a burning stick into a nest of fucking fire-ants. There has been word of an airstrike to take him down but his location means killing a shitload of civilians too, and it's unlikely to go ahead. He's put some thought into it—he knows we're after blood."

Hart's chest stung painfully. *Oliver.*

"But there's more," Walker added, "Intel has provided us with information regarding Taym's affiliation with an offshore organization that has the intention to spread the assault globally. It sounds like they plan to encourage young foreigners to join their group and then force them to wreak havoc on their own nations."

"Shit, Taym. Where did we go wrong with that kid?" Hart shook his head and wearily rubbed the side of his face. "You don't think he's got it in for America do you?"

Walker laughed softly. "Don't they all?"

Hart smiled into his cell, welcoming the humor, dark as it was.

"Are you ready for the rest of the recording?" Walker asked.

"Yeah."

Ivy stood in the dark, listening to the recording as she leaned against the wall outside of the study. She rested her head back and closed her eyes, trying to interpret what she was listening too. The men on the recording spoke in a language she assumed was Arabic, and she couldn't understand a word they were saying. Hart and Walker spoke the odd sentence to each other in the same language as the men, as if by habit. It was a side of them she had never thought about. They possessed exceptional knowledge of a terrifying world she knew nothing about. Oliver had never brought work home with him like this.

Ivy's heart thumped uneasily in her chest, overwhelmed by the seriousness of it all. She felt incredibly intimidated by the soldier who sat in the room behind her. Warm, loyal, gentle Johnny Hart, she told herself, but in the gravity of the moment, he frightened her unexpectedly. *Stay away from me, Ivy. You don't know me. You don't know what I've done.*

There was a loud knock at the front door, and Ivy gasped in response. She held her breath as she listened for Hart's acknowledgment of the unannounced visitor, but he was still deeply engrossed in the recording.

Ivy hurried to the front door and flicked on the outside lights. She opened the door a few inches and peeked outside.

"Hey, Ives," Tommy greeted her.

Ivy warmed in his familiarity despite his behavior at the Gala. Tommy's advances last night seemed to pale in comparison to the sudden uncertainty she felt toward Oliver's soldiers. Their talk of war provoked a fear that she had never felt before tonight. Ivy tried not to find comfort in Tommy's unexpected presence, but his apologetic expression encouraged a warm pity for the man.

He smiled at her sheepishly and fiddled with the camo baseball cap that he held in front of him.

"Tommy, what are you doing here?" Ivy whispered through the crack in the door.

"I came to apologize," he replied, dolefully dropping his gaze to his cap.

Ivy peeked back toward the study and quietly snuck out through the front door. She pulled the door so that it sat ajar behind her, still intuitively wary of Tommy's true intentions.

"Can I come inside?" he asked.

Ivy didn't want him inside with Hart. He didn't trust Tommy, and so she subtly ignored the question. "I should have introduced you to Oliver's friends last night, before you met them the way you did," she whispered apologetically. "Everything happened so fast yesterday, and it didn't even cross my mind that you might have seen them on your way out. I had no idea they were coming to San Diego to see me."

"Well, no matter, I heard they left this morning," he mentioned, rather pleased.

"Wow, news travels fast around La Mar," she frowned, keeping tactfully quiet about Hart's decision to stay.

"Why are you whispering, Ivy?"

She laughed sweetly. "Am I?"

"Ives, I'm here to explain what happened last night—"

"Tommy," she cut him off, hoping he would leave before Hart cottoned on to his presence.

"No, let me explain myself."

Ivy sighed impatiently.

"I wanted to show you how good we could be as a couple. I wouldn't have hurt you. Do you believe me?"

Ivy searched his face carefully for the truth. She remembered his eyes blackening with pleasure, visibly thrilled by her vulnerability. He'd had her right where he wanted her, and she couldn't do anything about it.

She leaned her head back on the doorframe and sighed resignedly, "I don't know."

"All I want is one chance to prove to you that we would be perfect for each other," he added in his defense. "You and me, Ives! Why won't you give us a chance? Come on, give me a couple of weeks to show you what an amazing boyfriend I can be." Tommy grinned persuasively. He pressed his hands together as though he were praying, and the baseball cap swung loosely off the back of his middle finger.

Ivy stared at the military camouflage print on the cap in his hands, and her brother crossed her intuitive mind. She took it as a sign.

"Look, I need to be somewhere," Tommy grinned, "but I'm going to interpret your silence as though you are considering it. One kiss before I leave?"

Ivy frowned at him.

"On the cheek at least? Come on," he added, seemingly irritated. "Shit, Ives, you sure know how to humiliate a man."

"I'm not trying—"

"No," he interrupted, pressing his hand against her mouth to stop her talking.

Ivy's eyes widened. His big hand pushed her head back into the door frame with enough pressure to cause concern, and she was grateful for Hart's presence in the house, though Ivy wondered if he even noticed her absence.

"I have all these women in La Mar who want me, but I keep rejecting them for you. They must think I'm insane!"

She rolled her eyes over the top of his hand.

"Sooner or later, I'm going to say yes to one of them, and we would never get the chance to see what might have been for us."

Ivy didn't believe him. Tommy wasn't the monogamous type.

"One kiss is all I need to open your eyes, Ives." His blue eyes darkened with lust as he leaned into her.

Ivy glanced at him nervously and mumbled her rejection into his hand.

"I didn't hear you say no," he whispered, curling back his lips to reveal a wicked grin.

She glared at him.

Tommy shrugged. "It may be a reluctant yes … but it is a yes, at least."

Ivy stepped sideways toward the door but Tommy was quick to respond, as though he had been anticipating her attempt to retreat. He leaned harder into her, pinning her against the door-frame, and laughed into his shoulder, his amused eyes returning to hers only seconds later.

"What's going on inside that head of yours? Being on your own for so long has made you crazy," he laughed. "Have you forgotten what it's like to be with a man, Ivy? A *real* man?"

She noted the genuine cheer in his tone, and she questioned whether he realized the effect of his actions. What seemed harmless to him, scared the hell out of her. It had been fourteen years since he professed his love for her, yet they had remained friends all this time. Maybe he really believed his actions were justified?

Ivy groaned again in his tight grip.

"You're making me out to be some kind of monster," Tommy growled under his breath. "It's one kiss! One fucking kiss … frigid bitch!"

Ivy tried to scorn him through his hand, but all she managed was an incoherent mumble.

His body pushed against hers, pressing her hard against the door frame as he twisted a lock of her hair beside her face with his free hand. His ravenous eyes took her in, and she thought about Hart. Tommy had no idea he was here inside the house, barely ten meters from where he had her pinned beside the front door. Nonetheless, Ivy was terrified. Tommy could assault her right here at her front door, beside the soldier who she felt exceedingly safe with, because Libya—and Taym—had Hart otherwise occupied.

Ivy's heart pounded fiercely with adrenaline, and she screamed desperately for Hart through Tommy's sweating palm.

"What the fuck, Ivy!?" Tommy growled, looking around nervously. He stopped playing with the lock of her hair and took a handful of it behind her head. He pulled her head back, forcing her to look up at him. Vulnerable and delicate, her eyes wide with fear.

Ivy felt him shaking with pleasure against her.

"Stop resisting me. Stop this," Tommy breathed.

He released her hair, then she felt his hand sliding up her inner thigh. He slipped his hand underneath her cotton dress, and Ivy panted frantically through her nose, catching her breath. She was growing dizzy with fear. She felt him rub his fingers against her through her underwear, and she whimpered under his unwelcome touch. Ivy writhed against the wall to set herself free, but she couldn't move. Tommy was too strong for her.

*"Hart,"* she mumbled through Tommy's hand. This would be the end of him, she thought. First Oliver, then this. Ivy's heart sank. He would never forgive himself. Her suffering had become tolerable after all these years, but Hart's torment was unbearable to watch.

"You feel so good, Ivy. Fuck, you feel good," he breathed insatiably into her ear, then he bowed his head and kissed her lightly on the cheek.

His fingers pushed her underwear to the side, and Ivy cried again for her soldier, but Hart didn't come. Tommy's fingers rubbed her ungently, then they entered her.

Ivy closed her eyes tightly. She cried out again, but this time to herself. *This is all my fault.* She had it coming, she thought. She should have been wiser about Tommy, but she was afraid of Hart. Caught off guard by a world she knew existed but had never witnessed so close to home. Hart was part of a dangerous world, but that didn't make him dangerous. It frightened her momentarily, and it was enough for her to seek comfort in the remains of her deteriorating friendship with Tommy. Now she was trapped, like a fly in Tommy's deceitful web.

Ivy closed her eyes. As Tommy helped himself to her with his wandering hands, she repeated Hart's name over and over inside her head, calling for her soldier, begging for his protection. When he didn't come for her, Ivy released her spirit and let it soar into the dark depths of the night.

At first, she thought Tommy had changed his mind. There was a quick scuffle and a faint grunt, then Ivy opened her eyes and saw Hart in front of her, holding Tommy.

Tommy bled from his nose. The blood stained his lips, and he had a glazed look in his eyes when he glanced at her. Ivy froze against the wall in his attention. She watched Hart pull his arm back and swing another powerful punch, sending Tommy tumbling gracelessly down the stairs behind him. Ivy yelped in shock.

Hart looked back at her, his shoulders bent with resentment, and Ivy sensed his rage. She was careful not to move. There was a distant look in his eyes, like his soul had left him temporarily, but he watched her long enough for his gaze to soften in concern. Ivy tried to smile, but a grating moan distracted Hart and the anger cloaked his eyes once again, pulling him back to the darkness.

Ivy took a step toward him but he threw his hand in the air and motioned for her to keep away. So she did. Hart tread swiftly down the stairs toward Tommy, and Ivy hurried after him, stopping at the bottom step. Hart lifted Tommy to his stumbling feet just to knock him down once again, and Ivy gasped. She watched Tommy writhe on the driveway in agony as Hart circled him like a furious predator, set to take him down at any second.

Ivy watched on in stunned silence.

Tommy pulled himself weakly to his knees, panting.

"You fucking son-of-a—"

"Don't speak!" Hart growled, his fists clenching and unclenching anxiously as he circled Tommy. "It's taking all of my strength not to do something I'll regret, so don't *fucking* speak!" His voice boomed through the stillness of the night.

Ivy jumped, startled by the authoritative command in his voice. She was afraid … afraid for Hart. Walker and Benji weren't here to help them if he suffered another attack, and the black of his eyes triggered a chilling reminder of last night.

Hart knew it was Tommy on his knees in front of him, but he saw Taym's face sneering back at him. He shook his head with the vision and growled at the frustrating instability of his thoughts. His superior intelligence fought madly with his anxiety, and Hart refused to bow down to the weakness that frantically tried to claim him. *Not while she was in danger.* The darkness clouded his judgment with a dense fog, one which he usually welcomed as a deserved punishment for being spared his life, but tonight he was mindful of protecting Oliver's sister. Hart ran his trembling hands through his hair and cursed to himself.

Tommy pulled himself to his feet in Hart's hesitation, and limped toward his BMW. Hart watched him shuffle away, remembering Libya, remembering his friend's death...*Taym's broken body shuffling awkwardly toward Oliver. His snapped elbow swinging loosely by his side. He leaned down and pressed the tip of his gun into Oliver's temple, and peered up at Hart and smiled … and then fired his gun.*

Hart exhaled suddenly. His blood ran cold, leaving him numb to all feeling except the sharp tingling that prickled the tips of his fingers. He held his breath and watched Tommy collapse into the driver's seat of his car. When Tommy slammed his door shut, Hart bent over and groaned into his hands.

"Hart!" Ivy called out, racing to his side.

She turned instinctively when Tommy's BMW snarled to life. She watched him swerve erratically away from the house and disappear into the darkness along the driveway. Then Ivy faced

Hart again and lifted his head to take a look at him. He was pale. His head was heavy and his eyes were lifeless, and Ivy's heart burst into an alarmed panic.

She exhaled a desperate whisper, "Oh God, Hart, please stay with me."

"Did he hurt you?" he asked weakly.

Ivy sighed in relief. "No … I'm fine."

"I was too late."

"No, you weren't. Come on, we have to get you back inside." Ivy pulled his arm over her shoulders and walked him up the stairs and into the house. She took him to the room next to hers and helped him lie down on the bed.

He was gone again soon after, somewhere deep inside his head. Ivy whispered soothingly to him until his trembling left him and the color had returned to his skin. She waited by his side for what could have been an hour, cooling the burning skin on his forehead with the back of her hand. She listened to his deep breath, slow with sleep. Then she rested her hand on his heart to ensure it had returned to its normal, steady rhythm.

Hart blinked his eyes open. Warmth flooded his sleepy gaze, and he stared at her intently without smiling.

"Ivy—"

"Shhh," Ivy shook her head.

She smiled at him with her crystal eyes, and he silently agreed. There was nothing to say. As long as she was safe. Hart succumbed to his exhaustion and fell asleep under her tender, watchful gaze, listening to the quiet whisper of Oliver's voice.… *Please protect her. If I don't make it home.*

Ivy took a long, deep breath and stared silently at the sleeping soldier. Tears filled her eyes. She rested her fingers on her quivering lip and breathed out slowly to gather her composure. She tried to imagine what it felt like to be conquered by your fear so completely. One minute Hart was fine, the next he was crashing in the dark. This was his second attack in twenty-four hours. Ivy dreaded to think how many attacks he'd suffered since Oliver died two months ago.

*Oh, Oliver.*

She needed him now. He'd know what to do. He knew Hart better than anyone, she thought, but then Hart wouldn't be here like this if Oliver had survived. Ivy contemplated this for a moment. She could never have imagined a world without her brother, and now she couldn't imagine a world without Hart. Had they not lost Oliver, the two of them may have never met. It was a web of thoughts that only confused her more.

Ivy whispered to him as he slept, "Once I only walked with you in my dreams."

The room was quiet. She laughed softly to herself and looked up at the ceiling, feeling rather silly for whispering to him in his sleep. Ivy looked back at his peaceful face and sighed quietly to herself. *He saved her.* Like he had saved so many in the past. Because of him, hundreds of hearts are still beating across the deserts of Libya and Afghanistan. Now she was just like them, forever grateful for this selfless soldier.

"Thank you for saving us," she whispered.

He didn't wake.

She smiled to herself, but it quickly faded. Guilt gnawed at her for doubting him just before Tommy had arrived. Ivy sighed and rested her hand on top of his. This time, his attack was all her fault.

## Chapter 10

HART BOWED HIS POUNDING head and glanced at his chest. The bullet wound had disappeared but the searing pain still ripped through his heart. Panting with rage, he watched blood drip from his mouth to the frozen bed of pine needles between his feet. The black of his soul leeched its way into his veins, and his body throbbed with the rich venom of pure hatred and revenge.

He sensed someone coming, a lurking threat among the trees. He kept a close eye on the forest around the clearing, then he growled heatedly through the crisp, still air. "Taym."

A face materialized in the fog between the trees, dark eyes glinting.

Taym laughed wickedly and stepped into the clearing with his rifle poised and ready. "You want me, Hart. I can see it in your black eyes."

Hart stood bare-chested in the clearing. Defenseless. His breath hung in a cloud on the freezing air, drifting past his unwavering glare as he waited for Taym. *Always waiting for Taym.* He could smell Taym's blood as he neared him, like a wolf scenting his wounded prey. Sensing his weakness. Sensing his vulnerability.

Hart peered down at his bare hands. He may have no weapon to protect himself, but he was armed with his swift perception and deadly agility. He presented his open hands at his side, luring Taym in with his defenseless façade.

"What do you want?" Hart puffed angrily. "Why are you

here?"

"You know what I want," Taym replied. "I—want—her."

Hart's eyes blackened. He swiftly grabbed the end of Taym's rifle and aimed it into the sky, striking Taym forcefully in the nose with the butt of the weapon before he'd even had a chance to react. Hart ditched the rifle into the forest and then growled as he tightened his fingers around Taym's neck. He forced his enemy backward across the clearing and slammed Taym's head against the trunk of a pine. He glared down into Taym's panicked eyes, listening to his breathless plea for mercy, but Hart had none. He didn't have it in him anymore. Mercy left him in Libya, when betrayal entrenched itself deep into his soul.

Hart focused on squeezing the life out of Taym's deceitful neck, and he waited for the pleasure in his death. He waited for the contentment, the liberation. But it didn't come. Hart leaned his head back and searched the sky, exhaling in his despair. Pleading to the heavens. Desperate for his release and still clinging to Taym, holding him captive until the devil came to collect him and the world forgave Hart of his sins. Of his ruthless guilt. When nothing came, Hart bowed his head slowly and closed his eyes. *What I deserve ... nothing.*

A few seconds later the sun's light appeared in a rich, dark-red glow behind his eyes, and Hart peered into the sky again. Behind a wispy blanket of mist, the sun was a white halo of light above the clearing. An immeasurable glory suddenly bore down upon him, and he felt the light pushing against the darkness inside him, attempting to free his tortured soul. Hart closed his eyes in its warmth. In its bright shelter, the dark could not reach him here.

"Please," he whispered.

A gasp forced his eyes open. He looked at the man he was choking, but instead of Taym he saw Tommy, struggling for air in his fatal grip. Hart shook his head in a moment of confusion, then he glared at Tommy through the fog.

"You keep the fuck away from Ivy! You hear me?" Hart ordered. The fear beat wildly through his protective heart.

Tommy didn't respond. He couldn't. His lips turned a gray shade of blue, much like the color of his eyes in the fog.

The sunlight seemed to grow brighter with Hart's anger, the

fog catching its white glow. Eventually, it became so bright that Hart could barely keep his eyes open. He squinted at Tommy until his blue eyes were all that were left of him in the fog.

Tommy whispered to him, *"Soldier, please … it's me."*

Hart tilted his head, confused. He blinked at Tommy a few times until the mist became so blinding that he was forced to close his eyes. A warm touch ran along the scar under his left eye, and he faltered in the tenderness. He sensed the ocean and the sand and the sky … and Ivy. *Oh Ivy.* Hart shook his head, feeling the cold air give way to the warm light. His enraged heart slowed to the sound of her breath, and he heard her sweet voice lull in the light surrounding him, *"Come back to me, Hart."*

The darkness suddenly swept in from the sky and landed on his shoulders with a crushing weight, wrapping its chilling wings around him and seizing the light. Hart gasped in the dark, feeling the claws sink into his flesh. A rush of hot blood streamed down his naked chest, then he was lifted into the empty night. The pressure of the darkness bore down on him from all directions until he couldn't breathe, and he fought desperately for his next breath. He fought harder than he thought he would at his end, but still the darkness won. His breath never came.


She hadn't tried to wake him. She knew it might be dangerous to wake a soldier of his caliber in the night. So Ivy stood at his bedside in the dark, helplessly watching him thrash about and call out to someone who wasn't there. Then he sat up and launched himself at her.

Ivy felt his breath against her neck, laden with rage. She sensed the desperation in his mumbling voice. His incoherent penance, heavy with guilt, heavy with fear. She felt all his strength and all his fury, shaking through the hands that held her throat. Now she choked in his powerful grip, feeling her life trickle away into the night. Ivy had never felt more fragile.

She reached out to him and trailed her fingertip along the scar under his left eye, like she had done earlier that day, pleading once again for this soldier to come back to her. To leave behind the self-inflicted damnation of his soul and open his eyes to what was standing right in front of him. *Open your eyes, Hart.*

*Open your eyes ….*

Hart heard a faint gasp from the darkness in front of him. He opened his eyes in time to see their crystal blue eyes closing in the moonlight. For the second time. He saw the compassion in them before they closed. No fear. *There was never any fear in those crystal eyes.*

"Oliver?" he breathed, disoriented and confused.

Oliver was gone, he remembered.

Hart shook his head to get his bearings. It took him a few seconds to realize that his strong hand gripped Ivy's throat. She gasped for air and stifled a small whimper before he released her, falling back onto the bed in the dark.

Ivy fell to her knees on the carpet and coughed the life back into her lungs. She held her throat and closed her eyes until the throbbing subsided. Hart flicked on the bedside lamp, and she looked up at him.

His eyes widened in sickening disbelief.

"Ivy? Shit, Ivy!" Hart stood quickly and ran his hands frantically through his hair. "What the fuck are you doing in here?" He wanted to lift her into his arms and assess the damage he inflicted, but he was too frightened to go near her. Afraid she might recoil from him. Afraid of hurting her even more than he already had. He was too dangerous to be around her in his condition. Hannah had told him he would get himself killed if he went back to the war, but she hadn't said anything about the risk he was to others if he stayed.

"This isn't going to work. I knew it wouldn't. Shit!" Hart paced the room. "I shouldn't have stayed. I shouldn't have fucking stayed!"

Ivy couldn't speak, but she wanted to.

Hart stopped pacing the room and rubbed his chest as he watched her, thinking frantically to himself. "I'm sorry, Ivy, but you are safer without me." He grabbed his bag from the chair in the corner of the room and lobbed it onto the bed.

"No!" Ivy gasped breathlessly from the floor. "No … Hart … don't leave." A sadness swept across her beautiful face.

"Look what I did to you! I told you I was dangerous!" Hart frowned dejectedly at her. He packed a handful of clothes into the bag. "I'm a fucking weapon of mass destruction in comparison to you. My mind, Ivy…it…it isn't right. What if I had killed you by accident? What if—"

"Stop it!" Ivy yelled. "Just stop! I know what you're doing."

Hart stopped talking. He held a jumble of clothing in his hand, and Ivy saw the anguish burning in his contrite gaze.

"Ivy—"

"No!" She stopped him. "You didn't know it was me."

"That doesn't matter," Hart replied. He paused in thought, then threw the clothes on the bed instead of in his bag.

Ivy sighed in relief, taking it as a small but promising sign he might stay. "I can handle it," she breathed.

"But I can't!" Hart looked at her. "Goddamn it, Ivy, if anything happened to you—"

"Nothing will happen—"

"Nothing will happen, if I am as far away from you as possible." He shook his head and cursed to himself. Hart picked up the clothes again and shoved them into his bag, angrily zipping it shut.

Ivy shook her head and thought about her brother, furrowing her brow in disappointment. "You are running away from me."

Hart didn't look at her. "I'm not running away from you, Ivy."

A hint of anger shaded her frown. "Yes, you are. You are running because you are frightened of me. Because of who I am to you."

Hart glared at her with an inscrutable expression that unsettled Ivy. Still, she bravely kept his gaze, breathing through the anxiety. She felt the tears well in her eyes. Ivy hated them for giving her away.

"I know there is something about me that hurts you," she breathed, "and I know it has something to do with my brother."

Hart breathed a long, slow sigh and rubbed his forehead. Trembling with the truth. *Oliver.*

"I am the one who hurts you, Hart," she breathed sadly.

"Ivy, please—"

"Stay with me," she pleaded, her small voice breaking. "Stay so there may come a day that you can look at me without pain. I can see his death in your eyes," her lip quivered, "… it breaks my heart."

Hart watched her bow her head into her hands and cry. His heart shattered in her sadness. She was still sitting where she fell, and he studied her with a dreadful anguish, reluctant to go to her. Ivy was right—he was afraid of her. He was terrified of her. She was the light leading him out of the darkness, and also the torturous reminder of what he had done. Ivy was saving him, yet killing him softly. She was becoming a piece of him that he couldn't live without, but in her presence, he was spiraling faster toward his ultimate demise. *Ivy Rose.* She really was his glorious misfortune. *Do you think the extraordinary journey through the sky will make it any easier for the fish to accept what is inevitably going to happen to him?* A small, resigned smile fell on his lips. *Yes, Ivy, if you let me die in your saving arms.*

Hart sighed into his hands. His compassion for Ivy soon superseded his fear, as it always did with him. He stepped over to Ivy, leaned down, and effortlessly scooped her into his arms. He felt her arm wrap around his neck and he waited for her to look at him before he spoke, "I'm sorry, Ivy."

She managed a small smile in response.

He lowered Ivy onto his bed and sat down beside her, searching her crystal eyes. She leaned back against the cushioned headboard of his bed and returned his gaze. He felt her inside his head, searching for answers.

"Can I take a look at your neck?" he asked.

"Not if you freak out like that again."

"I won't."

Ivy gave him a doubtful smile.

"I promise," he bit his lip and smiled in return.

"I don't want you to worry about me, Hart."

"It's too late for that. I'm in too deep," he smiled self-consciously. "I will *always* worry about you, Ivy Rose."

Her heart fluttered when her name left his lips. His pained smile was achingly beautiful, his brown eyes even more so. This soldier was rich with life, and yet so empty, intriguing Ivy to no end. She was irrevocably enthralled by him. His darkness frightened her, but his gentleness proved to her his true temperament. He was fighting an epic battle deep within and she vowed to stand by him, until the Johnny Hart in Oliver's tales had defeated his demons and remembered who he was before all of this had happened.

Hart stole a subtle glance at her legs as he leaned over her on the bed. Her tanned skin shimmered a summer gold in the lamplight, and he fought the desire to run his hand along her leg, to indulge in the warmth of her skin. To quench his parched, desert hands and satisfy his yearning ache for her. *If she were any other woman.*

"Please, let me look at your neck," Hart asked again, forcing the temptation out of his head.

Ivy saw his hand reach for her. She couldn't bear the nearness of him any longer, not if he didn't want her. She recoiled and rolled off the bed away from him. She turned to Hart and saw the concern in his liquid brown eyes.

"My neck is fine. Please stop worrying about it," she replied calmly. "Good night, Hart."

Ivy walked out of his room without another word.


Hart sat on his bed for a short while, and then decided to go after her. He found Ivy in the kitchen, leaning her forehead against the refrigerator. She had a dishcloth filled with ice pressed against her neck, with her other hand resting above her head. Blonde locks of hair curled down past her face, and she stood there with her eyes closed, breathing softly through her open mouth.

Hart shook his head. He stood in the doorway of the kitchen and rubbed his jaw, thinking. Reconsidering his departure.

"Hey," he breathed.

Ivy jumped, startled by his silent arrival. The dishcloth fell to the ground, and the ice slid in all directions across the kitchen floor. An ice block came to rest at Hart's feet, and he bent down to pick it up.

He took a step toward her, "I thought you said your neck was fine."

"It is." Ivy smiled, staying where she was. Stunned by his sexiness. A gray tank top hung loosely over his hard body, and she grew feverishly hot, inwardly begging him not to come any closer.

He took another step. "This is my fault. Let me help you."

"It's not your fault."

"It is. Why do people keep making excuses for my actions?"

Hart asked calmly.

"Because you keep blaming yourself for things that are out of your control," she replied, stepping away from him toward the kitchen island.

Hart stopped. He stood between Ivy and the refrigerator, and he thought about what she said. She didn't know the whole truth about her brother's death—maybe she wouldn't be so forgiving of him if she did.

Hart peered at her neck, but she bowed her head timidly. "Ivy, please!"

She gave in and lifted her chin without saying anything. Hart stepped toward her, and Ivy backed away unintentionally, overwrought with nerves. She bumped into the island bench behind her and yelped in surprise, cringing after with embarrassment.

"Are you okay?" he asked, keeping a straight face. He heard her muffled laugh through her hands, and he smiled curiously in response.

Ivy peered out from her fingers, and Hart raised his hands away from her and grinned. She caught an amused sparkle in his eyes, and she screwed up her face and laughed at herself.

"Yes, I'm okay."

"Yeah? Are you sure?" Hart laughed softly, charmed by her awkwardness with him. Her innocence never failed to astound him. He wiped his hands down his chest with a meekness that didn't escape Ivy's attention, and then he gave her a distinct look to prepare her for his second attempt at approaching her, "I'll be gentle, I promise."

Ivy blushed. His warm brown eyes dispelled her nerves and a curious smile curved up the left side of his face. Ivy liked it. When he got close enough, he looked down at her and gently lifted her chin with the side of his finger to examine her neck. Hart hesitated when they locked eyes. Fear flashed through his expression, and Ivy expected him to pull away from her like he usually did in these intimate moments ... but Hart didn't move.

She gripped his arm when he began to feel his way around her neck. It hurt a little, but he was gentle. His muscles moved beneath her fingers as he examined her; rock hard and determined, yet his hands moved over her with a delicate precision. She watched his brown eyes flick back and forth from her eyes to her neck, checking for any sign of discomfort. His hair was longer than she thought; shiny, with subtle hints of blond wisped throughout the brown. She wanted to run her hands through it, to feel the softness of his hair between her fingers. It took all of her strength not to reach out and touch him.

He smiled, conscious of her silent study of him. Ivy watched his eyes crease with humility, instantly melting her heart. She sighed soundlessly. The perpetually kind, compassionate, and patient Johnny Hart. Her beautiful, troubled soldier.

His smile faded and Hart pressed his lips firmly together in concentration. Sweat soon beaded on his forehead in the balmy midnight air. Ivy felt it, too, the sweat prickling her skin. Minutes ago she hadn't noticed the heat. Now she was dying of it. *Gloriously.* Hart was so close and achingly perfect. His earthy scent was intoxicating, sending her into a hot, dizzy spin. She grew flustered in the nearness of him, her breath growing heavier as he moved against her. Ivy begged the universe for his surrender so she could slake her insatiable desire for him. She couldn't go on like this—living in a constant state of desire. Ivy willed her wild heart to be still. She listened to his slow, tranquil breath, seeking stillness. She liked the way it sounded in his deep concentration, and Ivy closed her eyes peacefully … feeling his calm sweep over her restless soul.

Her body flinched now and then under his careful touch. Shades of blue had appeared around the sides of her neck, marring him with guilt. Hart wondered how much guilt one man could handle before it broke him entirely. His conscience was becoming so weighed down with his remorse that he felt like he might fall through the earth and land directly on the devil's throne.

Blood caught his eye when she turned her head. Hart sighed. Her soft flesh could never withstand his merciless grip. *Shit.*

"Band-Aids?" he asked reticently. "There is a bit of blood. I'm so sorry, Ives."

Ivy noted the unmistakable shame in Hart's expression. She pointed to the cupboard above the refrigerator, where he found a tin of adhesive bandages. He turned back to her, placing the tin on the island beside her. He gripped her firmly around the waist and lifted her off her feet, then sat her on the island's surface in front of him. Hart peered at the wound more closely.

He noted her silence. "How are you feeling?"

Ivy smiled nervously at him, battling her desire.

Hart tilted his head in concern when she didn't answer. "You're not going to pass out, are you? You *are* okay with blood, right?"

"Yeah, I'm okay with a bit of blood," she answered him. Ivy thought about it … *blood?* Blood was okay, if it were anyone else's, but there was something about her own blood that made her light-headed and wretchedly ill. Ivy felt the color drain from her cheeks and Hart looked at her, unconvinced. She was a terrible liar.

"You're looking pale, Ives. Do you need to lie down?" he asked seriously.

She stared back at him, suddenly lost in fantasy…*lying her down on the kitchen island…undressing her slowly…the stone cold against her burning skin. His gentle hands glide down her stomach, past her hips, casually slipping beneath her underwear—*

"Ivy! Answer me," Hart pleaded. "You're starting to worry me."

Ivy caught an intense seriousness wash over him suddenly. He was genuinely concerned for her. She blinked a few times before she answered.

"No, no …" she murmured vaguely, trying to recall what he had asked her. She considered blaming her unusual behavior on what happened earlier in the bedroom, but she didn't want him feeling any worse for what he had done.

"Ivy."

"No, really I'm okay," she smiled convincingly.

"Let me know if you're not feeling well, and I'll stop right away." Hart narrowed his eyes at her, still skeptical.

Ivy nodded. *Oh God, don't stop.*

Hart realized he was still holding her around the waist, her long, lean legs draped around him. He could feel her warm skin through the silk gown, and for a brief moment, Hart forgot why they were standing here like this. He held her crystal gaze for longer than he should have, those last few seconds robbing him of his rationality. His eminent valor weakened in response to his sudden yearning for her, and he welcomed the unfamiliar vulnerability of it. Hart knew she was beautiful, but everything about her at this moment in time consumed him entirely. She bit her bottom lip, trying hopelessly to disguise her pleasure, devouring his conscience with her sweetness. His strength bowed down in defeat. *You can take anything from me, Ivy. Anything you want.*

Hart swallowed and removed the Band-Aid from its wrapper. He lifted her face to the ceiling so he could apply it to the scratch on the back of her neck. Ivy's hair fell beautifully off her shoulders in long, glossy waves, and he admired it as he tenderly swept one of the locks from her collarbone. He rested one hand on the back of her neck to support her, then he gently pressed the bandage to her wound.

Hart looked at Ivy when he finished. He leaned into her without thinking, drawn in by her sweet coconut scent. Mesmerized by her parted, red lips. He stood close enough to feel her light breath, which shook with anticipation. He breathed her in, imagining the taste of her. Hart took his hand from the back of her neck and trailed his thumb across her cheek, exhaling slowly. He saw her close her eyes, her body trembling under his touch. Stirring something deep within him. Fate had shattered his heart into a thousand pieces, and in return, it delivered Ivy, this divine creature who effortlessly restored his tired, broken soul. Unknowingly. *Exquisitely.*

"I'm done, Ivy," he breathed, tearing himself from his reverie. "Are you okay?"

"Yes ... thank you."

"You have some color again. I thought I'd lost you for a moment there."

Ivy reveled in his nearness—he'd had every chance to move away. "I feel fine. Just hot—are you hot?"

"Yeah, it is hot in here."

An endearing grin swept across his face, and without thinking, Ivy reached out and lightly ran her fingers down the side of his face. Hart closed his eyes and turned his face into her hand, as if seeking her touch. Ivy brushed her thumb across his lips ... they were smooth and warm, and she forced herself to breathe, dizzy with desire. She slid her hand around the back of his neck and rested it there, rubbing her thumb along the hot skin of his neck. Hart's eyes closed tightly in response, desperately resisting her seduction. Ivy smiled faintly at her behavior. For the first time in her life, she preyed on a man's weakness. She enjoyed watching him fight the temptation of her. She could have any man she wanted, yet here she stood with a breath-taking soldier who begged her to keep her distance from him. Seduction had never been a necessary skill for her until now, and she was surprised by her raw pleasure in bringing this great soldier to his knees.

Ivy brought her other hand up to his face, her fingers delicately trailing across his skin. She breathed deeply, craving him, needing him, and with every breath she exhaled, she saw Hart melt just a little more. Every inch of her body cried out for him. She yearned for his strength. For his kindness. For the soldier she had heard of years ago and now knew. But most of all, she longed for the passion he refused her. Ivy rested both her hands on the back of his neck and pulled him slowly to her.

Hart opened his eyes and looked at her. *Irresistible, untouchable Ivy.* He rested his strong hands on the bench either side of her to support himself, weakening in her affection. His hands curled into fists around the wrappers of the bandage as he struggled against temptation. Hart knew it was wrong to love her, but he couldn't keep himself from her any longer; he wanted her. Her crystal eyes, her parted mouth, her long legs ... he wanted her divine body more than anything else he'd ever wanted. The desert. The sand. The scorching sun. They all floated away in her heavenly presence. He imagined how sweet she would taste on his lips. How soft she felt inside. Her thighs tightened around his hips, and all of a sudden the ties that bound his hesitant heart snapped under the pressure of his carnal desires.

Hart welcomed his victorious defeat as Ivy conquered him with her gentle, persistent heart. He felt her hands running along his shoulders, and the tenderness took him far away. Ivy was leading him somewhere safe. Somewhere peaceful. Somewhere he had never been before.

She looked up at him with wide eyes and nibbled at her bottom lip.

"*Oh Ivy,*" Hart exhaled in fevered desire. He ran his hands back through her hair, then pulled her toward him and kissed her.

Ivy groaned in pleasure at the warm softness of his lips finally on hers. The universe shifted around her as though every part of it turned in their direction to capture the glory of this moment. As if worshipping her divine victory ... *at last.*

Hart sighed into her neck and lifted her easily into his arms. Her long legs wrapped around him, and he carried her out of the kitchen and back to his room. He laid her down on his bed and joined her there, lifting her chin and brushing his lips along the warm, delicate skin on her neck. Kissing away the pain he caused her in his nightmares. Ivy closed her eyes, indulging in his passion. He untied her silk gown and his hand moved inside it and across her stomach. She melted divinely into him, breathing heavily under his warm touch, unsure if she could handle the pleasure. Then he kissed her passionately on her open mouth and groaned into her with heated desire. His heaviness weighed down on her, and she felt him tremble. It coursed through his body, into hers, and the bed began to tremor beneath them. *She saw him falling into the water in the moonlight, no one there to catch him ...*

Ivy exhaled sharply.

He looked down at her, his brown eyes drenched in an emotion she no longer recognized.

Hart leaned his forehead on hers and breathed into her with his eyes tightly closed. Painfully closed. Shaking uncontrollably. Feeling unsteady. Hazy. Disappointed. Defeated by his desire. He heard the ear-splitting sound of the bullet as it cracked through his memory, and the darkness closed its harsh, unforgiving iron fist around him, rapturously sinking its claws into his flesh until he bled. *My divine reprimand. Oh, Ivy.*

Hart opened his eyes to see her crystal eyes looking back at him. He quickly moved away and sat on the side of the bed with his head bowed into his hands, panting through the darkness that now clouded his mind. He randomly thought about his ex-girlfriend—how he had fucked her without feeling. Every day during his leave, until he returned to the war. She loved it, but there was never any love involved. *Never.* She had a black heart and a sinful tongue, and he had never wanted anything more than what they had. Until now. Hart shook his head, confused, wondering why she had even crossed his mind.

Ivy crawled over to him and wrapped her arms around his big shoulders. She rested her head on the back of his neck and breathed him in. All of him. His sadness. His broken soul.

"Everything will be okay. I promise," she whispered softly.

"How can you be sure?" He turned to her, asking the question with his eyes as much as with his words.

She looked at him in the light of the lamp. In his eyes she saw torment and painful sorrow, but she also saw love and fierce loyalty. She wanted to tell him all the stories she had heard about his courageous spirit. His unyielding chivalry. How he was the hero of Oliver's tales, and since meeting him, he had become hers also.

"I know, because there is something special about you, Johnny Hart," she breathed.

"No, there's not. My thoughts, my feelings, I can barely see anything through the darkness inside my head," Hart groaned, rubbing his eyes. "I'm so confused, Ivy. About life. About everything."

Hart looked at her with a resigned expression. Her heart broke for him.

"The darkness isn't always a bad thing," she replied. "Sometimes you need the darkness to help you find where the light is coming from."

Hart stared at her, unblinking.

Ivy got out of the bed and walked toward the door. When she reached the doorway, she turned and smiled reassuringly at him.

"I don't want you to leave," he breathed.

She studied him for a moment. "Then I'll stay."

"You're not afraid of me?"

Ivy shook her head. She climbed next to him on the bed, propped herself up on her elbow against the pillow, and grinned beautifully at him.

He smiled suspiciously in return. "Why are you smiling like that?"

"Like what?"

"Like you have forgotten about everything that has happened tonight."

"I'm smiling *because* I remember everything about tonight."

Hart laughed softly.

"Why are you laughing like that?" Ivy asked, happy for the small change in Hart's demeanor.

He looked at her with a sparkle in his eyes. "Because you're different, Ivy, and I like it."

Ivy's expression softened in his gaze. "You have no idea how quiet my life was before you arrived."

"Shit, I'm sorry," Hart frowned. He fell back on the pillow and covered his eyes with his hands.

"No, I like it. Phoenix soldiers, right?" Ivy grinned, remembering what he told her on the beach. "Things get interesting."

Hart uncovered his eyes and laughed warmly, "I tried to warn you."

Ivy laughed. Hart had turned her entire world upside down, and she loved every crazy minute of it. She stared at him while he smiled at the ceiling.

"He's going to be pissed," Hart said, more seriously.

"Who? Tommy?"

"Yeah," Hart rolled toward her onto his side, "he's going to come here again, but this time he'll be after blood. My blood."

Ivy frowned. "Tommy wouldn't be foolish enough to try anything. Not after tonight?"

His warm smile settled her anxious heart. He rested his head back on the pillow again and narrowed his gaze at the ceiling. "Trust me, Ives, he'll be back."

Ivy recoiled at the thought of Tommy forcing himself on her again.

Hart noticed a different tone in her quickening breath in the silence. He rolled toward her again, catching the unmasked fear in her crystal eyes. He remembered the young girl in Libya, held captive on the steps of the Exhibition Center. He remembered the mad glare in the insurgent's eyes, and his own defenseless vulnerability when the man was about to shoot him. He had offered himself to the heavens for her—he would have died for her that day. Then a realization swept through him as he stared at the beautiful woman lying next to him in his bed. Oliver's sister. *Ivy.* He would die for Ivy. He would protect her always, no matter to what end, and with this realization there rose a strength within him, stronger than ever before. Tommy would never touch her again—he would make sure of it. Ivy was under his vigilant protection now. Under the protection of Phoenix.

"Ivy, don't worry about Tommy," he told her, caressing her cheek. "When he comes back, I'll be right here by your side. Everything will be alright."

Ivy nodded and looked into his steely gaze. A fierce courage blazed within them, and his compassion overwhelmed her. She believed him. With all her heart she believed him. His soft smile exuded a warm, unswerving loyalty. The broken man in front of her transformed before her very eyes. The weariness faded, and suddenly, there he was, Commander Johnny Hart of Phoenix— one of the most intelligent and lethal soldiers in the world. Renowned for his expertise and for his noble, unwavering heart. The extraordinary soldier had finally returned.

Ivy lay her head on his shoulder, and he wrapped her in his arms. She fell asleep, untouchable by the rest of the world.

## Chapter 11

Ivy opened her eyes, and the morning sun greeted her warmly through her blinking eyelashes. Sunshine beamed in from the windows that opened onto the back of the estate, and she watched the dust float weightlessly in the air as she slowly woke up. Ivy breathed in deeply and stretched her long limbs. She ran her fingers through her hair and glided her hand across the warm, sunny sheets beside her. Empty sheets. Ivy sat up cross-legged in bed, her wavy hair falling all around her. She glanced around the room ... Hart's room. A sweet tingle rushed through her at the thought of him. His warmth. His body. His smile. That kiss. *I'll be right here by your side, Ivy.*

She fell back on the pillows, grinning happily.

The cool morning air wrapped around her when she stepped outside. She pulled a cardigan over her silk nightgown and walked barefoot toward the fire-pit and the stairs beside it that took her down to the estate's private beach.

The stone stairwell twisted its way through the trees on the descent to the sand below. The ocean swept out beneath her toward the horizon, and she could see the tranquil turquoise water in the shade below. Ivy stepped onto the cold sand and shivered slightly in the morning chill. She pulled her sleeves over her hands and enjoyed the cold, silky sand between her toes.

She walked idly up the beach twenty meters or so before she stepped onto the ridge of flat rocks below a cliff that divided her beach from the rest of the world. Ivy walked along a jetty of rocks across the water, hopping from one to the other until she reached the rock furthest from the shore, an island in itself.

The morning sun peeked over the cliff behind her and cast all its glory on the rock's surface, and Ivy laid back in its divine warmth. This secluded piece of shore was one of her most treasured places in the world, and it had been one of Oliver's, too. She thought about him as she laid there in the peaceful morning, remembering when he used to come home from the war. He loved to follow her down the cliff soon after she had left. He'd sit beside her on the rock in the sunlight, and they would talk for hours, but never about the war. It was an unspoken agreement. It became Oliver's place of refuge. His safe haven. Now this place meant more to her than ever before.

Ivy could feel him lying beside her in the golden light of the morning. She could feel him in the cool air that warmed with the rising sun. She could hear him on the gentle rush of the waves. She felt him radiating in the love that filled her heart. Ivy imagined Ollie's beautiful smile beaming down upon her from the cloudless sky on this beautiful morning. Then a hint of sadness stung her blissful heart.

The sunlight glistened on the water around her, and she listened to the sound of the waves lapping against the side of the rock. Ivy lay her arm along the rock's surface and dipped her fingers in the warm, soothing water. The salty air filled her lungs, and a stillness swept over her as she lost herself to the ocean. The water evoked a calmness in her heart, and she breathed in the world, remembering Helena's words in what seemed a lifetime ago ... *close your eyes. Be in this moment right now. In the sunshine. Let the universe carry on around you. It always will. Feel the earth beneath your feet. Its warmth. Its life. You are a part of this earth. Take your time. Follow the sun, and wherever you may be, be still.*

"Ivy?"

Ivy opened her eyes and leaned her head back to the soft voice behind her. He stood as a silhouette against the sun. She couldn't see his face, but Ivy could tell by his gentle approach that it was Hart.

"May I sit with you?" he asked.

Ivy squinted into the sun toward him, then sat up and shifted to make room for him on the rock. "Yeah, please."

Hart jumped effortlessly across the stones to her little island and sat beside her in the sunshine, wrapping his arms around his knees. She heard him take a deep breath as he took in the world around him. The stillness of the ocean washed over him, and then he glanced at her with his mysterious brown eyes.

He seemed different this morning, she thought. Confident.

Ivy noted his running shoes. "You went for a run?"

"Yeah, I did. I'm sorry I left you like that."

"No, that's okay," she blushed, thinking about last night.

Ivy looked back at him, catching his endearing gaze. He was smiling faintly, intrigued by her. A humble grin swept across his face, and his eyes creased with warmth.

"You always look at me like that, Ives."

"How?"

"I don't know, like I'm not really here with you."

He saw her tilt her head and consider it. There was a wistfulness in her eyes, as though she were waiting for him to grow wings and fly away from her at any moment. After everyone she had lost in the past, he understood why she expected him to leave, too. It was his own feelings he was trying to come to terms with—he didn't want to leave her. For the first time in his life, the war had never seemed so far away.

He flicked his nervous gaze to the water near his feet and then back to her beautiful smile. The morning sun caught her blonde hair, and her pale-blue eyes shimmered against the crystal ocean surrounding them. He thought about her spending the night in his room last night, sleeping peacefully by his side. He had barely slept last night, nor any other night for that matter. He didn't need it—especially if it only brought him nightmares. He had always been a light sleeper anyhow. In the war, his comrades depended on it. Hart was always the first to wake at any hint of danger. It was engrained into him to protect the people around him, the people whom he loved. Last night he came to the realization that Ivy now fell into that category. Oliver's sister. He had fallen in love with the one woman he couldn't have .... but he wanted her. God, he wanted her.

"It is hard to believe that you're here when Oliver isn't," she said eventually. Ivy looked at him and smiled happily, trying her best not to bring any shade of somberness to his bright mood.

Hart nodded. He understood.

"You were a superhero out saving the world, Hart," Ivy continued, "you didn't *actually* exist."

He laughed humbly. "Well, after everything that's happened over the past few days, I'm guessing I have distinctly assured you of my existence in this world."

She laughed, "Yes, I have to admit the past few days have been a tad more eventful than usual."

"Hey, I'm just trying to keep it light and entertaining," he teased. "I wouldn't want to frighten you off with all the excess baggage I'm carrying. I mean, we only just met, right?"

Ivy laughed, happily surprised by his careless boyish charm. It felt good to laugh with Hart. She could see the delight on his sweet face as he laughed with her, and for a moment he reminded her of Oliver, sitting beside her on their island in the sunshine. Maybe he was here after all.

"I'm glad you're here with me," she added, glancing at him. "It feels like Ollie didn't leave me entirely, like he left a little piece of himself with you, just for me."

Hart saw her blush. "I'm glad I'm here, too, Ivy."

She met his affectionate gaze, his expression still and thoughtful. She felt like she could say anything to this man, finding incredible comfort in his compassionate nature. This kind-hearted soldier—he who had witnessed humankind at its worst yet still managed to possess a soothing, pacifying influence over her heavy heart.

"So," Hart forced his lingering gaze from her, "is it deep enough to dive in around here?" He jumped to his feet and took off his shoes and sport tank top, dropping them on the rock beside Ivy.

Ivy looked up at him, wide-eyed. "You're going in? But it's so cold this morning!"

"Are you kidding?" He laughed. "It's beautiful. The water looks too good not to go in. Are you coming with me?"

"No," Ivy answered quickly, smiling as she shook her head.

"No? Come on. The water's warm," he coaxed. Hart stretched his hand down to her and encouraged her to take it.

Ivy looked at it for a moment, catching her breath when she

glanced over the rest of his body. The rippling muscles of his chest and arms crumbled her resolve. Her desire for him was unbearable, she could barely look in his direction, let alone take his hand.

She swallowed before she could speak again, "The water needs to be a little warmer for me to go in."

"Ivy Rose, the Earth's child, is afraid of a little cold water?" Hart shook his head and looked out to the horizon. "You hear that universe? The water is too cold!"

Ivy narrowed her eyes playfully at him.

"Someone's slacking off out there," he frowned, looking down at her.

She shook her head and grinned. Hart laughed beautifully, and it warmed her soul to hear it. Ivy reached into the water beside her and took a handful of water and splashed him. Hart laughed and dove off the rock into the ocean. She rolled onto her stomach and waited for him to reappear. He did—wiping the seawater from his face and sighing loudly with refreshing delight.

"Beautiful!" he called out. He smiled at her from afar and swam back toward her, taking in the beauty that surrounded him.

Ivy grinned with his pleasure. She rested her chin on the back of her hands and watched him enjoy a world he had lost all hope in. When he got closer, she caught a furtive gleam steal the softness from his eyes, and then he disappeared under the water.

"Don't you dare," she spoke to the water's surface where he left it.

Ivy waited. Anticipating his covert attack, but he didn't come to the surface again. Frowning, she stood to get a better view of the water beneath the surface, yet still he was nowhere to be seen. Her heart beat faster with agitated suspense. Ivy placed her sleeved hands over her mouth and leaned over the water, an intrigued grin creeping across her face.

"Where are you, soldier?" she whispered to the water.

"I'm right here."

Ivy gasped and turned to the voice behind her.

Hart had somehow managed to climb soundlessly onto the rock behind her. She had to admit, she was impressed.

The salt water dripped from his wet hair and rolled down his face, coursing over his glistening lips. He smiled deliciously and stepped toward her. A cheeky mischief still lingered in his expression, and Ivy took a step backward and shook her head.

"I know what you're up to," she told him, unable to conceal her grin. It really was too cold to get wet.

Hart laughed and wiped the water from his face.

He took another step toward her, "I would never throw you in the water. You can trust me."

Ivy couldn't step back any further without falling in herself, and Hart laughed again.

"I don't know …." she smirked, "Ollie would do it."

"Well, I'm not Ollie," he replied.

Ivy looked at his hand when he reached for her. She saw the sincerity in his eyes. After a contemplative pause, she placed her hand in his with complete trust.

She felt the electricity fire through their fingertips when they touched, as though the universe was caught off guard by their unexpected connection. An alarm of intimacy. A beautiful smile swept across his face, elated by her faith in him. Hart pulled her into him and wrapped his arms around her, and then he kissed her gently on the forehead. Ivy closed her eyes in the sun as it rose high above the cliff. She leaned into him and rested her parted mouth on his wet, bare shoulder, tasting his warm, salty skin on her lips.

A peacefulness embraced them as they stood in each other's arms over the water. Ivy felt his strong chest draw in the ocean air surrounding them, gradually succumbing to her world and her way of life. There was something different about Hart today—something had changed. Then for a brief moment, while her eyes were closed in the sunshine and the warmth of it kissed her skin, she felt Oliver's embrace in the light.

*Chapter 12*

Four months had passed since Walker and Benji had left for Monterey. Two months longer than originally planned. Hart didn't mind, all he wanted was his two best mates by his side again. The nightly phone calls with Walker had quickly evolved into an occasional update whenever some actual progress had been made on the Libyan or Taym front, which had been disappointingly slow for Hart. If Taym had not been under tight watch, his eagerness to return to Libya would be significantly greater than it was. Until the violent demonstrations eased off, no one was entering Tripoli. It became a waiting game involving the entire world, and Hart was quietly grateful for the timing.

On the odd occasion, General Garvey himself would touch base with him in pursuit of information regarding key players in the Libyan assault. Garvey personally assured Hart that his role within Phoenix was indispensable, which was exactly what Hart needed to hear. Being forced to take temporary leave due to his diagnosis of post-traumatic stress disorder was a huge blow to his confidence, but the thought of letting down his team mates is what hit him the hardest. Hart continued to be racked with guilt. He commanded one of the most elite teams in the world, yet he idled away his days in San Diego because of his psychological instability. This sense of failure had become a secondary vice to his culpability for Oliver. He felt he had abandoned his friends at a time when they needed him most, now his friends were coming

249

to him from Monterey, at a time when he needed them the most.

"Hey, hey!" Benji called from the front door.

Benji walked in with a khaki canvas duffle hanging over his left shoulder. His cap sat backward on his head, and he wore board shorts with a white tee and flip flops on his tanned feet. He looked like he had stepped off a flight from Hawaii, not a military base. Ivy was thrilled to see his gorgeous dimples and boyish good looks again. She was once again stunned by how incredibly handsome these soldiers were.

"Hart! Buddy! Look at you! Shit, man, look at that beautiful face," Benji hooted excitedly, affectionately smacking the five-week-old beard that Hart had yet to shave off.

Hart hugged him, "Hey, Benji boy, good to see you again."

Walker strolled in behind Benji, and Hart welcomed him with a hug as well. Benji dropped his bag by the wall as he took two quick steps over to Ivy and swept her off her feet. She wrapped her arms around his neck and laughed when he lifted her into the air.

"How are you, sweetheart?" Benji asked, returning her to her feet.

"I'm good!"

Walker dropped his bag beside Benji's and gave her a hug and a sweet hello.

"How was your flight?" she asked.

"The flight was quick now that we're based at the garrison in Northern Cali," Walker answered her. "I tried to borrow a bird, but they wouldn't hear of it." He winked at Hart.

"Garvey's been too bad-tempered these days to lend us a Black Hawk," Benji smirked.

"General Garvey?" Hart frowned. "He's a teddy bear."

"The General's gone into a deep decline ever since you've been MIA," Walker laughed softly.

Walker was even more handsome than Ivy remembered. Tall and strong, with dark hair and mysterious eyes. He was incredibly intimidating, and Ivy grew foolishly nervous in his presence once again. He wore a black tee and combat pants with his silver dog tags hanging over his shirt. Ivy glanced at the chain around Hart's neck. He wore his dog tags every day, but they remained tucked beneath his clothes. Ivy wondered whether he was ashamed to display them in his time away from base.

"We brought a case of Buds with us this time, Ivy, now we know they're your favorite," Benji grinned, heading back outside. He came back inside with the case of beer on his shoulder and walked past them toward the kitchen, "Let's get this business talk out of the way quickly so we can have a *real* holiday this time."

Benji disappeared into the kitchen, shaking his head.

Hart glanced at Walker. "Is he okay?"

Walker rolled his eyes. "Benji's not cut out for this nine-to-five bullshit."

Hart laughed. "I didn't think he'd cope in the office."

"Cope?" Walker laughed. "That kid comes into the office once a day for five minutes. He's coping, trust me."

"Why five minutes?"

"Why do you think?" Walker glanced apologetically at Ivy.

Hart grinned. "A woman?"

"Yep."

"Five minutes, eh."

Ivy smirked.

"Swift by name, swift by nature." Hart shrugged.

The three of them laughed and followed Benji into the kitchen.

Five minutes later they were lounging around the fire-pit with beers in their hands, talking about Libya. Ivy sat on the bench between Hart and Benji, listening to them discuss the civil war. She found their intelligence, their language, their knowledge of that world fascinating. She remembered her first night spent here alone with Hart and the fear that this side of him had induced. She knew him too well to be scared now. Four months spent lazing in the summer sun with this man had cemented a bond between them that was indescribable. Hart had kept his word and kept his feelings for her to himself. The raw desire between them was unbearable at times, but Hart would tear himself away to calm his carnal instincts, much to her disappointment. He still hadn't told her about what had happened in Libya the day Ollie died. The torment still lingered in his beautiful face, and it was this torment that kept a huge part of him locked away from her—the essential piece of Johnny Hart.

"Did they work out who the voice belonged to?" Hart asked.

"Not yet," Walker replied.

Walker sat with his bare feet up on the fire-pit, drinking his beer and looking utterly disinterested in the conversation. Ivy knew this wasn't the case because he had an answer for everything. She watched him smoke his cigarette, finding herself being turned on by the gentle, nonchalant attention he gave it. His dark eyes glanced at her now and then, and a wave of nerves rushed through her each time he did. His voice was husky and low, and when he smiled he looked contemplatively dangerous. Ivy dreaded to think what it felt like confronting this soldier as an enemy.

Walker caught her examining gaze and smiled at her, and Ivy exhaled the breath she didn't realize she was holding. She smiled back at him, glimpsing the attentive warmth beneath his steely exterior.

"So what's the latest on the Libyan assault?" Hart asked.

"Well, we have identified the specific groups who targeted Benghazi and managed to seize Tripoli. These were the groups who lost out considerably in the parliamentary elections," Walker spoke softly, "They figured the win was illegitimate and decided to fight for the leadership instead … literally."

"So, why doesn't the government take it back?" Ivy asked, trying to keep up with the conversation.

Hart glanced warily at her, unsure whether he liked her being a part of this discussion.

"It would seem a logical reaction," Walker replied, "but the risk lies in the wider region."

"You're worried the war will spread out of Libya?" Ivy frowned.

"What the Libyan government and the representatives of countries like the U.S. are worried about," Hart explained, "is that these extremist groups are backed by different states outside of Libya who are all in conflict with each other. It's a hidden power struggle behind the open power struggle."

Benji put his beer down and looked at Ivy. "We can't just send in military airstrikes to take these bastards down because the world is worried it may trigger a counter-strike from those states who have …," Benji paused to think of the right way to explain it, "undesirable intentions. If we deploy our troops to go and back up the Libyan army, we will inevitably end up fighting one or more of these other countries."

"So then, we just wait and see what happens?" Ivy twisted her face.

"If it gets worse, then we'll make a move," Benji replied.

"And the three of you will be sent back to fight," Ivy said. She dropped her gaze to her beer bottle and picked at the corner of the label.

The three soldiers looked at Ivy, then at each other—neither one wanted to be the one to reply.

"My brother was a tiny piece of a very large, complex puzzle." Ivy smiled faintly at the soldiers surrounding her.

"There are many reasons that contribute to these strains of conflicts, Ivy. They are like a chain of events," Hart told her. "Taym is one of the leaders of this breakaway regime, and his involvement in the capture of Tripoli has now made him one of the most wanted persons in the world. Oliver knew he was up to something before any of us did—he was a very significant piece of this complex puzzle."

Ivy nodded and gave him a small appreciative smile.

Hart smiled in return and then bowed his head. He thought about their days in Afghanistan spent training the local army in weaponry and tactics, and he remembered the day Oliver introduced Taym to him. He had his arm wrapped around Taym's shoulder, and the boy was wide-eyed and nervous, but Oliver had a way with the younger crew, always encouraging and brightly optimistic. Taym looked up to Ollie. He idolized him. Oliver never suspected Taym's betrayal until it was too late. He fooled them all. *But when exactly did it all go wrong?*

"What's the latest on Taym's whereabouts?" Hart talked into his beer bottle, then took a sip.

Walker sighed at the thought of him. "We've got him cornered, Hart."

"Britain has undercover ops all over that asshole," Benji added. "If he so much as steps a foot outside that building, a sniper will take him down. He knows that."

Hart couldn't decide whether he liked that idea. He wanted Taym for himself. There would be no reprieve, no release from his guilt, and no way out of the darkness if he were not the one to bring Taym to justice. His only path to absolution relied on his revenge.

"It doesn't make sense to me that he has holed himself up in an apartment block in central Tripoli," Hart replied, frowning. "He spent years moving with our team. Didn't he learn anything?"

Walker peered over his beer at Hart, and Hart stared back at him, thinking.

"Hey, I wouldn't say he's the smartest kid on the block," Benji scoffed. "You do remember that this is a guy who hopes to prey on the youth of our world and encourage them to wreak havoc on their own fucking nations, most likely killing themselves in the process."

Hart glanced at Ivy protectively and saw her breathe in deeply. It was a conversation she no longer needed to be involved in. She looked up at him and her crystal eyes filled with concern, and Hart smiled warmly to reassure her.

"Are you okay?" he whispered to her while Benji continued to talk. She nodded quickly.

Walker observed them subtly as he listened to Benji.

"Hart, you're the best soldier we have, and the garrison is just itching for your return, man," Benji continued. "Taym knows you're after blood after what happened with you and Ollie. It's almost like he's killing time, just waiting for you to come and find him. Everyone knows you have a score to settle with him."

Ivy listened to Benji speak, and then she turned to Hart, who looked up at Benji with wide eyes, hoping he would stop talking before she developed any further insight into the events surrounding Oliver's death.

Walker noticed Hart's concern. He leaned forward on his chair, realizing that Benji had forgotten Ivy had no knowledge of what had happened between Hart and her brother. The soldiers planned to keep it that way until Hart was ready to tell her.

Hart searched her face as she stared at him, anticipating the moment she would lose all faith in him. Waiting for the magic to fade from her crystal eyes. Waiting for her revulsion. Waiting for what was always meant to be. *Oliver should be here with you, Ivy. Not me.* She sat beside him in the midday sun and studied his reaction intently, as though she could see the whole truth in his guilty expression. Still, he couldn't tear his gaze from her incredible beauty. The light dusting of freckles across her tiny nose and the redness in her youthful, sweet lips, parted in anxious intrigue as she listened to Benji reveal Hart's deepest secrets. The fearful apprehension in her eyes triggered his protectiveness over her, and he could tell by her expression that she wasn't sure that she was ready to hear about the moment when Ollie died, the moment that imprisoned his soul so absolutely. He bowed his head and prepared himself for the fall.

Ivy saw the torment in his expression. Hart's eyes became troubled, and she recognized the disheartening guilt in him from when they first met. Reliving Oliver's death shattered his peaceful calm, and it broke her heart to see it again after these past months. Benji's revelation that Hart was there with Oliver when he died was too obvious for her not to say something—but she didn't. She imagined Hart watching her brother die. Years of friendship brought to a sudden end. A dreadful heaviness fell over her, and she forced herself to breathe through the sadness that struck her heart.

Ivy took a quick breath and turned away from Hart, finding refuge in the brilliant, blue ocean that rolled out before her.

"Benji," Walker warned suddenly, seeing Ivy's reaction. He motioned for Benji to stop talking before he revealed any more than he already had.

Benji looked up from his beer at Walker, who nodded in Ivy's direction. Benji rubbed his face when he saw her, feeling foolish for divulging more than he ever should in her presence. "Hey, I didn't mean to spook you, Ives. I apologize."

Ivy glanced at him and smiled sweetly, placing her hand on his back.

"No, it's OK, Benji," she lied, "but I'm going to leave you guys to talk. I'm having trouble keeping up with who is who anyhow." Ivy stood up and glanced at Hart as she walked past him. She managed a small smile as if to prove to him she was fine.

The soldiers watched her walk into the house, then Hart rubbed his jaw and groaned resignedly into his hands.

"Shit, that went well," he laughed wryly.

Walker laughed with him, lifting his feet back onto the fire-pit and relaxing again. "Ah, Benji boy …."

"Goddamn it, Hart, I'm so sorry!" Benji shook his head and placed his hand on Hart's shoulder. "I keep forgetting she doesn't know. Do you think she worked it out?" He twisted his face at Hart.

"I don't know. She's an exceptionally perceptive woman," Hart replied. "But don't worry about it, buddy. It's my fault. I really should have told her by now."

Benji sighed.

"Hey, she's a Rose," Walker added, "which means she is also exceptionally understanding, like her brother was."

Hart, Walker, and Benji sat wordlessly for a few minutes as they considered Ivy's feelings.

"Hey, guys?" she called from the back porch.

The three soldiers looked behind them and saw Ivy standing on the back steps with her canvas backpack draped over her shoulder. Her long hair glowed in the sunlight. She wore a white dress, which was semi-transparent in the sunshine. The silhouette of her curves took Hart's breath away. The dress flowed down past her knees, and she wore a pair of tan leather boots. The neckline of her dress plunged so low that Hart could see the white crocheted bikini cradling her breasts, and a fine, golden necklace fell suggestively between them—luring his eyes to a place that was mouth-wateringly tempting. He knew that his abstinence from Ivy was living on borrowed time.

Benji and Walker glanced from Ivy to Hart.

"Shit, I still can't believe that is Ollie's sister," Walker laughed gently, barely audible so Ivy couldn't hear him.

Benji and Hart laughed softly with him.

"She's sexy as hell," Benji grinned, patting Hart on the back. "I'm betting you've had a spectacular summer, my friend. I'm fucking jealous. I want all the details."

"You'll be utterly disappointed," Hart replied, grimacing and fidgeting with his empty beer bottle.

"I'm heading to Lights Beach. Do you guys want to come?" she called out.

The three of them looked at each other again, eyes bright at the prospect.

"I still haven't been to the beach after all these years," Benji said.

"Well, let's go," Hart replied, smiling. "You up for a hike, Walker?"

"Always," he replied, jumping to his feet.

"I saw Ollie's surfboards in the garage last time we were here," Benji grinned playfully. "You think he would mind if we took 'em for a bash?"

"I think he'd wish he were here," Hart replied.

"Well, do us a favor, big guy, and send us some waves!" Benji hollered into the sky.

Ivy grinned as the men walked toward her. Hart would never let her face the Ghost Trail alone with Tommy still haunting his thoughts, and she figured this was the best way to lighten the mood after their conversation about Libya. They had enough to worry about over there with Taym and the possibility of returning to the violence, and the last thing she wanted was Hart questioning her faith in him. She had learned her lesson that night with Tommy.

As the soldiers walked past, Benji threw his arm over her shoulder and pulled her into him. He breathed in the salty air and kissed her on the side of her head. "It is good to be home, Ives."

Ivy walked gratefully in the doting warmth of Benji's affection. She glanced at Hart and Walker beside her, and a tenderness filled her once lonesome heart. This was Phoenix. Here she stood in the place where her brother once did, and it was an honorable position to be in—under the protection and devotion of an unbreakable force. A friendship like no other. It was time for these soldiers to escape for a little while, and Ivy knew better than anyone how to block out the realities that had a damning effect on the hopeful heart. There was no better place for them to be than here with her in Oliver's home. In her world. Benji was right ... they were home.

With surfboards under their arms, the three soldiers cheerfully followed Ivy through the field of poppies that led to the Ghost Trail. The afternoon was hotter than Ivy had expected. The insects chirped blissfully around them, and she closed her eyes and breathed in the humid, coastal air that clung to the warm earth in the field. A slight breeze picked up when they reached the forest, a sign that the boys may be fortunate enough to find some good waves curling around the cliff on the south side of the bay. It was a surf break she and Ollie called Whiskey's, named after the renowned, boozy all-nighters that Ollie and his friends use to pull on summer nights back when they were teenagers.

She grinned as she listened to the men behind her, heckling each other about who was the biggest flop when it came to surfing. Seeing as none of them had surfed in over three years, Ivy guessed all three of them would be dismally surprised. She laughed quietly at their expense.

They dropped off the small waterfall and walked onto the silky white sands of Lights Beach. Walker and Benji searched the bay and realized this idyllic stretch of beach was exclusively theirs. The four of them walked side-by-side through the sun-bleached haze that covered the bay, and they were soon reminiscing about the good times, long before any of them were tainted by grief. Those were the days. Hot summers, wild nights, and careless fun. When being young excusably liberated you from the responsibilities of life. When no one expected anything from you until the day your better judgment kicked in, or when something happened that forced you to grow up quicker than you had wished. There was no going back to the reckless freedom after that, not without guilt contaminating your pleasure. Losing Oliver hit them all hard.

They walked through the hot sand beneath the swaying palms and the floating gulls, and they promised each other that today they would laugh without feeling guilty and live like all they needed for now was the perfect waves, crystal waters, and binding friendships.


"I'm going back in the water," Ivy twittered happily after the guys had returned from their second surf, exhilarated and exhausted.

The sun sat inches above the horizon, and the sunset was going to be spectacular. She didn't expect anything less on a day spent with Ollie's men. If her brother were out there, then the four of them would be his sole focus on this extraordinary day.

Ivy stood up and looked back to the men. She flicked Hart

an affectionate wink as she turned back to the sea. Her wavy blonde hair fell around her body, and she ran her slender fingers through it as she walked peacefully down to the water.

The three soldiers watched her idle gracefully down the sand toward the golden sky.

"So, Hart …," Benji's expression grew deviously wicked in the orange light of the sun, "have you fucked her yet?"

"Shit, Benji!" Walker scolded him. "She's Ollie's sister, you can't speak about her that way!"

Walker and Hart chuckled at Benji's usual, candid approach. His intentions were always harmless.

Hart leaned forward with a knowing grin. They had been eagerly awaiting the opportunity for Ivy to leave so they could inundate him with questions. Hart wrapped his arms loosely around his legs and glanced nervously at Ivy, who was barely out of earshot on the beach in front of them.

"Um," Hart hesitated, rubbing the back of his neck bashfully.

"Oh you lucky son-of-a-bitch!" Benji concluded delightfully from Hart's vagueness.

"No, Benji. Shit, no—" Hart replied quickly.

"No? Why the hell not? That right there is the perfect woman. What's wrong with you?" Benji frowned, directing his hands at Ivy.

Hart laughed humbly. He considered Ivy with a reserved gaze as she walked away from them. He thought about their last four months together, and a smile swept across his face. A lot had happened since he had arrived at Ivy's place on the night of the Gala. They had come achingly close to it, but no, he hadn't slept with her.

"I can't sleep with her, Benji." Hart picked up his shirt from beside him and threw it pointlessly on the sand in front of him. "She's Ollie's sister. It feels … *wrong*."

"Yeah, but you guys are hot for each other, it's intense to watch. Walker, come on man, you have to agree with me?" Benji shot a glance at Walker beside him.

Walker laughed. "There is definitely a spark."

"Hey, don't encourage him," Hart laughed, glancing at Walker.

Walker shrugged. "I'm sorry, but it's true."

Hart shook his head with a grin he struggled to contain. He grabbed a handful of sand and let it fall through his hand. These guys knew him better than he knew himself. They had been brothers-in-arms for over twelve years. There was no fooling them; Walker and Benji could read him like an open book.

"I've said it before," Hart added in his defense, "I'm not interested in falling in love. All I want is Taym."

Walker studied his friend quietly, and then he turned his gaze to Ivy, who had almost reached the water. "I'm going for a swim." He jumped to his feet and lifted his shirt over his head. "Go easy on him, Benji. Besides, when was the last time you slept with a woman?" Walker tossed his shirt at Benji and laughed.

Hart looked at Benji, surprised. "What about that woman back at Base? Five-minute-Swift?"

Benji recoiled sheepishly. "Nothing ever happened, she just wanted to talk."

Walker laughed.

"Don't laugh," Benji smirked. "I respect that about her."

Hart and Walker exchanged a perplexed glance.

Benji grimaced. "I haven't had sex in so long, it actually fucking hurts."

All three soldiers laughed at the truth of it.

Walker jogged toward the ocean. "Ivy, wait up!"

Ivy turned and waited for him, smiling beautifully when he reached her. "Hey, Walker."

"Hey, is it okay if I join you for a swim?"

"I'd love it." She smiled to herself. The three of them were always so polite.

Ivy tried to ignore the long scar carved across the top of his chest. He had just the one scar, whereas Hart had eight carved into his stomach and his chest. She had counted them.

Walker caught her inquisitive gaze. He rubbed the scar and smiled, his dark eyes softening with kindness.

"I'm sorry, I didn't mean to stare," Ivy looked away shyly, tucking a piece of hair behind her ear.

"Don't be sorry," he replied. "It comes with the job."

Ivy nodded soundlessly, lost for words in the presence of another ridiculously handsome soldier. He ran his hands casually through his hair when he spoke. He was rugged and sexy, and he was excruciatingly well-built. Ivy had to look away from him.

"So how has Hart been?" Walker asked her as they strolled down to the ocean.

Ivy gazed pensively at the soft sand that reflected the orange sky and thought about Hart.

"Hart has been ...," *charming, thoughtful, endearing, sexy, frightening, intriguing,* "okay," she managed.

"Just okay?" Walker frowned.

Ivy thought about Hart's nightmare that first night, pinning her against the wall in the dark with his strong hands wrapped lethally around her neck. She sighed. "He's got a lot happening inside that handsome head of his, doesn't he?"

Walker laughed at the obvious. "Too much."

Ivy considered Walker. There were many things these soldiers were keeping from her, but she didn't hold it against them. As soldiers, they had accumulated years of witnessing hardship and suffering, but when she looked into Walker's dark eyes, she saw nothing but kindness and genuine compassion for his friend.

"Are you guys ever going to tell me how he got like this?" she asked innocently.

Walker's brooding expression gazed down at her, thinking.

"He'll open up to you, Ives, just give him more time."

Ivy continued to watch Walker as they walked beside each other into the wet sand. He constantly seemed to be contemplating life. Always vigilantly mindful about what he was saying or doing, and Ivy sensed his heavy burden of concern for Hart. She wondered if all soldiers internalized what happened in the war. Did Walker suffer, too? She guessed they all did, in some way or another.

Ivy wanted to promise these men that there was far more good than evil in this world. They lived and breathed the deserts and the wars, and now Ivy wanted them to find comfort in her world of azure oceans and silky white sand. Where she walked through ancient forests and breathed in the fresh air that cleansed her weary spirit and awakened her soul. When on some days all she heard was the gentle breeze through the Torrey pines and the clicking of cicadas in the hot sun. With salty, sun-kissed skin, and bare feet, her tranquil summer days passed into balmy evenings with orange skies and burning bonfires under a blanket of stars. Then every night before she fell asleep, she thanked the universe for this part of the world that remained constant for her, no matter what happened in life. They would find peace here with her, just like Oliver always did. She would make sure of it. Her strength increased with their vulnerability. The more deeply she connected with her soldiers, the more she fell in love with each one of them.

"You three have a special connection," Ivy said. "It's beautiful to watch."

Walker glanced at her warmly.

"You're like a flock of birds; one flies off that way and all the others just naturally follow." Her arms swept gracefully toward the bright horizon.

"Ollie, Hart, and Benji know me better than I know myself," Walker smiled to himself. "After all this time together, the four of us behind enemy lines, we have naturally become pieces of one another."

Ivy listened to him, hoping he would go on.

"We were four separate pieces that were always meant to be together as one. That is what Phoenix means to us, twelve years operating as a single force. We're brothers-in-arms, we live and breathe each other day and night. That's why when Ollie died, a huge part of us died with him." Walker stopped talking and squinted his dark eyes at the golden sky.

She could see it hurt him to think about her brother. These men carried the world on their shoulders, but they carried it with extraordinary strength. She desperately wanted to reach out and take him into her arms, but she didn't know if he'd let her. Walker never gave much away, and right now he was bravely opening up to her, so Ivy remained thoughtfully quiet beside him.

"But Hart ... man, he took it the hardest," Walker added, dropping his gaze to the sand.

Ivy instinctively reached out her hand to take his. Walker's warm hand wrapped around hers in return, and they stared wordlessly into the spangled gold ocean in front of them, contemplating what had been and what was still.

Ivy blissfully soaked up the last of the sun's heat before she entered the cool ocean for a sunset swim. Terns glided along the smooth glassy water, and Ivy pointed out a school of bait fish that moved like a dark cloud across the water's surface. The air was still among the cliffs surrounding the bay, the breeze finally having died down for the evening. Ivy took a deep breath and filled herself with happiness. She glanced at Walker, and he smiled in return.

A wave rushed up the sand and washed over their feet with a cold, refreshing sharpness.

Ivy gasped. "Whoa, the water is colder than usual!"

Walker laughed. He pulled her over to him and lifted his arm, and Ivy ducked under him and faced the ocean again. He wrapped his big arm around her shoulders and leaned his chin on the top of her head.

"It's beautiful here," he said.

Ivy smiled into the sunset.

Walker let go of her and waded into the cool water. When he got a few meters in, he turned back to Ivy and shot her a breathtaking smile, and then threw his strong arms into the air beside him.

"Great friends, a perfect beach, and a stunning woman. *This* is paradise, Ivy!" Walker laughed beautifully and turned back to the water, wading excitedly into the ocean.

Ivy blushed. His body was incredible. He was tall and tanned, and his shoulders were broad and strong. She watched him wade through the water and dive beneath the sunset. Ivy tip-toed slowly through the shallow water. Not her usual style of entering the ocean, but she was suddenly feeling the cold now that the sun had half disappeared over the ocean. Walker had made his way back to her, and she could see his mischievous expression as he walked toward her through the shallows. She tried not to stare at his body. His washboard abs and toned arms sent a glorious shiver through her body, and the more she tried not to look, the more obvious she felt.

"Don't you dare splash me, Josh Walker!" Ivy shouted at him. "What is it with you guys?"

"Oh, come on, it's beautiful in here," he grinned roguishly, wiping his wet, dark hair off his forehead.

Benji came racing through the water from behind her. He splashed his way past her and dove into the refreshing, salty water. Ivy winced at the cold water as it washed over her from Benji's enthusiastic entry. She stood with her mouth wide open in surprise and wiped the water away from her eyes. She could hear Walker laughing, and when she opened her eyes, Benji emerged on the surface and shook the water from his golden hair like a Labrador.

"Thank you, Benji!" Ivy called out, sarcastically.

She felt herself lift out of the water, swept into Hart's arms as he ran into the ocean toward the sunset with the others. Ivy squealed when she realized what was happening, and she wrapped her arms tightly around his warm neck and braced for the cold. Hart jumped over a small wave and fell into the water with her clinging to him. The cold water embraced her, then his warm hands grabbed her around the waist and pulled her to the surface again.

"Hart!" Ivy spluttered. "You shit!" She wiped away the long, wet hair that clung to her face. The water wasn't as cold as she had anticipated.

Ivy could hear the three of them laughing around her, and it warmed her heart. She opened her eyes and caught their delight, and she couldn't help but laugh with them.

The boys swam further into the water to body surf the waves, and Ivy watched them from her knees in the shallow. For once she let herself feel happiness without guilt, and it revitalized her grieving soul. She allowed herself the divine freedom from despair in this rare and beautiful moment. Today had been a day like no other.

The three soldiers walked toward her from the ocean. Faceless silhouettes against a magnificent setting sky. Ivy's heart rose and fell at the bittersweet sight of Oliver's soldiers in the sunset, as if they had just stepped away from the orange sky. Then she remembered her brother's words. *Ivy, look into the orange sky, and I will be standing there. You will never be alone. I promise.*

## Chapter 13

THE GHOST TRAIL weaved a silver path in the light of the full moon. An eerie stillness hung in the ethereal glow that filtered through the canopy of trees on either side of them, which didn't go unnoticed by Hart. He watched Ivy's flashlight sway in the dark at her feet as the four of them headed away from the beach toward the poppy field. If anything, the flashlight spoiled the soldiers' night vision and made it difficult for them to see anything in the forest, including the trail. They preferred to move with the night, concealed by the dark, a practice learned from years serving in the military. But no one said anything for Ivy's sake.

Hart followed Ivy along the trail. He tactfully placed her behind Walker and Benji for the walk through the forest, a subtle protective measure. He walked at the end of the line, listening to the others as they chattered happily in front of him, much to his content. He willed their idle cheeriness to distract the alert soldier inside of him, but it didn't work. The trail spooked him. His imagination seemed to get the better of his intelligence when it came to this particular track, and he couldn't quite work out why. He felt pathetic. Past missions had necessitated an imperative sense of adrenaline and a driving determination to survive, but not this hiking trail. His anxiety evoked a vulnerability to ominous threats that didn't exist. Hart knew there was no one there, but he felt it. With every inch of his sharp, insightful soul, he felt it.

"Hart?"

"Yeah?" he replied.

"What's going on back there?" Benji asked. "Did you hear me?"

"Uh, no, sorry, I missed it," he laughed humbly.

Walker and Benji waited for him to catch up. Ivy stopped with them, turning around to watch Hart as he jogged toward them. She shone her flashlight in his direction to light the way, but also to read his expression.

"You're falling behind, soldier," Ivy teased him sweetly, thinking of the first time she brought him here.

"Do you feel it?" Hart asked quietly, looking over Ivy to Walker and Benji. He stood protectively close to her.

Walker nodded. His dark eyes searched the forest.

"Yeah, I feel it," Benji answered, considering Ivy.

"Like we're being watched," Walker added.

A chill ran through Ivy as she stared past the moonlit trees surrounding them. She didn't notice how quiet the forest was until just now. She tried to convince herself that they had made enough noise to still the creatures of the forest, but a glance at the soldiers made her hold her breath in their serious assessment of the woods.

A stick snapped on the trail near the beach. Ivy gasped and shot her flashlight down the track, but Benji swiftly took it from her and flicked it off, placing them in the dark quiet of the forest. She felt Hart's hand push her back toward the others instinctively, and a sense of danger overwhelmed her. Ivy opened her mouth to speak, but she had Benji's hand over her mouth before she could begin. She peered anxiously along the track into the darkness, then looked at the three soldiers who stood soundlessly around her. Walker's dark eyes squinted into the darkness. He had his arm reached out toward her with his body poised, ready to grab her and send her running at the first sign of danger. Hart stood with his back to her and his hand against hers; his gentle, reassuring touch a sign of his unyielding protection. It was his touch that kept her from bolting in panic. Benji stood against her with his hand still pressed against her mouth, his nearness warming her in the coolness of the night. They were impeccably silent, and unmoving, like silver statues in the moonlight. If she closed her eyes, she might believe the soldiers were gone.

Ivy couldn't see anything on the track. It was far too dark, but the soldiers peered into the black heart of the forest as though they looked directly into the eyes of the perpetrator. She held her breath behind Benji's hand, terrified of what she couldn't see. She imagined someone lurking in the concealment of the shadows staring back at them. Watching them. Waiting for her to breathe. Then Ivy forced herself to find comfort in the lethal force that surrounded her.

After a few minutes of deathly silence, Benji released his hand from her mouth and apologized, but she didn't speak. She listened to the pounding of her heart as she studied the soldiers who stood around her—each with their own wary expression, each scouring the dark forest that surrounded them. She had been down this track at night a hundred times before, most times on her own, guided by the music and the excited mumble of voices of Ollie's parties in the distance. Not once did she feel afraid. Not once did she think about any danger lurking in the forest around her. This was her home. Her place of refuge. Nothing could hurt her here.

"Stop it," she said quietly. "The three of you are freaking me out!"

Hart turned to her when she spoke, his familiar brown eyes staring at her in the light of the moon.

"It's the Ghost Trail, this happens to everyone," she continued. An agitated tone lingered in her voice. "Remember, Hart? I told you about it."

Hart narrowed his eyes at the others, thinking about the small light he had seen a few months ago in this same area. He held his tongue. He couldn't taint the forest that Ivy felt so deeply connected with. He wanted her to find peace here, always. Hart thought about her here alone once he had returned to Libya, and he found the thought disturbingly unsettling.

"I forgot about the ghost stories," he sighed resignedly.

"Ghost stories?" Benji smirked.

"Yes," Ivy exhaled. She turned around to face Benji, relaxing in his cheeky charm.

She laughed nervously. "You scared me. All three of you!

Shit!" She ran her fingers through her hair and smiled animatedly at the boys, her eyes widening in relief as the adrenaline waned and left her body.

"I'm sorry, Ives, I didn't mean to scare you," Hart said. He slid his hand into hers and started down the trail, gently pulling her along, desperate to get her out of the forest.

"So tell us about these ghost stories," Benji asked, discreetly changing the subject after catching the grave concern in Hart's expression.

Hart exchanged a wordless order with Walker when he passed him. Walker nodded in response, still warily mindful of the track behind them. He waited for them all to pass before he took his place at the back of the line, providing the rear defense. He peered at Hart ahead of him, holding Ivy's hand. Devoted to her safety, right where he should be.

Walker took another glance behind him into the forest toward the ocean and focused on a black area in the dark that his eyes frustratingly refused to adjust to. He trusted his friend with his life. Hart's sharp intuition had saved their lives on countless occasions when an attack was unanticipated, and if Hart sensed a threat where they least expected it to be, then it was there. Waiting for the perfect time to strike.

*Chapter 14*

Ivy and the soldiers walked into town, and instantly their concerns with the Ghost Trail were forgotten. The bar scene flowed seamlessly along the main street, making it difficult to determine where one bar finished and the other started. Tables dotted the sidewalks with cozy couples glowing in their candlelight, oblivious to the exuberance of the crowds around them. Ivy caught herself smiling at the endearing scenes as she passed them. The music and demographic changed from bar to bar, and Ivy couldn't help but be influenced by the liberating ambiance.

It was a Saturday night *and* a full moon, so the vivacious women of La Mar were out in full swing with their stiletto heels, mini-dresses, and abandoned inhibitions. They sipped brightly colored cocktails and blatantly eyed the opposite sex. Ivy smiled to herself as she made her way through a group of beautiful women on the sidewalk outside one of the most vibrant boutique bars in town. The women were tipsy and brazen, and Ivy thought about Hart, Walker, and Benji trailing behind her. Ivy laughed to herself. She was a shepherd leading her sheep through a starving pack of wolves.

Women embraced her as though they had been friends for years. Most of them she had known since high school, but they had lost interest in her friendship once Oliver left for the war. It had hurt, at first, but like everything else in her life, she wisely learned to distract herself from the obvious. The attention tonight didn't surprise her. Ivy had something these women didn't have ... three strikingly attractive men.

Dozens of lustful eyes honed in on the soldiers, and Ivy shook her head and laughed again. She expected the soldiers to be summoned into one of the bars, or maybe all of them. The women who lived in this town were confident, savvy, and outrageously gorgeous. Ivy always put it down to their exquisite summers and the exclusivity of La Mar. A hot, summer night held endless possibilities. The party only ended with the sunrise, and judging by the seductive gleams in their eyes, tonight appeared to be one of those nights. She felt a little concerned for Oliver's soldiers all of a sudden. These West Coast women knew how to handle a man; the question was whether these soldiers knew how to handle a West Coast woman.

Ivy stopped a few meters after she passed the group of women and turned. She was eager to catch a glimpse of the feast on her soldiers. She scanned the group for the boys and laughed heartedly at their predicament. The most chivalrous yet dangerous men she knew were held captive by a ravenous horde of women. A bold few refused to let them pass, and the soldiers had no option other than to oblige, too well-mannered to push a woman aside against her will. Ivy had expected it, and so she took the rare opportunity to sneak away without their attention on her.

Ivy winked at Hart, teasing him sweetly. She walked backward, casually slipping away from his watchful eye. His gaze was intense. Earth-shakingly intense. Hart shook his head when she refused to stop. A boyish smile swept across his face, and he furrowed his brow at her, pleading for her to behave.

*"Don't go,"* he mouthed to her through the women.

*"Sorry,"* Ivy shrugged. She grinned mischievously and gave him a small wave.

God, he was beautiful, she thought, trapped by a flock of provocative and stunning women, with his brown eyes fixed only on her. Ivy sighed loudly in coveted pleasure.

Hart's attention wavered for a moment when a beautiful brunette started talking to him. Ivy saw him bow his head and smile with a bashful humility that evoked a desire deep within her. The woman slid her hand down his chest after he politely refused her, and Ivy took the brief moment to disappear into the crowd while Hart wasn't paying attention.

She walked to the nearest liquor store, just a few doors down the street, taking a quick glance behind her before she stepped inside. *No soldiers.* After a few minutes, Ivy found the bottle she was looking for and walked toward the exit with her purchase.

"Well, if it isn't the elusive Ivy Rose!"

Ivy turned to the older man who had been idly sifting through the bottles of red wine. It was William, her father's closest friend. He was standing with open arms and an adoring grin, waiting for Ivy to hug him.

"William!" she replied excitedly, leaning into him for a hug.

"I haven't seen you since the Silver Moon Gala. How have you been since then, pet?" he beamed.

"I've been … good," she replied honestly, surprising herself. "Life has somehow found a way to keep me moving forward."

"I'm glad to hear it. Joyce has been a force to be reckoned with these past few months. She keeps pestering me about visiting you, and I keep telling her to leave you alone. Her curiosity is getting the better of her, I'm afraid." William grinned at her with a knowing twinkle in his eye.

A curious expression swept across Ivy's face. She narrowed her eyes at him and smiled. "And why is that Joyce wants so much to visit me?"

"Well you see, she's keen to meet some new friends of yours," William replied nonchalantly, plucking a bottle of red from the shelf and pulling his reading glasses back down to see the label. "She was feeling wretched about you sitting all alone in that big estate of yours, and so I may have mentioned to her that you had three of Ollie's soldiers staying with you."

William peered at her over the top of his glasses, past the bottle of red. There was an unmistakable sparkle in his wise old eyes.

Her brow furrowed curiously. "How did you know they were Ollie's men?"

"I worked with your father in the military for many, many years, my dear. I know people who know people," he grinned proudly.

"Are you watching over me, William?" she grinned charmingly at him, quietly touched by his concern for her.

"Maybe," he replied coolly. He peered at the bottle again. "Have you tried this?"

Ivy smirked at William's offhand, laid-back approach. He was just like her father.

She read the label of the bottle he held out to her, "La Rioja Alta, Gran Reserva. I never buy the Gran Reserva because I don't often have anyone to share it with me. Seems a crime, doesn't it."

"It's a beauty," he replied, "2001."

He stared at her for a short moment, studying her, and thinking to himself.

"The year my parents disappeared," she added, staring back at him.

William nodded and removed his reading glasses.

"So, these soldiers, how long are they sticking around for?"

"I don't know," Ivy replied truthfully.

He considered her for a second. "Well, they'd be fools to leave you, Ivy."

"Thanks, William."

"I hear they've left quite an impression on the rest of town. I don't think any woman in La Mar wants those young men to leave," he grumbled, rolling his eyes. "Including my wife."

Ivy thought about this. All of La Mar knew about the soldiers?

"Well, I'd better get back to Joyce. I'll be sure to tell her how happy you are," he said. He raised his eyebrows at the bottle she held tightly in her arms, then he grinned. "Gee, I miss those nights. Those times are long gone for me now. You have a lovely evening, Ivy. Be good."

Ivy stared at the bottle under her arm, and a wicked playfulness rushed through her, but it was short-lived. She absent-mindedly paid for the bottle and tucked it into her jacket, thinking about William's question. She had no idea how long the soldiers planned to stay with her, Hart included. She had been too afraid to ask. She left Hart ten minutes ago, and she already missed the soldier who stood unwavering at his sentry by her side. Once Hart was never here with her, now she could barely remember a time without him. She imagined her life once he had been granted the permission to return to Libya. Sanctioned to leave her sanctuary. What if Libya took his life, too?

Ivy stared vacantly at the ground outside the store, and a piece of her heart feathered down to the empty sidewalk in the soundless space that surrounded her.

"Hey," a gentle voice pulled her from the somberness.

Ivy looked up and saw Hart leaning against one of the trees outside the store beneath a halo of twinkling fairy lights.

"You followed me?" she smirked, walking over to him.

"Of course," Hart smiled warmly, his eyes softening at the nearness of her. He took her hand and ran his thumb tenderly across the back of it. "I told you, Ivy, right here by your side."

Ivy bit her lower lip and tried to conceal her delight. He smiled adoringly at her, and her cheeks burned in his gaze. She bowed her head in sweet shyness, and then he lifted her chin to face him. He didn't speak. He didn't need to. They were caught in a moment neither one of them saw coming. It was there in his dark eyes, eyes that were utterly incapable of veiling his deepest desires. Where would they be now, had he any control over them? She was grateful for his unyielding sincerity. His kindness. His warmth. The street's noise faded away, and Ivy caught her breath in his sudden solemnity. He was here for her, unquestionably, bound together by a loss that had shattered both their worlds.

Hart stepped toward her, and every inch of her melted helplessly in the divine nearness of him. After all these months resisting her, he was so achingly close. Hart bowed his head to kiss her, his lips yearning for the taste of her.

"Lovebirds!" Benji quipped as he passed them. "Get a room."

Hart opened his eyes and looked into her crystal gaze, and he smiled handsomely. He shook his head at Benji's terrible timing. Walker laughed and shrugged apologetically at Hart and Ivy when he passed them.

Hart rubbed his jaw and laughed, looking away from Ivy to regather his composure. "Benji, Benji, Benji …," he muttered to himself.

Ivy recovered quickly. She took a deep breath and laughed sweetly.

"I'm sorry, Ives," Hart smiled meekly.

"Don't be," she grinned.

"Like I've said before, we keep him around for the entertainment only."

Ivy laughed.

"So, what have you got tucked away in your jacket there? Looks suspicious. Did you steal something?" Hart teased.

"What? No! Of course not," she replied, pushing him away playfully. He laughed.

A mischievous grin swept across her face when she reached into her jacket. Her eyes widened with excitement and she presented the bottle to Hart.

"Tequila!" Ivy sang out delightfully.

Hart rubbed his chest nervously and took the bottle from her. "You want to shoot some of these bad boys tonight?"

"Tequila remedy," she twittered happily. "It's the perfect night for it!"

"Hey, I'm up for anything. It's Benji you'll have to convince."

"Do you think the guys will want to invite anyone back?" Ivy glanced at the women they had left behind, who were still spellbound yet discouraged by the soldiers' fleeting visit.

"Those women?" He grinned thoughtfully. "Walker and Benji aren't interested. Trust me."

"Why not?"

"Well, they're drunk for starters," Hart answered. He took her hand and walked beside her along the street.

"Most guys I know prefer it that way," she smirked. "Guaranteed she'll take you to bed without the challenge of the chase."

Hart looked at her thoughtfully. A raw sincerity sat in his handsome, retiring expression.

"We're past chasing one night stands, Ivy."

## Chapter 15

"OKAY ONE MORE, one more, come on, boys," Ivy laughed. She poured the tequila into the shot glasses they each held up around the fire outside.

The bright stars dusted the sky above them, and the ocean lulled soothingly in the dark below them. Ivy had turned on the stereo on their way through the house to the fire-pit, and music played from the speakers built into the patio benches.

"Walker, are you fading? Where's your glass?" Ivy glanced at Walker, who leaned forward on the sun lounger and casually flicked his cigarette butt into the fire.

"Hit me, gorgeous," he answered huskily, passing his shot glass around the fire from Benji to Hart so Ivy could fill it.

Benji passed the tequila back to Walker and grimaced. "Damn it. Here we go again …."

The four of them drained their glasses, and Ivy screwed up her face as the potent liquid burned its way down her throat. She sighed pleasantly to herself when the alcohol stirred a warm, tingling feeling inside. A gleeful giddiness that excited her. It was a feeling she had forgotten a long time ago. Ivy sensed a promising change in the air and a beautiful, reckless freedom blossomed in her soul.

"Holy shit, I'm out," Benji winced. "I haven't shot tequila in years."

Without looking, Benji threw his shot glass resignedly into

the air toward Hart who managed to catch it in his left hand.

"You have never been a tequila fan, have you, Benji boy?" Hart teased, patting him affectionately on the back.

Benji shook his head painfully. "Ives, there's nothing to you, sweetheart, how do you hold your liquor so damn well?"

"I think it may be genetic," she winked at him sweetly.

"It *has* been years since we drank tequila," Walker agreed with Benji, his dark, reminiscent eyes gazing into the fire. "Do you guys remember that time we all got shamefully drunk shooting tequila in Mexico?"

Benji stared at Walker for a few seconds before he answered. "If I was tanked on tequila, then I was most definitely passed out cold on a sidewalk somewhere."

"No, Benji, you were there," Walker assured him. He glanced at Hart. "Do you remember? We always hated the crowds in resort cities, but by accident we ended up in Puerto Vallarta one night in a hotel room with a pretty spectacular view." He laughed and leaned back in his chair.

Hart laughed. "Yeah, yeah, I remember, the four of us were sitting on the balcony having a quiet drink and realized we could see directly into the room opposite us," he smirked at Ivy, "Drunk spring breakers, everywhere."

"I wouldn't say that is spectacular," Ivy grinned, astutely aware the boys left out some specific details. She sipped on her beer, eagerly waiting for them to continue.

"No, these girls were topless, Ivy," Benji added once he remembered. "Breasts everywhere! They were touching each other and rubbing …."

"Okay, I get it!" Ivy interrupted sweetly.

Benji gave her a lascivious wink. His dimples sunk adorably into his cheeks as he leered ridiculously, and Ivy laughed at his menacing expression.

"I remember that night. Shit, I think we were about twenty-two years old." Hart shook his head and leaned forward on the bench beside Ivy, smiling fondly at the memory.

"The girls caught us watching them, and instead of being pissed off, they were turned on," Walker laughed.

That didn't surprise Ivy.

"Next thing you know," Walker continued, "after a few

tequilas too many, we're at a fucking foam party in some club at 4 in the morning."

"Foam party?" Ivy smirked across the fire-pit at Hart. "Not bad for a bunch of guys who hate resort cities."

"Hey, don't blame us, blame the tequila," Hart laughed, embarrassed.

"So where was my brother in all this?" Ivy asked.

Benji grinned. "Now that guy knew how to party."

"He was always, *always* the instigator," Hart added with a striking smile.

"That's doesn't surprise me at all," Ivy smiled to herself. "He was always throwing parties when my parents went away for the weekend. They became legendary. Kids would come from the neighboring towns just to say they had been to one of Ollie's parties. It boosted your street cred." She laughed.

Hart watched her carefully as she spoke about her brother. There was an unmistakable sadness in her eyes, even though she laughed. Her cheeks were flushed from the tequila and the heat of the fire, and her lips glistened in the firelight. She glanced at each of them when she talked, then she would dart her eyes timidly back to the fire. She was endearingly sweet. He loved the way she touched her mouth when she spoke, nervous in their attention. He fell harder and deeper for Ivy with every adorable trait he learned about her. Hart smiled to himself. The darkness inside of him had become shrouded in tequila and suddenly the vow he made to himself no longer mattered. He wanted Ivy. He wanted her love. Her innocence. Her body. Ivy was all he ever wanted.

"He told us about a party he threw in a fishing shack on the beach once that got a little out of hand?" Walker gazed warmly at Ivy, interrupting Hart's thoughts.

Walker's dark eyes flickered in the light of the flames, and Ivy's heart skipped a beat in their intensity.

"Yes, Ollie's notorious shack party," Ivy grinned as she remembered. "The first and the last party he had there. He told five of his friends to invite one extra person and to meet at sunset at the shack at Lights Beach."

The soldiers grinned as they listened. It felt good to laugh about Oliver without feeling sorrow.

"The invitation spread like a pyramid scheme," she continued. "Over three hundred people showed up!"

"So each time someone got told about the party, they were told they could invite one friend?" Benji asked, highly amused.

"Yes! It was wild," Ivy laughed. "There were helicopters, police, TV crews. He got in a lot of trouble, but it was worth it."

"So throwing parties also runs in the genes," Benji added. "The Silver Moon Gala was damn impressive, Ives."

"Thank you, Benji," she replied, glowing contentedly in the company of her thoughtful soldiers.

"You said there was a fishing shack at Lights Beach?" Hart asked more seriously.

"Yeah, it has always been there," Ivy answered.

"Where is it exactly?" Walker asked, glancing soberly at Hart.

Hart shook his head and shrugged, then looked to Ivy.

"Well, say you're walking toward the beach along the Ghost Trail. Maybe fifty meters from the beach is a small track that leads north for a little ways, just a minute or two," Ivy explained. She noticed the solemn shift in the soldiers' moods, but she continued. "There's an old fishing shack there. It's been there for forty, fifty years, maybe longer. It is nestled ten meters into the forest off the north end of the beach. It is pretty big, but a tight squeeze for three hundred people." She smiled, but the soldiers seemed distracted by this new information.

"We've never been to the north end of the bay before," Hart said, more to himself.

Hart, Walker, and Benji wordlessly exchanged concerned glances. It was only a few hours ago that the three of them had sensed something on the track, precisely where she mentioned. Hart still hadn't told Walker and Benji about the small green light he had seen. He thought about the ghost stories, but he was certain this was more than their imaginations. It was something the three soldiers had wanted to discuss in more depth, but there hadn't been a moment long enough where Ivy wasn't with them. The last thing they wanted to do was frighten her again.

"Hey, Ivy, it has been too long since I danced with a beautiful woman," Benji said with a tender, honest charm. "Will you do me the honor?"

Ivy watched Benji as he spoke to her. Studying him. The

fire flickered in his blue eyes, and he had a playful grin that was both boyish and cheeky, yet sweetly alluring at the same time. She loved his confidence. His mischievous and fun love for life. Then there was that body, those arms and his abs. Like Hart and Walker, Benji stirred feelings inside of her she knew were morally wrong, but Ivy didn't dwell on it for too long. Instead, she ran with it. Embraced it. These were Oliver's men and she adored them. She *loved* them. She had from the day they had first arrived at her front door.

Ivy reached for Benji's hand. "I would love to dance with you."

Hart glanced at Benji and Ivy who danced under the palm trees on the other side of the shimmering lap pool. He silently praised Benji's quick thinking, which gave him and Walker a chance to talk about this new information. They slow-danced amongst the candlelight that flickered in tiny glass orbs hanging from the palm trees. Benji appeared lost in the moment, with Ivy wrapped intimately in his arms, and a small wave of jealousy pulsed through Hart, but it was gone as quickly as it arrived. They seemed to be incredibly comfortable with one another, and the sight evoked Hart's genuine affection for both of them. To see them smiling together instilled a warmth in his soul that brought him pleasure, not pain. He saw Benji kiss her adoringly on the cheek beside her nose, and instead of concern, he felt relief in knowing that he was not alone in his quest to watch over Oliver's sister, to protect her. Oliver had been sorely missed by all three of them, and then they had met Ivy. She was everything they had never had in their lives, but now she was more; Ivy was all they had left of Oliver.

"So, I know you've seen something on the Ghost Trail before tonight," Walker mentioned, glancing behind him at Benji and Ivy to make sure they were still dancing.

Hart sighed. "Every time we're there I get this weird feeling that won't go away."

"Like what?"

"Like there is someone there," he frowned at Walker. "But why would there be, right? I think I'm paranoid."

"You don't let Ivy go there alone, do you?" Walker asked,

knowing the answer.

"Never. I didn't tell her that exactly, but I think she knows I'm not keen on the idea."

Walker nodded.

"I saw this light a few months ago, just after you guys left for Monterey." Hart leaned forward, glancing at Walker. "It was small and green, and I saw it in the exact location we heard that noise tonight."

"You think someone's living in the shack?" Walker frowned, pulling out a cigarette from the pack in his pocket.

Hart shrugged.

"Maybe it's all innocent, and this guy has nowhere else to live," Walker suggested, lighting his cigarette and inhaling it to life.

Hart thought about this.

"Should we check it out?" Walker asked.

Hart stared at Walker for a moment, thinking. He could see Walker's steeliness engraved into his dangerous expression. Walker would be up for anything. An expedition to the fishing shack tonight would excite him, not hassle him, especially on leave from the action in Libya.

Hart watched Ivy as he considered it. "No, it's fine," he answered eventually.

"Are you sure?"

"Yeah, I'm sure," Hart replied. "It's probably Tommy. That asshole wants Ivy, and he's not too impressed with me living here."

"You can handle him, can't you?"

"Of course. But I keep anticipating the worst whenever we are on that trail, and I don't know why. It's frustrating."

"I think all three of us feel that way these days," Walker answered. "What we went through with Ollie—fuck, man, that was intense for all of us. I'd say our instincts will always be on guard and we will always expect the worst. We're soldiers. We're Phoenix. Our instincts keep us ticking. They keep us alive. Listen to them, Hart—yours are always spot on."

"You're right," Hart nodded, rubbing his face.

Walker watched him quietly. He took another puff on his cigarette and thought about that night in the motel room before they arrived in San Diego.

"So how are your nightmares?" Walker asked.

Hart glanced at him. "Gone."

"Just like that?"

"It seems so."

"What about the anger? Do you think you'd attack the President's gofer again if you had the chance?" Walker laughed gently.

Hart rubbed his jaw, grinning reservedly. "No. I don't know what came over me that day."

Walker snorted. "Please, everyone hated that asshole. He had it coming."

"You knew him?" Hart asked, surprised.

"I had a debriefing with him only a few hours before you did. Did you see his suit pants?"

Hart grinned. "No."

"They were offensively tight. I copped a fucking eyeful of his baggage on the way in," Walker recalled, shaking his head. "Shit, I wanted to kick that guy's ass before the debriefing even started."

The two of them laughed.

"Yeah, but you didn't," Hart added afterward. They fell silent for a short moment.

"Well, someone had to do it." Walker smiled at him with a laid-back, nonchalant expression.

Hart leaned forward toward the fire. "Thank you, Walker."

"For what?"

"For sticking by me through all this mess. I know it's my fault the three of us are here." Hart spun his beer bottle between his hands. "Twelve months is a long time."

"You don't need to thank us," Walker replied, leaning in toward the fire with Hart. "Benji and I wanted to come with you. We didn't hesitate to leave. We'd stand by your side no matter what, Hart. You know that."

Hart frowned. "You weren't forced to leave?"

"Forced? Not at all!" Walker smiled. "We told Hannah we were going with you and she signed off on it as beneficial support."

A huge weight lifted from Hart's shoulders, and he exhaled loudly in relief. He buried his face in his hands to take in what Walker had told him, then he laughed. No matter who took them away from this world, the four of them remained resolutely intact. Brothers-in-arms. Brothers for life. Unbreakable. *Inseparable.*

"Hannah, Hannah, Hannah ..." Hart shook his head.

"She cares about you. Enough that it could get her into trouble one day."

Hart nodded as he thought about it. He didn't feel the same way, but he still cared for her.

"Talking about women falling for you," Walker smirked.

"Who, Ivy?" Hart sipped his beer.

"Ivy is worth the pain she unknowingly causes you."

Hart placed his empty beer bottle on the ground and stared into the fire, listening to Walker.

"You need to follow her, follow that light," Walker told him. He spoke to Hart with a determined expression.

Hart looked at him. "I try to. Believe me, I've tried," he sighed. Hart stared at his hands as he rubbed them together in front of the fire.

"This darkness that you feel, Hart," Walker paused, "it will consume you if you don't let her in. Listen to me—don't push Ivy away, you need her. You need each other. I have never been more certain about anything in my life."

Walker nodded at him, then he glanced over Hart's head and sipped his beer with an exaggerated casualness to warn him they were no longer alone.

Hart turned as Ivy and Benji came back to the fire-pit. They sat themselves down on the benches either side of Hart.

Hart's soul warmed instantly in her presence. "Hey, Ivy, can I steal you for a moment?"

Ivy remembered the night of the Gala when he asked her the very same question before he led her onto the dance floor. Hart didn't steal her away for a moment—he stole her away irrevocably. Everlastingly. She nodded breathlessly.

Hart slid his hand into hers and pulled her away from the fire.

He turned to Ivy under the palm trees and held her hands. A humble smile swept across his face, and he brushed a lock of her hair from her shoulder.

"Will you dance with me?" Hart asked.

"Hmm, I don't know?" Ivy grinned mischievously.

A curious smile curled up the side of his face. "You don't know?"

"Well, last time I danced with you, you left me alone in the middle of the dance floor in front of three hundred people."

Hart smiled meekly and looked away. He took her hand and ran his fingers through hers as he thought about that night. He looked into her eyes again and stepped toward her.

"I promise I won't leave you tonight, Ivy."

Her heart practically leaped out of her chest at the nearness of him. At his intensity and his innate charm. He exuded a warmth that quickened her pulse, yet calmed her racing heart. She smiled timidly and bit her bottom lip, hopelessly attempting to hide her weakness for him. Hart gently touched her face and ran his hand through her hair, then he pulled her toward him and kissed her on the forehead. He wrapped his arms around her and held her against his chest. Protectively. Ivy buried herself into him and rested her ear against his beating heart, and she listened to him, to his tranquil breath, to his soul. She closed her eyes tightly. The effect he had on her was overwhelmingly powerful. It was soul shaking, and Ivy hoped it never went away. Once these feelings had left her, then Hart would be gone, too.

He danced slowly with her to the music that drifted lazily from the house. He swept his eyes across the blanket of stars above them and thought about Oliver. It had been six months. *Today.* He wasn't sure if anyone even realized, but he did. His best friend hadn't been by his side for every minute, of every hour, of every day ... *for six months.* Hart closed his eyes and held Ivy to him, ignoring the grief that tried its damnedest to overpower him. Tears threatened, and his heavy heart crashed with torment. He breathed calmly toward the dark cloud that loomed over him, and he waited patiently for the anxiety to reclaim him. Hart braced for the fall ... but it didn't come. It was Ivy. She stood like a shielding light around his defenseless soul, deflecting the darkness of the demons deep inside of him. There was no trembling. No torturous flashbacks. Not while he held her in his arms.

With her shield of light against his darkness, Hart gathered the courage to think about his friend. *Oh, Oliver.* Hart exhaled into the sky. He remembered his sparkling blue eyes and his cheerful grin. His optimistic heart and his endless energy that burned like the sun by his side for all those years. Hart remembered the fun and the laughing and the good times spent with him on the streets of Libya and in the deserts of Afghanistan and Arizona. The constant witty banter between the team, mainly at Benji's expense, and the endless nights the four of them spent together under the breathtaking desert night skies. Hart smiled to himself and closed his eyes. He felt Oliver's light surrounding him. Radiating from the woman in his arms. Ivy Rose. The beacon of light that salvaged his withering soul from the black ocean all those months ago, when he was ready to die.

*This darkness that you feel, Hart … it will consume you if you don't let her in. Listen to me—don't push Ivy away, you need her. You need each other.* Walker's words replayed over and over in his head. Hart tightened his eyes shut. Walker was never one to tell people how to live their lives, but if he did, then you had apparently been heading down a treacherous path. In the war, Hart took his friend's rare advice whenever he offered it … to survive. Tonight was no different.

Hart peered down at Ivy in his arms. The tequila had settled in his blood like a dreamy haze that cloaked his fear. It felt incredible.

"Hey Ives," he whispered.

"Yes?"

"I've wanted to tell you something for a long time now and I…" Hart hesitated, trying to find the right words to tell her what happened. Desperate to get his secret out before his courage waned. "This is hard for me … but I …." He stopped dancing and rubbed his jaw anxiously. *"Shit."*

Ivy searched his face and frowned.

"I've never told you because … because I didn't want to frighten you any more than I already have." Hart pulled her to him again and rested his warm hand on her cheek. "I wasn't ready to lose you, Ivy."

She stared into his troubled eyes. "Are you ready to lose me now?"

"No! Never. That's not what I meant," Hart replied quickly. He searched for a way to explain why her brother was no longer here for her. For a way to confess his sins. He saw her crystal eyes fall from his gaze to the ground.

"Back when I first met you, I couldn't see what lay ahead for me," Hart breathed. "There was *nothing* when I looked into my future. I was blinded by the darkness, and by my suffering … and by everything that had happened in Libya."

He lifted her chin so he could look into her eyes. A rich intensity filled his expression and Ivy exhaled nervously.

"I couldn't see this, Ivy …," he continued. "I couldn't see moments like these that I thought I had lost forever."

His hands ran along either side of her face, and Ivy held his wrists, still concerned for what he couldn't tell her.

"Tell me what happened in Libya," she whispered. "I won't run from you, Hart. I promise."

Hart didn't say anything. He rubbed his thumbs back and forth across the smooth skin on her cheeks and thought about what she asked. The thought of losing her was too much for him to bear. He couldn't do it. He couldn't tell her. Hart bowed his head resignedly and leaned his forehead against hers.

Ivy's heart fell.

Hart could smell her sweet breath and her coconut-scented skin. He was never sure why she smelled that way, but it soothed him and turned him on at the same time. The candlelight flickered delicately around them, and Hart breathed in the salty, midnight air. The night was perfect, and so was Ivy. His troubles softened in her sweetness, then Hart leaned into her and kissed her gently on the lips.

He felt the world pause. The night stood still in hopeful anticipation. The music stopped. The ocean's purr faded. There was nothing but Ivy, her eternal light beaming in his arms. Her lips were soft and warm, and she tasted as sweet as he remembered from all those months ago. Hart pulled away slightly, their lips almost touching … both caught off guard by his sudden intimacy. Their spirits were spiraling pleasurably through the night, through the world that could be theirs, if only he weren't afraid. He sighed into her, closing his eyes to resist the temptation of her. *I shouldn't be here, Ivy …*.

"I want to show you something," she told him. Ivy took his hand and led him into the house.

Hart followed her to her room. She picked up a frame that was on a bookshelf, gazing at it lovingly for a moment. She handed it to Hart. He drifted to a corner of the room and held the photo she had given him. He numbly sat in the armchair behind him and stared at the picture in his hands. An array of emotions ran through him, but one stood out more prominently than the rest. Gratitude, for the time they had spent together.

Hart stared at the photo of himself and Oliver, sitting on a couple of army crates with their arms on each other's shoulders. Bare-chested and baby-faced without a care in the world. Hart smiled as he remembered that day. It was the day of their graduation ceremony in the Special Forces. They had been assigned to a twelve-man detachment team, the team that preceded Phoenix. It was the start of a friendship neither of them had ever expected.

He leaned back heavily in the chair behind him. He looked up at her with tears in his eyes, and Ivy hurried over to him and carefully took the frame from his fingers. She placed it beside her on a chest of drawers and turned back to him. He looked at her with a faint smile and leaned forward in his chair. He bowed his head and wiped away a tear that rolled down his cheek, then he laughed at himself, surprised by his reaction.

"I'm so sorry. I thought it might make you smile," Ivy apologized, frowning to herself.

Hart didn't look at her. "I don't have any photos," he breathed into his hands. "Thank you, Ivy."

Ivy twisted her face sadly to fight back her tears. She moved in front of him and bravely ran her fingers through his hair. Hart liked to keep his distance from her in these moments, but Ivy couldn't help herself. She cared too deeply not to go to him. Her blood warmed with the feeling of her fingers in his hair, still salty from the day at Lights Beach. When he looked up at her, she detected the sadness in his eyes, which seemed to welcome her affection, as though he approved of her intimacy. *Finally.*

Ivy trailed her fingers down the side of his face and through the short beard along his jawline, catching her breath in the sudden intensity that washed over him under her touch.

"They say only the good die young," he said quietly.

"So what about the good men who live?" Ivy smiled, her eyes softening with affection.

"I don't know," he whispered resignedly. Her tender hands ran over his hair, and his face, and his lips, and Hart closed his eyes. Her forwardness made him utterly powerless. For the first time since he arrived at Ivy's, he refused to resist her sweet seduction. It felt too good to push her away.

"Those men who live create a legacy for which the world can aspire to abide by," she said quietly. "Who can we model ourselves on if these men choose not to embody their virtuousness? The world will not benefit if you hide away from it, Hart."

He stared anxiously at her as she moved closer to him. Painfully close. Irresistibly close.

Ivy stood before him, straddling his knees. When she lowered herself onto him, he breathed out heavily. Lustfully. His hands slid around her waist, and he held her firmly. She looked down at him, adoring the surprise in his beautiful, brown eyes.

"The world doesn't need me anymore," he breathed.

Ivy leaned down to Hart and whispered into his ear. "Johnny Hart," she felt him quiver beneath her, "You have survived war, loss, and adversity. You can't give up now. The world will always need you. *I need you.*"

Hart exhaled loudly, feeling her hot breath whisper into his ear. He ran his hands up her back over her dress and through her long hair, and she leaned over him, responding to his touch. Her hair fell around him, and Hart grew dizzy in the intoxicating scent of her surrounding him. He groaned lightly, pulling her body toward his lips, hungry for the taste of her. He breathed into her neck as he fought his desire, but he couldn't resist any longer. He closed his eyes tightly in anguish and brushed his lips across the silky skin of her neck. Her ecstatic sigh in his ear sent his blood into a boiling frenzy. The feeling of her sitting on top of him was like nothing he had ever felt before. The Queen of Hearts. He had stolen her brother from her, and so he owed her everything. He was the dark knight kneeling at her gates, too ashamed to admit the truth of his guilt. Pleading for an undeserved forgiveness. He would succumb to her divinity—and then later to his atonement.

Hart gazed up at her hungrily as she kneeled above him, his beautiful eyes aflame with desire, sending a pleasant shiver through her body. He pulled her parted lips down toward his, and she breathed into him as he held her there, agonizingly brushing his lips against hers, hesitant to go any further. She saw the fear flash through his dark eyes before he clamped them shut and pulled away from her ever so slightly. Ivy's heart cried out desperately to the universe, pleading for this soldier's sweet surrender to her.

"Don't run away from me, Hart," she whispered against his lips, "not this time."

*"Oh Ivy, if only you knew …,"* he breathed painfully, kissing her lips softly and pulling away again. He heard her groan lightly in response, and Hart exhaled sharply. Overcome by her. Defeated.

*"If only you knew,"* she breathed, then he kissed her passionately and Ivy fell into an insatiable world where only he existed.

Hart groaned when he kissed her, sending a vibration through her mouth that tremored divinely into the depths of her sexual being. Ivy didn't want to come up for air. She wanted to die here, lost forever in Hart's unbridled passion. She couldn't get enough of him. His warm hands roamed her skin in places he had never touched her before, and she could feel him everywhere all at once, her hot skin tingling under his fingers as he explored her body. He slid his hand up the center of her dress toward her chest, his fingers grazing her breasts as they passed and Ivy trembled in response. He ran his hand up her neck, pushing her chin into the air, and she breathed toward the ceiling, closing her eyes as he gently kissed her neck and her collarbone. Hart ran his fingers down her neck and swept the straps of her dress from her shoulders, letting the sheer cloth fall to her hips. Hart effortlessly untied her swimsuit and groaned softly at the sight of her naked on top of him. Ivy panted with a sedated pleasure, watching his dark gaze take her in. She wanted him to see her. She wanted him to touch her. To have her. After everything she had ever come to know about this broken soldier, Hart deserved all of her.

Ivy expected him to be apprehensive with her body at first, but Hart was far from it. The voracious calm that lingered in his eyes made her realize he had done this a thousand times before. Hart moved around the female body with a proficient confidence that Ivy briefly considered being concerned about, but instead she was grateful for his expertise. It had been so long since she had slept with anyone that she worried she could only get them so far. But Hart … Hart knew exactly what he wanted, and Ivy sighed with pleasure when she realized it was her.

Hart paused for a moment unexpectedly, in awe of the flawless, naked beauty in his arms. Never had he seen a woman's body more perfect than Ivy's. He ran his hands up her body and around her face … pulling her to him again.

"You are so beautiful, Ivy … so beautiful it hurts," he breathed into her.

Ivy kissed him deeply, suddenly needing more of him. All of him. She ran her hands down his strong chest, and then along his stomach until she found the bottom of his shirt. His hands moved up and down her thighs on either side of him while they kissed, edging closer and closer to her but never quite reaching her, and Ivy groaned in desire. She lifted his shirt up his chest, feeling the incredible heat radiating from his body, then Hart grabbed the shirt from her hands and pulled it over his head. He threw it on the floor beside the armchair and lifted her dress over her head and tossed it behind her. He wrapped his hands around her bottom and lifted her as he stood up from the armchair, kissing her deeply as he did. Ivy groaned into him, turned on by his effortless strength as he walked with her in his arms toward the bed. She felt the muscles in his shoulders as he carried her, and she imagined him in the deserts flanked with heavy gear and weapons. The thought of his strength sent her blood rushing into a mad, feverish lust.

Hart listened to the ocean as it purred through the open balcony doors, but unlike every other night, it didn't soothe his avid soul. He longed to feel sheltered and gratified in the arms of beauty in its purest form, in the arms of this woman. Lost in the sweet taste of her, in the smell of her coconut-scented skin, in the feel of her silky hair against him. He groaned at the softness of her body. He bathed in her innocence. Bathed in her desire. *In her love.* He ran his hands up her smooth stomach and across her breasts, sighing into her with their soft, delicious suppleness in his hands. No rifle lay in his reach. No grenade. No handgun. No violent stranger. His once trembling hands found their reprieve in the splendor of her unfathomable beauty. Her divinity. Ivy was all he ever needed.

His passion bound her together in an unremitting state of tormenting pleasure, and she silently begged him to end the tantalizing torture. His heaviness weighed down on her, and Ivy felt the strength in him as he held himself above her, consciously trying not to crush her. He ran his hand over her breasts and across her stomach, then achingly down her hips. She leaned her head back and sighed into the air. Ivy remembered the night of the Gala when his fingers explored hers. She remembered the divine feeling of them running over her hands, and she couldn't believe where they were now. He slid her bikini bottoms down her legs, and as his hand moved up her leg again, she felt his fingers brush against her. Ivy moaned into him, and he kissed her hard, turned on by her pleasure.

He pulled away from her. A fierce passion drenched his eyes and overwhelmed her. Hart grinned beautifully at her; it was charming and reassuringly confident, and it sent a sweeping smile across Ivy's face. She didn't know whether to laugh or cry, then he leaned into her, and kissed her softly and slowly as he entered her.

Ivy watched him as he slept beside her. Studying his handsome, peaceful face. Everything about him was beautiful. He had come so far from where they were months ago. The nightmares and the attacks and the trembling had all just faded away. His demons were still there inside of him, haunting him from behind his heavily guarded walls, but for now ... Hart was okay. More than okay.

She moved her face closer to his on the pillow and stared at him in thought. This soldier had stepped out of her dreams and now he was here beside her. Stealing time. Hiding in the sanctuary of her love. She harbored him from the turbulent world until he was strong enough to face it again, and he was hers until that day. Until that day....

One day he would be stronger. One day he would choose Libya over her. One day he would choose Taym over her. One day he would leave her, and maybe never return. One day he was going to break her heart. *One day.*

Ivy sighed and closed her eyes, and fell asleep in the arms of her incredible soldier.

*Chapter 16*

"HART, my man! What happened to you last night?" Benji teased. "You two disappeared."

"Don't you start, you cheeky bastard," Hart smirked, rubbing his foggy head and regretting the last few shots of tequila last night. He lay back on a sun lounger beside the pool with Walker and Benji and closed his eyes in the sun's soothing warmth.

"You look different," Benji sniggered.

Hart smiled without opening his eyes. "Benji …"

"You didn't!?" Walker asked abruptly, almost choking on his coffee.

Hart rested his hand over his eyes and wished away his pounding head.

Walker sat upright all of a sudden. He ripped his sunglasses off and beamed at Hart. "You slept with Ivy?"

Hart looked at him, he had never seen him so animated.

"No fucking way!" Walker laughed.

Hart peered at Walker through the sunshine in his eyes.

"What are you talking about, Walker?" Hart frowned. "You told me to do it."

"Well, yeah, but I didn't expect you to take her straight to bed, you horny bastard."

Walker and Benji laughed.

"Shit, I didn't plan it," Hart replied. The reality of what he'd done suddenly hit him.

Walker leaned back in his chair with an unusually pleased expression. "That's great news. I'm happy for you two."

Hart watched Walker suspiciously, examining his expression and his tone. It was slightly out of character for him.

"No, I'm serious. Halle-fucking-lujah," Walker laughed, toasting Hart with his coffee mug and clinking it with Benji's.

Benji was grinning impishly beside him, anticipating Walker's celebration.

"I bet Ollie thought I would be the one to sleep with his sister," Benji teased.

"You know, it's funny you should say that," Hart laughed gently. "He did mention it."

"Mention what?" Benji frowned. "He thought I'd sleep with Ivy?"

Walker laughed. "You seem surprised?"

"I'm flattered," Benji replied.

"Flattered?" Hart replied, bemused. "Ollie was wrong. Shit, I promised him I wouldn't touch her."

"Hey, come on now, and I'm speaking on behalf of all three of us …," Benji stated calmly, "none of us knew Ivy was going to be so fucking gorgeous, am I right? So, if one out of the three of us were eventually going to sleep with her, and Ollie thought it was going to be me, then at least he expected one of us to do it." Benji winked at Hart.

Hart shook his head at Benji's straightforwardness and laughed softly to himself.

"Bizarrely, Benji's right," Walker added. "We're his best friends. I'm pretty sure he would have known there would be some magnitude of attraction between his sister and at least one of us."

Hart thought about this. He remembered his conversation with Oliver on the day that he died. *I think she'd like you. You two remind me of each other in a way. You both have a mysterious depth to your soul that is beyond me.* Oliver knew.

Walker saw the soberness in Hart's eyes as he lay on the sun lounger, quietly thinking to himself. "Hey, Hart," he added, "if it makes you feel any better, I don't know any man that could ever resist being seduced by that woman. I know I couldn't." Walker mused into his coffee. "To be honest, I can't believe you lasted this long."

Hart laughed wearily under the weight of the decision he made last night.

"If it were me, I'd blame the tequila," Benji grinned as he lay back on his sun lounger. He threw his hands behind his head and exhaled loudly in the tranquility of the beautiful morning. "Does it *ever* rain in Southern California?"

The week went far too quickly. Hart had just settled into his friends' companionship again, feeling something like the normalcy of his life before Oliver died, and now they were leaving. He walked Benji and Walker to the end of the driveway, where their taxi driver was having trouble punching in the code at the security gate. The dry Santa Ana winds blew through the trees as they strolled down the driveway, and their seeds fell like tiny helicopters to the ground around them. Hart appreciated their delicateness as they rode down on the hot wind.

"It is a beautiful day today," Hart said, staring wistfully into the trees.

Walker and Benji studied him for a few seconds, and then they glanced at each other and smirked.

"You sound more and more like Oliver every day," Walker grinned.

Hart looked at him thoughtfully. "Maybe it's La Mar? It is a pretty special town."

"Yeah, maybe it's the town," Walker replied wryly, his dark eyes narrowing with his smile. He glanced at a laughing Benji, and Hart grinned knowingly at his amused friends.

They all knew who was responsible for his brighter attitude toward life, and they were greatly indebted to her. Remarkably, she had puzzled his broken soul back together again, piece by devastated piece.

It was hard to say goodbye this time, harder than the last time. Their departure briefly reminded him of Oliver and how he left him permanently. They promised Hart they'd be home again soon, and it eased the anxiety in his heavy heart.

Hart walked alone toward the estate with his hands in his

pockets and stared at the sunlight that filtered through the trees. He thought about Ivy waiting for him at the estate's private beach and a warmth embraced his soul. He took a deep breath and smiled, then he closed his eyes and walked through the sunshine toward the house. He felt the sun on his face, warming his skin, warming his core. He listened to the dry leaves as they rustled in the wind above him. There was only peace here, surrounding him. The hot air rushed around him, and he could smell the ground beneath him in the heat. Its earthiness. Its richness. He heard the whispering on the wind; the same story conveyed over millions of years. He listened to it. He breathed it into his lungs. It was his for now. She had taught him how to hear the world. She had showed him how to find it, how to seek out what was always there ... an ancient world that paralleled the modern. A paradise that existed all around him that, with the complexities of life, he had come to overlook. Ivy was right. It was a refuge. A sanctuary for the lucky ones who knew where to find it. He was a part of this earth, eternally, because he had been born to it. He could find his reprieve in the little things, now that he believed. He searched his soul in the peacefulness that surrounded him and he found contentment. Liberation. He was free from sorrow ... for now, at least.

He saw her there, standing thigh-deep in the turquoise ocean facing the horizon. She ran her fingertips across the water's surface in big circles around her, and he could hear her humming to herself. Hart smiled. A wave of adoration flowed tenderly through his heart. He waded into the water behind her, and she turned to face him, her crystal eyes sparkling in the sunshine. There was no wind down here. It blew directly over the top of the cliff, allowing the two of them to swim in the glassy waters of her private beach.

"Hey," Ivy walked toward him. "How are you feeling?"

"I'm okay," Hart replied warmly. He tucked her hair behind her ear and ran his thumb across her cheek.

Ivy smiled at him. A glint of mischief flashed through her innocent expression; she could think of one way to take his mind off things.

"What was that?" he laughed.

"What?"

"In your eyes. What are you up too, Ivy Rose?" Hart grinned handsomely.

"Me? Nothing."

He was coming to know her too well, and Ivy blushed.

"I don't believe you," he laughed.

Ivy laughed and sunk under the water to hide her blushing cheeks. She smoothed her hair back when she came to the surface and opened her eyes.

"Do you believe in paradise?" she asked, looking up at him.

"I would like to."

She narrowed her eyes. "But you don't."

He looked away from her and his smile faded. "No. I don't believe in paradise. I've seen too many terrible things to believe there is a place where you cannot get hurt by the world."

"Wow." Ivy looked away from him and smiled.

"What?"

"You really do have a dark cloud over that handsome head of yours," she smirked.

Hart laughed humbly.

"I can prove to you that paradise exists," she said, biting her bottom lip.

"Oh, you can, can you?" Hart's intrigue swept over him cheerfully. "I thought this was it?" He raised his strong arms and gestured to the perfect beach around them.

"Well, it is a part of it," she smiled beautifully.

Hart's speechless expression entertained Ivy. She loved his fascination with her. He was wide-eyed and amused, astutely decrypting what she furtively conspired. God, he was handsome. Ivy let her eyes rove over his beautiful body and remembered the feeling of him inside of her. His power, his strength, his godliness. She sighed inwardly at the thought, her soul shaking with pleasure.

Ivy laughed and turned for the beach, suddenly breathless by him. Overcome by him. Unprepared for how confident she had become ... but Hart took her hand and stopped her.

"Don't go," he breathed.

"You want me to stay?"

"I always want you to stay, Ivy."

Hart grabbed her around the waist, and she wrapped her

arms around his shoulders, then he lowered them both into the water. He leaned into her and kissed her with a heart-aching tenderness, and Ivy felt herself spiraling madly in his unexpected forwardness.

She smiled wickedly.

"Paradise?" he grinned.

"No," she replied. *"This* is paradise ….." Ivy untied her bikini and threw it on the rocks beside them. She felt the cool water wash around her breasts and found it incredibly empowering. His eyes widened with desire, sending a ravenous rush of blood through her brazen heart.

"You're killing me softly, Ivy" Hart whispered, pulling her to him. "You know that, don't you?"

He pulled her onto him, and made love to her in the still waters tucked protectively under the Santa Ana winds, where a piece of Ivy's heart fell into the water and drifted away from her resolutely.

*One day.*

*Chapter 17*

Ivy sat on top of him in the warm sand, running her hands over the muscles of his chest. She slid her fingers down the silver chain of his dog tags, and then she leaned forward and kissed his smiling lips. Ivy lifted the tags over his head, to release him from his heavy chains.

Hart waited for her to lift her arms above him, then he glided his hands up her tiny waist and brushed the back of his fingers along the side of her breasts. He watched her eyes close with pleasure, and a hot sensuous breath escaped him. Hart rubbed his thumbs over her nipples, and Ivy groaned as she lowered the chain over her head, placing the tags snugly between her naked breasts.

"I'll keep them safe," she promised.

Hart watched her intensely. Unsmiling. "Do what you like with them, Ivy. You're all I need."

Her long wet hair surrounded him when she leaned in to kiss him. He pulled her off him and laid her down on the sand beneath him. Hart trailed his fingers down her sandy skin, past the tan lines on her naked hips and down her long legs, and he smiled. He saw her watching him, waiting for him with a smoldering sexiness that blazed in her hungry eyes. Hart's eyes followed his hand as he touched her, then he shook his head in awe of her pure perfection. A lustful breath escaped his lips as he ran his hand back up her thigh. She leaned her head back in pleasure and Hart bent down to her and kissed her open mouth. He tasted the warm salt on her lips, making him shudder as he slid himself inside her. Ivy moaned into his shoulder, sending his desire into a wild, fevered lust. *Paradise.*

The months disappeared quickly without Hart realizing. There were no schedules. No debriefings. No meeting points. No war. Libya? *Taym?* Everything from his former life had faded away. Hart spent his sun-drenched Californian days making love to Ivy all over her estate, from the private beach with the cool ocean lapping their hot, naked bodies, to the various rooms around the mansion. Here with Ivy, time stood exquisitely still.

Hart left Ivy at the estate's private beach. It had become one of the few places he felt comfortable leaving her on her own. The beach wasn't accessible from the north or the south, and the only way to get there was through the estate itself or directly over the water. Seeing as he stood between the security gate and the beach, it was impossible for anyone to reach her without his knowledge. He was her armor, her defender. Sworn to stand sentry in a fleeting promise to a friend. Bound to her by his loyal heart. His behavior seemed overprotective, but his instincts forced him to be. The memory of Tommy assaulting her only meters from him infuriated him. He relived that night over and over, so he never forgot what Tommy was capable of doing. Oliver would have sent that bastard to his grave, but Hart held back for Ivy's sake. The malicious contempt in Tommy's eyes exposed his dishonorable intentions, so Hart waited for his return; steadfast and fearless between the enemy and the girl he promised to protect ... because Tommy would be back, sooner or later.

Hart leaned into the refrigerator and pulled out a bottle of water. He took a few sips and then the security gate chimed through the intercom by the front door. He walked out of the kitchen and across the hall to the intercom. He stopped in surprise when he saw Hannah on the small screen attached to the wall. Hart stared, unsmiling, at the monitor. He cursed quietly to himself, and then he leaned reluctantly on the button to open the gates.

Hart opened the front door and stepped onto the porch to welcome his unexpected guest as she pulled up the long drive.

Hannah stepped out of the back of a black town car, and he caught a momentary hesitation when she looked at him. Her platinum blonde hair was tied back into a severe bun, and she wore a black suit and tall heels. She slung a black leather briefcase over her left shoulder. Her bright green eyes pierced the cool air between them as she walked up the stairs toward him.

Hart saw Hannah look away and take a deep breath before she reached him, and he could tell she was overwrought with nerves. When she looked at him again, he smiled.

A friendly smile swept across Hannah's face in response, and both of them visibly relaxed.

"So, this is Oliver's home," Hannah nodded her head as she looked around. "Impressive!"

"Hello, Hannah." Hart gave her a kiss on the cheek at the front door.

"Hi, Johnny, how have you been?"

"I've been good. Yourself?"

"Oh, good. *Busy.* My usual—buried beneath a large pile of tedious paperwork!" Hannah muttered quickly and nervously.

"Yet here you are in Southern California." Hart forced a smile, trying his best to maintain his courtesy.

Hannah glanced at him warily, sensing his subtle displeasure in her unannounced arrival. "I've been looking for any excuse to escape the daily grind. You know how it is." She ran her hand along her meticulously groomed hair. "Well, probably not lately. I'm sorry."

Hart laughed gently. "Don't be sorry. Life *has* been different."

"I guess it is different from your usual day-to-day," Hannah nodded, smiling. "Is it a good different? Or a bad different?"

"Good," Hart added. "It has been … humbling."

"Oh, please, Johnny, you are as humble as they come."

Hart smiled at her, but he didn't believe it. He thought about how Ivy breathed in the world whenever she reached the ocean, the way she walked the forest, the way she gazed into the orange sky.

Hannah stared at him curiously for a few seconds longer than necessary.

"Had you been here before with Oliver?" she asked, interrupting his thoughts.

"No, never," he replied. "We'd spent our leave in places like Mexico or Puerto Rico. Ollie would always return here alone." He could feel Hannah examining him already. Inspecting his surroundings and analyzing his progress.

"Well, it is marvelous, and you seem very relaxed here," Hannah grinned. "It suits you. I bet Ollie would have been very pleased you were here." She glanced at him out of the corner of her eye and peered past him through the front door.

"I hope so," Hart replied softly. *Were here?*

"So the boys returned to Monterey rather excited with your progress," she spoke politely in her eloquent British accent. "They told me you were living with a woman who seems to have made an extraordinary impression on you. I'd love to meet her." Hannah scanned the hall from where she stood outside the front door. "Is she home?"

He saw the intrigue in her expression, and a fierce protectiveness seized his heart. Hart hesitated before inviting her in. He didn't want her to meet Ivy or this new world he stumbled upon. Ivy's world ... the world he discovered and so desperately wanted to keep for himself. Hannah had some level of influence over his life in the army, but not here. Ivy had a life that Hannah had no part in, and he intended on keeping it that way.

"She isn't home, but you are more than welcome to come in," he said.

Hart wanted to escort her back to her car, to send her on her way before Ivy ever knew she was here, but Hannah accepted his reluctant invitation without a moment's thought. Her motive for being here was still unclear to him, but Hart concealed his concern when she stepped inside.

"So when did you arrive in Cali?" he asked, closing the door behind her.

"They flew me into Monterey a couple of weeks ago to assist in the resolution of a minor quandary, one with which I won't bore you," Hannah threw her hands in the air. "Honestly, the whole thing was a waste of my time." She walked a few meters into the foyer and then stopped, waiting for his direction.

Hannah cleared her throat nervously when he brushed past her. She could smell the sunscreen on his skin blended with the natural masculine scent that she had shamefully come to recognize over the years. She sighed inwardly at his flawlessness. He stood barefoot in a white tank top and a pair of board shorts, and she was quick to observe his lack of dog tags, but she didn't mention it. Hart was incredibly handsome, more so than ever before. His leave had allowed him to relax on the strict grooming standards that were required of a United States Army Officer, and she noted the subtle changes in his appearance. Hannah always preferred a rugged man. Hart's tan, beard, and longer hair made him look less like the clean-cut soldier she had always known, but more like a beautiful stranger she had met on an island vacation.

He waited for her at the kitchen's entrance.

"So you caught up with the boys then," Hart mentioned, hoping she would clarify the real reason for her visit.

"You needn't worry about Walker and Benji coming to me willingly. I practically backed them into a corner and forced them to talk under General Garvey's instruction." Hannah rolled her eyes.

Hart thought about Garvey and the last time they saw each other in the boardroom. He imagined his disappointment in seeing one of his Phoenix men being ushered away in handcuffs.

"He's devastated about you being on leave for so long. You know that, right?" Hannah asked.

"Hey, it's all in the past. After my appalling behavior in the boardroom, I know I deserved everything I got," Hart said humbly.

"You did what Garvey's been dying to do to that arrogant bastard for over two years now! Believe me, he doesn't care about Hanes," she smirked. "But he was very sorry to lose his finest soldier at such a critical time. Actually, Garvey is the reason I'm here."

Hart led her into the kitchen and listened to her marvel at Oliver's home. Ivy's home. She placed her bag on the island bench and rubbed her hands along its smooth surface.

"So, why *are* you here, Hannah?" Hart asked, his eyes searching hers.

"I knew you would want me to get straight to it."

Hart shrugged apologetically.

"I'm here because Garvey wants me to assess you so that you can return to active duty a tad earlier than the twelve months initially given," she spoke professionally and directly. "It is going against protocol, but the unrest in Tripoli requires us to get our best men back on the ground as soon as possible."

Hart felt the rapid beating of his heart all of a sudden.

"See … it was dreadfully unfortunate that things went down the way they did at your final debriefing," Hannah continued. "A bit of bad luck with timing, as you have it. Hanes was not supposed to have been at that meeting in the first place, and if he hadn't been there overlooking our procedures, then we do believe your leave would not have been quite so … excessive."

Hart stared at her but gave no response.

"Garvey assumed that if they sent you away, then you would be out of sight, out of mind," she grinned. "We decided that everyone would overlook what happened with you in the debriefing, and in turn regret your temporary dismissal at such a crucial time with all that is going on in Tripoli … meaning we could just pop you back into Phoenix earlier than intended and whisk you three away to all the action in Libya! Just like you wanted, remember?" Hannah grinned excitedly, but her enthusiasm quickly faded. She tilted her head at Hart's surprising lack of delight in her good news.

He leaned forward on the island bench. He thought about what she said. He felt her eyes on him, waiting for a reaction of some sort. She looked pleased to be sharing the good news, yet he sensed her confusion with his response. Hart frowned to himself. Returning to action was what he desperately wanted, and for the life of him, he couldn't work out why he wasn't thrilled about her proposal.

Hart nodded eventually, mainly for her sake.

"I expected a very different reaction, to be completely honest," Hannah said. She watched him carefully.

"I know, I'm sorry," Hart agreed with her, rubbing his forehead in thought.

"It's what you wanted," she frowned. "I thought you would be happy. Ecstatic, even."

"I am! Trust me, I am," he smiled kindly at her. "It's incredible news. Thank you, Hannah." Hart rubbed his jaw anxiously and glanced through the open doors behind him, hoping Ivy was still down on the beach. *Ivy* ....

Hannah noticed him checking the back of the estate, as though he were looking for someone.

"Okay. I get it. It's because of her, yes?"

"That I want to stay?" Hart asked.

"You want to stay!?" she replied, wide-eyed.

"No, no," Hart laughed off his unexpected honesty, surprising even himself.

Hannah twisted her face disappointedly. "You realize you don't get a say in the matter. If they ask for you, Johnny, then you must oblige. I'm sorry."

"I know! I know how it works, Hannah." Hart ran his hands irritably through his hair.

She studied him with a concern furrowed deeply into her brow.

"What I meant is that there are a few reasons why I need to stick around." Hart thought about Tommy. "It's hard for me to explain. I'm not comparing it with what is happening in Libya, but ..."

Hannah waited for him to keep going but he didn't. She considered him carefully. Something troubled that big heart of his, but he was being tight-lipped about it. As usual. Hannah never expected anything else from him. Whatever it was that concerned him, she trusted Hart's judgment. He was, after all, the most intelligent and esteemed soldier she had ever met ... plus she hopelessly adored him.

"You don't need to explain," she said in his silence. "How about we get this evaluation underway and then at least I have something to pass onto Garvey. I may be able to hold him off for another month or so, maximum, but when they leave for Libya, Johnny, you must be on that flight. That is definitely beyond my control."

Hart grinned beautifully. "Hannah—"

"Don't give me those eyes." She grinned bashfully. "Damn you for knowing how to melt a woman's heart."

Hart walked around the island and gave her a warm hug. Hannah accepted it happily.

"So, are you going to offer me a drink?"

"Anything you want," Hart replied.

"Is it too early for wine?" she asked, raising an eyebrow. Hart checked his watch and smirked. "3:30 in the afternoon. It's never too early for a drink around here."

Hannah laughed. He was not the soldier she sent away from Base eight months ago. Hart had changed. He was … *happy*.

"Hello," Ivy said softly behind Hart.

Hart tightened his eyes shut when he heard her, unprepared for the collision of his two opposing worlds.

Ivy caught Hannah's exploratory eyes looking her up and down. This woman was strikingly beautiful, in an immaculate, official sort of way. Her suit was impeccably neat, and Ivy instantly recognized the military in her commanding presence. In her self-assured expression. She had a towering confidence … or maybe it was the scarlet Louboutin heels she was wearing. She appeared clinical, but she obviously had a savvy flair for fashion. Her overt assessment made Ivy shift uncomfortably in her gaze, and she instinctively wrapped her fingers around Hart's dog tags, which still hung around her neck.

Hart turned to her, and Ivy caught a fleeting anxiety in his expression.

"You must be Ivy, Oliver's sister!" Hannah grinned, walking past Hart and taking Ivy's hand. "Oh, wow, I've heard so much about you! It is wonderful to meet you finally."

"Hello …." Ivy frowned apologetically, feeling terrible for not having the faintest clue who this woman was. She glanced up at Hart.

"This is Hannah. She is the army's clinical psychologist at the garrison in North Carolina," Hart told her.

"Hi, Hannah, it's lovely to meet you."

"Ollie always thought the world of you, Ivy. He would go on and on about how much he adored you," Hannah diverted her eyes to her wine and sighed. "It was terribly sweet."

Ivy smiled at the thought.

"Ivy, I hope you don't mind, but Johnny and I have a few matters of business to attend to. Can we leave you for ten minutes or so?" Hannah asked.

Hart and Ivy exchanged a fleeting glance.

"Of course," she replied.

"We won't be long," Hart promised. He winked at her and led Hannah into the study.

Ivy thought about him alone in the office with Hannah, the stunning woman she didn't know. She was poised and expressive, and perfectly polished. Ivy noticed the way she looked at Hart; the woman's desire for him was undeniably evident to her. She knew this because Hannah's desire reflected her own. She saw the way Hannah briefly touched Hart's hand as she passed him on her way out of the kitchen, covert but familiar. They were more than just colleagues. Friends? Former lovers? Lovers in waiting, perhaps? Ivy tapped her fingers on the island bench in a hurried agitation, and her thoughts raced through her head at an even faster pace. It was obvious that Hannah fancied Hart, but this wasn't the source of her sudden discomfort with the turn of events. Hannah could unintentionally reignite Hart's anxiety over Oliver's death. It had been months since he had suffered any anxiety attacks, and after this visit, Ivy predicted their unwelcome return.

She heard Hannah's laughter through the closed door, and Ivy rolled her eyes and smiled to herself. The woman was smitten.

Ivy pulled on a gray long-sleeved cotton shirt and walked back outside to the fire-pit. She looked out to the horizon and saw a line of dark clouds swallow the late afternoon sun. The wind crossed the graying ocean and brought with it a chilly bite to the air. The evening was rather cold, considering the morning had been gloriously warm. Ivy crossed her arms to keep warm and lifted her face to the wind that swept over the cliff. Another beautiful day had passed with Hart, but it was ending unlike any other since his arrival in La Mar ... it ended with another woman. A sophisticated woman. A woman who knew something she didn't. She saw it there in her excited green eyes. Ivy trusted her intuition. This woman was here for only one reason, and that was to take Hart away from her. What Ivy couldn't determine, was in what way she would take him away.

She looked around her as the wind caught the trees at the edge of the estate. The gusts were surprisingly powerful. Ivy frowned, sensing the disharmony in her surroundings ... it hung ominously in the cold tumultuous air. She rubbed the warmth back into her arms as the thick blanket of clouds headed angrily toward the coast. There would be no orange sky tonight.

"How are your nightmares?"

"I haven't had one for months," Hart replied, unsmiling.

"That's promising. What about the medication? Are you taking it? Did you refill the prescription I gave to you?" Hannah added, waiting intently for his answer.

Hart bowed his head and glanced at his hands momentarily, then met her gaze again. He remembered all sixty of the white pills sliding around the filthy, motel sink ... managing to catch just two of them in his fingers before the whole lot disappeared down the drain.

"Yeah, I'm taking the medication," he lied.

Hannah didn't notice. "Good."

"I don't need them," he added.

"Johnny, I told you before you that if we don't address your symptoms now, then you will be fighting a different kind of war for the rest of your life."

Hart didn't speak. He sensed her frustration.

Hannah tapped her pen frantically on the open notepad she had laid out on Ivy's desk. "Look, I know you don't want to believe that what is happening to you is real, but—"

"I know it's real," Hart interrupted, annoyed. "I just think it will lessen in time, like all grief."

Hannah shook her head, disappointed. "You're not making this easy for me, Johnny. I'm trying to get you back on Base so that you can return to Libya and find Taym Malak, but you can't even admit to me that you are suffering more than what is considered normal for—"

"Normal?" Hart laughed scathingly. "Who the fuck defines normal, Hannah? People like you!?"

She glared at him without speaking, more saddened than annoyed.

"When was the last time you saw your best friend get shot in the fucking head?" Hart leaned over the desk with two fingers pressed into his temple. A chilling darkness cloaked his eyes.

Hannah took a quick breath and lowered her gaze to her notepad.

"You're sitting here, telling me how I should feel in regards to circumstances that are beyond your capacity to even comprehend!" Hart growled across the desk. "How can you, or anyone, define what is normal after what happened to Oliver?"

Hannah didn't answer.

Hart cursed. "No one understands how I feel. No one understands because this type of shit *never* happens! Because it is not normal!" He leaned back heavily in his chair, feeling Hannah's eyes scrutinize him. She remained disconcertingly quiet, and Hart shook his head and looked away. "What does normal even mean anymore, Hannah?"

Hannah gazed wordlessly at the man sitting in front of her, spellbound, yet heartbroken for him once again. His suffering was excruciating to witness. Hannah tried to take Hart's anger with a grain of salt; soldiers often lost their temper in her inquisitive presence. She was never proud of her intrusion on their hearts and minds, but it was an occupational necessity. Unlike her other patients, however, Johnny's resentment was hurtful and unfamiliar, and Hannah's confidence plummeted in his sudden contrariness with her.

She swallowed quietly before continuing.

"What about Ivy Rose?" Hannah studied his reaction. "Does she understand what is happening to you?"

Hart met her gaze and studied her in return, analyzing her intentions. He didn't reply.

"Johnny, please, I'm trying to help you!" She remembered a time when she could barely draw a hint of displeasure from his lips. She always wanted it. Begged for it. As a psychologist, it gave her something to work with; a project that would keep her awake all night, rattling her perceptive mind for some brilliant solution. Johnny had never given her anything, nothing but a beautiful smile and an aching heart. Hannah placed her hand on her chest, feeling it thump madly and achingly in his forlorn desperation. This is what she had wanted ... and it hurt.

"Ivy," Hart said, thinking about the girl who took his breath away from the moment she opened her door to him. The world had taken so much from her, yet she handled it with a forgiving grace that inspired him. Her innocence was all he needed to mend his broken soul. "Ivy understands."

"Are you in a relationship with her?" Hannah asked seriously.

Hart looked at her coldly for a while before he answered. "What are you asking, exactly?"

"I'm asking if you love her, Johnny."

Hart hesitated. "Ivy has nothing do with any of this. Why do you want to know?"

"Why are you being so defensive?" she replied frustratingly. "Have you told her?"

"Told her what?"

"That Oliver gave his life for you," Hannah answered firmly. "I want to know if you have talked to her about this. I think it would establish whether you have forgiven yourself and have realized that you are not the one to blame for his death."

Hart shook his head.

"Is that a no?" Hannah concluded.

"I haven't told her."

"Okay." She scribbled down a few notes on her notepad, and the room fell quiet for a few minutes.

Hart was sitting precariously on the borderline of post-traumatic stress disorder. Hannah decided he was not definitively one way or the other. His recovery depended solely on one important revelation; Hart needed to accept that he was not responsible for Oliver's death. Once Hart realized this, she believed the rest would fall into place. All signs pointed to a full recovery if he found a way to forgive himself.

Hannah looked up at Hart, who had his face buried in his hands, patiently waiting for her to finish. She knew he needed Oliver's sister to help him find the answer he was searching for. His unwillingness to talk to her about Ivy proved to her that he had real feelings for this girl. He was protecting her. Gallant Johnny Hart. Ivy may be the key to unlock his heart and end his suffering. Perhaps Hart had found his sanctuary, just like she had instructed him to do. With Oliver's sister ... *of all people* ... Hannah took a deep breath with her revelation. Hart was falling in love with the one woman whom he believed he didn't deserve. Ivy had become his means of payback for his guilt for Oliver. He was in love with her, but her presence no doubt tortured him. For Hart, she presumed, it was a small price to pay for his survival. He couldn't leave her until his debt had somehow been repaid, until he had suffered enough to earn his right to live again. He hadn't done this yet. He was waiting, she thought—but waiting for what?

Hannah stared at Hart, who still sat with his head bowed into his hands. He needed more time here to settle the debt that his conscience had concocted. Oliver's sister needed more time.

She sighed resignedly and gently closed her notebook. "Okay, we're done."

Hart looked up from his hands, confused. "Done?"

"Yes."

Hart grimaced. "Things didn't go the way you expected."

Hannah smiled proudly, pleased with her discovery. "Actually, it went a lot better than you think."

A humble confusion twisted handsomely on his face, and Hannah closed her eyes as she walked behind him to the office door, lamenting her misplaced desire. She waited patiently in the foyer while Hart called out to Ivy in the yard. She came in quickly, looking lovely with her wind-swept hair.

"It was a pleasure meeting you, Ivy." Hannah squeezed Ivy's hand affectionately.

"Have a safe trip," Ivy replied.

"You look well, Johnny," Hannah said, as he walked her out. "Take care, and I will keep in touch. See you."

Hart thought about what Hannah had said as the town car pulled away. He could return to Base whenever he wanted. The decision was his. He thought about Taym holed up in the apartment building in Tripoli. *Taym.* He remembered Oliver lying on the hot concrete; he heard the bullet split through his pounding head, and he saw the crystal blue eyes watching him, but this time they didn't close....

Ivy stood before Hart, who was frowning and staring vacantly into her crystal eyes, evoking a cold fear that ripped its way through her aching heart. He wanted Libya. He wanted Taym. He wanted *blood.* She could see it there in his detached, determined expression.

"Are you okay?" she whispered to him.

"I'm okay," he smiled thoughtfully, his mind gradually returning to her on the driveway.

She sensed him reliving the torturous events that made him this way. "Does it hurt?" Ivy asked, looking up at him.

He saw the wind catch her hair. He saw the ocean in her eyes.

Then he saw her smile in his tender, lingering gaze, nibbling at her lower lip … reigniting his soul.

"Not anymore," he breathed, pulling her into his arms.

*Not when I'm with you, Ivy Rose.*

## Chapter 18

"You didn't hear me, did you?" Ivy breathed.

"No, I'm sorry, Ives," Hart replied, sitting up on the sand. He looked down at her beside him and smiled apologetically. "Something about dinner?"

Ivy sighed inwardly, concealing her disappointment. Hart was different after that psychologist's visit. More complex, if it were even possible. A piece of him had left her already, and Ivy knew it was only a matter of time before the rest of him followed. She guessed that Hannah had given him the permission to return to Libya. Hart hadn't said anything to her, but it seemed obvious. Ivy could see the war through his big, vulnerable eyes. The persistent anguish. There was a space she could no longer fill. A yearning. A hunger for the man who murdered her brother.

Ivy sat up and smiled reassuringly at him. "Do you remember Alex Gravelle? The chef from the Silver Moon Gala last year?"

"Yeah, vaguely," Hart replied, smirking with shame as he recalled the eventful night. He scooped up a handful of sand and let it trickle out of his hand.

"Well, he's asked if you and I would like a table at his restaurant tonight. Dinner is on him," Ivy grinned happily. "He's back in town, and he wanted us to try a few samples of what he's planning to serve up for the next Gala. How about it?"

"The Gala is coming up?" he asked, frowning.

"It's only a few months away, Hart. Where has that beautiful mind of yours been these past few days?"

Hart smiled, but it quickly faded. *Libya.* His mind had wandered thousands of miles to a buzzing apartment block in central Tripoli, hunting down Taym Malak. Plotting his revenge. Mentally he had returned to the war. For forgiveness. For mercy. To serve the guilty sentence he had bestowed upon himself. The answers were in Libya ... the answers *had* to be in Libya.

Hart sighed tiredly. He bowed his heavy head into his hands for a few seconds, forgetting Ivy was quietly watching him.

"Come here," Ivy cooed. She lay back on the sand, pulling him down to lay at her side.

Hart lay himself down beside her in the sunshine. He watched her run her fingers through the wavy blonde hair surrounding her as she leaned over him. She parted her red lips as she considered him, and so he rested peacefully in her thoughtful attention. He saw the sunlight glisten on her lips when she glanced up at the sea. He saw the dusting of freckles across her nose when she looked back at him. Her pale blue eyes smiled at him through her dark lashes, and Hart blinked in the fractured sunlight as it filtered through her golden hair and onto his face. It was Libya ... or the ethereal creature who bowed over him and lulled his heavy heart.

Hart knew what he wanted. He'd never been so sure of anything in his entire life. He wanted Ivy, and his fleeting honesty delivered him freedom for a few precious seconds before the freedom surrendered itself to guilt. *Oliver.* Hart looked into her crystal eyes and heard the bullet pierce the silence that surrounded them on the beach. Blood drenched Oliver's eyelids in a thick, scarlet mask. It flowed out of his shattered temple with the beat of his dying heart, and Hart exhaled suddenly ... it was a shard of a painful memory he had locked away. Too heartbreaking to relive. Too tragic to be real.

"Are you okay?" she whispered.

Ivy ran her fingers through his hair and frowned when he didn't answer. His color drained from his olive skin before her very eyes.

"Hart!?" she cried out, holding his face in her hands. Adrenaline stung her pounding heart.

Hart blinked his eyes a few times and then looked at her. He sat up and looked at the ocean. "Sorry, there have been a few things on my mind lately."

"You're thinking about Oliver, aren't you?" Ivy asked, sitting up beside him.

Hart stared at her for a few seconds and nodded. He smiled, embarrassed, and scrubbed his face with his hands.

"It's coming up on one year since he died," she mentioned thoughtfully.

"Yeah, it is."

Hart couldn't believe it. One year. Time was flying by at lightning speed, but with Ivy, time stood still. The war would come calling for him soon, and he would have to leave. Hart thought about Tommy. If that man knew he was leaving for Libya, then Tommy would surely bide his time in the shadows until then. Until the time was right. Until Ivy was left unprotected. News traveled too quickly in this town, and her safety lay in his silence. Tommy could never know he was leaving. No one could. Not even Ivy.

*Another secret.* He had so many. He looked at her beside him, and her trust in him broke his heart. He was never going to tell her the truth. His truths would break her, like they had broken him. He wasn't sure if it was right or wrong—all he knew is that he didn't want to hurt her.

Hart sighed resignedly at the ocean in front of him.

"What's going on in there?" she smiled with sweet concern. She tapped his temple lightly with her finger, then ran her hand down the other side of his face and gently turned his face toward her. Ivy took his hand in hers and held it tightly, binding his suffering to her strength.

Hart looked at her, his eyes filling with torment. "How do you do it, Ivy?"

"How do I do what?"

"How do you keep going?" he replied. "Ollie was your brother."

"Yes, but I didn't spend every day by his side like you did. I spent months away from him ... years, lately," she answered. "It's different for me. Whereas you two were inseparable."

Hart shook his head. "No, you look at the world differently.

You know he is gone, and you accept it. I see the way you look at the world around you, Ivy, like you can see past this life. What can you see? Tell me what you see."

Ivy looked away from him, unsure how to answer. Searching for the words to describe the strength she didn't feel. She had lost everyone, and if she thought about it too much, the grief would easily consume her. Ivy stared at the ocean as she considered his question. She watched the blue ripples on the water's surface in the distance, reflecting the few clouds that lingered in the pale blue sky. She saw the bait fish swimming in and out of the little waves that lapped the shore, their silvery scales gleaming in the sunlight. The terns sat side by side, peacefully tucked into the rocks and facing into the light breeze, unfazed by their presence only meters away from them on the shore. This was as much their world as it was hers. She found it humbling. Life was beautiful. Life was precious. There wasn't one moment when she didn't appreciate what she had before she lost it all. That's what got her through her darkest moments, knowing that she had valued their time together long before it ended. Still, it never stopped the pain. Or the grief. Or the loneliness. It just kept her moving forward at a bearable pace.

Ivy breathed in the world around her and felt her heart hesitate in somber remembrance, but her spirit remained steadfast, fiercely determined not to let her grief defeat her. She looked at Hart who patiently waited for her to answer. There was a softness about him. A deep compassion in his brown eyes as she rifled through her tragic past.

"When I look at the world around me, I see an abundance of natural beauty, which seems to bring me an inner peace." Ivy played with the sand as she spoke, then glanced up at him. "I struggle to look past the natural wonder that has always been here, and I feel like I owe it to the world to be the best person I can be, no matter what happens. No matter how scared or hurt I am. I dare not think about a future where I have given up, nor a world where I have lost all hope." She smiled at him and then looked back at the pattern she had been mindlessly scribbling into the sand.

Hart stared at her, unblinking, captivated.

Ivy bit her lip bashfully, feeling his eyes on her. She glanced at him again and laughed.

"Why are you looking at me like that?" she asked.

Hart smiled adoringly at her, his expression brightening with her magical charm. "When I first arrived, you told me that, when I went swimming," he smirked at her, "I was nothing but a creature on this earth just cooling off in the shallows of an incredibly vast ocean. Like an animal at a waterhole."

Ivy laughed, burying her blushing face into her hands. "Oh, I'm sorry," she laughed.

"No, I understand now." Hart warmed in her sweetness. "Your appreciation is not lost on a world that keeps letting you down, Ivy, because you have learned to strengthen yourself with the same world that weakens you. It's a balancing act of sorts. I didn't understand what you were saying because I let the war misconstrue my feelings for a world I had come to overlook."

Ivy smiled.

"Oliver *always* saw it. Like you. Back then, when you told me I was a creature of the earth … I had only just left the war, Ives. I thought you were crazy," he teased.

Ivy gasped playfully. "So why did you stick around!?"

"Because you were the sexiest woman I had ever seen," he smirked handsomely.

"I can't believe you!" Ivy laughed and pushed him away.

Hart laughed beautifully. He grabbed her resisting arms and pulled her closer to him, watching her with a delightfully wicked expression. He wrapped his strong arms around her, and he felt her lean into him and relax. He thought about the past nine months with Ivy. War could be ruthless and brutal, but nothing had prepared him for the year that followed Oliver's death. *Nothing.* One year ago he had never endured such intense, relentless grief. One heart-wrenching, torturous, beautiful, sexy, unexpected year. One year ago … he had never been in love.

Hart leaned into her and met her crystal gaze. He ran his fingers through her long hair and brushed his mouth across her smooth lips. He breathed in her sweet breath that effortlessly awakened his weary soul … *every time.* Hart sighed into her. He furrowed his brow and closed his eyes tightly; the full wonder of her was still unfathomable to him. He had never expected her. He had never expected La Mar. Hart ran his hand across her smooth cheek and held her close to him. He could feel his heart beating in his chest as he held her face to his, a profound heartbeat that thundered through his soul and stirred something deeper in a place where no one had ever been before, a place he had never known existed until now. Rousing something fierce. Something powerful. Overwhelming him and engaging his entire being and all that surrounded him. All that surrounded them. *Ivy. Oh, Ivy.* He had fallen deeply and irrevocably in love with her.

Hart kissed her lightly on the lips and sighed into her, "Ivy Rose … you are a divine tonic for a broken man."

## Chapter 19

HART AND IVY walked through a large parking lot in town and turned down a street in La Mar that Hart had never seen until tonight. Tree branches twisted elegantly above the street, and quaint boutiques sat nestled in the lush greenery beneath them. They dressed for the occasion; a booking at Gravelle's saw most people waiting well over two months for a table, however, Ivy was welcomed on any day she pleased. Hart wore a pair of beige chinos and a white linen shirt with the sleeves rolled casually to his elbows. Ivy wore a delicate silver lace skirt set, with a long sleeve lace crop top with a V-neckline and elastic bands at the cuffs. Both pieces featured a beautiful scalloped trim and the silver tone complimented her sun-tanned skin and her straightened, long blonde hair. The evening was busier than Hart had thought it would be. It was rather chilly for La Mar, but it didn't seem to bother the locals. The sky was clear and the air was still, and with Ivy smiling brightly by his side, life seemed relatively uncomplicated. For now. Hart ignored the niggling disillusion; welcome to the world of the living ... *but don't get too comfortable.*

He pushed aside a palm frond hanging across the footpath in front of them and ushered Ivy past. Her hand trailed across his chest as she walked by him, making Hart's stomach jump and igniting his desire.

"Gravelle's," she murmured, peering behind him.

Hart's eyes followed a line of lights along a boardwalk that led into a lush garden. Heliconias cascaded exquisitely over the railing, and he could smell the sweet scent of the flowers on the still air. He lost his bearings momentarily.

"I feel like we're in Mexico."

Ivy smiled at him. "Alex was born there."

Hart took Ivy's hand and led her along the boardwalk. The foliage eventually opened to a palapa-styled restaurant with mosquito lanterns that burned around the border of the tropical gardens, exuding a warm and inviting ambiance. A hint of nostalgia simmered contentedly within Hart.

Ivy squeezed his hand. "Nice, huh?"

"Ivy Rose! Eres tan hermosa," Alex beamed with open arms.

Ivy blushed. "Gracias. How are you?"

"Very good, very good." Alex leaned in and kissed Ivy on both cheeks. "You must be Johnny Hart." He turned to Hart with a bright, intrigued expression and held out his hand. "I am pleased to meet you finally. I have heard all about you."

"Pleased to meet you, sir," Hart replied politely, shaking Alex's hand. He looked quizzically at Ivy.

"I haven't spoken to anyone about you," Ivy shrugged. She recalled her conversation with William in the liquor store, but he had already known about Oliver's soldiers.

"No, not Ivy," Alex added with a faint accent. "The whole town talks about you. You were a friend of Oliver's, and everybody loved Oliver. I hear the folk whispering across the tables and don't worry—they like you." Alex pat Hart firmly on the arm. "Come, follow me. We have a beautiful night ahead of us!"

Hart wasn't sure how he felt about Alex's passing comment. He had been hiding in Ivy's pleasurable company for so long now, sailing through her soothing sanctuary of love and light away from the rest of the world ... or so he had thought.

Alex seated them at a private table under a cabana outside. "So the Silver Moon Gala is only a few months away."

"Yes. It snuck up on me this year," Ivy replied, biting her bottom lip and gazing seductively at Hart.

Hart narrowed his eyes at her and then smiled to himself.

"You have been busy?" Alex asked her.

"Very. I don't know where the days go." Images of her and Hart making love in the ocean flashed through her mind, and she glanced playfully at Hart. He shot her a breathtaking smile that warned her not to turn him on, and she repressed an ecstatic tremor.

"Ivy tells me you were born in Mexico," Hart mentioned, forcing his desire for Ivy aside.

"San Agustinillo. Are you familiar with it?"

"I surfed a break at Zipolite once before," Hart grinned. "Azure waters, fantastic food—"

"Yes, this is exactly how I was raised!" Alex interrupted, pleased with Hart's experience with his hometown.

"In fact, it is very similar to La Mar," Hart added, smiling at Ivy.

"I think so, too," Alex nodded. "That is why I opened a restaurant here. My home away from home. Azure water, amazing food ... and beautiful people."

Alex placed his hand affectionately on Ivy's back, and she smiled.

"Well, my friends, I want you to relax," he grinned. Alex turned to a waitress, who was standing attentively beside him. "You take good care of them, my dear."

The waitress nodded.

"I will check on you throughout the evening. Enjoy," Alex shot Ivy a wink and left. The waitress poured two glasses of wine and left them to their drinks.

"So the whole town likes you, eh?" Ivy grinned.

Hart caught the delighted sparkle in Ivy's blue eyes. "Yeah. It's strange."

"Strange?"

He looked at her as he sipped his wine.

"You know what's strange?" Ivy frowned. "That the only person who doesn't like you ... *is you.*"

Hart stared at her for a few seconds and then dropped his gaze to his wine. He swirled the warm red liquid in circles inside his glass, thinking. The folks in town didn't know him. They didn't have the faintest clue about him or what happened in Libya ... what he had done to La Mar's beloved son.

Hart sighed. "There are only a handful of people in this world who really know me, Ivy."

"I know you."

He looked up at Ivy again. Her mouth was slightly parted, and she considered him with a seriousness that panicked his guilty heart. Her wistful eyes saw everything for what it was. He thought his secrets were buried far beyond her reach, but the way she looked at him tonight gave him the impression that she had already unearthed them. He imagined her ethereal presence floating in the darkness within him, confronting the black heart of the devil and luring Hart's secrets from his craven claws. No one could withstand her blinding white light, not even the devil himself.

"I'm sorry to interrupt," the waitress said hesitantly. "Here is your first course." She placed two small plates on the table in front of them and hurried away.

Ivy caught Hart smirking at her from across the table, and she laughed, "Let's try and keep it lighthearted tonight, shall we?"

Her skin glowed warmly in the light of the lanterns, and Hart could barely take his eyes from her.

"Agreed," he laughed.

Ivy's heart floated in the gentle tone of his laughter. He was more handsome tonight than ever before; dressed neatly in his linen shirt and chinos. Hart's youthful appearance was hiding behind a beard inspired by their long idle days by the sea with stolen siestas beneath the palm trees. His hair had grown considerably longer since he arrived. Ivy trimmed it once, a few months ago, after a night of drinking around the fire-pit. Booze, bad lighting, and blunt scissors ... it was a disaster, yet Hart loved it. It was his first hair cut outside the army in fifteen years. For days afterward, he emerged from the bathroom holding out a piece of hair that was longer than the rest, and Ivy would blush in her failure and quickly snip it off. The thought made her smile.

"What is it?" he smirked.

Ivy grinned bashfully and tucked a long lock of hair behind her ear. "I don't know. I think I'm nervous."

"Yeah, I am pretty nervous myself." Hart rubbed his hands together and glanced at the other guests dining around them. "It feels like we're on a date."

Ivy bit her lip timidly. "Our first, official date."

"I'm sorry it took me so long. I'm a little out of practice." Hart's expression was soft and content in her company.

"I think you're doing just fine."

Hart caught her thoughtful gaze.

"So what are your instincts telling you, soldier? Do you think you'll make it to first base tonight?" Ivy giggled adorably into her wine and took another sip.

"I hope so," Hart replied unflappably. He held her gaze for a long while, and then he looked away and shook his head, smiling.

"What is it?" she asked.

Hart laughed humbly. "It's nothing."

"Nothing?" she smirked curiously. "Tell me. I want to know what you're thinking."

He slid his wine glass toward him on the table and smiled to himself before he spoke.

"I lost everything, Ivy. *Everything*," he said in disbelief. He turned his wine glass on the table's surface. "How did you and I come to be, when we began with the worst thing that could have ever happened to us?"

Ivy considered him. The pain was there behind his eyes again. It was never gone for long.

"Because we both loved him," she replied thoughtfully. "Grief is a lonely road to walk, but if I am on a journey down that road, then at least I have you walking beside me."

Hart stared at her, unsmiling all of a sudden.

"I've walked it alone before," she breathed.

Hart reached his hand across the table and rested it on hers. She felt his warmth settle inside her. His kindness. His compassion. She wanted to climb across the table and bury herself in his arms and never leave his embrace. She wanted to tell him that she loved him. More than anything in this world … she loved him.

"What is it?" he asked, noting her sudden silence.

"Nothing." Ivy blushed.

"Nothing, eh?" His striking smile gripped Ivy's heart. "Tell me. I want to know what you're thinking." He grinned playfully.

"Or does that only work on me?"

Ivy laughed into her wine, blushing fiercely. She saw Hart bite his bottom lip and narrow his eyes in desire. He was ridiculously attractive, she thought.

Ivy lay back in Hart's arms on the daybed that was nestled among the palm trees on the restaurant patio. Alex had left them there after he and his staff had finished for the night. It was after 11:30 when Alex left, leaving the keys to the restaurant with Ivy so she could lock up when they were ready to call it a night. The temperature had dropped considerably. Hart sat up and rolled down the shirt sleeves from around his elbows, and let them fall down the back of his tanned hands. He leaned back on the daybed and took Ivy's hand. He rubbed his hand down the inside of her arm and over her palm, and then he fanned her fingers open with his and traced small circles in her hand.

Ivy listened to his slow, soothing breath as he touched her. She looked up at him from his shoulder and cherished the rare contentment in his expression. At that moment, Hart was unafraid. It was an extraordinary moment of untainted ease, and Ivy immersed herself in the fearless freedom she discovered in his arms. His brown eyes were fixed on their hands, but a small smile acknowledged her attentive gaze. She ran her hand across his chest, gliding it through the buttons of his shirt to feel his hot naked skin beneath her hands. Ivy warmed with desire.

"So, it's now 11:45," Hart's voice was husky as he read the time on his watch. "It will be 3 a.m. by the time we get to sleep—"

"3 a.m.?" Ivy twisted her face. "We live ten minutes away."

"I know ... ten minutes too far." Hart ran his hand through her long hair and kissed her. A delicious grin appeared on his face when he pulled away.

Ivy dropped her head back on the daybed and failed to restrain her glorious smile. "Okay, let's go," she laughed.

Hart waited patiently beside her outside the restaurant, watching the street vigilantly. *Instinctively*. It felt like years since he had stood armed and alert in the streets of Libya—it felt like a past life. With Ivy, the memory was almost incomprehensible, but he felt closer to the war tonight than he had since arriving in La Mar.

He sensed something coming for them. A threat. Some kind of foreboding. He narrowed his eyes, remembering Walker's words. *Our instincts keep us ticking. They keep us alive. Keep listening to them, Hart—yours are always spot on.*

Ivy looked into the sky as she locked the gate. "I think it's going to rain."

Hart tucked his hands into his pockets and glanced at the dark sky with Ivy.

She slipped Alex's keys into her jacket pocket and smiled at Hart. "Let's go."

Hart took her hand, and the two of them walked side by side through the empty parking lot. He listened to the silence of La Mar at midnight. Everything appeared to be normal, but his instincts told him something else entirely. He slowed down as they crossed the center of the parking lot, and he pulled Ivy to a halt. Hart narrowed his eyes at the street corner ahead of them.

Ivy looked ahead where he was staring, but there was nothing there. "What is it, Hart?"

He rubbed his jaw anxiously. "I don't know."

She looked back at the corner where he was staring. "Can you hear something?"

"No ... but I feel it."

Ivy's heart beat faster. Hart had survived this long on his soldier's intuition. On his instinct to live. She fell silent, allowing the soldier to analyze his surroundings and their safety.

He pulled her to him when a group of young boisterous men appeared from around the corner. Tommy stood in the middle of them, exuding a smug arrogance that made Ivy sick with fear; he had come for them, just like Hart said he would.

Hart grabbed her quickly and ran back toward Alex's restaurant. She heard the men shouting behind them, hollering in excitement, their shoes pounding the asphalt of the parking lot. She could hear them closing in on them, and a breathless sound of fear escaped her lips. They weren't going to make it back to the restaurant.

Hart stopped her suddenly and pulled her to him. He pressed her against the brick wall at the far end of the parking lot and bent down to look directly into her eyes. Ivy stared back at him, panting through her fear.

"Stay behind me. Everything will be alright." Hart spoke to her with a calm and proficient confidence. His eyes were wide with grave seriousness, but Ivy found comfort in his composure. "Stay behind me, Ivy, okay?" he repeated, willing her to respond.

Ivy nodded out of breath. "Yes, yes … I will."

Hart turned to the group of men, who had formed a large semicircle around them, caging Hart and Ivy against the wall. They were armed with baseball bats and angry fists, and Hart analyzed each man who gathered around him. He stood in front of Ivy, unsmiling and unflinching.

One of the men to Ivy's right shot her a menacing smile and she exhaled in fear. She tightened her grip on Hart's shirt and leaned into him. Her brave soldier. Her shield of armor. The unwavering guard standing his watch.

*"Everything will be alright,"* she whispered to herself, clinging to her fleeing courage.

"So, how was dinner?" Tommy asked, smiling complacently at Hart.

His friends laughed.

"Not too bad," Hart replied, unruffled.

"My favorite dish is the sweetened quail." Tommy theatrically rolled his eyes back into his head and placed his hands on his chest. "To die for. I asked Alex to make it for me last night, but he was all out of quails. Fucking idiot!" Tommy looked at his friends for a laugh.

"You know, it's funny you mention it," Hart scratched his chin. "That was the first dish he gave us tonight."

Tommy glared at him, and the group fell silent.

"Then do you agree?" Tommy asked.

Hart considered Tommy's next move. Tommy didn't care about the quail—he was talking about Ivy. He recognized the thirst for blood in the men's eager expressions. It was ten against one, and they were here to fight, not talk about dinner.

Hart stepped backward and placed a protective hand against Ivy. He grinned dangerously, "Yeah, Tommy. *It was to die for.*"

Tommy glanced at two of his friends in front, and without a word, they pounced on Hart.

Ivy screamed at the sudden attack. Hart took on two men at once, and she pressed herself against the wall and tightened her eyes until they were almost closed. She squinted at the battle through her eyelashes and flinched when one of the men's hands came grasping for her past Hart. Hart elbowed the man in the face, then used him as a shield as the second man threw a roundhouse punch at Hart. The man gasped when his friend's head intercepted the punch, and Hart kneed the battered man in the groin before shoving him into the wall beside Ivy.

She threw her hands over her ears when the man crashed beside her. He fell unconscious away from her, but she could still hear the clashing of flesh in front of her. Hart moved swiftly. He was lightning fast, and Ivy knew that these slow-witted La Mar friends that Tommy liked to keep were no match for Hart's expertise. Once again, Hart showed her a life she had no part in, an elite soldier's life. She had spent a lifetime with soldiers, but only one was persistently challenged by the world around her. *What was it about Johnny Hart that the world so desperately wanted from him?* Ivy yelped when the second man hit the wall on the other side of her and slumped to the ground.

The fighting stopped momentarily, and Ivy dropped her hands from her ears. Hart panted in front of her, poised for another attack. His hands were out beside him, and his fingers were open and ready for his next opponent. His gentle, attentive, warm hands. Ivy's heart sunk.

"This ain't looking like some washed-up soldier!" said one of the men without taking his eyes off Hart, discernibly shaken. "I thought you said he was fucking weak with panic attacks or some shit like that, Tommy!"

"He was!" Tommy replied, baffled by Hart's calm composure after flooring two of his boys in less than fifteen seconds. "You saw him at the Gala!"

Hart glared at the rest of them with a steely expression that forced his third opponent to hesitate before he even reached him. Hart didn't move—he stood resolutely in his place in front of Ivy, examining the fickle group of men that surrounded them.

"I say we get the fuck out of here," another man said, his eyes wide with fear.

"No!" Tommy growled. "You stay right where you are, you fucking cowards! Cody, take him down!"

The men glanced at each other cagily, each one as petrified as the other. The man who had previously backed away approached Hart again, bolder under Tommy's direct order.

"Cody, please, don't do this!" Ivy pleaded from behind Hart.

"I'm sorry, Ives," Cody replied. "Forgive me, Ollie."

Hart hesitated. He frowned and shook his head at the man in front of him. He had already sized this man up for the fight; same height, same build, but there was something about Cody that looked disturbingly kind. Now Hart knew why … because once they shared a friend. Cody had a grim look in his gray eyes. This guy was here to prove himself to Tommy, so Hart pushed aside their common ground and braced for Cody's attack.

Cody reached into his back pocket and pulled out a thumb knife, and he flicked the four-inch blade open with a daring grin. The men cheered behind him. Their chances at bringing him down had just risen significantly, and Hart knew they all felt a little braver for it. It didn't perturb him. He heard a small sound of concern from Ivy and without looking, Hart pressed her against the wall behind them, shielding her as much as he could from the weapon. Cody's expression was proud and overconfident, but it was the tentativeness in his original approach that gave away his fear. Hart wasn't worried, just disappointed.

Cody lunged at him with the pocket knife, swinging it twice at Hart, who easily dodged the blade before Cody backed away again. Cody lunged again at an angle that meant Hart couldn't avoid the knife without harming Ivy, and so he took the blade instead. Hart groaned when the blade carved through his flesh.

Ivy cried out and reached for him, but Hart pushed her back with his firm, reassuring hand. The men grew louder with their thirst for blood. She watched them stalk Hart as though he were a dangerous animal, cruelly provoked for their sick enjoyment. Cody came for Hart again, and with a few swift moves from Hart, Cody hit the tarmac in front of her with a sickening thud, and she gasped. He was out cold, and for a few seconds, she wondered if Hart had killed him.

"Holy shit!" A man panted madly. He moved restlessly in his position among the other men. "Did you just kill Cody!?"

Hart didn't reply. He stared down each of the men around the dwindling semicircle and waited for his next contender.

"He's fucking dead!" The same man shouted.

"Will you stop losing your shit?" Tommy ordered.

"He just killed Cody!" he shouted, his voice breaking in panic. The man ran his hands through his hair, panting frantically on the midnight air.

His distress spread quickly throughout the rest of the group. Tommy cursed loudly, and from a safe distance he studied his friend's body, face down and motionless in the parking lot. The men glanced at each other with wavering confidence, waiting for the confirmation of Cody's death. Together, the men shifted their gaze to Hart, clearly unsettled by what they had seen so far.

Hart stared back calmly, giving away nothing, not even the fact that the knife wound hurt like hell.

"He's not fucking dead. Man up, boys!" Tommy glared at Hart. "This soldier is pathetic! I bet he's never killed a man in his life."

Hart tried not to think about the lives he'd taken, but he did think about Oliver. He had done more than just kill Ollie; he'd perversely taken it a step further and slept with his sister, without disclosing to her any of his accountability for her brother's death.

Tommy smiled at Hart. "This son of a bitch stole my girl. It will all be worth it in the end, boys, I promise."

Ivy shuddered to think what he meant, but before she had a second to question his intentions, Hart was fighting again. She heard their bodies hitting the ground around her. Tommy hollered orders to his friends with a voice that grew increasingly anxious under Hart's unanticipated charge. Hart was a powerful, fearless opponent and Ivy was grateful for it, but she couldn't let him fight to protect her any longer.

"Stop," Ivy whispered with her eyes closed. "Stop!" She considered her surrender for Hart's sake. She would walk into Tommy's arms, and this would all be over. Tommy had it within him to assault her again, but somehow, this was far worse. She had been a spectator of Hart's suffering for too long.

With her eyes closed, Ivy took a deep breath with her outlandish, reckless decision, and prepared to forsake herself for the soldier who proved to her over and again that he would gallantly fight for her until the very end. She gathered all her courage and stepped away from Hart, and then someone grabbed her before she could walk any further. Ivy gasped and opened her eyes.

"Are you okay?" Hart asked.

"Me? Yes, I'm fine," Ivy replied, confused.

"Good, let's go," Hart replied. He quickly took her hand and led her away.

Ivy followed him through the scatter of groaning bodies that were writhing on the ground. Her eyes widened in disbelief as he dragged her away from the dismal scene.

"You fought all of them!?"

"Hurry, Ivy," Hart replied, pulling her along behind him.

"How?" Ivy asked, stunned. She saw Tommy rise as Hart ushered her to the center of the parking lot. "Tommy …."

Hart glanced behind him. Tommy levered himself off the ground, using the wall to steady himself. The group of men gradually rose around him, except for a few who remained too dazed to stand.

"Shit," Hart breathed to himself. He rubbed his jaw and looked into Ivy's frightened gaze. "Go. You need to go. I'll hold them off."

"No, I'm not going without you, Hart!" She turned back to him after he pushed her away and followed him toward the men.

Hart turned back to her, growing frustrated. "Go, Ivy! I'm serious!"

"I'm not leaving you here with them!"

Hart sighed in frustration and looked back at Tommy against the wall of the parking lot. He had his hand behind his back, and Hart instantly recognized the motion. He turned to Ivy behind him with a panicked expression.

"Run, Ivy!" Hart's deep voice resounded across the parking lot.

Ivy froze with fear, alarmed by his sudden intensity, but Hart came for her anyhow. He grabbed her hand and pulled her toward the street at a frantic pace, and so Ivy ran with him.

Hart sensed the gun. There was no way Tommy could continue to fight after his thrashing, not without another card up his sleeve. One that could trump Hart's expertise and his speed. He had planned for Ivy to run—he hadn't planned for her not to listen. His next move was to get her to the cover of the nearest building, but an excruciating sound stopped him before they reached the edge of the parking lot. Tommy racked the slide of his pistol. The sound was torturously familiar, and Hart exhaled into the cold, night air and remembered the day that changed his life irreversibly. *Oliver.*

He pulled Ivy into him and breathed in her sweet, scented hair, desperate to block out the memories of his friend's death, but they flashed relentlessly through his mind. His demons rejoiced in the unexpected account, excitedly summoning the devil from the darkness that had almost left him entirely. The devil had been waiting for him. Waiting for his fear, no matter how fleeting it would be. Hart could hear him laughing—either Tommy or the devil—sniggering wickedly while his mind replayed the earth-shattering moment when he lost everything. His best friend … his world … his soul. He held Ivy close to his heart. The trembling shook his soul, but he fought off the urge to fall. Hart's strength grew exponentially in Ivy's illuminating presence, and he was not about to lose another Rose.

He quickly pulled Ivy in front of him with his back to Tommy. This time it would be different. This time he would do what he had ultimately come here to do … to protect Oliver's sister. To honor his promise to a fallen friend.

Ivy looked past him at the disgruntled men who were slowly regrouping.

"Ivy, look at me." Hart held her firmly, turning her face to him when she didn't listen. "Look at me, Ivy!"

She met Hart's troubled gaze. The seriousness in his expression frightened her. Ivy glanced behind Hart again, and Tommy's gun flashed dully in the glow of the streetlight. She stepped away from Hart.

"Oh god," she breathed faintly, going pale.

Hart stepped toward her and held her tightly.

"Hey, hey, Ives, don't you worry," he replied calmly, holding his big hands on either side of her face. He looked directly into her eyes, sensing her distress. "Everything will be alright. I am right here by your side, remember. I'll protect you, Ivy. I promise."

"I'm sorry, Hart," she replied, shaking her head.

"Don't be sorry."

"You told me to run, and I didn't," Ivy breathed. "What if

they hurt you?"

"Don't worry about me. I'll be fine," Hart smiled reassuringly at her. He ran his thumbs tenderly across her cheeks. "It doesn't matter what happens to me. I've been through worse, believe me." He looked into her crystal eyes and pictured Walker, Benji, and himself, bowed over Oliver's lifeless body.

Ivy trusted him with her life. His expression was dark and determined, yet he exuded a calmness that soothed her panicked heart. She took a deep breath, feeling the heat of his beautiful hands against her cheeks, then she nodded. Hart nodded back and turned to face Tommy, shielding her behind him once again. Most of the men were now shifting into a ring around the two of them in the center of the parking lot and Ivy reached for Hart's hand.

"I have to say, you knew that sound very well. I'm impressed." A revived arrogance consumed Tommy. "It makes me wonder, does the sound of a racking slide turn you on, Johnny?"

Hart didn't reply.

"I like to think it turns you on," Tommy laughed. He looked to his friends for some enthusiastic comradery. The men sniggered revoltingly through their bleeding lips and broken noses.

Ivy grimaced. She took a handful of Hart's shirt and leaned into him, losing her faith in the men she once knew.

"What do you want, Tommy?" Hart responded sternly, glaring straight past the barrel of the gun at Tommy's conceited face.

"You know what I want," he replied, waving his gun in the air as he spoke. "I want her! I want Ivy back!"

"No, you don't," Hart shook his head and smiled. "You can fool your friends here, but you can't fool me. What do you *really* want?"

Tommy stared at Hart, his expression filling with a distaste for the soldier. "You think you're better than me. Don't you, soldier?"

"Soldier?" Hart repeated, laughing to himself. He rubbed his chest and glanced at each of the men surrounding him. "See, I know men like you, Tommy. I get it all the fucking time. You don't want Ivy anymore, you want me. You have something to prove."

Ivy twisted her face behind Hart. She had known Tommy since she was fourteen … she knew how he felt about soldiers. Ivy cursed herself for not mentioning it to Hart earlier.

"My father was a soldier," Tommy stated.

Hart didn't speak. He shook his head tiredly and let Tommy continue. Altercations like these were old news for him, but he forced himself to remember this was a life-changing moment for his opponent. His patience bought him time to strategize.

"Let's just say we have a difference of opinion when it comes to the U.S. military getting involved in everybody else's business," Tommy added, nodding at his friends with a smug superiority.

Hart shrugged, indifferent to his opinion.

"What I fail to understand is why you choose to follow the orders of old men who sit around boardrooms and get off on the disillusionment of countries that are politically weak or unstable. It's intimidation. It's domination!"

"It seems I misjudged you, Tommy," Hart said dryly. "You are quite the emissary of peace."

Tommy tightened his lips, his face flushing with Hart's sarcasm. "We're here to fight assholes like you who raid innocent countries and occupy them as your own!" he shouted.

The men hollered in agreement.

"We fight assholes like you," Tommy added, "for our country—"

"I fight for my country!" Hart growled abruptly.

Ivy jumped in fright at Hart's sudden retaliation. She sensed his fury and his outrage, but only Ivy recognized the deep-set anguish in his voice. The disappointment at his failure.

She closed her eyes sadly behind his back. Hart's unrelenting self-contempt broke her heart.

"I fight for my country, and I fight for the people in other countries who are incapable of defending themselves." Hart continued determinedly. "I teach them how to protect themselves because they don't know how to. That is not oppression; it is liberation. Freedom comes at an extremely high price no matter where you are in this world. Someone inevitably pays for it, and that is where I come in."

Tommy shook his head unpleasantly. "See, like I said, you think you're better than me."

"I never said that." Hart shook his head, discouraged by their lack of tolerance. There would always be people who didn't agree with him, but Hart didn't ask for their support; he only asked for their respect, which they gave to anyone else who risked their lives to help others. He didn't fight because he had to; he fought because he wanted to. For his country. For his brothers-in-arms. He fought to protect the people he cared about so they could live their lives without the fear he confronted every day.

Tommy sent him a sinister smile. Hart recognized his real enemy. In countries like Libya and Afghanistan, the enemy was easier to identify because they wore their hatred proudly. Here in the United States, the enemy was harder to identify in the crowd. Hart glared at Tommy with his gun still aimed at his chest. There he was, the most dangerous enemy of them all ... concealed behind a prep boy façade and his freedom of speech.

"No one should fall on their knees and kiss the ground you soldiers fucking walk on!" Tommy smiled at his friends for support. "Look at you! You're not a hero we should worship, you're a fucking puppet we should piss on."

Hart felt Ivy lean her forehead against his back. He despised Tommy for putting her through this, forcing her to listen to his disillusioned opinion of soldiers, especially after losing Oliver.

"We never ask for praise, but we do appreciate respect. Like everybody else," Hart said judiciously, sensing the sudden rise in Tommy's volatility. "People are entitled to their opinion, including yourself, and I don't want to stand here with you splitting hairs and debating the decisions in which we have no say."

Tommy stared at him, unblinking and unimpressed.

"But if it is Ivy you want," Hart continued, "then I will stand here all night with you if I have to."

"Give her to me," Tommy replied.

"No."

Ivy gripped the back of Hart's shirt. He stood before her without fear. Hart's skills were extraordinary, but they were no match for a loaded gun. Hart would never give her up without a fight, and this was a fight he would lose. Ivy leaned into Hart and breathed him in. His soothing scent. His warmth. Then reluctantly, she stepped away from him, straight into the arms of the men behind her.

Tommy grinned at Hart. "You made the right choice, darling."

Hart narrowed his eyes, confused, and turned to Ivy. Immediately he went for her, but he was blocked by two men. Hart punched one of them in the face, and the man dropped like a lead weight to the ground. The second man went to hit him, but Hart grabbed his wrist and twisted his arm until he was forced to cry out and fall to the ground. Hart reached for Ivy—then the gunshot cracked the still, midnight air, stopping Hart and the rest of the men in their tracks.

Hart's dark eyes glanced ruefully at her. She shuddered in his black, lifeless gaze. Ivy heard her breath expel sharply from her lungs and she willed herself to breathe again.

Hart turned away from her to face Tommy, who had his handgun raised above his head and pointed proudly at the sky.

"Next one is on you, my friend," he smirked, lowering his aim at Hart again.

Hart bowed his head and sighed; crushed by her selfless decision to save him. He growled through his teeth into the cold air. *Not again ... not again!*

Tommy stepped away from Hart in response, fear marring his conceited exterior.

"Tommy, please!" Ivy cried.

"Move her out of the way, boys," Tommy ordered. "Set her up over here, that way she won't miss anything."

One of the men leaned into Tommy's ear. "Do this quick, Tom! The whole town would've heard that shot!"

Hart watched the men drag Ivy around the parking lot, and she stumbled as they pushed and pulled her into position. It reminded Hart of the young girl he had saved from the armed insurgent in Libya. Almost one year later, he was in the same predicament, but under entirely different circumstances ... because he was in America. He was *home*. Hart questioned the world he tried to protect. His country. The people. He blinked his eyes in confusion, temporarily disoriented by their hatred. The emptiness carved a fresh hole into his heart, and he recognized the emotionless calm take him over. The darkness ... and he welcomed it. Nothing could hurt him here.

He looked back at Ivy. He saw the ocean in her sparkling blue eyes. He saw the white sand on her sun-kissed skin. He saw the sunshine in her long, golden hair. He saw her smile at him and take him into her saving arms. *Ivy. My savior ... my punishment.* He had it coming, he thought.

Tommy walked toward Hart, who was now surrounded by five men.

"Get on your fucking knees," Tommy ordered, pressing his gun to Hart's head.

Ivy groaned as she watched.

Hart smiled as he dropped to his knees and then he looked up at Tommy. "Are you going to hide behind your gun for the rest of the night?"

Tommy laughed. "Not for too much longer."

Tommy threw a punch to the side of Hart's face, and Hart bowed his head as he recovered. He heard Ivy cry out for him. He wanted to go to her. To hold her. To remind her that this was okay. No matter what happened ... he had been through worse. He received another blow to the other side of his face, and Ivy cried out again. His ears thumped with the sound of his throbbing head, and instead of recoiling from the pain, Hart embraced it. He wanted it. He longed for the punishment; nearly a year of pleasure after promising himself pain. The guilt had festered inside of him all this time, and now he had the chance to pay for his sins. For Oliver, and now for Ivy.

Tommy hit him hard in the knife wound, and Hart doubled over in agony. He groaned loudly into the ground until two of the men lifted him again. Tommy hit him above the left eye with the hand grip of the gun. The force split the skin, and Hart crashed to the ground with a painful grunt.

Tommy bent down to look at him, and Hart smiled faintly at him through the darkness.

"What the fuck is wrong with this guy?" Tommy laughed. "Why is he smiling like that?"

The man holding him snorted. "Who the fuck knows?"

"He likes it," another guy laughed.

Hart pulled himself to his knees again and smiled at Tommy.

The blood pooled in the back of his throat, and he spat a mouthful of it at Tommy's feet.

Tommy grimaced in disgust. "Sick, masochistic bastard!" He kicked Hart in the stomach and nodded smugly as the soldier collapsed on the ground again.

Hart writhed on the cold tarmac and coughed the air back into his lungs.

"Stop!" Ivy cried out. *"Tommy, stop!"*

Tommy glanced at her. He tucked his gun into the back of his pants and pushed his hands into his front pockets. Then he dawdled cheerfully over to Ivy. She tried to move away, but two of his friends held her in place.

Ivy whimpered when he reached her. She could see them beating Hart in the background, and she finally succumbed to her tears.

"What's wrong, Ives?" Tommy asked. "You've seen enough?"

"Please," Ivy breathed, "someone will be here any minute. Let him go."

Tommy glanced behind him at Hart, who lay face down in the center of the parking lot. He laughed again and looked back at Ivy with an amused expression.

"What are you worried about? He fucking loves it!" Tommy beamed.

His friends laughed either side of her.

"Why are you doing this? He's been through so much. What you're doing is sick, Tommy! What happened to you!? What happened to the kind-hearted boy I once knew?"

Tommy grabbed her jaw aggressively, and Ivy gasped. He leaned into her and pulled her face toward his and she caught the desperate rage in his blue eyes.

"You, Ivy! You happened to me," he growled under his breath.

Her sad eyes filled with atonement. "You cannot force something that isn't there."

Tommy stared at her without blinking; searching her soul through her pale eyes. The anger faded, and his face softened, and for a brief moment, she recognized the fourteen-year-old boy whom she had once adored.

"Please," she whispered.

Tommy peered at the men holding her and nodded. They instantly let her go.

"Let's move," he ordered, glancing around at the other men. "Everybody, let's move!"

Ivy watched them leave, and then she ran to Hart's side. She kneeled down beside him and helped him to his knees. Blood dripped from his mouth, and Hart spat a mouthful of it on the ground beside him, away from Ivy.

"Here …." Ivy tried to help him to his feet, but Hart brusquely withdrew his arm from her and stood on his own.

He wiped the blood from his mouth with the back of his hand, and then he glanced fleetingly at her with dark, furious eyes.

Ivy stared back at him, stunned. "I'm sorry. This is all my fault—"

"Stop apologizing to me! Goddamn it, Ivy!" Hart shouted without looking at her.

Ivy winced in his anger.

Hart growled at his appalling behavior, but he was in no mood to explain himself. He lifted his shirt and inspected the knife wound across his stomach.

She watched him wipe the blood from his wound with his shirt and spit another mouthful of blood behind him. She didn't know how to help him if he didn't want her to. Ivy's heart beat restlessly. He glanced at her again, and she recoiled in the unfamiliar hostility of his dangerous black eyes. Ivy instinctively took a step away from him. She imagined him in the desert surrounded by the enemy. Commander Johnny Hart, a lethal force that you would be damned to mess with. Except for tonight. Tonight the enemy won because she disobeyed his command. She didn't stay by his side. She gave herself up … *for him*. Ivy saw the anguish cloak his eyes when he looked at her again. The trust that took months to build took only seconds for her to tear down.

Hart cursed in pain and inspected the laceration across his stomach, and Ivy gasped. Without thinking, she placed her hands tenderly around the wound on his stomach, but Hart quickly grabbed her wrists. Ivy looked up at him in surprise. He held her there for a brief moment, then he carefully pushed her away.

"Why won't you let me help you?" A frustrated tone lingered in her small voice.

"I'm okay, Ivy. Just leave me be," he replied, growing irritated.

"You're not, look at you!" she breathed. "Is it me? Are you angry with me?"

"I'm not angry with you!" Hart snapped.

He tore off a piece of his shirt, which hung loosely at his hips, and wrapped the piece of cloth around a deep cut on the palm of his hand. Another knife wound Ivy had missed during the fight.

Hart winced. "I knew Tommy would come for me. I told you he would. I fucking deserved it, too. It's fucking *karma!*"

"Karma?" She glared at him, baffled by his outburst. "What for?"

Hart turned his back on her and walked away a few meters and groaned, this time in frustration. *The truth.* It always came down to what happened in Libya.

"What? What aren't you telling me?" she asked walking after him. A nervous fear racked her heart. "Talk to me, Hart!"

He paced in front of her, breathing heavily and clenching his trembling hands by his side. He heard his friend's gentle tone through the white, anxious noise in his head ... *take me instead, Taym. Let Hart return home safely. Take me instead* ... Hart growled furiously into the sky, enraged with his uncontrollable thoughts.

Ivy's strength wavered in his anger. When she thought about it, she didn't want to hear what happened that day. If Hart told her why he was here, why he was *really* here, then she was terrified he might leave. She couldn't help but think Hart was biding his time here with her in La Mar until he was ready to tell her everything. Waiting for the right moment to tell her the truth, right before he would leave her forever.

Hart bowed his head into his hands and stood there, motionless. Thinking. He felt her there beside him, but he couldn't look at her. He sighed resignedly into the cold night air and turned to meet her troubled but compassionate gaze.

"They could have killed you," Ivy said before he could speak. She ran her hands through her long hair and stared at him. Studying him.

"They were never going to kill me, Ivy," Hart smiled dryly,

shaking his head.

Ivy didn't know. She shivered as she recalled Tommy's gun at Hart's head. It was the first time she had ever seen a gun. It would have been so quick, so final. If Tommy had wanted to kill Hart tonight, then he could have in a mere second ... and she would have spent a lifetime coming to terms with it. Like Hart was with Oliver. She thought about him watching her brother die, and Ivy bowed her head to hide her quivering lip.

Hart sighed. His brown eyes filled with a resigned guilt. "I'm not angry with you, Ivy."

Ivy stared at the ground, hiding her tears. Her shoulders rose and fell with her shallow breath.

"I could never be angry with you," he breathed agonizingly. His heart plunged in her silence. "The truth is ... I don't deserve you. I don't deserve to be here."

Ivy looked up at him. Her expression fell.

"To be completely honest, I never deserved to live," Hart hesitated. "Ollie should be here with you, Ivy, not me."

Ivy's heart beat madly in trepidation. "Please, Hart ... *don't speak.*"

Hart stopped talking and stared at her painfully. She breathed out in relief. His lip bled still, his soft, beautiful lips. Ivy closed her eyes despairingly when he opened his mouth to speak again.

"Ivy—"

"No. Please." She raised her hands to stop him speaking and stepped away from him toward the street.

"You need to know the truth."

"Not now, not after what happened tonight," Ivy pleaded. "You could have died."

Hart took a hesitant step toward her in the empty parking lot. He wasn't afraid to die—he had learned to conquer the fear of death long ago. He laid his life on the line for his country more times than he could ever recall. They all had. Walker, Benji ... *Oliver.* He regarded the rare sadness in her eyes, then a realization awakened inside of him. Hart recognized a new emotion in her that he was still coming to terms with himself ... *fear.*

Hart stared at her, unblinking. Almost one year ago he caught her in his arms at her front door; it was the only time he had witnessed the intensity of her grief. Ever since then, Ivy had become a beacon of light and strength in his darkness. Her crystal eyes carried the ocean and the sky and the forest and her love, but there was never fear. This was new. That was his mark on her. *His fear.* He rubbed his forehead and looked away from her in his dire revelation. Ivy had become too invested in him, scared he might be taken from her like everyone else she had loved. He made her vulnerable and susceptible to loss, again, and now his guilt for Oliver included the sister he was supposed to protect.

*What have I done?*

He slipped away to the black place inside of him, where his guilt manifested in its full glory. The devil opened his doors to him, and Hart walked in, world-weary and exhausted. Prepared for punishment. Ready to be defeated. He never deserved her love. Never. He remembered the night they made love for the first time, another deal made with the devil ... *he would succumb to her divinity, and then later to his atonement.* Hart closed his eyes with a resolute determination to make things right. It was time to say goodbye.

He looked into the black sky above them, and he sensed the rain before it fell.

Ivy felt his soul surrender itself in defeat. The emptiness suddenly clouded the warmth in his eyes, and the weariness reclaimed his jaded heart. She saw the soldier within him rise. He wanted the war. He wanted Taym Malak. Then once he had his revenge, Hart wanted to die.

Ivy lost her breath at the thought. The world shook beneath her feet and the rain began to fall. The sky wept for her broken soldier. Tears for her broken heart. Hart had made his decision. He was leaving her ... with no intention to return.

She looked up at Hart. "You don't care what happens to you, do you? You were ready to die tonight."

"Ivy, you don't understand—"

"No, I get it," she interrupted breathlessly. The parking lot spun in her anxious haze, and it dawned on her ... Hart needed the punishment to make him feel worthy again. To earn himself another day.

Ivy choked on her distress. The rain was cold against her skin, and she shivered on her own in the space she had now found herself standing, a thousand miles away from the soldier she adored.

"You feel guilty, don't you?" she asked. "Because you survived and my brother didn't?"

Hart stared at Ivy. He wanted to tell her it wasn't true, but he couldn't lie to her, not anymore. He wanted to pull her into his arms and let yet another storm blow over them, but he didn't. He had protected Oliver's sister. It was all he ever came here to do. He belonged to Libya now. To his duty as commander of the Phoenix unit. To his revenge. So he could repay Oliver's life with his own, because he was never meant to survive that day. Ivy was right.

Hart bowed his head and watched the blood drip out of his mouth and fall into the black puddle of rain beneath him, and then he closed his eyes.

"Hart?" Ivy's voice broke sadly. She waited in silence. His chest glistened through his torn shirt. His shoulders rose and fell in the light of the streetlamp. Drenched with rain. Burdened with contrition. Ivy shook her head sadly when he didn't answer. "You're making deals with the devil."

He looked up at her with a cold intensity that frightened her. "At least he understands."

Ivy exhaled, lost for words. His coldness drove a stake through her heart, and she felt it shatter to pieces. She shook again in the wet cold and bravely fought back her tears.

Ivy turned when a car pulled up behind her on the street.

"You alright, Ma'am?" The taxi driver called out through his car window, warily studying Hart who stood defeated in the center of the parking lot, physically and mentally.

Ivy nodded. "Yes, thank you."

"Is he causing you any trouble?"

"No. Never."

"You need a ride home then?"

Ivy looked back at Hart. She could hear her broken heart beating against the sound of the falling rain.

"Come with me," she breathed, miserably anticipating his rejection.

Hart shook his head. "Just go, Ivy."

Ivy breathed out slowly through her pursed lips, fighting

back her tears. He bowed his head in the falling rain, and she wished for it to wash away the sins he had assigned to himself. She begged the universe to release him from his survivor's guilt. To liberate him from the damning chains that shackled him to his best friend, the friend who would never get the chance to tell him it was okay that he lived.

Ivy sighed into the rain. She had shown him the life he deserved, and now it was up to him to decide if he was worthy of living it. She pulled her hood over her head and ran toward the taxi. Ivy climbed into the backseat and mindlessly wiped away the rain that pooled on her jacket. A lonely tear rolled down her dejected face, and she wiped it away without thinking.

"Where am I taking you, Ma'am?" The taxi driver asked her.

"Home," Ivy answered stoically. "La Jolla Estate."

Hart wiped his face and took a deep breath as the taxi disappeared down the street without him by her side. For the first time in years, Hart was truly alone. He looked up into the sky and watched the rain as it fell through the light of the streetlamp toward him. It soothed his broken, bleeding skin, and Hart closed his eyes and allowed himself to fall now that Ivy was gone. His wounds didn't bother him; he was well accustomed to these. It was the way she looked at him that cut him the deepest. The disappointment. The heartbreak in her crystal eyes. *Finally.*

Hart's hands trembled by his side, so he clenched them angrily and growled fiercely into the sky. His shoulders fell under the weight of Ivy's heavy heart. He couldn't do this to her anymore. She had suffered for him long enough.

"You're right. I was ready to die tonight," Hart whispered to her through the midnight air. He took a deep breath and sighed into the rain. "For you, Ivy ... I would have died for you."

*Chapter 20*

"You run into a mountain lion on your jog this morning?" Benji frowned at him.

Hart smiled at Benji, who sat across from him on the edge of the pool with his legs dangling in the cool turquoise water. Benji was shirtless with a baseball cap sitting backward on his head, and Hart could see himself in his friend's mirrored sunglasses. Walker and Benji had arrived from Monterey around 10 am this morning, and their company could not have come at a better time. His hostility with Ivy last night had earned him a deserved coldness from her, and he didn't have the heart to beg for her forgiveness. Not when he was leaving for Libya any day now.

The afternoon was surprisingly warm after last night's downpour, and the warming sunshine helped lift his dark mood. He pushed his sunglasses closer to his eyes and looked up at Benji.

"Not a mountain lion. Tommy," Hart answered casually, running his hand along the knife wound on his stomach. He had stitched himself up last night, aided with a bottle of scotch and one of Ollie's first aid kits. No one had even seen his black eye yet.

Hart removed his sunglasses and smiled meekly across the pool.

Benji's eyes widened. "What the …! What happened last night!?"

"Tommy threatened us with a fucking Colt. Right after I beat his sorry ass."

Benji shook his head and laughed in disbelief.

"And ten of his friends, too," Hart added, smiling.

"Ten? Damn." Benji brushed away an insect that landed on his forearm. The two of them seemed rather laid-back about the whole thing. "I've seen you floor eight men before ... did the extra two effect your performance?"

"Honestly, no," Hart laughed humbly. "Though it did prove more of a challenge with Ivy behind me."

"Hmm." Benji's expression fell. "Tommy's behavior is getting out of hand. Have you thought about taking this to the cops?"

"She called them this morning."

"We'll be heading back to Libya soon. Without you watching over her, it is probably best they are involved." Benji pulled his legs out of the water and stood. "That is, if you still want to go ...."

"Back to Libya?" Hart looked up at Benji, his wary brown eyes darkening.

"Yeah. Walker and I were thinking that maybe after all this time with Ivy, you may—"

"What?" Hart interrupted. "You think I've given up on finding Taym?"

"No, it's just—"

"I didn't choose to leave, Benji! Shit. They sent me away!"

"Hey, I know, I know, man." He threw his palms up in surrender. "Don't worry. We want Taym as much as you do."

Hart stared painfully at his friend.

"We'll get the bastard, too," Benji nodded.

Hart looked anxiously into the pool, feeling less confident about his skills these days, not to mention his temperament. He had felt constantly on edge these past few weeks, but he was assiduous in his restraint, careful not to lose his temper, especially around Ivy. Last night was an unfortunate exception, but he was paying for it today. He ran his fingers along the stitches across his stomach without a single thought for Tommy; it was Taym who plagued his mind.

He gazed determinedly up at Benji. "You really think we'll

get him?"

"Taym thought he brought an end to Phoenix," Benji stared at him, "but what happens to a Phoenix, Hart?"

Hart had never thought about it until now. "It is reborn."

Benji stared at him with an unflinching seriousness. "Taym Malak's days are numbered."

Hart nodded back, unsmiling, then Benji walked over to the fire-pit to sit with Walker and Ivy.

Hart lowered himself into the deep water. It ran painfully cold against his wounds at first, but the aching disappeared once his stitches were under the water. Taym entered his thoughts, but his mind drifted back to Ivy. He shook her out of his thoughts and focused on the shallow end of the pool, preparing himself for a grueling number of laps to clear his head and arouse his dwindling passion for returning to the war. Revenge … revenge is what he wanted. Libya … Taym … *Ivy.*

Hart closed his eyes and rubbed his foggy head. Her love continued to pierce the hatred he was trying to summon. She weighed heavily on his heart. He questioned his integrity if he chose to leave her. Was she safe? He had given himself as a decoy in Tommy's obsessive thoughts, but was it enough? If he were to be completely honest with himself, he couldn't say which decisions were right or wrong anymore. His moral lines were now blurred in the darkness that clouded his judgment, but he welcomed it back anyway. Hatred was powerfully addictive. Libya was finally within his reach, and he needed the rage. The fire in his blood. Last night his priorities dramatically shifted with his reignited accountability for Oliver, and a small part of him was grateful for Tommy's vilification. Ollie gave his life for him. It was a debt he may never repay, but he'd be damned if he didn't try.

Hart closed his eyes and groaned resignedly into the dark cloud over his head. There was no world in which he deserved Ivy. Not her innocence. Not her sweetness. Most of all, not her love. He took a deep breath with his final decision and sunk into the peaceful depths of the pool. He would forsake the purest love he had ever known … for the woman who gave it to him.

"I could cut the tension around here with a knife," Walker smiled warmly at Ivy. "Talk to me, Ives. What happened between you and Hart?"

Ivy took a deep breath and ran her fingers through her hair. She smiled nervously at Walker sitting beside her, watching her carefully. His dark eyes were filled with compassion and an indescribable intensity that, as usual, intimidated her. It was a waste, she thought, that these men weren't settling down and creating extraordinary offspring. Their big hearts and breathtaking good looks were being cast aside for honor, patriotism, and war. They were each remarkably outstanding in their own way, and she selfishly wished they could have it all. They deserved it all.

Ivy smiled sadly. "I don't know what happened."

"Were you two okay before last night?" Walker asked. He narrowed his eyes and extracted as much information as he could from her; through her words, to the way she gazed at the ocean.

"Not really." She twisted her face. "Ever since the clinical psychologist arrived that day, a large part of him shut down."

"Hannah?" Walker asked coolly.

Ivy nodded. Walker furrowed his brow and looked away from her. His dark eyes surveyed the ocean that rolled beneath them, and she sensed his sharp mind ticking avidly away. Ivy wondered what he knew, what he kept vigilantly hidden behind his piercing eyes.

Walker looked at her again. "When you say 'shut down,' do you mean he became depressed?"

"No, not depressed. More like he left, like his mind was somewhere else entirely." Ivy looked into Walker's examining eyes.

Walker nodded and glanced hesitantly at Benji, who sat down beside him.

"It is just one thing after another with Hart," Benji leaned forward and rubbed his face tiredly. "The guy can't catch a break!"

Ivy and Walker glanced back at Hart, who had set himself a mean pace in the pool.

"It's like the universe has had it in for Hart ever since Ollie died," Benji added. "Just chipping away at him bit by bit. We've survived so much shit in the past, but this is different."

Walker watched Benji intently as he spoke. He looked down at his hands and rubbed them together in thought.

"Has he had any nightmares lately?" Walker asked Ivy.

"None, but to be honest, I don't think he'd tell me anymore," Ivy sighed. "I feel like he's pulling away from me."

She peered at Walker, whose disheartening expression agreed with her.

Ivy sighed into her hands. She felt foolish for not seeing it earlier. Hart had been slowly preparing her for his departure, ever since Hannah's visit. She didn't realize it until this very moment, and she knew she was right—it was written all over Walker's contrite expression.

"Oh, I see," she breathed. Ivy met Walker's compassionate gaze, and her heart stung with the hurtful truth of it.

He considered her thoughtfully, his dark eyes full of apology.

"When do you three leave for Libya?" she asked reluctantly. Her heart throbbed painfully in her throat. The angst in his expression was killing her.

Walker didn't answer, but his eyes didn't leave hers.

"Walker?" She frowned.

He looked away and sighed. "Less than a week."

A wave of nausea rushed over her, and Ivy groaned into her hands. She closed her eyes and fell miserably into her breaking heart. She could feel her soul being sucked away, and a part of her desperately clung to it; she felt it there between herself and the emptiness that awaited her, stretching away from her, threatening to leave her forever. No one ever came back to her in the end. *No one.*

Walker's hand rested on her back. "I'm sorry, Ivy."

She looked at Walker and Benji and managed a small smile.

"We'll get the job done as quickly as possible, Ives," Benji smiled warmly. "We'll be back before you can miss us."

Ivy smiled weakly at him.

"Oh, shit." Benji's expression fell.

Walker and Ivy looked up at Benji, who stared straight past them toward the house. They turned to see what had caught Benji's attention, and standing on the pavers at the shallow end of the pool was a stunning woman in a red mini-dress and high heels. There was a suitcase by her side, and her hand sat on her hip as she glared into the pool where Hart was still swimming, oblivious to her presence. The woman shook her head while she waited for his attention, her fingers tapping agitatedly on her hip.

She had long dark hair, and her eyes were large and animated. Ivy had never seen a woman more beautiful, besides Hannah.

Ivy dropped her gaze to her hands, feeling foolish. Hart could have any woman he wanted. He didn't need to stay here in La Mar with her.

She sighed and got up to greet the stranger.

"Whoa, Ivy, sit down!" Walker grabbed her unexpectedly and sat her back down on the bench beside him. "Keep your distance. This one's a firecracker, and we don't want you getting caught in the crossfire."

"Oh, man, this is gold!" Benji laughed quietly.

"Here, I'm coming over to you, Benji boy, I can't see shit from here."

Ivy watched Walker change positions to the bench next to Benji. She glanced between the soldiers' eager expressions and frowned in bewilderment.

Walker reached to the wall of the fire-pit for his pack of cigarettes and eagerly lit one up. When he spoke again, his voice was low and husky. "You're in it now, Hart," he breathed coolly, exhaling the smoke.

Benji chuckled.

Ivy got up and sat between Walker and Benji. She felt awful for Hart, but her intuition told her not to go to him. "Shouldn't we help him? I mean, we were just talking about how the world seemed to have it in for him. One thing after the other, remember?"

Benji grinned at Ivy. "If *she* is here," he pointed at the woman, "then the world most definitely has a bone to pick with Hart. He is doing something wrong, that's for sure."

"Who is she?" Ivy asked.

"That woman there is pure evil," Walker replied.

"So we're just going to sit here and watch?" Ivy asked them.

"Yeah, this is different, Ivy," Walker twittered happily. "This is funny."

Benji and Walker chuckled like two naughty school boys.

Ivy turned her attention to the scene. A rare discord gathered in the pit of her stomach, and she realized then that her indefinable era with Johnny Hart had now come to its end.

Hart saw the red dress and dark hair from under the water. A wave of disbelief washed over him, right before vexation kicked in. He imagined the universe plotting his demise, asking what else could be thrown at him to make his fall from grace more entertaining.

Hart stood in the shallow end of the pool and wiped his face, then stared frustratingly at Nicole.

She smiled wickedly and spoke with a strong, southern tongue, "Good to see you, too, asshole."

Hart went to speak, but he couldn't. There were no words. He felt no emotion, or at least he thought so ... unless he could extract a more prominent sentiment from the senseless mess that scrambled inside his head. Resentment, maybe. Hart sighed. Resentment for the world, not for her specifically, though her presence was most undesired. Incredulous. *That* was how he felt. He could barely comprehend Nicole was here, at Ivy's. After four years.

Hart wiped the water off his face and moved toward the steps to exit the pool. He walked straight past her to his towel, which hung over the back of the sun lounger. He dried his face and then looked at her with an agitated confusion.

"Why, Nicole?"

"Why?" she replied, stunned. "Because it has been four years, you jerk! You didn't think to call me?"

"We ended it before I left for Benghazi," Hart growled. The darkness grew exponentially in her presence. "You broke up with me, remember? You said you couldn't do it anymore, that I would be gone for too long. Frankly, Nicole, it was the smartest decision you ever made."

"Yeah, but now you're home." Nicole smiled with her irritated eyes.

"Actually, I was just leaving." Hart laughed out loud at the absurdity of the whole situation. He glanced at Ivy and the boys around the fire-pit. He saw her there beside Walker. Her innocence shone like a beacon of light in the distance. Out of his reach ... where she belonged.

"What do you mean *leaving?* Where are you going?" Nicole asked.

"I'm leaving for Libya in a few days. It is bad timing, among other things," Hart muttered the latter under his breath. He glanced at her through the corner of his eye as he dried himself.

"That's me, eh, always with the bad fucking timing."

Her gaze dropped dolefully, but he knew her better than that; she was anything but sad. Nicole was already manipulating him. He could feel it.

"How did you even get in here? How did you get past the security gate?" Hart asked.

"I guess not all my timing is bad. My taxi pulled up as the gardener was leaving."

Hart shook his head. He glanced at her suitcase.

"I'm staying in a motel down the road," Nicole stated. "The place is a dive, but it'll do for now."

"For now?" Hart replied, throwing his towel over his shoulder.

"Well, I was planning on picking up where we left off, but if you're leaving in a few days ...," Nicole smirked, "then maybe we shouldn't waste any more time talking about it."

It was evident to Hart what she was suggesting. He watched her sashay toward him and for some reason he didn't move. Her body was still the same after these four years; she was still as sexy as the day he left her for the war. No less suggestive either. He had glimpsed her lacy underwear from the pool; no doubt all part of her cunning plan to lure him back. Her ample bust was bursting at the seams, as was her hunger for him. He remembered what she looked like naked on top of him, and once it was all he ever wanted when he returned from the war. Back then he couldn't even wait to reach the bedroom, so he would take her against the back of the front door, much to her delight. Hart felt a mild arousal, not for Nicole, but for the memories. Deep down he no longer cared for those either. Her black heart was darker than the devil's. Nicole was here for nothing less than to cause him more grief.

Her smoldering eyes did their best to bewitch him. He could smell her overpowering perfume as she trailed a bright, red fingernail down the center of his chest and down to his shorts. The palm of her hand flattened against his abs, and he heard her sigh. Her bright, red lips opened evocatively, and she breathed into his ear before she spoke, sending a hot ripple of goosebumps across his body.

"Do you remember what it was like?"

Hart didn't reply. He turned his face away from her and closed his eyes, breathing steadily under her touch. The darkness moved like a dense cloud inside his head. The dark was intoxicating. *Addictive.* He wanted to walk away from her, but he couldn't. She inspired the hatred, he needed to leave Ivy.

"You've never looked so good, Johnny," Nicole breathed into his neck.

Hart looked down into her dark eyes.

"I missed you so much, baby," she whispered. Nicole stretched up to him and lightly kissed his jaw, hoping for the lips he refused to give her.

He closed his eyes and looked away. "Stop it, Nic. I'm so fucking angry right now," his voice was calm, but his body was rigid with anger.

Nicole frowned in her appraisal of him, searching his face without moving away.

"You know I preferred you that way." She ran her hand up his chest, breathing heavily in sedated pleasure. "You always came back from the war so intense ... so hungry for me ... *so hard*...."

"Stop," Hart interrupted, glaring into her beautiful, deceitful eyes. The trembling shook his core. It swayed his selfcontrol.

She smiled in false sweetness. Her hand wandered further down his stomach and over the top of his shorts, and finally, Hart was able to pry himself away from her sinful lure.

"Nicole, things are different now. *Everything* has changed." The world was testing him, he thought; challenge, after challenge, after challenge. Or breaking him. His life, pre-Libya, had been a breeze in comparison to his life now. Long ago, Hart taught himself to abide by a solemn rectitude that defined his honor as a man. He never wavered in his integrity, despite life's trials and tribulations. It was humbling, yet victorious. It strengthened him. It made him a better man. But this past year had been incredibly taxing on his soul. On his humanity. He had lost a friend whose death forced him to question everything he thought he had become. Forced him to doubt all that embodied him. Hart didn't know who he was anymore ... and he didn't want to.

He glanced at the fire-pit, grateful that Ivy no longer faced him. Hart brushed past Nicole and walked toward the house.

Nicole frowned. "Where are you going?"

"Inside," Hart replied as he walked up the stairs. He led her away from Ivy before Nicole seduced the darker, primordial side of him that he had less control over lately.

Nicole followed him, as Hart expected.

"You aren't happy to see me, are you?" she asked, stepping inside.

"Are you fucking kidding me?" Hart shouted, turning around when he reached the kitchen island.

Nicole stopped abruptly in his anger.

"It's been four years, Nic! You threw a fucking vase at my head on my way out!"

Nicole winced apologetically.

"Shit, I can't believe this is even happening!" Hart rubbed his hands over his wet hair in distress.

"Yeah, but I missed!" she argued, baffled by his sudden outburst.

Hart rolled his eyes and leaned on the island, burying his head irritably into his hands. "That's not the point!" His voice boomed through the kitchen and out the back doors—no doubt they could hear him outside. He rubbed his face in frustration, concerned for Ivy more than anything. This was her home.

He looked up at Nicole, and she frowned at him with her dark eyes. She appeared confused ... and so she should be. There were a dozen things Hart was dealing with right now, and even he didn't have an answer for any of them.

"What's going on with you?" she asked. Nicole leaned forward on the island toward Hart with a seductive sparkle in her eyes. She couldn't help herself.

He leaned away from her against the counter beside the refrigerator and sighed.

"Well, well, well," Walker said from behind her. "Nicole,

what an unexpected ... development."

Nicole stood quickly and turned around. She groaned and rolled her eyes when she saw him. "Fuck you, Josh."

"Yeah, I missed you, too," Walker laughed.

He walked straight past Nicole with her suitcase in his hand and glanced with some concern at Hart as he passed. He placed her bag beside the doorway that led to the front entry hall and looked back at Nicole, who stared at him with a deadpan expression.

"Are you serious? It has been five minutes, and already you have your underling here trying to get rid of me. This is a new record, Johnny." Nicole looked at Hart with a displeased smile.

"Oh, no, I'm not trying to get rid of you," Walker grinned deviously, rubbing his jaw. "I thought if I left your suitcase alone with Benji, well, anything could happen. You know how he feels about you, Nic, and he's a pretty imaginative fella, our Benji boy."

Nicole glared at him, then turned to Hart. "Ben's here, too?"

Hart nodded, unsmiling. He was still contemplating how Nicole actually came to be here. He wondered if he had fallen asleep on the sun lounger ... surely this was another nightmare.

"Don't you guys get fucking tired of each other? Is the war not enough?" she scoffed. "I never get you to myself, Johnny, I always have to share you with these assholes!"

Hart didn't answer again, and Walker caught a disconcerting hesitation in his eyes. An anxiety he hadn't seen since that night in the motel room on their way to La Mar. Walker instinctively responded in Hart's apprehension, knocking his knuckles firmly on the stone surface of the island as he walked toward Nicole.

She stepped backward in his intimidating approach.

"Come on now. We aren't all that bad. You never gave us a chance. We could have been friends," Walker said, his dark eyes flickering with menace.

Nicole laughed dryly. "I had plenty of friends."

"Had?" Walker laughed at her aloofness and leaned into her. "I can't imagine why they didn't stick around."

"Oh, Josh, what are you laughing at?" she glared at him. "Last I heard, your ex-girlfriend was fucking Bobby Loons." Nicole grinned. "Engaged, I do believe!"

Walker's expression darkened.

Nicole relaxed, as she regained control of the conversation. Her aim was dead on, and she'd hit him where it hurt. Nicole smiled, utterly pleased with herself, and trailed her finger along the cold stone island as she made her way toward Hart.

"Y'all hear Bobby is a lawyer now?" She glanced back at Walker. "Hasn't lost a case, and he's swimmin' in his fortunes … we all know how much her mommy and daddy wanted her to marry into money. Of course, you would know that better than any of us, right, Josh?" Nicole laughed wickedly.

Hart saw Walker staring at her. He had regained his composure and appeared unfazed by her goading, on the surface at least. He knew how much Walker had loved a girl in his past. He also knew how hard he had crashed after she broke his heart. They had been madly in love, but it was her overbearing parents that ended it. Hart met her once, years after they broke up. She had bright blue eyes and a sunny smile. The girl was angelic, and Walker … well, he looked like trouble. Only his closest friends knew he was anything but.

"What about you? Have you done anything special these past few years, soldier?" Nicole looked at Walker with a raised, doubtful eyebrow. "I guess you haven't died yet, so you're kinda winning." She twisted her face, looking half disappointed.

Walker's eyes narrowed, and danger lurked in the smile that crept across his face. Hart sensed Oliver in Walker's thoughts, and he realized the peril Nicole had ignorantly placed herself in. Walker would never harm a woman, but the loathsome look in his eyes at this moment suggested otherwise.

"You know, I've never been able to get over how spectacular you are at being a Goddamn *bitch,* Nicole," Benji stated blatantly from the back door.

The three of them turned around, and judging by the horrified look on Ivy's face, she had obviously been standing there long enough to witness Nicole's malice.

"I was wondering when you'd slither in," Nicole hissed.

"A cold heart and a forked tongue," Benji smiled, "it's safe to say you're the only one who's slithering around here."

Nicole scoffed, crossing her arms. "Don't blame me, it's an adaptation I picked up in your loathsome presence. A means to survive in such a hostile environment, you son of a bitch."

"Darwin, I like it," Benji grinned deviously, rubbing his hands together in playful delight. "Well, I must say, you have quite the colorful array of adaptations." He grinned pleasurably, enjoying the despicable banter. The dimples pressed into his handsome face, and his blue eyes simmered with excitement and disdain.

Ivy's eyes flicked back and forth between the pair. If she didn't know any better, she'd say Nicole was thrilled with her opponent, as though he were worthy of her time. Her dark, shiny hair fell around her shoulders, and her skin was pale and flawless with mesmerizing red lips. Ivy was shocked that such a beautiful woman could be filled with so much animosity.

"That array of adaptations prevents me from dropping dead in your tedious fucking company," Nicole droned.

Benji laughed at her. "I take it Darwin's theory extends to your contemptible version of the English language?"

"Fuck you, Benji, you're one to talk," she lashed.

Benji laughed again.

Ivy took a deep breath. She had never witnessed this amount of hostility before, including last night's brawl. Walker looked like he were going to pounce on this woman, and Hart was dark with rage. Ivy could see it was a game for Nicole, but Benji was the only one of the men to see it that way. There was a plan, she thought. The universe *had* to have a plan for Hart. It was too much for one man ... all of it.

Ivy sighed and rubbed her forehead, and then the silence caught her attention. She looked up from her hand and saw Nicole's expression brighten with unexpected pleasure. Ivy felt Benji's hand rest on her back when Nicole strutted toward her. Hart stood to attention in the corner of her eye, but he seemed to place her safety in Benji's hands. The soldiers didn't need to worry. She was more than capable of standing her ground against a resentful female. It wouldn't be the first time. Besides, it wasn't Nicole's boiling temperament that concerned her, it was her being here at all that nonplussed her.

Nicole's face softened. She seemed friendly, sweet almost. A different woman entirely. Ivy glanced fleetingly at Hart.

"A beautiful Rose between all these thorns .... Hello, Ivy Rose," she twittered pleasantly.

Ivy smiled cautiously. "How do you know who I am?"

"Oh, sweet thing, you are so modest!" Nicole grinned at the soldiers in mock surprise and turned back to Ivy.

Hart narrowed his eyes at Nicole, more vigilant now that Nicole wasn't openly on the attack.

"You're all over the papers every July!" she continued. "I am a huge fan of yours!"

Ivy frowned, confused.

"The Annual Silver Moon Gala!" Nicole sang out. "I think what you do for those charities is awe-inspiring. The press in the Carolinas can't get enough of you at this time of year, especially after you raised awareness and profits for those poor, poor children in Charleston County one year. Do you remember?"

"Yes, I remember."

"You are a remarkable woman, Ivy, and so much prettier in real life. It is an honor to meet you." She grinned and took Ivy's hand tightly.

"So, how did you know Hart was staying with me?" Ivy asked, narrowing her eyes and prying her hand away.

Hart watched Ivy as she spoke. His darkness receded with Nicole's heightened intrigue of her. The woman he vowed to protect.

"Johnny? I saw him dancing with you on the front page of The Fayetteville Observer last week. They always hype up the event a few months before. It was taken at the Gala last year." Nicole glared at Hart, displeased. "'SOLDIER FINDS ROSE ON A SILVER MOON.'"

Hart and Ivy looked at each other. She tried to hide her sudden unease, but Hart was far too perceptive of her feelings.

"You said you were staying at a motel?" Hart asked, glancing at Nicole.

Nicole walked over to Hart. "Yeah. Why? You ready to *talk?*"

"Which motel?" he asked, indifferent to her flirting.

"Blue Bayou," she replied. "On the other side of town near—"

"I know where it is," Hart replied. He walked over to her suitcase and picked it up, and Nicole chased him across the kitchen floor like an excited puppy. He motioned her toward the front door, and once she was out of the kitchen, he turned to Ivy and the boys.

"I won't be long."

"You sure? Maybe we should order her a taxi?" Benji frowned. "She's up to something. I can feel it."

Hart gazed back at their pained expressions. "This way she's out of the house," he shrugged. "Hopefully I can get her on a flight home tonight."

"I'll take her," Walker told him.

Hart laughed. "She will never get in the car with you. You would have to tie her to the front seat once you got her in there."

Walker smiled playfully. "I could knock her out first?"

Ivy picked up the amusement in the soldiers' expressions, but they seemed to be seriously considering it.

Walker exhaled loudly. "Alright, but watch your back, man."

"I will. I'll see you soon," Hart nodded. He glanced at Ivy and then left the kitchen.

Ivy watched him leave. With a beautiful woman. A woman to whom he was clearly still attracted. She couldn't blame him; Nicole was all sex appeal. She thought about Nicole's hand running down his chest beside the pool, how he didn't stop it. It made her feel sick with uncertainty, and Ivy exhaled sharply. Her heart sped up suddenly, and she grew dizzy from its irregular, panicked beat.

"Hart," Ivy breathed. "Hart, wait!"

Ivy rushed past Walker and Benji into the entry hall. The front door was wide open, and she could see Nicole perched happily in the front seat of the Firebird. Hart stopped outside the front door and waited for her. Her heart thumped nervously in his presence as it did on that very first day she met him, right here at her front door.

"I shouldn't have kept my distance from you today. I'm sorry," she breathed. Ivy tucked her blonde hair behind her ears.

Hart studied her for a short while before he answered.

"Don't apologize. I deserved it, Ives." He glanced back at Nicole, waiting for him. "I should go."

Ivy lost her breath as he walked away. "Stay with me," she breathed.

Hart stopped walking. He turned to her slowly, and Ivy

sensed his torment deep inside, the torturous lashing of his love for her.

"Ivy, *I can't* ...." he replied agonizingly, tearing his gaze from her.

Ivy's broken heart trembled in her chest. Pieces of it plummeted through the depths of her soul. She could hear her breath shaking on the air between them. She couldn't help but feel Hart was alluding to their future, and she pursed her lips to control her sudden breathlessness.

Hart put Nicole's suitcase into the back of the Firebird and climbed into the driver's seat. She squealed delightfully beside him and waved to Ivy, standing in the large doorway of her estate. He turned the ignition and the Firebird roared to life, and its rumble seemed to confirm his decision; it was time to leave La Mar. Time to leave Ivy. Time to set her free. *Free of his burdens. Free of his weakness. Free of his darkness. Free of him.*

Hart frowned at Ivy in his rearview mirror as he drove away from her. There was a confused sadness written all over her beautiful face. Like their encounter with Tommy and his men last night ... they never saw this coming.

## Chapter 21

WALKER LEANED BACK IN THE office chair and glanced at the clock hanging in Ivy's study. He had been on a conference call for half an hour already with USSOCOM, and for the moment, he sat quietly and listened to the rest of the board plot the movements of Phoenix once they touched down in Libya. He mindlessly chewed on the end of a pen as he stared at the time ... 11:30 p.m. Hart still hadn't returned from dropping off Nicole. Walker considered every possible situation his friend may have encountered once he left the estate; this was out of character for Hart.

Benji walked in and took a seat opposite him. He leaned back in his chair and chewed anxiously on his thumbnail as he tried to listen in on the conversation. Walker took the phone out from between his ear and his shoulder, and sat it on the desk between them and pushed speaker. Both of them leaned in and stared soundlessly at the phone.

"… how can they be positive? Twenty of their men besieged the wrong apartment block just two weeks ago!" A man's voice spoke down the line.

"The British forces have given us confirmation, so we need to respond quickly. They raided the complex with the belief that Malak was in hiding with another leader of the group," a woman spoke confidently. "Turns out they were right about one of them. Ali Khaled. Malak and Khaled met four years ago, only weeks before Malak was deployed to Libya from Afghanistan. That was the start of their alliance."

*"Four years?"* Benji mouthed silently in disbelief. They stared at each other wordlessly, before Benji shook his head angrily and leaned back in his chair again.

"Ali Khaled is deceased?" a man asked.

"No," the woman replied. "Surprisingly, there were no casualties. Khaled was in hiding with his wife and two children, all of whom managed to flee undetected in the commotion. Their whereabouts are still unknown. He is regarded a high-value target, along with Taym Malak."

Walker chewed his bottom lip in anticipation of their deployment.

The woman continued. "We will drop Phoenix in Ras Ajdir on the border between Libya and Tunisia. It is a major transport hub, and their arrival should go undetected. It is approximately 110 miles from Tripoli. The rest of the operation will be discussed in tomorrow morning's meeting at 11 a.m. Sergeant Walker, do I still have your attention?"

Walker cleared his throat. "Yes, ma'am."

"You have four Mustangs who have been assigned to this operation. They have been thoroughly briefed on the information regarding Phoenix's history. This is a direct action and reconnaissance mission. Officer John Hart will remain in charge as Detachment Commander. Sergeant Walker, I am now promoting you to second in command. Congratulations."

Walker sensed the smile in her voice. "Yes, ma'am. Thank you, ma'am." He glanced at Benji, who grinned proudly from ear to ear, and Walker allowed himself a small smile.

"I expect to see you and Sergeant Swift in my office at 10:30 a.m. tomorrow morning before the debriefing. I suggest you hop on the next flight back to Monterey tonight. Your holiday has been cut short, I'm afraid."

"I understand."

"Commander Hart will be expected to join us over the next few days. He will be briefed on the operation before he leaves for Libya," she added. "Good night, Commander."

"Good night, ma'am."

Walker took his phone from the center of the desk and stared at Benji. "Libya, here we come."

Benji grinned. "Taym Malak. That bastard has no idea we're coming for him."

"He won't know what hit him."

"I'm sure Hart will give him a well-deserved moment to comprehend it all."

Walker's smile faded. "I'm sure he will."

Walker flicked through his phone and booked two seats on the next flight out at 5 a.m. The two of them left the study and walked into the kitchen. It was close to midnight, and there was still no word from Hart.

"Where's Ivy? She still outside?" Walker asked.

"Yeah, she is," Benji replied, tapping his fingers on the island. "She hasn't said anything, but I know she's gutted with Hart's prolonged absence. You think we need to worry about him?" He ran his hands tiredly through his hair.

"I don't know."

"It's Hart. He wouldn't do anything reckless."

"Hart wouldn't, no," Walker replied. He lingered in the open doorway that led outside to Ivy. "Nicole on the other hand …."

Benji and Walker sighed at the thought of her.

"He's a big boy. I'm sure he'll be fine," Benji said. "I'm going to bed, buddy, I'm beat."

Walker gave Benji a pat on the back and walked outside to find Ivy. He strolled down the stairs through the rippling reflection of the pool and saw her lying on the grass with her feet resting against the glass orb under the palm trees. Her legs were long and lean, and her blonde hair lay against the dark grass like a halo around her head. She was staring at the stars as the orb's light faded subtly from light to dark to light again … in an endless cycle beneath her bare feet. Walker stopped halfway down the stairs to admire her peacefulness. It was something he wasn't quite used to yet. Seeing her lie there, open to the stars, suddenly moved a mountain of uncertainties within him, and he discovered a sanctuary of freedom in her innocence. Everything about her in this moment captivated him. He took a deep breath and gazed into the thick blanket of stars above him, then he rubbed his hands nervously down his chest and walked over to Ivy.

He lay back on the grass beside her without speaking. Ivy looked at him with her piercing, crystal blue eyes, jolting his heart, and then she smiled at him when he lifted his feet onto the orb.

"You okay?" he asked.

Ivy nodded and shifted her gaze back to the breathtaking night sky. "I think so."

Walker looked at the sky. "They see it all," he said. "You can't hide anything from the stars."

Ivy turned her head on the soft grass and studied the soldier beside her. Somehow he never ceased to amaze her. Walker turned his head toward her again and smiled handsomely, and Ivy's heart skipped a beat in his mysterious charm. His eyes were black with the night, and the light of the orb sparkled brilliantly in their depths. Ivy felt herself being lured into them, blindly led by her curiosity. There was a hint of recklessness in his expression. Of mischief and thrilling danger.

Ivy forced her gaze to the stars again and smiled. "Fortunately, they keep our secrets to themselves."

She heard Walker chuckle humbly into the sky, and Ivy relaxed in his fascinating presence.

"So can I ask about your ex-girlfriend?" she asked hesitantly.

"Fiancé," he smiled. "I asked her to marry me ... on a night like tonight."

"Under a billion stars?" she grinned.

"Under a billion stars."

Ivy smiled at the thought of Walker in love and waited for him to continue.

"We didn't tell anybody we were getting hitched. We wanted it to be our little secret for a while. You know, before everyone told us we were too young." His dark eyes twinkled in the memory. "We had so many plans for the future …."

Ivy saw the distant look in his eyes. He propped himself up on his elbows and his smile soon faded.

"So what happened?" she asked thoughtfully.

Walker stared at the orb light as it changed shade, thinking quietly to himself.

"Her parents always questioned my intentions. She came from money, and I didn't," he smiled and shrugged his big shoulders. "Somehow they convinced her that her money was all I ever wanted." His dark eyes narrowed at the memory.

"I'm sorry," she whispered.

"Don't be," Walker replied, looking at her. "It was a long time ago."

"Do you think about her often?" she asked, studying his striking, dark features in the soft glow of the orb.

Walker considered her for a while, then he lay down on his back and stared at the stars again. "Lately I have."

"Why is that?"

He took a deep breath and hesitated before he answered. "I see a lot of her in you, Ivy."

Walker saw the wistfulness steal the curiosity in her expression. Her nearness was new to him. It was unfamiliar but extraordinary. He immersed himself in her beauty. Her lips. Her skin. The sweet freckles across her nose. Ivy was flawless. He saw her lips part to speak, but no words escaped them … so he laughed softly at himself and stared back at the stars. He brushed his hand through his hair and took a long, deep breath.

"I … I hope I don't bring you pain," she frowned.

A boyish grin swept beautifully across his face, and he looked into her eyes again. "You could never bring me pain, Ives."

Her heart beat excitedly in his company. He possessed a casualness that was so self-assured that she found it incredibly intimidating … and insanely attractive.

She smiled warmly at him.

"Bobby Loons, eh?" Ivy giggled. "He probably deserved to catch a break with a name like that."

"Yeah, maybe. The guy barely made it through high school," he replied. "Loony Bob." Walker grinned wickedly at Ivy.

"Josh Walker. I did not pick you as a bully!"

"Me? No, I never called him Loony Bob, I swear," he laughed, rubbing his chest.

Ivy narrowed her suspicious eyes. "Good."

"I ignored the guy completely."

Ivy hit him playfully, and they laughed. The sound of him warmed her heart, and she smiled into the sky.

"You don't have to feel sorry for him anymore, right?" He

smiled humbly at the stars. "He got the girl."

A thoughtful silence fell between them.

"Who hires a lawyer called Bobby Loons, anyhow?" Walker grinned, and Ivy laughed into the sky.

The two of them talked for hours into the night. Ivy glowed in Walker's presence. It felt good to laugh again, especially after last night, and she was grateful for his thoughtful company. He rolled to face her, propping himself up on one elbow, and Ivy did the same. His expression grew more serious, and he reached out and gently brushed the hair away from her face. She smiled sweetly in his attention.

"Ivy," he said, "Benji and I have to leave first thing in the morning."

"But you just got here."

"I know." He sighed and checked his watch. "Our flight leaves at 5 a.m., in two hours. We've been called back to the garrison up north. I'll have to wake Benji soon."

Ivy nodded gravely. She knew why they had been summoned. *Libya.* She didn't need to hear him say it.

"I'm sorry," he breathed. He saw a hint of fear cloud her crystal eyes as she stared at the ground between them. She ran her fingers gently across the tips of the grass and looked up at him. Her sweet, uncertain smile hurt his heart.

"Now that I've met you," she breathed, "I can't imagine life without you three in it."

"Please don't imagine that kind of life. You don't have to," he replied. An unsmiling intensity swept over him. "We will always come back for you, Ivy."

She smiled at the thought, but no matter what he told her, Walker could never guarantee their safe return. Their noble intentions were all she had to believe in. All she had to settle her restless heart and her unspoken fear ... *no one ever came back.*

Ivy looked up at him and smiled through the tears that threatened to fall. She smiled through the fear of losing her three soldiers. *Oliver's soldiers.* They were all she had left.

A tear rolled down her cheek. Ivy breathed herself through the sharp pain that broke her frightened heart.

"I'll miss you," she whispered.

"We'll miss you too, Ives. You have no idea."

Walker sighed. They didn't have a choice; they had to leave. It was an order. Ivy's sadness gripped his heart, and he winced at the pain. He rubbed his aching chest and thought about Oliver. Leaving Ivy behind stirred a similar unhappiness, like he was losing Ollie all over again. He leaned in to Ivy so he could wrap his arm around her and comfort her, but she stopped him. Walker frowned, disheartened by her rejection, then Ivy lifted her teary, crystal gaze ... and kissed him softly on the lips.

Walker didn't respond at first, surprised by the sudden encounter ... but he quickly lost himself in her impulsive sweetness. Her enchantment. Her eternalness. Her gentle tongue soothed hundreds of lonely past nights, and her sweet taste would keep him going for hundreds more. He ran his thumb across her cheek and through her hair, then he groaned softly into her mouth before he forced himself to pull away. Walker leaned his forehead against hers and closed his eyes. He could feel her light breath against his face, and he breathed her in. He wasn't sure how long they lay there like that, with their eyes closed and their foreheads pressed intimately together ... lost under the light of a billion stars.

"Stay alive, Walker, okay?" she whispered.

Walker nodded wordlessly. He saw her fighting back her tears when she went to stand, so he helped her to her feet and pulled her into his arms. He stood with her for a quiet moment, resting his face in her hair. He felt her crying in his arms, and he closed his eyes and shook his head. Leaving her would be hard for all of them ... especially Hart.

"I'll bring him home safely, Ivy. I promise."

Ivy bit her quivering lip. She wanted to speak, but no words came to her without a sudden rush of tears. *This was it.* Her time with Oliver's soldiers had come to its end. Libya called.

*"Ivy,"* he whispered painfully, desperate to comfort her.

She looked up at him.

Walker sighed. He couldn't tell her what she wanted to hear, and his heart crashed in her sorrow. Ivy smiled sadly at him, then she walked away and hurried into the house. He took a long, deep breath when she left and buried his hands into his pockets.

Walker leaned his head back resignedly and stared at the stars. They would leave Oliver's hometown in a couple of hours. Leave

America in a couple of days. He closed his eyes and thought about their deployment back to the place where they lost it all.

He had only one goal in Libya … and that was to bring Hart back alive.

Chapter 22

HART GLANCED CAGILY AROUND the empty motel parking lot as though just being here were a transgression. Everything felt different with Nicole. Everything felt wrong.

"One drink," Nicole pleaded, "for old time's sake?"

"I don't know, Nic. It's getting dark. They'll be wondering where I am," he replied. "There are a few loose ends I need to tie up before I'm deployed."

"Make me a loose end." She pouted her full red lips. Her behavior was over the top, but it seemed to be working.

Hart rubbed his jaw. He thought about Ivy at home and the gut-wrenching conversation they needed to have regarding Libya. Past and future. He felt nauseous just thinking about it. One drink seemed far too inconsequential at this time … compared to breaking Ivy's heart. He calculated the risk of staying for one drink, factoring in Nicole's reckless impulsiveness. Any plan she had concocted was surely substandard to what he had survived since he lost his best friend.

Hart sighed. "One drink."

The motel room was worn and dark, and a tangy scent underlying the cleaning solvents was a testament to the dismal assortment of guests over the past forty or so years. There was a tiled kitchenette to the right of the front door, with a small table and two chairs, and a bathroom at the far end of the room. A double bed sat in the center of the room with a flower-printed quilt draped across it and two towels folded neatly at the end of it. Hart walked to the window on the other side of the room. As he sauntered through, he wondered how many others had reluctantly entered its dispiriting walls.

"It isn't much," Nicole twittered happily from the kitchenette, "but the view is spectacular."

Hart heard her flick on the radio when he reached the window. He could see the graying ocean in the distance with the fading twilight sitting on the horizon. The sky above was dark and filled with stars; Nicole had taken longer in town than what she had originally promised him. He looked past his reflection toward the lights of La Mar in the distance. She was right, the view was spectacular. He could see everything from here. Hart looked to the hills to the left of town and tried to identify a piece of Ivy's walk to Lights Beach. He couldn't. He stared at the foot of the hills in the distance, examining a stretch of darkness between the gray sea and the hills, which he presumed was the forest they had hiked through. Hart frowned, still taunted by the tales of the Ghost Trail.

"Here you go," she spoke from behind him, handing him a tumbler of bourbon. "Cheers!"

Her treacherous grin didn't go unnoticed by Hart. He sipped the golden liquid and closed his eyes as he swallowed. A sweet warmth soothed his throat. He heard Nicole sit down at the table behind him and light a cigarette, but he continued to look over the town of La Mar as it twinkled sweetly in the dark. He thought about Ivy. She was down there somewhere, among the lights. They only spoke once today. A far cry from their days of making love in the warm waters off her shore.

Hart exhaled into his drink, then took another sip. Lines of repentance furrowed deep into his brow. The tremor started with its merciless indifference; he had tried his best to do what was right by Ivy, yet the darkness had prevailed in the end. Libya had him now. All of him. His anxiety. His weakness. His soul. He didn't have the strength to withstand his attacks any longer, not without Ivy. He was drowning in the deep, surrounded by the black emptiness. Ivy's light fractured along the dark surface of the water, but he would no longer reach for it. He waited for his deserved end … with her light dancing eternally in his eyes. *Oh, Ivy.*

Hart took another sip of his bourbon to dull the tremor and ended up draining the glass instead. The lights of La Mar began to sway in the distance, and he blinked his eyes to refocus.

He wondered if the world missed Oliver. Maybe he'd had the same effect on his natural surroundings, like Ivy. Hart remembered the way Oliver would smile at the sunset, as though he stood thousands of miles away from the war, then he bowed his head in thought. Oliver's heart had always been here in the land of long-lasting sunsets, azure waters, and white sands. He had always been here with Ivy, no matter where he walked in this world. No matter how far or how long he roamed, his heart had remained in this place where the ocean touched the orange sky. *Now he was gone ....*

Hart's stomach twisted as the bourbon settled inside him. It was painfully good. He quickly shook Oliver from his thoughts, but it was too late. The anxiety rolled through him with a wave of guilt and collided with the potent alcohol in his blood. The lights continued to sway in front of him. Unsettling him. Weakening his level-headedness, his judgment. No matter how hard he tried to convince himself that the lights weren't moving, he couldn't manage to keep them still. He ran his hands through his hair and blinked his eyes again. The lights drew him in. He felt himself fall into their abstraction, surrendering himself to his guilt and to his darkness.

Nicole appeared by his side and took the glass from him. "Here, I'll get you another drink."

Hart didn't respond.

"So, there is one thing about all this, which for the life of me, I cannot piece together." Nicole raised her eyebrow quizzically at him, oblivious to his silent struggle. "How did you, a soldier from North Carolina, end up living in sunny California with the famous Silver Moon Queen?"

Hart turned around and looked at her as she poured him another bourbon in the kitchenette. She leaned suggestively over the bench, and his dozy eyes wandered up the length of her legs. Nicole feigned her innocence and pretended not to notice. She glanced down at the drinks in front of her on the counter and smiled to herself.

"Did you know her before?" Nicole added in Hart's silence.

She turned to Hart, who no longer faced her.

"I knew *of* her," Hart answered, closing his eyes when he thought about Ollie. "How I ended up living with her is … complicated."

Nicole stared at him, waiting for him to go on.

"Oliver asked us to check on her if he died."

She walked over to Hart and handed him his drink, then sat down at the table again and picked up her half-smoked cigarette between her polished nails.

Hart breathed tiredly into his bourbon. He didn't want to talk about this with her.

"So why did Oliver care so much about Ivy Rose?" Nicole asked, screwing up her face when Hart turned to her.

"She's his younger sister," Hart replied with a frustrated tone. He shot her a disparaging look as though she should know this already.

"Okay, Jesus, Johnny, why are you lookin' at me like that? I've never even met the guy!"

"Are you fucking kidding me?"

"What?"

"You've met him plenty of times before!" Hart sat down on the end of the motel bed and glared at her.

Nicole tilted her head and searched her hazy memory. "I don't remember him at all. Maybe we were out, and I was drunk. Was I drinking?" she asked, draining her bourbon.

Hart narrowed his eyes at her. "Probably."

She slammed her glass down on the table and smiled beautifully. "Wait, I do remember! He was that guy with the bright blue eyes and that smile that just melted your heart. I remember him! *Oliver* …," she repeated whimsically in her southern accent. "What a shame he died, he was so handsome."

Hart nodded with a worn expression, then he threw his head back and finished his second bourbon in one gulp. He stared vaguely at the empty tumbler for a while and thought about Ivy and their past few days. He felt himself slipping into a numb, bourbon-induced exhaustion. Hart placed his empty glass on the table and lay back on the bed, then he sighed and rubbed his face tiredly.

Nicole took his glass to pour them another.

"What a waste of a perfect man," she declared. "Shame the reaper couldn't take Josh or Benji instead. They are such assholes."

Hart stared at her blandly as she talked. She glanced back at him now and then to confirm he was still listening, but Hart ignored her. How times had changed, he thought. He once appreciated Nicole's aloofness. For her uncanny ability to distance herself from everyone and everything. Once he needed that, grateful for her ability to prevent anything from touching her cold heart. It made coming home easier for him. Nicole never wanted to know about the war. Whatever was happening in her life was more important than anything he had experienced while he was away. Hart never wanted to talk about it anyhow. He liked to think that if it was left unspoken, then it was easier to leave behind. *Detachment.* Nicole became his vital tool for detachment.

He threw his hands over his eyes and thought about leaving, but he knew the momentary escape from his guilt for Oliver had already won him over. Hart groaned into his hands.

"Here, the third bourbon makes all the difference." She winked at him and held his drink above him in the air. "You are so tense, Johnny. I've never seen you like this."

He sat up and took it from her, and stared into it soundlessly.

Nicole sat down again and watched him.

"Drink it," she ordered.

He took a sip of his bourbon without looking at her, and her eyes narrowed in pleasure. Nicole placed her drink on the table and moved next to Hart on the bed, flicking her long, dark hair so that it cascaded in curls around her breasts. She lifted her leg and crossed it over the other and leaned into Hart, who still hadn't noticed her beside him. He was swiveling the ice gently around his bourbon, lost in thought.

She smiled. "Third one's the charm, right?"

Hart glanced at her beside him. "It's the last, too. I told the guys I wouldn't be long."

"Oh, come on, Johnny! When did you become so boring!?" Nicole stood impatiently and sat down next to her drink.

He rolled his eyes. "And there's my cue to leave."

Hart stood up from the end of the bed and lost his balance temporarily, long enough to concern him. He had barely touched his third bourbon, yet he felt like he'd been drinking all night.

His glass slipped out of his hand, and he stumbled when it bounced on the threadbare carpet, bourbon splashing against the flowered quilt. He tightened his eyes shut and cursed under his breath.

Nicole gasped theatrically. "Are you okay?"

"I—I'm not sure," Hart stammered.

"That worked a lot faster than I anticipated," she said, as if satisfied with herself.

He took an awkward step toward Nicole, who stood up and backed away from him toward the kitchenette. Hart fumbled blindly for the table where she had been sitting, and when he blinked his eyes open, he saw her standing in the kitchen with a wicked grin stretched from ear to ear. The light was dim, but he saw the thrill in her deceitful eyes, and he knew then what she had done.

He looked back at the bourbon-soaked carpet. It spun uncomfortably with the rest of the room, and he thought he might be sick. He leaned his hands on the table and bowed his head, then groaned quietly to himself.

"Hart?" she breathed.

He heard her come for him, but her nearness induced an enraged, thunderous growl. Hart struck the table powerfully with his fists, maddened by her insane behavior.

His deep voice boomed through the motel, "Nicole!"

Nicole covered her ears, terrified of his sudden rage. "Stop fighting it, Johnny!"

He felt her hands on his chest trying to settle him. He couldn't see much through the fading light, so he grabbed the conniving woman in front of him and pressed her hard against the motel wall. He heard her whimper in fright. His grip tightened around her upper arms—hard enough to intimidate her, but not hurt her.

Nicole exhaled sharply in Hart's iron grip. "I'm sorry!"

"Bullshit, Nic! You're never sorry!"

"I am ... I am! I thought you wanted this!"

Hart cursed again at her hollow apology. He felt her push against him to set herself free, and she succeeded in his spiraling blindness.

"Why?" he breathed.

"I thought I'd give you a little something to wind down! You were so uptight!"

She moved to the other side of the double bed near the bathroom, as far away from Hart as she possibly could in the tiny motel room.

Hart stumbled back into the kitchenette, knocking a picture off the wall as the room tilted under him. The glass smashed at his feet against the tiles of the kitchen, and he heard Nicole yelp in shock. He groped clumsily at the chairs around the table and finally managed to pull one out toward him. He sat down and leaned his spinning head into his hands.

"What was it?" Hart asked, squinting his eyes open and shut. "Did you give me Rohypnol?"

"Just one Roofie, Johnny, don't get mad!"

"Fuck, Nicole!"

"I'm sorry!"

"Shit ... *shit!*" Hart thought about Ivy. He pressed his fingers into his temples to stop the world swirling around his naïve, pathetic soul. His heart rate increased, and a sinister darkness fogged his mind. The barely audible music blared in his ears, and his heart thumped restlessly inside his chest, threatening to implode.

"It can be an aphrodisiac! I use them all the time, just ride with it," she breathed, doubting her decision momentarily.

Hart groaned again at Nicole's foolishness. Her selfishness. He needed to get home to Ivy before he would have to leave her for Libya indefinitely. Hart concentrated on Ivy's innocence, her tranquility ... and instantly his heart rate slowed to a more tolerable pace. He imagined her stepping into the soft sand and lifting her face to the sky, the eternal blue reflecting in her crystal gaze. Breathing in the salty air, breathing in the world. Hart took a long, deep breath as he thought about her stillness. Her gentleness. *Her love* ... and his soul settled.

Nicole approached him cautiously, now that he was calm. He was leaned forward with his elbows on the table and his face buried in his hands.

"Johnny?" she asked tentatively.

Hart didn't move.

"You still fightin' it, honey, or have you got it under control?"

Nicole walked toward him as though approaching a sleeping lion.

"Don't speak," he replied calmly.

"What are you worried about?" she smiled through her distress. "It's just like old times."

Hart rubbed his eyes open and glared at her.

"Old times?" he repeated. "You've never drugged me before, Nic. What the fuck is wrong with you?" The uncomfortable heaviness still lingered behind his eyes. Hart shook his head against a growing numbness.

She glanced sheepishly at him. "I saw you with her, with Ivy."

Hart didn't answer.

"I saw the way you two looked at each other. You love her, don't you?" Nicole dropped her unhappy gaze to her hands before she looked at him again. His expression gave her nothing.

Hart looked past her to the window.

"Should I be jealous?" she asked.

The room circled ominously around the red dress standing in front of him, and eventually he resigned himself to the spinning. Punishment for his pleasure with Oliver's sister. Punishment for his survival in Libya. The physical pain seemed to ease when he deserved it, but his guilt didn't.

Hart blinked in disbelief as the words spilled unbidden from his mouth, "I killed her brother."

Nicole's expression brightened, then she laughed.

"You're kidding? Oliver?" She didn't attempt to contain her excitement. "Does she know?"

Hart shook his head, unsmiling. "No. I haven't had the heart to tell her."

Nicole breathed out loudly in the delightfully scandalous news. Her eyes were gloriously wide. She sat down at the table next to Hart and stared at him with an open, confounded grin.

"She's gonna run for the hills when you tell her. You're gonna tell her, right? That would be the moral thing to do," Nicole challenged him brazenly, sliding her bourbon from hand to hand across the table.

"Moral?" Hart scoffed. "This coming from the woman who

just drugged a man in her motel room."

"Oh, please, you can't say you didn't need it," she puffed proudly. Nicole took a quick sip of her bourbon. "You looked like shit, Johnny."

Hart glared at her across the table. "Well, now I *feel* like shit also, so thank you, Nic."

He leaned his head into his hands again, feeling the slow, noxious sedation of the drug. There was no resistance from his body. He was floating outside of himself, watching the dismal scene from miles away. He was like a tiny, useless speck in a big, complicated world … and he was tired. *So tired.*

The stitches prickled under his left eye, and Hart felt a drop of blood glide down his cheek. He didn't bother to wipe it away, the sensation of the hot blood rolling down his skin felt good. It felt real. A lethargic weight fell upon him, and when Nicole spoke again, her voice was low and muffled in his ears.

"Oh, Johnny, you're bleeding," she gasped dramatically. She jumped up and hurried to the bathroom to fetch a cloth.

Hart rubbed the harrowing pain that gripped his heart. What would Ivy think when he didn't come home tonight?

Nicole returned with a wet cloth. "All those years coming home from over there, and not once have I seen you bleed!"

"That's because I never used to bleed." Hart bowed his head and thought about Ivy. "Now I bleed all the time."

Nicole's jaw dropped at the stoic soldier. She'd never heard him talk like this before.

"I've come to depend on it," he replied, looking at her. "I need it."

Nicole kneeled between his legs and grinned, enthralled by his darkness. "Like some kind of punishment?"

Hart nodded feebly, virtually defeated by the drug.

She dabbed the blood away softly with the corner of the warm washcloth, and he had no strength left to push her away. Nicole inflicted this upon him for selfish reasons, and the fact that he bled was an added bonus. There was an unmistakable hunger in her soulless eyes as she cleaned his face. She looked like a thirsty vampire who only barely restrained herself from licking his wound clean with her tongue. He thought about the confrontation with Tommy and his gang last night. Ivy gave herself up so he wouldn't have to bleed for her ... but he wanted to bleed for her. He owed her everything.

Hart groaned and drifted into a guilty, colorless haze.

"Bourbon fumes and a glorious masochist ... I want for nothing more," Nicole said from somewhere in front of him.

"That's because you're a sadist with a dark fucking soul," he replied with his eyes closed.

Nicole narrowed her gaze seductively, "And yet you're still willing to sleep with me."

He thought he felt her hands slide up the inside of his thighs, but it was too hard to tell through the numbness that had embraced him entirely.

"I'm not going to sleep with you," he whispered.

Hart dropped into the black abyss behind his tired eyes. The dark wings encased him once again, and he waited, until one by one the claws sunk into his bleeding heart ... and he roared in soundless agony. Nicole's husky laugh was the last thing he heard before the darkness defeated his soul.

## Chapter 23

IVY PICKED UP THE NEWSPAPER near the front gate and wiped away the dew from the plastic wrap with her fingertips. The mornings were getting warmer. It was that time of year again when she would count down the days until summer and the Silver Moon Gala. An excitement dashed through her heart, but it was more an ingrained sentiment than anticipation for the night. Ivy knew she wasn't looking forward to it this year. The Gala sat impatiently in the background of her mind, miles behind the welfare of her three soldiers. Once the Gala meant everything to her ... but that was before she had lost Oliver and gained his three soldiers, only to lose them again. She wondered how she could ever enjoy a night out again while her soldiers fought in a war across the world. Nothing seemed important to her anymore, least of all the Gala. They were going to risk their lives to hunt down the man that murdered her brother, and Ivy felt partly responsible. Losing Oliver made their return to Libya very real, and her heart was barely coping. Fractured by fate too many times.

She thought about Hart's absence last night. It still hurt ... losing something you never really had in the first place. Ivy took a deep breath and peered into the sky. She closed her eyes and thought about Hart, Walker and Benji. A timeless era had passed while she mourned her brother, and these soldiers brought Oliver home to her in their own distinct, charming ways. Walker said they had become pieces of one another over the years, and he was right. She thought about the way they watched over her with their unyielding devotion and protection, as though Oliver had sent them to her in his place. Ivy narrowed her eyes at the concept. She hugged the newspaper tightly to her chest and remembered Oliver's words to her on the beach all those years ago … *you will never be alone, I promise.*

"He sent them," she breathed.

The gates cranked open with a sudden *clang,* startling Ivy. The Firebird rumbled behind her, and she turned to the consoling sound. She stood in the center of the driveway and watched Hart's car roll toward her with a low purr. When he reached her, he came to a gentle stop. They stared at each other through the windscreen, both unusually tense. Hart had his elbow propped on the window, and he considered her with a thoughtful but unsmiling serenity.

Ivy fidgeted nervously with the newspaper in her hands and then moved toward the edge of the driveway, feeling rather foolish for standing in his way.

"Ivy, wait," Hart called after her, climbing out of his car without turning it off.

The Firebird rumbled deeply in the background with a gentleness that matched his soothing voice, and his calming presence overwhelmed her. She wanted to run into his arms and tell him that she missed him. No matter what happened last night … one night without him was too long.

He walked to her along the driveway with his hands tucked casually into his jeans pockets. His white shirt clung beautifully to the muscles in his chest, and Ivy grew more nervous the closer he got to her. His eyes weren't guilty. His expression carried no doubt. Hart was warm and adoring and nothing else.

When he reached her, he sighed apologetically. "Nothing happened, Ivy. I promise."

He searched her eyes, but Ivy felt too timid to hold his gaze. She ran her fingers through her hair and pulled it to one side and sighed loudly. Ivy looked back at him and caught the panic in his kind eyes. She managed a small smile in his unwitting vulnerability. His eyes … they still gave *everything* away.

Hart went to speak. "Ivy—"

"Don't. Please," she interrupted. "You don't have to—"

"Explain?" he cut in. "Of course I do. Ivy, I—"

"Stop!" She glanced up at him and shied away from his striking eyes; one night apart was all it took for her bashfulness to reclaim her. She breathed in deeply and looked up at him. "You told me nothing happened. I believe you."

Hart bowed his head and thought about last night. He left Nicole's motel room less than an hour ago, but he could not remember anything about the evening before. He recalled the splitting pain in his head as the drugs leeched through his veins, and then there was nothing after that. Nothing but a cold emptiness that sat uncomfortably in the pit of his stomach. He wanted to tell her about the Rohypnol, but he didn't, because she asked him not to.

Hart rubbed his chest with the palm of his hand, and a hesitant smile crept across his face.

"I missed you last night," he said.

"I missed you, too."

A glorious sincerity filled his brown eyes, but Ivy sensed the foreboding heartbreak within them. This was it. This was their final hours. The conclusion of their journey together. She heard the world whisper in her ear, telling her someone else would take him from here. Her assistance with this soldier was no longer required. Hart was leaving—but she wasn't ready to let him go.

"Come here." He reached out and pulled her into his strong body.

Ivy felt his big arms wrap around her, and suddenly her heavy spirit lifted weightlessly off the ground. She heard him take a deep breath of her hair and then calmly exhale into her. His breath was warm against the top of her head, and Ivy closed her eyes in his wonder. Falling irretrievably into his intoxicating scent. If only she could stay like this forever ... unreachable by the rest of the world, in the arms of her beautiful soldier.

Hart took her hand in his and pulled her toward the car. He picked her up and sat her on the hood with a roguish grin.

"What are you up to?" Ivy smiled, grateful for his unexpected playfulness.

"I'm driving you home. Lie down."

Ivy shook her head. "No, if I put a dent in the Firebird I'll feel awful. I know how much you love this car." She slid herself off the car, and Hart caught her.

"You're not going to dent my car, Ives. You weigh less than a bird." He slid her back toward the windscreen.

Ivy scowled at him playfully.

"Okay, okay," he laughed, "you weigh less than my rucksack, remember? I rest it on the car all the time back at Base."

She studied him carefully. "Okay. What about this?" Ivy held out the rolled up newspaper, and Hart rolled his eyes.

"Here, give it to me," he replied.

She passed the newspaper to Hart with an amused grin and he tossed it through the car window. Ivy held his hand as he leaned her back gently on the car. The black bonnet felt hot on her skin, and she melted into its soothing heat. She wore tiny silk shorts that she considered underwear rather than pajamas, and a see-through silk camisole that hugged her curves. Ivy could see her breasts beneath the white silk, and she made a conscious decision *never* to fetch the newspaper dressed like this in the future, should anyone other than Hart arrive unannounced at the gate. Judging by the delight that lingered in his adorable expression, Ivy assumed he was grateful for his well-timed arrival.

"Are you ready?" he asked from behind her.

*Ready?* The Firebird was hot beneath her, and the cold silk brushed against her nipples. The sensation sent a pleasant ripple through her body, and she warmed with sweet desire for the soldier who lay her down before him. Ivy looked up at him, her hooded blue eyes blinking sedately with pleasure.

"I'm ready," she said softly.

"Don't tempt me, Ivy." Hart breathed heavily.

She bit her lip to restrain her hunger for him. Ivy rested her head on the glass and gazed at the trees hanging over her. The branches cascaded around her, and Ivy sensed the peacefulness in the air. It was as if the world offered them this final, enchanting moment ... before everything changed. Before she lost it all, again.

Hart shifted the Firebird into first gear, and they rolled along the driveway at a gentle, purring pace.

Ivy smiled. She didn't mean to. It snuck up on her, and

suddenly she was grinning ear to ear as he drove toward the estate with her sprawled across the sun-warmed bonnet of his car. The sun caught the glossy leaves above her in the trees, and beyond the trees was the pale blue, cloudless morning sky. A still saltiness filled the air. Ivy imagined the mist hanging over the San Diego shoreline, surfers dotting the glassy waves. The engine rumbled through her body with a careless freedom that chased away the previous fear of his deployment, and with a long, deep breath, Ivy exhaled her heartache. She lifted her hands into the air and allowed the soft, leafy ends of the branches to sweep across her palms. She had never been here before. *In love.* Her feelings lay far beyond her understanding. Her spirit soared deliriously with the highest of winds, yet she was crash landing at a catastrophic pace. She carried an unfathomable longing for a man who would inevitably leave her, and the helplessness left a wretched, gaping hole in her happiness. It was like stepping off the edge of a cliff; one minute safe and still, feeling on top of the world … then suddenly falling through the air with the ground rushing fatefully to meet you. There will be no promise of Hart's return after he left for the war, so letting him go would be the hardest thing she had ever had to do.

Ivy rolled onto her stomach and leaned her chin on the back of her hands and watched Hart through the windscreen as he drove. He stared back at her with a beautiful grin, but Ivy could see the gravity of their circumstance weighing on his mind. Oliver. Libya. Taym. It was all there in his silent solicitude.

Hart saw her smile fade. A wistfulness shaded her sweeping eyes, and he felt her inside him, searching his soul. He sighed to himself inside the car, then parked the Firebird alongside the bottom step and turned off the engine. Ivy didn't move, so he remained in his seat, spellbound by her pensive, crystal gaze.

"You're leaving … aren't you," she breathed. Hart nodded his head reluctantly. She saw his big shoulders rise and fall soundlessly inside the car.

A shallow breath escaped her lips. Ivy rested her forehead on the back of her hands and listened to her shaking breath against the bonnet of the Firebird. She pleaded silently for a world where she could keep him. For a world where there was no war. A world where she didn't lose everyone she loved because they possessed the strongest and bravest of hearts.

"Ivy," he murmured. He got out of the car and stood beside her.

She slid off the bonnet and looked up at him.

"They've summoned me, Ives. I don't want to leave you, but I have to."

"I know." Ivy twisted her face miserably without looking at him, unable to speak through her sadness. She walked up the stairs, and when she reached the top, she turned to face Hart. "I've been around soldiers long enough to understand the difference between duty and love."

Hart looked up at her. "I'm so sorry."

Ivy smiled faintly through her tears. She considered the angst in his vulnerable eyes. "As long as that's the real reason you're leaving."

Hart stared at her as he thought about it. She had a fragile aura about her, and Hart knew she was referring to his role in her brother's death. She stood above him in the grandness of her estate with an extraordinary presence that moved him. Ivy Rose. His Queen of Hearts. Hart knew he was only inches from the gallows where he truly belonged. He was leaving because he wanted Taym Malak dead. Gone. Eradicated from this world. It was necessary, and it was justice. *So he thought.* After all this time, drenched in Ivy's sweet perception of all things, even he questioned his own conviction. He didn't belong here with Ivy, nor did he belong in Oliver's home. He felt like a fugitive in disguise, stealing time with her before she discovered who he really was. Before the world made a final verdict on his guilty soul. It was finally time to serve his life sentence of penance and atonement … without Ivy.

Hart rubbed his jaw but quickly stopped when the trembling visibly shook his hand. He did his best to conceal it from her. He denied himself of her compassion because he was on his own now. His future lay with Libya, not Ivy. He would fight until the day he died, and on that day he would succumb to it gladly. There would be no pain or fear in his death because he had died once before … the day he left Ivy Rose. The divine being who saved his weary soul from the living dead.

"Ivy, I want to tell you everything but I …," Hart paused. He rubbed his jaw and looked at her again. The truth about Oliver sat anxiously in his chest, and he willed for the words to roll off his tongue once and for all. He yearned for her anger with him. Her revulsion.

Hart groaned lightly, feeling his head spin, desperate to tell her everything.

Ivy shook her head while he suffered in his unspoken words. The way he always did. The past year flashed tenderly through her thoughts, and a small, sympathetic smile appeared on her face … before she walked inside.

Hart turned toward the driveway and cursed. He ran his hands through his hair and blew the air out of his lungs with a long, tired breath … mentally fatigued with his conflicting thoughts. He didn't want to go, but he loved her too much to stay. Hart sighed into his hands and leaned on the roof of his car. He stared intently down the driveway, wracking his mind for a clear path through the constant convolutions of life. Decisions were always a matter of the mind in the war, but here with Ivy, his heart complicated everything.

A taxi appeared in the distance on the driveway. Hart studied the car as it approached the estate. He walked into the center of the drive and stood in its path, and the taxi came to a halt when it reached him.

The window behind the driver's door opened. Hart walked toward it and peered in.

"Hey, Johnny, I couldn't leave without apologizing," a voice said from inside the car.

Hart wiped his hands tiredly down his face. He leaned on the open window and glared at Nicole in stunned frustration.

"I know! I get it! You're pissed at me!" Nicole threw her hands in the air. "Just let me explain myself, okay."

Hart groaned irritably. "No! Goddamn it, Nicole! No!"

"Five minutes! Just give me *five* minutes!"

Hart ignored her. He moved to the driver's window and motioned for him to open it. The driver peered nervously at Nicole before reluctantly opening his window.

"Get her out of here. Now!" Hart growled.

The taxi driver was rather young, and he glanced uneasily at Hart. He turned to look at Nicole and slowly lowered his foot on the accelerator.

"Don't listen to him! You stay right here!" Nicole commanded. The taxi stopped again. "You can't send me away like that!"

Hart didn't look at her. Instead, he read the driver's name on the information card, plastered to the dashboard. Considering the pronunciation of his surname, Hart assumed the man was Italian.

"Parli Italiano?" Hart asked flawlessly.

A wide grin appeared on the driver's face. "Sì!"

Hart shot the driver a friendly, charming smile. Gaining the trust of foreigners was a necessary skill for Phoenix, and Hart genuinely enjoyed the process. He sensed the sudden shift in his own confidence.

"Hey, no, no, no, don't you dare!" Nicole called out from the backseat. Hart and the driver continued to talk without taking any notice of her. "Don't you use your soldier antics to flatter my driver, Johnny, stop … stop it!"

Nicole hit the driver's shoulder in the front seat to stop him from conversing with Hart in a language she didn't understand. She was positive Hart was conjuring up a phony story to encourage the taxi to take her away. She saw the laidback charm exuding from Hart. His smile was breathtaking. She mindlessly tapped the driver as she gawked at Hart from the backseat in hopeless infatuation.

The taxi driver continued to ignore her attempts to thwart their conversation, so she exited the car before they finished.

"Idiots," she whispered under her breath, making a beeline for Ivy's door.

"Hey!" Hart ran after her. "Where do you think you're going?"

"Ah, excuse me, Signora! You haven't paid!"

Nicole paused and rolled her eyes. She rifled through her handbag and trotted delicately in her high heels back to the taxi. She threw a handful of notes into the driver's lap and turned to the estate again.

"This isn't my house," Hart grumbled under his breath as he followed her. "You can't just waltz into Ivy's home and cause her unnecessary trouble."

Nicole's expression remained apathetic toward Hart. She set

her sight on the estate and hurried toward it with a zealous haste.

Hart's anger with her sparked a renewed sense of unrestrained fury. Taym Malak flashed through his thoughts and Hart grabbed Nicole's arm firmly and forced her to stop, making her gasp. He hadn't left for Libya yet, and Ivy was still under his vigilant protection.

"How the fuck did you get in here anyhow?" he growled.

"Let go of me … that hurts! What is with your behavior lately?"

Hart laughed, bemused by her ignorance. "I don't know, Nic? Maybe I'm coming down off the drugs you slipped into my drink last night!"

Nicole scoffed and rolled her eyes. She ran up the stairs to Ivy's front door, but Hart beat her there. She curled her lip and shot him a sneering glare, then she peered curiously past him into the house.

Hart threw his arm up in front of her and pulled her away from the door.

"Johnny!"

"You didn't answer me, Nic! How did you get past the security gate!?"

"I let her in," Ivy replied from inside.

Hart looked to Ivy, who was standing in the center of the entry hall, watching them with her curious, blue eyes. She wore cut-off denim shorts and a white tank, with an oversized knit jersey tied loosely around her hips. Her long tanned legs were planted in light-gray hiking sneakers, and Hart immediately searched the hall for her backpack. There it was, sitting beside him at the front door. He knew immediately where she planned to go once he left her this afternoon. The thought of her on the Ghost Trail alone troubled him deeply, and his heart leaped into a sudden panic. There was a coolness in her expression that anyone else would misperceive as casual disrespect. But not Hart. If she weren't solely led by her innocence, he would have conceived her plan as payback for his departure.

"Please, don't," Hart begged her, forgetting his vexation for Nicole.

Ivy didn't reply. She recognized the pain that drenched his brown eyes. She knew he didn't want her going to Lights Beach alone, but it was her sanctuary. Her place of refuge. Later, when he left her for Libya, she would go there to survive the world as it fell to pieces around her. Like it always did.

Nicole and Ivy walked into the living room and sat together on the sofa, while Hart stood in the kitchen and watched the two of them carefully.

"So, I have the donation for the Gala right here," Nicole said cheerfully, pulling a small envelope from her handbag.

Hart shook his head when he heard her. This was Nicole's way in, but her actual motive remained unclear to him.

"Thank you. It is very kind of you to make such a substantial contribution to the cause."

"Oh, no, I love it. Honestly, it is an honor just to be here with you, Ivy. I read about it every year. You're a huge celebrity!"

"I'm not a celebrity," Ivy blushed, dismissing the thought quickly.

Hart listened to Ivy from the kitchen. He closed his eyes, feeling guilty for leading Nicole straight to her.

"Your dress is beautiful by the way," Ivy added, changing the topic.

"Thank you!" Nicole ran her hands down her skin-tight black dress.

Ivy dropped her gaze in a rare moment of doubt and thought about Hart with Nicole last night.

Nicole turned to Hart in the kitchen. "Don't you have things to pack? Places to go?" she said dismissively. "You told me last night you were leaving for Monterey today?"

Ivy shuddered sadly.

"Not while you're here," he replied blandly.

Ivy caught his protective gaze. She admired Hart's selfless guardianship of her. It wasn't conditioned, or learned. It was an instinct. An inherent virtuousness that all three of Oliver's soldiers gallantly possessed. But today Ivy felt numb to it.

Hart's cell rung in his pocket, but he let it go unanswered.

"You should get that," Ivy suggested. "It might be Walker."

"I'll call him back."

Hart leaned against the island and rubbed his forehead with a weariness that caught Ivy's attention. She frowned to herself and thought of Walker trying to reach him. Since Hart was leaving today, Walker most likely had some vital information concerning their mission in Libya. Hart had never deliberately missed a call in the past, and she had a feeling that this was the phone call he had been waiting for all year. *They have him. They have Taym Malak. Oh, Oliver....*

The ringing ended, and Ivy glanced at Nicole, who was silently examining their behavior. Hart's concern was merited, she thought. The gleam in Nicole's eye illustrated her pleasure in their misfortune.

"Please, call him back." Ivy held his gaze. The trouble was gravely anchored in Hart's expression as he remained unmoving in the kitchen. She nodded at him to leave, managing a small smile to ease his concern with Nicole.

With apprehension, Hart walked toward the front door and glanced behind him to assess Ivy's feelings. Having not spoken to her about what happened last night, he was a little anxious to leave her alone with Nicole. He had no option other than to put his trust in Ivy's sharp intuition and pray she didn't fall victim to Nicole's wicked games. Hart could only think of a handful of people who were immune to Nicole's bewitching allure. She relished in the art of seducing the innocent, man or woman, captivating them with her lascivious, devilish charm. She conjured a darkness within even the brightest of souls, and Ivy's blinding light stood perilously close to Nicole's insatiable black hole. He considered the pair as they sat side by side on the sofa ... the two women couldn't be more opposite. Hart stood indecisively at the door while holding the handle, then without reassurance from his thoughts, he left them.

Nicole listened for the door to click shut. She found his protectiveness over Ivy tedious, and she rolled her eyes at the monotony of it all. She did her best not to snigger aloud at his cynical behavior. Hart's reluctance to trust her only encouraged her to rebel against him, and Nicole smiled ever so slightly. Her dark eyes smoldered with wicked anticipation for revenge on Commander Johnny Hart. Ivy was all alone without the protection of her soldiers, and Nicole was eager to conjure up some trouble.

"You have quite an impressive view here," Nicole beamed.

Ivy smiled and relaxed. "Not a day goes by that I don't appreciate it."

Nicole leaned forward and slid out a cigarette from the open pack she had placed in the center of the coffee table. Her slender fingers guided it to her bright, red lips, and with a flash of the lighter, she gently inhaled the cigarette to life. She offered the box to Ivy, who politely refused.

"You don't mind, do you?" Nicole breathed out huskily. "I can go outside, if you prefer?"

"No, it's fine."

"They're the non-filtered type," Nicole continued calmly, in her cool, southern accent. She raised her eyes to meet Ivy's. "Gives me more of a buzz, you know, a spinning sensation … a light-headedness." She waved her hands around in circles above her head with a gorgeous smile and sinful eyes.

Ivy laughed timidly.

Nicole closed her eyes and tilted her head back and slid her body divinely down the sofa, sighing with pleasure as she did. Her black dress slipped slowly up her thighs, and her long, dark hair fell beautifully around her flawless, porcelain skin.

"Hmmm, I love it when I'm spinning," she breathed. Nicole stayed there for a short while, allowing her consciousness to indulge in the easy high she had waited for all morning.

Ivy furrowed her brows, perplexed by Nicole's behavior. This woman had to be riding on more than just a cigarette. Ivy snuck a quick glance at the door and wondered how long Hart would be.

Nicole sat up and peacefully spun the pack of cigarettes on the table, and considered Ivy beside her. There was a beautiful innocence about her that nauseated Nicole, but she couldn't deny the burning sense of envy she felt toward her. These soldiers were the most resilient, good-looking men Nicole had ever known, yet Ivy somehow managed to reign the hearts of all three of these unattainable men. She looked away and wrapped her pouty lips around the end of her cigarette. She took a long draw of it and shifted her covetous, dark eyes back to Ivy. Hart was the most desirable, impressive man Nicole had ever had. She refused to compete for his affection.

Ivy ran her fingers through her hair and pulled it down to

one side in front of her, forcing a smile when Nicole looked at her.

"Damn!" Nicole exclaimed, startling Ivy. She watched Ivy's hair fall like golden silk and the jealously snapped against her insecure heart, making her laugh unexpectedly. "These poor soldiers didn't stand a chance when they met you, did they?"

"What do you mean?"

"Well shit, Ivy, look at you! You're the perfect woman! I can't decide if I love you or hate you!"

Ivy's sweet expression dissolved with cynicism.

Nicole took a quick puff of her cigarette, growing excited with the unexpected pleasure in provoking Ivy. If Hart wanted the Silver Moon Queen instead of her, then there was only one thing left to do before she left La Mar; sabotage the relationship.

Nicole cut Ivy off before she could respond. "So, tell me, how do you keep all three soldiers so devoted to you?" she grinned.

Ivy thought about it. She understood the bond between herself and her brother's soldiers; it was deep and trusting and powerful. The four of them share a loved one who was now beyond their reach, and this is what bound them together in the very first moment they met. Their devotion to her was a manifestation of love. Indescribable, incomprehensible ... *love*. But she wasn't ready to disclose their relationship with just anyone. A huge part of her lay burdened with superstition, terrified she might lose it all should she admit to anyone how happy she was in their attention.

"I wouldn't say they are *devoted* to me ...," she managed eventually.

"Of course they are." Nicole stared blandly at Ivy. Unconvinced. "Those men are in love with you, Ivy."

Ivy laughed. "No, it's not like that."

"It is!" Nicole laughed bitterly. "All three of them! I see the way they look at you. Josh, Benji ... *Johnny*." She took an impatient puff on her cigarette and looked away to conceal her resentment.

"They care about me," Ivy added. "It's not what you're thinking—"

"Honey," Nicole interrupted, "those soldiers want to fuck you."

Ivy smiled through her frown, taken aback by Nicole's frank

attitude.

"They're men. What do you expect? Simple, Goddamn men." She leaned into Ivy on the sofa and parted her lips seductively. "So what's your secret? How does one woman please three men all at the same time?"

Walker and Benji flashed rebelliously through Ivy's thoughts, gloriously drenched in sunlight as they emerged from the waves of Lights Beach. She was a terrible liar and the truth blushed shamelessly in her cheeks—the idea of being with either of them had undeniable appeal.

Nicole's eyes widened when Ivy didn't respond. She chuckled proudly.

"Shit, I've got you all wrong!" Nicole exclaimed. "You do please all three soldiers, don't you? Damn, Ivy, I expected much less from someone like you. I'm impressed."

"What? No, I—" Ivy hesitated. She rested her cold fingers on her burning cheeks. The thought of Hart inside her sent a shooting warmth through her body, forcing her to stop talking.

"Okay, now we're getting somewhere!" Nicole inhaled powerfully on her cigarette and glared at Ivy with a roguish, reckless grin. "So how do you do it exactly? Do you fuck one for breakfast, one for afternoon tea, and the lucky last for dinner?"

Ivy regretted her decision to convince Hart to leave, but she regained her composure as Nicole went on.

"Oh, no, wait, wait!" Nicole continued, waving her hands at Ivy. "Then you fuck all three together for dessert!" She slapped the table with her hands and laughed gloriously to herself. The ash from her cigarette scattered across the glass surface of the table in her excitement and Ivy watched on in stunned silence.

"Oh God," she added, sighing pleasurably, "… imagine a tiny thing like you with those three, huge, *delicious* soldiers, all at the one time." Nicole rolled her eyes back and fell back into the sofa, quietly considering herself in the same situation with not one, but all three men. As much as Walker and Benji irritated her, she couldn't deny her attraction to their mouth-watering physiques and beautiful faces.

Eventually Nicole stood up from the sofa and ran her fingers through her hair. She smiled down at Ivy. A breathtaking, beautiful smile. A distrustful smile. "Oh Ivy, I don't mean any harm ... I'm just fucking jealous."

Ivy forced a laugh, trying to ease the awkward situation. "Well, don't be," she replied. "You make it sound far more ... *enthralling* ... than it actually is." Ivy fought off the thought of Hart's sculpted body above her while they made love. His strength. His attentiveness. His soul-aching tenderness. She tried not to recall her kiss with Walker and the heart-melting warmth of his lips against hers. The way Benji's dimpled grin and twinkling blue eyes whisked her breathlessly off her feet every time he smiled. As much as she hated to admit it, Nicole's ludicrous impression of her relationship with these men was far more accurate than Ivy originally thought. In fact, two days ago, she slept with Hart for breakfast, lunch, dinner, *and* multiple times for dessert.

Never all three soldiers at once.

"But it has crossed your mind, right?"

Ivy looked up at her. "What?"

"All three at once!?" Nicole asked with excitement, gleaming at Ivy with anticipation.

"No. *Never*," she dismissed, avoiding Nicole's burning curiosity. She desperately wanted the conversation to end.

"Come on!" Nicole jested. "Not once? Gee, Ivy, learn to take an opportunity when it's presented to you. I always do."

Ivy laughed awkwardly and glanced at the door again. Hart would despise this conversation.

Nicole walked over to a tray of spirits standing on a wooden cabinet at the bar on the far side of the room.

"You don't mind if I help myself to a bourbon do you?" Nicole asked.

"No, go ahead." Ivy glanced at the time in the kitchen ... 10 a.m.

"You want one?"

Ivy thought about the long, dreadful day ahead and sighed. "I'd love one."

Nicole strutted happily across the room with their drinks in her hand. Ivy could tell she was delighted with her unexpected drinking partner at such an unusual hour in the day. Nicole was exceptionally beautiful when she was happy, and Ivy wondered when she had grown so insecure in this life.

"Bourbon makes me a better human being," Nicole sparkled mischievously. "Without it, I am simply unbearable." She passed

Ivy one of the tumblers and sat down beside her again on the sofa.

Ivy took a large mouthful of bourbon, quickly followed by another, and another, and Nicole looked on, impressed.

"So, you and Johnny, are you two an item?" Nicole asked.

An exaggerated indifference in Nicole's expression revealed her desperation, and Ivy considered her cautiously. "No. Not really."

"Not really? I don't understand. You're either together, or you're not," Nicole replied smugly. "Have you fucked him?"

Ivy choked on her bourbon.

"No," Ivy lied. A light, awkward breath escaped her lips before she sipped on her bourbon again.

"Johnny thinks I have a jet black soul," Nicole smiled sadly. She placed her glass on the table and turned to face Ivy. Her expression was serious but still beautiful. "He never said it exactly, but I know how he feels. He once told me to let a little light into my heart ... but there was never a lot of light around me to let in."

Ivy smiled politely. She didn't want to listen to Nicole talk about Hart on a day like this, so she finished her bourbon to deflect the pain. She looked past Nicole at the bottle of bourbon on the bar.

Nicole turned to look at the bar where Ivy had her eye. "Anyhow," she continued, "I kinda like the dark. Everything I do is done best in the dark." Nicole grinned into her bourbon, then finished it.

Ivy shrugged her shoulders. "Like they say, that's when the stars shine their brightest."

Nicole's eyes twinkled with an indescribable evil. "I like you, Ivy."

Ivy bowed her head and smiled hesitantly into the empty glass sitting on her lap. There was something unbalanced about this woman, and she hoped the encounter would soon end. Walker was right. Nicole was a firecracker. Or more like unstable dynamite. Ivy's heart was telling her to run for cover, but she remained unwisely in her position.

"You want another drink?" Nicole asked.

"Please."

Nicole fetched the bottle of bourbon. "So, did Johnny talk to you about what happened last night?"

Ivy sighed inwardly. "No, he—"

"Good!" Nicole stopped her. She poured the golden liquid into the two tumblers that sat on the coffee table and then sat down. "There's something special about that soldier. He's a true gentleman. You can always depend on him to never kiss and tell."

Ivy felt a wave of nausea rush over her.

"Everything about that man is godlike," Nicole continued. "And I mean … *everything*!"

Ivy exhaled sharply. Hart told her nothing happened, and she believed him. At least, she wanted to believe him. The truth dangled precariously in her reach …all she had to do was ask.

"Nicole, last night…" Ivy hesitated.

"Mm-hmm?"

Hart gave her his word, and now she felt like she was betraying him. A dreadful heaviness bared down on her heart. She trusted him, yet somehow the question slipped past her lips. "Did you sleep with Hart?"

Nicole's eyes narrowed in delight.

Ivy held her breath as she waited for her answer … then Hart walked into the room.

## Chapter 24

"EVERYTHING IS IN MOTION, dead on schedule. If we leave on Thursday, then Taym is ours," Walker said down the line. "Two more days and that bastard is ours, Hart. Finally."

Hart sighed in relief and stared into the blue sky. "That's good news, buddy. Shit, I can't wait to bring Taym to his knees."

"I have a bunch of maps in front of me that intelligence dropped on my desk earlier today."

"You have a desk now?" Hart laughed.

"I do! They're actually not as bad as you think."

"Yeah? We'll see," Hart smiled. "So why do we need maps? We're central Tripoli. We spent three years over there."

"They insist we use them. The maps are fucking inaccurate as hell, but we'll humor them," Walker laughed. "Hang on, Hart ...."

Hart waited as Walker spoke to a colleague. He rubbed his jaw and glanced back at the house, thinking about Ivy on her own with Nicole.

"Sorry, man," Walker said eventually.

"No problem."

"I have Benji sittin' on my fucking lap here. Get your ass off my desk, man."

Hart sensed the smile in Walker's voice, and he laughed. "Hey, Benji boy!" Hart called out.

"Hey sweetheart," Benji replied playfully.

"Some Mustangs joined Phoenix," Walker continued. "They've been debriefed on the op and the unit's history over the past twelve years, with a little extra time spent on 2014. They endured a three hundred twenty-five-page document on what happened in Libya last year. Poor bastards."

Hart didn't reply. He rubbed his forehead wearily and wondered how they interpreted the circumstances of Oliver's death through black and white print.

Walker listened to Hart's silence on the other end of the line. "Look, I read it, Hart. It states the facts. Nothing more, nothing less. What's important here is that they have an in-depth knowledge of the target. They want Taym too, not as badly as we do, but they do nonetheless. Plus, we need them. They're good guys. You'll like them."

Hart thought about it. "If you two are okay with it, then so am I."

"How's Ivy taking it?" Walker asked casually.

Hart stared back at the house and sighed into the phone. *Ivy.*

"You have spoken to her right?" Walker added, concerned. "You have told her you're leaving?"

"She knows."

A quiet moment had passed before Walker spoke again.

"I'm not sure if you are aware of this, but our presence is not compulsory on this mission. Not after what happened last year with Ollie. Benji and I have been talking, and we think—"

"Don't even say it, Walker," Hart interrupted. He rested his hand on the back of his head and closed his eyes tightly. "Don't tempt me. Shit!"

"Phoenix will find Taym whether the three of us are there or not," he added cautiously. "We're worried about Ivy. I don't think Ollie meant for us—"

"No! We are going to Libya for Oliver. We owe it to him to bring Taym to justice," Hart reaffirmed. "I'm on my way. I'll see you in a few hours." He heard Walker sigh through the phone without pushing the matter any further.

"Alright," Walker replied. "We'll see you soon, buddy."

Hart tucked his cell into his back pocket and wiped his face tiredly. He leaned his head back and closed his eyes, and exhaled into the sky. He thought about Ivy. It was his decision now. He could stay with her here in La Mar, living out his days in her divine wonder … but he would never stop battling the demons that riddled his guilty soul.

"Shit," he breathed.

The war had called for him at last, and he would leave her willingly. It was his duty as a soldier and an officer. His honor as a friend. Taym Malak plagued his thoughts and revenge overruled the declarations of his heart. He groaned into his hands as he walked back to the estate. This was goodbye.

Hart opened the front door, and Nicole's laughter rattled the emptiness in his trembling soul. The darkness instantly embraced him, and he welcomed it with open arms. He needed it if he were to going to fight Taym … if he were going to kill him. The darkness would bring pleasure in Taym's dying breath. Hart craved the untainted sweetness of his reprieve. His release from the devil's merciless grip. He could already feel the razor-sharp claws being pulled one by one from his heart. Hart pushed Ivy far out of his head and out of his soul. Her light was too bright. She blinded his hatred with her uncorrupted heart. She was too good for him. She always had been. All he ever wanted after losing Oliver was death … and Ivy wanted life.

He walked into the room where Ivy and Nicole were sitting.

"Hart!" Ivy jumped up in surprise.

He looked at her across the room, and a flood of anxiety filled his heart. "I have to go," he said softly.

Ivy exhaled sharply. "Right now?"

Hart nodded unhappily. He saw the color drain from her cheeks. He wanted to go to her and wrap her in his arms, but then he would never let her go. Time seemed to stand still as they stared at each other soundlessly through the room. He felt himself watching them from afar as though he had already died in the war; floating through an empty, black void without her eternal light by his side.

Hart tore his heartbroken gaze from her and left the room to gather his belongings, leaving Ivy with Nicole.

"Wait, Hart!" Ivy left Nicole and ran after him down the hall that led to his bedroom. Her stomach was rolling in the suddenness of Hart's departure, and the bourbon only made her wretched unhappiness worse. The foreboding loneliness. The helpless despair. There was nothing she could do to keep him from leaving her. Hart already had his bag on the end of the bed, and Ivy stood in the doorway and watched him toss his clothes from the drawers to the bag with a sudden urgency. He seemed desperate for a quick exit.

"Who called?" she asked quietly. "Was it Walker?"

He paused with a handful of clothes in his grip. He took a deep breath and eventually dropped the clothes into his bag, and pressed them down gently in thought. He closed his eyes with a disheartened expression etched into his face.

"Yeah, it was Walker," he responded without looking at her, then he continued to pack.

Ivy's stomach twisted in his unfamiliar aloofness. She peered down at her shaking hands and bit her lip in the frightening silence between them. Ivy exhaled slowly as the pain bled through her sad heart. A sickening wave rushed over her, and she waited in silent agony as another soldier she loved delivered himself to the war.

"They need me back there," he spoke indifferently. He zipped up his backpack and threw it over his shoulder, and walked toward her in the doorway. He stopped when he reached her.

She looked up at him.

"Ivy...," Hart sighed. All his determination faded in her nearness. There were expectations required of him as a commander in the army, but he would give it all up for her in a second if he didn't feel so guilty about Oliver. He fought the urge to let the backpack fall off his shoulder. To resist the urge to fall to his knees and tell her why he was here with her. Why he was *really* here with her. That painful truth.

Ivy stepped out of his way. He stared at her unblinking for a few moments, before he stepped by her and headed toward the front door. Ivy followed him. He walked outside without a single glance back. She stopped at the top of the steps and watched him toss his backpack through the open window of his car. She felt cold in the warm sunshine on the porch.

With his back to her, Hart leaned on the car and closed

his eyes. Last time he was deployed, he returned home three years later. He couldn't promise Ivy his early return, nor his safe return; she had been through too much for lies. His life was no more significant than any of the others whom she had loved and lost to the war, including his best friend. Hart groaned into his hands and wiped his face, fighting back the tears. He took a deep breath and turned to face Ivy, who stood on the top step with an innocent sadness that shattered his heart.

"Ivy," he breathed painfully.

"Don't go, *please*," she said breathlessly. "If anything happened to you, I wouldn't survive it this time. I can't do it anymore. I'm not strong enough to go through it again."

Hart walked to the bottom of the stairs and gazed up at her. Sweet tears welled in her eyes, and he felt his own gather unexpectedly. He imagined her on the warm white sands after he left, strengthening her soul in the natural beauty that surrounded her, her pale blue eyes gazing past the ocean as she talked to the orange sky. He had witnessed her do it once before. She had smiled at the sunset as though someone was there, smiling back at her. Then she whispered onto the wind, and he lost himself in her compelling conviction.

"You're the strongest person I know, Ivy," Hart smiled faintly.

"No, Hart, if you died...," she hesitated, struck all of a sudden by the heartbreaking thought. Ivy breathed out a long, ragged breath through her pursed lips and gathered what little strength she had left.

Hart bowed his head. Then he looked up at her with a warmth that filled her heart and emptied it all at once.

"Here, I got you something on my way home this morning." He jogged back to the car and reached through the open window, then returned to the bottom of the stairs. From behind his back, he revealed a long, bright red poppy.

A beautiful smile swept across his face, and Ivy's heart swooned as he climbed the steps toward her with the fragile flower pressed gently in his fingertips.

"It took me some time to find the tallest, strongest looking poppy in the field," he grinned. "Then I saw this one in the distance ... *reaching for the sky.*"

Ivy smiled at him. She took the poppy when he handed it to her. His fingers brushed against hers, and Ivy caught his gaze in the unexpected, intimate moment. She twisted the flower in her fingertips, and her eyes softened with love for the selfless soldier who stood in front of her.

A gentle smile curved his lips handsomely. "The weary, wounded ones are stronger than you think."

Ivy brushed the silky petals across her lips.

"Their strength never changed ... their world did," she replied.

Hart smiled, and then frowned to himself, pleasantly mystified by her pure heart. He stepped toward her and ran his hand down her face. He breathed in her coconut scent and fell unwillingly into the eternity of her compassionate heart. He felt powerless against her beauty. Against her sweetness. Her love. He sighed at the feeling of her warm skin against his hand, then he closed his eyes and leaned his forehead against hers ... fighting the urge to kiss her. Hart brushed his lips against hers. Her pleasured breath caused a deep yearning within him, and he stifled a groan before tearing himself away.

*"Oh Ivy ...."*

"You don't have to go," she breathed, dizzy with desire.

Hart sighed. "I have no choice."

"You always have a choice."

"I don't, Ivy. I am the Commander of Phoenix." Hart stepped away from her, slightly irritated.

"You are choosing Libya," she frowned. "You're choosing Taym. He won, right?"

A coldness clouded Hart's eyes. Ivy's hand dropped to her side, and the poppy hung ruefully between her fingers. He took a step away from her down the stairs, and she noticed the distance he consciously put between them.

"What did he win exactly?" Hart asked her coolly.

"The battle inside of you," she replied. "I have been watching you fight your demons all year, Hart. You're giving up the fight. You're letting him win." Ivy began to tap her fingers nervously on her thigh, fearful of the direction she had taken in their final moments together.

Hart didn't respond.

"It was Taym Malak ... or me," she added weakly. "I understand. I know why you're afraid of me."

"I'm not afraid of you, Ivy."

"No, you're right." She took a nervous breath. "You are afraid ... to love me."

Hart narrowed his eyes with an emptiness that frightened her.

There it was. *The fear.* The darkness behind his eyes. Hart rubbed his jaw and backed away from her down the steps. Ivy heard her breath growing louder in his retreat.

He smiled wryly to himself and stopped near the bottom of the stairs. He remembered bowing over Oliver's lifeless body, feeling utterly helpless. Feeling like his soul had been ripped clean from his body by a friend who turned out to be his worst enemy. A traitor who drove off to a famous victory, gaining worldwide recognition for bringing down the commander of what the world thought was America's most impenetrable force. It was now his duty as commander to find Taym and make him pay for his betrayal. For his treason against the United States of America. Against Phoenix. There was only one clear path forged ahead for Hart ... and Ivy didn't belong on that road to retribution.

"I have to go. I'm sorry," he breathed.

Ivy bowed her head in thought ... maybe he didn't love her.

A lock of hair fell in front of her eyes, and he wished he could go to her and brush it tenderly from her face. To feel the silkiness of it in his fingers. To feel it fall softly over his naked body when they made love ....

*"God, I'm so sorry,"* he repeated, holding himself back from her saving arms.

Ivy looked up at him, suddenly angry in her grief. "Why are you going back? Oliver is *gone.*"

Hart dropped his gaze and nodded unhappily. He slid his hands into his pockets and turned around, and walked down the rest of the stairs. He turned to face her again once he reached the driveway.

Ivy followed him, defying his retreat. "You're chasing ghosts, Hart."

"Walker, Benji, and I are going back because Taym murdered

Oliver in a heartless, cowardly attack. He betrayed us, Ivy! We were his brothers-in-arms! His friends! We trusted him with our lives because that's what we do in Phoenix!" Hart laughed at the ludicrousness of ever trusting Taym. "We had his back … and we thought he had ours."

Ivy frowned sympathetically.

"He took him from us, Ives. From all of us, including you!"

"I know what he did, but nothing you do in Libya will bring Ollie back!"

"Damn it, Ivy! You think I don't know that!?" He threw his hands in the air and groaned angrily.

Ivy flinched in Hart's frustration. His eyes frowned at her apologetically. There was desperation in his expression, and conflict. Then he turned his back to her and groaned again.

Ivy exhaled and looked at the ground. Nervous of what she glimpsed in his eyes.

Hart turned to look at her again. He was rubbing his chest anxiously, and Ivy frowned. She always wondered why he did that. Why he rubbed his chest when they spoke about her brother. His brown eyes were drenched in agony. Was he soothing an unbearable ache in his heart? It saddened her when he did it because it was a wound she could not heal. A deep wound he kept concealed from her, along with the rest of the secrets that hurt him the most.

He walked toward her and stopped. "I need to be there when they find him. I owe it to your brother to … to …"

"To what? To kill Taym?" Ivy laughed at the incredulous thought. "A life for a life? This isn't you, Hart!"

"This is all I am, Ivy!" Hart shrugged his shoulders at her and held his hands out despairingly by his side. "I warned you! I told you I was no good for you! Shit, there is so much about me that you still don't know. You don't know what I've done … what I've done to you!" Hart panted heavily. His eyes were wide with torment, and he considered her carefully.

He ran his hands through his hair and thought about Oliver giving up his life for him. Giving up Ivy. Knowingly forfeiting this incredible world that he shared with her, so that Hart could see it for himself, which made *everything* worse.

"Damn you, Ollie," he muttered.

Ivy glared at Hart when she heard him. "What happened over there? What is it about Oliver that hurts you so badly?"

Hart didn't respond. He glanced at her warily and then turned away.

"Talk to me, Hart! There's nothing I can't take," she pleaded. *"Nothing!"*

Hart looked at Ivy, who shook sadly on the steps. Her trembling dissolved all of his strength, his brave façade. He was falling fast into her sweet, breathless voice. Losing himself in her everlasting love. Her beaming light. Queen of his heart. She had conquered his guarded walls with her persistent heart and now he was at the gallows, falling to his knees. Waiting as the seconds passed with their excruciating timelessness. Hurry up. *Slow down.* The rope tightened around his neck with its promise of finality. Ivy would rescind her love once she discovered the truth about him ... and Oliver would forgive him his sins for deceiving her.

Hart sighed, defeated. "I promised Ollie I would check on you if ... if ..." he hesitated, unsure how to say the torturous words out loud. *If he died. He should be here with you. Not me. Oliver sacrificed himself for me. I should have died that day in Libya. It should have been me, Ivy.* "If he died," he breathed finally.

Hart met her compassionate gaze, and the two of them stared at each other, wordless and worlds apart.

Ivy walked over to him and stopped when she reached the beautiful soldier who was still broken in so many ways. He held her gaze, unblinking. She sensed his soul searching for forgiveness. From her. From Oliver. Forgiveness from himself. He was going to Libya to find a release from his relentless guilt ... for surviving. Ivy peered down at her poppy and took a deep breath, then she looked up into the eyes of the man she loved more than anything in this world.

"Ollie loved you," she breathed. "You were his best friend. You meant the world to him. He told me so many times."

Hart buried his eyes in his hands and bravely fought back his tears. He remembered Oliver's smile. His laughter. His friendship. It hurt to think about him still.

Ivy watched a tear roll out from under his hand, breaking her heart with its authentic sorrow.

She bowed her head and exhaled. "I know what happened

in Libya."

There was a short silence, and Ivy looked up to see if Hart had heard her. He had. The confusion swept over his expression. The usual anguish. The torture. The truth he thought she didn't know.

"No," he replied, looking away from her. "Not everything."

*"Everything,"* Ivy whispered reluctantly.

He looked at her and shook his head with a slow, dazed denial.

Ivy exhaled sadly. "I have been waiting for you to open up to me, but you couldn't do it. You didn't want to hurt me."

Hart heard the fear on her shaking breath. He recognized the truth in her innocent eyes. She could never lie to him.

"When?" he breathed, almost inaudibly.

Ivy breathed in deeply. Her lip quivered when she went to speak, but her voice failed her. He looked puzzled. Dumbfounded by her knowledge. She hadn't seen him like this before. She felt like she was betraying him. Lying to him all this time.

The poppy spun mindlessly in her fingers. She noticed him staring at it while he frantically searched his memory for that exact moment when she discovered all his secrets. Ivy took a deep breath and revealed his unwitting confessions in an eloquent, gentle tone. The realization swept slowly through his wide eyes as she spoke his own words back to him ….

*"I am broken, Ivy. Shattered. I will never be the same man I was before he died. I have done something terrible. Unforgivable. Ivy, you are my divine reprimand. My savior, my punishment. You remind me that he died saving me. I am the reason he is gone. I killed your brother. I killed Oliver. I'm so sorry. Let the water take me, Ivy. Let me die, too. If only you knew."*

Ivy stopped and bowed her head.

The pain gripped her heart, and she closed her eyes and waited for their end. She heard him exhale suddenly as if he had been holding his breath this whole time … but he didn't speak. Ivy peered up into his eyes and willed him to respond, terrified by his silence.

Hart turned away from her. He remembered the night she found him in the water at the Silver Moon Gala, ready and willing—hoping—to die. It was the first night they had met, and she had heard it all. Every word.

"Hart?" she said nervously behind him. "I'm sorry I didn't tell you sooner."

Hart panted loudly, shaken by her revelation. He ran his hands over his hair and stared along the length of the driveway in stunned silence.

"Say something," she whispered.

Hart turned around and studied her carefully. She didn't recognize what she saw there in his eyes. Concern? Regret? Betrayal, maybe?

"You knew all this time?" He laughed at the absurdity.

Ivy nodded apologetically.

He rubbed his face anxiously with both hands and then glared at her. "You should have told me."

"I didn't know how to tell you—"

"You didn't know how!?" Hart interrupted angrily. He threw his hands out beside him in utter despair. "Shit, Ives! It's all I've been thinking about since the day we met!"

"I'm sorry!"

"Why didn't you say something!?"

"I ... I don't know ...."

"Ivy!" Hart growled impatiently. He bent down to look directly into her eyes, and she looked away. "Ivy? Answer me, pl—"

"Because you wanted to die, Hart!" she shouted loudly in her defense.

Hart fell silent, taken aback by her distress. Guilt festered deep within, twisting his stomach.

"You begged me to let you go! You begged me to let the water take you! But I couldn't ... I couldn't let you go." She sobbed at the memory.

Hart glared at her. His brown eyes were cold and furious, but not for long; a tormented sadness arrived with her tears.

"I couldn't tell you the truth because I was scared," she continued. "I was scared you would leave me. I couldn't lose you, too, not after Oliver."

Ivy let her tears roll down her cheeks and stared at Hart. She thought about the night she had found him in the water. When he reignited all the gut-wrenching pain from when she lost her brother. She couldn't let him die. She remembered it clearly like it was only yesterday, Hart's soft voice begging her to let him drown. His beautiful, lamenting tone. She almost did, convinced by his suffering. By his torment. As though it were heartless of her to save him. As though she were without mercy.

"I had no one left," she breathed.

Hart's eyes softened with sorrow, and for a brief moment, she saw the soldier who saved her life in more ways than he would ever know. The vulnerability in his gaze ripped straight through her heart, tearing down every pillar of strength she had left. His sincerity was heartbreaking.

Hart closed his eyes. Her suffering hit him hard, and at that moment he realized the weight of what she carried since that night at the Gala. His pain was tolerable and deserved, but her pain was excruciating for him. His stomach twisted agonizingly, a pain like no other he had felt before. Not in all his days of service.

"I wanted to tell you …," he breathed.

Ivy nodded wordlessly.

His heart plummeted to the driveway at her feet, and this was where it would rightfully remain; scattered on a road that led to his sanctuary. To his eternal beacon of light. *To Ivy Rose.* Oliver's sister.

Hart reached for her, but he didn't touch her, "I have to go."

He waited in her presence for a few more seconds, then his apologetic expression faded to disappointment, and he turned to his car.

Ivy assumed he wanted her anger. Her hostile admonishment. He was never going to get it from her.

"There is nothing you could say or do that would make me think less of you," she called out after him. "I know you, and I know my brother … you are not responsible for his death."

Hart stopped before he reached his car, but he didn't turn to face her. She could see his burdened breath in the rise and fall of his broad shoulders. He had his head bowed, and she couldn't see it, but she knew he was rubbing his jaw, thinking, the way he always did. Then he continued walking to his car.

Ivy whimpered when he reached the Firebird. "Oliver died because he wanted you to live, Hart! Why can't you see that?"

Hart turned around quickly. He ran his hands over his face

and back through his hair in frustration. It hurt him to have this argument with her. This wasn't them. His hands trembled fiercely beside him and Hart clenched them into tight fists and looked into the sky, and then growled into it with overwrought despair.

"Damn it, Ivy! I was there with him when he died!"

Ivy recoiled in his anger. She narrowed her eyes at him and gripped onto the poppy as though it were all she had left in this world.

"Oliver was my best friend, and I watched him die! I watched him take his last breath and then leave this world forever!" Hart panted. "You have no idea how things went down that day in Libya!"

"No, I don't, but I know my brother. Ollie knew us better than anyone. Don't you ever wonder why you are here with me in La Mar?"

Hart stared into the sky as the memory of his best friend's death struck his desolate core. He sighed into his hands and looked at her again.

"That's the thing, Ives … I shouldn't be here."

"I know it was an easy decision for Oliver that day, to save you instead of himself," Ivy said softly, approaching him carefully. "I know this because … because I would do the same for you."

Hart stared at Ivy, unblinking. Her long, wavy hair fell off her shoulders as she walked toward him. It took all his strength not to run to her. To put all of this behind them. To go back to the way things were.

"There is no one else quite like you, Johnny Hart, and you are the only one who refuses to acknowledge how incredible you really are."

Hart shook his head.

"Stop falling," she pleaded. "Hold onto something. Hold onto *me*."

Hart hesitated in her nearness, quickly losing himself in her intoxicating enchantment. "I can't," he replied, stepping away from her.

Ivy stepped toward him again. "You put everyone else's feelings before your own, and this whole thing with Ollie is crushing you because he put *you* first. Don't blame yourself for what happened."

"There is no one else to blame," he sighed dejectedly.

"Then don't blame anyone."

The tears sat in his heart-broken brown eyes, and her own tears rolled down her cheeks for him. "One thing led to another that day, and it ended tragically," she continued. "It was a chain of events that ended with Oliver wanting you to walk away from Libya. He wanted you to live—"

"But I'm not living, Ivy!" Hart interrupted. He glared at her … desperate to hold her and desperate to run. "All I have left inside me is revenge. I literally tremble with *fucking* revenge!" He panted as he watched her, torn with the instability of his emotions. There was no other place he would rather be than here with her. Bathed in her love. Bathed in her glory. But there was a rage swimming hazardously in his darker depths, and he put her future at risk by staying here. He was becoming too volatile with his anxiety and his thirst for blood. The darkness won. Ivy was right. The thought devastated him. It crushed him. It maddened him. Death was easy—living was hard.

"I'm going to Libya to find Taym." Hart sighed into his hand. "And if I die in the process … then so be it."

A weak sound escaped Ivy's lips. She swallowed the bulging lump in her throat and willed herself to take a breath. The air hung silently between them as she processed what he was saying to her; he had no intention of coming home. The moment felt excruciatingly final, and it frightened her.

"Then I am sorry," she said ruefully, looking up at him. "I made the wrong decision on your behalf."

Hart looked at her.

"I should have let you drown that night at the Gala." Ivy twisted her mouth unhappily and looked away. Tears rolled down her cheeks, and her breath shook before she spoke again. "Maybe my brother made the wrong decision, too. He should have saved himself."

Hart nodded and bit his lip in bitter acknowledgment.

Ivy's panicked breath grew louder in his silence. He believed her, even though she didn't mean a word of it. His defeated gaze reduced her to tears. He looked broken. Where was the heroic soldier she knew was there inside of him? He had been with her all these months, but where was he now? She needed him to save the day before their ending. Her heart thumped fearfully against her chest as she waited for him to speak. For him to respond to a cruel comment she wished she could take back. She waited for him to move. To come at her. To leave. To do *anything.*

Hart turned and opened the door of his car, and Ivy's heart leaped into her throat.

"No! Hart!"

"Taym is dangerous, and I have to stop him." Hart sat down and slammed the door before she could reach him. "If I let him get away with what he did to us, then there will only be more people like you and me, Ivy. More death and more suffering. I cannot let that happen. I am the Commander of Phoenix."

She stood there helplessly and watched the very last of her soldiers leave her for the war. The losses in her past seemed to overpower any strength she had left, and Ivy's heart plunged into the depths of the dark, empty pit that had swallowed what hopes she'd had left in life, loss after loss.

"I thought you had left the war behind you," she whispered weakly.

Hart's eyes blackened with hatred. "The war never leaves you, Ivy."

"*Stay for me,*" she breathed.

"Ivy," Hart closed his eyes and sighed. "You are the reason I am leaving."

He heard her breathe out suddenly, then Hart turned the ignition and pressed his foot hard on the accelerator with the clutch down, revving the rumbling Firebird to life for the drive north to Monterey. His heart ached with a sickening intensity that physically weakened him. He glanced at Ivy, taking in the very last of her beauty. Her divinity. Consciously carving her innocence into the depths of his memory for a time when he would most need her glorious light … in the absolute darkness of war.

Hart shifted the car into gear and let her step away. He had a long, lonely road ahead and he'd be damned to let her follow it with him. As he drove away, a furious rage fueled his thirst for the blood of a man who had caused him all this pain. Hart growled and hit the steering wheel powerfully with the palm of his hand. He was angry with Taym Malak. Angry with the war. Angry with Hannah for diagnosing him with post-traumatic stress disorder. Angry with USSOCOM for enforcing his leave in the first place. He was angry at Oliver for sending him to Ivy because he knew what he would find here with her. But mostly, he was angry with himself. His only peace lay with his future ... and he couldn't wait to accept his sentence.

## Chapter 25

Ivy LEANED ON THE DOOR FRAME, feeling her broken heart pound feebly against it. He left. *Hart left.* She breathed raggedly, stunned. A sickening wave rushed over her, and she bent over and buried her face in her hands. She stayed there for a short while, waiting for the nausea to pass. She could see her backpack in the corner of her eye, and as she leaned back against the door frame she thought about Hart's insistence that she never go there alone.

Ivy bit her lip and considered her trek to Lights Beach. It would be going against his wishes, against his judgment. Hart sensed danger on the Ghost Trail … but her backpack beckoned her to leave. *Run to Lights. Run to safety. Seek refuge from the pain.* Ivy kneeled beside her backpack, and with a hurried urgency she double-checked she had everything for the hike.

"Ivy? Where are you going?"

"Nicole!" Ivy gasped, having forgotten she was here. "I'm sorry. I have to go."

Nicole studied her warily. "Johnny left, didn't he?"

Ivy paused without looking at her, then nodded.

"Hmm, that doesn't surprise me at all. Don't hold your breath for his return, Ivy. I know I won't." Nicole replied dryly. She watched Ivy and waited for a reaction. When Ivy didn't respond, she rolled her eyes and shrugged her shoulders. "Okay, I guess I'll be off then." She collected her bag from the living room and returned to Ivy with a satisfied grin.

Ivy narrowed her eyes as she studied Nicole's disquieting mood swing.

"That man will always be a mystery to me, but there is one thing I know for sure about Johnny Hart," Nicole smirked.

Ivy stood and looked at Nicole. "And what is that?"

"He knows how to break a woman's heart."

Ivy dropped her gaze to her hands and fidgeted anxiously with the strap of the backpack. Her heart was definitely broken.

"Still," Nicole continued coolly, "it was worth it."

"What was?" Ivy asked, regretting it instantly.

"Coming to San Diego," Nicole smiled beautifully. "One night is all we needed. Johnny and I just seemed to pick up right where we left off."

Ivy felt a black shadow cast itself over her in the open doorway. Nicole's confidence sent a chill down her spine, and she remembered what Hart had told her earlier on the driveway, regarding his absence last night … *nothing happened.*

Nicole stepped into the sunlight spilling in through the open door and ran her polished nails through her long dark hair. She stood opposite Ivy and leaned her head back against the doorframe, closing her eyes with a low, pleasured hum. Ivy held her breath. This was it. Nicole had her right where she wanted her. The truth about last night was already rolling off her wicked tongue. Ivy felt powerless, anticipating the strike that would end her once and for all. She raised her chin and waited for the crushing truth. Ivy could see it sparkling ominously in Nicole's dark eyes.

"Love is like a sin when you're lying beneath that god-like creature," Nicole breathed huskily.

Ivy exhaled sharply. Time stood dreadfully still. The air hung unnaturally around her, and she struggled to breathe it in. Nicole continued to speak, but Ivy couldn't hear a word she said. Her heart was slowly pouring out everything she had ever experienced with Hart.

"Oh, who am I kidding?" Nicole continued, rolling her eyes. "He is not all to blame. I've always been his little harlot, shamelessly anticipating the next time he's overcome with the desire to fuck. No woman in her right mind would deny that man, am I right?"

Ivy turned away from Nicole and leaned on the foyer table, catching her wretched reflection in the mirror.

"Oh, I'm so sorry," Nicole frowned. "Earlier you asked if Johnny and I slept together last night, and I was just answering your question."

Ivy didn't respond. She focused on her breath, trying her best not to let Nicole see straight through her. To witness her foolish heart crumbling to pieces. She was falling through the depthless pit of grief inside of her, where everything precious in her life had disappeared, including her soldiers. She saw them as she fell through the darkness. He was there … with his beautiful smile and warm, brown eyes. Watching her fall through her eternal, empty abyss.

"I thought after everything he did to your brother," Nicole continued, "I assumed you two never stood a chance. I didn't realize you had feelings for him, Ivy. I promise I would not have allowed last night to go as far as it did if I knew." She glanced outside to hide her lying eyes from Ivy's gaze in the mirror.

Ivy turned to face her, and Nicole studied her displeased expression.

"Hart told you what happened in Libya?" Ivy asked. Her eyes narrowed suspiciously.

Nicole nodded, watching her with feigned pity.

A new feeling simmered deep inside Ivy. It was a feeling she wasn't familiar with. She stared at Nicole in disbelief. In utter bewilderment. Ivy shook her head in confusion, and then realized she was furious. Seething with distrust. She couldn't decide what it was exactly that Nicole still wanted from her, especially now that Hart had left *both* of them behind.

"Why are you even here?" Ivy frowned, rubbing her forehead gently with her fingers. She lifted her tired gaze to Nicole.

"I gave you money for the Gala, remember?"

"No," Ivy replied, annoyed. "I mean, *why* are you here? Why now? Why are you doing this?"

"Doing what?"

"This! Everything!" she shouted, throwing her hands in the air. "I don't understand why you are here in California. Is it because you wanted to sleep with Hart!? Did you fly over two thousand miles just to fuck him?" Ivy ran her fingers through her hair, staggered by the immoral woman in front of her.

Nicole nodded without smiling.

Ivy threw her hands over her face and tried not to cry in front of Nicole. She thought about the past year with the three men who had healed her heart and enriched her world. Then she thought about Oliver.

"We had come so far," Ivy lamented to herself, hoping something or someone out there was listening to her, besides Nicole. "After everything that we went through with Oliver. All the suffering, all the pain. Why is this happening? Why?"

Nicole didn't speak. She looked down at her bag with an uncomfortable silence.

"I feel sick," Ivy breathed. She leaned over slightly and held her stomach. She could guarantee this reaction was the exact response Nicole had been longing for since her arrival yesterday.

Ivy walked outside to gather her strength, but mostly to deny Nicole the satisfaction of her victory. She took a long, deep breath and stared down the driveway.

"My intentions were purely innocent," Nicole spoke demurely, following Ivy outside.

Ivy laughed softly and shook her head.

"It's those soldiers you need to be concerned about, especially Johnny." Nicole waved to the taxi waiting for her by the fountain. She stepped carefully down the stairs in her heels, then turned to look at Ivy once she reached the driveway.

"Walker, Benji, and Hart, they are good men," Ivy replied.

Nicole laughed. "Take the soldier away from the man ... and all you are left with is a man. Johnny was always going to break your heart, Ivy."

Ivy stared at her silently in thought. The past few days with Hart *had* been challenging for both of them, she couldn't deny that, and it was these latest hindrances that caused her to question his intentions, not his character. It was possible that Nicole was telling the truth about last night. Life had become complicated for Hart, even more so than usual. Sleeping with another woman would simplify things—it could end everything they had shared since he arrived on her doorstep almost one year ago. He could walk away from La Mar knowing he could never return, because this time, he had genuinely betrayed her. Nicole was simply the naïve messenger. Hart knew she would tell her what happened. That he slept with Nicole. *He slept with Nicole. He lied to me ….*

Ivy groaned quietly, growing dizzy with her shallow breath. She forced herself to breathe in and out, but the disturbing image of Hart and Nicole overwhelmed her. She could feel the tears threatening her composure.

"Good-bye, Ivy." The taxi pulled up beside Nicole, and she climbed into the backseat without glancing back.

Ivy waited for the taxi to disappear down the driveway before she let her sorrow defeat her. She sat herself down on the top step and groaned into her hands. The world thundered off its axis and everything she believed in started to slide away from her in slow motion. The pain was suffocating. She grabbed her chest and willed her lungs to take a breath, stifling a small cry of distress. Her heart pounded uncomfortably within her, and soon it was all she could hear. Everything began to fade away, and she wondered how she remained sitting, instead of crashing to the marble of the porch, where she felt she belonged. She remembered the only time she had fainted; it was right here at her front door, and Hart had scooped her into his arms and saved her from the fall … but there was no one here to catch her now.

*Hart.*

Ivy wanted to hate him, but she couldn't. How could he ever love her when the heaviness of her brother's life weighed down on him so unforgivingly? She was a living memory of that day.

Ivy looked up into the bluest of skies and shook her head sadly. Hart's plan didn't work … she still loved him.

## Chapter 26

IT IS PEACEFUL IN THE DEEP. Tranquil. Unaffected. The perfect place for a hesitant heart. Ivy didn't want to come up for air, not when there was uncertainty drifting darkly on the surface. A frightening, debilitating doubt. Her faith dwindled, and Ivy sheltered the few remnants she had left in the quiet of the water's depths. If only she could lie down on the sandy seabed forever, amid the infinite, silent, crystal blue, where nothing ever changed.

A sad tremor rippled through her soul. Somehow she had convinced the world that she was impervious to suffering. Immune to the merciless grief that tirelessly sapped her strength. She was losing her determination to fight, and Ivy considered defeat. She knew more than anyone the risks that came with giving in … there was no feeling worse than that of lost faith.

She remembered Hart asking her how she did it, how she managed to stay strong after everything that had happened to her. *I see the way you look at the world around you, Ivy, like you can see past this life. What can you see? Tell me what you see.*

She had an answer then.

*I don't know anymore.* Ivy cried inwardly under the water. *I can't see anything past you, Hart!*

His beautiful face rushed through her thoughts. The kindness in his gentle gaze. The charm in his handsome grin.

The strength in his body. She felt his warm fingers run across her face and through her hair, and Ivy groaned at the pain that suddenly gripped her broken heart … then her breath was spent and her body screamed for air.

She pushed off the ocean floor and swam quickly to the surface, gasping for air when she finally reached it. She wiped the saltwater from her face and choked on the small waves splashing against her as she wept. After a few minutes, Ivy swam back to the shore.

She lay down on the warm, soothing sand and stared at the hazy sky. There was no one here. There never was at Lights. The bay was hers, and she found peace, at least, in the solitude. Ivy took a deep breath and exhaled slowly. She closed her eyes and just laid there … exempt from life.

Ivy listened to the water as it lapped the sand. She listened to the familiar call of seagulls in the distance. She felt the trapped heat of the earth as it rose around her through the cool mist that had settled in the bay. Often, if she lay still enough, she could hear the ocean's eternally beating heart. She couldn't hear it, not today. Today she found no comfort in her surroundings. No clear perspective. No release from her concerns. No reassurance from the world. Ivy drifted in and out of her troubled mind, struggling to notice anything past the relentless pain in her chest. Her heart was immune to her place of refuge. To her sanctuary. The beauty surrounding her couldn't ease the hurt she felt inside. No matter how hard she tried, there was no escape from what Hart did to her.

She sat up and stared at the blue horizon. Ivy couldn't remember the last time she saw the sunset, but she needed one now. One so spectacular that she forgot she was alone. It was easier to imagine them beside her in the sweet memories inspired by the burning, orange-colored sky. A time when she once surrendered herself to the raw veracity of the earth and appreciated that the world had its own plans, no matter her own or anyone else's. She bowed her head in resignation and ran her hand mindlessly through the warm sand, grabbing handfuls of it and watching it glide out between her fingers, hypnotized by the way it fell across her knee in all different directions. Hypnotized by its whiteness. Its pristineness. Ivy peered up at the sky again in thought. It was too perfect here in paradise, it didn't match reality. No gray skies. No squalling winds. No rain. She imagined a storm to reflect her sorrow.

Ivy sat soundlessly under the perfect sky. Lost in her restlessness. Lost in the hopelessness. Her soldiers left her to chase the ghosts of their past ... and one of them was her brother.

She looked to the horizon.

"They are coming to you, Ollie," she breathed, biting her quivering lip. "I'm so sorry. *I tried.*" Ivy stared at the glassy ocean with a courageous façade to keep herself from falling to pieces, then a small sound of defeat escaped her lips. She bowed her head and closed her eyes. "Please, show me the rain."

Ivy walked absently through the wide creek back to the Ghost Trail, stepping mindlessly over the stones under the water. When she reached the bank, she sat down and pulled on the sneakers she had dangling in her fingers. The sun's reflection danced in her eyes and across her skin as she stared blindly at the water. She lay back on the bank and stared vacantly at the sunlight flickering through the leaves above her. She felt nothing for it. A numbness cloaked her emotions, and Ivy liked the way it felt. It felt ... *safe.* Time drifted by. Neither fast nor slow. There was nowhere to be. Nothing to do. No one to return to. So Ivy remained there by the river in the silent heart of the forest, lost and impassive to life.

A flock of birds flew past, rousing Ivy from her cataleptic state. She stood quickly and glanced in the direction the birds had flown, but they were gone almost as quickly as they had appeared. Ivy squinted her eyes through the trees, surprised by the darkening light in the woods. A thick carpet of storm clouds had rolled in from the ocean and threatened the blue sky with its inexorable approach.

Ivy peered pensively into the gray sky.

There was a sudden stillness around her. A soundless void filled the air. There were no bird calls. No insects. No sounds of life. Just the sound of her light breath among the trees on the trail. An icy breeze swept across her skin. She sensed a presence in the forest around her, and the thought sent an unsettling chill through her body. Ivy removed her backpack and pulled on the jersey she had tied around her waist. She rubbed her arms to fight the chill and peered up at the trees, which remained disconcertingly still despite the wind.

"Damn you, Hart," Ivy murmured, shaking her head. The Ghost Trail. Hart did this. He spooked her with his unremitting demons.

All of a sudden, she sensed a shift in her surroundings. Something urged her into the forest. Her instincts were telling her to move, so Ivy tied up her hair into a long ponytail, secured her backpack, and made her way up the trail through the forest toward home.

As she walked, she thought about Hart and the way he searched the forest whenever they came here. His vigilant heart had never wavered, until today. He felt less like a soldier after Oliver died, but Ivy failed to see him as anything else. She was grateful for it. For his awareness. For his sharp intuition. She thought about him in the parking lot a few nights ago, staring at the empty street corner in the distance where Tommy eventually appeared. Hart felt the threat coming for them even though she hadn't. No matter how perceptive she thought she was, she couldn't match Hart's uncanny sense for danger. He begged her not to come here alone, yet here she was ... more alone than ever.

"They are not my ghosts," Ivy whispered to herself, slowing down. She frowned and glanced around the forest that stretched out either side of her along the trail. The sun disappeared behind the clouds, and the forest fell a darker shade around her.

Ivy stopped walking.

She sensed someone following her, but she refused to turn around. She didn't want to give in to the panic ... to encourage her doubtful soul. Fear tapped its claws on her wary heart, but Ivy consciously ignored it, clinging desperately to the little faith she had left. This was her forest, nothing could harm her here, and so she took a deep breath and kept walking.

Ivy had only taken a few steps when another icy wind brushed past her from the ocean. She stopped again on the trail.

The presence was there still. Behind her. Waiting deathly still in the forest when she stopped. Watching her. Wanting her. She never understood why Hart felt so protective of her on the

Ghost Trail, until now. All this time, they were never alone.

"Shit!" Ivy breathed, giving in to her fear.

She bit her bottom lip and slowly turned around, reluctantly peering down the trail that had gone dark in the overcast sky … but there was no one there. Just an empty track that led to the creek and on to the ocean.

Ivy took a deep breath and leaned her head back, feeling foolish but relieved.

"Keep it together, Ivy," she whispered.

She turned up the trail again and thought about the soldiers as she walked. Walker, Benji, and Hart once stopped her here in the darkness. Maybe in this exact spot. They surrounded her protectively as though there truly were a threat lingering in the distance. All three of them sensed it, and she frowned as she thought about it. It was their instincts that stopped them that night. Phoenix instincts. Elite soldiers who had walked behind enemy lines most of their lives. She now regretted coming here alone.

Ivy stopped walking and exhaled a long, weary breath, fed-up with the mind games that wreaked havoc on her rational perception of the forest. She looked up into the treetops and laughed at herself. Her childhood trail had been tainted by the suspicious minds of Oliver's soldiers. The concept of someone following her was rather outlandish—even the ghost tales seemed more plausible to Ivy. She still sensed the unusual silence of the forest, but she tried not to take it as a warning. As if it were the forest's way of speaking to her … its silent deterrent. If anyone should notice the subtle variance of the forest, then she should. Ivy stood between the trees on the trail and listened carefully ….

She could hear it, the lack of solace in the stillness of the forest. Its voice was suddenly loud and clear in its silent frenzy, and it was telling her to hurry. Telling her to *run*. Something was coming for her. Ivy groaned without turning around. She sensed their eyes on her. *Many* eyes on her. She peered anxiously at the forest around her with wide eyes. Then she heard it … a clear, distinct sound on the track behind her. One she couldn't ignore. Ivy turned instinctively on the spot, and saw him in the distance, quietly watching her.

She gasped in the silence. The fear paralyzed her momentarily. He stood on the trail and gently pulled a rope from one gloved hand to another, with a disturbing, unhurried patience. A balaclava covered his face, but his empty black eyes watched her with a chilling serenity. He didn't move, so Ivy remained in her place in the terrifying stand-off. She wasn't ready to run. She wasn't ready to be chased. Her breath was all she could hear in the deafening silence, and it shook as it left her lips, quickened by adrenaline. Ivy watched him wind the length of rope around his right hand, the subtle action unleashing a stomach-churning fear inside of her. Then it happened ... the man took a slow, deliberate step toward her along the trail, and Ivy turned to run.

The air seemed to thicken, slowing her down. Her legs failed her in her stunned panic, and she cried out breathlessly and willed herself to run. Ivy could hear him coming for her along the track. The terror sent her racing up the Ghost Trail, hurdling swiftly over rocks and logs and ducking under branches that hung in her way. Her heart beat at a wicked pace, flying high on sheer panic. She heard his breath behind her. His boots on the track. He was gaining on her, and she had little hope of outrunning him. The old redwood log lay across the trail in the distance, and Ivy was grateful for it. She had been climbing this log since she was a child and she knew she could scale it with little effort, maybe giving her an advantage in his pursuit. Ivy hurried toward it with a small glimmer of hope, but it was shortlived. A second man in a balaclava walked along the top of the log and stopped in the center of it, his gloved hands clapping with anticipation.

Ivy came to a sudden halt when she saw him. Her sneakers slid across the dirt and out from underneath her, and she fell on the track, breaking her fall with her hands. She anticipated his assault while she was down, but he remained standing on the log, still clapping his hands as if eager to join the hunt. Ivy shot a glance behind her along the trail; he was still there, not far from her, but he had stopped running. He stood sideways on the track and stared at her with an unsettling silence, his lean shoulders rising and falling with his heaving breaths.

Ivy panted as she pulled herself to her feet. She removed her backpack and dropped it on the ground resignedly. Fifteen meters of Ghost Trail was all that separated her from each man. Ivy looked from one to the other. She wondered if there were more of these men waiting for her in the flanks of the forest, and her eyes frantically searched the trees around her. A halo of sunlight appeared on the forest floor in the distance, and Ivy considered running to it. She knew she wouldn't get far through the trees before they caught her, but she only needed a short distance to achieve her plan. She reached into the back pocket of her denim shorts and pulled out her cell phone, keeping it concealed within her hand. Without looking, she unlocked the phone with her thumb and pressed down the voice dial button. She thought of the only person she knew would find her eventually ... dead or alive.

Ivy took a deep breath and spoke toward the forest in an articulate, assertive tone, "Call ... Hart." She turned on the speaker phone and looked up at the men.

They hesitated either side of her once they realized what she had done, and then the man on the trail behind her came for her again. Ivy launched off the trail into the forest toward the sunlight that filtered through the trees on the forest floor. The cell phone was gripped tightly in her hand and rung unanswered by her side as she ran. Ivy looked to her right and saw the man sprinting along the top of the log in her direction. He moved faster than she did, without the bushes and the rocks to maneuver through. She looked to her left, and the other masked man was sweeping through the forest like a black shadow at a frightening pace toward her. They were closing in on her fast and Ivy listened helplessly to the ringing of her cell ... she wasn't going to make it. She whimpered over her frantic breath and begged Hart to answer.

A low-hanging branch whipped her face and Ivy grimaced at the pain. She grabbed her cheek and glanced behind her as she ran. Both men were only meters away, moving in on her and preparing to take her down ... then her cell stopped ringing.

*"Hey, you've reached Johnny Hart. Please leave a message."*

Ivy cried out when she heard Hart's gentle voice as she finally reached the circle of sunshine in the forest. The two men threw themselves on top of her, and she fell heavily under their weight. They grappled with her arms as she fought against them, but they quickly managed to subdue her. Ivy held onto the phone for as long as she could, desperate for the beep of Hart's voicemail as the automated voice ran through the options of leaving a message. One of the men pried it from her fingers, and she shouted wordlessly in dismay when he managed to free it from her grip.

Ivy saw him glance at the photo of Hart on the screen, and he hesitated briefly. His dark soulless eyes widened with an unmistakable fear. He showed the screen to the other man, who snatched the phone from his hand and lobbed it into the air in front of them. The cell beeped as it left his hands. The phone spun away from her through the sunlight, and she took a deep breath and cried out Hart's name as loudly as she could into the forest. Seconds later, a glove was shoved roughly into her mouth. Ivy gagged on the thickness of it as it slipped down the back of her tongue, threatening to suffocate her. One of the men pressed her head forcefully against the ground as they tied her hands behind her back. She groaned against the dirt, her eyes blinking in the bright sun, and she wondered if she would ever see the sunlight again.

A black cloth was pulled over her face, and by the musky scent of it, she guessed it was one of the men's balaclavas. Ivy stared wide-eyed into the woven balaclava as they lifted her effortlessly to her feet. She hobbled between them as they headed back toward the beach.

The wind picked up all of a sudden. It felt cold against her skin, and Ivy predicted it would rain any minute now. She could hear the terns' haunting shrills in the distance, and she imagined their snow-white bodies floating against the dark gray sky. The waves were crashing against the shore with a fierce strength, and even without seeing, Ivy knew a storm was almost upon them. It was what she had wanted, what she had asked for. The universe responded to her plea. *Someone was listening.*

"Show me the rain ...," she whispered to herself.

Large drops of rain landed on her skin, and Ivy leaned her head back to face the sky. She closed her eyes behind the balaclava and took a long, deep breath to calm her fear. Ivy sighed sadly. She had one final request before she left this world forever ... she wanted to see them, one last, beautiful time. Walker, Benji ... *Hart.* She could see him in the darkness in front of her. His handsome smile. His warm eyes. His kind, shining soul. She could feel his gentle touch on her hot skin. His breath against her neck. His lips brushing against hers. Hart stood right there in front of her, in the infinite dark.

Helena's words whispered through her thoughts …. *Feel the sun. Feel the light. See the dark. Contemplate in the darkness, as it is here that you can see everything most clearly.* Ivy narrowed her eyes as she thought about it, and suddenly, what Hart did with Nicole didn't matter to her anymore. She didn't care. He did it to push her away. To save her from his inevitable fall. If he didn't die chasing Taym, then his soul would yield irretrievably to the darkness once he returned to the news of her disappearance, or worse, her death.

Ivy closed her eyes and begged the universe to find the soldier she loved more than life itself. To bring him back to her before it was too late for her to save his heroic yet broken soul. She whispered her plea inaudibly through the black of the balaclava, onto the wind that swept through the silence of the forest, and into the soaring gray skies above her … and deep into the heart of her brave soldier. *Johnny Hart.*

# Part Three

## - CALIFORNIA -

*"The wound is the place where the light enters you."*

Rumi

1207 - 1273

## Chapter 27

# - MONTEREY COUNTY, CALIFORNIA -
## May 2015

THE FIRE IN HIS MUSCLES burned agonizingly in his physical being, but Hart pushed himself harder, breathing fiercely through the pain that ripped through his lungs. Her innocence flashed through his thoughts, blinding him temporarily, and he groaned in the suffocating guilt that bore down on him. Hart clenched his teeth and ran faster along the redwood trail, setting himself a cruel pace in his desperation to leave her ethereal presence behind him. Her crystal eyes blinked open, and he hesitated in her sweeping, seductive lure. Lustrous blonde hair fell all around him, and he felt her with him in the forest. Her light. Her *magic*. Hart pushed himself even harder, yearning for the indomitable strength he once had but no longer felt.

Pain hit him like a bullet to the chest, and he finally gave in to his need to rest with a raging howl that resounded through the ancient air of the redwood forest. Hart bent over in exhaustion. He leaned his hands on his knees and panted toward the ground, grimacing at the pain that burned relentlessly in his chest. He stared at his boots planted firmly on the bed of pine needles, and watched his breath as it hung in the cold air. He stood and rubbed the throbbing area over his heart where Oliver had shot him in his nightmare, and he cursed under his breath in the silence of the trees.

Hart waited there for a minute to catch his breath, then he rolled up the sleeves on his combat shirt and removed his backpack. He took off his cap and tucked it into one of the large pockets on the side of his combat pants, and reached for his water bottle inside his backpack. He took a desperate, breathless mouthful of water, breathing out in relief once it soothed his burning throat, and then he placed the bottle in his pack and swung the bag onto his back, tightening the straps.

Hart checked his watch. 05:30. He was due at the General's office at 0800, sharp. He tried to calculate the time it would take him to return to Base from where he was, but his thoughts shifted to the pines. They were oddly distracting, arousing an unexpected anxiety in him. They were too familiar. Familiarly dark. He had been here before … but only in his sleep. He thought about Taym pressed against the pine tree—*or was it Tommy?* Hart groaned and held his forehead. He wiped his hand down his face and stared into the towering heights of the redwoods. Tommy. Taym. He couldn't decide who troubled him more.

Hart jogged at a more leisurely pace back in the direction he had come. It didn't matter how fast he ran … he would never outrun the memory of Ivy. He didn't want to. He was being pulled to her as though she had enchanted the forest around him. Her illuminating light was in everything. Ivy was everywhere around him.

Hart ran through a patch of sunlight that fractured through the pines. He stopped in its glow unintentionally. He lifted his chin and faced the shards of sun piercing through the soaring canopy. Hart leaned his head back and closed his eyes in its warmth … and he felt her light radiate from within him. He felt her soft lips against his, and her sweet taste still lingered on his tongue. Her blonde hair glowed in the sunlight as she leaned over him on the sand … and he heard her laughing beside him in the crystal water of Lights Beach. He saw the dusting of freckles across her nose. The sparkling sea in her blue eyes. He reached for her sandy skin and kissed the tan lines on her hips, and he felt her enticing warmth beneath his lips. Her eternalness in his heart. Her light, pleasured breath on his body ….

Hart tightened his eyes shut behind his hand.

"Ivy," he whispered.

A cold wind swept past him as though it had been waiting for him to speak her name. So it could carry it back to where she was … back to La Mar. Back to the ocean. Back to the setting sun. *Back to Ivy.*

He sighed into the sunshine.

Ivy was a divine daydream in the nightmarish reality of war, but he forced himself to set it aside. He had chosen to leave her, and Hart rubbed his face tiredly at the thought. He had left Ivy to hunt down Taym and avenge his best friend's death. This is what Oliver would have wanted for him. For Phoenix. Oliver would never have left Libya had Taym murdered any of his men, he would have hunted the traitor down and killed him in his sleep, robbing Taym of the satisfaction of dying with purpose. It's what Hart wanted, too. Yet his instincts were holding him back when he so desperately wanted to return to Libya.

Hart peered up from his hand. He heard someone's panicked breath on the still air … and then he realized it was his own. The sun disappeared behind a cloud, and the shade stole the sun's warmth from him. He wiped the sweat from his forehead in the cold. It was a peculiar feeling. One that made him feel restless and nauseous. He felt nothing and everything at once. Hart clenched his fists by his side to stop the trembling that threatened him once again. To resist the merciless shudder that rattled his intellect. *Not here.* The forest picked itself up and spun around him, and he grimaced in the face of his vulnerability. Overwhelmed by the enormity of the redwoods surrounding him—their sheer size belittling his existence—he needed direction. Perspective. He needed peace. Hart thought about Ivy. The way she whispered on the wind to someone who seemed to listen. They *had* to be listening. Her magic lay in her allegiance with the earth, and someone was there, protecting her from afar. *Guiding her.*

He needed guidance … now more than ever.

Hart looked into the misty sky above the pines and listened to his shallow breath on the air. He closed his eyes and released his tightly clenched hands, and slowly opened his arms to the world around him. He bared the darkest depths of his soul to the bright sky, and he pleaded for Oliver's forgiveness. For his mercy. He begged his friend to release him from his guilt for surviving that tragic day. His guilt for living. His guilt for coming home.

For laughing. For falling in love. For wanting what Oliver no longer had … *life.*

Hart groaned and fell to his knees in unbearable sadness, and pleaded for his friend to hear him. He opened his eyes and stared at the sky through his tears …

*"I'm so sorry,"* he exhaled, his breath shaking. "You know I would trade places with you if I could … but I can't. Please forgive me, Ollie … *I can't.*"

Hart cried on his knees and confessed the sins that crippled him so completely. Baring his grief. Baring his fear. The world stood still around him. Impassive to his tears, yet somehow sympathetic to his sorrow.

"I'm sorry for what happened in Libya." Hart closed his eyes, lowering his head, feeling his tears fall. "I'm sorry you never got to come home. We were so close to going home …." He clenched his jaw and tightened his eyes, "I'm sorry I didn't come with you when you left this world. We did everything together … *but not this.*"

Hart exhaled sadly and stayed there on his knees, waiting in the silence. Waiting for something. Anything. A whisper … the wind … a reply of any kind ….

He blinked his eyes open when he felt them there. Listening. Hearing his heartfelt plea on the still air. He felt stronger in their presence. Safer. Less afraid. Almost as if … he could smile.

Hart took a deep breath before he spoke again.

"I want to thank you for being my best friend while you were here." He smiled to himself. "You knew me better than I knew myself …. you knew exactly what you were doing when you sent me to Ivy. You knew what would happen, you bastard."

Hart laughed softly to himself and rubbed his jaw.

"Thank you," he looked into the sky again, "for showing me a life with her that I never dreamed existed. Thank you for sending me home. Thank you, Ollie … for saving my life." Hart exhaled loudly and fell back on the heels of his boots, and bowed his heavy head. He sat there for a short while, with his eyes closed, listening to the world around him with an open mind like Ivy had taught him. With an uninhibited heart.

He whispered with his eyes closed, "Tell me what to do."

The sunlight fell upon him again, and he felt the warmth

of it on the back of his neck. Hart lifted his face toward it. A weight lifted from his shoulders, and he breathed easier in the tranquility of its light. Hart felt himself being pulled to his feet by the rays of sun. He instinctively rubbed his chest where Oliver had shot him in his nightmare, but he no longer felt the pain. No bullet in his flesh. All he felt was the pounding of his heart against his chest as it embraced the unfamiliar reassurance of the world surrounding him. He listened to the forest as it whispered in his thoughts….

*I promise I'll check on her, and I promise I won't leave her until she's begging me to go.*

*No, Hart, she would never do that … she will ask you to stay.*

*So I'll stay. Whatever she wants, Ollie, you have my word.*

Hart's shoulders rose and fell as he sighed heavily at the memory. He leaned his head back and closed his eyes peacefully in the sunlight, and smiled in its soothing solace. He knew what he had to do.

## Chapter 28

HART OPENED THE DOOR slowly and carefully. The dormitory room was dark despite the height of the morning sun in the sky. The building belonged to the Phoenix unit, but only Walker, Benji, and Hart occupied this room. The recruits claimed the dorm room next door, meaning Hart's absence remained undetected by everyone, other than his two friends.

The bathroom light cast a thin yellow line beneath the door, catching Hart's eye. He could hear the shower running, so he closed the door softly behind him and snuck soundlessly past Benji, who was still snoring in bed. Hart smiled as he passed him. He reached his own bunk at the far side of the room and threw his backpack on the bed below, then climbed effortlessly to the top bunk and laid down. He pulled his cell out from under his pillow and read the screen:

Wednesday at 12:33 pm: one missed call from Ivy Rose
Wednesday at 12:33 pm: one message from Ivy Rose

He tapped the side of the phone, thinking. The missed call was from yesterday, so he decided to call her back later today at a more appropriate hour, worried he might wake her. He laid his head back on his pillow and stared at the ceiling.

Walker came out of the bathroom with a towel wrapped low around his hips. His dog tags hung down his strong chest, and he was rubbing his wet hair with his hands, oblivious to Hart's presence in the room.

Hart rolled onto his side and propped himself up on his elbow.

"Hey, Walker," he spoke quietly, mindful not to wake Benji.

Walker glanced up at Hart, surprised to see him. He stared at him thoughtfully before he responded. "You took a little longer than I expected."

"I know," Hart replied. He sat up with his legs hanging over the side of the bunk. "I'm sorry, I didn't expect to be gone so long."

"You said a couple of hours," Walker smiled faintly, as he walked toward Hart.

Hart rubbed the back of his neck. "Yeah, I did."

"You're lucky I know you as well as I do," Walker said, leaning against Hart's bunk. "If anyone else knew about your absence, you'd have the entire garrison out there looking for you."

"Shit, I know. Thanks for not saying anything," Hart nodded at him.

"You know we wouldn't."

Walker took Hart's hand and clapped it between his, then he turned to the window beside them and swept open the curtains. The two of them stared out the window into the morning sun, and they welcomed the new day with a nervous breath. Today was their last day in the Californian sunshine. Deployment for Phoenix was scheduled at 23:00 tonight from Fort Hunter Liggett, Monterey County, bound for Ras Adjir, Libya.

Benji stirred and rubbed his face wearily. He glanced up at Hart through his sleepy eyes and grinned as he threw off his sheet to sit up.

"God, you're even more beautiful in the morning," Benji mumbled happily.

"Good morning, sleeping beauty," Hart replied, smiling.

Benji stood slowly in his boxer shorts and routinely scratched and readjusted himself. "Where'd you end up last night?"

"Where *did* you end up?" Walker asked, glancing from Benji to Hart. "Did you sleep in your car?"

"No. I slept in the Los Padres National Forest outside the military reservation," Hart replied. It was further away than any of them had anticipated, but somehow he'd just ended up there… in the forest.

Hart jumped off the top bunk and walked over to his bag of clothing in the corner of the room. He hadn't unpacked since arriving yesterday morning. He knew the guys were watching him, waiting for a more informative reply than the one he had given. He left them yesterday to clear his head after leaving Ivy, and he noticed their tactful silence as they each considered his state of mind. He unbuttoned his combat shirt and removed it, along with his military tank top. Bare-chested, with his dog-tags hanging brightly against his sun-tanned chest, Hart dug through his bag until he found his black t-shirt. He pulled it on then took his cap from the pocket of his combat pants and placed it backward on his head. Hart sat on the bed beside him and glanced up at the boys.

Both Walker and Benji were studying him with a contemplative silence.

"I'm okay," Hart answered, forcing a smile. "Really, I am."

"No, you're not," Benji replied. "There's no going back to her once you're in Libya, Hart. It will be too late then."

Hart didn't respond. His smile faded. He rubbed his jaw and nodded wordlessly at Benji's comment. Walker continued to analyze him.

"So what did you decide?" Benji asked, dressing in a similar black tee and combats pants. "I mean, that is why you left yesterday … for some clarity."

Hart sighed into his hand and stared back at the concerned gazes watching him from across the room. "I don't know," he breathed. "My mind is telling me one thing. My heart is telling me another …."

"Go with your heart," Walker replied without hesitation.

Hart looked up at him in surprise.

Walker shrugged. "When do the three of us ever make a decision with our hearts?"

"He's right," Benji added. "We're soldiers; we go where they tell us to go. We do what they tell us to do. We follow our gut. We follow our instincts. We follow our intelligence. We *never* follow our hearts."

"I can't." Hart shook his head. "I can't let you guys face

Taym without me. If something happened to you, then I would never forgive myself."

"So, what's new?" Walker grinned, his dark eyes narrowing at Hart.

The three of them smiled.

"Fuck Taym," Walker added casually. "He took Oliver from you, don't let him take Ivy, too."

Hart stared at him, thinking, then he shook his head. "No, I can't go back. It is my duty to go with Phoenix to Libya."

"What about our duty to Oliver?" Benji asked. "We promised him we would keep her safe and now we've left her vulnerable to that dick, Tommy."

"Tommy shouldn't hurt her again," Hart replied hesitantly.

"Shouldn't?" Benji frowned.

Hart looked up at him. Benji's blue eyes were troubled, and it was a sight that Hart had become sadly accustomed to with him this past year. Ivy seemed to stir a fierce protectiveness in Benji that Hart admired. In Walker, too. He frowned to himself and thought about Tommy. He would always be a threat to Ivy. Hart knew that. He had experienced Tommy's aggression firsthand, and the guy was mentally unstable. Irrational with his obsession, to a dangerous degree. Considering this, Hart still couldn't deny the military if they summoned him. He was the Commander of Phoenix. He had responsibilities. Men to protect. *Friends* to protect. He had done everything in his power to prevent Tommy from further pursuing Ivy, even using himself as a distraction. Tommy needed a win to back off, and now Hart was no longer a threat to his ego. If anything, it was his own relationship with Ivy that made everything worse for her. Going back to La Mar might bring her more harm than good, forcing Hart to reconsider the decision he made in the forest this morning.

Hart sighed. "I can't go back to Ivy."

Walker shook his head in quiet disapproval. He pulled his jocks up and unwrapped the towel from his hips and threw it on his bunk. He walked over to his locker and pulled a black T-shirt over his head and dressed in his combat pants. The three of them were due in the General's office in ten minutes.

Hart watched Benji and Walker pull on their boots and tie them up, then the two of them stood in front of the door. Hart stood and walked over to meet them.

"When did Garvey arrive from North Carolina?" Hart asked, pushing aside his aching heart by changing the subject.

"Yesterday afternoon," Walker replied.

"Did he notice I was missing?"

"He had his suspicions," Walker smiled.

Hart checked his cell phone and nervously twisted his mouth.

"What is it?" Walker frowned, glancing at the cell.

Hart looked at him. "Nothing. I had a missed call from Ivy yesterday."

"Did you call her back?" he asked.

"No, I was going to call her after the meeting."

"Well, did she leave a message?" Benji asked, stepping toward Hart.

"Yeah, she did." Hart tucked the cell into his pocket and walked toward the door, but Benji stepped in front of him to prevent him from leaving. Hart stopped in surprise, then cast a rare, authoritative look at his friend, a silent order to move out of the way.

"Did you listen to it?" Benji asked, unfazed by Hart's reaction.

"No, I haven't had a chance."

"What if she's in trouble?" Benji asked. "What if Tommy's hurt her?"

Walker watched his friends cautiously.

"Tommy won't fucking touch her, Benji," Hart replied. "Now let's go."

Benji looked to Walker for his support.

Walker nodded. "Listen to Ivy's message, Hart. We'll meet you at Garvey's office," he suggested warmly, pulling Benji out of Hart's way.

Hart stared at the door, but he didn't move.

"What's wrong?" Walker asked, detecting Hart's uncertainty.

"I don't think I can," Hart breathed, rubbing his face tiredly. He moved back into the room. "Shit!"

"Of course you can," Benji exclaimed. "It's Ivy!"

Hart didn't respond. He felt Walker's sympathetic gaze on him.

"It's like that fucking doorbell moment all over again," Benji remarked.

Hart shot a disapproving glare at him.

"Whether you choose Libya or La Mar, we're here for you, buddy," Walker said, easing the friction between his friends. He walked over to Hart and rested his hand on his shoulder. "Listen to the message, for Ivy's sake, and we'll meet you outside Garvey's office in five minutes."

Hart met Walker's compassionate gaze and nodded.

"Five minutes," Walker smiled. "Don't be late or Garvey will lose his shit." He grabbed Benji on his way out and guided him toward the door, leaving Hart alone in the room.

Hart waited for them to leave, then he closed his eyes and rubbed his forehead with the back of his hand. He looked at his phone, and a sickening anxiety swept over him all of a sudden. Her voice was too sweet. Too gentle. It would break his heart to hear her. He remembered her raw, breathtaking grace on the beach, the day after they met. The image danced through the chaos in his mind until Ivy was all he could see … walking into the sea. Her blue eyes watching him follow her to the water. Leading him out of his darkness with her light. With her love. Her liberating enchantment. Ivy's words resounded through him. *It is not about there being something or someone bigger out there that you should believe in. It is believing there is something bigger inside of you. If I ask the universe for help with something that is troubling me, then deep down, I know I am really asking this of myself.*

Hart sighed into his hands. He had chosen Ivy in the forest this morning. It was his heart that told him to go back for her, not the trees of the forest or voices in the universe. His strength suddenly wavered at the thought of her alone. Out of his reach. Out of his protection. He glanced down at the screen of his cell with a disturbing feeling that nestled itself in the pit of his stomach, and the darkness unsettled him once again. Something was wrong.

He stared determinedly at the phone and slid his thumb across her voicemail message on the screen without another thought. He pressed the phone to his ear and sat down on the end of the bed, breathing calmly through his disquieting concern. He waited patiently for her sweet voice to lull softly down the line.

He listened to his cell as it diverted him to Messagebank,

feeling the anxiety wane. Hart leaned his forehead into his hands and recalled the relief in Oliver's eyes when he realized he had saved him. The distinct elation that his friend would go on living, even if he, himself, would not. It was the ultimate sacrifice ... then Oliver died with the sunset in his eyes.

Hart frowned curiously.

Every day Oliver would wait for the desert sun to sweep across the sky and fall onto the horizon. Watching it paint the evenings with its burning colors, just like Ivy. She always talked to the sunset. Hart's eyes widened. Ivy had been talking to him. To her brother. She knew Oliver was where he always wanted to be ... *standing in the orange sky.*

Everything fell into place. It all made sense. Hart sighed into his hands as the revelation unwrapped the chains from his tortured heart. Oliver wanted them to check on her. He wanted them to protect her. He *wanted* them to love her in any possible way. Oliver sent them to her, foreseeing their reluctance to leave her behind. Predicting their love, so she would never be alone. Oliver wouldn't condemn him for falling in love with Ivy; he would condemn him for leaving her behind.

*Tommy.*

The past year had tested Hart in ways like never before, but he would be eternally grateful for the one good thing that came from his devastating heartbreak: Ivy Rose. He would protect her because his best friend asked him to. But he would do *anything* for her ... because he loved her. With a revived determination, Hart closed his eyes tightly with the phone against his ear and waited for Ivy's voice. Instead he heard the distinct sounds of a struggle on the other end of the line. Hart's eyes shot open.

He stood and gripped the cell tensely in his hands, then Ivy screamed his name down the line and Hart's adrenaline ignited the fearless soldier within him. He held his breath as he listened vigilantly to the rest of the recording. He heard a painful gasp from Ivy ... then the message ended.

"*FUCK!*" Hart shouted abruptly.

His eyes narrowed as he contemplated his options. Hart hadn't felt this kind of control since Libya. He tapped his cell against his bottom lip while he analyzed what he had heard on the other end of the line. He quickly dialed Ivy's number. It rang until her voicemail picked up. He dialed it again … and it rang again until voicemail picked up. Tommy plagued his thoughts.

"What have I done?" he breathed.

He checked his watch—he was due at General Garvey's office in two minutes. Hart hurried over to his backpack and rummaged around inside it until he found his keys. He picked up the bag and ran out the door, heading toward his Firebird.

Hart had been driving for ten minutes before he finally picked up his cell off the passenger seat and dialed Walker. He had the accelerator pressed to the floor, and he was speeding down the highway at a furious pace. Purple-flowered fields surrounded him, and the Firebird dashed between them with a determination that snarled defiantly through the still air, spoiling the serenity. Hart propped his elbow up on the window and held the phone to his ear, and happened to glance at himself in his rear-view mirror. His sunglasses reflected the world in front of him with their mirrored lenses, and Hart recognized a soldier whom he had thought was lost forever. He sensed a sudden confidence that he had been missing all year. He felt unconquerable. *Fearless*. Driven by an essential, indomitable determination that strengthened his mind and fortified his soul. He thought about the man he had left behind in Libya; Commander Johnny Hart, the soldier who defined him. He had walked behind enemy lines for over twelve years without fear. He was a desert rat. An elite force. A weapon. He was Josh Walker. Benjamin Swift. Oliver Rose. He was *Phoenix*. The final decision to go back for Ivy was made with an unwavering certainty because of his devotion to a fallen friend. To his brother-in-arms. There would always be a Rose in Phoenix … he would make damn sure of it.

As he waited for Walker to answer, he remembered the girl in the marketplace. He remembered how it felt to give up his weapon and offer his life for hers. It was his duty to protect those who needed him. His honor. Hart narrowed his eyes down the highway and shook his head, regretting the way things ended with Ivy.

"Hart!" Walker snapped anxiously down the line. "Garvey's pissed you're late! Where are you? Wait … are you driving?"

"I'm going back for Ivy!" Hart replied, shouting over the wind that rushed through his open window. "Her message. Something's happened to her …!"

"What did she say?"

"She didn't say anything! She fucking screamed my name, Walker! Someone has her, and I think it is Tommy. I *know* it's fucking Tommy!"

Hart heard Walker curse on the other end of the line.

"If he's forced himself on her, I'll kill him!" Hart continued. "She called me yesterday! He's had almost twenty-four hours to do whatever the hell he wants to her!" He imagined her with Tommy, petrified and vulnerable, and his stomach twisted painfully.

Hart listened to Walker's silence. He knew he was formulating a plan of attack, so he waited for Walker to speak.

"Get to Ivy," Walker agreed. "I'll take care of Garvey. Call me as soon as you arrive in La Mar. I'll wrangle us a bird."

Hart laughed. "Garvey isn't going to give you a Black Hawk, man."

"Are you underestimating my influence on the General?" Walker responded wryly. "You know me better than that, Hart."

Hart sensed Walker's dangerous grin down the line. "Ah, you're right. If there is anyone who can bend that man's ironclad will, it's you."

"Damn straight. Look to the sky, my friend!"

## Chapter 29

# - SOUTHERN CALIFORNIA -
## May 2015

HART PUNCHED IN THE SECURITY CODE at the estate's entrance and waited for the rambling iron gates to crank open. He tapped his fingers impatiently on the steering wheel and glared down the driveway with a steely expression that reflected his determination to get to Ivy. The weeping trees along the driveway cast a grim picture for him as he waited. They blew wildly in the hot Santa Ana winds, and the air was hazy with smoke from the wildfires he had seen burning in the San Diego East County on the drive down. The smell of smoke permeated everything. The fires cast an auburn pall over the afternoon sun in La Mar and an irrefutable shadow over his heart.

Hart floored the accelerator as the gate opened just wide enough for his Firebird to pass through, and he shot through the opening toward Ivy's house. The Firebird came to a skidding halt at the bottom of the stairs, and Hart hurried up to the front door with the engine still rumbling contentedly behind him.

He saw a white envelope sitting on the door mat with *Ivy Rose* written in blue pen across the front of it. Hart picked it up. He knocked loudly on the door and pressed the doorbell twice. Without waiting, he turned the door handle, but it was locked.

"Ivy!" Hart bellowed, his voice booming off the estate's walls. He stepped backward and waited a few seconds before he called for her again. "Ivy!"

Hart ran his hand through his hair and over his face in distress. He glanced at the envelope he was still holding in his hands and tucked it into his back pocket. Hart moved quickly to the study window, to the estate's left. He peered into the room, then hit the glass with a frustrated grunt. Hart walked down the stairs, then stepped backward toward the fountain in the center of the driveway, looking up at the estate's façade. He put his hands up to his mouth and called out her name one more time, but there was no reply.

Hart gripped his hands on the back of his head and walked back to the Firebird in frustration.

"Where are you, Ives?" he breathed, staring at the empty estate from beside his car.

He pulled the envelope from his back pocket and leaned against the right fender of his car. Hart stared at Ivy's name on the front of the envelope. It looked like Nicole's handwriting. He narrowed his eyes at this and opened the envelope. Had the circumstances not been so disconcerting, he would have left the envelope untouched. Hart slid out a small piece of paper and read the note:

> *Ivy,*
>
> *I wanted to apologize to you before I left town. I said some things to you with the intention of deliberately hurting you. It sounds heartless, I know, but in the big scheme of all things, who can blame me? I still love the guy. I always will. Yes, I tried to win him back, but I couldn't sway his feelings for you. Johnny loves you, Ivy Rose. You win.*
>
> *It is not like me to feel the need to clear my conscience, but there was something about you that made me feel like I had to. Don't get me wrong—I expect I'm going to hell, and I'm sure I deserve it, but after deceiving you … well, it felt like I was heading someplace worse.*
>
> *The truth is … I lied. Johnny didn't fuck me. Call me a fool for asking for your forgiveness, but I just had to try.*
>
> *Sorry.*
> *Nicole*

Hart dropped his hands, still holding the letter, looking into the sky in sudden disbelief. "One fucking thing after another," he growled.

Hart crumpled the letter and tossed it into the fountain

behind him. He rubbed his hands wearily up and down his face, fighting the fatigue after the all-nighter in the woods and the long drive from Monterey. He had spent the entire night running away from his feelings for Ivy … and now he was chasing after them. He imagined how Ivy felt after hearing about his betrayal from Nicole. Nicole was a vindictive liar. A master of deceit. No one was immune to her wiles, not even Ivy. Hart imagined Ivy's broken heart being ground to dust by Nicole's lies, and he felt her pain in his soul. Ivy's image wavered in his mind, as if she were drifting further and further away from him, out of his reach. *Untouchable.* Only this time, he wasn't pushing her away.

Hart leaned over, his hands on his knees, and exhaled a long, controlled breath toward the ground. He would never do it to Ivy. *Never.* His loyalty was all that remained unbroken after losing everything last year. His abiding disposition that saw him through to today. Now he was back, stronger than ever, with a determination that pledged a deadly force against anyone who stood between him and the woman he had sworn to protect.

Hart stepped quickly around the car and slid into the driver's seat. He floored the accelerator and disappeared in a cloud of burning rubber. He glanced at his cell on the passenger seat; he still hadn't called Walker since he arrived in La Mar. Garvey was probably reeling with frustration, but he would have to deal with Garvey at a later time. The Firebird screeched its tires furiously on the asphalt outside the gate, and Hart sped down the hill toward town. He had never been to Tommy's house, but he knew where it was. Everyone knew where Tommy lived. Over half the women in La Mar had visited his place at least once, falling for his exaggerated, artificial charm. Hart shook his head at the absurdity of Tommy's popularity with women. He had done nothing except cause immense trouble for Ivy, including assaulting her at her front door. She swore to him that Tommy didn't touch her, but he had his suspicions.

He rubbed his chest and thought about the coward who had held him at gunpoint only days ago. Tommy had used her as a means to constrain Hart's lethal skills; it was Ivy's safety that hindered Hart's fight. She gave herself up, and Hart was forced to accommodate Tommy's demands after that. Tommy's ego gave him an unrealistic portrayal of Hart, and things were drastically different now … Hart no longer had Ivy. Tommy had no idea he was coming for him, and Hart tightened his fingers around the steering wheel in front of him, smiling dangerously at the thought.

Dusk had set in by the time he pulled into Tommy's estate. The sunset had been foiled by a blanket of smoke that glowed a brilliant orange along its edges, setting a red haze over the rest of the sky. Hart walked from his car with his hands tucked casually in his pockets. He gazed contemplatively at the sky and primed himself for his confrontation with Tommy. He ducked through an impressive archway covered in bright pink bougainvillea, and in the midst of his agitation he couldn't help but think how Ivy would have appreciated them.

Hart approached the front door confidently. There was an unfeigned coolness about him that caught the attention of two young maids who were collecting flowers from the lush garden beside him. Hart nodded and smiled at them in greeting, and they smiled warmly in return.

A large, cast-iron fist hung at head height in the center of the wooden door, and without hesitation, Hart knocked it against the strike plate three times. He took a step back, slipping his hand back into his pocket, and studied the grand, Spanish-inspired mansion in front of him. As much as it displeased him, Hart couldn't deny the remarkable architecture of Tommy's home. La Mar truly was home for the luxuriously rich.

A beautiful young woman answered the door. "Can I help you?"

She wasn't at all what he was expecting, though when he thought about it, Tommy was far too pretentious to answer his door, especially when someone else could do it for him. She was dressed neatly in a black and white dress, and by the looks of the linen apron wrapped around her tiny waist, Hart assumed she was also a maid. Her blushed cheeks and timid grin instantly warmed his heart.

He smiled with an effortless charm. "I hope you can help me. I'm looking for Tommy. I was hoping to catch him before I left town."

The maid tilted her head, and Hart caught her delighted eyes drifting unintentionally down his body. He bowed his head, restraining a self-effacing smile.

"Is he home?" he added, peering up at her again.

The maid gazed at him with a vague, open-mouthed expression as she reiterated to herself what he had asked. "Yes. Wait here," she replied, embarrassed. "I'll let Tom know you are here to see him."

Hart went to speak as she walked away, but she paused on her own accord and returned to him.

"Was he expecting you?" she asked.

"Uh, no," he replied hesitantly, grateful for her return. Hart smiled and ran his hand along his jaw, then he bit his bottom lip and glanced up at her with big, brown eyes. "See, I was hoping to surprise him. We haven't seen each other in a while."

"Okay," she smiled, bowing her head bashfully. "Follow me."

Hart knew he had won her affection, but he didn't have time to feel ashamed about his behavior. He pressed his hands together and mouthed a soundless thank you to her before she led him inside.

He followed the maid deep into the mansion. They walked through spacious marble halls and past extraordinary wall-sized pieces of art that unfortunately impressed him. The home boasted a level of sophistication that baffled Hart. For an arrogant, pompous brat, Tommy still had taste.

Hart refused to believe it. "So does Tommy live alone?"

The maid turned her head and furrowed her dark eyebrows at him, as though his comment were humorously absurd. "Tom still lives with his parents."

Hart cursed silently to himself. "Are they home, too?"

"Yes, they are. Tommy is having afternoon tea with them outside in the center courtyard as we speak." She had turned to him before she walked him outside. "Shall I bring you something to drink?"

"No. No, I'm fine. Thank you," he replied, re-strategizing his meeting with Tommy.

The maid went to turn toward the courtyard, but then paused in Hart's warm gaze. "Are you a friend of Tom's?" she asked, narrowing her eyes with a curious smile. "I probably should have asked you before I invited you in. I could lose my job, and you …

well, I was distracted," she blushed.

"I … uh …," Hart sensed her suspicion and a wave of shame washed over him. He ran his hand through his hair and stifled a small, ineffective mumble before he looked at her and smiled.

The woman bowed her head apologetically. "I'm sorry. Of course you are."

Hart breathed out noticeably.

"It's just that you're not at all like the friends Tom likes to keep."

Hart's smile faded. "I'm not his friend. I'm sorry, I don't want to get you in any trouble."

The maid shook her head and smiled at him, evidently intrigued by his confession.

"Look, I need to talk to him about something. It's important," Hart told her.

The maid nodded and turned toward the courtyard. "He'll know…."

Hart frowned. "Who?"

"Tom's father. He'll see right through those eyes of yours."

Hart didn't respond.

She looked back at him with a beautiful smile. "Don't worry. William is harmless."

Hart followed her outside. His plan to confront Tommy had been unexpectedly hindered. Before he had any more time to consider a new strategy, they entered the courtyard.

"I am sorry to interrupt, but you have a guest." The woman bowed her head and smiled sweetly at Hart before she left.

Hart locked eyes with Tommy, who sat on the opposite side of the table from where he was standing. He watched Tommy's face turn a sickening shade of gray. Hart smiled, pleased with the ill effect he had on Tommy. He wanted to walk over to him and wrap his hand around his throat, so he could drag him to his feet, kicking and begging for his release, just like he did in his dreams. He wanted to hear him gasp for air and in the breath that escaped his deceitful mouth, he wanted Tommy's apology. His regret for threatening Ivy. Hart wanted the truth of what happened yesterday in his absence … and he wanted Ivy back, safe and unharmed.

Tommy's father stood with his hand outstretched eagerly

toward him. Hart blinked his eyes in disbelief and pushed aside the image of Tommy, focusing on the older man in front of him.

"William."

"Commander Johnny Hart," he replied, shaking Hart's hand firmly between his own. "It is a pleasure to meet you finally."

Hart glanced at Tommy's mother, Joyce, speechless as he continued to shake William's hand mindlessly. He recognized them through Ivy. She pointed them out to him once in town, explaining to him how they were her parents' closest friends. Hart knew everything about these two gentle souls, yet Ivy failed to mention one significant detail ... they were also Tommy's parents.

Once the shock subsided, Hart glanced warmly back at William. "It is a pleasure to meet you also, sir."

"Joyce," William called, motioning for his wife to come over. "This here is Johnny Hart, the man who stole our young Ivy's heart." William looked back at Hart and winked at him.

"Hello, Johnny," she smiled, taking his hand affectionately. "Will you join us? I can have the girls bring you some tea."

"No, thank you, ma'am," Hart answered politely.

"I've heard a lot about you and Phoenix, Commander," William spoke proudly, tucking his hands into his pockets. "You're a hero of this country, son. I am honored to have you in our home."

"Thank you, sir." Hart bowed his head humbly.

"I served my country for over thirty years," William nodded. "I have a lot of friends who are still in the service. They're scattered all over the country, and they can't speak highly enough of the legendary Johnny Hart."

Hart rubbed his jaw with a bashful smile. "Thank you, sir."

"William, please. Call me William." He placed his big hand on Hart's shoulder. "Ivy couldn't be in safer hands. Her father would have liked you."

Hart's expression softened. He had never thought about her father's approval, only Oliver's. It felt good to hear it, relieving almost. He smiled gratefully at William, taken with the old man's authenticity, and William nodded back at him with an approving, reminiscent gaze.

"That means a lot to me. Thank you, sir," Hart replied.

"William," he reminded him. He patted Hart a few times on the back and gestured toward Tommy. "No doubt you've met my son?" William glanced at Tommy, who sat meekly at the other end of the table.

Hart nodded. He had done far more than meet him; he had witnessed Tommy's abhorrence. He had suffered the brunt of his bitterness toward soldiers. This father and son couldn't be more different.

"Yeah, we've met," Hart replied.

Tommy recoiled in Hart's lingering, perilous gaze, and William detected the sudden frostiness between his son and the renowned soldier.

"Actually, Tommy is the reason I'm here," Hart added, analyzing the weakness in Tommy's refusal to acknowledge his presence.

"I see," William replied, seemingly disappointed with his son. He glanced apprehensively at Tommy, then twisted his mouth and looked back to Hart. He nodded with quiet approval, as though he knew all too well what his son was capable of. "Well, we'll leave you two alone to talk."

William turned to his wife. He glanced disapprovingly at his son one last time and led Joyce inside.

Once they were out of sight, Hart shifted his gaze back to Tommy. His charming behavior dissolved into a calm that belied the rage burning fiercely in his eyes.

"You can't fucking touch me here. Not in my own home." Tommy stood from his chair and threw his hands in the air. "Not in front of my parents."

"I don't know, Tommy." Hart glanced toward the door. "The way your father looked at you … I'd say he's hoping I beat the hostile, intolerant ass of a man right out of you." He kept his voice low and subdued, so as not to warrant any unwanted attention from inside.

"You know what, fuck you," Tommy retaliated, stepping away from the table.

Hart laughed to himself as he strolled across the courtyard, strategically placing himself between Tommy and the safety of his house.

Tommy backed away at his approach and managed to get

himself entangled in a wall of white bougainvillea. He carefully
unhooked his polo shirt from a thorn on the vine, and when he
turned back to look at Hart, he was standing right in front of
him.

"Shit, man!" Tommy jumped. He leaned his head back
against the thorns and winced in pain. "What do you want from
me?"

Hart's eyes darkened. "Where is she?"

"Who? Ivy?"

"Where is she?" Hart growled.

"I don't know where she is!" Tommy stared into Hart's
infuriated glare. He was terrified by the dangerous and volatile
look in Hart's eyes. Tommy swallowed awkwardly and glanced
at the house.

Hart took another step toward him, hands still in his pockets.

"I haven't seen her! Honestly! I haven't seen Ivy since …
since that night in the parking lot," Tommy admitted reluctantly.

"You're lying."

"I'm not lying!" Tommy nearly shouted. He nervously rubbed
the side of his head with his hand. *"Shit!"*

Hart exhaled loudly. His soul suddenly darkened with
anxious uncertainty. He clenched his hands inside his pockets
and breathed himself through the weakness of his trembling soul.
He grew angry. Furious with his vulnerability. Hart blinked his
eyes tightly to focus his blurring vision, and Tommy's sneering
grin appeared in front of him.

"You forget to take your meds this morning, soldier?"
Tommy chuckled in relief.

Hart narrowed his eyes, and with lightning speed, his left
hand flew from his pocket and wrapped itself around Tommy's
throat, forcing him back against the bougainvillea.

Tommy grunted in pain when the thorns pricked his flesh.
He tried to speak, so Hart gripped him even harder.

Tommy gasped for air, and Hart smiled as the darkness
enveloped him. He leaned into Tommy and listened to him
splutter a few words of surrender before he spoke to him again.
"I'm only going to ask you one more time," Hart whispered.
"Where is Ivy?"

"I … don't … know."

Hart bowed his head without loosening his grip. Ivy's voice screamed through his memory and he narrowed his eyes. He looked up at the coward in his hands, tightening his grip again to distract him from the pain that twisted his stomach. Tommy gasped painfully, and Hart watched his lips turn a satisfying shade of blue. He examined Tommy's bulging eyes, but sadly for Hart; the truth sat worryingly in Tommy's petrified gaze. He didn't know anything.

Hart growled angrily and released his grip.

Tommy gulped air into his deprived lungs. He slumped forward and groaned the life back into his body.

"What the fuck is wrong with you!?" Tommy stumbled over to the table and nursed his neck, wincing at the throbbing pain. He groaned again and glanced fearfully at Hart when he stepped toward him again, flinching instinctively in fear. Tommy threw his hands up in surrender, panting. "I told you already! I told you I don't know where she is! I'm telling the truth, Goddamn it!"

Hart dropped his gaze in confusion.

"She's your fucking girlfriend," Tommy continued, sensing Hart's uncertainty. "Or is it ex-girlfriend?"

Hart looked at him.

Tommy chuckled painfully, expecting Hart had finished with his interrogation. "Little birdy told me you banged a prostitute at the local inn."

"Prostitute?" Hart repeated. Local inn … motel … *Nicole.* Hart frowned. "That wasn't a prostitute, that was … an acquaintance," he added, looking away.

"Hey, if she does it for loot," Tommy shrugged his shoulders.

Hart glared at Tommy, who immediately stopped talking. The two of them were silent for a short while. Hart inwardly deliberated on Ivy's whereabouts.

"You never deserved her," Tommy said into the table, still nursing his neck. "I did. I wouldn't have left, and Ivy wouldn't be missing."

Tommy's complacency struck Hart hard in the chest. Or was it the truth that hurt him more? He rubbed his eyes to focus his vision.

"Look at you. Fucking washed up soldier," Tommy snarled. "What more would you expect from a man who killed his best friend?"

Hart slowly raised his head, staring dead-eyed at Tommy, who instinctively recoiled from him. He took two quick steps to Tommy and lifted him until he was standing straight, then he pulled his fist back to silence the witless son-of-a-bitch. He caught William in the corner of his eye, silently witnessing their altercation from the window adjacent to the courtyard. William still had friends in the military. He probably knew everything. Tommy must have overheard him talking.

Hart held his shaking fist in the air while Tommy cowered in his hands, anticipating the blow with his eyes clamped shut. Hart hesitated and glanced back at William. The older man watched him with an expressionless calm, then he lowered his eyes and let the curtain fall in front of him.

Hart stared at the swaying curtains behind the window and forced himself to remember who he was and why he was here. He looked down at the pathetic man he held in his grip, and Hart growled irritably and shoved Tommy a short distance away from him. He turned and ran his hands through his hair, frustratingly disoriented in his quest to rescue Ivy. If Tommy didn't have her, who did? The world began to spin around him, and Hart held his head to keep his balance. He could hear Tommy panting heavily beside him in the silence somewhere. He felt William's impassive eyes burning through him from the empty window. The bright bougainvillea swirled around him as he rummaged through a thousand thoughts that eventually led him to one unanswered question. *Where was Ivy?*

Hart left the courtyard quickly. He hurried through the mansion, desperate for the isolation of his car. Hart ignored the concerned expressions from William and Joyce as he passed them in the corridor. He ran past the artwork and under the marble archways that led to the front door, and on his way out, he glimpsed the young maid who now looked disturbingly like Ivy. Hart grabbed his chest and ran beneath the bougainvillea and the auburn sky, and when he finally reached the Firebird he threw himself into the driver's seat and slammed the door behind him. Once he caught his breath, Hart held his hands above the steering wheel and watched them shake uncontrollably. His fingers tightened into a fist. Hart threatened to punch the steering wheel in front of him, but instead, he closed his eyes and leaned his head against it. *Ivy. Ivy, talk to me. Where are you?*

His cell phone shrilled beside him on the passenger seat, startling him. Walker's name appeared on the screen and he answered it. "Hey, Walker."

Hart leaned his head back against the seat, relieved to hear from his friend.

"Hart, you in La Mar yet?"

Hart could hear the concern in his voice. "Yeah, I'm here, pulled in less than an hour ago. Sorry, I didn't call. How was Garvey?"

Walker chuckled grimly. "You don't want to know."

Hart sighed aloud, relaxing in his friend's usual, laid-back response.

"Actually, things have changed significantly since you left." Walker paused. He sighed and then spoke again. "Garvey could not have you in a more ideal position."

Hart closed his eyes and rubbed his jaw. "Why am I getting a bad feeling about this?"

Walker didn't respond right away.

"You were right, Hart," he said down the line.

"About what?" Hart opened his eyes and stared, perplexed, at the town of La Mar twinkling in the distance.

"About the mechanical noise in the background of the recording," Walker answered. "The recording from the night we were extracted from Libya … the one with Bar Rafid?"

Hart remembered the recording. It was the anxious tone in Walker's voice that had his attention.

"The other guy was on an American Airlines flight," Walker continued.

Hart could tell he was reluctant to go on.

"Keep talking, Walker," he encouraged, troubled by his friend's uncharacteristic distress. "Did we find out who it was?"

"Yeah, we did. You were also right about the voice in the recording. He was using a device to mask his voice. They didn't pick it up because the recording was of such poor quality, but you picked it up, Hart. They should never have sent you away …."

Hart narrowed his eyes and waited for Walker to continue. His fear for Ivy combined with his alarm at Walker's behavior wreaked havoc on his mind, but he forced himself to keep calm.

"If they had kept you at Base, then I don't believe we would be in this position right now. The President is pissed. He arrived today, along with a swarm of officials."

"The President?" Hart asked, rubbing his chest nervously.

"I've got some bad news, buddy, but we're packing the birds as we speak," Walker spoke reassuringly, easing him into it.

"Walker, just spit it out, man! You're making me fucking sweat here!"

"I hope you're sitting down."

"I am." Hart looked around his Firebird still parked in Tommy's driveway.

"Good. The voice on the recording ... ah, man," Walker hesitated. "Hart, it was Taym."

Hart must have misunderstood. "Who was it?" he asked.

"Taym Malak."

Hart held his breath. Stunned. The last twelve months were starting to fall together like pieces of a puzzle. He stared, unblinking, at the world in front of him. Ivy's world.

"Hart? You still there?"

Hart blinked his eyes in disbelief. "You said he was on an American Airlines flight—"

"He boarded a flight from Tripoli, bound for Los Angeles," Walker interrupted with a sudden urgency.

"LA? What the fuck, Walker?" Hart repeated, exasperated. "How? When?"

"Last year. He boarded the flight at 5 a.m., the same night we were extracted out of Benghazi. This happened before they even had a chance to revoke his passport."

"So he came into America as a citizen!?"

"Yeah, he did," Walker answered. "Benji and I were pulled in to identify him on LAX security footage because we refused to believe what they were telling us. He had it all planned, Hart."

"Are you positive it's Taym?"

"Broken leg, broken arm ... it's Taym alright," Walker replied. "Benji leaped out of his chair like he'd seen a fucking ghost." Hart groaned into his hand. He couldn't believe what he was hearing.

"Bar Rafid revealed Taym's plan to establish a clandestine terrorist organization within America. I don't know why he's opening up about this shit all of a sudden. We think something is about to go down, Hart. Something big. Los Angeles has been placed under a serious and imminent terror attack," Walker spoke precisely and efficiently. "Taym is not working alone either, another extremist they call, Omen, left Sirte a few days ago for America. We don't know a whole lot about this guy yet. All we know is that he is extremely dangerous and he fucking *hates* Americans."

"Get in line."

"It seems we're not that easy to love," Walker said lightheartedly.

Hart imagined the smirk on Walker's charming expression.

"Hey, listen," Walker continued, more upbeat, "you need to watch Ivy until we get there, she'll be—"

"The girl ...," Hart interrupted, remembering the recording. The sharp sting of adrenaline pierced his heart. "They're talking about Ivy on that tape, aren't they?"

"Yeah, buddy, they are. Oliver killed Abad. We believe this is a personal vendetta against Ollie that he planned to undertake before taking any major action in the United States. After Taym had landed in LAX last year, footage has him boarding a flight fifteen minutes later," Walker paused and sighed, "... to San Diego."

Hart clenched his fists and cursed under his breath. Taym was *here.*

Walker continued in Hart's stunned silence. "I know you won't let Ivy out of your sight, and you need to keep it that way until we get there—"

"I don't know where she is, Walker!?" Hart exclaimed abruptly. "She's gone! No one's seen her since I left La Mar!" He ran his hands through his hair in distress as he thought about Taym with Ivy. Oliver flashed through his mind. He didn't want to believe it ... Libya couldn't possibly be here in California. Taym and Ivy were two pieces of entirely different worlds, and now they were colliding catastrophically before him.

Walker sighed down the line.

"Taym has Ivy," Hart thought aloud, forcing himself to

believe it.

"You are the only one on the ground in San Diego. You can get to her before the rest of us."

Hart didn't reply.

"Hart?"

"He was waiting for me to leave." Hart ignored him. His eyes narrowed with hatred for the deceitful coward who had stolen everything from him. Now he had Ivy.

"I need you to think," Walker spoke calmly. "Her security is pretty tight. I don't think he would have taken her from the estate? Do you?"

Hart heard Walker give the 'okay' to someone. He hoped it approved their departure from Monterey any minute now to assist him in his search for Ivy. He swapped the cell to his other ear and turned the keys that were dangling impatiently in the ignition. The Firebird rumbled to life again, and Hart drove in a slow circle on the driveway outside Tommy's home, the gravel crackling beneath his tires. His hand mechanically turned the car onto the driveway so that he faced the road in the distance, but his mind was a million miles away in thought.

"You're right, the estate seemed untouched," Hart replied, driving slowly away from Tommy's. "If he took her from town, people would notice. I mean, it's Ivy, Goddamn it, half of America knows who she is."

He heard Walker breathing calmly on the phone.

*Ivy.* He remembered the heartbreaking sadness in her eyes when he told her he was being deployed back to the civil war in Libya. He recalled her fear when he admitted he was leaving her to avenge her brother's death. Off to hunt down a man wanted for the murder of a United States Special Forces soldier. Wanted for treason. For blood. She was a ray of light in his rearview mirror, as he drove away into his deserved darkness. Hart groaned as he recalled the agonizing moment between them on the driveway.

"Focus, Hart," Walker encouraged warmly, hearing his friend's familiar suffering. "She must have been taken from somewhere quiet. Somewhere where no one could witness her abduction."

Hart twisted his mouth in thought. Where would she run too after he broke her heart? He imagined her running inside after he left.

"The backpack," Hart muttered distantly. He remembered their silent argument in front of Nicole once he realized she planned to go to Lights Beach without him. He felt foolish for thinking she would listen.

"Backpack?" Walker repeated.

"I saw him," Hart remembered, "at Lights Beach." He had convinced himself that his mind had simply played a trick on him, too many years spent walking in the war, besieged by the enemy. But it was him all along. Taym. He wasn't a ghost—he was real.

"Remember I told you about the green light in the distance that night on the Ghost Trail?" Hart asked Walker, pushing the light on his military watch and watching it glow a bright green in the fading daylight.

"Yeah ..."

"Shit, I can't believe I didn't put it together sooner." Hart hit the steering wheel when the light disappeared on his watch. "It's identical to ours," he panted. "He's living at Lights Beach. He's in the fishing shack in the forest."

"You think he's been there this whole time?"

"I do. Ivy put it down to the ghosts ... a fucking figment of my imagination. I knew someone was watching us. You were there, Walker! We all felt it! Tell me you felt it, too?" Hart asked ardently.

"Yeah, I felt it." Hart heard a knocking sound on Walker's end of the line. "Hold on, Hart," Walker said, his voice was muted as he held the phone away from his mouth.

"What is it, Sergeant?"

"Sir, the Black Hawks are good to go. We're ready to leave when you are, sir."

"Thank you, Sergeant." Walker's voice returned to the phone. "Hart?"

"Yeah, I heard."

"Get to Lights Beach and hit me with the coordinates. I'm walking to the birds as we speak. You think you can handle Taym until we get there?"

"I can handle Taym. I have been waiting for this moment, Walker."

"I know you have."

Hart heard the smile in Walker's steely tone. This was Phoenix. The action excited them. The hunt thrilled them. Hart could already smell Taym's blood. The sweet scent of revenge.

The noise of the Black Hawks' blades grew deafeningly louder as Walker approached them, and Hart was forced to hold his cell away from his ear.

"Don't be long!" Hart called out, his smile fading.

"Go get your girl, Commander!" Walker shouted, "And look to the sky!"

Hart threw his phone on the passenger seat and headed for the poppy fields out of town, racing down the main street of La Mar. There were a few angry outbursts regarding his speed, but Hart took no notice.


Dusk had given way to the twilight, and the sky above the hills surrounding the poppy fields was a sullen, smoky gray. The wind was strong and unusually cool after the Santa Ana winds. Hart pulled over near the gap in the wire fence and reached into the glove box for his flick-knife. It was all he had. He tucked it into the back pocket of his pants when he stepped out of the car. He stared across the poppy field at the dark entrance of the forest. Ivy was in there somewhere, he could feel it, but it was the danger he felt first … like a sixth sense.

He leaped effortlessly over the fence. Colorless flowers swayed around him in the dim light of the moon that struggled to pierce the smoky haze. He heard Oliver's gentle voice lull across the poppies on the wind … *promise me you will check on her for me, Hart. Please protect her. If I don't make it home.*

He looked up at the moon. "If you must take a life tonight, then take mine. Sacrifice the darkness, not the light … not Ivy," he breathed. "Take *me*."

Hart ran through the poppies toward the forest. He imagined how the moon saw him, carving a dark trail through the moonlit flowers. Running toward his beacon of light … to his bright sacrifice.

*Chapter 30*

HART MOVED SWIFTLY IN THE DARK, keeping away from the trails. So far, there had been no one guarding the forest; either Taym was foolish enough to think Hart wouldn't find him here, or he was anticipating their fated reunion.

Hart stopped a safe distance from the fishing shack, close enough to hear the wind rattling the loose planking. Light from the windows cast a pale glow into the forest. He crouched in the dark to study the fishing shack and its armed occupants. The structure was small, much smaller than he had imagined it to be. He thought of Oliver's parties and guessed maybe twenty people might fit inside, and even that would be a tight squeeze. Hart couldn't imagine a couple hundred teenagers scattered around the decrepit cottage ... but if anyone could pull it off, it was Oliver.

Silhouettes sauntered around the outside of the shack, oblivious to Hart. Their cigarettes flared bright orange in the dark, and he could hear their laughter on the blustery wind. They appeared nothing more than a handful of harmless teens hanging out in the woods, except for the shadow who was itching his crotch with a handgun. Hart shook his head and smiled. The scene reassured him. Their casualness announced their inexperience. Their minds weren't in the game, just their depraved hearts. Which was enough for Hart to justify their worth.

He did a quick head count; seven men around the perimeter, and one or two inside. A tall shadow cast itself across a sandy patch of light to the left of the shack, catching Hart's vigilant eye. He moved silently further toward the beach so he could see inside. This side of the shack was actually all window—the view of the bay would have been spectacular. Looking into the shack through, however, he saw Ivy. Hart sighed in relief at the sight of her ... *alive*. Her long hair fell around her and glowed exquisitely in the room's light, and his expression softened. A few seconds later, an armed man walked into the room and approached Ivy with a directness that troubled Hart.

Hart squinted through the forest into the window, eager to recognize the man. Desperate to confirm the sighting of a wanted man for treason, homicide, and terrorism, which in turn gave him the permission to kill. The man's face was thick with hair, making it difficult for Hart to identify him, but given the wiry black hair and sinewy frame, he assumed it was Taym. The twins had been smaller in stature than the rest of them, but it never hindered their accomplishments within Phoenix. It was their unencumbered spontaneity that earned them a position in the elite unit. Their ability to think creatively under pressure. The twins were exceptionally resourceful and cunning. USSOCOM never once considered how it might work against them. None of them had.

The man leaned over Ivy and spoke to her, but she refused to acknowledge him. Hart watched her carefully, his chest pounding with protective fury. Hart could sense the man's anger with her reaction, and when he spoke to her again, he raised a threatening hand to the side of her face. Hart's lips curled in a silent snarl in the dark. Ivy turned her head defiantly toward the window, with her eyes closed tightly in fear, and waited for the infuriated response to her rejection. The man grabbed her chin, forcing her to look at him. Hart leaned forward in the dark in response, ready to run to her. The approach would not be ideal for a victory, but watching Taym threaten Ivy was too much for Hart to endure. He watched them, unblinking, until the man took a step away from her.

Hart relaxed his tense muscles and evaluated his final opponent. His body thrummed with impatience, but he knew he would get to Ivy through the barricade of dark strangers. He had studied the men for a few minutes now, and they were no match for his expertise. Yet a vague fogginess worried at him when he envisioned what came after her rescue. An uncertainty plagued his confidence, and it flourished in the darkness he thought had left him.

Hart withdrew from the shack's light, and crouched behind the closest tree, terrified of his incapability. He wasn't afraid to die. He was afraid he might not rescue her before it happened. He rubbed his chest where Oliver shot him in his nightmare and grimaced at the pain. Hart sensed his ending with Ivy because he had been there before with his best friend; the circumstances were painfully similar. A tremor quaked in his depths, and he shuddered in its unnerving presence. He stared at his shaking hands as he squeezed them in the dark in front of him. He was being summoned. Summoned, once again, to the darkness inside his soul. This time it felt different. Stronger. Harder to resist. Hart leaned his head into his trembling hands and groaned through his clenched teeth, willing himself to fight the fall ... but he was already falling ....

*The devil waited patiently for him. Foreseeing his weakness, as always. He sat there in the dark surrounded by his sycophants. Eager to make another deal with the tired soldier who always had nothing left to lose ... until now. He tapped his claws in sweet anticipation for the soldier to arrive, to make him an offer he couldn't refuse. "Soldier, on your knees."*

*Hart heard the raucous shriek of hell on the devil's tongue when he spoke to him, and he bowed his head in disheartened surrender. He did what he was told.*

*"Take what you want from me," he breathed, "but I must warn you, there is not much left of me to take. All I have to offer you is my loyalty. My truth. I swear to you my eternal allegiance. However, I ask of you one thing before I die. Help me save her. My soul is worthless to you until then ... until I fulfil my promise to a fallen friend. Help me save her life, and I will go with you anywhere."*

A soundless soliloquy, validating the deal he made earlier with the moon. Hart wished for the night when Ivy pulled him from the water. Oh, to begin again. To know then what he knew now. He breathed into the sky with a reassuring acceptance of his fate. His darkness would finally forsake itself for her light, and he would take it with him to wherever he was going once he left this world. Her light was everlasting.

Hart blinked resignedly at the sky. He caught glimpses of the stars behind the smoky haze that filtered the moonlight. He felt their light reach him and sink into his soul. He felt their assurance and their abiding strength, and so Hart surrendered himself to them. To the universe. To the devil. To anyone who saw worth in his feeble soul. He would leave this world for Ivy, his glorious misfortune, because he was always heading gloriously to his demise with her. There were far worse ways to go.

"This will be the end of me," he breathed into the sky, and a small smile curled humbly on his face.

Hart reached into his back pocket with a revitalized determination and pulled out the flick-knife. He glanced over the blade, glinting in the silver moonlight. His steady brown eyes narrowed, and a shroud of detachment cloaked his concern for Ivy. He fostered an icy indifference toward the men who surrounded her. They were insignificant. A triviality that stood between him and his objective. Ivy would survive—the lives of these men were irrelevant. As was his own. His unwavering fortitude returned, the drive to do what needed to be done. Fear had no place in him anymore.

Hart took a deep breath and turned toward the fishing shack. He counted the men twice more and reached seven both times; one man inside made eight in total. Hart waited for any he may have missed. Their nonchalant silhouettes hadn't changed. They weren't expecting him. Adrenaline rushed into his body, and Hart welcomed in its stinging presence. He longed for the fight. He longed for the action. He longed for Ivy.

She turned her head toward the window. Her piercing blue eyes shot open, and Ivy stared at him in the forest. Hart paused in her crystal gaze. Temporarily lost in time. He knew she couldn't see him ... but he saw her. The past year with Ivy all came rushing in at once, and he saw the sea, and the sand, and her naked sun-kissed body, and Hart hesitated in her beauty. In her wonder ... then a small *click* sounded at the back of his head.

"Oh, you don't disappoint, Commander," a lucid, amused

voice spoke from behind him.

A noisy gust of wind squalled through the tops of the trees, and Hart peered into the sky. He stood slowly and turned around with his hands in the air until he faced the man behind him in the forest. Hart looked him dead in the eyes and then shifted his gaze to the gun fixed on his chest. He didn't recognize the man. He had a broad smile and large, dark eyes that blinked excessively. His fidgety fingers drummed the gun in his hands, making Hart nervous standing in his line of fire. The man was disturbingly skittish, or unhinged, but there was a hardness in his expression that spoke of his grim fanatical past, and Hart knew instantly who he was.

"They know you are here, Omen," Hart told him. "They will be arriving any minute now to take you down."

"You are bluffing!" Omen's shifty gaze darted back and forth from Hart to the fishing shack. He stepped toward Hart and motioned with his gun for him to start walking. "Now move!"

With his hands resting on his head, Hart turned and walked in the dark toward the fishing shack, fixing his gaze on the light surrounding Ivy. She looked wistfully through the window to where he walked, and with a small, content smile, Ivy closed her crystal eyes. Those blue eyes he may never see again ...

*Oliver.*

Hart exhaled loudly, remembering the day that brought him to his knees. His dark eyes remained unblinking on Ivy. His strong shoulders rose and fell with every enraged breath he took. Taym took Oliver from him, and he'd be damned to let him take Ivy, too.

Hart prepared to strike the assailant who held him at gunpoint.

"Hey, Omen!" A voice shouted from outside the fishing shack. "You got someone with you?"

Hart glanced at the silhouettes in the distance as they began to gather in a line next to the window. They swayed beside each other, straining to see past the darkness of night.

Hart ignored them ... *six, seven, eight men. Omen makes nine.*

"I have the Commander!" Omen howled.

The men cheered riotously. Omen laughed to himself and then brusquely shoved his prisoner toward the men with his handgun.

Hart closed his eyes appreciatively in response, calculating the distance between himself and the weapon. He took a slow, deep breath, and as he exhaled, he swiftly spun around and knocked the handgun from Omen's unsuspecting hands. He pounced on Omen in the same motion, dragging him to the ground.

Hart listened to the men calling for Omen, confused. He was wrestling with him in the shadows of the night, and Hart was grateful for the darkness. Hart reached for the handgun, which lay just out of his reach. His fingertips grazed the grip, but Omen threw himself on top of him, and the two of them fell back through the trees.

With a few deft moves, Hart positioned himself on the top of his opponent. He pressed his knee to Omen's chest and used his other leg to maintain his position while Omen thrashed madly on his back. Hart wrapped his hands around the man's neck and pushed his thumbs into his throat, waiting for the sickening crunch of his neck, but Omen struck back, jabbing Hart's knife into his stomach. Hart grunted through his teeth at the pain, feeling the throbbing heat of the blade in his flesh. He released Omen's neck, quickly disarmed him, and sunk the knife into the man's neck. He watched Omen's eyes roll into the back of his head, feeling him shake underneath him.

Hart rolled off the man, stooping tactfully low. He retrieved his knife and grabbed the handgun lying on the forest floor. He pressed his hand against his wound and ducked behind the closest tree to catch his breath. Hart gritted his teeth under his panting breath, careful not to attract attention.

The men's voices were still calling from the shack. Hart held the gun by his cheek and stole a glance at them; they were still beside the shack, oblivious to his victory. He winced in pain when he hid behind the tree again. Hart lifted his shirt and inspected the wound, which was only centimeters above the stitches he had sewn into himself the other night. He sliced a piece of his shirt off with his flick-knife, and then bit down fiercely on its grip to prevent him from making any noise as he firmly poked the piece of fabric into the bleeding wound with the tip of his finger. Pain flashed white behind Hart's eyelids, and he stifled a groan. Breathing hard, he pocketed the knife and glanced again at the men.

Hart couldn't help but notice how perfectly positioned these men were; lined up in a row like sitting ducks along the trail to the shack. He was astonished by their lack of experience, but he was grateful as well. They stood idly dumbfounded in the distance with no idea how to react should anything not go in their favor. Hart chuckled to himself, his blood racing with adrenaline. He leaned out from the tree and shot the silhouette furthest from the window of the shack, the first in a line they had so nicely assembled for him.

Hart tucked himself behind the tree and stared into the forest in front of him.

"Two down, seven left …," he whispered to himself, then he waited for their haphazard retaliation.

The men watched their friend's head loll back and forth on his neck before he fell lifelessly to the ground. They gawked at each other in stunned silence, and then all six men began shooting aimlessly into the forest.

Hart waited for the gunfire to stop, and without hesitating, he leaned out from the tree trunk again and shot the next silhouette in line.

"Six."

He heard their panicked voices shouting madly behind him, and then the gunfire started again. Hart waited for the bullets to stop shrieking past him in the forest. Then he leaned out from the tree and shot the next man in line.

"Five."

Hart pressed himself against the tree trunk in the dark. Their reaction was quicker this time, but they were still lined up beside the window. He gazed fondly into the endless, black depths of the forest as he waited. *Ivy's forest.* He found it comforting and familiar. He remembered the conversations, and the laughter, and the flirting with her along the Ghost Trail … the beginning of a love he had *never* expected.

When the shooting stopped, he snuck a quick glance at the men to ascertain they were still assembled into a neat line. Hart shook his head when he saw them, smiling at their dim-wittedness. He leaned out from the tree for the last time, he hoped, and shot the next silhouette in line.

"Four."

Hart sunk to his knees and waited, ready to make a dash for Ivy, putting his faith in these strangers' fear. When there was no comeback with gunfire, Hart peeked toward the men. He saw the next silhouette in line make a beeline for the fishing shack, and the last two didn't hesitate to follow. Hart glanced through the window at Ivy, who sat alone in the room. She was perched in the light almost purposefully to lure him out of the darkness … and he would go. He was a moth to her flame. A moth that was laden with tenacity and unmatched skill. He was not going down without a fight.

He set his sight on the right side of the shack and took off soundlessly through the forest, keeping low and out of sight. When he reached the wall on the other side, he pressed himself against it, then tread through the sand toward a side door. Hart tried to enter, but the handle had rusted through, cementing the door to the wall of the fishing shack. He wasn't getting inside without throwing himself through it and attracting unwanted attention, so Hart kept moving along the wall in the dark toward the front of the fishing shack.

For a moment, he thought he was back in Libya, but the terns shrilled hauntingly in the distance and the sound brought him back to the beach. Hart looked into the wind toward the beach. He could just make out the white sand in the moonlight, simmering between the trees with the ocean's fury, then a large, faceless stranger suddenly shuffled around the corner in front of him, and Hart ran to him instinctively.

The man raised his gun to shoot, but Hart managed to deflect the weapon away before he fired. Hart elbowed the man in the face, then struck his head back hard against the weathered boards of the fishing shack. The man didn't fall, as Hart had expected, instead he came back at him with two-fold force. They wrestled with each other against the shack, their powerful bodies cracking the timber with each blow to the building's weathered exterior. Eventually, Hart managed to maneuver the large man into a headlock, using the shack's wall as leverage and waited for the struggling stranger to fall limp in his arms.

"Three," he panted.

A voice in front of the shack forced him to move before his opponent's body had even dropped to the sand. He darted around the back corner and ran along the length of the shack toward the window on the other side, keeping a vigilant eye on his surroundings. When he reached the far corner, Hart peeked around the edge of it and saw two men standing outside the window with their handguns raised and poised nervously into the forest. Hart ducked behind the wall again and searched the moonlit sand at his feet. He found a piece of wood that had fallen from a pile stacked high against the back wall. Hart hefted the wood to find a better grip and the right balance, then he hurled it into the forest in front of the men.

It crashed through the branches in the distance, and as he expected, the men shot aimlessly in the direction of the sound. Hart stepped out from his concealment while they were distracted and walked confidently toward them. He lifted his gun and shot the closest man in the back of the head. The second man turned to him, and when Hart pulled the trigger, there was nothing but an empty *click*. Hart didn't pause for even a moment. He used his empty weapon to knock the gun from the other man's hands, but the man fought back with a determination that Hart wasn't expecting. The two of them struggled on the sand outside the window beside Ivy. The light inside the shack cast a spotlight on them, making the fight harder for Hart. He had grown accustomed to the dark, and tonight, it seemed to work to his advantage.

Hart took a blow to his left cheek, and his vision blurred. He shook his head to collect his spinning head, then retaliated with a swiftness that signified his patience had come to an end. The stranger had no chance of matching his deadly skills. Hart hit him repeatedly until the man's hands dropped and he swayed in place, unconscious on his feet. Hart's chest heaved with exhaustion. He thought about leaving him there to fall in his own time, but Hart struck him one last time across the face with a frustrated growl, panting as the man slumped to the sand.

An unfamiliar wave of emotion swept over him. Hart looked down at the man's lifeless figure against the white sand, and he frowned to himself. He almost felt sorry for him.

"One left," he said breathlessly, spitting a mouthful of blood onto the sand.

He wiped the blood from his lip with the back of his hand, wincing as he did, then turned to Ivy behind him in the window.

A faceless silhouette stood between them with his handgun raised. Hart squinted into the light to determine if the man stood behind the glass or directly in front of him, and the silhouette started to laugh. The spiteful tone in his laughter gave away the man's identity, and Hart's eyes narrowed at the familiar sound.

A deep growl rumbled on Hart's breath. He felt contempt and disappointment … *and rage*. The fire in his blood burned through his veins with such intensity, such insufferable pain, that Hart was forced to breathe himself through the darkness that threatened to consume him. Oliver's warning resounded through him; he had known before anyone ….. *It's Taym we need to worry about. I don't trust him, Hart.*

Hart smiled dangerously in the pale light, "Taym."

## Chapter 31

THE GUNSHOTS EVENTUALLY STOPPED, but the eerie silence outside kept her crystal eyes glued to the window beside her. A gust of wind brushed the hair off her shoulder, and she shifted her attention to the open front door; the shack was unmanned for the first time in two days.

Ivy twisted her hands in the air, trying to maneuver them out of the rope that bound her wrists together. It wasn't the first time she had tried to escape. She had lost count sometime yesterday. Ivy had given up on freeing her ankles; they were bound so tightly to the legs of the chair that she had lost all feeling in her feet shortly after they had tied her there. She pulled on the rope that attached her hands to the steel railing on the side of the countertop and held her breath as she writhed her hands around within the knot. But it was no good. The knot wouldn't budge. Ivy cried out in pain, bowing her head in hopelessness … there was no way out.

Ivy stared blankly at the blood-soaked rope around her wrists. She blew on the raw flesh beneath the rope and grimaced at the pain … then another gunshot broke the silence. Ivy looked at the window and desperately searched for what lay beyond her reflection in the darkness. Her breath quickened, panicked by the change. Something had disturbed the men's usual confidence and smug superiority with her. By this time last night, all nine of the men had paid her an unwelcome visit. The thought made her shudder in disgust. Not one had forced themselves upon her, but she knew it was only a matter of time before they turned on each other. Tested the ranks … and tonight felt like one of those nights. There was friction among the men. A chaos barely held in check by Taym Malak. Ivy expected one of the men to enter the front door any moment now and take advantage of her lack of guard. Taym. He had stood at her side almost the entire time since she'd been brought here, and he had protected her on more than one occasion. She knew that he killed Oliver, but she was somewhat grateful for his authoritative presence. It was a peculiar feeling she tried to ignore.

Another gunshot rattled the air, then a loud *thump* shook the window beside her. Ivy yelped in fright. She stared nervously at her reflection as it bounced back and forth from the impact. She tugged on the rope again with a sudden urgency. A loud scuffle outside caught her attention and Ivy stood from her seat and looked at the window again. With her feet bound to the chair, she shuffled herself backward into the kitchen as far away from the window as possible, sliding her hands to the end of the steel bar. The steel railing was screwed into the side of the wooden counter, but it was loose enough to encourage her not to give up entirely. It had seemed a misplaced hope until now, with no one here to spoil her attempt to escape.

"Come on!" Ivy pulled violently on the rope, sliding her hands up and down the railing to find a point of weakness.

The bar rattled on the screws, giving Ivy hope. The rope burned her bleeding wrists, but she held her breath and pushed through the pain. She grabbed the bar in frustration and shook it as hard as she could, but it failed to come loose. Ivy cursed sadly. Another blow of bodies hit the glass beside her and she ducked instinctively. She looked up at the window again and waited in the harrowing silence. The stillness was unsettling, and Ivy watched the window reluctantly, unable to look away. She gasped and recoiled when a shadow behind the window seemed to lunge at her, and with a deafening crash the window exploded inward, shattered glass flying into the room with a gust of icy wind.

Ivy winced and buried her face in her arms to protect herself from the glass. The noise deafened her momentarily and she felt the glass land around her like falling rain. She waited for it to settle before she looked up again, pieces of glass falling from her hair to the floor. She stared wide-eyed at the room in front of her; the shattered glass seemed to cover the entire fishing shack, including two bloodied bodies in front of her on the floor. Ivy gasped at the sight of them. A man lay at her feet face down and mumbled incoherently into the ground. His hands were cut, and he writhed slowly in the broken glass while he regained consciousness. She fell into her chair and shuffled as far away from him as the rope allowed her to move. Ivy glanced over the second body which lay further away from her. He wasn't moving. She couldn't tell if the man was unconscious or dead.

She leaned away when the man at her feet began to rise. He propped himself on his elbows in the glass and growled in gut-wrenching pain. Ivy winced and tried to look away. He pulled his legs up under his body and kneeled on the ground, then he leaned his head back and cursed wearily at the ceiling.

Then she saw him. His brown eyes flicked to her, and her heart leaped in her chest. "Hart!"

"Ivy!" Hart whispered, his expression softening at the sight of her. His wounds immediately forgotten, Hart lurched to his feet and ran his hands down the sides of her face, and immediately he began to untie her hands.

Ivy grimaced at the pain.

He frowned. "What have they done to you? Have they—"

"No," she replied quickly. "Nothing like that."

Hart met her gaze fleetingly, then looked back to the knot between her wrists. She saw the relief in his expression. The knot that had held her for nearly two days came free quickly in his deft fingers. With his flick-knife Hart cut another two pieces of fabric from the bottom of his shirt and gently wrapped the pieces of fabric around her wrists to stop the bleeding, tucking the loose end into the make-shift bandage to keep it from coming undone.

Ivy looked at him in disbelief as he tended to her wounds—*his lips, his hair, his beautiful warmth.*

"You came back," she breathed. Ivy ran her hand across his face when he stopped to look at her. His skin was so smooth. So warm. He looked into her eyes with a solemn expression that saddened her.

Hart turned his face into her hand. "I should never have left you."

Ivy bowed her head. "I know why you did. Nicole told me

what happened."

Hart frowned and shook his head at her. He lifted her chin so that she could see his truth. His unwavering loyalty. *His love.*

"I didn't sleep with Nicole. She lied. I would never do that to you, Ivy," he breathed.

Her eyes filled with sweet relief. Ivy bit her lip to restrain herself from grinning ear to ear, and Hart smiled at her. It was beautiful ... *breathtaking.* She wanted to pull him into her arms and fall hopelessly into his kind heart. Surely by now he belonged to her. Her soldier ... kneeling at her feet and offering her his unyielding protection. His eternal devotion. She could see it there in his eyes, they revealed all his secrets. They always had.

Hart leaned into Ivy and brushed his lips against hers, sending Ivy's head into an intoxicated spin. High on the sweetness of his breath. Dizzy from the smoky, earthy scent of his skin. He ran his hands through her hair and kissed her softly on the lips, and Ivy closed her eyes and melted into his heavenly warmth. His soft tongue lulled away the world around them. His tenderness consoled her racing heart. Ivy felt everything inside her dissolve into a hot pool of pleasure.

"We're going." Hart pulled away and looked at her seriously.

Ivy blinked her eyes open, drowsy with desire.

"Taym will come to any minute now, and I need you as far away from here as possible." Hart lifted her to her feet. "It's you he wants."

"Me? Why?"

"Oliver killed Abad, Taym's brother. This is his payback. You need to get out of here, run to Tommy's. William will know what to do."

"It sounds like you're not coming with me," she breathed, "you are coming with me, right?"

Hart looked down at her and frowned.

"Hart?"

"I have to finish things with Taym. You know I do."

Ivy opened her mouth to speak, but she stopped herself. He was right. Hart would never rest until he had his revenge.

Hart smiled reassuringly at her. "I'll catch up to you, I promise. I won't let you go, Ivy."

When Hart bent down to cut the rope around her ankles,

Taym was standing behind him with a boat oar gripped behind his right shoulder like a baseball bat. Ivy cried out, but Taym was already swinging the oar, striking Hart across the back of his head and sending him unconscious to the floor.

Ivy stumbled on the chair behind her and fell onto it to prevent herself from falling. She watched Taym toss the oar away from his bleeding hands without taking any notice of her. He paced a loop around the room, and another loop, then another loop, all the while tapping his fingers on his chest and seemingly deep in thought. Conflicting thoughts, judging by his torn expression. Ivy looked to Hart, who was struggling to get off the ground.

"Hart! Hart, get up!" Ivy shouted.

Taym shot a maddened glare at Ivy from across the room. He pointed at her and made a beeline for her recuperating soldier, as though it were her fault that he was going for Hart again. Ivy wished she hadn't said anything. She crouched in her seat and untied the rope around her ankles, desperately fumbling with the knot so she could protect Hart. She managed to set herself free, and Ivy stood up from her seat to run to him, but it was too late. Taym took a long stride from the center of the room and kicked Hart hard in the chest. Ivy stopped suddenly at the horrific sound of Hart's ribs cracking.

Taym's black eyes considered Hart, who writhed on the broken glass between a scatter of chairs, coughing the life back into his winded lungs. He paced back to the other side of the room and leaned his hands on a long bench beside the front door. He hung his head and stared at the bench before he looked back at Hart.

"Stay down, Hart," Taym growled. "My fight has never been with you."

Hart groaned into the ground, and Ivy looked at him, her crystal gaze pleading for him to rise.

Taym shifted his wily gaze to Ivy. "He'll do anything for a Rose."

Ivy backed away in Taym's attention. She wanted to talk to him. Reason with him. He wanted her dead because Oliver killed his brother, but what was the sense in that? She could spend a lifetime tracking down the people who took her family from her, but when would it end? Resentment was easy. Forgiveness was harder. It was found within only the strongest of hearts. He was angry. Hurt. She knew how it felt to lose a loved one. Her empathy exceeded her current predicament and she felt sorry for him. Taym could not forgive, because he didn't know how to.

Ivy saw Hart rising from the ground. He crouched unsteadily on his feet, but Taym's penetrating eyes stayed on her as he walked toward her. His hatred bore a tunnel across the room, preventing him from seeing anything but her. Ivy stopped retreating, finding comfort in Hart's stealthy recovery.

"Please, Taym just wait," Ivy begged. She threw her hands in the air, and Taym stopped on cue, smiling pleasurably with intrigue.

Hart slammed himself into Taym with a growling fury, pushing Taym back across the small shack, slipping and sliding across the shattered glass. Hart positioned himself in front of Ivy again. He held his ribs and glared at Taym, then he dropped his hands into a fighting stance. Seconds later, Taym lunged at Hart.

Ivy ducked and waited for their powerful bodies to come crashing toward her, but Hart's strength kept them from falling. She couldn't see Taym past Hart's strong frame, but the sound of clashing flesh proved he was still there, fighting. Ivy backed into the corner of the kitchen counter. She fumbled through all the drawers until she found a tarnished butter knife. She frowned as she pulled it out. She grasped the handle determinedly as Hart and Taym wrestled around the main room of the fishing shack, then something further along the counter caught her eye. A *gun*. Ivy ran to it. She threw the knife away and picked up the gun … wrapping her fingers awkwardly around the grip. It felt strange in her hands. Unnatural. There was a slide on the gun, but she didn't know if she needed it to fire the bullet. She couldn't even tell if there were any bullets.

Ivy aimed the gun at the shattered window beside her. She clamped her eyes shut and racked the slide on the weapon, half expecting it to fire without her pulling the trigger. A cold gust of wind blew her hair across her face, and she glared back at Taym and curled her finger on the trigger. She raised the gun in front of her with both arms outstretched, centering her aim on Taym's chest.

Taym ripped up a loose plank from the shack's floor and swung it at Hart, striking him across the bleeding wound on his stomach. Hart roared in agony as he fell to his knees, pressing his hands into the knife wound that was now bleeding profusely through his fingers.

Hart groaned in pain, but Ivy's eyes were fixed steadily on her target. Taym stood over Hart with the sharp end of the timber raised above his head, and Ivy knew he planned to bring it down on Hart. The stake would kill him. She saw the feral look in Taym's eyes; he wanted blood. He'd already taken Oliver's. Ivy held her breath as she pulled the trigger, but it needed more force than she thought. Taym clenched his teeth together and smiled wildly in the wind, and then thrust the piece of wood down toward Hart….

Ivy screamed when she pulled the trigger, but she didn't hear it, the sound of the gunshot deafened her momentarily. The recoil of the gun made it jump in Ivy's hand and she lost her grip on it. It bounced along the counter, and she blindly chased it as it slid away from her. Taym cursed at her from across the room, and Ivy looked up in surprise. He was nursing a small nick in his shoulder, and her eyes widened with fear. *She missed.*

Taym looked up from his wound and set his sights on Ivy. A black emptiness cloaked his eyes, and she knew she had exhausted the patience of the man who had spent the past two days reluctantly protecting her. He hurried to the front door and smashed a weak, inconspicuous timber board on the wall beside it, then he reached his arm into the hole and pulled out another handgun. Taym turned back to face Ivy with a dull expression on his face, but his eyes were animated and dark and sweat dripped down his temples in his fury. Ivy backed away from him until she came up against the wall behind her, and she closed her eyes. Taym took a few steps toward her, raised his gun, and without a moment's hesitation, he fired his gun at Ivy.

Ivy held her breath, feeling the blustery, icy wind embrace her. She waited for it to carry her away. She waited for the pain. The breathlessness. The unfamiliar sensation of the bullet entering her flesh … but she didn't feel it. She didn't feel any of it.

Ivy blinked her eyes open and saw Hart standing in front of her, facing Taym. She ran her hands across her body, certain she had been shot. She looked up again at Hart, who was holding the gun she had dropped. Ivy realized then, that it was Hart's gun she heard fire.

His gun was raised straight out in front of him and aimed at Taym across the room. The muscles rippled along the length of Hart's arm with a tenacious vengeance. An unbending grit. His heart and soul were riding on the bullet he fired, and Ivy knew he wouldn't give in until Taym had taken his last breath. Hart's powerful frame heaved with exhaustion, and she could hear his panting breath over the wind whistling through the shack. The wind rushed through the window beside her and Ivy huddled against the back wall of the fishing shack, with Hart unflinching before her.

The two men faced each other in a stand-off ... exactly how it all had begun a year ago around the table in Il Liberta Square. Taym and Hart held their position, their guns fixed and unmoving. Their dark eyes burned with an unbendable will that hinted at a stalemate ... neither one was giving in.

Hart glanced at Taym's chest, waiting for the crimson confirmation of his bullet. He never missed. When the blood began to pulse through Taym's jacket, Hart felt grateful more than relieved. Grateful to the moon and the stars. Grateful to the devil. He felt Oliver all around him suddenly—his demanding, bright presence filled the air, and Hart's chest burned torturously. He felt Ivy's light drawing out the devil inside of him, and he felt forgiveness. Mercy. *At last.* The sweet relief from his culpable guilt. Finally ... he was free.

Hart's voice was authoritative, but gentle when he spoke, "It's over, Taym."

Taym coughed on his blood and spat a thick mouthful of it on the floor. He looked up at Hart and began to laugh.

"Phoenix will be here any minute." Hart motioned his chin to the sky.

Taym laughed again. "I am not scared of Phoenix."

Hart watched him carefully without blinking. Taym's hand slid into his left pocket, and Hart narrowed his eyes. He stepped backward away from Taym until he had Ivy tucked safely behind him. He kept his gun fixed on Taym's menacing expression and Hart considered a second shot to end it once and for all. Taym was dying, but not quickly enough for Hart ... he didn't trust him.

"Keep your hands where I can see them, Taym, or I'll shoot you between your eyes, you son of a bitch."

Taym chuckled and slowly started to remove his hand from his pocket. "Ah, Johnny Hart. We know each other well, don't we?"

"Not well enough." Hart's grave eyes didn't waver from Taym.

"Ah, yes ... Oliver." Taym nodded to himself. "Opportunities presented themselves to me, and I—"

"You betrayed us, Taym!" Hart cut him off. He clenched his jaw and waited for Taym to respond.

Taym stopped talking and glared at Hart.

"You are here to get your revenge, but you've already had it," Hart growled. "You killed Oliver."

"Ollie was going to die whether he killed Abad or not."

Hart shook his head. "Ivy had nothing to do with your brother's death."

"Ivy Rose needs to *die.*"

Ivy tightened her eyes shut and remained quiet. She listened to their conversation and imagined their world before she knew them ... a darker world filled with death and betrayal. The luxuries of La Mar seemed offensive in comparison.

"You killed her brother, Taym!" Hart shouted.

"And Oliver killed *my* brother!"

Ivy jumped in fright. She rested her hands on Hart's lower back and thought about her brother and Taym in their final moment together. No soldier was without wounds.

Taym pulled a device from his pocket and held it weakly in the air. A red light blinked between his fingers, and Hart took a deep breath and pressed his lips together to tame his fury. He was too late—the device had been activated.

"Don't do this," Hart told him. "She's done nothing wrong. Let Ivy go ... take me instead."

Ivy felt Hart's body grow tense. The sudden change frightened her.

"Oliver Rose murdered my brother," Taym wheezed, "so I

will take his sister with me to hell."

Hart shook his head. "No."

"No?" Taym laughed.

"Not this time," Hart replied calmly.

Taym spat another mouthful of blood on the ground beside him and glanced at Hart's chest with a thin, smug grin. "You are running out of time, Hart."

"A Rose for a Rose," Hart replied. "I made a deal."

Ivy looked up at Hart and frowned. He bowed his head to his shoulder, and Ivy knew he was talking to her.

He sighed, then spoke again, "I made a deal with the devil."

Ivy narrowed her eyes sadly.

Hart looked back at Taym and caught his calm, intent consideration, almost as if Taym understood where he was coming from. Hart frowned curiously, but Taym was quick to dismiss the exchange as he slid the device back into his pocket.

"You know what this is?" Taym asked.

"I know what it is."

Ivy wanted to look, but instead she closed her eyes and leaned into Hart's back. She longed for the peacefulness they once had. For their long, lazy summer days. For the sun. For the ocean. The hot sand and salty, sun-drenched skin. She longed for the water that lapped against her as she made love to her soldier in the crystal shallows. She had never taken one moment of it for granted.

Taym gurgled and spat another mouthful of blood on the floor, then looked at Hart. "You showed me how to build this. Do you remember?"

Hart nodded.

"I added a few extra minutes because I was feeling nostalgic." Taym tried to smile.

"You knew I would find you."

"Sooner or later." Taym coughed. "You always cared too much. For everyone, including myself and Abad." His musing gaze lingered on Hart as he worked up the strength to speak again. "To this day, I bear no ill feeling toward you. You loved Abad and me like we were your brothers. I was *fourteen* years old."

Hart shook his head with frustration. He wanted to hate

him. He *tried* to hate him. Taym took everything from him … but he saw the innocent fourteen-year-old boy in front of him, and he felt nothing but forgiveness.

Hart groaned and tightened his grip on his shaking gun, but Taym didn't flinch.

"Hart, you haven't changed."

"What are you talking about?"

"You want to hate me, but you can't …"

Anguish racked Hart's expression as he listened.

"Your love is what separates you from the rest of us," Taym managed, "but it has always been your biggest fear."

Ivy tightened her eyes shut in reluctant agreement. *Hart's light was also his darkness.*

"Love is pain. For the ones that feel it the most." Taym lowered his gun and smiled. "You were always going to come back for her, Hart."

Hart nodded at Taym and waited patiently for him to die.

Ivy heard Taym's rasping breath and her eyes shot open. Taym's handgun thumped onto the floor amid the shattered glass, and she stared at the weapon and processed the promising sight.

"How did you find this place?" Hart asked.

"Oliver told me all the stories," Taym paused, out of breath. A small smile faded on Taym's lips. "Do you want to know, why Oliver?"

Hart remained impassive to Taym and waited for him to speak. Ivy willed Taym to go on.

"The depot."

Afghanistan. Hart remembered that day well; the raid, the explosions, the destruction … and the fourteen-year-old twins who were collected by Phoenix on their exfiltration from the depot. They could have left them there to die, but Oliver insisted they take them back to Base, against the orders of their superiors. He was never going to leave them in the middle of the desert without water or shelter, and the rest of them agreed to take them in and share the impending reprimand.

That was the only decision Oliver made that day that was his and his alone.

It wasn't Oliver's decision to raid the depot. It wasn't his decision to reduce it to rubble. It wasn't his decision to bring any harm to the twins' parents. He was a soldier, and he had his orders. Oliver was there for the same reason Hart was, and that was to fight for the lives of the men who stood beside him. To fight for the ones they left behind. They fought so that their loved ones back home never witnessed what they saw every single day in the war. The suffering. The privation. Death.

Hart exhaled loudly in exhaustion. He dropped his arm so that his gun hung loosely by his side. Then he watched Taym's body collapse lifelessly to the ground.

Hart closed his eyes and bowed his heavy head.

Taym's body slumped to the ground, and Ivy gasped. She rushed around Hart and lifted his head. He looked at her with his warm, adoring eyes, and Ivy smiled beautifully.

"Hello, Ivy," he breathed in relief.

Ivy cried happily and pulled his face to hers, enjoying the smoothness of his freshly shaven skin. She gazed into the brown depths of his eyes and smiled. It was finally over.

Hart leaned his forehead against hers and breathed in her sweet coconut scent, then he held her out in front of him and looked at her.

"What is it?" Ivy searched his concerned expression.

"I don't want to alarm you, Ives, but there's a bomb hidden somewhere inside the shack."

Ivy's eyes widened. "A what?"

"I designed it myself on one of our *quiet* days in the desert. We have approximately twelve minutes," he said, glancing at his watch, "if Taym actually added the extra few minutes."

"Right, okay," Ivy replied, breathlessly stunned. She couldn't process what he'd just said. It was hard to be afraid again, with Hart right there beside her. The thought of a bomb in the fishing shack at Lights Beach was preposterous.

Hart looked down into her crystal eyes and saw Oliver. He knew they didn't have a lot of time and he needed to honor his promise to a fallen friend. He grimaced at the piercing pain over his heart, where Oliver shot him in his nightmare. *Until the day I die defending her ... a Rose for a Rose.*

Hart groaned suddenly.

Ivy frowned in his pain. "Does it hurt?" she asked.

Hart watched her hands run across his skin. Her fingertips were tenderly brushing his surface … searching him for any serious injury. He felt her light entering him at each wound, bringing him to life even though he felt much closer to death.

"Don't you worry about me," he replied softly, smiling.

His eyes blinked uncharacteristically slowly, and Ivy tilted her head and studied him. She noted his pale complexion, until the thought of the bomb distracted her. She slid her hand into his and pulled him toward the door, but Hart stood heavily behind her, anchored to the floor.

She turned back to him. "We have to go … the bomb."

Hart blinked his eyes lethargically, and a beautiful, broken smile lingered on his handsome face. Ivy's breath began to shake nervously. She stood in front of Hart and let him run his hands across both sides of her face.

"Hart, please, let's go," she breathed. "You're scaring me."

Ivy grabbed his hands on either side of her face and encouraged him to move, but Hart shook his head.

*"What's wrong?"* she whispered, afraid.

"Remember the fish in the osprey's talons?" he asked in a low, lamenting tone. "It was the first time you brought me here to Lights Beach. Do you remember?"

She searched his eyes for an answer she didn't want to know. "I remember everything."

Hart smiled. "Ivy, you are my glorious misfortune."

A light whimper escaped her lips. The fish flew to its consequent death, but the journey there was unlike anything it had ever experienced before the osprey found it.

She felt an ominous cloud engulf her ecstatic heart, but Ivy decided to disregard her intuition. Hart was fine.

"Let's go," she repeated.

"I'm not coming with you," he breathed resignedly … then he fell to his knees.

Ivy grabbed him as he fell, falling with him to the ground. The cold wind rushed around them on their knees, and she lifted his heavy head and cried out his name. She looked into his eyes— their disheartening emptiness frightened her. She remembered the night she found him in the water at the Silver Moon Gala.

Now here they were again, almost one year later.

"Hart? Hart, talk to me ..." she pleaded.

Ivy lifted the hand she had resting on his heart and gasped when she saw the thick, scarlet liquid that coated her palm ... *blood.* She examined the black T-shirt over his chest.

"Ivy, go," he whispered.

"You've been shot...," She pressed her hand over his bleeding chest and groaned, trying to keep the inconceivable truth from rushing to her surface. *"Oh God, you've been shot."*

Hart moaned under his breath. He blinked his eyes a few, lazy times ... then he closed them.

"Hart, please open your eyes," she begged, holding his face to hers. "Open your eyes!"

Hart opened his eyes, just a crack, capturing just enough brown to recognize the life within him still. She glanced around the fishing shack from where she kneeled with Hart on the floor, frantically searching for anything to help them. *Anything.* Ivy searched his pockets for his cell phone.

"I lost it, Ives," he said weakly. "While I was fighting in the forest."

"Okay, you'll be okay," she responded reassuringly. Ivy pressed her hands firmly on his chest to stop the bleeding.

"You're so beautiful," he breathed, running his thumb across her smooth cheek. Hart smiled warmly at her. "So beautiful it hurts."

Ivy couldn't smile. She bit her quivering lip to fend off the devastating heartbreak as the universe prepared to steal another soldier from her heart.

Hart felt them before he heard them—the thundering beat resounded through his soul and he knew they had finally arrived. *Black Hawks.* Walker was here. A sweet feeling of relief masked his pain ... Ivy would be safe now.

"Look to the sky," he said fondly.

Ivy looked to the ceiling when he said this, listening to the heavy thumping above them. "What is that?"

"Black Hawks," he managed. *Walker ...*

He pulled her lips toward his and breathed her in. *His divine reprimand. His punishment. His savior.*

"Ivy," he said, with his lips on hers, "Ivy, I'm sorry this is happening to you again." Tears rolled down her face, and Hart ran his thumb through their sweet, wet warmth.

*"No, Hart ...,"* Ivy shook her head. It was inconceivable to her that she could lose him like this.

"I'm so sorry," he whispered. The eternal beacon of light in his darkness. Her light would never fade. Hart looked into her crystal eyes, and then kissed her.

Ivy groaned sadly, feeling the strength wane from his body.

Hart whispered his dying breath on her lips ... and closed his eyes with its abiding truth, "I love you, *Ivy Rose."*

She felt his lips leave hers, and he fell away from her again. She cried out when she caught him, his weight pulling her down to the floor with him. He looked up at her one last time, and she saw the warmth fade in his eyes. Ivy leaned over him and pleaded for him not to leave her, but he watched her soundlessly with his pensive, brown eyes ... breaking her heart with their inconceivable truth.

Hart listened to his beating heart. He heard it thunder through him with the blades of the Black Hawks. He saw her sweet face leaning over him, and he saw the blue ocean in her eyes. The white sand in her blonde hair. The sunlight on her glowing skin. The tan lines on her naked body. He lost himself in her divinity. He lost himself in her light. Then she was gone ….

Hart lay there in the darkness, listening to the blades beating laboriously slower, in time with his dying heart. *Let the water take me, Ivy. Let me die, too.* Then he drifted into the silent darkness, holding her light resolutely to his soul.

## Chapter 32

Ivy glanced behind her and saw a group of men with rifles storm through the front door of the fishing shack. They wore black from head-to-toe with flashlights beaming from their headgear, and they approached her with a swiftness she had now become quite partial to in a man. *Phoenix.* She had heard about them in stories and dreamed dreams of them at night, but they were now missing the hero she fell in love with many years ago. Ivy bent over Hart and held him close… not ready to let him go.

"We have a confirmed sighting on the Commander and the Queen of Hearts."

Ivy breathed into Hart and tightened her eyes.

"Get her out of here, boys!" A voice shouted over the noise of the Black Hawks.

Ivy heard the order. She buried her face into Hart's neck before she was scooped into the arms of one of the soldiers. She cried out as he carried her away. Reaching for Hart. Calling for him. Begging him to wake up from his eternal sleep. She saw them kneel over him and check his pulse, but when another group of soldiers raced past her through the doorway, she lost all sight of him.

The fear struck her suddenly, and she groaned into the cold wind outside. The soldier stood her on the beach, and a couple of armed men escorted her across the moonlit sand to the helicopters. One of them placed her on a seat inside the closest Black Hawk and fastened a strap across the front of her, then he nodded at her and ran back to the fishing shack.

Ivy rested her hand on her heart to calm its pounding fear. She exhaled slowly through her pursed lips to stop herself spinning with grief and wept soundlessly into the deafening noise of the Black Hawk. She jumped in fright when someone tapped her on the shoulder. Ivy turned to the soldier beside her. He pulled his gloves off and grabbed a set of headphones from a hook set in the ceiling, then positioned them carefully over her ears. He adjusted the microphone so that it sat on her lips, and then he threw his thumb up to see if she was okay. Ivy wasn't sure how to reply, but he didn't wait around for an answer. He sat in his seat beside her and calmly strapped himself in.

A composed, husky voice spoke through her headphones soon after. "Fox, is she secure?"

Ivy heard the voice and she glanced quickly at each of the armed soldiers who surrounded her, overwhelmed by the chaos of the frenzied ocean and the beating Black Hawks. She could hear her breath panting through the microphone on her lips, and the sound unsettled her.

"Affirmative, the Queen of Hearts is secure." A different voice replied in her ears.

"Roger that. The Queen of Hearts has been extracted. One man down."

*One man down.* Ivy's heart sank. She thought she might be sick. The Black Hawk's blades beat even louder as they lifted off the ground, and she stared at the fishing shack through her twisting hair. Ivy wished she were still with him. In his warmth. *In his love.* It felt wrong to leave Lights Beach without him. She looked down at her wrists and ran her fingertips tenderly along the pieces of Hart's t-shirt, deep in thought. What would Hart have done if she died? Would he have left without her?

Ivy began to pull at the restraints that strapped her to the seat.

"Uh … that is not a good idea, ma'am."

Ivy glanced into the night goggles of the soldier sitting beside her, then turned back to the complicated buckles.

"Ma'am, we are off the ground. Please stay in your seat."

The same husky voice spoke through the headphones after him, and Ivy guessed it was the pilot, "What's going on back there, Fox?"

"I'm not sure, sir. I think she's trying to leave."

"Well, that is not an option, Sergeant. Don't make me come back there."

Ivy noted the humor in his tone. She vaguely recognized it, but the soldier beside her was desperate to keep her restrained, so she fought against his hands as he prevented her from freeing herself.

"Ma'am! Please!"

Ivy managed to undo her buckle and remove herself from the straps. She stood up from her seat and grabbed the handle beside her, and faced the open air above the beach. She lost her balance momentarily when the Black Hawk stopped and lowered itself to the sand again, as though the pilot half-expected her to jump. Ivy looked down at the beach below her and tightened her eyes. It was an intimidating drop, but the pilot was right, she *would* jump.

The squalling wind pushed against her when she leaned out of the chopper. She looked up into the blades and kept mindfully low as they carved the night sky with their impressive speed.

"Keep her secure, Goddamn it!" The pilot ordered through her headphones.

Ivy felt the soldier grab her arm. She looked at him, standing behind her with open-mouthed bewilderment, seemingly half-amused by her attempt to escape.

"Ma'am! We're in the sky! Where are you going?"

Ivy took a deep breath with her decision and brushed his hand from her arm. "I can't leave him."

"Ma'am!" he replied.

"Grab her, Fox! Now!"

Ivy ripped the headphones from her ears and launched herself into the air beneath the blades. She dropped onto the beach a fair distance below the Black Hawk, then hurried back to her soldier through the whipping sand.

She didn't get far before she was lifted effortlessly into the arms of a soldier running toward her from the shack. Ivy cried out when he carried her back to the Black Hawk. He fastened her more securely to her seat and Ivy watched him tie her hands together with a cable tie thrown to him from the pilot. He looked up at her, and Ivy peered into his goggles.

The soldier shouted over the noise of the blades, "I'm sorry, it's for your own good!"

He carefully positioned the cable tie over the pieces of Hart's shirt still wrapped around her wrists. His touch was gentle and attentive, as though he knew Hart had tied them there himself.

"Here, Ives, put these back on before you lose your hearing!" The soldier placed the headphones back over her ears.

*Ives?* She frowned curiously at the soldier kneeling in front of her, then he lifted the night vision goggles from his face and shot her a handsome, dimpled smile.

"Benji?" Ivy breathed in surprise.

He finished tightening the cable tie, picked up his rifle, and nodded at her as he pulled the night vision back over his eyes. Benji leaped out of the chopper and headed back to the fishing shack.

The helicopter grew increasingly louder. It lifted from the beach with a sudden urgency and Ivy was forced to hold on to something. She glanced at the pilot and assumed it was due to her previous escape.

"We are in the air," his calm voice echoed through her headphones again. "See you back in Monterey."

Ivy considered the pilot for a few seconds, and then she looked out the open hatch. She took a nervous breath as they rose above the ocean, and she watched the silver shoreline fall away as they lifted weightlessly into the sky. Ivy rested her hands on the window and stared where she imagined the shack to be in the black forest below her.

"Benji will take care of things on the ground, Ives," the pilot's voice lulled reassuringly through her headphones. "He'll do everything he can for Hart. We don't want to lose him either."

Ivy peered at the pilot in the dark. *Walker* ... he was flying the Black Hawk. He turned to look at her and when they locked eyes, the steeliness in his expression softened instantly. His dark eyes smiled at her in a way that broke her heart and reassured her simultaneously.

Ivy wanted to tell him that Hart died in her arms, but she couldn't. She couldn't bear to witness his heartbreak. Instead, she gave him a small, sympathetic smile and turned away from him.

Walker frowned. "Are you hurt, Ivy?"

"No."

She listened to his discerning silence. She watched him in her peripheral vision, then she sat up in sudden alarm, her eyes wide with fear. The soldier beside her reacted swiftly, ready after her reckless exit.

"Walker! The bomb!"

"They are disarming it as we speak. Try not to worry, Ives." He smiled warmly at her and faced his controls again.

Ivy's unconvinced gaze lingered on him for a short while, then she turned back to the window. She examined the beach in the distance as they flew away from it. The second Black Hawk was still perched on the shore, and she wondered if the group of soldiers was still inside the fishing shack. Along with Benji and Hart. Ivy swallowed the lump in her throat and watched on anxiously. Hart had said twelve minutes—surely the time was up by now? She studied the area of the forest where she had spent the past couple of days ... when Hart was alive. Her life had been at risk, but it didn't matter to her because *his* heart was still beating.

A giant fireball exploded into the sky above the fishing shack. The forest, the beach, and the Black Hawk on the sand were instantly illuminated in orange light from the blaze. Ivy threw her hands onto the window in breathless fear.

"Hold on!" Walker shouted.

The Black Hawk rolled sideways through the sky, reeling from the force of the bomb. Ivy clung to the handle beside her, feeling her stomach turn over. She looked out into the moonlit clouds to her right and held her breath, then looked past the soldiers to her left and saw the wild ocean rolling beneath them. Ivy closed her eyes until Walker managed to regain control over the chopper. When they were flying steady, she glanced appreciatively at Walker, then turned to the fireball that rolled around itself into the sky. It lit the clouds and the forest with its burning, orange glow, and she couldn't help but wonder if Oliver was there ... leading his friend into the orange sky.

"Swift, this is Walker, do you read me?"

Ivy stared at Walker as he waited for Benji's reply. He shot her a quick glance then glared at the fireball that had now settled itself on the wind. His anxious expression panicked her. Walker was anything but anxious.

"Swift, this is Walker, do you read me?" he repeated. "Swift!"

Ivy waited breathlessly in the silence. She glanced at the soldiers seated around her, noting their unsettled distress in their shaking heads and cursing mouths.

"Shit, Benji! Do you read me?"

"Why isn't he answering?" Ivy yelled.

Walker's dark, sober eyes flashed at her from the front of the Black Hawk, but he didn't respond.

Ivy exhaled sharply. She leaned her head against her seat and stared into the darkness that had resettled over the bay. *Her* bay. *Her* beach. *Her* forest. She closed her eyes and thought about a time when this was paradise ....

*"So, I'm in your world now," Hart grinned beautifully at her, "where you get to keep what you ask for?"*

*Ivy laughed. "Something like that."*

*He laughed humbly, "You could have anything you want, and you asked for us, the jaded remnants of war?"*

*"Yeah, I did." Ivy curled her lip in jest.*

*"Hey, no, I get it," he teased, scanning the pristine bay around them. "Living in paradise must get pretty monotonous after a while."*

*"It can be a little repetitive," she laughed, playing along. "Now you are here, and suddenly things are alluringly enchanting once again."*

*He looked up at her, his brown eyes ablaze with desire. "The enchantment around here is all your doing, Ivy."*

*Ivy blushed. "I meant to say interesting ... things are interesting again. Good interesting, though. You know, different," she mumbled nervously.*

*Hart laughed softly to himself.*

*"Well, trust me, it always gets interesting with a Phoenix soldier hanging around." He grinned. "There hasn't been a time in our lives that the world didn't throw a curve ball at us, good or bad. I hope you're ready."*

*"I am," she grinned happily at the thought.*

When Ivy opened her eyes, her world had disappeared into the darkness.

## Chapter 33

# - MONTEREY COUNTY, CALIFORNIA -
## July 2015

"Sir."

"At ease, Commander."

"Thank you, Sir," Walker replied. He relaxed in Garvey's calming presence and sat down when the General motioned toward a chair.

Garvey dropped a folder on his desk and leaned back in his office chair with a heavy sigh. He removed his reading glasses, rubbed his tired eyes, and put the glasses back onto the bridge of his nose.

"I've been sitting here all day reading paperwork," Garvey stated casually. He glanced at Walker with a nostalgic grin. "I envy what you guys have ... or had, I should say." He sighed sympathetically. "The action. The comradery."

Walker gazed thoughtfully at the General as he spoke, then he bowed his head and stared at his fingers, interlocked in his lap. He nodded wordlessly in understanding. He knew what he meant.

Garvey leaned forward and considered Walker quietly.

"I miss it now and then," he added in Walker's silence. He tapped his finger on the folder and studied the soldier who sat uncharacteristically subdued opposite him. Garvey narrowed his eyes. "You alright, son?"

Walker sighed, and then answered. "Yes, sir, I'm alright."

"You know, it's been a couple of minutes, and you haven't

asked me for anything yet," Garvey spoke warmly. "First time in thirteen years."

Walker smiled faintly.

"Or is this a social visit, Commander?" Garvey grinned doubtfully. "Another first."

Walker ran his hand through his hair with a coy smile. "Well, there was *one* thing …."

Garvey removed his reading glasses and leaned back in his chair again. "Wait, let me guess. The Night Stalker needs a bird?"

Walker grinned mischievously. "Yeah, I need three, actually."

"Three!?" Garvey replied, wide-eyed. "Shit, I can't just give you a bird whenever you need to be somewhere, Commander! Have you got something against commercial airlines? Geez, I'm not that keen on airplane food either, but let's be real."

"I have nothing against airplane food."

"No? What about those green eggs you get sometimes?" he asked with a hint of distaste.

"Green eggs, sir?"

"Yeah," he frowned to himself. "My scrambled eggs came out green once, for breakfast. Why do you think that was?"

Walker's dark eyes squinted in amusement. The General was in a peculiar mood.

"I have no idea," Walker laughed gently. "The question is, sir … did you eat them?"

The General shrugged and nodded apologetically. "It was a long flight."

Walker twisted his face slightly in disgust, then tapped his thumbs together nervously, anticipating an answer to his request.

"Last time I gave you a Black Hawk was for a good reason." Garvey's expression grew serious. "There was a terrorist threatening the life of an American citizen …."

"American citizen?" Walker interrupted. He leaned forward in his chair. "It was Oliver's sister."

Garvey sighed and nodded without speaking.

Walker stood from his chair and leaned on Garvey's desk. "I have three Black Hawks prepped with another two pilots ready to leave on my command."

Garvey twisted his mouth in thought. "Who have you got?"

"Lachlan and Smith."

"You taking Swift?"

"Goes without saying," Walker replied, unblinking.

The General smiled dryly. He rubbed his temples and closed his eyes, as though he were nurturing a sore head. "I don't know...."

"Think of it as a training exercise," Walker encouraged. "It's San Diego. It's only a few hundred miles from here. We'll be back by midnight."

The General wiped his hands down his face and stared resignedly at the gritty, untiring soldier in front of him. Josh Walker was one of his finest.

"Okay," Garvey affirmed. "One bird."

"Three."

"*One* Black Hawk, Commander," he replied sternly, pointing at Walker.

Walker rubbed his hands together happily.

"I recognize that look in your eye," Garvey responded authoritatively. "I mean it, one Black Hawk, or I'll kick your Phoenix ass back into the Night Stalkers."

"You'll kick my ass, sir?" Walker grinned cheekily.

Garvey rolled his eyes. "You think an old man like me can't kick your ass?"

"I'd like to see you try, sir."

The General shook his head and carefully placed his reading glasses back over his eyes. He picked up the folder again and opened it, then sighed into it with a trace of a smile. "Twenty years ago I could have kicked your ass."

Walker laughed harmlessly and walked to the door of the General's office. He pulled it open, then paused in the doorway. He glanced back at the General, who still had his eyes in his folder, and Walker's smile faded.

"Thank you, General." Walker frowned suddenly, his dark eyes softening. "She needs to know the truth. It's been six weeks."

Garvey looked up from his folder and nodded stoically at Walker.

"One Black Hawk," the General reaffirmed.

"Yes, sir. I heard you," Walker replied. "One Black Hawk."

Garvey shot him an unconvinced smirk, then Walker left.

*Chapter 34*

## - SOUTHERN CALIFORNIA -
July 2015

IVY RUBBED HER WRISTS in a slow, musing manner. There was nothing there anymore. No rope burn. No tenderness. Not even a scar. Six weeks had healed her skin completely, as though all of it had never happened.

She fastened the gold bracelet around her wrist and looked into the mirror in the foyer of her estate. She wore a sheer, off-white gown that plunged between her breasts and hugged her waist, falling away from her hips to the marble floor in an elegant, sweeping organza silk. Delicate straps trailed over her shoulders and crossed beneath her hair, which cascaded in blonde waves down the length of her back. She gazed into the mirror, indifferent to the gown. She made a routine twist from side to side to examine the dress, but her mind sank into the layers of silk that flowed weightlessly around her. Ivy slipped into a dream-like haze. She saw nothing in the depths of her gown. No grief. No anger. No confusion. *Nothing.* The dress was enchanting and romantic and seductive … everything Ivy had not felt in six long weeks.

The Silver Moon Gala had finally arrived, but her mind was miles away with her soldiers. Six weeks had passed since that night in the forest. Six weeks without a word from the military. Six weeks without a word from the United States government, including the President, who according to the newspapers, seemed to have known her personally since she lost her renowned father in her teens. Ivy had never met the guy. He owed her nothing. An innocent notion that contradicted how the media construed his role in her kidnapping. They had been relentless in their approach, desperate for her recount of the terrifying night, but Ivy had said nothing. The story's end had yet to be confirmed, so she wasn't quite sure where to begin.

All she wanted was one phone call to end her suffering. One phone call to pull her from the despair that she knew all too well. Unfairly well. Where were her soldiers? No phone call. No text. No message of any kind to let her know they were okay. They were resourceful fellows; they could find a way to reach her. If they had the opportunity to do so.

Ivy sighed at the thought. The military was still hunkered down in the aftermath of what happened with Taym Malak that night. News of a terrorist group and an explosion in La Mar, outside San Diego, had spread like the wildfires that had since been extinguished. America needed someone to blame, and rumor had it both the government and the army were scrambling to get their stories straight with one another before they commented on the incident that stunned the rest of the world. So Ivy remained in solitude behind her iron gates and waited for the military to enlighten the world about what happened that night on the Ghost Trail. All without knowing, still, the fate of the three soldiers who changed her life irrevocably.


Ivy walked into the kitchen and stood at the island bench. She stared at the pool outside in the summer heat, the dazzling blue catching her eye. She watched the bright blue ripples glisten across the surface of the water. It soothed with its rich hue and gentle movement, and she felt his calming presence surround her tortured soul. His gentleness. *His warmth.* Filling her heavy heart with a love she could no longer keep. She closed her eyes and leaned forward on her hands, suppressing the overwhelming urge to cry. Hart had whispered his love for her in his dying breath. It was a sweet but terrible moment she could no longer bear, and yet she had no choice but to endure the relentless anguish of it all. Ivy took a deep breath and buried her grief in the nonsensicality of what happened with Taym, like she had done a hundred times since that night. Was any of it real? Six weeks had passed without any confirmation of Hart's death, and she desperately needed it, to quell the innate flicker of hope that still burned for him inside her. Hopelessly awaiting his return. It wreaked havoc on her heart … and Ivy worried that she was slowly, inexorably, losing her mind.

The soundless emptiness of the estate suddenly caught her attention. Ivy looked around the kitchen, tapping her nails on the island's cold surface. *Tap-pi-ti-tap. Tap-pi-ti-tap.* She listened to the sound of its lonely rhythm in the silence. It emphasized the isolation and the cruel sense of loss she felt she no longer deserved. Quiet voices mumbled in the living room in front of her and Ivy tilted her head and frowned, dubious of her state of mind. She walked out of the kitchen and caught the television's reflection in the windows overlooking the ocean. She recalled leaving it on this morning, to fill the grieving silence of her home. When she picked up the remote from the coffee table to turn it off, Taym Malak's grim face appeared on the screen in front of her.

Ivy gasped instinctively. His dark, hollow eyes prodded the still-fresh wound in her heart, and she groaned in fear. Not of Taym, but of the potential for new information in this news coverage.

"*…notorious terrorist, Taym Malak, was able to enter the United States with a valid American passport and live here undetected for almost one year.*"

A female news anchor appeared on the screen. Her expression was rather somber, and it cast a dreadful shadow over Ivy.

"*Days before his death, he kidnapped a Californian woman and held her hostage, with the grave intention to have her carry out a mass homicide against her will, sometime over the next week. There has been no word on where the attack was planned, but fortunately, the young woman, Ivy Rose, is now safe and recuperating with family after her terrifying ordeal.*"

Ivy closed her eyes. She was safe, yes … but alone.

"*You may recognize her as founder, and hostess, of the renowned annual Silver Moon Gala charity event, held every July in San Diego.*"

Ivy stepped away from the TV in surprise; a photo taken of her a few years ago at the Gala was displayed on the screen in front of her.

"*Ivy lost her brother, Commanding Officer Oliver Rose, just over one year ago to Malak. The attack on Ivy Rose seemed to be a personal vendetta for Malak, and with further investigation, it has been confirmed that he plotted to create his very own terrorist organization within California, so far recruiting more than twelve Americans who were radicalized by Malak through social media."*

She frowned and shook her head. If there was anyone who hadn't learned of what had happened to her six weeks ago, they knew now. The woman took a deep breath and looked up at the camera from her notes with a subtle expression. Ivy frowned curiously.

*"The three soldiers who coordinated Taym Malak's capture have yet to make any appearances or statements since their disappearance after the raid on the clandestine terrorist group. They remain under tight security at a training base in Monterey County. There have been reports that a soldier died on the night of the raid; however, there has been no official confirmation regarding who, of these three incredibly brave men, survived that calamitous night."*

Ivy couldn't listen anymore. She rested her finger on the power button of her remote, then a photo of her brother, Hart, Walker, and Benji appeared on the screen. Ivy pressed her hands to her mouth and held her breath. They were so handsome, with their dazzling smiles and green berets. The four of them stood arm-in-arm between a dozen other soldiers, all of them laughing. She managed a small, sad smile when she thought of them together, all those years ago.

The woman was back on the screen and smiling brightly. A protectiveness awakened in Ivy all of a sudden. She wasn't ready to share these soldiers with the rest of the world.

The woman took a deep breath and continued. *"We cross live to a Public Affairs Officer for the Army base in Monterey where these soldiers are currently residing. We hope he can shed some light on the wellbeing of the three soldiers who have captured worldwide attention with their heroic actions. Officer Cross, thank you for taking the time to talk to us."*

A staid, gaunt-looking man stood uncomfortably in front of the camera. *"Good evening, ma'am."*

*"America just can't get enough of our new heroes, Joshua Walker, Benjamin Swift, and Johnny Hart. We can't help but feel exceedingly proud of these men. Has there been any word on their recovery from this whole ordeal?"*

The man had taken a contemplative breath before he

answered. *"The United States Army is extremely sympathetic toward the tribulations that these soldiers have endured over the past twelve months, including the original loss of their particular unit's commanding officer in Libya this time last year. Unfortunately, due to the extraordinary circumstances of this incident, we have not been able to comment on the situation."*

*"We understand that the assailant, who was born in Afghanistan, was given a United States passport by government officials, which allowed him to enter America and put our country directly in danger. Should we be concerned that there may be others around us with arrangements similar to Malak's, who may take advantage of such an incredible privilege?"* The woman's eyes widened with incredulity.

*"Look, ma'am. The decision to provide a foreign soldier with a United States passport is one that we are exceptionally meticulous about. It is a very rare occurrence and one that is made within a strict, measured environment—"*

*"Yes,"* the woman interrupted, *"but there are reports that Malak always intended to enter America and had already recruited twelve American citizens before he arrived, all of whom were radicalized through social media. How was this not foreseen? These citizens didn't even have to leave America to be a part of this organization. The organization came to them! We dread to think of how many more Americans may have died from a wrong decision made by the very people who were supposed to be protecting us."* The woman frowned and shrugged her shoulders.

Ivy was stunned. Hart was right. All this time he wanted to return to Libya to find Oliver's killer and prevent something like this from ever happening again. She remembered their argument on the driveway before he left her. When she accused her brother of making the wrong decision when it came to saving Hart's life instead of his own. The sorrow in Hart's eyes now struck her breaking heart, and Ivy groaned, ashamed of her ignorance. Hart was too kind to retaliate. Too wise in the progressions of war. It was too late to apologize to him now.

*"The decision was made by a number of respected authorities within the Defense Department and the United States government,"* he continued. *"It was not a decision made lightly, nor a decision made by one person alone. Currently, there is an inquest into how this tragic event unfolded, but in the meantime, we can assure you and the people of the United States that this will not happen again."*

*"You said 'tragic,'"* the woman's tone saddened. *"Are you confirming the death of a soldier on the night of the raid?"*

A sickening wave of fear nearly wiped Ivy off her feet. A dreadful heaviness gathered in her heart, and she silently prayed to the universe, shaking weakly in fear. Ivy closed her eyes and held her breath, and listened for the man to reveal what America had been suspecting for six weeks.

The man looked into the camera with a steely, emotionless expression. He put one finger to his ear and glanced away from the camera momentarily, before returning his impassive gaze to Ivy. *"I have been given authority by the United States government to inform you and the world, that, unfortunately, we did lose one of our soldiers six weeks ago on the night of the raid."*

Ivy's heart shattered into a million pieces. She felt the breath sucked from her lungs and she bent over and moaned in gut-wrenching pain. The remote fell from her hands and hit the carpet, and the muted thud of the bullet that buried itself into Hart's chest replayed over and over in her mind. She hadn't heard it at the time, but now she recalled the moment all too easily. She remembered his blood on her hands and the sweet contentment in his smile. Their lives were tragically ripped apart in the deafening silence of that moment … then she remembered the fading warmth in his beautiful brown eyes as he fell away from her. Drowning with the emptiness he thought he always wanted.

*"That is terrible news,"* the woman's face fell. *"Can we ask which one of these brave soldiers gave his life for Ivy Rose, and ultimately for the people of America?"*

*"His family was notified immediately following his death. Right now it is up to the government to decide on when the soldier's name will be released, but I do believe this may be as early as tonight."*

*"Well, again, that is heartbreaking news, Officer Cross. Can you tell us what will happen to the Americans who joined this dreadful organization?"* The woman shook her head in contempt.

*"I can safely say, ma'am, that they will always regret the day they decided to turn their backs on their country."* The man smiled sternly.

*"Thank you, Officer Cross. I think we can all rest a little easier tonight, knowing that this group is no longer a threat to the people of America, but the world still holds its breath as we wait for the name of our fallen hero. Thank you for your time."*

*"Thank you, ma'am."*

"Breathe," Ivy whispered, forcing herself to take a breath.

She turned off the television and breathed quickly and mechanically in the silence. A small groan escaped her lips as she felt herself hyperventilating.

*Foolish.* Ivy hated herself for the huge part of her that wanted to believe. The hope that she tried to ignore, but was too frightened to let go of. Foolish to think that it wasn't possible for this to happen to her again. It was unfair. Hart came back for her because he loved her, and now he was gone. Another soldier she loved … *gone.* Ivy fell to her knees and buried her face into her hands. Then she lay down on the carpet, and cried.

## Chapter 35

EVENTUALLY, THE TEARS STOPPED. It was not for lack of grief, but she had learned long ago how to put grief into an isolated place within her. She was otherwise empty, utterly spent of hope, confidence, and love. She imagined herself in the near future, still anchored to the carpet in her misery. No one to check on her. No one to lift her from the floor. No one to make sure she didn't die from her broken heart. It was possible, she thought. It was tempting to lay here until the world had moved on from what happened, or until malnourishment replaced her grief, whichever came first. Ivy stared at the thick, woolen weave of the carpet as she considered it. When would that be, she wondered. *Days? Weeks?* She rolled onto her back and sighed, resting her hands over her eyes. Ivy cast away her feelings for one crucial reason ... so she could pick herself up off the living room floor.

She drifted mindlessly back to the kitchen and was startled by a firm knock at the front door. Ivy walked to the entry hall and then stopped, fear freezing her in place. She stared at the back of the door and waited for her courage to catch up to her from the kitchen. This time last year, she expected her driver to be standing behind the door, and in his place were three breathtaking soldiers. Ivy knew they weren't there today. She was surprised to feel the hope that flickered inside of her.

Ivy almost smiled, then she bowed her head and took a deep breath. *Foolish.* She summoned the emptiness she had felt only moments earlier, but it didn't come. Ivy wiped her wet cheeks and took a deep breath to compose herself, and then she carefully opened the door.

*Maybe, just maybe …*

The driver smiled when he saw her. "I am here to take you to the Silver Moon Gala, Ms. Rose."

Ivy's heart sank and settled comfortably in a place she knew she would never go looking for it.

"Hi," Ivy managed a small smile.

"You are captivating, Ms. Rose, as always."

Ivy locked the front door, then turned to him. "Thank you."

She climbed into the backseat of the town car, and the driver closed the door gently behind her. She noted that he had turned the air conditioning off, knowing her preference for open windows and the fresh air. She was grateful for the unassuming friendliness of the older man. He'd been her father's driver, and she always asked for him for the rare times she needed a car because he reminded her of happier times, before her loved ones had left her.

The seat's leather was hot on the back of her legs, but it was a feeling that aroused a summer nostalgia instead of discomfort. Ivy relaxed into the warm seat with a long, weary sigh; the night ahead was going to be her toughest yet.

The driver pulled away from the empty estate. Ivy stared at the weeping trees as they rolled slowly past. She listened to the birds twittering happily in the branches outside her window. Everything in her life had changed, yet the world around her remained the same. It didn't recognize her broken heart. It didn't darken its bright blue sky in mourning. The sun still flickered through the trees, and she still felt its divine warmth on her skin. The flowers still bloomed, and the bumblebees still hummed within them. The ocean still sparkled in the distance, and the crystal waves still lapped the perfect white sand. All of it remained unchanged and unaltered, no matter what happened to her. Ivy faced the sun that shone through her window, then closed her eyes and sighed to herself.

"You have lost faith, my dear."

Ivy caught the driver's old, compassionate eyes watching her in the rearview mirror.

"I'm afraid I may have, this time around," she replied,

forcing a smile.

The driver shook his head. He watched the road ahead of him with a pensive silence, and Ivy took a deep breath and turned back toward the world outside her window. There was nothing to say. Everyone knew about her soldiers. A love story that was once exclusively her own was now a touching tragedy that belonged to the world.

"I will not leave tonight."

Ivy looked at him again.

"If the night is too much for you, Ms. Rose, I will be waiting for you outside."

"No, you can't wait for me all night. It is too long for you."

He nodded at her. "I will wait, my dear. All night."

Ivy exhaled slowly through her pursed lips, fighting back the tears that threatened her guarded composure. Over the past six weeks, she had taught herself to ignore the sympathetic words of strangers, pretending they were just that … *words*. Ivy nodded at her driver and brushed away her tears. It is when they truly cared that it hurt the most.

## Chapter 36

# - SILVER MOON GALA -
## July 2015

"THERE ARE TWO MOONS this month," Taylor told her.

"Are there?" Ivy peered pensively into the sky. A blue moon, she thought to herself.

She felt Taylor's eyes on her, but the two of them stood together silently as Ivy contemplated her feelings on the rarity of the event, then she frowned unhappily into the sky.

"Maybe it's a sign," Ivy breathed, leaning into the balustrade.

Taylor looked from Ivy to the afternoon sky. "Tonight is the night, huh. I overheard the staff talking about it earlier. Are you okay?"

Ivy shrugged without looking at her friend. She twisted her face to stop the tears.

Taylor frowned. "Oh honey, I'm so sorry."

"They're going to release his name, Taylor." Ivy groaned and laid her head on her forearms, breathing slowly and deliberately toward the ground.

Taylor's hand rubbed her back in small, soothing circles and Ivy appreciated her friend's fleeting soft heart. Her hesitant but comforting presence. Taylor always had a callous, uncaring exterior, but over the past few years, Ivy's misfortunes had uncovered her softer, more sympathetic layers.

"It's been six weeks," Ivy breathed.

"I know, honey."

"I can't do this anymore. I don't have the strength. If they say his name out loud ... I can't ... I ... *ugh* ...." Ivy stopped talking, worried she might be sick. She stood and glanced at Taylor, who was wiping away her tears and shaking her head, seemingly embarrassed by her own behavior.

"I'm sorry," Taylor sniffed. "I promised myself I wouldn't cry in front of you tonight, and now I'm crying. Look at me!"

Ivy smiled at Taylor's unguarded heart. It was a blue moon after all. She turned around and watched her guests gradually fill the Gala, passing her with their apologetic gazes and shaking heads. Ivy bowed her head to avoid them. She closed her eyes and pressed her lips together, forcing herself not to think of him. It was so hard. He took her hand here once. He led her onto the dance floor. He led her innocently to the end of his love. *Oh, Hart.* Barely a minute passed she didn't think of him. *His breathless fall ....*

A small whimper left her lips, and Ivy opened her eyes in time to catch Taylor's concern.

"I'm sorry for your loss," a young voice said.

Ivy blinked and peered at the gorgeous brunette who stood in front of them. A young, good-looking man stood beside the girl with his hand around her waist, and Ivy found herself staring at the baby-faced couple with an unexplained feeling of irritation. She recognized the young woman. She was a local girl ... twenty-one, maybe twenty-two years old? She had talked to Hart once, in town. Most of the girls would stop him if they had the chance, but Ivy liked it. She enjoyed watching him pry himself away from them with his impeccable charm. She loved his humble smile when he eventually caught up to her. The way he rubbed his jaw and apologized for their unsubtle dismissal of her. Ivy would laugh, and Hart would roll his eyes, and then he'd wrap his arm around her shoulders ... until the next woman along the street took advantage of his courteous nature.

Hart's absence from La Mar had created a whirlwind of speculation, and Ivy overheard the whispers on the odd occasion. It was one of the reasons she had started to avoid town. *He died saving his one, true love.* They called it tragic but hopelessly romantic, shamelessly swooning over America's latest hero. Her hero.

The girl's eyes were big and doleful, and Ivy couldn't bear the sympathy any longer.

"We read all about it in the paper," she continued. "You two deserved a happy ending. Commander Johnny Hart died a real hero."

There they were again. *Words.*

Taylor looked at her. "We still don't know for sure that it was him."

Ivy smiled politely. She knew.

"Oh," the girl replied. "I'm sorry, I assumed it was—"

"Please stop talking," Taylor spoke abruptly. She glared at the couple and then turned to Ivy.

Ivy felt the color draining from her cheeks. "I'm sorry. You will have to excuse me, I have to, uh ...," she trailed off.

"Ivy?" Taylor frowned.

Ivy rubbed her forehead and walked to the stairs that led from the dancefloor to the beach. *"Breathe ...."*

"Ivy?" Taylor called after her.

The girl followed her a few steps. "I'm really sorry—"

"It's okay," Ivy interrupted her.

Ivy hurried down the stairs and started to run. Taylor called after her again, but she didn't stop. She slowed down to kick off her heels. Her bare feet sunk into the warm sand and her heart pounded with a sense of sadness that threatened to take her down at any moment. *Not here, not at the Gala.* Ivy stifled a small cry and raced along the shore in the golden sunshine. She headed for the cliffs at the end of the bay, where one year ago today in the light of the silver moon ... she had saved a broken soldier.

Her sadness trailed behind her in the distance. It was never far from her these days. She ran from her grief. From the pain. From the torture of not knowing. When she reached the sand below the cliffs, Ivy fell to her knees with exhaustion and stared agonizingly at the spot where she pulled him from the water. She had saved him, and one year later he had died in her arms. When she loved him even more.

Ivy's panting breath grew shallow, and she looked up at the sparkling ocean through her tears. She whispered Hart's name into the sky, feeling the sound of it roll across her tongue, and when his name left her lips onto the balmy ocean air ... Ivy closed her eyes and cried.

She wasn't sure how long she cried. Ivy wiped her tears and glanced back at the Gala along the beach. Her guests were dancing, thankfully oblivious to her misery. The bonfires blazed in the sand. The music floated in the salty air. The ocean glistened peacefully in the late afternoon. Her tanned skin warmed in the summer sun, and Ivy relaxed in these familiar things. It was nice to escape the whispering crowd for a while. She worried that her presence at the Gala would cause a somberness she didn't wish upon anyone.

Ivy pulled herself to her feet and sat on a nearby rock. She gazed into the west as the sun lowered spectacularly in the sky, casting a rich, golden hue across the mist-covered shore. She felt oddly peaceful, contrary to her tears. His beautiful calm fell over her with the falling sun, and Ivy imagined him there, standing beside her brother in the sky. She remembered the words he spoke to her as he kneeled in the wet sand, his painful, unconscious lament. Confessing his sins and baring the sincerity of his soul. Hart was never to blame for her brother's death. *Never.* He was her savior. He was Oliver's savior. Walker's savior. Benji's, too. Hart was the center of their worlds, their unwavering pillar of strength. Their selfless saint. Hart was the beating heart of Phoenix, and she loved him for it. *God, how she loved him.*

Ivy exhaled sharply. She pressed her shaking hands against her chest to ease her aching heart. Oliver sacrificed himself for Hart because he couldn't bear to see Hart leave this world before him … and it really was unbearable, she thought, walking this world without Hart in it.

She gazed wistfully at the horizon as the water and the sky primed themselves for yet another breathtaking sunset. Ivy looked back at the Gala with a pang of guilt. She should be there for the sunset, at least. She took a deep breath and gathered the pieces of her heart, then stood to face the sea. The breeze picked up her hair and cast it off her shoulders. She closed her eyes and listened to it whisper past her ears, soothing her restless soul.

"Take care of him, Ollie." Ivy whispered sadly to the horizon. Then she started back toward the Gala, to wander aimlessly through a crowd of condolences and empty embraces.

Ivy reached the stretch of beach in front of the Gala. She waited for a small wave to rush up the sand and wash over her feet before she returned to her guests. Wasting time. There was already a few dozen commiserating eyes watching her from the dance floor, and it grew exponentially the longer she stood there. Ivy bowed her head and closed her eyes, feeling the panic rise nauseously within her. She focused on the world around her to calm her fleeing heart. The salty scent of the summer ocean. The terns' shrills in the golden sky. Her feet in the warm sand. She listened to the cheery music drifting on the breeze. The excited mumble of voices on the dancefloor. She listened to the laughter and the delight of her three hundred guests who were enjoying the Silver Moon Gala …. She tried to connect with these elements of her world, to find some peace in them, but her mind wandered anxiously …. *What if they released his name while I was gone? I missed it, the official confirmation of his death. That's why there are a hundred solicitous eyes on me.*

Ivy looked at the dancefloor and clenched her jaw in frustration, then closed her eyes. *Focus* ….

She listened to the gentle purr of the ocean behind her. Its tranquility. Its reassurance. Its eternal heart beating steadily in time with hers. The music, and the voices, and the terns all seemed to fade from Ivy's hearing. She listened for the Gala, reluctant to open her eyes, but she could no longer hear it. Only the ocean's heartbeat remained, and it grew stronger and louder with its earth-shaking rhythm. She felt it beat with her own heart until it became too intense to be the ocean's pulsing heart. Ivy placed her hands on her stomach, feeling it vibrate through her entire being. She frowned at its strength, then her eyes shot open.

"Black Hawks," Ivy whispered suddenly. She had heard them before, on the night Hart died. *"Look to the sky,"* she remembered.

Ivy looked up at the dancefloor and the steps to the beach were now overflowing with guests, all eyes fixed on the sky behind her. She didn't turn around. She was too scared to surrender herself to hope yet again. Her anxious breath quickened as the Black Hawks grew closer, filling the sky with their commanding presence. Ivy looked up at the dancefloor again and saw her guests gathering excitedly, their smiles glowing in the orange sun. They pointed at the sunset and shouted to one another over the sound of the rotor blades splitting the sky, clearly in awe of the rare spectacle. Then the phones and the cameras came out, and soon all eyes were on her. Ivy turned her face away from the cameras, attempting to catch her panicked breath.

The news crews dashed around each other on the sand just south of the Gala. Ivy caught their frenzied commotion in the corner of her eye. They arranged their assortment of cameras to face the setting sky. All but one. She felt it on her as she stood alone on the shore in front of the Gala ... the world's prying eye. Ivy swallowed the sickening lump in her throat. The force of the blades beating against the sky became too much for her. She sighed resignedly in the thunderous sound, then turned in the sand and lifted her face to the wind that swept off the sea, peering hesitantly into the sky. Sitting in the sunset were three Black Hawk silhouettes, flying majestically toward her out of the orange sky. *Oh, Oliver.* Ivy groaned weakly into the air. Too heartbroken to have hope, but too hopeful not to believe. Adrenaline burned fiercely through her veins, and she grimaced in its nauseating presence. She couldn't decide whether she was overcome with joy or infuriated with herself for believing it could be him, coming back for her one last time.

She stared breathlessly into the air, her crystal eyes reflecting a deep, wistful orange as the three Black Hawks filled the magnificent sky with their presence. They had succeeded in capturing the cheering hearts of the Gala behind her, and everyone believed it was the soldiers. Ivy wanted to believe. *She so desperately wanted to believe.* She pressed her hands to her chest again to calm her trembling heart. The thunderous beat of the rotors turned into a body-shaking roar as the sound reverberated against the cliff walls with the approach of the low-flying helicopters. The sensation of the blades booming through her body became too overwhelming, and she groaned soundlessly into the deafening sky. She gave in to her hope ... clinging to her deteriorating faith. Ivy fell to her knees when the Black Hawks slowed as they passed above her and the Gala, and she watched them disappear over the top of the cliff, leaving a stunned silence in their prodigious wake.

The music started up again moments later, and the excited crowd made their way back under the pavilion. Ivy blinked her eyes and looked at the sand. Time seemed to slip away too easily from her these past six weeks, and still, somehow, it moved excruciatingly slow.

"Need some help?"

Ivy looked up at Taylor, who stood beside her on the sand. Her dark hair fell in beautiful waves down her shoulders, and she had a small smile that was neither excited nor sympathetic. She seemed rather stunned by the whole ordeal, much like Ivy.

"Yeah. Thanks." Ivy reached for her friend's hand.

Taylor pulled Ivy to her feet and brushed the sand from her gown.

"So, I didn't order the military helicopters, but they were a massive hit with the guests. No one can stop talking about it! You really should have run it by me first," Taylor teased.

Ivy glanced at her friend and tried to smile.

"Are you okay?" Taylor asked.

"I don't know. My head is spinning," Ivy replied, holding her hand to her forehead. She closed her eyes, feeling the beach turning in circles. Overwhelmed with the unknown.

"Do you think it was them?" Taylor asked.

Ivy glanced at Taylor, tragically disheartened by the reality of Hart's death. "Walker, maybe. Benji. But probably neither, not after all this time."

Taylor looked away and ran her hands awkwardly down her dress.

Ivy frowned. "Taylor? What's wrong?"

Taylor cursed under her breath and then turned to look at Ivy. "I should probably tell you about the statement the President released about ten minutes ago."

Ivy stared at her, unblinking and terrified.

Taylor nodded gravely. "I'm sorry, Ivy … they released his name."

"*No* …," Ivy breathed out uneasily. "No, it can't be."

"I'm so sorry."

A wave of nausea rushed over Ivy, and she began to shake. "Don't say his name, Taylor. I can't bear it. Please don't say his name out loud."

"No! No, I don't know! I haven't heard," Taylor replied quickly, keeping Ivy from falling to the sand again. "No one wants to know. Believe me. Your guests have agreed that tonight was not the right time for you to hear it."

Ivy closed her eyes with a fleeting relief. For now she could survive in her ignorance, however short-lived it may be, but her heart sank when she thought about him. It would end with Hart how it all started ... in her dreams.

"I think I'm going to be sick," Ivy groaned weakly. She faced the sunset and breathed slowly and carefully into the wind.

"Maybe it was Walker up there in those Black Hawks?" Taylor offered, dropping her gaze to her feet in the sand. "He cares about you, too. I saw the way he looked at you, Ivy. He adores you."

Ivy closed her eyes. She was appreciative of her friend's concern, but hoped she would stop talking.

"I'll go and get you a drink," Taylor added in Ivy's silence. She walked away from Ivy a few steps and then paused. "Hey, Ives?"

Ivy combed her fingers through her long hair and turned to look at Taylor.

"Do you want me to find out who it was?" Taylor hesitated. "Maybe it's better if I tell you. You know, instead of you being on your own at the estate if ... if he ...."

Ivy contemplated the inevitable pain either way. She nodded emotionlessly at her friend and then turned to watch the end of the sunset ... and it was beautiful. More beautiful than any sunset Ivy had ever seen. It cast a captivating enchantment over her weary soul, and Ivy breathed in the salty breeze when it brushed her cheeks. She thought about Hart. His unwavering kindness and his fierce heart. He defended her until the very end ... and then she watched him die. Any minute now, Taylor would be back with the news of his death, and her world would shatter once again. This time, it would break her absolutely.

Ivy cast her lonely heart into the ocean and let it drift into the sunset. To the soldier who stood there with her brother in the orange sky. She breathed out slowly through her pursed lips, fighting back the tears. Fighting back the grief. The wind caught her hair and she closed her eyes as it whispered past her ears. She heard it this time, speaking her name. Telling her to be strong. Encouraging her to be brave. Ivy smiled sadly at the world's compelling, impassive consistency, then she heard her name again ....

*"Ivy."*

She opened her eyes and looked at the ocean.

"Ivy, you are here," a gentle voice whispered on the wind.

She heard him again. The gentleness. The tenderness. The unmistakable warmth.

"Ivy Rose."

Ivy buried her face into her hands. She could hear him behind her ... calling for her ... but she couldn't turn around. Too defeated to believe.

"Ivy, please," his voice broke.

Ivy turned in the sand, her breath shaking as it left her lips. She peered up at the soldier who stood on the sand like a god bathed gloriously in the radiant, orange glow of the sun. His dress uniform dazzled in the sunset with the military's colorful badges, ribbons, and pins, and when she met his warm, brown eyes, a gorgeous smile suddenly swept across his face.

Ivy exhaled suddenly through her trembling hands.

"Oh Ivy ...,"

"No ... you've been dead for six weeks," she breathed weakly. Her heart pounded against her chest, still too hesitant to believe.

Hart could see her slipping into shock. Her breath was quick and shallow, and he was afraid she might hyperventilate in her distress. Her color faded in front of him on the beach, so he gathered all his strength once again, and pushed through the excruciating pain so he could wrap her in his arms and never let her go.

"I'm alive, Ives. I'm here," he answered, concealing his pain as he shuffled through the sand. Her heartbreak hurt him more than his wounds ever could. "Walker, Benji, they're here, too."

Ivy shook her head in disbelief. He limped toward her along the beach with a cane in his right hand, and his right leg moved awkwardly, the cast showing beneath the cuff of his olive pants. The contortion of his beautiful face gave away the true depths of his pain. Still, Ivy couldn't go to him. She remained in her place by the ocean, stunned with her fear. Terrified that he was nothing but a cruel apparition.

"I don't understand?" she cried. "They said someone died. I watched you die, Hart!"

"It wasn't me," Hart breathed. His eyes saddened when he

thought about the soldier who lost his life that night.

Ivy saw him grimace, struggling torturously to reach her. "Please, don't," she said, throwing her hands in the air and motioning for him to stop walking.

Hart looked up at her, disheartened by her rejection. He sighed and stopped. He saw the unmistakable grief in her eyes. Six weeks with no word of their well-being had taken its toll on her heart, and he understood her reluctance to take him back. Their silence in the military was enforced, but now he wished he had disobeyed protocol, so she felt for him what he had always felt for her. After everything they had been through ….

"I can't bear to see you suffer anymore." Ivy buried her face in her hands. "Not for me … *please, not for me.*"

Hart smiled. Relieved.

"Don't you worry about me, Ivy … I'll be fine," he said, smiling warmly.

"What happened?" she managed, gesturing at his cast.

"Oh, this?" Hart pointed at his right foot. "Uh, I broke my ankle."

Ivy gasped incredulously. For six weeks she thought he was dead. "The fishing shack exploded, Hart! I watched it obliterate the forest around it … and you walked away with a broken ankle?"

"Well, I didn't *walk* away." Hart ran his finger across his bottom lip and laughed softly.

Ivy missed the way he laughed. He purred with humility, and she felt her body ache for him. It was a feeling she thought she would never feel again, and it felt incredible. Ivy watched him rub his jaw in his usual unassuming manner. His beard was shaven. She wanted to trace her fingers along the smooth olive skin on his handsome face, but still she couldn't go to him.

Hart limped toward her again with an amused grin.

"I also broke three ribs," he added with a light-hearted humor. He spoke warmly, studying Ivy's reaction. He hoped it were enough to justify his disappearance, or at least bring a smile to her sweet face.

Nothing.

"And I dislocated my shoulder," he added. Hart fanned out his left arm to show her it was healed.

Ivy frowned, horrified by the number of injuries inflicted on him because of her.

"There were a couple stab wounds." He grinned. He tilted his head toward her, searching her for a smile. Hart continued to justify her worries by humoring her with his injuries instead, and he could see her crystal eyes melting in his approach. It was working.

"I went into surgery three times. I have well over a hundred stitches." He ran his hand across his stomach and continued toward her.

Ivy gasped quietly.

Hart nodded, watching her intently.

"I had one bullet removed." He rubbed the wound over his heart and bowed his head in shame. It was the one that had finally brought him down. The one he had felt in his chest all year ... long before it embedded itself there six weeks ago. The bullet that prevented him from saving her.

Hart stopped in the sand in front of her as he recalled the devastating frustration that shattered his dying soul. Taym. *The bomb.* The night he drifted helplessly away from her to his death, before she was safe from all harm.

Ivy saw something holding him back. She recognized the torment in his eyes. "It wasn't your fault," she breathed.

"Which part?" he replied, looking up at her with a faint smile. "When I lost Oliver? Or when I nearly lost you, Ivy?"

She shook her head.

He looked into her blue eyes. A warm wind shifted her hair a little, and he tucked a blonde lock of it behind her ear. Ivy tucked it in again with a small, bashful smile. He saw her cheeks blush and suddenly she was grinning up at him and embracing him with her eternal light. There she was ... his divine angel. His queen. Hart's eyes softened, and he smiled adoringly in return. He moved closer to her, his approach gentle and slow. Her hand slipped under his jacket, and she ran her fingers over his chest. Over the bandage that covered his heart. She looked up at him and he tightened his eyes and sighed heavily at the long-awaited tenderness of her love.

"Does it hurt?" she asked.

"Not anymore," he replied. "Not when I'm with you, Ivy."

She placed her hand on his heart, and he caressed the back of it with his thumb. She melted under his warm touch, a warmth she thought had left this world forever.

"Ivy. All along I believed you were brought to me as a divine reprimand for the death of your brother. A gloriously cruel torture that was both insufferable and heavenly all at once," Hart spoke gently. "My head was a mess. I no longer had the strength to resist you, yet it was inconceivable to me, after everything that happened in Libya, that I was the one for you. Going back to the war was the only way I could give you the life you deserved. That is why I left you. I'm so sorry. Please forgive me."

A tear rolled down her cheek, then she blushed and glanced at her bare feet in the sand. Hart lifted her chin with the side of his finger and took a deep breath when the orange sky caught the smooth, flawless skin of her cheek. He saw the light freckles that dusted her nose, and he sighed with sweet relief that he was here with her once again ... alive in her breathtaking divinity.

"I know that Oliver sent us here for a reason," he continued. "He sent us here because he knew there was always a chance he wouldn't make it back to you. This was his way of protecting you, of protecting all of us. He knew what we would find here with you. He knew we needed you, Ivy, more than you will ever know."

Another tear rolled down her cheek. He held the side of her face with his big, gentle hand and tenderly wiped away the tear with his thumb.

"What about Phoenix?" she asked.

"Phoenix," he repeated fondly, glancing at the sunset. "Walker, Benji, Oliver, and I ... we *are* Phoenix. We always will be. We risked our lives for our country, and we lost a life for our country. We have nothing to prove to anyone anymore."

"You're not going back to the war?" Ivy asked, surprised.

"It's been fifteen years, and we're tired." Hart shook his head with defeat. "So tired."

Ivy looked at him.

"We thought we'd confronted everything in those wars. We thought there wasn't a force that could ever bring us down. We knew we weren't invincible, but ...," Hart dropped his gaze momentarily as he thought about his best friend, "but losing

Ollie made us realize we weren't as strong as we thought we were."

"You are the strongest men I have ever met," Ivy breathed. She ducked her head to meet his gaze, which now lingered on his feet.

"Yes, we're strong." Hart looked up at her sincerely. "But you, Ivy … you are invincible."

Ivy considered him with her musing, crystal eyes, which reflected the light of the world around them, and Hart breathed in deeply, overcome by her unassuming innocence. The wind caught her hair and swept it from her face, and she smiled at him. Hart knew then that he was right … her light was everlasting.

He sighed happily, "We're staying with you, Ives."

Ivy bit her lip and smiled. She thought about being bound to her three soldiers for the rest of her life. Unbreakable. *Inseparable*. A Rose in Phoenix … just like her brother.

Hart took her hands in his, and they stood face-to-face in the light of the golden sun.

"The world stole something from me that I wasn't expecting, and in return, I received the same," he said, shaking his head in disbelief. "I never expected you, Ivy. *Never*."

The warm, salty air moved gently around their bodies and the peacefulness embraced them. A lopsided grin swept across his handsome face, and Ivy felt her body tremble with desire.

"You were the bright light leading me out of the darkness, and I am so *fucking* glad I followed." Hart grinned deliciously at her.

Ivy laughed. "You didn't always follow," she teased him.

"I didn't know what was good for me," he replied, smiling playfully.

"Oh, and you do now?" she smirked.

"I will never forget."

Ivy saw him glance hungrily at her lips, and instinctively, she leaned into him so that only a few centimeters separated her from the soldier she thought she had lost forever. She trailed her hands down his chest, and Hart pulled her to him. He ran his hand along her cheek and pulled her lips toward his … and then he stopped.

Ivy breathed into his mouth, lightheaded, feeling him brush

his smooth lips against hers, as he always did, and she groaned into him. His eyes closed tightly, reveling in her pleasure, and Ivy smiled.

"You saved my life, Johnny Hart," she whispered to him, frowning at the intensity of her love for this selfless and courageous soldier. The beating heart of Phoenix.

Hart shook his head humbly. He slid his hands through her hair and pulled her lips to his once again, and he remembered the night they met, one year ago today. When the darkness seemed unending, and she was there, the light he thought he no longer deserved.

"No, Ivy," he breathed softly on her lips, "you saved mine."

Then he kissed her, underneath the orange sky.

*"Ivy, if I die ….*
*then look into the orange sky and I will be standing there.*
*You will never be alone.*
*I promise."*